WHISPERS OF GLORY

GUSTAV S. FAEDER

Hamilton Books
A member of
The Rowman & Littlefield Publishing Group
Lanham • Boulder • New York • Toronto • Oxford

Hamilton Books
4501 Forbes Boulevard
Suite 200
Lanham, Maryland 20706
Hamilton Books Acquisitions Department (301) 459-3366

PO Box 317
Oxford
OX2 9RU, UK

Library of Congress Control Number: 2005935414
ISBN 978-0-7618-3349-9

To Marjorie, my very good friend, whose love,
perseverance and encouragement
made this book possible.

With additional thanks and
heartfelt appreciation to Tracy and Erica
whose yawns, pushes, suggestions and
encouragement are on every page.
And to Eric for his
haunting title.

I

THE SECRET
OCTOBER, 1860

Sarah Morrow followed her husband through the center hall of their ample home, "Henry, do you have to go? All this talk of a Republican President and secession worries me."

"Be back day after tomorrow, with horses and maybe a new coach. No need to worry. I'll be fine."

"I hope so," Sarah gave in, her arguments exhausted over the last two days. "There's bread and meat packed for two."

At the front entry, a double door of chestnut-wood, elaborately carved, Henry turned to kiss his comely wife, "Ezekiel thanks you, too."

"At least, you're not going alone."

Down gentle steps and across the herring-bone brick walk, the iron gate was cold to his touch as he lifted the latch. He turned, knowing she waited to return his wave.

The little exchange had started early in their marriage, and quickly became a sign of deep affection, to Henry, a devotional to their love of twenty-five years. To Sarah, the opportunity for a brief prayer for his safe return.

This morning, she waved, too, to Ezekiel Brown who sat his horse holding the reins of Henry's roan mare.

Ezekiel and Henry had been brought up as brothers in Washington, D.C., crying for milk and clean diapers at the turn of the century, studying their numbers, and working in the Morrow warehouse that backed the canal in Georgetown. Leaving Washington in 1832, Henry had promised they would be together again as soon as he was settled. Four years later, he redeemed his pledge from Winchester, Virginia.

Before he mounted the roan, Henry checked a saddle bag for his matched pair of derringers. Though he had never found cause to use them, he always made them part of his travel kit.

They rode west on Wolfe Street, which showed on the first plan for Winchester town, a dirt surface packed hard by wheels, hooves and feet, just wide enough for two wagons to pass. Brick sidewalks, substantial houses and century-old shade trees made it a very pleasant street indeed, one of the town's nicest.

They savored the bright autumn day, breathing deeply of the mountain air, taking in the vivid colors of stately trees, "You serious about goin' t'Moorefield, Henry? Jed didn't say nothin' else, just be here ready t'go to Moorefield."

"Heard about a stage line selling out, Zeke. Hope to pick up horses cheap, maybe even a coach. Besides, we both need a ride through the mountains before the color fades."

They reined north on Stewart Street for a block then west on Boscawen to the Northwest Turnpike.

"Take it we're goin' through the mountain at Petticoat Gap."

"Yup."

Through toll gate and gap, they left one turnpike for another that branched south to Moorefield. Never had they seen the trees more glorious, oaks and maples, russet and orange, yellow aspens, shades of reds and gold, all the more dazzling in the year-round greens of the pines and firs.

At the Poplar Run ford they stopped to let the horses drink. "You picked a fine day for ridin', Henry, clear and peaceable."

"Some different than what we knew in Washington. Never knew how crowded it was until I saw The Valley."

"You're right about that. Too many people even back then. What it must be nowadays! Whooo-ee!!"

Testing girths, they mounted up, rode on toward Wardenville where they planned to spend the night.

"Henry, whatta you make of all the hullabaloo 'round the country? Seems ever since John Brown got himself kilt at Harper's Ferry people been het up an' ashy."

"You're right, Zeke. Almost a year since Old Ossawatomie got himself hung and nothin's any better. All the shouting and name-calling'. Too busy running their mouths to listen to each other.

"I say stop the squabbling and work to build the country again. Nobody seems to give a damn about the country anymore."

"Sure seems so, don't it. Not like it used t'be."

They rode in silence, each with his own thoughts.

"You think there's gonna be a war, Henry?"

"Who knows? North and South been quarreling forty years or more, and always been able to find a way to come together.

"But it's different this time. Mean. Angry. Lucky if we get through the election without someone getting shot."

"You really think so?"

"Wouldn't say it if I didn't. You ought to know that, Zeke. Lincoln will win with the democrats divided like they are. The South won't sit still for Lincoln."

Again they lapsed into silence, letting the horses laze along at their own pace.

Abruptly, Henry spat, "Democrats better get their ass together before it's too late."

"Too late? Sounds like you're answerin' my question."

"What question?"

"About war. I take it you're sayin' it's mighty close."

Henry scowled, "I guess you're readier than me to say so, Zeke. Damned if I want to see that."

Reading the look, Ezekiel knew more was coming. He waited.

"With David up there at West Point and graduating in May, he's sure to get into it first crack. Jed and Brian'll get caught in it, too. They have good prospects, Zeke, Jed knowing farming so well, thanks to you, the other two with college educations.

"Goddamn," Henry's anger bubbled into a thunder clap, "We raised our sons for more than getting shot in somebody's fool war. They want a war, let 'em fight it their damn selves."

Pushing the long shadows of sundown, they approached Wardensville, "Supposed to be a tavern right on the highway," Henry mumbled, "maybe those men up ahead will know."

He motioned toward a wagon on the side of the road. It sat lopsided for a broken wheel, the rear right. Two hard-looking men stared at it, one scratching his unshaven chin, the other cursing their bad luck, "Sum bitch was awright when we left."

"Well, it ain't now. You shoulda seen it an' fixed it."

"How the hell could I tell, Paw?"

"Don't you git biggity with me, boy! We musta broke forty jars, 'most whole goddamn load." The older man kicked the forlorn wagon, "Sum-mumabitch."

Henry reined up, still out of sorts. He tried to override his mood, "Evening. My friend and I are looking to spend the night. Understand there's a place up ahead."

"Got misery 'nuf wit'out no damn questions f'um strangers."

Sensing trouble, Henry eased off, "Just lookin' for supper and a bed for tonight. If there's anything we can do to help. . ."

The older man worked his cud of tobacco. He spat close to Henry's boot, squinting to calculate the effect. His eyes turned bright and sly, never leaving Henry's, "Mebbe they is."

He sidled closer to the wagon, suddenly snatching an ancient muzzle-loader from under the seat. He pointed it directly at Henry, "This here gun's double-loaded with buckshot. You wanna he'p, y'kin git off them horses an' carry the rest uh these jars inta the woods afore the sheriff comes along."

"No need for the gun, friend. Be glad to help. Sometimes, sheriffs can be a nuisance," Henry forced a laugh.

He and Ezekiel dismounted.

The moonshiner scratched his hairy belly, then his crotch. He shuffled closer, smelling of filth and evil.

Henry knew there would be no placating him.

He worked the tobacco into his cheek and spat brown juice again. He peered at the two travelers. For the first time he acknowledged Ezekiel's color, "You, you tomcattin' nigger, you a slave? You wanna run, run. Don't mean no anyways t'me."

Ezekiel answered slow and dignified, "No, sir, I am a free man and I do not want to run."

Tobacco-chewer half-turned to his son, "He ain't just any ol' black-stick. He a biggety nigger, too." He whirled, driving the butt of the heavy gun for Ezekiel's side. The blow would have broken ribs had not Ezekiel re-acted to deflect it.

Henry hit the musket, too, knocking it to the ground, attacking the man at once. Ezekiel rubbed his arm, thanking God it wasn't broken, and tangled with the son as he moved toward the sudden melee.

Henry and the moonshiner, separated, circling for an opening. When hairy-belly aimed a kick at tender parts, Henry caught his shoe and twisted, setting him in the dirt. Sprawled awkward in the roadway, he wiped his nose on a sleeve.

Henry eyed him closely, tried once more to calm him, "I have no quarrel with you. I want no trouble."

"Well, I do," the other screeched, "got no use for niggers ner anyone travellin' with 'em." Guardedly, he heaved to his feet, poised to renew the fight.

Henry tried a final time, "My offer to help you still stands. If you don't want it, we'll just be on our way."

"Summumabitch." His attack was as ungainly as his language.

Sidestepping, Henry smashed him full on the nose and snarled, "You ignorant bastard."

Blood spurted and Henry bore in. Clumsy-ass bear-hugged him and they fell to the ground. Henry struggled to break the iron hold, strained against it, knowing he was fighting for his life. The other squeezed and Henry fought to breathe. He gouged for an eye, missed, pushed a palm into the battered nose.

The punishing hand, finger nails dangerously close to the moonshiner's eyes raised a feral howl, but he held his death grip, squeezing, squeezing.

As Henry was fighting, Ezekiel sparred with the younger man, landing blows with his good right hand. Driven by the coarse epithets hurled at him, he called on lessons learned in Washington's streets.

Ezekiel broke him down bit by bit. Buried him in a fury of blows and epithets, "bastard, peckerwood, trash, puke, shit-face" and more. He beat him to the edge of consciousness until he staggered into the trees and disappeared. Ezekiel slumped in the roadway, his chest heaving, his bad arm throbbing.

Henry wriggled and strained for each tiny breath; gradually, he squirmed a forearm under the fat chin, into the sticky mess of warm blood. Working his other hand for leverage, he pushed the shaggy head back. Back, slowly back, more and a bit more. A final shove and the deadly bear-hug was broken. Panting, they jumped to their feet and glared across the inches that separated them, just the two of them, Henry and the man of many descriptions, all unsavory.

Shaggy-head backed gingerly for his musket there in the dirt locking his eyes on Henry's, toe-testing the ground behind him for each small step. Henry stalked him.

Moonshine backed until his foot touched the musket. For long moments, they stood wary, eyes locked, chests heaving, waiting, waiting for opportunity, seeking the tiniest edge. Neither blinked. Neither moved, except for pumping lungs.

Henry saw the degenerate eyes flick to the gun, sensed the intent, the villainy. He was ready for the lurch to retrieve it. Evil-eye's position made him vulnerable.

Henry's kick from behind was hard and true, sending him sprawling face first beyond the gun, into the broken glass. He yowled in pain, clawing at the shards in his face. Closer to his horse than to the moonshiner, Henry snatched at the saddle bag.

Both derringers were ready to fire, he knew, for he had cleaned and loaded them this morning. This morning! Years ago. Tearing at the oil rag wrapping, he cocked the hammer. The click filled the roadway like a long-barreled bird gun.

His opponent was crouched over the musket, one hand only inches away, the other still clawing at his tattered face. Hot eyes flashed cold hate as he took Henry's measure, calculating his next move. His glance dropped to the derringer in Henry's right hand. A derisive sneer twisted his mouth.

Henry warned him one more time, "I wouldn't go any farther, if I was you."

"You gonna stop me with that dofunny?"

Henry closed half the distance.

They stared, revulsion from one, derision from the other; bodies posed in the falling darkness, in the sour smell of sweat, the pungent scent of fear.

Ezekiel crouched, ready to spring.

"You and your goddamn nigger friend! Ha! And that li'l ole thing in yer hand. My pecker's bigger'n it.

"Here's a real gun."

He grabbed for the musket, turned to fire.

The derringer fired and smoked.

Henry saw the flame, smelled the acrid smoke of black powder. The moonshiner knelt in the road by his long musket, surprise on his face, a round hole under his left eyebrow. New blood flowed over old and dripped onto fingers raised for the last time. Where the bullet went in, an eyeball protruded. It fell to the ground.

He toppled onto his face, dust to dust, blood to dirt. Henry shivered from cold sweat. It could have been him.

The wagon with the broken wheel sat where it had sat, disabled, worthless, indifferent that its load had been lightened, no happier to be rid of its cruel master. Smashed jars glittered in the road. White mule soaked the ground dark.

"Dumb," Henry whispered, "dumb as secession. Stupid as war."

They stared at the crumpled body for long minutes, numb, knowing full well what happened, but not understanding.

"He's dead, Ezekiel," Henry spoke in a monotone, dull, out of character, "we'll have to find the sheriff."

The lack of emotion stirred Ezekiel. He came close, put a hand on Henry's shoulder, "Before you start lookin' for the sheriff I want you t'count to ten."

"Zeke, we have to find the sheriff."

"Not now." The words were an order, emphatic and final. Ezekiel Brown was the only man on earth who could talk to Henry Morrow in such a tone.

"Now," he continued in a gentler voice, "count to ten."

Henry obliged.

"Now breath deep. Five times." As he did, Ezekiel took a canteen from his saddle bag, "Drink."

Henry obeyed, as a small child would obey.

"Now we have to talk. Sens-ible."

"We have to find the sheriff."

"Sens-ible. We got to talk sens-ible. First, I know all about the law, man's law and God's law. . ."

"But. . ."

"But—nothin'. Man's law and God's Law says, Thou Shalt Not Kill. But another law says protect yourself."

"That's just what I did. The sheriff will see that and a jury will, too, if it comes to a trial. I have to report what I've done."

"Henry Morrow, y're a smart man, but there's times you make a man doubt it. Thirty, forty miles from home, and you still think you're in Winchester. We're in the mountains, Henry, with people we don't know. You're an outsider here, a nobody. I'm double nobody 'n they don't know my name or yours, not your family or reputation or mine. They don't know either of us for honest or crooked as a barrel of fish hooks.

"You just killed a man with family and friends all 'roun' here'bouts. A moonshiner at that. If his family and friends don't get you, th'other moonshiners will, figgerin' you for a revenooer. Anybody travellin' with a negro gotta be th'enemy, you heard how he talked."

"Zeke, stop your carrying' on. My duty is to find a sheriff."

"You ain't listenin', Henry. They don't give a shit for you. An' that don't begin to explain what they think of me."

"And one more thing, Henry. That young'un I near kilt will be tellin' tales that could get us both hung before mornin'. No judge. No trial. Nothing but a rope an' a horse whacked on the ass."

For the first time, Henry realized the killing involved both of them; furthermore that Ezekiel could well be subjected to more than a simple hanging. He gave in.

"I wasn't thinking clear, Zeke. You're right."

"You were thinkin' clear 'nuff for Winchester."

Once again, as he had seen so many times over the years, Henry Morrow saw his friend reduce a problem to its bare-bones, "Simple fact is we're not in Winchester."

They galloped north for their lives, thoughts of a good supper and bargains in a coach and horses replaced by the secret they would have to guard for as long as they lived.

Yes, for as long as he lived, Henry Morrow thought. But he was wrong.

II

WINCHESTER, VIRGINIA
NOVEMBER, 1860

In a foul mood, Henry Morrow stuffed his vote into the ballot box and headed home. The national split in the democratic party bothered him. The fight and killing on the Moorefield Road ate into his guts. Even the sidewalk with its uneven bricks irked him. He ate his supper in silence and left the table for the privacy of the front room, his office and sometime sanctuary. His behavior signaled to all that this was a door-slamming night: the louder the slam, the greater his displeasure with the world. To his credit, most evenings saw the front-room door left open, an invitation to all to share his good humor.

Henry Morrow was a proud man, proud of his accomplishments, his family, and not least of all, his Virginia heritage, even though he was born and raised in Washington, D.C. In the nation's capital and for the last 26 years in Winchester, the head of the Morrow family had lived rigorously by his personal creed: tell the truth, keep your word, pay what you owe.

Since last month's killing in Moorefield, Henry despaired, for even though he hadn't lied about it, he felt his silence less than honest, unworthy of himself. his wife, and children. He saw it as a taint on future Morrows and those gone by: on great grandfather Ephraim who trekked into the Shenandoah Valley when it was the western frontier, on grandfather Jedediah killed in the battle of Brandywine in '77, on his father, Jeremy who followed his star to Washington, D.C. All had ventured into the unknown, and Henry Morrow saw himself as the guardian of their proud heritage.

Henry was a large man, broad, muscular, barrel-chested from years of labor. By 1860, at age 61, he had thickened a tad about the middle, not paunchy but enough to extend his belt to the next notch. The extra girth wasn't really necessary, he had mumbled cantankerously to his pretty wife Sarah, only a bit more comfortable when he sat.

His hair was full, still thick and long, white and gray streaking the dark brown. Younger, it had been next door to black, the color of long-roasted coffee beans, almost burned. It had taken on the look of old sterling, confirming its dignity through the tarnish.

His eyes could flash fire or express sorrow, as dark as his hair had been, the same coffee-bean hue almost one with the pupils. His open face and broad hands suggested trust, one lined by the weather, the other square, calloused by years handling stone, brick, lumber, and rough, leather reins. A man of his word, he could be tough or generous as needs be.

When Henry puzzled a problem, a calloused hand massaged a sharp scritch-scratch across his chin. The more difficult the problem, the slower the rhythm as he rasped along the stiff stubble. To intrude provoked scowl lines between glowering eyebrows, and a selection from his notable collection of grunts.

Henry's normal behavior was one of brusque impatience, not surprising for an energetic man with much to do. Those close to him tolerated his sharpness for they knew his gentler side to be close to the surface.

He ruled his family with the same intensity he applied to himself, instilling his values, protecting his wife and daughters in a world that could be dangerous for women. His paternalism partook of the times, tuned to the notion that men worked outdoors while women's responsibilities were in the kitchen, the nursery, and the bedroom.

Yet, unlike many, his beliefs embraced not only love but a heart full of tenderness for his wife and children. Knowing she had a good man, Sarah could smile at his irascibility and stand up to him without fear.

On their first night together, she had discovered a gentleness to him that transformed her initial apprehension and inhibition into joyous abandon. Their exchange of gifts had produced five healthy, promising children. They lost Andrew, their youngest, before the war was a year old.

Ruth was the oldest, passionate as her parents. She lived just around the corner, trapped in a disappointing marriage to the son of a local banker; Sarah fretted the situation. Grace was the youngest at seventeen, sometimes called Racey. Her frivolity distressed her father despite Sarah's faith that she'd come around.

Both parents felt less anxiety with the boys. The oldest was David, a first-classman at the United States Military Academy; soldiering had been in his head and heart as a small boy. Brian, a year older than Racey, studied at Washington College in the upper Shenandoah Valley. Jed, twenty-three, 'born to farm' Ezekiel always said, would take over the family farmstead eight miles south of Winchester.

Ezekiel Brown, who ran the 150-acre farm with his wife, Mattie, and his mother, Mam, who lived in the Winchester house, completed the family. Ezekiel and Henry had been friends ever since they were toddlers in Washington. With pleasure did Henry Morrow reminisce those early days before Winchester, before the farm and Sarah.

He had met her in 1835 when he held a door into the dining room of Taylor's Hotel. She smiled her thanks. He was taken at once with her natural beauty, eyes brown as his own, perky nose, full lips, and a smile that said work alone was an incomplete life. An unassuming innocence lent grace to her eye-catching curves. She felt the attraction, too, accepting him within the year. He purchased the farm for their first home.

Of native limestone, the house looked blue on cloudy days and reflected flecks of silver in the sunshine. A guest house, where Ezekiel and Mattie lived, was of the same stone.

The big house faced east, well off the center of the property, favoring the eastern and northern boundaries. Two and a half stories high, it had fourteen rooms, four unadorned Doric columns between verandah and roof extension. A balustraded balcony divided the columns, marking the second floor with its six bedrooms and wide, airy center hall

Sarah loved her new home, especially the wide verandah that looked south over a gently sloping carpet of cut timothy. Maple trees, dogwoods, and redbuds flourished at the field's edge and in a picturesque copse in the center. Beyond, purled Opequon Creek, fresh from the mountains, lined with willows; beyond it, the unfinished Valley Turnpike. Henry's wagons had hauled much of the stone for the newfangled surface. Oak and chestnut trees and an apple orchard stood toward the mountains.

By 1840, they had three children, Ruth, David, and Jed; the Valley Turnpike was completed; and Henry had established himself as owner of the Shenandoah Stage Company. He celebrated the completion of the Valley Turnpike Company job by inviting his six drivers to dinner and tankards of beer at the Red Lion Inn.

"You can continue working for me without losing a day's pay. The wagons and tack need working on. By then I'll have loads to haul, or my name isn't Henry Morrow." He made no mention of his plans for a stagecoach line.

In 1848, the Morrows moved to the large, brick house in Winchester with all its conveniences, shops, first-rate schools and the stage terminal. Ezekiel and Mattie remained at the farm, running its orchards, fields, and livestock. Sarah and Henry had insisted they live in the big house, but to no avail.

"What'd we do in that big place!" Mattie sniffed, "this jus' suits us fine. Big enough an' cool in summer, warm in winter.

"An' Ezekiel," she said coyly, "don't have ta chase me too far when we feel like leggin' down t'gether."

The Morrows and the Browns had a dozen productive years, happy and peaceful until a presidential election changed it all.

Henry watched with increasing anxiety as election day approached.

The rhetoric had a new harshness, and Winchester was dividing as the country was dividing. Crossroads of the lower Shenandoah Valley, Winchester was practically a border town, closer to Washington, Baltimore, even Harrisburg in Pennsylvania than to Richmond. Many of its settlers had come from across the Potomac, from Maryland and Pennsylvania and further north. Substantial family lines and business connections to the north still existed.

Casting his ballot on November 6, Henry Morrow thought again of the trip to Moorefield, not only the killing but the talk with Ezekiel about the split in the Democratic party and Lincoln's election. Feeling none of the gaiety of previous elections, he grumped as he had before, "Democrats are torn apart. There's trouble ahead, serious trouble."

He and Sarah waited for the election results in John Linn's tavern bordering Courthouse Square. She drew attention, along with envy of her husband's good fortune.

By midnight, the news was in, "Lincoln wins 180 electoral votes to 123 split by four democrats. Gets less than forty percent of popular vote." The first Republican President!

"I'm worried, Sarah. The South won't stand still. There's already talk of secession."

"We've heard that kind of talk before and worked it out. We'll work it out again."

"I hope so but it's different this time. The talk is meaner, fighting mean."

Sarah took his arm, pressed close to him as they turned off Loudoun Street onto Wolfe, "It will work out, dear."

"Our boys will catch the brunt of it, that's what worries me. Our boys and the stage line."

Henry held the wrought iron gate for her.

Turning on the brick walk, Sarah touched his face lovingly. Dark eyes sparkled, her long, chestnut hair flowed as she stood on tiptoes for a quick kiss, "I'll make us a hot toddy and then we'll go to bed."

"Damn fools," Henry muttered, "better they put their differences aside and turn to building the country again."

Then he caught her invitation.

He took her arm. And smiled.

III

DISSENSION AT WEST POINT
NOVEMBER, 1860

As Henry and Sarah Morrow in Winchester and citizens across the country waited anxiously for the election results on November 6, so too did the cadets at the United States Military Academy. High above the Hudson, they ignored the melancholy bugle triplets of Taps, and filled the Plain with their cheers and catcalls.

A broad-shouldered cadet, an inch over six feet tall, led a group of Southern cadets to an ancient elm tree outside the barracks. In the darkness, his resonant voice rang, his shadow body moved with vibrant grace and agility; only these were evident, not his chestnut hair, dark brown eyes, generous mouth, strong jaw, or sculpted cheeks of the Morrows, not the elfish grin or tanned face or thin nose with the slight flare.

"String him up here," ordered David Morrow, and they hanged an effigy of the president-elect.

Cadets from the North cut the grotesque figure down. Tensions crackled, but the cadets averted the vitriol of abolitionists and fire-eaters across the land.

South Carolina's reaction to Lincoln's election was immediate: on the day after the election, a defiant Palmetto flag was raised in Charleston; the following day, the *Charleston Mercury* read, "The tea has been thrown overboard, the revolution of 1860 has been initiated": two days after that the legislature called for a secession commission.

On December 20, the commission threw the gauntlet, breaking the Union asunder:

> "We the People of the State of South Carolina . . . do declare and ordain
> . . . that the union now subsisting between South Carolina and other

States, under the name of 'The United States of America' is hereby dissolved."

At West Point, David Morrow castigated Lame Duck President Buchanan for his inaction, "The hotheads are taking over. He needs to get off his fat ass and find a compromise." James Buchanan wasn't hearing David Morrow.

The next two months saw the demise of compromise: five states joined South Carolina, seizing federal properties; Southern congressmen resigned; the germinal confederacy adopted a constitution; Jeff Davis became provisional president; and Charleston fire-eaters threatened Fort Sumter.

In March, Lincoln took the Presidential oath. Within the hour, he filled the Buchanan void.

"I hold . . . the Union of these States is perpetual . . . It follows from these views that no State . . . can lawfully get out of the Union . . . I therefore consider . . . the Union . . . unbroken."

In Winchester, Henry Morrow steamed, "What the hell's Lincoln going to do, Call out the army?"

Back at West Point, David Morrow had no question, "He's drawn a line in the dirt. He's ready to fight."

Henry recognized serious trouble, but missed its vast scope as his son did not. Associating with cadets loyal and disloyal to Lincoln and the Union, David heard opinions from Maine's pine forests to Florida, Michigan, and the Texas plains.

From Nat Turner's Rebellion in '31 to *Uncle Tom's Cabin* he heard the prejudices, repeated and reiterated, lily-white truths for the tellers, soot-black hyperbole for the listeners. Lost in the shouting were the loyal blacks in Turner's Rebellion and the compassionate whites in *Cabin*.

One month into Lincoln's presidency, Cadet David Morrow looked furtively over his shoulder and slipped through the side door of Benny Havens' tavern. He squinted through tobacco smoke layered in the flickering light of oil lamps. Finally he spied his friends at an obscure table near the door to the kitchen, a quick exit should a patrol come snooping.

Benny Havens was his own man, shrewd, independent, suspicious of authority of any sort. Snow-white hair lent a disarming dignity that left one unprepared for his quick temper, profanity, and sharp wit. A beak of a nose fit his personality; sleepy eyes did not. Siding with the cadets and all others badgered by officialdom, he had fought the civil authorities and the fancy officers on the hill for forty years to serve the locals, and the ill-fed, thirsty, restricted cadets.

Stealthy night–figures raised stories of illegal booze and rentable women, but neither the town of Buttermilk Falls nor the Military Academy had been able to shut him down. The Academy did declare his ordinary "off limits."

Benny came to the table as David sat down, "Evenin', sir. Hot rum flip to chase the chill? First one's on me tonight."

"Sounds good, Benny. I thank you," David laughed, "and the United States Army thanks you."

David sniffed toward the kitchen, "Smell hot biscuits, Benny, but there's something else. Peppery. Spicy."

"Eldest daughter's stewed chicken. From supper servin'."

Knowing the mess hall's poor food and young appetites, Benny added with a twinkle in his eyes, "If y're hungry."

He headed for the bar, knowing the answer would catch up.

"Great, Benny!! I could eat double."

The innkeeper acknowledged with a lazy wave.

Texan Tom Rosser set the trap, "You're late. We thought you had trouble with the guard."

The eldest of Henry Morrow's sons smiled a greeting around the table, "As a matter of fact, I was challenged. Damn, if I ever heard such strange talk from a sentry! I froze in the shadows."

The group roared laughter.

George Custer, known to the cadets as "Fanny," raised his pewter tankard, his blue eyes sparkling. Fun lover and practical joker, he pitched his voice high in a dialect of his own.

"Ah dew mean it, Mista, halt yo' beeg feet wheah they is."

"Custer, it was you! Why, you skunk!"

Custer laughed, "Just got here myself."

"You're all skunks," David laughed with the rest of them, "You all were in on it."

"Benny," he signaled, "need another round."

He turned to Rosser, "Tom, you realize we-all may never be together again?"

The others quieted, for David had won their respect.

"For a hundred years," he continued, "the North and South have been building a country. My Pa says stop the damn shouting and get to building again."

All but Rosser nodded agreement. His quick temper flared, "Except they won't let us be, screaming about slavery, yapping how sinful we are, how the North is doing God's work."

Another cadet spoke up, "Tom, Lincoln only wants to keep the Union together. He doesn't care a dead fish tail for slavery, one way or the other. He said as much in the campaign."

David broke in, intending to be calm, but emotion took over.

"We know the negroes as individuals, respecting some, disliking others. Yankees love them all and don't really know one of them. I played with them growing up. We worked side by side. I had a black Mammy I loved like a mother. Still do. Outsiders don't see that side of things, only what they want."

He raced on, steel in his voice, "People like Garrison and Stowe hate the South. They insult Virginia, my family, and they insult me." David slammed his pewter cup to the table.

Nearby tables looked up to see what the ruckus was.

Custer broke in, "Dave, no need to get hot."

"Yes, I am hot, goddamn it. My grandfather had slaves, and treated them right. Didn't sell them. Never beat one. He took care of them when they were sick, gave them a place to live, food to eat when they were too old to work. And a Christian burial when they died."

He paused, but for only a moment, "He bought two from their black owner and manumitted them. My father did the same."

"Dave, we all know. . ."

"Not from that vile book you don't know, and that trash newspaper! I don't like being painted with the sins of some renegade overseer who should be strung up."

A rough voice boomed from across the tavern, "Maybe we oughta string up a loud-mouth soldier boy."

"You tell 'em, Bull."

Big Tom Rosser, six feet two inches tall, 240 solid pounds, jumped up, shaking his fist, "That's what the country needs. Advice from shitasses like you."

The one called Bull, flabby-big but still imposing, made for the brawny Rosser. Men were standing now, the tavern close to flash point. The North/South argument had exploded again, just as it had uncounted times in the countryside around.

Benny Havens rapped on the bar, "Gentlemen," speaking evenly, authoritatively, "I suggest you mind your own tables. You want to fight?" He surveyed the room for affect, "go outside."

Bull stopped in his tracks.

Rosser taunted him, "Come on shitass, outside."

For a full minute, Benny scowled around the room, pausing to lock eyes with the one called Bull until he wavered and returned to his table.

"Anyone have a question?" Benny eyed his silent domain.

Gradually, the tavern resumed its conversational buzz.

Custer spoke up, hoping to soothe his friend, "I'm a Yankee, Dave. I believe like my father. I come down on the side of democrats and state-righters. I think negroes. . ."

"You're damn right, Fanny," David interrupted angrily, "and that scurrilous newspaper and book say you're wrong to think that way. They'd have you believe all states-righters, democrats, slave owners, and Southerners consort with the devil."

Custer grinned impishly, "Damn! that's what's niggled at me so long. Dave Morrow, you are in cahoots with the devil."

Perturbed as he was, David missed the intended humor, "What the hell's that supposed to mean?"

"It means," Fanny Custer pointed a crooked witch-finger, "that you, David Morrow, are a friend to the devil. You have friends not in high places, but in low."

The cadets, including David, roared at Custer's antics. He bowed theatrically, became serious again.

"As I was saying, the negroes need to be slaves because they can't take care of themselves. My Pa believes that, and so do I."

David chuckled humorlessly, "You from Ohio, talking like that? I think more of them than that and I'm from Virginia."

Custer looked up quickly, "Don't get me wrong. I'll honor my cadet's oath. It's as simple as that."

David's bitterness erupted again, "Oath be damned. I swore the same as you, but their actions nullify it. No black Republican is going to set me against my family and Virginia."

The tavern clock bonged midnight.

David caught Benny Havens' attention, waved around the table for a final round. They toasted their friendship solemnly.

Leaving by the front door, they returned to the barracks pensively for they sensed a parting of the ways, farewells to good friends and the end of revelries at Benny Havens. They walked together, yet, in their heartache, they walked alone.

At half past four that very morning, the bombardment of Fort Sumter flooded West Point with talk of war, David, Rosser and Pelham were ready to leave at once. Others prevailed on them to delay, "Maybe it will go no further."

Rosser's quick temper flared, "The hell it won't! Too many have careers at stake to stop now. They don't care horsecrap for anything else." He jumped from his chair to tramp the room one side to the other, his swarthy skin showing anger, "I've spent five years of my life here. All for nothing, damn it.

"Shit!" his voice rose, "just plain shit."

"I'm with you," echoed Pelham as angry as his friend but more in control, "my fondest dream was to be an officer in the army. Now they're about to tell me to fight my own people."

David hurt, too, "My great grandfather fought with General Washington. I grew up on stories of him, stories of his father, Ephraim, fighting Indians in the Shenandoah Valley. They risked their lives for freedom. I'll do the same."

Rosser halted his pacing, "My grandfather fought in The Revolution, too. He lost an arm at Guilford Courthouse. Our families already fought to live free. Now we have to fight the same goddamn battle."

Pelham cut in softly because he was a gentler man than either of his friends, "It does seem we are being cut out to do it all over again. Like we're fighting the second Revolution."

"One thing's sure," David closed the discussion, "nothing will change for all we talk." He smiled wanly, "Like Napoleon observed at Waterloo, 'its time to go home'."

The three penned resignations. On April 22 they left their friends and the long gray line. Sad handshakes, back-thwacking hugs and manly tears marked their leaving.

"I'll miss you, Fanny. And the times at Benny's."

"Dave, I'll miss you, and your help in the ring. I thought I was a good horseman but you showed me things I never knew."

"We shouldn't be fighting one another."

Tears filled Custer's eyes. "That's so. We shouldn't."

To hide his own emotion, Rosser turned away.

The three descended the hill, boarded the side-wheeler for the trip down river. They slumped to a wooden bench on deck.

Halfheartedly, David drifted to the rail. He clutched at it, stared downstream, "Damn, damn. . ."

He cursed no single discontent, but a combination of personal and national issues. Mixed in, from deep inside, was a vague uneasiness at forsaking his cadet oath.

Pelham joined him, ramrod straight from years of training, "Going home to our own kind is a good thing. There's no way we could have stayed.

"Dave, I'm going to introduce you to the prettiest little bundle you ever saw. My cousin'll take your breath away."

Looking over his shoulder, he called his ex-roommate, "Tom, come over here. You are going to meet my cousin, too. She has eyes blue as an Alabama sky, and hair like the silk of new corn shining in the morning sun.

"Stop your moping, Tom. We all are going home!"

Thus, the effervescent John Pelham, the handsome, boyish John Pelham who young ladies found irresistible, helped his friends out of the doldrums.

In New York, they bought a copy of the *New York World* hawked by an urchin warbling the singsong call of all newsboys, "REBELS INVADE NORRR-FORK." Scanning columns under black headlines of ENEMY, TRAITORS, HANG JEFF DAVIS, they realized the depth of the hostility pervading the country.

David broached the subject on the southbound train, "We need to be careful. Let's face it, we're in enemy territory!"

"Dave, I agree. There's a heap of high-temper out there."

In Philadelphia, another newspaper rekindled their anxiety: a Lieutenant Walter Jennifer was clamped in irons by Governor Curtin for resigning from the army to join the Confederacy.

They caught the first train south, a freight.

"From Baltimore to Harper's Ferry. We can join up there," David suggested, "it's only twenty-five miles to Winchester."

With a smile to Pelham he added, "I can show you some pretty cousins, too. Sociable Virginians."

"Montgomery's the place to go. The capital and quickest place to get an appointment," said Rosser the practical one.

"Tom's right, Dave, the capital is the best place to go."

"You may be right, but for me it's Virginia. That's where the fighting will be. Besides, Winchester's only six hours."

"But first is to get an appointment," Pelham offered, "and to meet my blue-eyed cousin you have to go where she is."

"Right," Rosser agreed, "first thing is to get appointed the highest rank we can. In Montgomery, they could make us captains. Three bars are better than two—or one."

David Morrow stretched out his hand, "I guess it's goodbye then, at least for now.

"The years at the Point were good ones. The best part was that I met you two. If this turns into a real war, I hope we get a chance to fight together."

"I, too, Dave. It has been a real honor to count you a friend." Unexpectedly, Pelham snapped to attention and saluted. Never before had he saluted with tears of sadness.

"Tell that pretty cousin my heart belongs to her already."

David turned to Rosser, extending his hand, "Tom, I hope you get those three bars. I'm not saying goodbye to either of you, because I know we'll be together again.

"Like the three musketeers," he laughed, and walked into the station house to wait for the Harper Ferry cars.

IV

ARGUMENT AT WINCHESTER
MAY, 1861

"Damn it t'hell," Jed pitched redolent horse manure into the wagon, "he won't listen t'me any more'n a forkful of shit."

Muscles glistened as he worked the pile down, arms, legs, and shoulders, all in sweaty harmony with the job.

Jed Morrow was a strapping man, six feet tall plus a couple of inches, 220 pounds, broad-shouldered, thick through the chest. He was built for the outdoors, the open spaces of plowed fields and hunting grounds, for the heights of Little North Mountain and the Alleghenies, for forests and sky and free-flowing streams. He was a child of them all, with his generous smile, his father's square farmer's hands, permanent crow's feet and bronzed skin. Irrepressible eyes of brown and full hair of darker brown, as his father's at age twenty-three, cried out for the freedom of the wind.

Pitching manure was not his favorite job, but neither was it the worst. As a youngster, he had learned from Ezekiel that you don't fight physical work; you break it into parts and learn its rhythms. "Work smart," Ezekiel had taught, and Jed Morrow had listened and learned to use his body with ease, without apparent effort. He seemed slow—until one matched his effort and soon found himself exhausted. Jed could work the day long, with pleasure in place of tedium. Today, however, there was no joy.

"Damnit, Pa, why won't you listen t'me? It's not that I'd never come back." He jabbed his pitchfork into the pile.

"Jed, dinner's ready." Sarah's call went unanswered.

Louder this time, "You hear me, Jed, dinner's on the table."

"Yes, Ma."

As it had for several days, the stalemate between Jed and his father killed the customary dinner conversation, giving Sarah hope they could finish without another slam-bang row. Grace stole glances, one to the other as she ate, waiting for an argument—like yesterday when Ma had gotten into it. It was not often she could listen to Ma and Pa quarrel.

"Pa, I wish you'd. . ."

"Jedediah, I told you. No more of this at the dinner table. Go along t'my office and we'll finish it once and for all."

Sarah glared at them, ignoring her unfinished plate, reached for dirty dishes and silver, piling them with a clatter. She never stacked her good dishes like that. Still out of character, she snapped at her daughter, "Grace, help me clear," and without controlling her exasperation informed the two men, "The pie will be on the kitchen table."

She pushed from the table, reached with both hands to the piled plates, askew with the remains of dinner. She paused at the kitchen door and turned. All she saw was the top of Henry's head.

Legs hidden by the mahogany table, he was lifting from his armed chair, not in it, not quite out of it. Seldom did she see him so off balance and, it occurred to her, so defenseless. In spite of her irritation, she smiled at the thought of pushing him back into his chair and saying, "Relax, dear, it's not the end of the world."

Instead, she spoke across the table, "Now, Henry, you listen to him. He's a grown man, with his own ideas."

Henry shoved roughly from the table, "He may be, but sometimes he doesn't act his years."

Jed scowled and crossed the room with his plowman's strides.

Grace stood watching and listening.

"Grace, get on with your clearing. Then wash your hands, and use the brush on your teeth."

"Yes, Ma." Reluctantly, she went about her chores.

"Now, Henry, I know how you feel, but you have to realize Jed is old enough to go where and do what he pleases. He's. . ."

Henry cut in, "He's still got responsibilities here."

In his father's office at the front of the house, Jed stared vacantly through the wavy glass. Had he been interested he could have seen through the budding leaves to Loudoun Street, or Main as some oldtimers still called it.

He wondered if there was anything at all he could say to convince Pa. Ma understood, even though she didn't agree, but Pa, he just held to his own opinion, hell or high water.

Just like great gran'daddy Ephraim, he thought, who had run his string out a century ago. Jed's fingers worked involuntarily as he waited.

Henry stormed into the room, attacking the cherrywood door. Its crash reverberated through the house, delaying him a critical moment. He had wanted the first word to set the tone.

"Pa, I've told you how I feel and I hope for your blessin'."

Henry rumbled ahead as though Jed had said nothing, "Jed, we talked enough. You aren't going and that's that."

"But, Pa, I told you. I'm suffocatin' here."

"I don't want you here. I want you down the road, on the farm. You know the plan t'clear more acres and expand the herd. Ezekiel can't do that by himself. He needs you t'help. You leave and our plan is shot t'hell."

"Pa, this war changes all that. Everybody. . ."

Henry shouted, "You're vexin' me, boy. I don't want t'hear anythin' more about this ruction. Dammit, it's all I've heard. War this, war that. It fills the courthouse, the street and John Linn's Tavern," he pounded his desk, "and by God I won't listen to it in my own house."

"Pa, I have t'get out of Winchester. I need. . ."

"Don't tell me what you need, boy. I need you right here. We already have two soldiers, one too many by my calculation. Your brother David is the only one who belongs in the army. When he left for that military school up there on the Hudson River, we were happy.

"That's what I mean. I. . ."

"Don't interrupt, Jedediah. I'm not close t'finished. David was gone for a soldier, but now Brian is in the army, too. This letter came," He assailed papers on the desk.

"Your brother joined up in Lexington. They call themselves the Liberty Hill—Liberty Hall—whatever the damn name is—Volunteers. My smartest son, a year from graduating from Washington College. Enlisting, for God's sake!"

Jed took a deep breath. He'd give it one more shot, "Pa I know you been upset, but you've got t'sit still just once and listen. You've lived in Washington and seen somethin' of the world. I want the same thing. I want t'see Washington and Philadelphia where Gran'daddy lived, and New York. I want t'join the army and see somethin' of the country. Maybe the ocean and sailin' ships, see what's across the ocean."

"ACROSS THE OCEAN!"

"Yes, Pa, across the ocean. And when I do I'll be back t'work with Ezekiel, but that's what I want first. T'see the world, just like my gran'daddies. Ephraim had his chance comin' t'the Valley. Old Jedediah followed George Washin'ton. Your daddy left Philadelphia and you left Washin'ton. You—all had your chance and now I want mine. And I guess that's all I have t'say."

Henry Morrow's brow wrinkled, his eyes narrowed. He looked ready to explode, "Well now, I guess you've had your say and I listened. Now you listen t'me. You say you want your chance, and I say your chance is right here. You want t'run off on some damned wild goose chase and you don't even know what you want. Talking about joining the army one minute and sailing ships the next. Jedediah, you may have been born twenty-three years ago, but I'm telling you here and now that you're not that old. You are thinking like a child all steamed up over a picture book."

Henry was almost shouting, "All I can tell you is t'grow up and forget this childish nonsense. You think the sail ships are all sunshine and adventure, but I'm telling you they're nothing but hard work and danger. With disease, bad food and bad water. I knew them on the Potomac. I knew the sailors. And this war your brother Brian thinks is so important?

"It's nothing but the doing of greedy politicians from the North and narrow minded politicians from the South. One's as damn bad as the other. So you forget enlisting in the army. It's mostly white trash and fornicators who don't care if they get their ass shot off. Jedediah Morrow, I won't have you with them.

"I'm telling you one last time, your place is on the farm."

The tirade was too much for Jed. "Goddamn it, Pa, I knew you wouldn't listen. You never have. You never will. I want your blessin' but I'll leave without it if I have to. I'm tellin' you one last time."

Sarah pushed through the door, "What is it with you two. I can hear the shouting all the way to the kitchen, shouting and vile language such as I've never heard in this house."

"Sarah, maybe you can talk some sense into your son."

"Ma, maybe you can tell him t'shut up one time and listen."

"Jedediah, don't talk disrespectfully to your father. I don't understand either one of you."

"Ma, I—I—I'm sorry." Jed kissed her on the cheek, glaring at his father, turned on his heel. If you can slam the door, he thought, so can I. Again it echoed through the house.

Glowering at a spot on the rug, Henry clenched his teeth.

"Henry, my mother used to say if you grasped too tightly on anything you would lose it."

Turning to leave, she reached for the door latch, had a second thought, turned back, "If the war is driving this family apart what in the world will it do to the country?"

Henry Morrow sat lonely in his front-room office trying to hold to a time when sweat and hard work solved problems. He never in his life was so tired, of Jed's arguments over and over, of Brian's enlisting, of the talk of war, war, war.

Friends had become problems, too, for Winchester was divided, and the whole Shenandoah Valley, North and South, arguing about who was right. How the hell can God be on both sides? Henry wondered.

"Dammit!" he growled to himself, "I don't care what side you're on. Valley people have always been divided, but never like this. In December, everybody talked about South Carolina seceeding from the Union, arguing if Virginia should do the same. Now all I hear is fight 'em if that's what they want, no mind which side they're on. Nothing but war. God, I'd like t' hear some crop talk or weather talk. Somebody talking about horses or the stage coach business or even who's messing with who's wife."

V

LEXINGTON, VIRGINIA
MAY, 1861

Toward the middle of May, Brian Morrow signed the muster and was sworn into the Liberty Hall Volunteers, a company of Washington College students and graduates in Lexington.

The youngest of the Morrows' sons, Brian had the family eyes and hair, dark brown. Unlike his brothers he was less than six feet tall, two inches less, and weighed some sixty pounds less than Jed. He was well-proportioned with good shoulders, narrow waist, coordinated and graceful in his actions. Brian was the scholar, more the deep thinker than his brothers, less the doer.

Early on the morning of June 8, The Liberty Hall Volunteers formed precise lines for muster and inspection. Liberty Hall was the original name of Washington College when it opened in 1749,

White gaiters and white crossbelts with brass buckles set off gray, woolen uniforms sewn by local ladies. Caps were adorned in front with intertwined brass initials, LHV; in back with white havelocks all precisely aligned. A slight breeze lifted the havelocks, rolling them like an ocean wave down the line. A virginal battle flag rippled lazily. The same intertwined LHV adorned the stocks of shouldered muskets. James White, scholar, respected professor of Latin and classics, served as captain.

At the courthouse, citizens of Lexington oohed and ahhhed at their sudden soldiers, applauded patriotic speeches, bowed heads as Captain White's father, The Reverend Dr. invoked God's blessing. Mothers patted tears, and the Liberty Hall Volunteers were off to muster into the Army of Virginia.

Private Brian Morrow and his friend, Lieutenant John Lyle, climbed aboard one of the stage coaches hired to carry the company to Staunton, the first leg of their journey to Harper's Ferry. Brian had studied the maps.

"Too bad the railroad doesn't go straight down the Valley," he said, "we'd have only 150 miles instead of 300. What a waste of time, crossing the Blue Ridge twice, east, then back west."

In Staunton at 10 o'clock that evening, they slept on the floor of the freight depot.

Their first breakfast on the road was bread and coffee. Brian's friend, Lieutenant Lyle, wrote of the bread in his journal, ". . . India rubber. It could be stretched into ropes and pressed into balls."

They lingered three days in Staunton, regaled with all sorts of treats recorded by Brian: "baked wheat bread, coffee, beef, fresh strawberries, pies. Cake served by the townspeople and their daughters . . . Prettiest girls I ever saw. We were sorry to leave."

Sorry, indeed, as they crowded into the boxcars. All night long, they squirmed and shuffled for space in the rattly cars.

"Your musket's in my face."

"I'll move it if you take your feet off my stomach."

"Damn I'm hungry."

"Be quiet, for God sakes."

They chugged up the grade of Rockfish Gap in the Blue Ridge and careened down the eastern slope. Queasy in the swaying car, Brian vomited.

Too close to him, Ted Barclay cursed, "Damn! You and the guy that's been farting all night oughta ride on the roof."

Brian had no interest in Charlottesville as they went through. They stopped in Gordonsville, where he found a stream and a rock to beat the vomit out of his shirt and trousers. Fresh air helped. He felt better as they pulled into Manassas Junction.

Boarding a third train, they puffed westerly now through the Piedmont and the Bull Run Mountains, up the Blue Ridge again. Hurtling precariously into The Valley, they clanked past Front Royal, across the Shenandoah's South Fork, along the narrow corridor at the base of Massanutten Mountain into Strasburg.

The final leg was in farm wagons down the Valley Pike, the road Henry Morrow built twenty years ago. When they passed the area of the Morrow farm, Brian shouted excitedly, "There it is. The farm where I grew up! Over there, beyond the trees."

A voice boomed from across the wagon, "You just call it the farm? Doesn't it have a name?"

"No. Guess Pa never thought of it."

"No name! Where Ah'm from, ever'thin's got a name. Dawgs, plantations, even trees—'spesh'ly the plantations."

Shouts filled the air, "What'll we name it?"

Yells came from wagons ahead and behind, "What's the excitement?"

"We're naming Brian's farm," they shouted back.

A cacophony of names erupted, "Magnolia. Confederate Acres. Mary Anna," the last for a friend made in Staunton.

"Sweetwater."

"Liberty Hall," cried another.

A chorus spread up and down the wagon line, "Yeah, Liberty Hall. That's it, Liberty Hall. LIBERTY HALL."

Brian balanced uncertainly in the jolting wagon, "Liberty Hall it is then, for our college and the army's best company!"

"Three cheers for Liberty Hall and Washington College!"

Hoorahs rang up and down the turnpike. The Morrow farm had a name, whether Henry Morrow liked it or not.

At the outskirts of Winchester, the young soldiers cleaned shoes and muskets in the late afternoon sun, straightened havelocks, gaiters, belts, and marched proudly into town.

Many waved at cheering citizens who lined the road, and grinned all the way to the fairgrounds where they camped. The date was June 13, five days to go 300 roundabout miles.

"Captain White, request permission to leave for the night. I haven't seen my family since the Christmas holidays, sir."

The fatherly commander knew Brian well, for three years his professor, friend, counselor, and father figure.

"Permission granted, Brian. Be back for morning muster."

Brian saluted, "Thank you, sir."

The captain's orderly called, "Visitor, sir. Name's Morrow."

Elated that Pa had come, Brian saluted again and was gone.

Standing erect outside the tent, he scarcely had time to look around when a whack on his back sent him reeling.

"Briney, I been lookin' all around this camp for you."

Inches taller, pounds heavier, Jed blanketed his brother in muscled arms and his farmer hands. They pounded each other on shoulders and backs.

"Jed, Jed, it's so good to see you. I thought maybe you'd be in the army. How's Ma, Pa, Ruth, Racey. Everybody? What about David? And you? Captain White gave me a pass. Did. . . ?"

"Whoa there little brother. One thing at a time. All the folks are fine." He stooped to retrieve Brian's cap that he had knocked to the ground. Bashfully, he handed it back.

"Guess I got carried away."

"Where's Pa?" disappointment shadowing the happy reunion, "let's get started. I'm so anxious to see everybody."

They turned down the company street, one heavily muscled, broad of torso, with dark brown, unruly hair and thick eyebrows; the other, slighter, lithe. Jed trudged, as though plodding through newly turned soil; Brian walked with a spring, graceful and light. His dark hair had a soft wave in front. Jed was the Percheron, Brian the racehorse.

As the two brothers neared Winchester town, Jed threw an arm around Brian's shoulders and drew him closer. From an erect, soldiery stride, Brian's gait became an unbalanced combination of hop on one foot, limp on the other, halfway up Loudoun Street.

Two blocks before Wolfe Street and the Morrow house, Jed stopped.

"Briney, let's stop at John Linn's. I'll buy."

"All right, but just one. I am anxious to see Pa."

Once inside, they drew benches up to a trestle table polished smooth by a half century of use. A very attractive server bubbled to their table, John Linn's niece, Betsy.

While many men had mistaken Jed's perseverance and stamina for dullness, Betsy had been more discerning. She saw at once his intelligence, sensitivity, and latent gentleness that encompassed nature and all living things.

"Hello, Jed," she cooed, "beer?"

"Evenin', Betsy, this here's my brother. He wants one, too." He patted her lightly on the backside as she turned.

"Jed Morrow, you keep your hands to yourself," she flirted boldly, "a body'd think it was Saturday night."

She flashed a smile that added, "And we were alone."

He smiled back, thinking of a night not so long ago.

Lying side by side under the stars on that crystal clear night, he had shared with her his fondest fantasies of sailing a golden ship with snow-white sails, of living the rest of his life with her. He had pointed to Polaris, the North Star.

"Take my hand, Star Queen, and we'll fly to it."

He had reached for her. Engrossed in his childlike suggestion, she had taken his calloused hand in her own. They lay there, touching only fingers until Polaris faded in the dawning sky.

He raised his tankard to clunk Brian's and drank heartily.

"Pa thinks it'll be a long war, Briney. You think so?"

"Most would disagree. Folks in Lexington see a quick end to it. Same in Staunton. Didn't talk to anyone in Gordonsville," he added with a memory of vomit and sour clothes.

"But what do you think?"

"Me? I'm not sure. No one really knows a thing like that."

Jed caught Betsy's glance, raised two fingers.

"Except for one thing, England and France joining us. Already Northerners are saying, 'Let the South go its own way'.

"Mr. Lincoln can't stand opposition from his own people, England and France, too. I'd say a short war if we get help from them, a long one if we don't."

He drained his first tankard, "Now tell me all the news. How is everything at home, at the farm? We named it Liberty Hall when we went by." He reached for the pewter tankard, "Start with yourself. I take it you haven't enlisted yet?"

Preoccupied with Brian's observations, Jed didn't hear the question. Pa talked of a long war, too. Enlisting in the army to get out of Winchester might not be such a good idea after all.

"Ought to think on it more," he thought half aloud

"What did you say, Jed?"

"Just tryin' t'figger somethin'," he countered the question. "All this talkin' and listenin' is dryin' my throat. I need a brew. You want one?"

"All right, but what are you trying to figure?"

"Briney, I'm thinkin' on enlistin'."

"That's great, maybe we can be. . ."

"But it isn't," Jed cut in quickly, "that's the problem. Pa is madder than hell about it. Just keep workin', he says, t'improve the farm. Build it bigger.

"Briney, I got this dream t'see things. Enlist. Maybe get a job on one of those big sailships."

"I'll be! I thought you'd be a farmer forever. You been learning that from the time you were little."

"Pa thinks so too. He's madder than a tree'd 'possum. All he can do is yell when I try t'talk to him. Won't even listen."

"Maybe I can talk to him. He'll listen to me."

"I don't think so. He's mad with you too."

"With me! What in the world for? He's proud to have me going to college. You sure he's mad?"

"I'm sure, Briney. He's mad with me for wantin' t'leave home And he's mad with you for joinin' the army."

Jed called for two more brews.

"For joining the army! Not Pa, Jed! He can't be angry with me for that! Why, he used to tell us stories, about granddaddy fighting with General Washington. He was so proud of him fighting for what was right.

"This time it's our own people telling us how to live. That's not right, Jed, and I enlisted to stop it. Why is Pa angry with me? It's the same thing.

"I thought he'd be proud of me," Brian ended solemnly.

The two sat silent, staring into their beer, taking long quaffs. Jed repeated his signal to Betsy. When she brought full tankards, she began a small flirtation, "Jed, maybe we could. . ."

Seeing their changed mood, she thought better of it. She served her next few tables in silence, not at all like her.

"And there's still more, Briney. You and me aren't the only ones Pa's mad with. He's been shoutin' at Racey, too."

"At Racey? You serious? If Pa had any favorite, it was his li'l—his little girl Ger—Gracey." Brian felt a fuzziness in his head and lost his train of thought.

"An' I 'member the day when—Jed, who b-broos this stuff? It's stronger'n what I've had in Lexington."

Ignoring Brian's wooziness and his question, Jed plowed on.

"He's more'n upset, I'd say, from how he's treatin' her. And I have t'agree. She's headin' for trouble, Briney."

"Naw, Jud, no trubble, no trubble."

"She's kickin' up her heels is what she's doin'. Every time a soldier walks down the street, she finds an excuse t'be out in the yard and an excuse t'begin talkin'. And I've seen her flirtin' with soldiers around Courthouse Square.

"Briney, maybe you can talk to her."

"Y'er talkin' 'bout—about ar li'l shish—shishter. Not like that, Jud, not like that.

"But she ish mighty pretty."

Brian smiled vapidly. His head flopped to one side. He would have toppled off the bench had Jed not caught him.

Serving the next table, Betsy sprang to help, supporting Brian by an arm as Jed held his shirt front.

"Briney, you ain't drunk that much. Wake up!"

Betsy was more realistic, "Maybe not, Jed, but he's gone for the night. You'd better get him home."

"Home! Pa'd kill me. Got t'get him back t'camp."

"Take him to my place first and make some strong coffee."

Preoccupied, he never saw the sparkle in her eyes.

As he stepped around the table still holding Brian by the shirt, he brushed close to Betsy. She leaned into him, pressing even closer, "You know where my place is, don't you, Jed?"

An hour later, when she joined them, Brian was sprawled on her bed, unconscious, breathing heavily. Jed slumped in the large rocking chair by the window, staring into the night.

"Didn't you make coffee for Brian?"

Getting no answer, she asked again.

"Couldn't wake him up."

"Would you like some?"

Jed looked up for the first time. His tone lightened.

"Some what?"

"Some coffee, of course. I'll put the pot on."

Betsy turned to the counter to grind the aromatic beans.

Jed stood up, approached her from behind. He put his arms around her waist, pressed into her. His hands slid upward lifting her ever so slightly. He bent to her ear to whisper.

"I'd rather have a poke."

"Jed Morrow, the coffee'll be done soon. And I've had a long day." Her voice reflected fatigue.

"When are you going to romance a girl again?"

"That's what I'm doin'! Leastways I thought I was."

"I mean with words and sweet talk that make a girl feel special, like a queen."

"I remember one night when you held my hand and told me about the North Star. You said we'd fly to it and you called me your Star Queen. We didn't do a thing but look at all the stars. They looked close enough to reach out and touch. I'll always remember that night, Jed. The happiest night of my life."

"I remember, too. Y're still my Star Queen."

"But you haven't talked that way lately, Jed,—like—like you lost a dream and can't find it."

Betsy ended in a sob, for Jed and for herself. She continued sadly, as if she, too, had lost a dream, "You'd think I was one of your cows to be mounted, and you the bull. Just paw once, snort twice, and put it in. A cow doesn't need to be romanced, Jed. And a cow doesn't need love."

She sniffed into a dainty handkerchief, dabbed at moist eyes to regain her composure, "But a girl does."

"Betsy, you mean more than that to me. I don't have t'tell you that."

"But you do, Jed, you do."

Taking her by the hand, he urged her toward the rocker. She held back momentarily, and Jed glanced at her uncertainly.

With feigned indifference, she let him lead her toward the chair. Still peevish, she halted abruptly, jerking his arm. She withdrew her hand from his, whisking imaginary soil from her skirt. Her ploy forced him to make the next move.

When he reached for her, she very deliberately picked at a last bit of lint, keeping him waiting a few seconds more before he sat. Only then did she perch stiffly on the very edge of his knees. Folding her hands in her lap, she held herself rigid and aloof.

Jed charged ahead, "I'm no good at word-romancin'—that night I was just talkin' about myself and what was important t'me. I just kind of got carried away I guess."

"Just carried away! Jed Morrow, I thought I meant more than that to you!"

He looked at her blankly, puzzled by her coolness, upset that his words had somehow made her unhappy, "More than what? I never told nobody all those things before. Nobody but you."

Thinking he had settled the issue, he nuzzled Betsy, kissing her ear and neck. His pensive mood lightened.

"But doin'-romancin' that's somethin' else. Damned! if you aren't a better romancer than me. All that cow and bull talk!

"Oh, Jed, that's just what I mean! You don't. . ."

Her voice caught and she buried her face in her hands, sobbing softly.

Sorry that he had somehow caused her more unhappiness, he ventured no more conversation.

Instead, he massaged her neck and shoulders, softly at first, clicking and popping tense muscles. He kneaded each sore spot, adjusting the pressure until the winces became purrs. Gradually, he worked across her shoulders and down her back, purposely decorous for he wanted this time to be her's, not his, not their's, but her's alone.

He sensed her disquietude drain away.

Tenderly, he asked, "That feel better?"

"Uh huh."

He pumped the rocking chair in small arcs, push back, rock forth, push back, rock forth.

She let her head fall forward as she relaxed, and yielded as he turned her and drew her close against him. He shifted in the chair to reach her more easily. Contentedly, she relaxed against him as his fingers worked, more slowly, yet more slowly.

"Oh, that feels so good," she murmured.

In peace and comfort, she moaned. Her eyelids closed sleepily. She quivered, just a bit, nestling into the hollow of his shoulder, cherishing his tenderness. Relaxing her softness against his chest, she drifted, vaguely aware that soothing fingers moved more and more slowly, then, not at all. She knew only that he held her, and she was safe forever.

The chair drew and redrew its peaceful arc, forward and back, in complete peace, forward, back, to and fro, to and fro.

Eyes still closed, Betsy lifted her face to his and kissed his cheek softly. With her lips she caressed him, cheek, eyes, and nose. When she reached his mouth she entangled her fingers in his unruly hair and pressed his head to her, whispering.

"I love you, Jed, I love you so much."

He held her in his arms as he rose smoothly from the chair, and carried her to the bed. He bent slightly to catch up the thick comforter folded there; it was all they needed. He let it fall beside them to the floor.

He loosened the first of a dozen tiny buttons that closed the bodice of her dress, fumbled with the next few that were stretched tight over her breasts.

"It's a shame the strain you put on these little buggers."

Betsy stood quiet, smiling at the temporary obstruction, at Jed's humor. Only he would say it that way. She remembered the desire of their first night together, hers apprehensive and timorous, his frightening at first, then restrained for her.

He fumbled more with the confining buttons, giving up momentarily, to squeeze her breasts gently, two breasts, two hands. She pressed her own hands onto his, trembling with expectancy as she whispered, "Let me help."

In seconds, Betsy had her bodice open. She let her dress drop, and two petticoats. She stepped out of her pantalets.

With growing urgency, she unbuttoned Jed's shirt, slipped it from his shoulders. She unbuttoned his trousers and let them fall away. Then his drawers. They stepped together, sharing softness and hardness. They kissed gently, passionately, pressed together, and whispered their love.

Gently, Jed lowered her to the comforter. In their offering and accepting, the world vanished with its war and country noises, its sailships and foreign lands, and the coffee pot's boiling and steaming over the open fire.

The word-romancing was not important any more, nor Brian, not three feet above them. Everything was gone, everything but the flood of their overwhelming love.

He entered her without urgency, fully for himself, gently for her. They pressed together, pressed together again and yet again, into their own world of star queens and north stars. Again and again until the stars exploded into shapes, colors, melodies, and fragrances that filled their heavens and secret places.

"I do love you, Betsy, more than you'll ever know."

Satisfied, she smiled dreamily, and they held each other on the comforter for many minutes.

"And I love you."

She cuddled into the protection of his arms, sighed, all tension gone, all pretenses and feigned indifference set aside.

"Jed Morrow, if you were as good at word-romancing as you are at doin'-romancing, you'd drive a girl crazy wondering which it was she wanted first."

They crawled into the bed with Brian for the short time until dawn, curling their bodies together, Betsy between the two brothers, her back to Jed. She was warm against him, secure in his encircling arms; and he, not nearly as sure that he wanted to leave Winchester.

She was the first to waken, as the first light eased the darkness. The discovery that she had slept between two men brought a smile to her lips, then a chuckle, and finally laughter enough to waken the both of them.

"Jed Morrow, you're the only man who's ever been in my bed, and now you must be the only man in Virginia to share a girl's bed with his brother."

Catching the humor as she had, Jed laughed with her.

"Come on, Briney, get up! Time t'get up."

Brian moaned a beery hangover, pulled at the single coverlet. He rubbed his eyes, covered a yawn, blinked blindly into the growing light. Gradually, he took in the situation. The three of them in bed together.

"Jed! What!!"

Betsy teased, "It was a short night, wasn't it?"

Brian, who was completely uncertain of his behavior since the conversation at the tavern, could only imagine.

"Brian, you've got to hurry to make roll call."

At the doorway, Betsy hugged him and kissed him on the cheek, unable to resist the opportunity in his perplexity. She put her lips to his ear and whispered loud enough for Jed to hear, "Thank you, Brian. I had a wonderful time."

Understanding her prank at once, Jed shook his head slowly, astonished at her rowdy teasing.

Her good-bye to Jed lingered. While the words were the same, she whispered them very differently, "I had a wonderful time."

Betsy waved, watching them disappear down the street.

"Jed, what did she mean about a wonderful time last night?"

"Just that, I guess. Just what she said." Jed wasn't about to let his brother off so easily.

"Come on, Jed, you know what I mean. I'm really embarrassed. I don't know what hit me last night, but I can't remember a thing after we left the tavern."

"That there college didn't teach you much about drinkin' beer, that's for sure."

"But I'm still embarrassed. I know that Betsy means a great deal to you, and I wouldn't do anything to—"

Jed didn't let him finish, "Forget it, Briney. Betsy was happy and that's what counts with me."

"Yes, but—"

"But nothin'. You have t'hurry t'be there for muster."

"You're right, for now. But this conversation isn't over. "And, Jed. don't tell Pa I was in town. He'd kill me!"

Five minutes late for muster, Captain White gave him extra duty.

On the 19th of June, the Liberty Hall Volunteers joined Jackson's Brigade, as Company I in the Fourth Virginia Infantry commanded by Colonel James Preston. Ordered north, Jackson's regiments pitched tents four miles north of Martinsburg in a place they dubbed Camp Stephens. Rumors of Yankee activity kept them on alert for two weeks. Jeb Stuart's horsemen patrolled toward the Potomac.

VI

HARPER'S FERRY
MAY, 1861

When David jumped from his rattly car at Harper's Ferry, he was shocked to see the U.S. Arsenal in ruins. Even now, one week after the Yankees burned it, the acrid smell of scorched timbers pervaded the area. Virginia militia had fought the flames to save machine tools and small arms worth $2,000,000.

David wasn't surprised that Union troops had left, for The Ferry was impossible to defend, a shooting gallery almost surrounded with high ground. However, he was surprised at the number of slovenly soldiers slouching through the streets. The place cried out for training and discipline. Even more disappointing was his encounter with the colonel he met, an old militia officer from the War of 1812.

"Colonel Harper, I've just come from West Point, ready to serve in any position commensurate with my training."

"You say your name's Morrow?"

"Yes, sir, David Morrow. From Winchester."

"Just pick your company. Everyone signs as a private."

"Colonel, I'm qualified for more than that. I've had five years training at the Academy. I'd hoped for a captaincy."

"Captain!" exploded Harper, who wore his half century of militia service as a medal, "we have captains twice your age with years of service, elected by those who know them best."

"I'm familiar with company elections, General, and I also know that Virginia is in need of trained officers."

"That may well be. But even as commanding officer I have no authority to appoint anyone to the commissioned ranks."

"No authority, sir?" David's sarcasm seethed.

Harper looked up sharply, "Young man, you are close to insubordination. West Point has not given you the right to. . ."

"Begging the colonel's pardon, SIR, but since I am not in the army, the threat of insubordination is meaningless."

They locked eyes. David wanted to add, "You old fossil."

Harper knew the accuracy of David's riposte, and could do nothing more than work his gums in a futile attempt to reply.

Recognizing the inevitable, David Morrow ended the interview, "Thank you, sir, for your time."

He turned on his heel and stamped out, muttering to himself, "Damnit! I should have gone to Montgomery with Rosser and Pelham."

Early that evening, David guided his rented mare onto Wolfe Street, galloping the last hundred yards to the generous, brick home of the Morrows. Had he seen the upstairs curtain flutter, he would have been better prepared for Racey's unbridled welcome.

His younger sister came flying through the front door, taking the brick steps two at a time.

"David! David! I can't believe it's you. What are you doing here? I thought you were still at West Point."

He swung a leg over the saddle, slid to the ground, just in time to catch her in mid-air. She snuggled against his cheek, her arms about his neck as he swung her in circles that took her feet off the ground, lifting her long, chestnut hair to the wind.

When finally he stopped, she leaned back, looked at him adoringly, and kissed him hard on the mouth.

"Racey, you are a pleasure to these hungry eyes. How you have grown in two years."

He set her on the ground, holding her right hand high. Taking the clue at once she twirled on tiptoes, her head arched back as far as it would go, her mouth wide in laughter.

"My brother's home! My brother's home," she sang, absolutely radiant, "My brother's home! My brother's really home!"

Holding his hand, she danced around him up the boxwood-lined path. At the steps to the wide verandah, she stood close hugging him about his middle, "The best brother in the whole world."

As they stood together, the resemblances stood out: the same dark hair and eyes so dark that iris and pupil melded; straight nose, softened in profile by a slight tilt at the end; sensual mouth, lower lip generous almost to a pout; strong jaw line; high cheekbone; cheeks carved elegant concave.

"And I have the best sister, Racey! Oh, it is good to see you, sweetheart! Is Pa home?"

"Yes, he's in his office. Remember where his office is?"

"I certainly do. With the Dutch tiles around the fireplace, showing the dog from puppy to old age. At The Point, I thought of them often, and I'd be a different tile during the day—puppy when we were off duty, old dog at taps."

"You couldn't be an old dog if you wanted to."

"Grace! in the name of all that's holy, what's the commotion out here?" Henry Morrow came onto the verandah, staring for a moment at his two children,

Skirts flying, Sarah rushed by him, down the steps.

"Oh, David, it is good to see you! Let me look at you. Have you eaten? You must be hungry," her last words were muffled against his face as he hugged her off the ground.

He never had a chance to answer the questions.

"David Michael Morrow! What in tarnation you doing home? You wrote graduation was a couple weeks off."

Henry narrowed his eyes, quizzical, suspicious, "You fail your classes up there?"

"Let me enjoy my son's hugs, Henry, before you get your report. Davey, you take my breath away. And I love it!

"Oh, it is so good to have you home."

Henry was wise enough, considerate enough, too, to let his wife have her moment. It was David who broke the spell.

"No, Pa, nothing like that, nothing like that at all."

"Then what in blazes you doing' home? Grace, stand straight like a lady—and keep your feet together."

"Yes, Pa," Grace murmured as her brother answered.

"No, I wasn't failing. As a matter of fact I've been in the first section."

"Don't give me fancy talk."

"It's not fancy talk, Pa. The first section is the top of the class, the highest grades."

"Then why the hell are you home?"

"Henry," Sarah intoned, nodding significantly toward Grace.

"I came home to join the army."

"Join the army!! Last I heard you were in the army."

"I came home to join Virginia's army."

"David Morrow, you better get yourself back before they throw your ass out."

Grace covered her mouth. Sarah erupted.

"Henry Morrow!"

"I can't do that, Pa. I resigned."

"RESIGNED!! Of all the. . ."

Catching himself on the verge of another impropriety, Henry looked at Grace, headed for the front door, "This is man's talk, and I have a feeling it's gonna get worse.

"Into the house, Grace. Into my office, David."

Sarah interrupted, "First, into the dining room, all of you. Supper's ready. You can talk later." She left no choice.

At the door, Mam, Ezekiel's mother, held open arms to David, her eyes aglow. She caught her breath, "You'll squinch me plum' t'death."

"Mam, you get prettier every time I come home."

"Gwan wiv' your foolishment!"

The supper table buzzed with questions and answers, Sarah's about his health and well-being, Gracey's about his cadet friends. Henry tended to his food. Finishing first, he sat impatient amidst the happy chatter.

David had a second piece of rhubarb pie, tart and flaky, "Mmmmm," he smacked his tongue at its rousing tang, "Nobody makes rhubarb pie like you, Ma. My favorite."

Satisfied that her family was fed, Sarah gave her blessing, "Now you two go have your talk."

Henry settled in his chair, the prime leather molding its surface cracks and permanent wrinkles to its long-time master. Despite its age, it had lost none of its seasoned fragrance.

"Now, let me get this straight. You left? Quit?"

"Pa, I didn't quit. I resigned. I resigned to fight for Virginia. It was either that, or fight against her."

"Fight against Virginia? That doesn't make any sense."

"It didn't to me either, Pa. That's why I left. And I didn't quit. I was near the head of my class. I could have graduated in a few days. But I didn't want a commission signed by Lincoln.

"This isn't our country any more, Pa. The Black Republicans have taken over, and they won't be satisfied until we kiss their ass and say 'Yes, Your Excellency,' and 'No, Your Highness'. I want no damn part of that."

Henry raised eyebrows at the earthy language, but said nothing. Over time, he realized, David had changed. He had found himself listening to his oldest son with a confidence he had never felt in Jed or Brian. West Point had given David self-confidence, taught him to observe and analyze, to articulate.

"David, I agree with you except for one thing."

"What's that, Pa?"

Turning slowly in his chair, Henry spoke quietly, "You said you wanted nothing from Lincoln," his words came more slowly, each a nail to be driven home, *"but you should have stayed to graduate. And got the paper."*

"Pa, I want you to understand why I left the Academy."

"What's done is done," Henry interrupted with the last words he ever said about West Point, "you did what you had to. I just hope you are wrong about this country.

"It's good t'have you home, son."

"It's good to be home, Pa. Tomorrow we'll talk more."

David climbed the front staircase with light heart, thrilled to be home, with his family again. He smiled softly at Racey's irrepressible greeting, at Ma's joyous tears, and yes, at Pa's impatience, too, for it rose out of a deep concern for his family. He fell asleep at once and slept almost until noon.

For the most part, David's first full day at home was a pleasant respite. He spent two hours in the big kitchen with its homely cooking smells, greeted again by Mam, served smoked ham, fresh eggs, yellow-rich milk from the farm, Mam's beaten biscuits with peach preserve put up almost a year ago.

Sarah sat with him while he ate, talking family.

"Jed practically lives at the farm, working with Ezekiel.

"Ruth has a new baby since you were home, a boy one year old. I wrote you that. Ruth and Jonathan adore him, but they have changed. Sometimes I think she isn't very happy.

"Grace has been studying at home since the Female Academy closed. She has a tutor but isn't too happy about it. She's also studying music— piano, and for the last six months, guitar.

"Brian's enlisted."

"Enlisted! Brian's no soldier."

"He felt he had to. He was studying to be a professor. Pa thought he ought to be a lawyer, more money in it he said, but now he's angry with him for joining the army."

"Brian's too serious for his own good."

"Yes, he is. Ezekiel runs the farm as if he was born there.

"Mam, you can see," Sarah smiled at her, "young as ever."

"I want to see everyone while I'm here. Maybe I can visit Ruth this afternoon, and the farm tomorrow."

At that point, Grace came bouncing into the kitchen. She tugged at his arm,

"C'mon, David, let's go up to the courthouse. Another company of soldiers is coming. From Rockingham County. Besides, I have to show you off."

"Grace, you know your father doesn't want you up there when it's full of soldiers."

"Oh, Mumma, I'll be all right. Besides, I'll be with David. He'll protect me! Won't you, David."

"David, that reminds me. Your father left a message for you. He'll try to be home early so as to spend some time with you."

He hugged his mother, "I haven't eaten a breakfast like that since my last visit. Delicious!" He hugged Mam, "thank you, Mam."

Grabbing his hand, Grace hauled him out. Loudoun Street was full of militia troops who impressed him no more than those at The Ferry, nondescript or plain filthy with few exceptions.

Here and there, they met a friend of Gracey's, and she introduced him grandly, "My brother was in the first section."

He saw at once the soldiers' interest in her, smiling, touching their caps in informal salutes. Her varied reactions fascinated him. She was not the little girl he remembered.

She ignored an unkempt soldier, glanced through long lashes at another, stared blankly at a foppish officer preening for her, greeted cheerfully a young soldier with the look of a lost puppy, and for a ramrod lieutenant in an immaculate uniform, a look that could have meant nothing or everything.

David knew the young officer would remember her for a while, "Racey, what makes you smile at one soldier and ignore another?"

"Why, David, I don't do that. Why do you ask?"

She looked at her brother with a fleeting pout and a languid look through upper lashes. She purred affectedly, soft, slow, "Ah have bin raised uh lady, suh, an' would nevah dream of bein' so bold. The question, suh, is foah anothuh."

She burst into laughter, and David never did sort out her portrayals. He knew only that soldiers thought as they would.

Soon after, he pleaded weariness and they started home. His concern persisted. She was all too attractive to be playacting to strangers. Such theatrics were for cousins and friends who knew the rules of the game.

"Racey, I enjoyed being with you, and meeting your friends. It was a good afternoon. But I have to be serious for a minute."

"Serious? About what?"

"Be careful of the soldiers. Some have no respect for young ladies. Some will read what they want in a friendly greeting."

"I know that!"

"Just be careful around them. Most are decent fellows, away from home and just lonely to talk, best to a nice-looking girl.

"But they're all stronger than you. Some are downright bad. To them, you're only a pretty girl to use and throw away."

"Oh, you're just being a big brother."

"Racey, it's more than that. You could be hurt bad. Be careful, honey, be very careful around them."

"Thank you for worrying about me, David. You're the best brother in the world. And you needn't worry so."

"But I do. I've seen what can happen. They get drinking and think the world belongs to them. Some don't need the drink."

They walked the rest of the way in silence, holding and swinging hands, Grace celebrating their being together, David still concerned with her innocence.

After supper, David and Henry talked again, David relating his experience at Harper's Ferry. Henry listened carefully, stroking his chin as usual when he pondered a problem, "Hmmmmm."

Recognizing the preoccupation, David said good night. He collapsed on his bed and was asleep within minutes.

Sometime after midnight, he wakened.

Moonlight outlined the furnishings of his room, the spooled footrail of his bed, the night stand of tiger maple, the chest-on-chest with its golden birdseye, the ash and pine rocker. The large oak tree etched by the moon's back-light filled the open window. As a youngster he had climbed the oak, up and down. Being home with family and familiar things was good, to remember younger days, and simply to have the time to enjoy it all. He would sleep in again, as late as he wanted.

"David! David! Pa says to get up." Racey jumped and spun, landing seated on the bed. "Wake up! David, wake up! Pa says its important."

He was alert at once, the habit of five years, "What time is it?"

"Ten o'clock. I put clean clothes on the chair."

"Thanks, Racey, I'll be down in a minute."

"I'll wait outside. I hope you don't have to leave."

In the kitchen, David kissed his mother on the cheek. Henry answered before he could ask the obvious question.

"Heard this morning that colonel you saw at Harper's Ferry was the wrong man to talk to. What's his name?"

"Harper, Pa, Kenton Harper. Same name as The Ferry. Sounds like you been scouting."

"He was replaced last month. He only commands a regiment."

"That scoundrel! He let me think he was C.O."

"Well, he isn't. His boss is a colonel name of Jackson from the military school in Lexington. Hear he's a real soldier, West Point, made a name in Mexico. Sounds smarter than Harper."

"He must be, Pa, graduating from The Point. This Colonel Jackson will find me a position." David's zeal was back, "Thanks, Pa, you'd make a good spy. I'd like to take Sable if you can spare him."

"Good choice, son. You ride him easy, he'll run all day."

Sarah insisted he have breakfast before he left, "Everybody needs a good meal to start the day."

"All right, Ma, just like yesterday's. With extra biscuits?"

"I'll do that and more, dear. I'll pack some to take. with Ezekiel's smoked ham."

"Oh! David. I wish you didn't have to go. We've had so much fun," Moist eyes made Racey's smile all the more radiant.

"You remember what I said about the soldiers."

"What's that about the soldiers!"

"Nothing, Pa, just between Racey and me."

Henry frowned, "Secrets between my own children. Bah!

"David, I hope it doesn't, but if it comes to fighting, you're with the right people. I'm proud you're siding with Virginia. I want you t'know that, son." He extended his hand.

"Thank you, Pa. That means a lot to me."

Sensing a run through the countryside, the coal black stallion pranced east on Wolfe Street. At the corner, David turned in his saddle, right hand stretched high, then stiff and straight at his cap, his very best cadet salute.

Excited, the big stallion, half a hand over 16, celebrated his own freedom as David saluted, rising magnificently on hind legs to dance a half circle, shaking his mane to the wind. Settling weightlessly, he shook his head in regal abandon.

With a touch imperceptible to anyone watching, David reined Sable onto Main Street, and north down the Valley.

Through Redbud Run to the Charlestown Road, he crossed the railroad tracks. In Harper's Ferry by mid-afternoon, an alert guard challenged him, and directed him to brigade headquarters.

The sentry, who knew horses well, took special note of this one, smiling approval when Sable turned gracefully to the right and trotted off proudly. He had seen no sign, not rein, spur or knee, but somehow the big black knew what his rider wanted.

VII

SALUTED BY A GNAWED PEACH
MAY, 1861

A man in a nondescript, dusty uniform squatted on a camp stool in front of the commander's tent, chewing a bite of peach. He wore a threadbare tunic of the U.S. Army, Mexican War vintage, a size too small. Erstwhile gold maple leafs suffering a dozen and one years of tarnish and disintegration added to the seedy appearance. The major's insignia was matched by a forage cap perched forward on his head, its cracked visor aslant over a prominent, aquiline nose. A full beard framed his face, temples to chin.

Looking up sleepily, he emanated melancholy as though he had lived through, perhaps was still suffering, a deep personal tragedy. The cheerlessness was only a part of this complex man with the deepset eyes, gray some said. Others saw blue.

Despite his appearance, he hadn't missed a detail of the rider and his stallion. As the guard had done, he noted David's peerless seat, and as the guard had not, the tiny flick of wrists that brought the horse to an immediate halt. David saluted.

The seated officer acknowledged it with a vague motion of hand toward his cap, the first time David had ever been saluted by a half-eaten peach. The man in the shabby uniform continued to study horse and rider. He said nothing.

David sat steady, returning the gaze man to man, long enough to show he was not intimidated, not so long as to start a contest of wills. That challenge would have been rude, and he knew would have served him badly.

He dismounted, "I'm looking for Colonel Jackson."

"Nice horse."

"Yes sir. Foaled on our farm near Kernstown."

The other bit into the peach.

"Good for the innards," he volunteered, inspecting it closely and gnawing at it again without hurry. He looked up from under the cracked visor.

"West Point?"

Surprised, David braced in approved Academy style, chin and stomach sucked in, chest out, shoulders back, spine ramrod stiff.

"YESSIR—David Morrow—SIR."

"The Point marks a man. I am Colonel Jackson."

Such was David's roundabout meeting with the tender warrior who gloried in battle and yet hated it, the devout Christian who fought on the side of slavery, and yet gave money for a Negro Sunday School.

"Yes, colonel, it does indeed."

"Stand easy, man." He sucked on the peach again.

"Yes, sir. Thank you, sir."

David paused, deferring, then taking the colonel's silence as permission to continue, "I was at The Academy until earlier this month. My class graduates in a few days."

Thomas Jonathan Jackson, Colonel, Virginia Volunteers, had liked what he saw, the soldierly bearing, the straightforward manner, the open face and dark eyes that held his own without wavering. A taciturn man, the former professor had made a judgment and found himself using more words than was his wont.

"Two classes this year, I understand."

"Yes, sir, May and June."

"Had you been a cadet under my advisement, sir, I would have told you to stay on. A presidential appointment and a diploma comprise an important accomplishment, not to be taken lightly."

"My father said the same thing, Colonel Jackson."

"Your father is a smart man. He looks to the future."

Despite the paternal warmth in Jackson's words, David wanted to be understood.

"Had I been studying under you in Lexington, colonel, I surely would have followed your advice. But I wasn't at Lexington, sir, and accepting a commission at West Point was quite a different circumstance.

"It would have meant taking an oath against Virginia."

Standing, Jackson stretched his left arm high above his head, "And why, I ask, did you not take the oath, and resign? Others have and more will, I am sure."

"I have no argument with the decisions of others, Colonel, but I felt I would be accepting it under false pretenses. I will not lie to a friend or to the government. Sir."

Jackson recognized his own sense of integrity, as well as the strict honor code of West Point and Virginia's military academy where he had taught. This young man lived that code to the letter.

He warmed to the thought of his initial judgment.

"I salute your respect for the old standards, David Morrow. If we don't have a place for you, I'll make one. We can ill afford to be wasteful, sir."

He bit again into the peach, extracting the stone for the final drops of juice.

David wondered which Valley orchard furnished him his peaches.

"Corporal," Jackson called his clerk, "kindly record in my book that David Morrow, Cadet, USMA, has joined my staff as a volunteer.

"And prepare a letter to General Lee for my signature. I need an appointment of first lieutenant for Mr. Morrow. Get the personal details from him."

Turning to David, "That puts you on the roster until I decide final assignments in my command. And, believe me, sir, that will be done very soon.

"Until then, you will be busy. This place needs discipline and organization and drill, sir, drill, drill, drill."

Then Colonel Jackson appeared uncertain of himself for the first time, "Unofficial service is necessary for the time being. There is no position, and no pay."

"Your confidence is sufficient, Colonel," chancing a smile, David relaxed his Academy formality, "Until I run out of money, at least."

Jackson chuckled deep in his throat, "We'll have you on the roll before that.

"Until then, and," he added wryly, "maybe afterwards, I want you to drill these men until they can march in their sleep. We must train them for harsh things ahead.

"Train them, train them, train them," he added with increasing emphasis, pounding a fist into his palm three times.

"Yes, sir." David saluted his cadet's best.

For two weeks, he followed Jackson's regimen, drilling fifty minutes of each hour. resting ten. He taught some right foot and left foot. He shared with them five o'clock reveilles, dust, and dawn-to-dark workdays.

He instructed them through The School of the Soldier, and marched them through the company drills, relating the evolutions to battlefield situations. "I want more than blind obedience. You need to understand the whats and whys of columns, lines, wheels, obliques. Your lives may depend on it.

"Attention COMPANY—right FACE—about FACE—left FACE.

"Forward. Common time MARCH—company HALT—about FACE—forward Common time MARCH—company HALT." David stood in place.

The company was back where it began, fifty men in all their diverse glory, homespun shirts and trousers of forty different dyes, shapeless hats, indifferent boots, many still caked with manure, men with ragged beards, a few boys still to feel their first razor.

"Column forward Guide right MARCH—Left turn MARCH— Right turn MARCH—Double quick step MARCH."

Thirty-three inch steps, 165 a minute. The men broke sweat. "Company HALT"

He covered the manual of arms, taught them to load a musket in nine steps.

The order "Tear CARTRIDGE" was his favorite, for the tearing was done with the teeth, and loose powder caused the black stains that marked a soldier.

They drilled with muskets and bayonets until they ached. "Care for your musket as you would your woman," he said, "take care of her and she'll take care of you."

He gave a spirited bayonet demonstration, "Lunge, parry, club up with the butt, slash down. Lunge, parry, club, slash.

"One more thing, yell like banshees, screech and howl. Cold steel rattles them. Cold steel and shouting rattles them more. Now pair off and practice." David saw the uncertainty, "Without bayonets for today. Just the moves."

Intermixed were lessons in military courtesy and custom, how to salute, pack a knapsack, pitch a tent, read a compass, care for blistered feet. He described and demonstrated the details of standing guard, and then had them repeat the routine.

He had them dig a trench line with shovels, and then traverses with bayonets and tin cups.

"Now you're beginning to look like soldiers," he said one day to his trainees after a musket-loading session, "you've smelled powder and tasted it." He laughed in good humor, intending no ridicule, "You're black around the mouth."

He heard a muffled sneer, "Damn Wes' P'inter."

He spun back to them instantly, his humor gone. His dark eyes flashed black, "Is somebody unhappy?"

No answer.

He snapped again, "Bitch on your own time. Not mine. Any questions?"

Still no answer.

He looked up and down the rigid line.

The guilty soldier kept his secret.

David double-quicked them for the subsequent fifty-minute period, up and down, through their own dust. Timing Jackson's ten-minute rest precisely, he barked them into formation.

"In place REST." The men relaxed with one foot in place.

"Are there other observations you have concerning your officers, your duties, or the requirements of this army?"

Not a soldier moved a muscle.

He paced slowly along the lines.

"Now's your time to speak up."

Standing straight without the exaggerated cadet brace, he waited. His dark eyes stared others into the ground.

"Good." He dismissed them.

The next day, he drilled them as usual, as though nothing had happened. They bit cartridges and looked at each other black in the face. When they laughed, he knew yesterday's episode had its effect. They were becoming soldiers. The grousing continued, but not within David's earshot.

Soon they were drilling as regiments, and one day all five were brigaded, raising more dust than they had ever seen before.

Colonel Jackson had been busy, too. He put the arsenal to work, and sent the armory's surplus machinery to Winchester for transshipment to Richmond.

He tricked the Baltimore and Ohio Railroad out of engines that he sent south and rolling stock he destroyed. Citizens cheered as each locomotive inched through Winchester by mule power and rolling logs. Soldiers cheered when flaming cars hurtled into the Potomac to sizzle and settle.

He sent details into Loudoun County to requisition horses for the artillery with orders to "buy them if you can, confiscate them if you can't."

He sent troops to the heights commanding Harper's Ferry, others down the Potomac to guard the railroad bridge at Point of Rocks, and still others, upstream to Sheperdstown and Martinsburg to watch for Yankees.

David realized he was contributing to the change, but turned anxious for more action.

Late one afternoon, he received an order to report to headquarters. He had heard nothing about his appointment since his interview with Colonel Jackson.

To his great disappointment, the colonel wasn't there. Major Massie, brigade inspector general, greeted him, "Colonel Jackson would have seen you himself, but he had business downstream.

"I've just returned from Richmond and bring you good news. General Lee has endorsed the colonel's request. As of yesterday, you are 1st lieutenant, Virginia Volunteers.

"I was assured your papers will be here within the week.

"Congratulations, lieutenant," the major thrust out a hand.

"Thank you, major. That is good news."

"I think a celebration is called for. Something on the order of a ride to Halltown? Or Sheperdstown?"

"Sheperdstown sounds good to me."

"Do you know, by any chance, a lieutenant by the name of Randolph? William Randolph the Third? Bill is cavalry, and good company. Might ask him to join us."

"No I don't know him, Major. Haven't met many for the time I've spent drilling. But ask him, by all means, ask him."

"You have been busy. It's time for a breather."

"Indeed I have, long enough to develop a mighty thirst. And, major, I—uh, I don't quite know how to put this, not knowing you very well, but—uh—."

"Just say what's on your mind, lieutenant. Don't stand on ceremony with me."

"Well, sir, it's just that I'm not sure what you mean by celebration. I don't even know if you're married or single."

"What does that have to do with it?"

"Well, sir, I know this young lady in Sheperdstown.'

"I understand."

"And, if I might presume—if you—she has sisters."

All three enjoyed their night in Sheperdstown.

The next morning, Major Massie saluted Jackson's chief of cavalry, the ebullient, full-bearded James Ewell Brown Stuart.

Jeb Stuart's eyes twinkled, "You-all had a bad night? You don't look too good."

The major ignored the observation, "May I present Lieutenant Morrow. I believe you've been expecting him."

"Halloo, lieutenant, glad to have you in the cavalry. Name your price and I'll buy that big black you're riding."

David caught his admiring glance and glowed through his miseries, "Afraid he's not for sale, sir."

"Call a price and I'll double it," Stuart pressed with joyous abandon.

David bent to Sable's muzzle, caressing the sleek neck. The big stallion answered the familiar touch, lifting his head and neighing.

"What's that, old friend?" David cocked an ear.

"I see. You want to stay with me.

"Sorry, sir, Sable refuses to leave me."

Always ready for a laugh, Stuart touched fingertips to his broad-brimmed hat in appreciation of David's skillful parry. Its ostrich feather, black as Sable, caught the wind.

Jeb Stuart laughed heartily.

"Understand you've given the recruits a taste of The Point."

"Yes sir. Afraid I'm not cut out for a drillmaster."

Stuart pretended surprise, "Not a drillmaster! Hmmmm. You and I will have to talk. Reminisce The Academy."

"Yes sir, I'd like to hear about your class of '54."

Stuart was pleased, "You just happen to know that. Right?"

"Just happen to," David grinned, "yes sir."

"Colonel Jackson speaks highly of you. That right, major?"

"Yes sir, 'a good one' is how the colonel puts it."

"Well, lieutenant, welcome to my command."

"Glad to be with you, sir," David said sincerely, for he felt an immediate rapport with this laughing cavalryman with the red-brown beard and ready sense of humor.

Leaning toward David and lowering his voice confidentially, Stuart added, "Colonel Jackson told me not to be surprised if he recalled you. Told me you were doing too good a job to waste on cavalry picket. Said he needs a permanent drillmaster."

Then, seeing the alarm in David's eyes, Stuart laughed his hearty laugh again. He walked over to stroke Sable's muzzle.

"If you're planning to throw your lot in with me, you've got to learn when to relax and join the fun. I take my laughs where I can, and make my own enjoyment. If I don't, nobody else will."

"Yes sir, I surely will remember that. In fact, I take it as an order. Sir!"

Stuart chuckled at the small joke and turned instantly serious, "Had a company come in from Washington County a couple days ago. The Washington Mounted Rifles, Captain William Jones. Old West Pointer. Resigned. He raised a company and came back in. He's ten years older than I am, and graduated from The Point six years earlier. He's not happy at all to be under me, but he's a good man to learn the trade from. Right off a sourapple tree, Jones. No jokes, no laughs, but a good man.

"He probably won't like it, but I'm assigning you to him."

Momentarily, Stuart tried to appear stern, but he couldn't control the insistent smile or his laughing eyes, "I've a mind to assign you to my staff so's I can keep an eye on that talking stallion of yours.

"But I suppose it's better you watch Jones and learn your trade from one of the best."

VIII

EZEKIEL'S STORY
JUNE, 1861

Leaving Brian after the night at Betsy's, Jed headed south, up Loudoun Street and the turnpike. Near the toll gate, he chose the Middle Road that passed closer to the Morrow farm.

Dog-trotting most of the way for the exhilaration and freedom it gave, he also was anxious to talk to Ezekiel. He knew, too, that Mattie would hustle up one of her special breakfasts for her 'growin boy'.

A mile shy of the wagon-worn lane to the house, he cut cross-lots, through a hay field to a gentle hill, likely a frost heave of the Ice Age. Renewed to a rich green by the night's rain, the ground was spongy, the uncut hay still wet, soaking his boots, darkening his trousers to the knee.

On top of the rise, he stopped to wipe forehead sweat with a sinewy forearm. He took in great gulps of rain-washed air, relishing its fragrance, clean and sweet.

He wiped again, thrilled, as he always did looking over this generous land, Pritchard's Hill interrupting the line of the turnpike to the east, the western mountains ghostly in dissipating fog. It had lifted enough to reveal Opequon Creek spilling to the valley floor, hugging a small knoll for half a circle. The vista filled his eyes, for this Valley was a part of him, he a part of it.

From his hilltop, Jed Morrow looked down the easy slope on fields of patterned furrows, some straight, some curved to the land, fitting one to the other as a puzzle of the playful gods.

He would carry this land in his heart wherever he went; even now, as he knew he would leave, he was certain he would return. He breathed it in, treasured and celebrated it.

He blinked to clear his eyes.

The fields abutted outbuildings and the stone house in which he was born. Approaching the back of the house, he saw its soaring chimneys that guarded the sides, and a plain porch without the pillars and portico gracing the front. Fifty yards off stood the house of Ezekiel and Mattie, smaller, of the same stone construction.

The two houses glistened clean in the morning sun, preening their designed angles, lines, and planes of wall and roof. The houses contrasted neatly with the panoramic irregularity of foothills, creek and meadow; man's order and nature's, one compulsive, the other constant, somehow related, coming together to beget mongrelish orchards and fields.

Jed absorbed the harmony, awed as always by the evidence of change that left things the same. People need to accept change as nature does, he conjectured, Pa especially.

In the distance, he saw Mattie, a tiny figure at the well in the yard. The well-house was of the same limestone, built by Ezekiel to replace its crude predecessor.

"A good well deserves a good home," he had said with simple elegance.

Waving and shouting, Jed loped the downhill grade and the flatland to the house.

"Mornin', Jed. Knew you'd be comin' along," Mattie gave her biggest smile, broad and white.

"Let me carry the buckets."

"All right. I don't need ta look twice ta see y're more than ready ta eat."

"I am, for sure, Mattie. How'd you know?"

"I can smell hungry, that's how, I can smell it in my nose."

"Where's 'Zekiel? I need t'talk to him."

"First you eat. A full belly makes good talk better."

Mattie's husband appeared from the recesses of the barn, stood for a moment, blinking at the bright sunlight, a lean man of average height, wiry and sinewy. He had the calloused hands of a workman and the disposition of a saint. The Valley and Nature were as books to Ezekiel, books he read with ease.

"Thought I heard your voice, Jed. G'mornin'."

In the kitchen, Mattie busied herself at the iron cookstove. Jed moved a chair from the table and straddled it. Ezekiel filled mugs from the fire-blackened coffee pot. He slid a tin of sugar and a crock of fresh milk across the table. Mattie stirred grits and turned slabs of hickory-smoked bacon in the iron spider. She cracked a half dozen eggs into sizzling grease, served up two heaping plates, each edged precariously with a pair of over-sized, beaten biscuits, Mam's recipe.

"For my growin' boys."

"Mattie, y're a good woman."

In no time at all, the two men were swabbing remnants of eggs, grits and bacon drippings.

"Mattie, nobody can make biscuits like you. Mmmmm!"

Without asking, she served each of them another on a singed stove-cloth, "Apple butter's there. An' strawb'ry jell'."

"I'll have t'go halfn'half," Jed laughed, "unless you have another one." Grinning, she obliged.

"Mattie, I don't know how you do it!" Jed admired.

"That's for me ta know and you ta aks," she answered pertly.

"Can I talk with Zeke now?"

"Only if you got enough t'eat," she replied seriously.

"All that and four biscuits! I've had more than enough."

"That's all I need t'hear."

"No, Mattie, there's one more thing."

"What's that?"

"Thank you. For breakfast and that big smile."

Her sparkling grin filled the kitchen again, "G'wan with you, Jed Morrow, I know you an' your moon talk."

"I mean it, Mattie. I wouldn't prank you like that."

He turned to Zeke, "What do you think of this war?"

"Don't rightly know, but a man has t'protect what's his."

"I'm signin' up!" Jed blurted impulsively.

Zeke saw the crucial question at once, "Henry know?"

"Not yet."

"He oughta know before me."

"I tried t'tell him, but he won't listen. 'You have t'stay here,' is all he says, 'need you on the farm'."

"Henry can be stubborn," Ezekiel nodded, "sometimes stubborn as a pointy-eared mule turned deaf. But he still has ta know. Better he know before you leave than after."

"He just gets mad. He doesn't want t'hear nothin' about it from me. Will you tell him, Zeke? He'll listen to you, Zeke."

Ezekiel pondered, rubbing his chin as Henry did. Mattie started to say something but noted his concentration. She covered her impulse by refilling the coffee mugs.

"Jed, when you were a shirt-tail boy, I did somethin' like y're aksin'. You remember the day you came down here instead of goin' ta school? Your daddy was gonna wallop you in the woodshed. We got into it, him and me.

I told him you were gettin' grown t' where you needed t'be let go a bit. He said he'd think on it."

Jed brightened, "That's what I mean. He listens t'you."

"But that isn't what I mean," the older man corrected gently, "what I mean is you aren't a young'un now, and you gotta talk for yourse'f. Nobody else can do it, Jed."

Jed started to reply, but Ezekiel held up a work-hardened hand. He studied his coffee mug, took it between both hands and sipped. His voice was serious and gentle.

"Jed, I've known your daddy a long time, from way back in Washin'ton when we were both young'uns. Raised like brothers we were. No black. No white."

Jed slumped in his chair, "Zeke, I heard this before."

"Maybe so, but you gonna' hear it again. Maybe you learn somethin' new."

"When his daddy died, the four of us kep' right on livin' in the same house. Henry took over the warehouse and the haulin' business, an' Mam tended the house. You an' me kep' on like we was doin' learnin' ta read an' figger. Still just like it was, es'ept Mister Morrow, your gran'daddy, he's gone.

"I ever tell how come Mam and me was livin' there in your gran'-daddy's house in Georgetown?"

"No, Zekiel."

"Mam was a granny-woman. Come in ta help birth new babies. She was there t'help birth your daddy. Your gran'ma died and ole Mister Morrow he aksed her t'stay and keep house."

"Mam said she'd like that but she wasn't free t'choose. So Mister Morrow, he bought Mam and me from a man we belonged ta."

"You were slaves!?"

Ezekiel ignored the question, "He aks him, 'How much you want for them?' And that old nigger man who owns us names off his price. Mister Morrow, he knows it's too high but he don't blink an eye. 'Done!' he says.

"And he give Mam a paper sayin' she's free. And he give her one for me, too."

"Slaves! You—were—slaves!? I never knew that."

"See? Sometimes when a man listens he get ta learn somethin'."

Mattie moved toward Ezekiel.

Still shocked, Jed looked wide-eyed from one to the other.

"That's how it was—Ole Mister Morrow, Mam, and me and you growin' up t'gether. Mister Morrow he built a house on Rock Creek Park and bought farmland in Ten'llytown. When his Pa died, Henry got it all. He ran the business until he got ailish and the doctor told him ta leave Washin'ton. He left the business with me and ole Arthur t'keep books. And the house for Mam and me."

Ezekiel continued his story, telling how he and Henry had spent their last night by the Chesapeake and Ohio canal where it runs through Georgetown, looking at the river and the rowdy sunset beyond, watching a mule skinner and his team, listening to his obscure words hummed into a workaday rhythm.

"Sittin' there by the canal, Henry says t'me, 'Zekiel, we been friends a long time. I'm gonna miss you'.

"Hate t'see you leavin', Henry. We had some good times.

"He says 'I told Arthur t'give Mam regular house money and whatever else she wants so all she got t'do is let him know.

"'She's been a lovin' ma ta both of us,' Henry says, 'and Pa loved her, too. Before he died he told me t'take care of her there's money enough so's she don't have t'want for anythin'.'

"And then Henry showed me the will he made, in case he put the rug."

"Never heard that before. You mean died?"

"Yup. He give the Georgetown house t'Mam and the farmland t'me and the warehouse and haulin' business t'me and old Arthur t'gether.

"Then Henry says, 'I'm sendin' for you both soon's I'm able'. And he did when he bought this here farm. When he knew Mattie and me was almost married, he said bring her, too."

"I wrote him back that I couldn't because she's not free.

"And that Henry! Next thing I know, a man comes in and says 'who owns this slave name uh Mattie?'

"Who wants ta know I aks him?

"When he says 'Henry Morrow' I told him, and next day he comes back with Mattie and a paper. 'I'm from the bank,' he says, 'and Henry Morrow wired ta buy this Mattie and bring her here with a paper sayin' she's free'."

Ezekiel finished his story with tears in his eyes. He looked into his coffee mug again, studying it as if to find more words to tell better what was in his heart.

Mattie came closer to touch his shoulder. Love was in her moist eyes, and in her touch.

Ezekiel looked directly at Jed, saying very softly, almost in a whisper, "There's no man I love more than Henry."

"Zeke, I understand," a subdued Jed answered, "I shouldn't have asked. I'll find a way t'talk to him."

IX

A COLD MORNING
IN JUNE, 1861

Ruth Morrow Brighton squirmed in her bed to her husband, pressing her softness to his back and buttocks. She moved a hand to his ribs and let tapered fingers creep across his chest.

"Just one time before you leave," she whispered, "Jonathan. don't leave me like this."

Getting no response, she let her fingers wander across the valley of his navel. She pressed closer.

"I need you, Jon. Please, please love me."

In her rising passion, Ruth undulated against him, pressing, withdrawing, pressing. Touching him tentatively with feathery fingertips, she curled her fingers and stroked softly, ever so softly.

With a start, her husband pulled away from her, "Ruth, for god's sake! You know I don't like you to be so bold." Henry Morrow's eldest daughter shriveled inside.

No stranger to rejection, she had promised herself many times to let her husband be, but her passion swelled each day and then by the minute, destroying her determination. This morning was particularly difficult. She was at flood tide and he was leaving for the war.

Jonathan swivelled to a sitting position on the edge of the bed. Thirty-one years old, six years older than his wife, he was showing signs of a middle-age paunch. His sedentary teller's job in his father's bank showed. Physically and mentally it showed, not only in his middle, but in eyes blunted by boredom, enlivened at times with anger, more often numbed in sadness. It was the latter now as he felt Ruth's hurt and hesitated, wishing for words that would make everything right.

None came.

He stood on spindly legs, prudishly turning away. He pulled drawers and trousers into place before shedding his nightshirt. Not before his shirt was fully buttoned did he turn to her, his face showing premature middle age too, as did his thinning hair and retreating hairline, as did the loose skin along his jowls and under an indifferent chin.

Unwilling to leave without an attempt to make amends, he said softly, "I'm sorry I can't give you what you want. If only you wouldn't be so—demanding."

Ruth turned into her pillow, fanning long, auburn hair across it, sobbing as she hadn't since her nuptial bed.

In five years, that night had never faded. Nor had the previous one that began as an innocent stroll to Town Run, the stream between Wolfe and Boscawen streets where they had played as children.

They had sat quietly that wedding eve in a hidden place on Town Run, her long legs toward the purling water. More open with each other then, they had talked of important things and trivial. Ruth lay back, letting her arms fall carelessly over her head, "I could stay here forever."

"I could, too, Ruth," he leaned over her, and kissed her gently on the lips. The veneers of instilled inhibitions fell victims to their embraces. She arched her back, swelling her breasts with each breath, shaping against him, flat and curved. He kissed her cheek, her neck, her shoulder. She murmured as he explored her.

Her own explorations told him patience was unnecessary.

That first love-making was quick for him, uncomfortable for her. She cried out just once, a sharp, little scream subdued behind a clenched fist. A moment later, he gasped and was finished, wondering how this had happened. She wondered too, if there wasn't more to it than that.

They lay side by side without words but not without embarrassment. Little by little the chagrin dissipated.

There must be more to it than that, she thought, there has to be. Her whisper broke the silence, "Asleep?"

"No."

"That's good."

"Why?"

She rolled on her side, wriggled closer and rolled another quarter turn onto him, front to front.

She undulated against him, "That's why."

This time was better, less urgent for him, more promising for her. The groom-to-be was marrying a very lively lady.

On the walk back from the creek, she had cuddled against him, an arm around his middle, "Tomorrow night, we'll do it all again, in a soft bed. And I'll make it even better for you."

On the following day, Winchester people filed into Christ Episcopal Church, immediate families, cousins, cousins removed, friends and business associates of Henry Morrow and Jonathan's father, owner of The Valley Bank of Winchester. Each side of the aisle was seated tight with a backdrop of standees.

"Wilt thou have this man . . . so long as you both shall live?"

"Oh, yes! Yes!."

Surprised at her ardor, the minister glanced up, fortunately unaware of the fantasy that engulfed her.

'Oh yes! Jonathan! With this body I will have thee . . . with my body, with my body.' She heard only bits of the ceremony, "pledge thee my troth . . . of the Holy Ghost . . . and so fill you. . . ."

'So fill me!! Oh, Jonathan!'

Guests invited to the wedding celebration filled Taylor's Hotel. Ruth greeted them all, flushing with the effort. Without her veil, she felt exposed, disrobed, and colored more with remembrance of yesterday's lovemaking. Remembrance of yesterday's and anticipation of tonight's.

Disquieted that her daughter might be feeling poorly, Sarah spoke to Mattie, "Does Ruth look feverish to you?"

"I'd say so any other day," Mattie replied, "But not on her weddin' day, Sarah. Nothin' the matter won't get fixed t'night."

"Oh, Mattie Brown, you!"

In a quiet moment after a lilting quadrille, Ruth stretched on tiptoe to whisper to her husband. She couldn't resist brushing his ear with her tongue. Soon afterwards, and perhaps a bit earlier than custom would have it, the newlyweds bid their guests a good night. The new Mrs. Brighton was ready for bed.

Jonathan kissed her lightly, "I need a tot of rum. I'll be along in a minute."

"One minute, no longer." Ruth ran a finger along his lips, and crossed the reception room. She just knew that everyone in the room was looking at her, staring with knowing smiles.

Their bridal room was lighted with a single candle, lit specially by a romantic maid. Ruth pirouetted across the large room, dancing shadows about the walls and ceiling. From the long window, she looked down on the street for dreamy minutes, then turned to the high bed. She disrobed, hanging skirt, bodice, shifts, camisole, corselet, underwaist, pantelets, all in the massive armoire. Lastly, she peeled stockings over thin ankles.

Draping her nightdress over the footboard, she stood exposed and accessible in the soft light. Her lissome figure lifted as she stretched wide toward the ceiling, standing for a moment as the lovely Psyche awaiting her Eros. She shivered expectantly. Fingertips ventured immodestly. She turned down the coverlet. Climbing the step stool, she threw her arms into the air and collapsed onto the high bed. Embroidered linens were cool to her body as the singing waters of Town Run had been cool.

She quivered again, remembering, anticipating, hugging herself for control. She caressed last evening's lovemaking, 'Jonathan, I adore you. I adore everything about you. I love the way you touch me, and the things you do to me.'

She dozed.

Sensing Jonathan astride her, she smiled in her sleep and opened her legs to receive him. She came awake.

Sitting up, she moaned and wiped perspiration. Jonathan was not there; she was alone. For the entire night she was alone.

In the months that followed, she tried repeatedly to arouse him, with discretion and without, demurely at first, then boldly. Confidence waned but was renewed by desire. At best, her infrequent successes left her only partially fulfilled for his comportment was mechanical, without excitement. Despite his ineptness, they produced a girl and a boy. Pleased to be a mother, she had come to an intermittent acceptance of his indifference.

On this last morning together, Ruth remembered her joy of five years ago, the ecstasy that preceded her wedding. Tears welled again.

"Jonathan, please don't leave, I beg of you. Stay and we'll make things different between us. Please, Jon."

"It won't be for long."

With that he pressed his lips to her forehead, lingering longer than he intended to finger through her auburn hair.

"I love you, Ruth. I do love you, but you smother me. Just like the colonel and my mother."

A half hour later, Jonathan and Jed were two miles north of Winchester, their stride jaunty, their talk full of enthusiasm. The army was at Bunker Hill, named erroneously as it had been in Massachusetts. Five miles out, they came to Littler's Run.

"Jed, I am ready for a rest."

"I can stop or keep goin'. Walkin's easier than workin'."

They walked several yards upstream to fresh water, drank deeply, and splashed cupped handfuls over head and neck.

"Might as well enjoy it," smiled Jed as he shed shoes and long stockings. Jonathan tugged at his own boots.

"Makes me think of the creek at home."

"Town Run," said Jonathan turning melancholy, "I used to walk there—with Ruth."

Back in Winchester, Henry took his place at the breakfast table and called gruffly. "Sarah. where's that son of yours."

Sarah came from the kitchen, wiping hands on her apron. Near forty-five years old, the few pounds she had added were in no way unattractive. Heads still turned when she walked into John Linn's tavern with her husband.

She pushed wisps of brown-gray hair into place, "Call him again, Henry. Just waiting for the biscuits to brown."

"Already did. Looked all over and he isn't here.

"Don't know what's got into him. He knows the rules and he isn't here. Just like that time when he was a tad!"

"Now, Henry, don't get upset. I'm sure he's around here someplace. He'll be along."

"Somethin's eatin' at that boy. Ever since the war started, he hasn't been himself, telling me he had to leave Winchester."

"Is that all? He must have said something else."

"Just that he was suffocatin' and needed to get away."

"And how did you answer him, Henry?"

"I just told him we needed him at the farm."

"And what else, Henry? I know you didn't stop there."

"Last time, I said I didn't want t'hear any more about it."

"Henry Morrow, you didn't!"

He looked sharply at his wife, "Dammit, he vexed me, Sarah. I didn't want t'hear any more, and I told him. Now don't you—"

Sarah sniffed the air, "My biscuits!!"

She rushed through the kitchen door into Mam's smile, "Already got 'em out, Misarah." Mam used 'Misarah' easily, the name of a longtime friend.

"Thank you, Mam."

Biscuit emergency over, Sarah felt the irritation again, murmuring, "Why can't he accept the fact Jed is twenty-three years old?"

"His pa was the same way," Mam offered knowingly. adding wisely, "prob'ly his pa before him."

Sarah speared thick slices of ham from the black skillet and slapped them impatiently onto a hot platter. How could Henry be so insensitive? Telling Jed he didn't want to hear any more.

She spooned portions of fluffy, golden eggs onto another serving dish. How could he do that?

She flicked the long-handled spoon. Its contents splattered the edge of the plate and divided. Most dropped inside, but a portion missed the mark and landed on the hot surface of the cook stove.

"God bless it!!" she hissed aloud, red-faced and irritated with the kitchen heat in addition to all else.

The errant eggs sizzled and smoked black as charcoal.

With a serving dish in each hand, Sarah stomped across the kitchen, backed into the dining room door, sending it swinging with a switch of her hip. She announced curtly, "Breakfast is ready," and louder, "breakfast, Grace."

Henry held his wife's chair as he always did in the dining room. Without a word, he marched around to his own place and sat stiffly. They ate quickly and in silence.

They went to church in silence, parroted the liturgical responses and prayers and returned home without a word.

"Change your clothes," Sarah said to Grace, needlessly for she was already half way up the staircase.

Henry changed clothes, too. He needed to work, to sweat, to get away from people, people like headstrong sons and ministers who didn't know enough to stop talking. Like wives with tears and you didn't know why.

Woodpiles were different. They didn't talk for an hour and a half every Sunday morning, or want to leave home, or carry on. Henry attacked the logs with buck saw and axe for three hours and felt better. He even waved at Sarah who he thought just happened to be standing in the window.

North at Littler's Run, the silence between Jed and Jonathan was interrupted by an army wagon rattling south, up the Valley. The muleskinner perched on the high seat looked worse off than his team, shapeless felt hat, threadbare trousers, and shirt of worn homespun that gapped wide where it had lost the fight with his belly. A stubble of beard, mostly gray, some black, covered his face. He slacked the reins for the mules to drink.

"Howdy," he greeted them, confidently sending a stream of tobacco juice past the whiffletree between the mule team. It spattered into Littler's Run and was washed away.

"Mornin'," Jed greeted him, "nice day. Not too hot."

The old mule skinner climbed stiffly, rump first onto the wheel rim and hub to the ground. "Yup. Where you boys goin'? Couple nights past old Patterson was headin' fer Williamsport ta cross inta Virginny. You two figgerin' on stoppin' him?"

The old teamster cackled staccato at his country joke. He spat amber again into the run.

"No, not us. We're not in the army yet."

"Well, Cun'l Jackson is down the road a bit and he'll stop them Yankees before they git too far."

"You say Colonel Jackson is up ahead? How far? We're looking for him so's t'join the Winchester Rifles."

"The Rifles! Ah know them. Cap'n Clark's Company. Cap'n Bill Clark. Mighty good man, Bill Clark."

The old mule skinner pointed, "Jus' keep ta the road an' y'll run right inta 'em. Jus' ask fer the Second Virginny. That's the regiment where The Rifles are."

"Thank you kindly, old timer. Appreciate it."

"But you boys be keerful uh Old Jack. He's been drillin' the b'jesus outa them boys. He got a new man, uh West P'inter that's bin givin' them fits. They'll fight when the time comes, but they don't think too kindly on drillin'. 'Ain't no sense t'it,' they say, 'war'll be ovah 'fore we git the hang of it'.

"Tell Cap'n Bill y'run inta me. Skinner Thomas, that's me. Own a farm in Fairfax County, near Vienna. Hired fer a couple months between plantin' an' harvest. Hard money—no scrip fer me. Prob'ly do the same nex' year if the war ain't done with."

Skinner Thomas retraced his two-step ladder to his seat spat again over the wiffletree, flicked the reins, lifted a lazy arm in farewell, and resumed his rattly ride.

Jed and Jonathan watched as he drove off, his rounded back moving easily to the lurches of the springless wagon.

"That Skinner Thomas must need the money bad," Jed pulled on his shoes, "seems a fellow old as him oughta be home scratchin' in his garden or playin' with his grandkids instead of bouncin' along behind a mule team. Must be older'n Pa.

"Y'know, Jon, I feel right bad sneakin' out on Pa. But there's no way I coulda stayed. I was plain suffocatin'."

He needed to be understood, "When I was a little kid, the school room suffocated me, too. I just wanted t'work with Zeke, out in the open. Then one day I saw a picture book of sail ships and other lands and I wanted t'see for myself."

"Jon, how come you just up and leave so suddenlike?"

They walked along in silence for several minutes.

"Jed, you're not the only one. I know just what you mean by suffocating. All day in the bank with my father watching every move. He knew everything I did, and everything about everything. And his stories of the war with Mexico! Over and over. He was a colonel and you would think he won it by himself."

They covered some distance before Jonathan continued, "I remember one time when I was a little boy. I ran into my parents' bedroom and my father was on top of my mother. I can see him now, looking over his shoulder, his face red as a beet, and him sweating and shouting to get the hell out of there.

"Ever since then, they were at me. Jonathan, stand up straight, Jonathan, study your lesson, go play outside, Jonathan, say 'sir', don't run in the house.

"When I went to work in the bank, it was worse, bring me the ledger, write your figures plain, show more respect.

"I thought Ruth would be different, but she was always picking at me, too, especially. . ."

He stopped abruptly, blood rising in his face. He looked sheepishly at Jed who knew better than to press him.

A half hour later, they were at Bunker Hill challenged by a cavalry lieutenant with a six-man detail returning from a scout over Apple Pie Ridge, "Lieutenant Rando'ph, First Virginia Cava'ry. State yoah business."

"Yessir. We're from Winchester, up here to enlist in The Winchester Rifles. This here is my friend, Jedediah Morrow."

"Howdy, lieutenant. Got two brothers up here somewheres. Brian Morrow, he's younger than me, private in the Liberty Hall Volunteers. You know him?"

"The Libuhty Hall Volunteahs? Doesn't ring a bell."

"My brother was in Winchester four days past and he said they were headin' for Harper's Ferry."

"Army left The Fay-ree to stop Pattuhson. Yoah brothuh's probably out hunting Yankees."

"My older brother's around here, too. David Morrow."

"Dave Morrow! Well, Ah'll be!" Randolph leaned in his saddle to shake hands, "A pleasure t'meet a brothuh of Dave's. Yessuh, Ah know Dave. Know him well, and that's a fact."

He threw a leg over the pommel of his saddle.

"Dave and Ah have had a coupla times togethuh. One night in Shepuhsdstown—what's the name of that Winchestuh comp'ny?"

"The Winchester Rifles. With the 2nd Virginia."

"That's Jackson's. Hold to this road," Lieutenant Randolph turned in his saddle and pointed, "their camp's not moah'n a mile. Ah'll tell Dave Ah saw you."

Jed and Jonathan found the campsite just as Jackson's vanguard marched in, "Lookin' for The Winchester Rifles."

"Stay where y'are an' they'll be comin' along. They was marchin' right behind us."

Before nightfall, they had signed the company muster as privates, joined friends at the campfires, listening to stories of the army, Harper's Ferry, and Colonel Jackson.

"You shoulda seen them engines sizzlin' in the river."

"Old Jackson, he's a hard man. Looks it, too, hardscrabble uniform an' all, but he's a real soljer. An' that loo'tenant uh his, whoo-ee! Like t'kill a man marchin' and drillin'."

"Day before yesterday, it was. We was ready for 'em but old Patterson he never came. We was marched one way and th'other. No sense t'it, no sense atall."

"Yesterday we was at Williamsport. Patterson fell back and Ole Jack had us smash up the B & O, rollin' stock, repair shops, storage sheds, the whole shootin' match. Damnyankee cowards."

"Marchin' fer nothin'," one complained, "Ah didn' join up t'wreck railroads. Joined up t'whip the Yankees and git home."

"Jed, your brother's with us. First lieutenant. He's 'nother hard sonofabitch, tough as Ole Jack. One day I seen 'im march uh comp'ny right inta th'ground. They was plumb fagged out. But most the men like 'im, say he knows what he's doin'."

They also learned of Jackson's anger with his commander for leaving Harper's Ferry without a fight, listened to complaints about maggots in the biscuit, Yankees across the Potomac; and painted women easy to bed down.

They talked with their friends until the bugles blew, and continued in hushed tones afterward. Gradually, it died out.

Jed turned to Jonathan, "Haven't seen you so easy since we left home. You and the army will get along fine."

"Everything will be all right. I can feel it."

X

"SEEING THE ELEPHANT"
AT FALLING WATERS
JULY, 1861

At early dawn, David Morrow was up and ready, impatient to be off on his first patrol, anxious that nothing go wrong. Information was that Yankees were about to ford the upper Potomac. His job was to observe and give timely warning. With him were a sergeant he did not know, Corporal Tom Rafferty whom he regarded highly, and nine privates.

He waited on those late for his muster. Ex-West Pointer David Morrow steamed, chafing to be gone. He paced the ground. He inspected gear and weapons, his own three times. He examined Sable from bridle to hooves.

Finally, the malingerers appeared, three of them, as slovenly in attitude as in appearance. Their swagger reeked insolence. In no mood to let the challenge slide, David grimaced fiercely at the foulest one. He let fly.

"Dirty, foul, grimy, filthy, rusty! You, your horse, tack, weapons. You, SIR, are an insult to the army!

"SERGEANT," he bawled, "escort this individual to the provost marshal. He is to remained confined until I return."

The sergeant glared for the culprit was his cousin, "What's the charge, sir?"

"Charge? You need to ask the charge, sergeant? Absent from muster. Disobedience of orders. Conduct unbecoming a soldier. A hazard to this patrol. Silent insubordination. Buttons missing. Snotty nose. Pick your own charge. You get me!"

"Yessir." He marched the man off.

With the second of the culprits, David went eyeball to eyeball, "The order ATTENTION does *not*, I repeat, *NOT* mean slouch. It means shoulders *back*, guts *in*, heels *together*.

"NOW!"

He approached the third, "You have anything to say, Mister?"

"Me? No sir. Not me, sir."

David scowled up and down the line, had more to say, decided against it, "Prepare to mount in one minute. REST!"

The formation dissolved, and the soldiers bitched.

"He sure het up this mornin'."

"Threw a double duck fit, he did."

"Got a damn bug up his ass!"

Corporal Rafferty intervened, "Like last week when he found the rag in your musket, eh. Coulda blown your face off."

"Sure'n hell somethin' make him complainy."

"Parade-ground sonabitch."

Corporal Rafferty knew the boundaries, "Can it, Gibson, that's goin' too far. One a' these days, we're gonna meet up with Yankees. The lieutenant knows what he's doin'."

"Mount up," David yelled impatiently, "the order is to find them and report. Avoid contact. Rafe, you ride with me." He vaulted into the saddle, arm signaled, his irritation waning now that he was on his way.

"HeeYaaa! Go, boy, go!!" Spurred by David's excitement, Sable lifted his fore legs and took off at a gallop. Atop the first rise, David awaited Rafferty and Princess. Sable shook his head as if to say, ' Why are we stopping?"

Rafferty queried opposite, "Why the hurry, lieutenant?"

"Come on! There's Yankees out there."

Sable caught the smell of Rafferty's mare. "You hear me, Sable, there's Yankees ahead." David sidled him into the breeze.

He and his corporal trotted north, David wary, edgy, leading the patrol by 100 yards. Abreast them at the same distance were two outriders, one to either side, swallowed and regurgitated by patches of trees and dips in the ground.

David scanned the ground ceaselessly, stopping, starting, twisting in his saddle, stopping again. He fidgeted with his weapons, loosening the saber, spinning the cylinder of his revolver. He dismounted to inspect Sable's hooves. Rafe had never seen him strung so tight.

"Problem, Lieutenant?"

"Just checking."

"He looks fine t'me, sir."

"Two months is a long time to wait for some action."

He fretted the next fifty yards, "Hell, it's longer than that! I've been training five years.

"Where's that goddamn flanker?"

The one on the right, the critical side toward the Yankees, had been out of sight overlong.

"Damnit! Rafe, ride over there, see what's happened to him."

The missing rider came into view.

"Prob'ly just stopped t'water the weeds," Rafe suggested.

"He should have pissed before we started. Christ! five years training, and we get bushwhacked because he has to piss."

David settled into his black hole, scowling, watchful, searching, searching, seeing nothing in the rolling countryside. They picked their way through Falling Waters, toward Williamsport and the Potomac crossings.

"You think we'll find 'em today, lieutenant?"

"I'm sure. I can smell it. You loaded and ready?"

"Sir, I thought the orders were to avoid contact."

"Maybe theirs are different."

"Yes, sir. Six and one in the chamber. Mind a question?"

"Keep it short."

"Why are. . ."

Raising a hand to halt the patrol up the road, David spoke quietly, "Rafe. you hear that?" He squinted into the gentle rise ahead. He stood in his stirrups, "There it is again. Take a look. Stop short of the top. Keep low."

Rafferty reached the military crest. The urgency of his signal said it all, "Yankees!"

David signaled a new direction to his flankers and diverged right for a copse of trees on the ridge line. Rafferty angled down the slope to follow him. From the far edge of the trees, they looked onto a fragmented column halted on the highway, not a thousand yards off. More Yankees than either had ever seen.

Most sat alongside the road, some stretched out, a few on their feet. Around the perimeter, others relieved themselves, some standing, some squatting elbows to knees. Here and there, one smiled relief and heisted his britches.

"Rafe. We've got the vanguard, damn it, we've got 'em."

"Yes sir," Rafferty felt relief, too, for the lieutenant's pique was gone. He had recovered now that the waiting was over.

David squinted furrows and crows' feet at a group of officers. One saluted and rode off, back toward the river. "Rafe," he even sounds happy, "that looks like staff. Enough for a general. What do you think?"

"Looks so from how they're trucklin' t'that one officer. A brigade, two three regiments. Don't spot but two flags, though."

"Rafe, you've got a good eye. Maybe 2,000," With controlled excitement he studied the column, "Anything else?"

"A couple a' flashes across the river. Could be the sun reflecting off guns or limbers. Or off muskets. Could be infantry and last night's rain keeping the dust down."

"They're waiting for them to cross and close up, I'd bet a paymaster's lockbox. Could be a division in all."

They observed a few minutes longer, then withdrew through the trees to the patrol halted in the roadway.

Dancing Sable up to the sergeant, David spoke rapid-fire. "There's Yankees halted on the road. About 2,000, more ready to cross, maybe artillery. I want to report this to Colonel Stuart myself, so the patrol is yours.

"Sergeant, keep close scrutiny. Scout around them, to the ford. Report every twenty minutes, sooner if you think necessary, road, direction of march, progress, or no change. Also when that other column crosses. I'm taking Rafferty with me."

"Yes sir."

"Good. Repeat it."

"Road, direction, location, crossings, no change. Every twenty minutes." David noted the sergeant's efficiency.

"Or sooner. And tell them to be careful. No heroes."

"Yes sir. And, lieutenant . . . ," the sergeant hesitated.

"Yes?"

"You were right back there at camp. Those three were way out of line."

"Why, thank you, sergeant. Lives are at stake. And duty.

"Rafe, I want you to follow me at 75 yards. If I run into trouble, hightail it for Colonel Stuart and report what we saw."

Rafferty looked puzzled, "But the road's clear, sir." He paused, "You expectin' a ruckus?"

"Not expecting. Just preparing for."

Rafferty took note and was impressed, "YesSIR."

By 7:30 A.M. Jeb Stuart had relayed David's information to General Jackson at Camp Stephens, and passed orders for his men to saddle up. He called for David.

"General Jackson wants to hear about the Yankees firsthand."

"I'd like Rafferty to accompany me. Your permission, sir?"

"Granted. I'll go with you too."

The corporal was happily surprised, not every soldier had the opportunity to meet the general face to face.

"Morning, general," David snapped a parade ground salute to Jackson. Rafferty saluted, too, trying to match it.

"I hear Stuart's been working you and that stallion."

"He has indeed, sir. This is Corporal Rafferty. general. He saw them first." David gave his report.

Jackson nodded to Jeb Stuart, "Same as your messenger, colonel. Anything to add, corporal?"

"No sir, the lieutenant covered it all."

"It's got to be Patterson," Jackson said softly to himself, punching fist to palm, "Major Massie, I want a regiment ready to move at once, and Captain Pendleton with one battery. The others to load wagons and stand by to move. Stuart, you know what to do. I've waited a long time for this day."

Leaving headquarters, Jeb Stuart complimented David, "A good report. Just what he likes, short and to the point. Stay close to me today. And keep your eyes open."

"Yes, sir. And thank you, colonel."

David had made a friend of Rafferty, too, "Thanks for including me, lieutenant. I saw the mess at The Ferry before the general took over. He knows what he's doing."

"That he does, Rafe, that he does."

"Did you see his eyes shining? He's a fighter."

David couldn't miss Rafferty's zeal. He liked it well.

Stuart's bugler blew "boots and saddles," mounted troopers formed companies, captains to the front. David cantered over to the Washington Mounted Rifles.

"Captain Jones, the colonel ordered me to ride with him."

"H'rrumph," growled the irascible Jones, called "Grumble."

David saluted, smiling as he rode away, not meanly for he liked the old curmudgeon. He reined up alongside Stuart.

"Two of your patrol came in. One reported 'no change' and the other that they were moving toward Falling Waters. With more fording the river. Infantry."

"I'd like to talk with the couriers, sir."

"Sent them to the general."

"You know how old Patterson is?"

"No. But he fought the British in 1812."

Stuart took note, "Lieutenant, you ever unprepared?"

"Like everybody else, sir. But not if I can help it."

Meanwhile, Jackson was riding north with Kenton Harper, Colonel, 5th Virginia Infantry, the same Harper who had told David to enlist as a private.

The regiment contacted the invaders in the fields of a farmer named Haines, two miles south of Falling Waters. To get a better view of their first Bluecoats, men climbed trees and rail fences. Jackson put a quick end to it.

He sent snipers to Haines' farmhouse and outbuildings, the rest of the regiment into a woods, where each man found a tree, rock, or bush for cover. He ordered Captain Pendleton, a 52-year old Episcopal priest to advance one of his four guns.

A courier galloped up on a lathered horse, "Colonel Stuart's compliments, sir. The Yankees look more than reported earlier. Three, maybe four thousand. And they're all moving this way."

"You see them, soldier?"

"Yes, sir. I scouted to the river. Road is full of them."

"How many flags? Did you count flags?"

"Yessir. Six."

"Thank you. Your horse needs attention, soldier."

"Yessir, right away, sir."

The Yankee battle line advanced across farmer Haines' land. Snipers in the barnyard opened fire. The battle line came on. The snipers fell back. Bluecoats pressed, firing blindly into the trees. Hidden at the wood's edge, the 5th Virginia was about to fight its first fight, to see the elephant.

The Yankees came toward them. Soldiers of the 5th glanced expectantly at their officers.

They waited the order to open fire.

They sweat. They twitched nervous in the dry leaves.

Still no order.

The Yankees came on.

They itched. They scratched. They chewed. They spat.

"Steady, men, hold your fire!"

More waiting. Restless seconds.

"For Chrissakes, cun'l!"

The Yankees were close.

More sweat.

"PREPARE TO FIRE BY VOLLEY."

"Thanks be to God."

"AIM!"

"FIRE!"

Flame flashed from the tree line.

"RELOAD AND FIRE AT WILL."

Smoke from black powder puffed and drifted into the open.

The Reverend Pendleton patted his 6-pounder and shouted, "The Lord have mercy on their souls! FIRE!"

The little gun spewed fire and canister.

Bodies fell, some still, others twitching, cursing. The Yankee line hesitated, closed up the holes. It moved forward again. The 6-pounder boomed a second time, and a third. A Federal gun returned the fire. For one hour they fought, biting cartridges until mouths were black.

The 2nd and 4th Virginia, having loaded the wagons, double-timed into position by Pendleton's 3-gun reserve.

Patterson took his losses and extended his line beyond the Confederate flanks. Jackson saw the danger and ordered Harper back on the 2nd and 4th. He waited confidently, but Patterson lost heart. Jed and Jonathan with the 2nd, and Brian with the 4th had an easy introduction to hostile gunfire.

During the action, David lost Stuart, but caught up to get a lesson on boldness. There was Stuart ordering Union infantry to dismantle a rail fence, 49 Pennsylvania volunteers, who mistook him for one of their own until he ordered them to surrender.

"Halloo," Stuart boomed merrily, delighted with his catch.

"Too bad you didn't have a pack of hounds, Colonel, you could have rounded up the whole column."

Jeb Stuart's hearty laugh rang raucous.

It was two weeks later that Brian found his brother.

"David! I've been looking all over for you."

Private Brian Morrow immediately assumed a charade of regret, "Beg the lieutenant's pardon, sir."

His salute was parade-ground, worthy of General Lee himself, but his acting skills failed. The merriment in his eyes and the tomfoolery that played around the corners of his mouth gave him away. David played along, delaying his return salute.

"The lieutenant accepts the private's apology. . ."

Brian compressed his lips to control the smile.

"accepts with the stipulation that the corporal will. . ."

Brian stifled the rising laugh, showing pink.

"will refrain from unsoldierly familiarities with . . ."

Dark pink, cherry, vermilion, purple.

"unsoldierly familiarities with officers."

With exquisite timing, David returned the salute slowly, very, very slowly, letting the pressure grow. Until, like a blowhole Brian burst, spraying sparkling droplets.

"Should have known better than to start a contest with you."

"Don't feel bad, Briney. I was at the end of my string, too."

"Have you seen Jed? He's close by."

"No, let's get him."

"Get him? Do you mean what I think you mean?"

"You've got the picture, private. Lead on."

Nearing the bivouac of the 2nd Virginia, David dropped behind, his kepi low over his eyes. Brian hailed his brother.

"Jed, come over here to meet one of our officers."

Supine against the smooth bark of a wild cherry tree, Jed yawned, stretched and looked up at the silhouette of his brother against the bright moonlight.

"Hello, Briney."

"Want you to meet my lieutenant, Jed, we shared a room at college. And we're still good friends even if he is an officer."

Jed saw only a chin, a mouth, the tip of a nose, and the top of a kepi. It could have been anybody. He yawned, "Hello, David."

Disappointed, Brian grumbled "How'd you know?"

"He's my brother. I ought to know him. And if I di'nt, I'd know Sable. I fed him and curried him enough to recognize him a mile away," he laughed as he stood up, "from any angle."

Accepting the collapse of their little balloon of a joke, the conspirators threw up their hands.

"David, I am glad t'see you," Jed bear-hugged him. "We been hearin' how you drilled men into the ground at The Ferry."

"I wasn't that tough, Jed."

"Not t'hear some of 'em tell it. I said you belonged t'the horse thief branch of the family."

"Sorry if they were friends, Jed. I had a job to do."

"They weren't. Some men aren't happy 'less they're gripin'."

Brian broke in, "I hear it in my company, too."

"Same in Captain Jones's Mounted Rifles," David offered, "the men complain about him, and you can see why. He's a cantankerous, sour old man everyone calls 'Grumble'."

"I've heard stories of him, mainly how jealous he is of Colonel Stuart," Brian added.

"He is that. Calls him 'that young whippersnapper'. Stuart likes to enjoy himself. Captain Jones hates it, rather sit alone in his tent. But his men will follow him anywhere. He knows his job and they respect him."

Jed spoke up, "You have t'take to a man like that. I'd be in his company in a minute. Should be more like him."

"You're right," agreed David, "a mean spirit can make life unpleasant, but incompetency can get a man killed."

Washington headlines shrieked, "FORWARD TO RICHMOND." General Irvin McDowell pleaded for time, "My men are green. They are untrained."

President Lincoln replied dryly, "So are the rebels."

McDowell saluted and marched west for Manassas Junction, an important rail center, and the first Confederate defense line on the road to Richmond.

The Southerners' line was a broken one on the right bank of Bull Run, covering the fords from Stone Bridge on the Warrenton turnpike to the railroad bridge downstream at Union Mills Ford. Limited manpower made the steep banks of the muddy little stream an important part of the defense.

On July 18, Confederate troops left the Shenandoah Valley to reinforce their compatriots in Manassas, too late for the Federal reconnaissance at Blackburn's Ford, upstream of Union Mills.

The skirmish was a small one, its 150 casualties paling before the 4,900 killed and wounded three days later. To the one hundred and fifty, though, it was a very nasty affair indeed.

Jackson's brigade marched through Winchester and out of the Valley, 2,600 Virginians in five regiments, the 2nd Virginia Infantry, Brian and the Liberty Hall Volunteers, the 4th Virginia and Jed's Winchester Rifles, and the 5th, 27th, and 33rd.

"Any idea where we're going, Brian?"

"Can't tell. Maybe to flank Patterson. If we cross the Blue Ridge we could be going to Washington, Manassas Junction, Fredericksburg, or farther south to Richmond."

"How do you know all that?" one challenged.

"Studied Captain White's maps."

Jackson's Brigade marched through Winchester at 3 P.M. through Ashby's Gap at midnight, and halfway down the eastern slope of the Blue Ridge to Paris by 2 A.M. on the 19th.

Bringing up the rear of the 2nd Virginia, The Liberty Hall Volunteers made camp. In the dark, Brian's friend, Lieutenant John Lyle, found a ground contour that fit him like a glove he said, and dropped off to sleep.

Dawn reveille revealed a cemetery.

In the half-light, Brian was the first to see that Lyle's cozy nest marked a grave where the soil had settled, "I'm happy you're getting another chance, John."

"What do you mean, another chance?"

"Looks to me you're rising from the dead, sitting up in that grave."

Lyle looked around to see the small headstone staring him in the face, and scrambled as though his life depended on it. The men joshed him all the way to Manassas Junction.

"Lieutenant, you heerd 'bout the man who couldn't die?"

"Or the ghost who wouldn't stay buried?"

The young officer could only grin sheepishly and take the raillery in good spirits. The macabre humor ended three days later when they looked on hundreds of corpses on Henry Hill.

A half mile ahead, Jed wakened to less humor than Brian, "Damn, it's hardly light. Ole Jack, he hasn't any mercy."

Jonathan stretched and yawned, "My God, he'll kill us marching, before we fire a shot."

Regimental and company officers shouted up and down the roadway. Sergeants bawled orders.

"Form up, men, time to move out."

"Shake those men awake. Get 'em up. Get 'em up."

"Into line, men, into line. The General's ready to move."

Sleepily, the men stumbled south toward Piedmont Station.

"Jed, how long will it take to get to Manassas?"

"Hell, Jon, I don't know. It's just one foot ahead of the other, same as plowin' a field."

As they marched, Jed Stuart remained in the Valley drawing a cordon around Patterson so tightly that he was unaware of Jackson's march for three days, until the 21st when the battle for Manassas was already in progress.

At Piedmont, the men loaded into boxcars of the Manassas Gap Railroad, the mainline into the Shenandoah Valley. Some climbed to the roofs. The more astute among them recognized the importance of Manassas Junction when they saw its network of rail connections to Alexandria, Fredericksburg, Richmond, to Gordonsville and the upper Valley. They rattled into Manassas Junction in mid-afternoon.

The regiments camped near Blackburn's Ford, scene of the previous day's action. Pine groves gave shade for comfort and needles for a bed. Five miles upstream was Stone Bridge and the hill where the aged Widow Henry lay helpless in her bed.

As Jackson's Brigade was arriving in Manassas, Jeb Stuart and his cavalry departed The Valley, having successfully screened the infantry's move.

"Sergeant," bellowed Stuart, "Lieutenant Morrow is to report to me until further notice. Inform Captain Jones."

"Lieutenant, you may have surmised that we're taking the blinders off Patterson. We're off to the east and glory."

"Yes sir. Smells to me like the real war."

"Looks so. I want you on my staff. Choose your title, aide-de-camp, assistant adjutant, secretary."

Stuart drew a turnip of a pocket watch from his waistcoat, clicked the cover, "You have twenty minutes to get your gear."

XI

PANIC ON BULL RUN
1861

Saturday, July 20, was a day for Jackson's soldiers to rest. Some slept; others wrote letters; still others played brag, a poker game with three wild cards. Several curious of Longstreet's skirmish on the 18th, walked the Bull Run ford called Blackburn's. They stood on the banks of the muddy stream with men who had fought there, blooded veterans now. Their skirmish took on new and newer dimensions as they explained and pointed.

"Here's where they cum across."

"That's wheah Ah seen 'em fust."

Brian headed for the ford with Ted Barclay and John Lyle, happy with a duty-free day, excited to be exploring the scene of Longstreet's action. Their talk was cheery, steps springy, three boys on a lark, their muskets incongruous.

Brian and his friends stood thoughtfully at temporary burial mounds, lonely holes, lonelier bodies. The glory of war became more complex. Could this be me? In a month? Next week? Tomorrow?

Their questions remained unasked, still too alien, too private. Innocence lingered uneasily.

Brian tarried at one unwanted mound, reflecting that two days ago its occupant was full of life, walking the woods, wading the sluggish stream, suddenly stumbling awkward, without answers to questions that came too late to ask.

Brian was touched, imagining a family as his own, sad that their son was away, mercifully ignorant of his death for now. He reflected that Northern families would grieve as those in the South, just as those in The Valley, in Winchester. On Wolfe Street perhaps?

The morning's enthusiasm shriveled.

Brian, the young scholar, became less scholarly in the woods at Blackburn's Ford, less ingenuous, even more thoughtful. School and philosophy books faded. "How many angels on the head of a pin" became irrelevant. He called after his friends.

They had gone on ahead, leaving him with his soldier ghosts, alone in the piney woods.

Sunlight filtered through the trees. A passing cloud raised slithery shadows from the forest floor. He called again, anxiously. Anxiously, he started after them.

Up ahead, the undergrowth took on eerie shapes. Thorns and branches grabbed as he went by. The humidity closed about him. The air weighed heavy, morbid. Sweating now, his fright mounted. He conjured hidden Yankees and long gun barrels aimed at his head.

He craved silence and invisibility, but needed his friends, "Ted, John, helloooo."

No answer. He called again. Nothing. He ran after them.

Then he remembered an expression from back in The Valley. "Scheisskopf, you stupid scheisskopf," he chastised himself, "skittish as a spooked horse. Spooked by your own imagination."

He fought the incipient panic. He hastened on.

A few feet from the muddy stream, his boot tangled with a leather strap attached to a canteen he knew was Yankee, quite different than his wooden one. The intricate swirls and designs in the strap caught his attention. He reached for it.

Suddenly, he sensed movement behind him, nothing more than a current of air. A warning crashed into his mind. Too late!

A muddy boot crushed down on his outstretched hand. Rough leather rasped tender skin, forced him belly down, face to the mire. In one compressed moment, conjurations of Yankees became one man, close up, real, knife-sticking close. He had time only for his soul.

'Our Father who art in heaven . . .'

He saw Ezekiel and the hog. Ezekiel plunged his blade. Into throat and belly. His throat. His belly.

'Hallowed be thy name . . .'

Ezekiel pulled the blade. Syrupy blood spurted and spilt, spoiled and desecrated.

'Thy kingdom come . . .'

Hopeless, Brian collapsed, face deep into the muddy clay. He felt its silkiness along his cheek, smelled its wild sweetness.

'Thy will be done . . .'

His mother ministered to a small boy. Taking a giant mote of dust from his eye.

MUMMA I NEED YOU NOW. ITS GETTING BIGGER!

'on earth as it is in heaven.'

He clamped his eyes tight to ward off impending doom.

'Give us this day our daily . . .'

He clawed the buttery clay desperately, without purpose.

"If I was you, I'd leave that canteen set."

Still holding the tooled strap, Brian heard the words, hollow and distant. He lay brainless, empty, dangling. A chill washed his body. No knife thrust came. Nothing. Nothing but time, a single distorted second that refused to tick.

"May be it's full of Winchester brew. And you know what happens when you drink Winchester brew."

The words emerged, taking shape as a ship slipping a fog bank, the intonation and cadence, a familiar drawl. By degrees the terror subsided, slowly at first, more rapidly as terror does when the unknown becomes known. The crushing boot relaxed.

Reason filled the void. The second ticked away, making time for the next and the next. Brian rolled onto his back. He blinked against the bright sunshine streaking through the trees. A familiar outline silhouetted in the back light, came into focus, shaggy head, wide shoulders, deep chest. Details emerged, the open grin, dark hair, big hands.

"Jed! Jed! You damned—You—You—Jed! What did—What were . . .?" Furious, he flung red mud at his brother.

"You like to scare the shit outa me, Jed. Goddamn, I almost shit in my pants. Jed, damn you, you 'most made me shit my pants."

Speechless for a moment, Jed chastised his brother gently, "Never heard you talk like that."

Brian dug a toehold for leverage. He drove a shoulder sharply into Jed's thigh, throwing him back, onto the ground. The two of them grappled in the slippery clay there at Blackburn's Ford, rolling over and over. Brian thought only of hurting his brother, to get even, to cleanse his fear.

He grabbed for Jed's throat, but was no match. Jed easily muscled him helpless, and cooed to break the anger.

"Simmer down, little brother. I'm Jed. Remember me? I'm the one you grew up with. The one that taught you t'ride, and which end of the horse t'put the bridle on. Cool down, Briney, I didn't mean t'scare you that much."

"Well, you did, goddamn it, you scared the shit outa me."

"Tsk, tsk, such language."

"I never had such reason to use it before, you big—you—you—you big brother."

Sitting there in the mud, the two stared at one another. Brian reached for the Yankee canteen with the tooled strap, "I'm not about to leave this behind after all this."

Jed smiled. Brian's eyes softened. Jed chuckled softly. In a moment, their laughter filled the woods.

"Jed, what are you doing here?"

"Got here yesterday. Jon's over yonder." He waved to him. "He wanted ta give us a chance ta—t'talk.

"We've been trackin' you for a while. Saw you lag behind and I figgered it time t'teach you t'guard your rear."

He lowered his voice. "Briney, there's people around here that don't wish you any good. Better you learn it from me. And just so's you understand proper language, guard your rear means protect your ass."

Jonathan reached them, "I told him not to be too rough on you, Brian. It's good to see you."

"Hello, Jon," he wiped the clammy clay and perspiration of fear, "never expected to meet you here."

Jonathan offered his hand and said proudly,

"Company F, better known as the Winchester Rifles. We wanted to be with people we knew."

Further exploration of the site of General Longstreet's skirmish was forgotten. The three of them sat in a pleasant glade talking for the rest of the afternoon.

"Did you get to see Pa before you left? Or Dave?"

"No and yes. Pa's still mad. But General Jackson took a liking to Dave for the way he ran bayonet drills. Some girl in Sheperdstown took a likin' to him, too, I heard."

"Since you brought it up, I need to talk to you about another girl. Betsy?"

"Jon, you have to excuse us, but this is important."

Jon left them to sit meditatively by Bull Run.

"What did happen that night we were in Betsy's room, Jed? You have to tell me, whatever it was."

A month ago, it had been good fun to let Brian stew in his uncertainties, but the casualties at Falling Waters had disturbed Jed, and now these at Blackburn's Ford. Brian could die with the guilt of betrayal on his soul. The charade that Betsy had launched in good humor was no longer funny.

Even so, Jed wasn't averse to a brief postponement.

"Like I told you that mornin', Briney, it doesn't make any difference. Betsy was happy and I'm satisfied with that."

"That isn't an answer and you know it. Betsy loves you. And you love her. That's pretty obvious. I didn't realize that at the tavern, not until the morning we left.

"Now, I have to know if I said anything or did anything at all that was objectionable to her." Brian hesitated.

"Or if I—or if—Jed, did I . . .? I was in her bed, for God sakes. I have to know if I did anything to hurt her or you." He pleaded, "If I did, I'll get on my knees and beg forgiveness. I'll do the same with Betsy. Tell me the truth, Jed, please."

"Briney, whatever you think you did that night, forget it."

Jed paused, watching his brother's discomfiture, toying with him for a few more seconds.

"Jed, for God's sake . . ."

"You didn't do a thing. I dumped you on Betsy's bed, and you were out cold until mornin'. You couldn'a got up if you wanted.

"And you couldn'a gotten nothin' else up either."

Jed roared at his earthy joke, but Brian was too preoccupied absorbing his innocence. He looked up quizzically, failing to understand the laughter. Jed put his arm around his brother's shoulders, "You didn't do anythin' that Betsy took offense at."

"You sure you're telling me the truth?

"So help me, Briney, it's the honest truth." He raised his right hand. "You couldn'a done anythin' even if you wanted to."

"I'm surely relieved to hear that. It really bothered me."

"I know it did. Betsy is sorry as I am. It kind of got out of hand. Before I left, she told me she shouldn't have teased you that way. But she couldn't help it, she said, you were such an easy mark.

"She really likes you a lot, Briney. She said that, too, and if she didn't, she wouldn'a done it."

"She is some woman, Jed. You hold on to her."

"I like that holdin' on t'her and I plan t'do a lot more. Soon as this war's done with, we're goin' t'cut the cake, get ourselves hitched. I told her that before I left."

On the road back to their camps, Brian attempted his own joke, "Jed, you don't suppose Betsy wanted to dump you for me and that's why she said what she did?"

"Could be. Yes, it surely could be," Jed said thoughtfully. He paused several seconds, then added,

"Except for one thing, little brother. Y're forgettin' what started the whole thing."

"I could never forget that. It was Betsy whispering to me that she had a wonderful time.

"That's right! And she did. Takes two t'have a good time like that. I was the other one, little brother, not you."

"Just the way it should have been, Jed, just exactly the way it should have been."

XII

CARNAGE
JULY 21, 1861

The day after the brothers' reunion in the mud of Blackburn's Ford dawned clear and warm. Ordinarily, its being Sunday, the soldiers would be at leisure, or as General Jackson, communing with the Lord. The Sabbath, he believed, was a day for churchgoing, reading the Bible, meditation and prayer.

By dawn, he was up and about, knowing he would deny his holy obligations and the Lord's peace this Sabbath day.

Those sleeping into the dawn were routed out by gunfire from Stone Bridge, Yankees feinting an attack to cover the real assault a mile west, down Sudley Road and Matthews' Hill, past the Stone House where Sudley Road crossed the Warrenton turnpike. Fighting grimly against superior numbers, the Butternuts fell back, fought again. Yankees pursued them onto Henry Hill. Jackson's Brigade double-quicked to stem the tide.

He deployed his Virginia regiments to receive the onslaught, using to advantage an unimposing but critical hollow in the ground, Brian's 2nd Virginia on the right toward Bull Run, Jed's and Jon's 4th on the left. Jeb Stuart's cavalry extended the left some 500 yards at Sudley Road. David shadowed his new commander.

The infantry regiments hugged the ground, cringing at whining shells from guns on Matthews' Hill. Jed nudged his friend, "Ain't this somethin'. Clawin' the ground like moles."

Jon spat dirt, "Yeh, maybe it was a mistake to sign up."

Another shell exploded above them, scattering lethal shards of iron. Blood stained Jon's sleeve. It oozed down his arm, along his hand. It dripped onto the ground.

"Y're hit, Jon! Y're hit!" Jed tore open the sleeve, felt through torn flesh for broken bones. Ripping off the damaged sleeve for a make-do bandage, he bound the wound tightly.

"We're goin' t'the rear. Your arm needs a doctor."

Jed stood up.

"Git yer ass down, soldier. 'less ya want it shot off."

Jed dropped. He threw an arm across Jon's shoulders.

"The sergeant's right, Jed. I'll be all right."

Bluecoats advanced behind their own cannon fire, bobbing, weaving, taking cover, running low again. Down Matthews Hill and across Sudley Road they poured, many into eternity, a few to flag rank and fame.

West Pointer George "Fanny" Custer was one of them, with the cavalry supporting the field guns. Now a lieutenant, he had reported to the adjutant general in Washington for assignment. "Company G, 2nd Cavalry," the officer said and took him into the next room to meet General Winfield Scott, General in Chief of the army since 1841. "Provide yourself with a horse, if possible, and call here at seven o'clock this evening," Scott said, "I have dispatches for General McDowell at Centreville—want you to deliver them." Horses were hard to come by, but with "Custer luck" he found one and was on his way in high spirits. McDowell commanded the army south of the Potomac and meeting him could be a boost to his career. His luck ran out, however, for an aide insisted the dispatches be given to him. A disappointed Custer joined his company.

Artillerymen careened down Sudley Road, precarious on their high seats, white-knuckling handholds. Drivers lashed frenzied horses up the hill toward Jackson's line. In seconds, guns were unlimbered, loaded, and firing at short range.

Men fought amongst the cannons, clubbing with muskets and rammers. Virginians shot the horses to immobilize the guns. New York Zouaves in red shirts and blue pants shot the Virginians.

Brian and the Liberty Hall boys ran to help, whooping enough for the whole regiment. They crashed into the Zouaves in their fancy uniforms and tassled fezzes. They fought bloody, hand-to-hand.

Brian caught the glitter of a bayonet and side-stepped, twisting as one Zouave lunged. He felt the blade inside his arm, felt it twist, seeking a soft spot between his ribs. He jammed his musket into the softness beneath the fellow's chin, squeezed the trigger. The smoke cleared, revealing a head with no face. It was blown to hell.

The explosion sprayed Brian with bone and bloody tissue. He screamed crazily. Running after his comrades, he found himself alongside William Paxton, his corporal and friend.

"My God, Brian, you've been hit bad. Get to the rear."

"Not me, Bill, I'm fine," Brian yelled wildly, wiping at the filth on his face, now viscous sticky. His sleeve came away red and foul. He looked at it blankly. It meant nothing.

"Brian, you sure you're . . ."

A minie ball smacked. Corporal Paxton fell dead.

Jeb Stuart with 150 troopers debouched from woods across Sudley Road. Mistaking the Zouaves for a Louisiana battalion with a similar flamboyant uniform, he shouted encouragement. A breeze caught the Zouaves' flag.

Alongside, David yelled, "Stars and stripes, sir! They're Yankees."

"Charge," boomed Stuart, and 300 rowels kicked horses' flanks. David and his colonel raced in front. They flew through a break in one rail fence, galloped for another, shifting weight, urging steeds. Feeling Sable gather for the leap, David leaned into it, holding with his knees. Stuart was on his left.

They took the second fence together, soaring side by side, stirrup to stirrup, floating, suspended in air, horses' forelegs tucked daintily, hind legs extended, tufted manes and feathered tails frozen in time, two men and two gleaming horses creating a flash of synchronized beauty in the pandemonium.

David and his colonel were as hinged extensions of their mounts, closing tight to the withers, opening again as the horses rotated through their exquisite leaps.

Into the Yankee line they pounded, David guiding on Stuart. In the melee they were separated.

Men faltered. Men went down. Horse pistols popped. Sabers hissed. Carbines flashed fire and became clubs. Wild-eyed horses with empty saddles reared and snorted. Zouaves fired and reloaded with an efficiency that confirmed their training.

David spotted one loading his musket. He put the spurs to Sable. The Yankee pulled the ramrod. David saw the black hole of the muzzle, a perfect circle. He gave Sable his head. The black hole doubled in size. David screeched, HeeeYaaa."

Time expanded and the black hole expanded, cannon-muzzle big. In its center, David caught a flash of golden flame, and felt a tug at his forearm.

Sable bowled into the fancy uniform. The lead bullet ripped through David's sleeve. Eyes and mouth agape, the Zouave screamed maniac-mad at a black demon with iron for feet and fire for eyes. Sable veered left. David swung his saber. They were behind the Yankee line.

He caught the flash of Stuart's blade, swinging circles overhead, pointing toward Jackson. The two of them rallied scattered troopers into a tumbleweed formation.

Stuart's big blade hissed its message, "Follow me."

Back they raced to safety, David and Stuart side by side, black flank to chestnut, driving through the remnants of the Federal line, through the debris, through the screaming wounded and the silent dead, through the danger of those still alive. David slashed right; Stuart, cross-handed to his left.

Some of the troopers kept on going, east on Sudley Road. "Get them," Stuart yelled. David and an adjutant wheeled and brought them back.

Meanwhile, a few hundred yards to the west, Yankees pushed across Henry Hill, unaware of Jackson's men behind a wave of ground, waiting, waiting, dry-throated, cussing empty canteens. On order, they stood up, appearing to startled Yankees to have risen from the ground itself.

A volley rolled down Jackson's line. Federals recoiled.

A Confederate officer commented on a Yankee's valor.

"Kill the brave ones," Jackson growled, "and the rest will give up."

Deep in Jackson's soul lurked the warrior he was, an age-old strain of Celtic savagery from the highlands of Northern Ireland: "Kill! Kill the enemy before he destroys you."

Confederate leaders bawled and croaked drily, "Forward." Bayonets glinted in the afternoon sunlight. Bearded men in slouch hats shifted tobacco from one cheek to the other and spat into their future. For some, this chaw was the final fragment of life, its juices the final ejaculation. They pulled at hat brims and squinted at forever.

They moved out, straight here, bowed there, obliquing around obstacles, left and right, stretching and squeezing as bellows on a giant accordion. All day, Bluecoats had driven them across the fields and woods of Manassas; they would be pushed no more.

The tide had changed and they knew it. The momentum was theirs. Near the center of the line now, Brian felt it and cheered, free of yesterday's terror, exhilarated by the sense of victory. Off to his left Jed sensed it, too, and stepped off waving his company forward. Jonathan walked next to him, like a man in a dream, looking neither left nor right.

From somewhere in the line came a piercing scream, perhaps a soldier remembering David's bayonet instruction at Harper's Ferry to "yell like furies." Another and another joined in, each declaring his own battle cry, pulsating, eerie, feral howls. Others picked up the wild yells, their voices clashing and grating in a wild cacophony of wailing and keening, of Furies and Banshees, ghouls and pagans. Others and still others, right and left, joined voices until the entire line was caught up in it.

The rebel yell had been born.

On the right, Jed fired his musket, ran forward, "Come on, Jon, we got 'em."

Jon waved his wounded arm, "Let's go! They been pushing at me all day. Now it's my turn." He screamed the banshee yell.

"Father," he yelled, "you hear that, colonel father? You and your damned Mexican War. Did you hear that? Did you?

"Now, damn you, it's my turn to stand up and push back."

For the first time ever, he was in complete control of his life. Free to do as he chose. Free to curse his father. Free to kill. Free to be killed, by God.

A Yankee loomed in front of him, two huge chevrons on his sleeve. Jon fired pointblank. Transfixed, he saw the black hole appear and the spurt of blood from the Yankee's neck, wasting the last efforts of a pumping heart. He saw it all, precise and magnified.

He thrust his bayonet into the gut of another Bluecoat, twisted it with a snarl, "Don't tell me how to use my fork, goddamn it." He clubbed another alongside the head.

Jed caught up with him, "Jon, Jon, don't get too far ahead."

"Don't you nor nobody tell me what to do," Jon snarled, swinging his musket at Jed, "nobody tells me what to do.

"NOBODY!"

"Jon! Jon!"

Stopping as suddenly as he had gone berserk, he cocked an ear to the familiar voice. Uncertainty clouded his face.

Recognizing his friend there in the middle of chaos, he spoke from his very soul. For a moment, it seemed to Jed, his words stopped the war.

"You never had people like I did. People running my life. They kept at it, Jed, kept at it and at it, never satisfied. I never learned how to handle it without hurting them.

"It's like being castrated by someone you love and needing to blame someone else."

"Jon, this will be over soon. Then we'll build a campfire and write letters home about bein' heroes." He offered his canteen, "Take a swig of corn. It'll do you good."

Jon ignored both suggestions, "I thought everything would be good with Ruth, but it was too late. She deserved better."

He turned to go, stopped, turned back, "Tell her I love her. You've been a good friend, Jed."

Jed reached a friendly hand.

Unprepared for Jon's sudden dash, he stood witless. For one critical moment he remained rooted, hand extended, feet anchored heavy to the ground. He screamed.

"JONNnn!! NO! JON! IT ISN'T TOO LATE. WE CAN FIX IT."

But it was too late.

Across the plateau Jon ran, slashing with his bayonet, clubbing with his musket, through the small cornfield and apple trees near Mrs. Henry's house. The clapboard house was in shambles, cannonaded by Union guns, and old Mrs. Henry was dead. Killed by strangers trespassing on her land, by a cannon ball violating her bedroom.

Jonathan stopped. Raising his face to the sky, he shouted across the battlefield, "This is my day, colonel father. Your goddamned bank clerk is celebrating. I'm free of all of you. Free to do whatever I goddamn please!"

Soldiers nearby stopped in their tracks. They watched as he loaded his musket, leisurely tearing the paper with his teeth, pouring the powder, deliberately ramming the lead slug home. They saw him throw the ramrod, he had no more use of it, watched as he scanned the battlefield, defying some one, anyone, to shoot him. Again, he lifted his head to the heavens.

"Curse them, O Lord, for they know exactly what they do."

He charged past the Henry house and the pitiful remains of its owner killed in her bedroom. Past the crest of the hill he ran, down the west slope, directly toward stalwart Yankees struggling to form a defense line between Young's Branch and the Warrenton turnpike.

Jed saw his furious attack. Saw him clutch at his chest. Saw him stumble forward on his face. Watched as his friend reached a hand toward a small cedar tree, and lay still.

Jed marked the little cedar that survived where men died.

He chased down Henry Hill, angling toward Jonathan. He had fallen, one arm trapped under, the other stretched toward the little tree. A supplication. Had he lived another heartbeat he would have fallen close enough to touch God's little tree and perhaps found what he sought.

Jed rubbed tears from his eyes and dirt from Jon's. He closed his friend's eyelids, brushed at scratches and dirt ground into his face, pathetic, little wounds that mocked the butchery of his chest. He found the musket with no ramrod, jammed its muzzle into the ground as a marker. Jonathan's passion was over.

Jed wiped a sleeve across his eyes, "Why, Jon? Why?"

"Move yer ass, soldier. We ain't stoppin' yet." It was the sergeant who had yelled on the hill during the bombardment. He never used names. Just told them all what to do with their ass.

McDowell's whipped men made for Centreville and beyond, all the way to Washington. With a few exceptions, Sykes' Regulars for one, his army was without organization or honor, a veritable mob.

Civilian spectators from Washington, here to see the war won by this one battle, were caught up in the tumult with their picnic baskets and French wine. Men with wives, men with lady friends, all dressed to the nines to attend the outing, in cravats, stovepipe hats, and morning coats, ladies in hoops, ostrich-feathered bonnets, and colorful parasols to shade delicate faces. In the crush of the retreat, their expensive clothes were ruined, their fancy carriages wrecked.

David, with the troopers, chased Yankees north on Sudley Road, collecting flags, arms, prisoners, equipment. He wore a matched pair of Colt revolvers taken from an officer en route to Libby prison. Night came. They returned to safer ground.

Jed returned to the little cedar tree and Jon. The indignity of soiled trousers paled at the desecration of heart and lungs and innocent fields. Unashamed, Jed wept over his friend at the little tree, wondering why some seemed more unlucky than others. And why parents did what they did.

'Do better by my children, by God, if I live to have any.'

He hailed lanterns swinging on the hill, a detail searching for equipment or human casualties he didn't know which, "Halloo. Need your help." They ignored him so he went to them. "Need help for my friend. Need to take care of him."

"Cain't do it. The loo'tenant would skin us alive. Leave 'im an' we'll bury 'im in turn, er mebbe y'kin find a undertaker at the hospital across the pike."

"Didn't know there was one."

"At the toll house. Where Sudley Road crosses."

Jed had no trouble locating the hospital, a Stone House with a veritable signboard of amputated limbs under a smashed window. Even as he approached, a leg came flying through to build the pile higher. He found no undertaker at the make-shift hospital, but he did learn of a church not too far away.

"Sudley Church. 'bout a mile north," his informant pointed up the road the Yankees had poured down earlier full of piss and vinegar. The same one they covered later with energy but no vinegar.

Jed borrowed a horse, "Have t'come back this way. I'll return him tonight."

He rode off, Jonathan across the horse's withers, his arms and legs swaying stiffly to the horse's gait.

"Why'd you do it, Jon? Things were workin' out. Why?"

At the church, he found badly wounded Yankees left behind, and a resident of Sudley Springs who said he was "the sexton, kind of." He assured Jed the preacher would bury Jonathan in the churchyard cemetery, mark the grave with a wooden marker, name, date, and 2nd Virginia Infantry.

"That's all I have," Jed handed him 11 crumpled bills.

The kind-of sexton waved him off, "That's not necessary."

"I appreciate it, but want you t'have it. Don't know a church can't use extra money. If it's more, write my sister. Ruth Brighton. Winchester," pointing to the body, "she's his wife. His pa owns the bank."

"Too bad. He had a good future."

David spent the early hours of darkness with Sable. He removed saddle and blanket, meticulously inspected him, running hands over the sweaty back for hot spots, and rippled fingers down each leg. Lighting a candle to clean and examine vulnerable fetlocks, to look closely at hooves and shoes. He brushed dirt away and picked at a tiny pebble caught in the curve of the iron.

He scratched Sable's face, combing his fingers through the long forelock, caressing the big, black cheek. The stallion turned his nose into David's head, nuzzling his own affection. The huge eyes were quiet.

"You saved my life, old friend. You saved my life today."

Sable nuzzled again.

Hand-feeding him the last of the oats he carried, David cooed and found a bit of sugar. He lit another candle in the perforated tin holder to curry and brush the great horse, and then a third. The candle flickered, sputtered out. David stayed with his horse the night through.

With too little energy and too many visions, Brian looked half-heartedly for Jed. Failing to find him, he walked toward Bull Run and collapsed in a quiet place untouched by the battle. He saw Bill Paxton fall again and again, just fall, never rise to his feet. Bill's last words had been of concern for him.

Brian heard the words again, the final words of his friend, "You've been hit. Get to the rear."

"Bill, you should have looked to yourself instead of me," Brian whispered, "If only I hadn't stopped you there."

Then he saw the Zouave with a lopsided head and no face. A fancy uniform laughed hideously. Lopsided heads, no faces, empty uniforms. Brian knew and felt the guilt. He had killed the Zouave. He had killed his friend

He cried his nightmare and splashed again into Bull Run. In the muddy stream, he washed his hands and washed his face, his friend's blood from one, the Zouave's gore from the other. He soiled Bull Run and wished he were dead. Above, on the high bank, he saw the apparition, the soldier with half a head and no face cackling wildly, "Get to the rear, Brian, get to the rear."

XIII

AFTERMATH
JULY 22, 1861

Yesterday's battlefield wakened soggy in God's pure rain, washed by gentle raindrops, but not cleansed. Henry Hill, where the Morrow brothers had fought, was dotted with debris: muskets, smashed equipment, used-up clothing, used-up soldiers thrown into graves too shallow to hold them in the rain.

Silent soldiers gleaned the far flung arena, appearing like wraiths, vanishing in the mist. Quartermaster details collected weapons for another day; others, more fortunate, sought souvenirs to show the home folks. Or sell! the bloodier, the better. Burial parties dragged stiffening bodies and shoveled wide trenches, pulling rags high on their faces. Some vomited. All swatted glutting flies.

A greater number, searching missing friends, moved slowly among the still forms, occasionally stooping to turn a face. Rain soaked them equally, the soldiers and the corpses.

Among those searching were the three Morrow brothers, drawn irresistibly, unable to stay away. Yesterday's brittle grip on life demanded they view this ground again.

Jed walked the small cornfield near the Henry House, seeing again Jonathan's frenzied flight through the field and down the hill. 'Why, Jonathan? Why? I would have helped you work it out.'

Beyond the cornfield, he walked the tall grass, uncut hay that lay in ruin, trampled flat as the corn stalks. The Widow Henry's house, used by Confederate sharpshooters, had collapsed onto its foundation stones. The ground about recorded more near misses than hits, untidy furrows plowed by solid shot and scars of exploding shells. The debris and damage saddened Jed as he walked, such a waste. The unlucky ones, lugged by the burial parties, thought nothing at all.

David and Brian visited their own part of the battlefield along Sudley Road, south of Jed. There at different times, each stared at bodies in fancy blue and red uniforms, David searching for the one Sable trampled, Brian hesitant for fear of finding one with no face. Each walked among the prone bodies, rain-soaked horses still in harness, rain-soaked men beyond caring.

On the plateau to the north, field pieces glistened wet and dripped the rain, abandoned, waiting indifferently for whoever would haul them away. Some were askew, impotent on broken wheels.

Later, David huddled in his tent, writing.

Dear Ma and Pa and all, By now you must have heard of our victory here at Manassas. We fought them all day, and finally they gave it up and ran for home. Colonel Stuart was madder than h—that we didn't chase them farther. He said if he was general he'd have driven them until they surrendered. As it was, we did pursue them a good piece, until it got dark and we had to give it up. We captured many prisoners, I have no idea how many, or how many flags and wagons. I took two Colts off a Yankee I caught. They were too good, anyway, for that Larracks officer. If the rest of them give up as easy, the war won't last long. Pa, Sable is in fine shape. He's eaten his share of fresh grass and for the last couple of weeks I've been able to find corn for him. I brush him every day. He is a real war horse. The Colonel took me out of Jones' company and made me his aide-de camp. Fancy title, isn't it? He's always in the thick of things, the Colonel is, whether in a set-to or in camp. Racey, you remember what I told you about the soldiers. Study hard on your lessons, and I'll bring you a Yankee sword. Your son and brother Lt David Morrow

Brian couldn't bring himself to write until the middle of the week and even then took two days to finish.

Dear Ma and Pa, I have just returned to my tent and will try again to write you a letter. I wanted to write yesterday evening, but was too tired. Since the battle on Sunday, we have been busy collecting muskets and all sorts of equipment. We are camped here near the battlefield in what we call Camp Maggot. The name is appropriate, and everyone is happy that we'll be moving soon. At least that's the way rumor has it. Last Sunday's battle was a great victory for us. We chased Yankees across the creek, and we heard two days later they were back in Washington. Many of the men are saying that this will end the trouble, that the Blue-coats won't fight any more. I don't think Lincoln will let them give it up. I hope I'm wrong.

(later) You will be happy to know that Jed and I spent several hours together the day before the battle. We had a free day after the march from Winchester. We stumbled across each other looking at one of the fords where there had been some skirmishing. That scoundrel! He scared me half to death. After he had his little joke, we spent a good afternoon together. I almost forgot, I found a Yankee canteen with a beautiful, leather strap. Somebody spent a lot of time tooling a fancy design on it and interwoven initials. The initials made me think of Pa's gold ring that he wears. They told me that David was around here someplace with the cavalry. I keep looking for him, but I haven't seen him yet. I did see Jed briefly the day after the battle, but not to talk to. I shouted and waved but he didn't see me. I didn't see Jonathan. That's strange because they seemed to stick together. Pa, I'm sorry I didn't see you when we were near Winchester. Most of the time we were on alert and restricted to camp. I know you are not happy that I enlisted, but I hope you can understand why I did. I hope to get home soon for a few days, and we can talk about it then. I am fine and in good health. Please send two pairs of socks, a shirt, and some soap—and three dollars. We haven't been paid yet. Your loving son Corporal Brian Morrow Write to me Company I, Fourth Virginia Infantry, Jackson's Division.

Jed wrote to Betsy as well as his parents. He tried three times to write Ruth but couldn't.

Dear Pa and Ma Well we bin in our first big batle and Im fine. I guess by now you know what hapened Jon got kiled after we had the yankees on the run. All of us were chasin them, sort of excited like and Jon was out in front of us all, shoutin and wavin. Tell Ruth Im sorry. I feel right bad because we bin good friends since we got in the army. I marked him by a sedar tree and found a church near the batlefield that said they'd bury him in their graveyard. They said theyd mark it. Sudley Church its called. Pa I never thawt much about dying and geting kiled until I saw Jon shot. On the farm I saw you and Zeke butcher hogs and chop heads off the chickens but I never conected it with peepul dyin. Seems now that its all the same hogs chickens and peepul all dyin the same an all goin to the same place like they talk about in church. Animals have a right to go to heven just like peepul some of them are beter than some peepul. I hope you arent stil mad for leaving the way I did. Im just not very good at teling how I feel about things I guess. Tell Ma and everyone I love them—and you to Pa. Tell Ruth I'm sory about Jon. This was suposed to be a letter for you and Ma but I guess it turned out to be mostly to Pa. I didnt meen it that way and hope you know it. I love you to Ma. Your son Jedediah Morrow

Dear Betsy Well we bin in a big batle, and Im fine. I guess by now you have all the news about it. Betsy I mis you I have only bin away a month and it seems like a thousand yeers. I think of you all the time and the way you look and feel all prety and softlike. Even in the midle of the fitin on Sunday I was tl inkin of you Then I figered I beter tend to biznis or I wont be thinking of you very long wich I did. Last nite I was rememberin the nite you and Brian and I were al. in your bed. Well I met up with Brian and told him all about you jokin him. He was so upset that he did somethin he shouldnt I had to tell him. And he told me to hang on to you and never let you get away becuz you are such a nice person. Well he didnt need to tell me that because I knew it alredy but he's rite and I told him then and there that I was going to mary you as soon as I got home and I hope you feel the same way. May be you cud go over and visit with Ruth. Jon got kiled and may be you can help her. I tried but cant write her. Tomorow I will ask Capn Clark for a pass to go home sos we can get maried if you want to. I want to ask you properlike first. I heer that Genl Jackson said no passes but it can't hurt to try. With love to my Star Queen Jedediah Morrow.

XIV

NORTHERN VIRGINIA
JULY 23, 1861

Two days after the battle at Manassas, David rode east to Fairfax Courthouse with Stuart and the regiment. The road was pleasantly free of dust after the rains, fields on either side sparkling in the morning dew, a glorious morning marred by war. The litter of McDowell's routed army was everywhere.

David rode silently, still annoyed with the failure to destroy it completely. For a day and two nights, he had chafed that Joe Johnston had not administered the coup de grace. The mistake was a critical mistake, he felt, a gift of time to rebuild and fight again. He had put it succinctly, "The general quit before it was finished."

Stuart's adjutant, William Blackford, trotted alongside, "Morning, Dave. Beautiful day for a ride through the country."

Lost in his blue funk, David never heard him.

"Hey there, David Morrow. Wherever you are, come back. I said 'it's a nice day for a ride'."

"If you say so," David grumbled.

"Do I detect a note of discord? Or a night without sleep?"

"Unfortunately, the former. How can we beat them and let them go? Damnit, Johnston only needed to give the order."

"I'm not sure it was that simple. Our boys were tired, hungry and without water."

"That's excuses, just bullshit excuses. Sure they were, but the Yankees were too. All we had to do was go after them. The colonel had us chasing them. And we captured a bunch."

"But we had horses."

"The horses were beat. And so were we, but Stuart kept us going. Too bad he wasn't commanding the whole damn army."

"Dave, I'm just giving the general the benefit of the doubt. But, we've talked all that for two days. It's done and over."

"You're right, Will."

"Even if Johnston was wrong, he's still the general."

They rode in silence, accepting yet rejecting.

"Dave, it is a shame to waste a beautiful morning on the general. I'm sure he isn't moaning about us."

"You're right." David brightened, "Without Johnston, I wish I did have a night without sleep. I might have something pleasant to think about."

"You know we've been friends almost a year. I knew we'd be friends when you said you liked Captain Jones."

"I said I respected him. Because he knew how to command cavalry. He stood out in that ragtag militia at Harper's Ferry."

"I knew him in Abingdon. He wasn't enthused about rejoining the army, but said he'd take the company if I'd raise it and be lieutenant. I was happy to find somebody else who accepted him."

"I saw right away he was a real commander. Then I did come to like him, the old curmudgeon. I wondered about him."

Blackford picked up this opening, and told how Jones had lost his new bride at sea, en route to duty in California.

"I've heard that and wondered if it was true."

"It's true. He never got over it."

By the end of Blackford's story, they had ridden into Centreville and beyond. A few miles north they overtook Yankee stragglers along the road, loners and groups of sullen soldiers.

David relished the diversion, trotting close to them and giving Sable freedom to toss and shake his head. The huge horse enjoyed the game, adding his own snorts and neighs that showed teeth. One look at him convinced weary Yankees to give up.

When one group was not adequately impressed, David reared the big stallion and fired a newly acquired revolver. Flailing hooves convinced all but one who raised his musket. David shot him. Through the head. Another moved to help him.

David roared, "Let 'm lay," and herded the rest to the provost guard, sidling Sable into the slow ones.

They were at Fairfax in midmorning, opposite the picturesque courthouse where the Little River Turnpike crossed Ox Road. The lovely building stood on a slight rise at the corner, red brick, two floors high, graced in front with an arcade, topped with an octagonal cupola. Stuart summoned them.

"Since you two are together, you might as well stay together. Scour the town for whatever you can learn. I'll be up there." He pointed down Little River Turnpike toward Washington.

"Let's start at the tavern," David grinned, nodding to the corner opposite the courthouse. They roamed the public houses and streets, querying citizens, "Where's McDowell's camp? How far? How many men? Artillery, how many guns? Any cavalry?" They washed dusty throats with dark ale.

Meticulously they paid for newspapers to glean later.

Their information was in Stuart's report to Johnston: 'McDowell's retreat continued in utter disorder into Washington City . . . there is no force this side of Alexandria.' Also, that three-month enlistments for 50,000 Federals would expire within 15 days, that Patterson in The Valley had been replaced by Banks, and rumors that McClellan was about to replace McDowell.

"When he reads this," Stuart said, "we'll see some action." He, too, was unhappy with Johnston's failure to pursue.

"Colonel, he'll get Johnston to move. Those three-month soldiers won't fight. Washington's ours for the taking!"

They fully expected the war to be over soon. One private wrote his sister, "Nobody thinks the war will continue longer than a few months. We will clean them out in two more battles."

Johnston, however, did nothing. He was satisfied with Jeff David's orders to assume a defensive posture.

"We ask only to be left alone," Davis had said ingenuously, hoping that his words would be respected across the Potomac.

Stuart occupied Falls Church and three hills beyond. From them soldiers could see the unfinished dome of the Capitol and Bluecoats at Bailey's Crossroad.

He established a line of outposts closer to the Potomac to warn of Yankee activity. Boredom was the lot of the outpost details, sweat in summer, shiver in winter, sheer boredom jolted now and then by the zing of a rifle bullet. Even the small comfort of a campfire was forbidden, ever since a trooper was spotted in the circle of firelight and shot dead.

Captain David Morrow, promoted for service at Manassas, spent days in the saddle in a repeat of his activities at Harper's Ferry under Jackson. Only now he drilled horsemen instead of foot soldiers. He was delighted one day to hear a story about Tom Rosser, his old friend from West Point.

"Yessirree," a young subaltern was saying, "that Yankee balloon was floatin' up there as pretty as could be. We could see someone in it lookin' through the biggest binoculars I ever saw. Countin' us I guess. Soldiers shot at him but didn't do any good.

"Then I hear this artillery officer cussin', 'Sonofabitch! that gun ain't near high enough.' Then he shouts for a shovel.

"Well, sir, he dug a hole, dropped the trail of his howitzer into it, lined up that gun by eye and fired. Next thing we know, the basket is hangin' crooked and swingin' like it's ready to bust loose. The Yankee in it is wavin' like a crazy man and they haul him down. Damned if that Tom Rosser didn't almost shoot that balloon from the sky."

David found his friend at once.

"Tom! Tom Rosser!" David shouted from a distance. "What are you doing up here with the cavalry?"

"Same as you, whatever the hell it is that you're doing," responded Rosser in his resonant voice, "how about a drink? My tent's right over there."

After crushing handshakes and back thwacks, their reunion was conversation with Rosser's usual bourbon and cigars.

"Try one of these Cuban beauties." They sniffed the heady aroma, bit the ends, and lit up.

"Now tell me what the hell happened to you since May," David encouraged.

"First, tell me how you made three stripes so fast."

"I was as surprised as you. After the battle, Colonel Stuart says he's requested I be made captain. Then yesterday he hands me the paper. That's all I know."

"You must have made a helluva impression. Congratulations, Dave."

"Now, tell me about the last two months. After I left you in Baltimore. What happened to you and Pelham?"

"Well, we reached Montgomery, Pelham and me, and had a bit of a time. As you can see, they made me a first lieutenant in the Washington Artillery just in time for the ball at Manassas. Was downstream at Union Mills Ford until it was almost over. Then we chased Yankees. Got prisoners, flags, you name it."

Rosser roared laughter, "After the battle, Beauregard took one look at our Yankees and their flags coming down the road and thought he was being attacked. He kicked spurs and his horse took off like a scared deer."

Both of them rocked helplessly at the imperious general fleeing from his own men. Their raucous laughter and knee slaps broke up Rosser's narration, "The general's hat flew off—his sword flying—elbows flapping—Damn what a sight . . .—"

Rosser made a partial recovery to finish, "I sent Dearing to apologize and I'll be damned if the general doesn't arrest him," rollicking laughter again, "for howling—like—an Indian."

They broke out again in shrieks that brought tears to their cheeks and aches to their belly muscles.

When they recovered, David had a West Point story.

"Remember that lieutenant that had quarters near Old North Barracks? You know. The one Custer stole the chicken from."

"Indeed I do, and roasting it in Custer's fire place. Best meal we had all month. Then, they found feathers under Custer's bed and he got demerits."

"Yeh, I felt bad about Custer taking the rap, but it wouldn't have done any good to speak up."

"Me, too, but you're right. It wouldn't have helped him."

"Well, I never told anybody this before, but Custer wasn't the only one scouting the lieutenant's house. If you remember . . ."

Rosser held up a hand, offered the bottle, "This sounds like a long, thirsty one." He filled tin cups.

"If you remember, his wife had her cousin living with them. She was about twenty and always in a dress that pulled her in and pushed her out in all the right places. Well, I can tell you it wasn't just the clothes, Tom, she had all the parts underneath."

"I remember her. Long blonde hair."

"That's right. She acted so sedate at the soirees with every cadet at her feet. Damned if I was going to be the same."

"Come on, Dave, you were no different than the rest of us."

"I don't say I was different," he grinned, "just smarter."

"What do you mean—just smarter?"

"Well, for one thing, I kept my distance. I nodded and smiled, but I kept my distance. I could tell she liked that.

"The first time she smiled back, I went over to her and just took her arm. The guys around her were madder than hell.

"We really hit it off, right from that first dance. After that we met as often as we could. For weeks, we strolled Lovers' Walk and Crow's Nest, holding hands and looking at the river.

"One time, she asked me if I could meet her at the back of the chapel after taps. That was the first time I ever kissed her, really kissed her I mean. Then she said I was more mature than the rest, and I suggested we might be even more mature in the barn back of her house. She thought so, too.

"The first time she was soiree-sedate but after a few minutes, I don't know how but, we were saying how much we loved each other. From then on, she wasn't sedate any more.

"She used to put a vase in the window with two dried flowers in it and I'd know to meet her."

Tom Rosser exploded, "A vase with two flowers! In the first window. Upstairs. Right?"

"That's right. A little glass vase—about so high."

"So that's what the two flowers meant! I used to see that damn vase and wonder about it. She had the same damn signal for a friend of mine, except his was one flower. He told me about it.

"But then there were two flowers and I never did know why. I never knew there were two of you."

"There weren't two of us, Tom. She told me about this other guy, no name. She met him through fancy friends of her aunt, and for a lark arranged the signal. Then she met me and cut him off."

"That sounds right to me. I only saw the single flower a few days and then it was gone. Dave, why the hell didn't you introduce me. Afraid of competition?"

David became very serious, "No, Tom, you wouldn't have been any competition." He looked sad. "We became very fond of each other, and had plans to be married when I graduated."

"You never told me that."

"No, I didn't because I didn't want anyone to know until the time came. Anyway, none of you would have believed me."

"Well what happened? You just resigned and left her there?"

"No, Tom. Her aunt found out about us and sent her away."

"Geez, that's right. One day she was there and then she was gone. And no more vase. I wondered what happened to her."

"I talked to her aunt, but she just said they sent her away to protect her from the wilds of Virginia, as she called it."

"I'll be damned."

"Then she said something about Harvard and somebody studying medicine there. Only she said it 'Hahvud' and 'docta'."

"Anyway, she was packed off, and I never knew where. I even asked her uncle, the lieutenant, but he'd got his marching orders and wasn't about to cross his high-falutin' wife.

"Too damn bad. They had no call to treat you like that."

"Well, they thought they had good reason. I may look for her one day. It's probably just as well, with the war and all."

They drank, smoked, and talked far into the night. And paid for it the next day. David nursed a throbbing head as he rode the morning inspection of outposts.

Back in Winchester, Ezekiel Brown was troubled, too, as he rode down the Valley Turnpike and reined west onto Wolfe Street.

"Mornin', Henry. Figgered you could use some pickin's from the garden. The corn is sweet as sugar. You heard from the boys?"

Henry gave Ezekiel a sagacious smile, "No need t'bring table vegetables every time you come lookin' for news of the boys. Ever since Manassas we've had more vegetables than we can eat."

"I know, Henry, I know. Just seems more dignified this way.

"You got a letter. I can tell by your face."

"That I have, Zeke, that I have."

Henry reached into a pocket for Jed's letter.

"Read it yourself. Jed's got somethin' about you in it."

Ezekiel plodded carefully through it so as to miss nothing. His progress was apparent through a variety of murmurs, exhalations, and exclamations.

"H'mmm."

"Uh huh."

"Lawdamercy."

"My, My, if that don't beat all."

He stood quietly when he finished, just looking at the single page, thinking of a time when life was simpler and Jed a schoolboy anxious to grow up. He folded the letter gently, respectfully, re-using the existing creases to avoid corrupting it with new ones. Ezekiel was touched by Jed's words, enough to claim a share of him.

"You and me have raised a fine boy, Henry. A fine boy with a good brain. Not afraid of workin' neither."

Henry had no trouble sharing Jed, for a joint fatherhood had indeed developed as his son had worked with Ezekiel.

"Yes, Zeke, we did that. You're a good teacher."

The two men remained silent, each with his own memories of a younger Jed, serious and eager to learn. Zeke broke the spell.

"I remember talkin' ta him one day while we were workin'. We done a heap of talkin' we did, some serious, some just for fun. And the questions that boy had—Lord save us!

"Questions about farmin', about the crops—specially about the animals. I remember the day he saw his first birthin'—how'd he get in there how'd he get out why's he all wet? Lawdamercy if he didn't aks a passel of questions.

"Times he aks about the weather and Washin'ton and sail ships—all sorts of things. Then, questions about women. Some I could answer and some I couldn't."

Ezekiel paused and smiled his gleaming smile, "But I guess I answered more than I didn't."

He posed coyness in a sideways glance at Henry, "Did the best I could. Maybe you answered the ones I just guessed at."

Henry simply smiled. He listened patiently for his friend to go on. Sometimes, he thought, Zeke comes up with a real gem, lots of wild ideas but enough gems to take the time to listen to him.

"That young'n 's comin' into his own, Henry. Goin' off ta war is the best thing he ever did. If he doesn't get hurt."

"If he doesn't get hurt! Zeke! You gone crazy in your head? Best thing he could have done was t'stay home. Of all people, you ought to know that. Y're workin' your ass off without him."

"But I'm not talkin' about me. I'm talkin' about Jed. He's smart, Henry, not book smart like Brian, but common sense smart. He needs ta see how the rest of the world works."

"You always looked at him different than me, Zeke. I remember when he ran away from school t'work with you. You said t'loosen the reins. You were right then, Zeke, I know that now. But this time y're wrong as hell. Jed's place is with you."

They had had the same discussion before, always without resolution. Henry cut it off, not unkindly.

"Zeke, seems Jed got two Pa's who can't agree."

Ezekiel smiled at the warmth and humor in Henry's voice.

"Time ta get back ta work."

He couldn't resist the urge to match Henry's wit.

"If I don't bring veg'tables you still show me the letters?"

"With or without, Zeke," Henry waved good-naturedly.

Ezekiel raised his arm in good-bye and headed for the farm.

XV

NORTHERN VIRGINIA

After their first meeting, David and Tom Rosser spent a good deal of time together, talking the war. Women. The Point, their families. Women. The Yankees . . . Women. Frequently, in the evening twilight, David curried Sable as they talked.

Rosser never failed to admire the shining black stallion. One evening, he blurted out, "I'll give you $500."

"I'll take it first and thank you second," David held out his hand, "but what in the world for?"

"What do you think for? For your horse, of course."

"Five hundred dollars!" David scoffed without intending to.

"Eight hundred," the other raised the ante.

David saw he was serious, "He's not for sale."

"Just about everything's for sale. Give you a thousand."

"Tom, I mean it when I say he's not for sale."

David walked the length of the big horse, stroking the gleaming coat and bulging shoulder muscle, finger-combing strands of mane.

"What do you think, old boy?" Sable snorted.

"Just as I thought, Tom. He wants to stay with me."

"You and your humor! He doesn't know what the hell we're talking about," Rosser was sorely disappointed. No one refused a thousand dollars for a horse, except to bargain it up. He swung an arm in disgust and tramped off.

A few nights later he was back, "Sorry about the other night. I didn't mean to lose my temper."

"Forget it, Tom. I've seen your short fuse before."

David suggested a respite from their all male routine,

"Let's ride over to Falls Church. I know a young widow there with a friend. And we can stop at Taylor's for a drink."

"Okay," Rosser laughed, "she have a vase in her window?"

Riding toward Falls Church, David did most of the talking, "You've never been to Taylor's?"

"Heard talk of it, but I've never been there."

"You won't believe this place, Tom. The only place that serves soldiers from both sides. Be ready to see blue uniforms."

"I've heard. Wondered if somebody was pulling my leg."

"They weren't. Mr. Taylor has worked a miracle with his one rule. You come into his place you leave the war outside."

"You mean that no one argues about what Lincoln's doing?"

"That's right, everyone respects Mr. Taylor's rule. I have seen only one fight, a troublemaker mean with whiskey."

"There have to be more. Someone says 'Lincoln' or 'Davis' and all hell would break loose."

"Not as easy as you might think, Tom. The fight I saw was broken up by men from both sides. They escorted the culprit out—sat on him until he quieted down.

"I'll be damned."

"When they came back inside, everybody cheered, Yankees and Confederates alike. They all like the place as it is."

"The proprietor must be a magician."

"He's a real character. Reads Shakespeare."

"He does!"

"Not only that, but when the mood hits he'll quote him at length. He can draw tears with Hamlet and laughs with Petruchio. He laces his talk with Elizabethan. He should have lived 250 years ago in England and run a pub alongside the Avon.

"If Falls Church had a river it would be called Avon, like in Stratford town. There's his place now, at the crossroads."

A short canter downhill brought them to their destination.

They surveyed the public room, groups of gray uniforms, groups of blue. In a corner were two in blue, one an officer back-lighted by a dim oil lamp on the wall.

David indicated a table near a side door, a sturdy trestle with years of nicks, "Quick exit, just like Benny Haven's."

The table had character that comes only with the years, its edges rounded, its top burnished by barmaids' wiping and customers' bending elbows in homespun, linsey, and velvet.

At the end of the bar, Mr. Taylor surveyed his domain from a high stool. Seeing them enter, he alighted with a grace beyond his Falstaffian girth. In his own eclectic style of fleeting burrs, rhythms, and poetic anachronisms, he welcomed them in a voice resonant and full.

"How now, kind sirs? My guests please be." He marked the entire room in an easy wave, "and share my humble inn with me."

Rosser's expression conveyed, "I see what you mean."

"I've chicken and biscuits, apples with spice, whiskey and bourbon mulled or with ice. Good talk, good food, good drink my rule. Enjoy yourself, my second rule. To eat and drink in peace my law. For sleep, a bed with good clean straw."

Intoned by a master performer, the greeting was more than a businessman's appeal, an entertaining welcome, warm and sincere.

"Evening to you, Mr. Taylor. Bourbon for my friend and me. Fairfax County bourbon."

"Anon, good sirs," Mr. Taylor was off to the bar.

"You won't find anything smoother this side of the Blue Ridge," David crowed, "but there's as good in Winchester."

Rosser looked around at the tables, "How did he ever get Bluecoats and Confederates to sit down together?"

"That's quite a story, Tom. I've heard our host tell it a couple of times. He makes quite a show, like he's on stage."

Mr. Taylor set firing cups before them, small glasses with short stems and bases with flared rims like little saucers.

"Your health,"

"And yours, Tom."

Sipping, they savored the liquor's smooth pungency. Its velvet warmth soothed their throats and caressed their bellies. Tom twirled his cup impatiently, "Well?"

"Well what?"

"The story. How did Mr. Taylor get them to stop fighting?"

"Oh. It seems that two scouts came in for a drink, a Yankee through the side door, a Confederate through the front. They stood surprised, ready to draw revolvers. They might have, too, but for their love of bourbon. It was stronger than their politics and military training put together."

Mr. Taylor came back to the table, "Another cup, gentlemen?"

David, "Why not?"

Tom, "Better still, bring us the bottle."

The proprietor was back in an instant filling their glass cups, "Couldn't help overhearing my story, good sirs.

"They, fine gentlemen, were ordered the same amber nectar ye're imbibing. 'Fairfax County bourbon,' one said, and t'other, 'Fa'uhfax Counteh bub'n.' Zounds! if they didn't look t'one another and banish the differences between them. The fraternal love of dedicated bourbon drinkers overcame all enmity. Poof!" snapping a finger off his thumb, "just like that."

David toasted, "To the good health of all bourbon lovers."

Mr. Taylor caught a signal from another table and excused himself. David continued the story.

"As our host tells it, one was from Leesburg, and the other from Maryland. They found they were blood-related. Real cousins, each father the other's uncle."

Mr. Taylor hustled between tables and bar for several minutes, pouring, chatting, patting a shoulder here and there. David saw him lean toward the officer at the corner table and nod his head affirmatively. Returning, he wiped their table, more of habit than need and put down clean firing cups. He hit one on the table with a crack like a small pistol. Soldiers in the room jumped.

"Be at ease, gentlemen. Just a bit of a demonstration for them that don't know the firing cup. That's why they're called as they are." And he banged it again, sharply, base down.

"The gentleman in the corner saw that you were officers and expressed an interest in buying you a drink."

Tom Rosser reacted quickly, "He's Yankee!"

Mr. Taylor came alert at once, "I don't think . . ."

David interrupted, "Neutral ground, Tom. Remember?"

"Yeh, okay, neutral ground."

"But first," David invited Mr. Taylor to sit with them, "I want you to finish the story for my friend. I'd like him to hear the end from you. From where they bought the two bottles."

Their host beamed, "Ahhh, me old da, God rest his soul, used t'say 'tales are like women, both unfold and blossom when a man picks his words with skill. And, good sirs, both need t'be heard.

"I speak truly now without beguilement, for, lo, there's but a mite left to tell. The gentlemen bought two bottles of Fairfax nectar, one each, and they came behind the bar there and put the bottles on the shelf so's all could see them. Exactly where you see them now." He pointed.

" 'Leave em stay til we come back,' one said.

" 'Yessuh,' the other agreed, 'leave em sahd by sahd, frien'ly-like provin' we-all kep' the waw cleah outa this peaceluvin' tav'un'.

"The Maryland cousin said, 'We'll be back for 'em, God willin', and buy drinks for all'."

David and Tom Rosser applauded so that all in the room turned toward them.

"That is one story I'll always remember," Tom said.

"And your rendition adds to it," David said.

Mr. Taylor bowed his head for his bubble moment, then pushed back from the table, "The officer in the corner, sir?"

"Yes, thank you. Ask him to join us—bring another cup."

"By your leave, good sirs," and he moved through the tables, holding up a single finger to those who would delay him.

The officer from the corner did indeed wear Yankee blue, lieutenant's silver bars, and the yellow piping of cavalry, "Couldn't help but note your order when you came in. I'm a bourbon drinker myself."

"Appreciate your generosity," David tilted the bottle, "Like you to sample this one. Made right here in Fairfax County."

The Yankee accepted the glass, "I could have asked our host, but to be honest I wanted to meet you. I've not had a chance to talk to a Confederate officer."

"Curious?" Tom Rosser bristled, "we're just like you except for knowing what's right."

David headed off potential friction as he filled the cups, "You must be a stranger to these parts."

"Yes sir. Originally from Philadelphia. More recently from Massachusetts—Williamstown. Graduated from Williams College, was on the faculty there. Name's Matt Garland. Company C of the Lincoln Cavalry, officially the First New York."

"Dave Morrow, captain with the First Virginia. This is Tom Rosser, Washington Artillery."

"My pleasure, gentlemen." Lieutenant Garland held the firing cup for the bouquet, then sampled the amber liquor.

"Mmmm. Real sipping bourbon. I'll remember that label."

He twisted the glass cup between thumb and forefinger, raised it in salute, "In your debt, sir."

"I've just been telling how this place came to be neutral ground," David fished for the appropriate reassurance.

"Yes, I heard the story just recently, from Mr. Taylor himself. His incredible tale of sanctuary evokes Notre Dame cathedral and Victor Hugo's hunchback. A born raconteur, Mr. Taylor."

"Indeed he is, but living on a slippery slope. The slightest action could destroy what he's created, or rumor even a false one. His sanctuary depends on faith."

Matt Garland nodded in disbelief, "It is an aberration indeed here between the armies."

"Had trouble a few weeks ago. A soldier with too much pop-skull started a row. Whether he was North or South is immaterial. What is important is how the trouble stopped."

"And how was that?

"Strangely enough," David continued, "one of his companions who tried to quiet him was shoved onto a soldier at the next table. That turned out a bit of luck because the two of them had an instant understanding. Together, they subdued him. His friends took over and hauled him outside to cool off."

"You leave me puzzled. What's so unusual about that?"

"Only that one table was Southern soldiers and the other Northern They found grounds to cooperate."

Matt Garland thought for a moment then smiled broadly, "You have not told which uniform the troublemaker wore."

"I have told you that men of hostile armies saw eye to eye and worked together. That's what's important."

Matt Garland brightened with understanding, "Captain, you are a subtle man. Our leaders should be as acute."

"And you, lieutenant, I take for thoughtful. Most would have pressed for an answer out of sheer curiosity."

Lieutenant Garland turned to his companion still in the corner, "Sergeant, come over and meet these gentlemen."

Sedge Folsom, with three huge chevrons on his sleeve, downed his drink and rose ponderously to his feet. He slouched toward them, carrying rounded shoulders as a burden. Deepset eyes ranged the entire room, the eyes of a man who had been hunted. Thick eyebrows and uncombed hair narrowed a beetle brow. The rest of his face was askew with a splayed nose broken once or more, repugnant with badly formed, tobacco-stained teeth. Black stubble held it all together.

David disliked him half way to their table. The hairs on the back of his neck sent their warning shivers.

Behind the bar, Mr. Taylor sensed a threat to his covenant.

Folsom's eyes flared challenge, as did his jaw working his chaw of tobacco.

"This is Captain Mor—" Garland started the introduction.

"Want no truck wi' rebels," Folsom growled in his throat.

"Sergeant, this tavern's neutral ground."

"Jus' don't want no truck wi' no rebel sonsabitches, 'specially no fuckin' Black Horse sonsabitches."

His snarl was palpable, mean, suffocating, emitting putrid miasma. He hadn't been at war long enough, nor had the war become that vicious, that it affected him so strongly. Sedge Folsom had hated the whole world for a long time.

"Folsom! That's enough!" bellowed Garland, "wait outside!"

The sergeant edged around the table toward the side door. He stopped in front of David, not two feet away. Very deliberately, he worked his tongue and jaw to shift the wet tobacco, pursed his lips, and spat a stream of brown juice toward David's boots.

David was on him in a flash, drawing his revolver, grabbing a handful of long hair and pulling down and forward. The front sight of his revolver disappeared into Folsom's ear.

"You filthy bastard," David growled low, and very, very slowly, "Now clean it up. Boots and floor."

The room froze, thoughts half said, laughs half laughed, pewter tankards suspended between table and gaping mouths. Near the bar, Mr. Taylor stood nailed, one hand extended in supplication.

A small click crashed ominously, David's revolver hammer.

His voice lashed, "The—boots—first—BASTARD!!" Staccato words of cold steel, perched on the rim edge of violence.

Matt Garland edged toward him in an instinctive move to side with his own. Six feet two inches, 200 pounder Rosser moved, too, restoring the balance. They locked eyes. Rosser nodded ever so slightly, left, right, "Stay out of it. Your man's in the wrong."

Matt Garland's eyes flashed. He mumbled limply, "I know it."

"Zounds! Gentlemen, remember where you are," Mr. Taylor pleaded, "no fights in the tavern, please!"

David never heard the plea, hissed, "Slow and easy. NOW!"

Folsom stooped gingerly to one knee, lower still to the boots, David bending with him to keep his handful of hair and the revolver in his ear. Folsom wiped the boots clean on his sleeve. David nudged with the steel barrel, edging him to the slime on the floor. His eyes wild, Folsom blinked from trigger finger to cocked hammer, forth and back. He balanced awkwardly on a forearm to clean the floor.

David was a sculpture, knees flexed, ready for anything.

"Marry, I pray thee," Mr. Taylor begged, " No fights in the tavern, gentlemen. Remember the covenant."

David heard. The voice came from all directions, as though through a sea-fog. The voice was right; this was neutral ground.

"You filthy bastard," David hissed, "get up."

Still clenching the handful of hair, he backed Folsom slowly around worn, pine tables, between benches, slowly toward the open door. Folsom caught his heel, regained his balance.

"Out!"

With gun to Folsom's ear, David steered each toe-searching step back, down one step, another, a third, to the ground. He stopped, reining in his prisoner by the handful of hair. He stared contempt; Folsom, contempt and fear.

For the second time, David moved too fast for him, yanking again at black hair, down and forward. The sergeant stumbled off balance, vulnerable, exposed. David's cavalry boot exploded in his crotch, and sent him reeling into the dirt. Yelling agony, he grabbed himself with both hands, drawing his legs tight.

David aimed the revolver. Folsom tightened his clutching hands for protection, and involuntarily the muscles in his rear. He cringed, equally fearful of death and loss of manhood.

A single shot echoed into the tavern.

Folsom felt heat and pressure zing alongside his head, gone in an instant. He spared one hand to discover an ear shortened by the grazing bullet. He knew the shot had gone exactly where it was aimed. Hard pressed to ease both ear and groin, he struggled to his feet, bent double, limped and groaned into the night.

Three men in the tavern rushed to the open door, Rosser and Garland shoulder-tight, Mr. Taylor stretching to see around Rosser's big shoulders. David pushed brusquely through. Matt Garland struggled with humiliation and anger, "Captain, I am sorry as hell. I am shamed. He's an unprincipled renegade.

"This should never have happened, especially in the tavern."

David needed time for tension to drain. He had killed men on the field at Manassas, but this effort to avoid killing cost him more. Trembling, he took a long pull at the bottle. He poured the rest on his boots and scrubbed them clean. He looked up slowly, his voice hoarse and minacious.

"You're goddamned right it shouldn't. Virginia doesn't need animals like him running loose."

Genuinely saddened by the episode, Garland attempted to make amends. He wanted desperately to let these two Confederates know that he was closer to them than to the Folsoms of the world.

"I've been fortunate teaching at Williams, able to live outside this barbarity. Seems war is for the most brutish among us. I detest that, and am not proud to be a part of it."

David called for another bottle, "I've no quarrel with you, Matt Garland, except your choice of drinking companions."

"He's hardly that, captain. We were inspecting pickets. The tavern seemed like a good idea. Folsom's no friend of mine."

"I'll kill the bastard if I see him again."

"I understand. I am truly sorry because I think we could be friends. I hope we meet again under different circumstances."

Lieutenant Garland wanted to say more. Instead, he saluted another apology and left the tavern.

Tom ordered clean glasses, filling them from a new bottle. Two drinks later, David had regained his composure.

"God help us if Lincoln's got many like him. Can you imagine what'd happen if he's turned loose on the women, Tom?.

"My mother and sisters, Zeke's wife and mother. There's no way they can defend themselves. And my youngest sister, Racey, she doesn't even see the danger."

The visions infuriated David again. He grabbed the other's shoulder, "We have to stop 'em, Tom, we gotta stop 'em!"

"Take it easy, Dave. You know most of those people aren't like him."

"The bastard. I should have blown his goddamn head off."

David tossed off another drink, "Let's go find the sonofabitch, Tom, and string him up."

"He's not worth the trouble. Besides, Garland might have caught up with him. He seemed like a good sort. I wouldn't want to force him into a fight."

"I want no trouble with him. But what the hell's he doing with that animal?" David clung to his waning fury, "I could kill that one with pleasure."

Tom pressed his advantage, "Let's have one more drink and head for camp."

In the excitement, they forgot about visiting David's young widow and her friend, and all about vases in windows.

XVI

FREEDOM HILL

"Detail! Halt!". Lieutenant Matt Garland dismounted, "sergeant, dismiss the men."

An orderly took the officer's horse.

"Thank you, Roberts."

Tired from a long patrol beyond Falls Church, Lieutenant Garland headed for division to make his report to the provost marshal. He was a civil man by nature, inclined to treat his men with respect, leading instead of driving them. Not that he scorned discipline, or the line between officers and their men. He could read a man off, as he had Folsom at the tavern.

Garland was assigned to 1st New York Cavalry, Company C. detailed as provost guard, Franklin's Division. His company commander, Captain William Boyd, was Provost Marshal.

Being policemen had its lows, but the men liked the looser schedule and freedom from regimental duties. A few felt immune to control. After all, who was to arrest them?

Sergeant Sedge Folsom was one who found the assignment much to his liking. He had time for women, booze, and entry into all sorts of places under the pretext of official duty.

While other soldiers of Company C whiled away their off-duty time with letters, poker games or local strumpets, Sergeant Sedge Folsom prowled the countryside with a false rank and a false name, Corporal John Smith. His tattered shirt had two chevrons. He'd have worn mufti but for the risk of being hanged for a spy.

Folsom ridiculed the thought of paying for either a woman or booze, preaching his beliefs to any who would listen, "Why pay fur it win ya c'n take it fur nuthin'.

His vulgar bragging alienated all but a few toadies.

"Ain't seen no whore yit what was wu'th the price, not fur a half a dollar 'r even two bits like most a' these c'untry bitches is askin'. They ain't got no spirit fur it. Jus' hike up their dress an' take it without pushin' their ass once.

"Only times whores is wu'th a shit is when they's th'only ass aroun'. 'Druther fuck uh sheep."

He roamed beyond Alexandria County into Fairfax, to Great Falls, Tyson's Corner, Vienna, Hunter's Mill, and Frying Pan. Only once did Folsom ever revisit his victim.

Freedom Hill was a pretty farm, its gentle fields sloping toward the village of Vienna from a crossroads known as Tyson's Corner. The house was off the road, partially hidden by the contour of the land. In this season of the year, corn planted almost to the house itself was tall and green.

From the cover of the cornfield Folsom watched a young black girl working over a wash board in the yard, her shapely arms thrusting down against the board, easing upward. The rhythmic motion of her body fired him, rounded hips contouring again and again against her thin skirt, breasts swinging firm. The girl hummed a lyrical combination of moan and chant, rising and falling in the same erotic rhythm. Absorbed, Folsom kneaded himself.

The dark body and earthy voice became prey in his personal jungle where wild creatures bellowed and mounted with fury.

The girl stopped to rest. She squeezed a forearm between fingers and thumb to drain the soap and water. Then the other. She stretched high against the aches, arching her spine to ease the weariness. She flexed again, feet wide.

Folsom consumed her, drank her in, piecemeal and altogether, stroking fingers, stretches, breasts, legs spread wide, ass taut as a bow ready to fire. He fixed on her dress, where it stretched tight, where it fell loose, hinting at hidden joys, inviting explorations, his prey to hunt, to use, to devour and throw away.

Raising first to one knee, he stood ever so warily to his full height. A bull cat afire with hunger and desire, he stalked her from the rear, never taking his eyes off her, never blinking, yet, he never saw her for the lust in his heart.

Step-stop-drool-wipe-step-more quickly now!

The girl sensed danger at the last instant, as a doe upwind of the hunter, startled, no time left.

Folsom moved in close, one arm a vice holding her body tight against his, back to front.

"No noise now, li'l nigga girl. Inta the barn, jus' you an' me an' m'frien'."

She felt him through her thin dress, opened her mouth to scream. His hand flicked. She caught the glint of a knife. Felt its cold edge at her throat. The scream froze.

He rubbed his free hand along her hip, snaked his fingers around, and grabbed roughly into her.

Eyes rolled white with alarm, half closed toward the glistening blade. She had been attacked twice before, but never like this, never by knife and such foulness. She felt the evil, smelled it, too terrified to scream, to fight back, to plead as she had before with success, "Ah've got tha diz-eeze."

Nothing she could do would make a difference, she knew that. Her eyes rolled back in her head. She went limp.

He dragged her into the barn, dropped her into a dark corner. Tearing her dress top to bottom, he pulled at her breast, dug into it with vile fingernails and scratched across, sternum to ribs. Blood welled along the nail tracks and ran its course down her brown skin.

Fumbling now with his false uniform, he attacked her in the hay, spearing her, ramming into her mercilessly. No difference that she just lay there, without moving her ass. Just like the whores he hated.

In a frenzy of absolute power, he pounded at her brutally, crushing, grinding her helpless body, raping her vilely as he always did, woman, man, or animal. He burst into her, then slapped her face, once, twice, three times for not showing more spirit. He got off her and spewed wet tobacco.

Cackling his amusement, he warned her, "Stay put, bitch, I ain't done yit."

Then he ransacked the house, finding nothing but two bottles of apple-jack, one full, one opened. He gulped the one, smashing the empty bottle against a wall. Angered at the meager loot, he returned to the barn, ready again for the girl.

Only her rag of a dress was there on the scattered hay, only that and the stains of her wasted blood. He searched the stalls and the hay and the loft. She was gone.

"Sonofabitch!"

Pulling the cork with his teeth, he took a long pull from the full bottle. And raged. Already determined to return despite his own once-only rule, he shouted around the empty barn, "I'll be back, bitch. So's you an' me c'n do the fancy stuff. Ya hear me, bitch? I'll be back."

He attacked the bottle, dribbling to his shirt, left the barn and the girl. He lurched up the hill to the crossroad.

Standing there in the dark where Chain Bridge Road and the Leesburg turnpike mixed, he tilted the bottle again, draining it, drizzling down his stubbled chin to older stains on his shirt. He belched. He tipped the bottle again, cursed its emptiness and flung it into the night.

He howled a whiskey-yell, "Fuck you all, white, black, north, south. Sedge Folsom hates all ya goddamn bitches."

He stumbled east along the turnpike past Taylor's tavern where he cursed vengeance on the cavalry officer who had cost him part of an ear. Detouring around guards at Bailey's Crossroad, he found his tent on the grounds of Alexandria's seminary. Sedge Folsom was safe again, with General Franklin's provost guard, charged with enforcing the army's regulations.

XVII

BETSY AND RUTH

Betsy crossed to the west side of Main Street to avoid the bold soldiers at Courthouse Square. Even so, they whistled their eagerness. One shouted a brazen invitation. She walked two blocks down Boscawen Street, preoccupied with Jed's letter of Jonathan's death, apprehensive of meeting Ruth. Whatever would she say to the new widow whom she had never met? In all her 20 years, she had never faced such a task.

What if it were Jed? How would she react if a stranger came to her and said, "I was his friend and I've come to help you?" She crossed the street to Christ Episcopal Church.

She attended Christ Church regularly, sensing promise in its Roman arches and strength in the Norman bell-tower that left one feeling it should lift higher in a steeple. Finding peace in the quietude and in the liturgy and words of The Reverend Meredith, she came to the church often, to kneel and pray for Jed's safety. She had first seen him at Christ Church, across the nave.

Betsy crossed the narthex, laced her fingers and stepped the length of the center aisle. She paused respectfully before the altar and the massive, hewn cross. She moved into the pew, knelt and bowed her head to reverent fingertips.

"Heavenly Father, protect your son from those who would do him harm, sustain him in his faith, and please bring him back to me." She paused. "Guide me and the words of my lips as I speak to Ruth." She paused again, "In Jesus' name. Amen."

She remained kneeling in private sacrament, eyes closed, head bowed, praying no more, asking no other favor.

Somewhere a timbered door swung on its hand-wrought hinges and boomed shut. It was time to leave.

She walked the block to Ruth Morrow Brighton's house with its elegant door of walnut. To her third knock, it opened slightly.

Betsy controlled her surprise at the face in the narrow opening, for Jed had said his sister was 25 years old. Before her was a woman, wan, drawn, her pallor the more stark for the redness of a thousand tears. The eyes were lusterless, the auburn hair, dull and unkempt. The voice cracked, "Yes?"

"I'm—I'm Elizabeth Dearing."

The dismal voice croaked again, "I know no one with that . . ." The door moved on its hinges.

Betsy stepped forward, reaching a hand, "Please. I'm Jed's friend. He said he would write you."

"Jed . . ." the ghostly figure gasped, hand to mouth, "Then you must be—oh no—I . . ." Tears welled in her eyes. Indecisive she stood holding the door, unable to open it more, unwilling now to close it. Betsy smiled to reassure her.

They stood in silence for a long minute, Ruth struggling to make a decision. Betsy broke the mounting discomfiture.

"Jed wrote he wants us to be friends. I know it's a bad time, but . . . ," she stepped forward, just a bit, touching fingertips to the door's walnut panels.

Ruth said nothing, only looked to the floor, stepping back in wordless gesture.

"Please call me Betsy."

"Just for a moment," Ruth whispered, "did he write about Jonathan?"

"Yes, a beautiful letter. I have it if you'd like to read it. Parts are personal."

"I'm really not up to it. Maybe tomorrow?"

The next day, Betsy passed the gawking soldiers again, prayed at Christ Church, and waited before the elegant door. Ruth opened it, wider this time in silent invitation. An older woman entered the foyer.

"Ah could get the doah, Miz Ruth."

"Hello, Ruth," Betsy looked at the other, "you must be Mam."

"Ah shuah is. Mam Brown."

"Jed has told me about you."

"Ah raised him. And his daddy before him. Ah don't know you, but you are pretty as a picture. Red ribbon an' all!"

Pleased with the compliment for she had taken special care to look bright and perky this morning, Betsy cooed, "Why, thank you, Mam, thank you very much."

Ruth wore a calico dress patterned brightly with small blue flowers. Clean and pressed neatly, Betsy noted. She had brushed her auburn hair. Her face still held the indoor pallor.

She beckoned toward the parlor.

"Want to read my letter from Jed?" Betsy offered it.

"Not now. Maybe later."

"When were you and Jonathan married?"

"1856"

"Did you know him long?"

"About five. . . It's not important."

Hoping to stumble onto something to pique Ruth's interest, Betsy chattered about herself.

"I had a brother and a sister. Both younger. I pretended to be their mother, feeding and dressing them, tucking them into bed. I loved taking care of them."

No response.

Betsy continued, "I taught Jesse to throw sticks for our dog to run after. He always giggled." She laughed uncertainly, "Jesse, not the dog."

Ruth remained silent.

"And I took care of the baby. Mama had a bad spell after she was born, so I did everything. Everything but feed her, of course. I couldn't do that."

Betsy turned thoughtful, lost in a story she had tried to keep light and happy. Melancholy gathered, stealing the joy from her account as a fog stealing blue from the sky.

"Jesse had just started to run about when the house burned. Mary was still an infant. Mama died, too, rushing into the flames to save them."

Ruth stifled a gasp behind sharp knuckles.

"Oh, I shouldn't have. I'm so sorry."

But Ruth was touched by the tragedy, "No. Please go on."

"Without Mama, Pa seemed lost. He left me with Uncle John."

"That's awful, to leave you like that."

"He didn't mean to. He said he'd come back for me. I know he would have if he was able. He loved me."

The two sat silent for several minutes, before Betsy continued, "Uncle John loves me, too. He's always been kind to me. He sent me to the Winchester Female Academy."

"I remember it, on the corner of Main and Peyton Streets."

"After that, I felt I should help in the tavern. One year turned into two, then three. I met Jed and the war came along."

"But the tavern. And all those rough men!"

"Only a few are rough. Uncle John doesn't stand for any shenanigans. Most are local folks. I've served your Pa, your Ma, too, and Jed. She always has wine."

Ruth spoke wistfully, "I've never been in Linn's, or any other tavern. The Colonel would be shocked."

"The colonel?"

Ruth stiffened, "Jonathan's father. I daresay Jonathan would have been, too. Damn him!"

She sprang from her chair.

"Ruth, what is it?"

"Leave! You must leave."

"I can't leave you like this."

"Leave me alone."

"Tomorrow then?"

"Just leave." Ruth ran from the room, up the wide staircase.

Betsy found Mam, "Miss Ruth's upset. Please look in on her."

Quietly, she let herself out.

The following day, Betsy visited again. Rather than risk more talk, suggested they bake for the children.

They worked along, one dispirited, the other looking to break the solemnity by talking of oatmeal cookies as if the whole world existed in them. As they stored the last of the utensils, Ruth volunteered an apology and an invitation.

"I'm sorry I behaved so childishly." She put her fingers to her mouth, "It was only yesterday wasn't it?"

"Don't apologize, Ruth. You were upset."

"It was a stupid thing, acting the ninny like that."

"We all do things like that, one time or another."

"I suppose," Ruth replied absently.

Over the next few weeks, Betsy visited often. Ruth regained something of her spirit and color. A mutual affection grew between them. She even smiled, and one day laughed aloud, recalling the first day they baked together, "Oatmeal cookies! How seriously you did discuss them."

She seemed to have something else on her mind, not quite sure of her words, "Betsy, I'd like to ask you something."

"Yes?"

"I'm not quite sure how to say it. I don't want to impose."

"Just say it flat out. If you're imposing I'll tell you."

"Well, I thought it would be nice if—if you stayed overnight."

She raced on, "I have so enjoyed our talks. We could pretend we were girls again, talk all night. Have cookies and milk. Or wine. I'd like to be a girl again, a young girl with no worries."

"Except for Jed, I had more worries then than I have now."

"Your story of course. But it's nice to think otherwise. "Will you do it? Maybe you could stay two nights. Or three."

"I'd have to let Uncle John know, else he'd have the militia combing the county."

Betsy stayed not one, but several nights with Ruth. Sharing confidences and embarrassments, they cemented their friendship.

"Did you meet Jed at the tavern, Betsy?"

"I saw him in church first. Then one day he came in and asked Uncle John to introduce us. Very proper he was."

"He was right."

"Yes, he was. Uncle John was so impressed that he escorted me to Jed's table."

Imitating her uncle, she continued, " 'This here's m'niece Betsy,' he said, 'you treat her polite becuz she's uh good girl.'

"I can't say it the way he did, but the words are right," Betsy giggled, "then he said, 'an Betsy, this here's Jedediah Morra' who sez he's gonna marry ya'.

"Uncle John!!"

" 'That's what he said, didnya, Jed?.' And Jed says, 'Yup'.

"Ruth, I was so embarrassed. Jed was looking into his beer so that all you could see was the top of his head."

Ruth covered her mouth to keep from laughing. "Oh, I'm sorry but I can just see you. A school girl and her first beau."

"It wasn't funny, Ruth," Betsy started peevishly, until she was caught up in the humor, first a giggle then full-blown laughter for several minutes. Even after they gained control of themselves, spasms of giggles broke out.

"Uncle John likes Jed. He told me later he likes your Ma and Pa as well as anyone in Winchester. 'Henry keeps his word,' he said, 'and Sarah's good as gold.

" 'They raise their children right,' he said."

"I never thought of us that way. Raised right."

"His very words."

By the last night of Betsy's visit, they had become very close. After supper she encouraged Ruth to talk about Jonathan, "You can't keep it bottled up forever, Ruth."

Ruth did talk, momentarily happy to have a confidante, needing to talk of her confusion and disappointment.

"I just don't understand why he left. He had everything right here, and he ran away from it. Was it my fault?"

"No, Ruth, Jed wrote his last words expressed love for you. Something else must have bothered him."

Reluctant to talk more of embarrassing marital problems, Ruth backed away, "I'll miss our talks."

"We can do it again."

"I am so happy that Jed asked you to call."

They sat quietly, comfortable in their new friendship. For the first time since Jonathan's death, Ruth had found a smidgeon of peace and felt an incipient hope for the future.

"You know, for all our talk, you haven't told me much about Jed. Are you two courting?"

"Oh, Ruth, he's so wonderful! I just love him so much." Betsy bubbled spontaneously, waiting for that very question.

"What about him? Does he feel the same?"

"Yes! Yes! He calls me his Star Queen." Betsy lowered her eyes modestly, blushing her embarrassment, "I shouldn't have told you. It sounds silly, saying it like that.

"But it isn't when he says it. He wants to get married."

Ruth glanced up quickly, her eyebrows drawn together in a silent combination of surprise and disapproval, "Oh."

"Yes. But then he said we should wait until the war is over. He's afraid he'd get hurt and be a burden the rest of his life."

"My brother showed good judgment, Betsy."

"I tried to change his mind," Betsy said softly. Her eye lashes traced with tears as she whispered, "I'd take care of him no matter what happened."

Abruptly, Ruth changed the subject, "Jonathan should have been as considerate. He said he loved me, too. But then he ran off, leaving all that great love of his in a heap like dirty clothes. Sometimes I think he did it in spite."

"I'm sure he thought well of you, Ruth."

"Maybe. Before we married." Ruth's eyes filled, "Oh, Betsy, he left me so many times after."

Betsy touched Ruth's arm empathetically.

"He was so cold. Never intimate." Ruth clenched her hands in her lap, stared at them.

Betsy waited. Ruth would say more if she wanted to.

"He just left—when I needed him most." Her sobs took over.

Betsy came to the love seat, comforting her, rocking her gently until the wave of hurt passed, "How terrible."

Ruth dabbed with a dainty handkerchief, "I'm all right now."

"It seems you and I can be steel and flint."

"We do seem to strike sparks. Please, what I've said is not for anyone else."

"Of course, Ruth. I would never betray your trust."

In bed that night, Betsy thought long of Ruth and Jonathan. She had to let him go, she concluded, in an angry, calm, happy\sad goodbye, a final, shutthedoor farewell. They needed to talk more.

"Good morning, Betsy. You look as though you didn't sleep much."

"I didn't. I was thinking."

"About what?"

"About you. Ruth, I'm going to strike one more spark."

"So early in the morning?"

"Best time for me. When I'm," she yawned, "wide awake."

"Coffee first?"

"How about coffee during?" she smiled.

Ruth poured two steaming mugs, "Go ahead. Spark."

"You have to go to Jonathan's grave."

"I have to—what!"

"You have to go to Jonathan's grave. Jed wrote where he was buried. Ruth, you have to go there—make your peace with him. Otherwise, you'll live the rest of your life with a ghost. Bring him back, bury him in Winchester, or leave him where he is. You have to let him go so you can live your own life. Forgive him in spite of the hurt you feel."

"Betsy, I couldn't do that. Leave Winchester? Find the church? How would I get there?"

"For heaven's sakes. Just go. Find him. Mourn him if you will. But say goodbye, forgive him. He's never coming back, Ruth. He will never come back."

"I know you mean well, but I can't do it. Papa would never let me. How could I ever travel all those miles alone?"

"I'll go with you. I'll ask Uncle John to find us an escort."

"I don't see how in the world . . ."

Betsy interrupted, "Don't try to figure all the details. They will fall in place. If you can think of a better way to make peace with Jonathan, do that instead. You have to do it sooner or later. Better to start sooner."

"Just promise me you'll give it serious thought."

"I can do that, Betsy. I will think on it."

The more she thought, the more she realized that Betsy was right. She had to say goodbye to Jonathan.

XVIII

FOLSOM'S RETURN

A week after he was at the house on the Vienna road, Sedge Folsom was still flaunting his escapade, "Gonna git me summore a' that southron black meat. Be better now it ain't virgin."

As before, he lay at the edge of the cornfield of Freedom Hill watching. No one was in the yard. Nor in the barn. He made sure of that. He skulked to the house, into the kitchen.

Female voices came from the front of the house, one he recognized, the other soft and innocent. Folsom leered.

"Damn, if it ain't gonna be two fur one."

Slouching across the country kitchen, he paused. Turned.

No one.

Stealthily now into the hallway. A quick glance up the stairway. Another into a room to the left. An office.

Another look back. He peered into the parlor.

The black girl stood near the window seat alongside the other. Folsom stepped into the room addressing her first.

"If it ain't m'nigga frien' from the barn."

The two girls jumped.

"It's him, Missy, it's him!" The black girl moved closer to her mistress who stood rigid, one hand in her apron pocket.

Folsom showed his teeth, a penchant he thought a smile.

"It sure'n hell is. I come back like I sed."

He took Missy in at a glance, skipping blonde hair and blue eyes, down the cotton, summer dress that covered, but could never hide the sweetmeats underneath. He slobbered tobacco juice.

"Missy, you got a treat comin'. Ain't she, nigga gal?"

He moved forward.

"Papa! Papa!," the blonde girl screamed.

"Now don't you go pretendin'." Folsom closed in, inflamed by their panic.

The white girl tugged at the tight pocket of her dress, but the little gun was caught. She squeezed the trigger anyway. The explosion rocked the room. Smoke came from the pocket, mostly from the open top, a small puff from the bottom through a powder-blackened hole. The ball ricocheted off the floor into his ankle.

Shrieking, he backed to the center of the room, "You goddamn bitches! You near shot my foot off."

He grinned his curse through yellowed teeth and foul breath, "Nobody shoots at Sedge Folsom, without he pays. An' you two bitches is gonna pay!"

He swayed toward them, panting hate and lechery. Feinting left and right, he herded them back, back toward the window seat.

The girls clung together for safety. Folsom reached for their throats, one black-nailed hand for each.

"But, first. . ." He cocked his head.

The click behind him was familiar. Head down, ready to charge, he turned.

There in the doorway was a smallish man with a shotgun ready to fire. Folsom saw at once its black muzzle and cocked hammer. He saw, too, the bull whip coiled loosely over the man's shoulder. Spreading his arms and extending his fingers wide, he stood perfectly still.

"That's raht smaht," the old man smiled without humor.

"Fust, you jus' unhitch that theah gun belt."

Folsom"s eyes went to slits, calculating, sizing him up for guts and quickness. He hesitated.

"Now! You Yanky divil!

The belt, holster, and gun clattered to the floor.

The old man moved to one side and jerked the shotgun.

"Outsahd! Me an' you got business. Jus' move slow an' easy-like. An' git yer hands up. Way up! You divil."

Folsom did exactly what he was told. He had been in tight situations before, and had escaped. Be patient, he told himself, watch your chance. His eyes went narrower, blacker. His chances were best here in the room, up close, but the old man seemed to know that too, keeping his distance.

"Now git on tha road. Down tha hill inta Vienna. We gonna string you up, fer thievin' an' disrespectin' women.

"An' jus' so's ya know. My gun ain't loaded fer birds."

Folsom sagged hopelessly through the kitchen into the yard. Head, shoulders, arms wilted and drooped. His entire demeanor shouted surrender, dejection, resignation to defeat. To look at him was seeing a whipped man, just what he wanted. Act out the illusion. Wait, spider-like.

He had come out of many a scrape this way. Conniving for the gift of a brief second. In his violent lifetime, he had learned to snatch these unintentional offerings.

Furtively, from under his hat brim, he measured the other, watching, waiting.

He took his chance when his captor stumbled momentarily in the late evening twilight. The muzzle of the shotgun went skyward. Its single barrel exploded.

He ran for the old man, and was surprised at the agile sidestep that avoided his bull-like rush. When he turned back for another attack, the old man had flicked the horse whip out in the dirt behind him.

"Deefile my girls!!" he shouted, "Uh good whippin's wot y'need—like a dadgum mule."

He snapped the leather at this evil man who would defile his granddaughter. It cracked like a pistol shot, slicing into Folsom's forearm. The old man worked his whip as an artist his brush, drawing back for each stroke, laying it on with confidence and precision. Sedge Folsom's efforts to move in close were rewarded with a pattern of red stripes. For the first time in his life he took to his heels. The old man followed, not far before his grandfather's lungs rebelled, but far enough to paint three more stripes.

Folsom reached the cornfield. He lay still, listening to the crackle of dry stalks. Lying perfectly still, he could hear the farmer over to his right, moving toward the road.

Beyond the reach of whistling leather, the raging sergeant snarled, "I'll be back, old man. Fur you an' them two bitches."

The old man cackled, "Jus' tell yer Yanky fren's y'met up with Skinner Thomas."

The old muleskinner reloaded the shotgun and sat in the shadows, watchful and hopeful, angry with himself for losing his captive.

XIX

RUTH'S MIRACLE

"Yes, Ma, if Mam can take the children that's what I'll do.'

"Your father will have a fit."

The front door slammed shut, "Fit. Fit. Who'll have a fit?"

"Why, Henry, I thought you were at the courthouse."

"I was, but they couldn't find the right paper. They never can find the right paper."

Leaning toward Ruth, Sarah whispered, "I don't think this is the time to bother your father."

"It has to be, Ma."

"What are you two connivin'?"

"Not conniving, Pa, planning a short trip."

"A trip! Who's going on a trip?"

"I am, Pa. And I want you to listen to . . ."

"Ruth, I'm not listenin' t'anything about a trip. I have enough trouble with people that can't find papers. Sarah, there any coffee on the stove?"

"Yes, and I think you should hear Ruth while you drink it."

"Don't have to. It doesn't make sense."

Ruth would not be put off, "Pa, I've thought this out. If you'd listen it would make sense."

"You aren't going anywhere."

Losing her patience, Sarah shook a finger, "Henry Morrow! Just because you're upset with somebody who can't find a paper you don't have to treat your daughter like a child. Ruth and I have talked about this. I think she's right. I don't like her out on the road either, but this might be just what she needs.

"You and I have talked about how she's avoided everybody since Jonathan's death. Living like a hermit."

"All right, where do you want t'go and why?"

"It's not that I want to, Pa. I have to go to Manassas."

"Why in the world Manassas?"

"Jonathan is buried there."

"So?"

"I have to say goodbye to him."

"Goodbye! T'say goodbye! Doesn't make sense."

He hesitated. Maybe he had missed something, "Is it t'bring him home you want to go?"

"No, Jonathan has had a Christian burial. He will stay where he is. The colonel won't like it, but I really don't care."

Henry nodded slowly, side to side.

"If that means you won't let me go, I'm going anyway."

"No, I was thinkin' how much like your mother you are."

"It was really Betsy's idea."

"Whothehell's Betsy? I never heard of any Betsy."

"John Linn's niece. She's Jed's friend. He wrote her to visit me. We've become very good friends."

"That Betsy! Friend of Jed's? Hmmmm!

"Is that all of it? Just go t'say goodbye? Hardly seems worth the bother. Won't do Jonathan any good, that's for sure."

"Pa, it's not for Jonathan that I'm going. It's for me. To say my farewell. Say my forgiveness. Let him go."

"Forgiveness? For what?" Henry snapped.

For dying and leaving me alone," Ruth thought but didn't add, "in my bed for all those years."

Nodding approval, Sarah cut in, "I agree. I have friends who suffered the same. Widowed and living a dream the rest of their lives. This niece of Mr. Linn's is a thoughtful one."

"That may be so, but there's details t'consider. How you gonna get there, for one?"

"By wagon. We'll hire a driver."

"What if it breaks down? There's bushwhackers and thieves and worse—seems you're askin' for trouble."

"Pa, I have to go whatever the risk. Betsy said she'd go. Her uncle could get a driver."

Henry grumped, "I'm not lettin' you ride off with somebody John Linn picks. Betsy goin' just means two women in danger instead of one."

"Henry Morrow, get off your high horse. Mr. Linn is your friend. His niece is a smart girl. Now let's get down to business. What about Ezekiel? I'm sure he would be willing,"

So simply did Sarah wipe out all Henry's objections.

And he knew it.

"Well, I don't know," cradling his chin in his hand.

Sarah knew the signs. After a decent interval, he would agree, then make Ruth accept a long list of conditions. But that was all right. He was only trying to protect his daughter.

"Ruth, you know how I feel. But I guess it's somethin' you have t'do. I'll agree if 'Zekiel goes with you, if you don't travel after sundown, stay nights with decent people, avoid public rooms caterin' t'soldiers, and don't talk t'strangers."

"Henry, for goodness sakes! Ruth's a grown woman. She can manage your list and whatever else you haven't thought of yet."

"Pa," Ruth leaned to kiss the top of his head, "it's nice to have a father so concerned. We'll be fine. Honest we will."

Henry motioned Ruth to follow him across the room. Unlocking the tall gun case he reached for two boxes of black walnut.

"Matched derringers," he said, "Remember how t'shoot?"

"Yes, I do, Pa, and how pleased you were the first time I hit the little cloth you hung on the fence post."

"Give one of them t'John's Betsy. And keep them handy."

"Thank you, Pa,"

"Get close and aim for the middle. Remember hearin' that?"

"I do, Pa. You also told me something else. After my first shot. Do you remember?"

Henry knitted his brows, but brightened quickly, "Yes, I do. Don't pull the trigger. Squeeze it."

"So's it goes off before you know it."

"And don't blink," he embraced his firstborn, "God keep you, Ruth."

"And you, Pa. I love you."

Two days later, they left Winchester, Ruth, Betsy, and Ezekiel driving one of the farm wagons, a plain wagon and ordinary horses. "Not worth the stealin'," Ezekiel had said.

At the corner, Ezekiel and Ruth turned to wave to Sarah and Henry. They were standing very close together.

Betsy was at the tavern, dressed plainly in a saggy, brown dress to help hide her fullness. She carried a reticule and an unadorned bonnet. A small trunk was beside her, worn leather studded with brass.

"Hello, Betsy. Ezekiel, this is my good friend Betsy Dearing. She's Jed's good friend, too."

"G'mornin', Miss Betsy, happy ta make your acquaintance."

"Thank you, Ezekiel. I feel I already know you from what Jed has told me. He said you were a second father to him."

Ezekiel beamed, answering modestly, "I do what I can." He jumped from the wagon as she stooped to pick up the little trunk.

"Don't you go liftin' that, Miss Betsy.

"I've put straw in the wagon, and Mattie stuffed flour bags ta sit on if you want. She put in some hams, too, in case we need 'em. 'Never can tell' she said."

He turned the wagon around, clattering south on the turnpike. All three of them looked up Wolfe Street as they passed. It was empty, except for a lone dog tagging a tree.

A half mile on, they pulled up at the toll gate.

Ezekiel reached in his pocket, "Henry gave me money ta take care of things."

"We're really on our way," Ruth gushed, "I can hardly believe it." She turned to Betsy.

"Papa gave me something for you," offering one of the derringers, "he said you should carry it. Keep it handy all the time. Do you know how to shoot it?"

"Not really. Just that you pull on the trigger."

"Here, I'll show you. First you don't pull on the trigger. It spoils your aim. You squeeze it, more and more. If it goes off before you know it, you've done it right."

"I'll keep it in my reticule."

"If it's handy there. I have one, too, here in my pocket. It's no good if you can't get to it."

Crossing Ashby's Gap through the Blue Ridge, they drank in the view to the east. Two hours later they forded Goose Creek.

"Wanna get out and stretch? I'm gonna water the horses." Ruth and Betsy walked a short distance upstream.

Ezekiel was checking harnesses when a shot rang out, from the direction the girls had walked.

"Oh, my God!" He took after them as fast as he could run.

Ruth saw the alarm in his face, "Oh, Ezekiel, I am sorry. I was showing Betsy how to shoot Papa's derringer."

"Miss Ruth, I'm not one ta find fault, but you sure gave me a conniption. Henry said ta turn around and come back any time I thought it best.

I espect there won't be any more reason ta do that. Will there, Miss Ruth.'
It was not a question.

Ruth touched his arm affectionately, "Ezekiel, I was forgetful. Forgetful and wrong. I'm truly sorry."

Approaching the tiny village of Upperville, Ezekiel found a tidy farm
at a fair price for the night. Immediately, he declared, "I'll sleep in the wagon
so's ta be with the horses."

The farmer's wife was a jolly sort, obviously one who enjoyed her
food, "Supper'll be ready soon. Make yourselves comfortable in the parlor.
Would you like tea? Or coffee?"

"No thank you. I would like to wash though."

"Of course. Mr. Toler just put a pump in the kitchen so you won't have
to go outside. There's hot water on the stove."

"The pump will be fine."

"The privy's out there to the left. The door swings shut by itself, so
you can't tell if it's in use. Just rap on it. Or better still, give a yell from the
back porch."

Betsy spoke for the first time, "I could use it now."

"It's milking time so it should be empty. Give a shout if you like."

Amused, Betsy caught Ruth's eye, "I'll just knock on the door."

"Supper's not fancy, but there's plenty of it. Chicken left from dinner,
beans from the garden. They're the last fresh ones for this year, and tending
toward stringy."

"I'm sure they'll be delicious. Please, no bother."

At the supper table, Mr. Toler proved as congenial as his wife, "It's nice
to have guests. Mostly soldiers now."

He poured wine from a dark bottle, "Scuppernong. From our own
grapes. Would you care for some? Mother?" He queried Ruth and Betsy
with his eyes as he asked.

"Then I'll have to drink my toast alone."

He raised the glass, "To a pleasant and safe journey."

Later, as they prepared for bed, Ruth suddenly broke down.

"Ruth, what is it? What's wrong?"

"I don't really know. Now that we've started I'm not sure I want to go
through with it."

"I think I would feel the same way. Disloyal to someone who was close."

"Betsy, how can I close the door like that!"

"You'll find a way when the time comes."

"Oh, I don't think I can. I was so sure that this was the right thing to
do, but now I don't know. I just don't know."

"We've had a long day, Ruth—we're both tired. You'll feel different in the morning. I know I will."

"I hope so. Good night."

The second day, they went through the pretty town of Middleburg, over the Bull Run Mountains at Aldie, onto the Little River Turnpike that ran straight across the piedmont for twenty miles.

"It's pretty, but I'd miss the mountains," Ezekiel mused. He swayed on the high seat, humming softly in a sonorous baritone, a soulful melody in a rhythm that matched the horses' gait. Caught up in the lamentation, the girls realized that he was singing words and a repetitive refrain.

"I can't make out most of it, but it seems to be a story, a sad story," Betsy whispered so as not to interrupt him.

"And wisps of celebration pop up. I thought at first it was all sad, but it isn't. I wonder what it is." They listened to uncounted verses, enchanted with this musical side of Ezekiel.

"I've heard Mattie sing since I was a baby and she put me to bed, but never you, Ezekiel. What was it you were singing?"

"I used ta listen ta the mule skinners on the canal in Washin'ton. They'd walk along the tow path as if they were in another world. Just singin' ta themselves. And their mules."

"So many verses."

"Mam taught me a lot of them. Make up the rest."

At the toll gate coming into tiny Arcola, he asked about a place to stay for the night.

"Half mile down the road," the gatekeeper pointed, " y'll see a house on the right. The doctor's house."

Ruth was delighted to learn that Dr. Weeks knew Henry.

"So you're his daughter? I rode his stage up the Valley Turnpike, to Lexington to visit my sister. Almost a year ago. Mr. Morrow spoke of President Buchanan letting the country drift into trouble. Yes, I do remember him. A man of strong opinions."

"He is indeed, Dr. Weeks," Ruth added with a surge of pride, "my Pa helped build the Valley Turnpike."

Later, in their room, she told Betsy, "Pa is a remarkable man, the things he's done. I never thought much about him.

"I'm sorry if I was difficult last night. Thinking of Pa has helped. Like he's given me courage."

"I'm glad."

"Something else. Ezekiel's song reminded me that you keep going no matter how much trouble you have. Today, Pa and Ezekiel came together, just for me it seems. Like a miracle."

"You never know about miracles, Ruth. One comes into your life. For a moment you see the hand of God. Then you explain it away. God gave us brains. We use them to deny Him."

"Betsy, so serious?"

"I'm sorry."

"Don't be. I can see why Jed is attracted to you."

The third night, they stayed at a tavern near Centreville, Ruth's idea, "Tonight let's stay in a public place where we can have a glass of wine with supper."

They did. In fact, they had three glasses of wine, one before supper and two with.

They questioned the innkeeper as to Sudley Church.

"Go west on the turnpike across Bull Run. Then through the toll gate at the stone house and turn right, up the hill about a mile. That's Sudley Road. Y'll see the church on your left."

"Thank you. We'll be staying again tomorrow night. Please hold our room for us. No one else. We'll pay the difference if you turn anyone away."

They found Sudley Church with no difficulty.

"I'd rather do this alone."

Finding a pleasant spot under a huge oak, Betsy and Ezekiel watched Ruth as she headed for the small burial ground.

Betsy mused, I would like to help you, Ruth, because you're my friend. Just ask me, and I'll come running. But I can't unless you ask.

"This here tree must be a hundred years old. White oak, they're tough old trees. Like some people."

"Tell me, Ezekiel, is Mr. Morrow one of your oak trees? Mrs. Morrow, what's she like?"

"Miss Sarah? She's a worker. She gets her eye on somethin' and there isn't any stoppin' her. I've seen her work alongside the men in the fields, then tend ta her own chores in the house. Yes mam. She doesn't take no sass, not from anybody."

She watched Ruth walking toward the simple burial markers. Newly turned dirt, reddish and lumpy, marked recent graves.

She saw Ruth pause at each one, reading the inscriptions, contemplating each. Across the rows she made her silent way, reading, pausing, reading, pausing. She went on to one marked with a broken musket.

"Miss Betsy?"

Startled, Betsy jumped, blinked, touched fingertips to brow, brushed lightly, one time across. She murmured vaguely as she came back to Ezekiel, "Oh, I'm sorry. I was anxious about Ruth."

"You were a hundred miles away."

She held up a hand, "Shhh."

By a small, wooden cross, not weatherbeaten as some, yet not new, Ruth had stopped, reading, reading, her hand lifting to her mouth. She kneeled. Betsy knew she had found what she had come to find. Ezekiel's voice came back into focus.

"—Henry in Washin'ton. Those were good days."

Ruth still knelt by the grave.

"When was Jed born?"

Still kneeling, Ruth touched the little cross.

"Was in '38, two years after we came ta Winchester."

Ruth was standing now, staring down at Jonathan's resting place. She stood ramrod straight, controlled, determined, yet, a lonely figure above the modest gravestones and crosses.

"Miss Ruth be comin' now."

She had left Jonathan's grave, walking very slowly, preoccupied, head bent low. Betsy felt the despair.

At the edge of the little burial ground, Ruth stopped, lifting her face to the sky. A radiance came over her there at the little church, destroying the darkness in her bearing. Suddenly, she was buoyant, free, alive in a new day. Auburn hair reflected the sunlight, and her face, the goodness of God. She threw her shoulders back, and headed for the wagon.

"Betsy. Ezekiel. Our business here is done." She climbed to the high seat alongside Ezekiel.

Back on the Warrenton road, the same man raised the toll gate, "Find the church all right?"

Ezekiel answered, "Right where you said. Thank you kindly."

"Lookin' for family?"

"Yessir."

"Find him?"

"Yessir," Ezekiel offered a coin.

"No charge," the gatekeeper knuckled his cap to the ladies. Ruth to Ezekiel, "I want to see the battlefield."

"You're on it, mam," the gatekeeper said respectfully, "if you look at the front of the house there, you'll see a cannon ball still stuck where it hit. House was used for a hospital."

"Where did Jackson's men stand? I want to stand where Jonathan stood," Ruth demanded.

"Yes ma'am. If you go up that road," he pointed to the continuation of Sudley Road across the turnpike, where it led to New Market and beyond into Manassas Junction, "At the top of the hill turn left into the field and you're there. Be sure to turn into the clearing before you come to the trees. If you look back this way, you'll be looking exactly as General Jackson's men did, right at the Henry House. All wrecked now, shot to pieces except the chimney. Jackson's men ran past that house, leavin' it to their left, and down the hill to the turnpike here."

Ezekiel swung the wagon around, turned left up the gentle rise of Sudley Road. Worn lower than the fields by years of traffic, it had eroded even more at the sides where rain water had carved its own channels. Ezekiel considered the ditches.

"Better leave the wagon here. I'd hate ta break a wheel."

The violated field formed a low plateau connecting the Warrenton Pike and the vale to the east. Once ripe with hay and corn, it was stained with holes from exploding shells and scars from rolling, bouncing solid shot; defiled by marching boots, horses' iron shoes and the iron-rimmed wheels behind them; trashed with the debris of equipment worthless even to the scavengers. Here and there a small patch of rich grass stood undisturbed, a pitiful reminder of what had been destroyed. Overlooking it all stood a sentinel of a chimney, rising from the rubble of boards that had been the Henry House.

Ezekiel surveyed the ruin, saddened and angered by the tragedy that had come to the land, "Isn't enough ta march from Washin'ton shootin' people. They have ta tear up the land, wreck the houses. Why don't they just burn it? Burn it all up."

"It's terrible to think what happened here, Ezekiel, enough to last a lifetime."

"It surely is, Miss Betsy. God's good land and they treat it so bad. And all those boys gone."

Ezekiel shook his head slowly in disbelief. When he spoke again, the anger was gone and the words were subdued, respectful. "This land is different from what it was, changed now. No longer just hay and corn fields. It needs ta be cleaned and cared for now so's people can see it a hundred years from now. See where my boys fought. And Jon'than, too."

Silent the whole time, Ruth lagged behind as they crossed the plateau to the house, almost to the sloping ground beyond. Without warning, she started to run, to catch up, Betsy thought, until she ran by them, out of control, screaming, her hair streaming wildly. Ezekiel ran after her, past the house, to the crest of the hill where he caught her. Holding her gently, respectfully, he intoned over and over, "It's all right, Miss Ruth, it's all right. Everythin's all right."

She struggled to break away. Ezekiel was too strong.

Giving in, she trembled. Gasping for breath, she looked up at him with great, fearful eyes.

"Miss Ruth, it's ok, it's ok."

Almost a whisper, soft, soothing, reassuring, his singsong gradually took effect, as it had a hundred times to calm an alarmed animal at home. Ruth quieted enough to relax her head against him, great tears coursing down her face.

"You all right now?" Ezekiel loosened his hold, she slumped to the ground, sobbing her distress, whispering, "I just need to rest."

"What is it?" Anxiety flooded Betsy's voice as she caught up, "What's the trouble?"

Ezekiel dropped to the ground beside Ruth, sighing to ease the tension, "I could use a rest, too."

He pointed north, "That's Centreville over there," and east, "that's Manassas," and around to the west, "that's the toll gate and the Blue Ridge." Transparent, childlike though his effort was, his stratagem worked.

Ruth, strung taut since they had left the burial ground at Sudley Church, regained control. Betsy's concern eased. All three were willing to do nothing, just look across the open land and let their minds relax.

At the bottom of the hill, a small cedar tree reminded Ezekiel of Jed's letter. He wondered if Ruth knew of the little cedar that marked where Jonathan had fallen. He started to point it out, thought better of it. Then he noticed another cedar and a third and fourth, and was glad he had kept quiet.

Ruth looked down the hill, too, staring intently as if she saw something not really there. She stood, shaded her eyes to see better, compressing her lips into a bloodless line, clenching fingers, unclenching them, all the while whispering, "It's wrong, it's all wrong.

"I've been to his grave. He's dead. But only a few minutes ago I saw him, here on this hill. Jonathan was alive and running. He ran with me. But, he's dead. For certain, he is dead.

"This is the hill where he died. He ran down this hill and fell near the bottom. Pa told me that, from Jed's letter he said, ran down a hill chasing Yankees. Only a brave man could do that."

Betsy and Ezekiel listened. She fell silent but her mind raced on.

How could you face such danger, Jonathan, and yet run away from me so many times? I wasn't dangerous at all. You ran away from me, and here on this hill you ran straight into Yankee soldiers shooting at you. The children will have to know about you, Jonathan. You were a good soldier and a courageous man. You did what you had to. As we all do.

I wish I knew exactly where you fell. No, I'm glad I don't.

She stood in the same spot motionless, staring down Jonathan's hill, lost in reverie. It's over, Jonathan, it's over. Betsy was right.

You were right, Betsy, about coming here. You are wise, Betsy, like Mama. For your years, very, very wise. Now I understand, not everything, but more than I did. Thank you, Betsy, thank you.

Her satinet skirt rippled and snapped in the west wind. Ruth Brighton lifted her head toward the Blue Ridge and its Valley, toward Winchester and home. She shook her long hair loose, and like her skirt, it too caught the western wind.

Patiently, Betsy and Ezekiel waited, sensing an elemental undercurrent too precious to disturb. However obscure it might be to them, the interlude belonged to Ruth, to extend or to end as she would. After several minutes, she did end it, turning to them drained of emotion and energy.

"We've had a long day. It's time to leave."

"I could meet y'all at the toll gate. It's not so far that way, straight down the hill."

Ruth's voice reflected fatigue, "We have followed Jonathan far enough." She pointed to the turnpike where Sudley Road crossed it, "We'll wait there. Betsy, you ready?"

"Yes." Her voice was almost a whisper.

Back at the inn, Ruth ordered wine with their supper, "Red," she told the proprietor, "a bottle."

Preoccupied with the emotional events of the day, she sipped thoughtfully and ate her supper in silence. Betsy did the same, sensing that Ruth had need for a quiet time before talking of the day. Leaving the public room, she asked the bartender to send the rest of the bottle to their bedroom, upstairs.

"Yes ma'am." He called a barmaid to escort them up the dim, narrow stairway.

By a single candle, they finished the bottle.

"I will never forget this day," Ruth said finally, as they prepared for bed. Her eyes were bright, catching the light of the flickering candle, her face, tinted blush with the wine. The day was indeed unforgettable. She had reached the time to talk of it, to share it, to express her thanks.

"You were right about forgiving Jonathan. I never imagined I would be able to do that, but when I was kneeling by his grave this morning something came over me. All at once. I realized that Jonathan was not bad, Betsy. At heart, he was a good man. Whatever it was that bothered him was not his fault. When he left, he said he loved me. I never believed him until this morning. He really did love me."

"Jed spoke well of him in his letters. He always wrote what good friends they had become.

"This morning at the church, I prayed for him, then I said good bye. Last of all, I said my forgiveness. I thought that was the end of it, but then, I asked the same of him. I asked him to forgive me. I don't know why I did that, I hadn't thought of it until that moment, but it seemed—it seemed . . ."

"Appropriate?"

"Yes. Appropriate. That's exactly it. As soon as I did that, I had the strangest sense of peace. I could think of Jonathan without ill feeling, without rancor.

"Then, later at the battlefield, I realized that Jonathan had to be a courageous man to do what he did. He ran down that hill, Betsy, into all those soldiers. He believed in what he was fighting for, and gave his life for what he believed. I'm proud of him for that. I'll tell the children to be proud of their father. Going to the battlefield was another of those little miracles we have talked about.

"He's at rest, Betsy. So am I. At rest with his memory. At peace with myself."

"Ruth, I prayed for that. I am so happy for you," Betsy's smile turned to concern, "but whatever in the world happened to you on Henry Hill?"

"I really don't know.

"I felt Jonathan alongside me. He was just there, walking with me, not saying anything. Then he was running, his hand on my arm hurrying me along, shouting. 'This isn't any place for you, Ruth. RUN! RUN!' I could feel his hand—heard him yelling—I saw him there by my side. He pulled me along faster and faster and I ran with him. Until Ezekiel caught up and stopped me.

"So real that moment was, Jon with me, trying to save me, Betsy. He was trying to save me.

"We were in the battle but nobody else was there. Just the two of us. The field was empty, not even any grass or dirt, only covered in waves of smoke. He was shouting for me to save myself, but there wasn't any sound. Everything was quiet, even Jon. His mouth was screaming at me, yelling, but he had no voice—even so I could hear him. Then he stopped and held me close. His lips said, 'I'm sorry I hurt you. I love you, Ruth, I will always love you.' He said that—I heard it, but there wasn't anything to hear."

She paused.

"And nobody else was there.

"Except there was a soldier sprawled sleeping near a little cedar tree. Somehow, he's Jonathan. He was with me. He was down there at the bottom of the hill, too. Then the soldier was gone. Jon was gone. And Ezekiel sat down beside me.

"How can you explain something like that, Betsy?"

"I don't have the faintest idea. Unless it was from last night's wine," she smiled coyly.

"Oh Betsy, it couldn't be that!"

"What else then?" She blew out the candle.

Ruth's voice floated through the dark, filled with wonder.

"A miracle? Betsy, do you suppose it was a miracle?"

The question lingered on the tendrils of candle smoke.

XX

A CHANGE OF PLANS

The following day, Ruth had already dressed when she heard the bed creak and Betsy's sleepy, "Good morning.

"Guess it's time to get up and start back."

"Betsy, not yet. Not for a few days."

"But we said we'd be back as soon as we could."

"David wrote last that he was in Northern Virginia, near Fairfax. The proprietor said it's only seven or eight miles."

"But, yesterday you seemed exhausted. Ready to go home."

"Yesterday I was, but not this morning. Oh, I had such a good night's rest.

"I'd like to see David. And maybe we can see Jed."

Betsy bounded out of the bed, "Do you think we could? But we have no idea where he is. What about Ezekiel?"

"Do you know who you sound like?" Ruth smiled

"No. Why do you ask that?"

"You sound like I did a week ago," she smiled again, amused at their reversed positions, "all questions and doubts. Jed is in Jackson's Brigade. It's easy to ask where Jackson's Brigade is."

The innkeeper knew exactly where the brigade was, "A mile east of town. Camp Harman they call it." Betsy was ecstatic.

Ezekiel was less than enthused, "Henry'll be espectin' us home." But Ezekiel was no match for the two of them.

"We been more'n a mile, Miss Ruth. I don't see anythin'."

"Strange. Let's continue a bit. It might be just ahead."

Ezekiel drove on, stopping at a farm house to ask.

"They said Gin'l Jackson was there, but left yesterday."

Betsy stifled tears, "We missed Jed by one day?"

Ruth commiserated, "That's a shame. But we can still see David."

They headed for Fairfax Courthouse, Betsy very quiet.

At noon, they rattled into Germantown and on to the county seat. It throbbed with soldiers, wagons, and horses.

Ezekiel spotted a lieutenant with a long cavalry saber and yellow piping on his uniform, "Escuse me, sir, can you tell me the whereabouts of Gin'l Stuart?"

The young officer looked at the wagon as if its occupants were either Yankee spies or camp followers.

Ruth stared back, "My brother is with General Stuart."

His skepticism showed, "And who might that be? Madam!"

Ruth skewered him with sweetness, "Captain Morrow, sir. Captain David Morrow."

The young officer crumpled, "Captain Morrow. Of course. He's ADC—that's aide-de-camp, ma'am, to the general."

"How nice of you to recognize the name."

Eager to make restitution, "The general's at Munson's Hill, ma'am, near Falls Church. I'd be honored to escort you."

He braced, saluted as respectful a salute as Fairfax Courthouse had ever seen, "Lieutenant Hollins at your service, ma'am. I'd rather a proper introduction, but . . ." He flashed an engaging smile and threw up his hands in mock despair.

"We're also looking for General Jackson's Brigade. I have another brother with him."

"Ma'am, I'm not sure where he is, but I can find out." He took off like a schoolboy playing hooky.

Betsy was delighted; Ruth, still miffed but succumbing to the lieutenant's efforts to make amends.

Ten minutes later, he was back, "Good news. General Jackson is not far down the road. He just arrived yesterday."

Betsy squealed in happiness. "How far? How long will it take to get there?"

The lieutenant hesitated, "Probably half an hour. But I'm embarrassed because General Stuart expects my immediate return."

"Think nothing more about it. If you'll just point our direction."

He was genuinely sorry, "No, by G—, by golly, I'll escort you as I said I would. With your permission of course." His eyes begged for the chance to redeem himself. "Ruffians are about, and the route can be confusing."

Ruth relented, enjoying for the first time in years the attention of an attractive man, "I'm Ruth Brighton. I lost my husband at Manassas."

"My sympathy, ma'am," respectfully he touched his hat brim.

"These are my friends, Elizabeth Dearing and Ezekiel Brown."

Lieutenant Hollins touched his hat again.

A half hour later he was inquiring in order the whereabouts of Colonel Allen's Second Virginia, the Winchester Rifles, and Jedediah Morrow. To Betsy, it seemed hours before they found him.

She was in his arms in seconds, "Jed, Jed, . . ." She could say nothing more.

He couldn't believe what he saw, "What? How'd you get here? Where'd you come from?"

"What's the difference, sweetheart, I'm here and that's all that counts."

"Y're right, Star Queen, right as rain."

"We're going to Falls Church to see David. I so hoped you could go with us."

Jed scowled, "No passes. General Jackson even refused an officer with a sick wife—about t'die they said. Hell, I'm not stayin' here. You can bet on that."

"Sounds like something I don't want to know about," Lieutenant Hollins rode off. To let his horse graze, he said.

Enveloped in a big bear hug of an embrace, Betsy's voice was muffled, "But what can you do?"

"Maybe you can use this, Jed," taking it all in at the back of the wagon, Ezekiel held up one of the hams Mam had packed.

Jed lit up, "Zekiel, you some kind of magician?"

He gathered them close, "Go toward Falls Church. Out of sight of the tents and wait for me."

Betsy waivered, "You'll get in trouble, Jed."

He hugged her hard. Kissed her again, "I'll be along soon." Taking the ham from Ezekiel, he headed for the tents of the Winchester Rifles.

Ezekiel snapped the reins and clucked his tongue at the horses. Lieutenant Hollins fell in behind.

Behind them, Jed greeted his messmates, "Look what old Jed's got." He held the ham high.

"MMmm uh. We eatin' good tonight!"

Squatting in the middle of them, he motioned them all in close, conspirators all, "This here's a special ham from the best smokehouse in Frederick County. It's yours for a small favor."

"What kind of favor, Jed?"

"Just stand muster for me until I get back. Today. Tomorrow. Maybe next day. Nothin' I haven't done for you buzzards."

Ten minutes later he vaulted into the wagon to join Betsy. They rode backwards, legs dangling, carefree as children. Betsy leaned against him, inside the arc of his arm, yielding happily as he pulled her still closer. An hour ago, neither would have given a plugged nickel for their chances of being together.

"Jed, what did you do?"

"Do for what?"

"To leave camp. You said you couldn't get a pass."

"I took care of it."

"But what did you do?"

"Messmates'll answer for me at muster."

"Won't you get into trouble?"

"Maybe," Jed smiled his big grin as he pulled her closer, "if I do, Star Queen, it'll be worth it."

Betsy frowned her worry. He relaxed his hold on her.

"Old Jack's stingy with passes. He ought t'know men are gonna go French leave. Anyway, he can't do anythin' now."

He turned to the high seat in front, "Zekiel, thank you. Sorry I couldn't enjoy the ham, but I'd rather be here."

"Figgered you had good use for it back there."

"I did that, Zeke, turned it into a three day pass."

"Got three more. Anybody hungry."

Lieutenant Hollins made his contribution, "There's a small creek up ahead. It's a pleasant place to stop if you want."

Five minutes later, they pulled up at a shallow ford. Ezekiel watered the horses and walked upstream to fill the canteens they carried. Jed cut slabs off Ezekiel's second ham. The sun was low to the western hills.

Betsy and Jed had walked the last mile, hands around each other's waist, lagging behind, talking and laughing together.

"Betsy, we just gotta get by ourselves tonight."

"I've missed you, too, Jed. But—"

"But what, Star Queen?"

"I'm not feeling just right."

"You aren't sick! Betsy, you all right?"

"Oh, I'm fine. It's not that. It's just that it's—it's not the right time. Jed, you know what I mean."

"Oh."

"I'm so sorry, Jed. We should have left last week. I never dreamed I was going to see you."

"Come on now. No tears. I'm just so happy t'see you. It doesn't make any difference."

Betsy couldn't resist the chance to tease, "No difference! Jed Morrow, that's not very flattering. How can you say that?"

"Aw, Betsy. It does and it doesn't."

"I'm sorry. I didn't mean to make you feel bad."

"I don't feel bad. Not about that, but because it isn't easy t'explain. May be it's like Sunday dinner at home, everythin's so good, then you have dessert. Then you want more dessert. Betsy, I already had dinner, dessert too just walkin' together like this."

She snuggled close as they approached the wagon, "Oh, Jed, you can romance a girl can't you! I do love you."

The sun disappeared as they rattled into Falls Church. They took Lieutenant Hollins' advice and stayed at Mr. Taylor's, the same Mr. Taylor who served soldiers from both sides of the line.

"Pick where you want to stay," the lieutenant had said, "with a family or at an inn. It's your choice. I like Taylor's Tavern myself, clean rooms and the best food in town. The owner is an unusual host."

He hesitated, "Mrs. Brighton, I am truly sorry for my bad manners at the Courthouse. I'd like to stay but—General Stuart, you know."

"You were unspeakably rude," Ruth flirted, "if the General is angry with you, tell him it was his aide's fault for having a sister that demanded your services."

Beaming at Ruth's turnabout, the young officer saluted her gallantly, "I hope we meet again." He nudged with his spurs and galloped off with his delayed papers for General Stuart.

Mr. Taylor greeted them as they entered his public room, "Welcome ladies, welcome lucky gentleman, welcome to my humble inn. I've chicken and biscuits, a side of pork roasted crackling brown, and apples fried hot and spicey t' tantalize yer tongue. I have subtle wines for ladies, red and white and burnished gold mellowed in oaken casks. For you, sir, the best bourbon this side of Mr. Washington's own river. Or my own nut-brown ale if that's your preference."

Setting plates and glasses he embellished his greeting, "Y're not from these parts, that I can see. Whatsoever I can do to ease your journey, just ask and ye shall have."

"Why thank you, sir, that is kind. I am Ruth Brighton of Winchester. My friend, Betsy Dearing. My brother, Jed Morrow."

"Morrow? Morrow? That mark has a familiar ring, begorrah. Let me think now. Hmmm! Morrow. Morrow.

"Ahhh, I have it. An officer, a handsome gentleman. He always comes in with a giant of a friend. A month ago, mayhap less, he throttled an uncouth soldier and was a flea jump of profanin' the sanctuary of my modest establishment. As ye may have heard, I welcome both North and South askin' only they get on without hostility. I remember Captain Morrow well restrainin' himself at the very last instant and preservin' our peace."

"That sounds ominous. Whatever did he do?"

"He took the lout outside, out that very door," he pointed. "before he shot him."

"Shot him!!"

"Only to give his ear a bit of a nick, exactly what he intended. A grand officer, indeed.

"Captain—ahhh yes, I have it—Captain David Morrow. He's often here. May be here tonight before I close."

"Oh, I hope so. You'll let us know if we're in our room."

"That I will. His sister, ye say?"

Ruth looked up sharply, "His sister and his brother, sir."

"No offense, good lady. Yer resemblance supports yer words."

They ordered pork and spiced apples, with wine, ale for Jed, and a fourth plate with chicken and pork for Ezekiel who insisted on guarding the wagon and horses.

An hour later, two officers reined up at the tavern.

"Tom, look at that wagon back there. Looks familiar. Only one wagon I know has a seat like that. Built big for comfort."

"Just an ordinary farm wagon, far as I can see."

David Morrow inspected it more closely.

"Who's messin' around my wagon?" Ezekiel came from behind it, brushing straw from his clothes. In the dim light, he recognized the big stallion, "Y'gotta be Sable. No other horse is that big and that black."

"And only one voice like yours, Zeke Brown. Whatinthehell are you doing here?"

"David, y're a sight for these old eyes."

"This is unbelievable. Zeke, what in the world are you doing here in Falls Church? Where's Pa?"

"Back in Winchester, I guess. He ain't here."

Ezekiel related the story of their trip, to Centreville, to the cemetery and battlefield. "Miss Ruth, Miss Betsy and me. This mornin' we got Jed."

"So. Jonathan killed. I'm sorry to hear that. Must have been a shock to everyone. A shame.

"But tell me how's everyone at home? And who's this Betsy?"

"Jed's friend. More'n a friend is my guess."

"They're all inside now?"

"Sure are. Prob'ly eatin' supper."

"Zeke, this is my friend, Captain Rosser."

"Pleasure, Ezekiel." Tom Rosser held out his hand.

"Friend of David's a friend of mine, sir."

"Come on inside. I'll buy you a drink."

Ezekiel hesitated a moment, "David, I better not."

"Nonsense, come on."

Ezekiel resisted, "David, it's better if I don't. You know it and I know it. It ain't that important."

"Damn it, Zeke!"

"Some day. Not now. Maybe your son and mine. Maybe you and me one day if we're lucky."

"Damn it!" David kicked open the side door, remembering the night he tussled with the boor of a sergeant and herded him through this same door. He shouted toward the bar, "Mr. Taylor, three pints. Bring them out here."

The proprietor carried the three pewter tankards in one huge hand, fingers laced through the handles, "Evenin', gents. Drink inside if that's your pleasure."

"My good friend here is reluctant."

"Not for my doing, sir, I welcome all in my tavern, all that can conduct themselves as gentlemen as ye know."

Ezekiel spoke up, "Y're a generous man and I'll return the kindness by stayin' out here. I want no trouble. And I want ta make none for others."

"The hell with that, Zeke. Come on."

A lone horseman rode up to the hitching rail. Heading for the door, he spied the three men drinking ale, "Captain Morrow. Is that you?"

"Yes. The light has me at a disadvantage."

"Matt Garland. First New York Cavalry. Lincoln's own. I met you here about a month ago."

"I remember it well."

"I apologize again for . . ."

"No need. Wasn't your doing. You remember Captain Rosser? And this is my friend Ezekiel Brown."

David noted that Matt Garland held his hand to each of them.

"Captain Rosser, pleased to see you again. And you, Mr. Brown."

Ezekiel smiled.

"My sister and brother are guests of Mr. Taylor tonight. I was just going in to join them. Want to come along?"

"I don't want to interfere with family."

"Nonsense. I want you to meet them. Especially my brother. He's in Jackson's Brigade.

"Come on, Zeke."

"David, I don't think so. 'Nuff trouble around, without stirrin' it up."

"Zeke, you're probably right. But I don't like it."

Ezekiel laughed, "See? Y're part of the problem. You don't like it. Somebody else like what you don't like. And boom! Trouble. I'm fine, David, don't you worry. Somebody has to be with the horses."

Inside, David squinted into the dim light. He made out Jed near the wall, and two women across from him, backs to the door. Left hand on his saber against its rattling, the other to his lips signalling Jed to remain silent, he crossed the room.

Quietly, he stood behind the women. For one uncertain moment he waivered, decided hell I've taken bigger chances than this. He picked the one to his left, tipping her backwards, half off the bench and kissed her full on the mouth. He looked into hazel eyes that definitely were not Ruth's, neither angry nor friendly, but wide in surprise and innocence.

"Oh! I'm sorry."

Jed roared his hearty laugh.

"You're not my sister," David apologized still holding her.

"I'd like to be," Betsy looked him square in the eye as she reached a hand for Jed.

"You must be Betsy."

"You must be David."

"I'd like to say I'm sorry."

"Well, aren't you?"

"To be truthful, no. I'm not sorry at all."

Betsy felt the warmth in her face as she recognized the compliment. She glanced at Jed.

Ruth reached for him, "David, just the same old David. More enthusiasm than caution. It is good to see you." Betsy wriggled toward the end of the bench, still holding Jed's hand. David embraced his sister as he squeezed between them to sit, and she, him. Jed glowed as if he had arranged the entire meeting.

"Jed, I might be giving you some competition."

"You haven't a chance."

Betsy let her eyes dance through dark lashes, first at one, then the other, "Maybe not. But then again . . ."

Enjoying herself lightly, she became serious, then merry again, "I'm not sorry either. It was a nice way to meet my new brother. It seems, Jed, that meeting your brothers is always fun. First, Brian. Now David."

"Betsy, welcome to the family," David turned to his two companions, "Please meet my two sisters," he smiled, "Ruth, Betsy. Tom Rosser and Matt Garland. And my brother, Jed.

"Tom and I were friends at The Point. He's artillery. Matt's a professor at Williams College, now with the First New York Cavalry."

To Rosser the greetings were warm, accepting: from Ruth, "It is an honor to meet you, sir"; Jed, "Howdy, captain"; Betsy greeted him with, "It is nice to meet you." She turned at once to the Yankee officer, smiling graciously, "And you, professor."

Jed said nothing to him, simply half raised a hand. Ruth was ice, nodding stiffly, "My husband was killed at Manassas. Shot by Yankees. Perhaps by you, sir."

Matt Garland winced at the attack. He softened his resonant voice, "My sincere condolences, ma'am; I am truly sorry.

"It may be worth nothing to you, but it's important to me that I tell you I wasn't there. I find little to be thankful for these days, but I do give thanks that I was still in Philadelphia on that sad day. I arrived in Washington with my regiment on the day following the battle."

"You are absolutely correct, sir. What you say is worth nothing whatsoever."

As soon as the bitter words were out, Ruth regretted them. They were so inconsistent with the feelings flooding over her. *Why am I saying this? It's none of his doing. He's following orders same as Jonathan did. He's handsome.*

She addressed him again, with as much fire, but with less ice.

"If you, sir, are so blameless then why do you come into Virginia to fight people who want only to be left alone?"

"Hardly blameless, good lady." Matt Garland's answer was unmitigated sorrow, "as most, I have let others lead me. Others without vision, humanity, or generosity. Now it is too late."

Matt Garland was having another problem, starting with a sense of kinship with David. Now, since she first spoke, something even closer with this beautiful sister. The two of them, brother and sister, had an intensity about them, David honorable, principled, of sincere words. He had seen that one in action, morally unable to ignore the baseness that was Sedge Folsom. Now, he was seeing the same passion in the sister who had suffered great loss in this quagmire brought on by fools.

God knows, the whole country has gone topsy turvy, beyond fixing short of bloody war. She's powerless in the middle of it, paying the tolls for screeching demagogues.

"Why am I in Virginia?" His blue eyes darkened toward purple, "Because our forefathers believed in a united country."

The straightforward answer impressed her, not only the words, but a sincerity that couldn't be denied. Intuitively, she knew he could never dissemble. His eyes could never hide subterfuge. Here was a man of character that marked him substantial, of dreams and expectations that touched eternity.

The soldier receded and the teacher emerged as he had spoken, a teacher in the broadest sense, concerned with others and the future of his country, a teacher fighting to protect his standards in an imperfect world. An uncommon man, and, Ruth had to admit to herself, an attractive one at that.

She had little to say after their brief exchange, but she watched him closely, unobtrusively she hoped. As he watched her.

Despite her initial reaction, despite the blue uniform, she felt herself drawn to Matt Garland. Soft golden hair, an innocent, little-boy smile were part of his appeal, and those eyes. Already she had seen the telltale darkening toward purple, now the sapphire blue as he laughed at a story David told.

He reminisced, "Makes me think of a class I had at Williams. A student was less than excited in our academic investigation, so I asked the lad next to him to nudge him out of his reverie." Ruth noted the soft melancholy in his tone and knew at once the army wasn't his first choice. He wore the Yankee uniform only because he felt a responsibility.

'You would rather be there wouldn't you?' She almost said it aloud. His lips were alive as he formed the sounds, his whole mouth was alive, drawing her in, attracting, exciting.

" 'Wake him up, yourself' I heard, 'you put him to sleep'."

Laughter around the table forced Ruth to relinquish Matt Garland's sensual mouth, to make a pretense of laughing with the rest of them, as she had heard nothing of his story except 'put him to sleep'. For a moment their eyes locked. He raised a hand as if to touch her fingers.

Just before midnight, they broke up, the three officers to their respective commands; Jed and Betsy together in the same room, he on the floor close to Ruth and Betsy sharing the bed.

He had just dozed off when the bed creaked and Betsy whispered in his ear, "I'd like you to hold me—just hold me."

They stayed together there on the floor almost until dawn. wrapped in each other's arms, sleeping lightly and waking to enjoy their closeness, Betsy secure, Jed satisfied to be with her. At dawn she left him for the bed, whispering again, "Jed, it probably would be all right if you want to."

"You make it tough on a man, Star Queen, but I'd rather wait until probably becomes certainty. There'll be another time."

As Betsy eased into the bed, Ruth moaned, turned toward her. She had not wakened the entire night to dream of Matt Garland.

XXI

DINNERS, UNEXPECTED
AND FORMAL

Brian Morrow, now First Corporal Morrow after a chain of promotions when Captain White had to resign, had the duty. Detailed as division guard company, he and the Liberty Hall Volunteers were free of daily drills and the picket duty that was a lopsided combination of sheer boredom and mortal danger.

Jed rushed breathlessly into the guard room, "Briney! You heard yet? We got marchin' orders."

"Jed! It's good to see you. Whose got orders?"

"All of us, Briney. The whole brigade's leavin' t'morrow fo⁻ Winchester. We're goin' home! Briny, We're goin' home!"

"I heard a rumor, but it didn't make any sense. Why didn't Jackson just take us with him three days ago when he left?"

"I don't know anythin' about that. The army does things different than I would."

"By golly, that explains our orders to return to regiment today. That Old Jack!. He's gone three days and got us back."

At Manassas Junction, three regiments including Jed's waited for trains the whole night in cold rain and no shelter. Fires sputtered weakly. At 9 in the morning, they boarded, wet, tired, without food since yesterday's breakfast.

Brian's 4th Virginia and the 33rd, were ordered to stand down for twenty-four hours, waiting for the cars to return.

In Strasburg, the Liberty Hall Volunteers found a hotel that fed them supper at a dollar each. They cleaned out the kitchen. The next morning, the brigade marched north down the Valley Turnpike, bivouacked four miles short of Winchester, close by the wagon road that led to the Morrow farm.

Yielding to the temptation, Jed and Brian took French leave after dark
to visit Ezekiel and Mattie. The door was barred.

"Who's out there?"

"Ezekiel, open the door. It's us, Brian and Jed."

The door swung wide, "If this don't beat all! Come on in."

A surprised Ezekiel continued to block the doorway, a loaded shotgun
at the ready. Behind him, Mattie held an oil lamp high.

"Ezekiel, move your backside so these boys can get on around. An'
Lawdamercy, put that gun down!"

Handshakes might do for the men, but she needed to hug them and
be hugged after most half a year. She brushed at tears.

"Now sit down an' I'll get somethin' ta eat."

"How are the folks, Zeke? Glad to see General Jackson back, I'm sure."

"Sure are. Y'all been home?"

"Not yet. We just marched from Strasburg, and bivouacked on the
pike." Mattie looked puzzled as she filled plates with cold chicken and fresh
bread. She clucked disapproval.

Jed broke in, "You were closest. Is Pa still mad with me for runnin' off
like I did."

Mattie teased, "And we thought y'all wanted ta see us."

"We did, Mattie. We wanted to see you as much as Ma and Pa."

"And you could tell us about Pa," Jed added ingenuously.

"Boys," Ezekiel obliged, "your Pa was, ta put it blunt, mad as hell. But that
was then, and now is now. He's beginnin' ta understand. Just the other day, he
was talkin' about you two. Not mad like he was. Just sorta complainin'."

Well, that's an improvement," Brian offered.

Mattie took advantage of the pause that followed, "What's this
bee-whacked you said, Brian?"

"What?"

"Bee-whacked. You said y'all were bee-whacked on the pike."

Ezekiel's laugh was chopped short, "Ezekiel Brown! Don't you be so high
an' mighty with me. I aks questions ta learn. And I was not addressin' you."

She tilted her chin haughtily, looked a 'So there!' toward her husband,
turned to Brian for the answer to her question.

"It means to camp for the night, Mattie."

"Why don't they just say 'campin' for the night then'? Like regular
folk. No need for fancy talk when regular words'll do."

Mattie glared at Ezekiel, "An' no need ta git high an' mighty like some
folks around here. Some of us don't know everythin'. An' one of us don't
even know that."

"An' one of us need ta be reminded now and then, Matty." "Yes, sir, Mr. Ezekiel Brown, one of us sure do."

He came close to his wife, "I was wrong ta laugh."

That very evening, the Morrow dining room glowed warm with candlelight. Tapered flames danced in tiny air currents, and wicks sputtered occasional annoyance. Single candles in sterling holders graced the Hepplewhite sideboard, and a candelabrum, the dining table. Henry and Sarah sat opposite, General Jackson to Henry's right. Next to the guest of honor was Ruth, across from Racey. To Henry's left was Alexander Boteler.

"It is such a relief to have you back in Winchester, General Jackson. When you left in July we were beside ourselves. Oh! the thought of the Yankee army in our town!"

"Now, Sarah, don't you add t'the general's burden."

Jackson raised a hand, "Worry not, sir. With The Lord's help we'll win this war. He knows what each of us can carry."

"That he does, general, that he does."

Sitting diagonally from General Jackson, Racey hung on his every word. Imagine! The hero of Manassas right here in their dining room, the man who protected Winchester and the whole Shenandoah Valley! Yet, she was surprised, he seemed so gentle and kind. She thought he looked sad in the candlelight.

Sarah ignored Henry's message, "Burdens aside, general, I am very happy you're here. I feel safer than I have for months."

"Your kind words are gratifying to an old soldier. But we still have much work ahead of us." He turned as Henry spoke.

"A few months ago, general, I would have argued the point. Matter of fact, I did, with our sons. Told one of them, 'Stay right here ta build the farm. That's where the future is,' I said. Next mornin' he was gone.

"The oldest just showed up one day and says he's joinin' the army. I told him t'finish up his schoolin' at West Point, but he didn't listen either.

"Youngest son enlisted in Lexington before I could talk to him. All three are in your army, general, one with General Stuart. He's a captain."

Jackson brightened, "Of course. Captain Morrow. Did good service at Harper's Ferry. General Stuart speaks highly of him.

"You'll be happy to know I advised him as you, to stay at The Point and graduate. But he felt that was taking a commission under false colors. Felt it dishonorable.

"You can be proud of your son, Mr. Morrow, proud indeed."

Jackson turned toward Sarah so that she could share the compliment, "He's a fine young officer."

The general changed the conversation before it turned to military matters he would avoid, "A fine dinner, Mrs. Morrow. My compliments, ma'am."

"But you ate so little, general. May I help you to turkey? Or ham, you haven't sampled our ham."

"Perhaps another serving of spoon bread. Very small, mind you. It is delicious."

"Thank you kindly, sir," she said with pretended coquetry, "some buttermilk to go with it?"

Jackson held out his glass, "I have found buttermilk a fine potion for the dyspepsia."

Sarah poured from the ironstone pitcher.

Across the table, Racey consumed Jackson's every word, every move, noting that he sat perched like a bird on the edge of his chair, his back perfectly straight.

"Brandy, general?"

"Oh, no!" he exclaimed in surprise for he was accustomed to eating with people who knew of his aversion to liquor.

"I promised The Almighty years ago to forego the pleasure."

"I'm sorry, general. I didn't know. Your stomach?"

"HENRY MORROW!" Sarah rapped out.

"No offense," Jackson smiled, "May I tell you why?"

"Oh Yes! Yes!" Racey looked ready to bounce in her chair.

She had idolized him from the moment she had been presented to him, captivated by the gentleness in his gray eyes as he had said, "Mrs. Jackson prays for a daughter like you."

Henry glanced sharply at Gracey, visibly upset by her lapse of decorum. Sarah, seated across the table, leaned forward, half raised a hand in a gesture of restraint. It was Henry who spoke.

"Grace, the general doesn't want . . ."

For one of the few times in his life, Henry was ignored by one of his children, his youngest at that, "Why do you dislike it, general?"

"I didn't say I disliked it, Miss Grace. Quite the contrary. Once, many years ago, I sampled spirits, and discovered I liked it very much. That discovery convinced me to do without."

Racey pushed further, "But why? If you liked it so much."

"I simply treated it as an exercise in self control, Miss Grace. A man must know how to control himself before he assumes control of others."

He turned to Henry, "Please continue pouring, sir. I know Colonel Boteler will accept a glass. He tells me you two have been friends for many years."

"Indeed we have, general, since 1834. It was the first night I had ever stayed in Winchester. I was enjoyin' the late evenin' on the veranda of Taylor's Hotel when he introduced himself. As a matter of fact, he influenced me to settle in Winchester."

"Tell me, Mr. Morrow, how did that come about. The colonel can be persuasive, I know full well."

"Well, sir, I simply mentioned I was lookin' for a place t'call home. He jumped at that and said as close as I can remember, 'By a fortuitous turn of fortune's wheel, you have come to God's own country. A man can live a lifetime here and each day find something new to thank Him for'."

General Jackson nodded, "Our good colonel has a way with words."

"Not only that, general, but he gave me the idea that launched the Shenandoah Stage Coach Company."

"And what was that, Mr. Morrow?"

"That I haul stone for the Valley Turnpike Company. By offering to haul it for ten percent less than their cost, I convinced them to try me. Wound up with six wagons."

"Sounds simple enough."

Henry laughed heartily, "Do you know those scoundrels gave me a cost estimate that did not include grain for the horses or blacksmiths or stable expenses. Then they tried to get me to go to fifteen percent, failing that, thirteen."

"How did you answer them?"

"Straightforward, sir. Give me an honest estimate and I'll give you an honest day's work."

"And the bargaining on the percentage?"

"Said I'd take another look at the end of the month. But they knew my first offer was a good one and never brought it up again."

"I can see why Alex spoke so highly of you."

"Our friendship is one of mutual respect, general." Henry poured, handed the glass to his friend, "Sippin' bourbon, Alex, made right here in Frederick County."

Colonel Boteler raised his glass, considering its contents with respect, "As I've said, there's something here every day worthy of a man's thanks. To your very good health."

An ardent Whig, Alexander Boteler had recently been elected to the Confederate Congress and appointed Colonel, part-time aide to General

Jackson. It was he who had been responsible for the dinner party, planting the idea with Henry, then encouraging the general to accept. He waved the glass appreciatively under his nose and sipped.

"Your statement of enjoying liquor interests me," the colonel nodded toward Jackson, "I tasted it, too, and as you yourself, sir, I liked it very much.

"But, alas! It was at that very point that you and I part company, completely and unequivocally part company, sir. While the discovery convinced you to leave it alone, it convinced me of quite the opposite!

"Mind! I'm not an advocate of overindulgement."

Laughter exploded around the table, except for Ruth who veiled an insistent smile with her dinner napkin. General Jackson laughed in his strange way, a silent kind of panting with his head thrown back, his mouth open in enjoyment.

When the hilarity subsided, Jackson made his own joke.

"The difference between a politician and a military man, sir. They ponder identical facts, and reach antithetical conclusions."

Laughter broke out again, Boteler in a deep belly laugh.

"But let me extend my observation to the war," Jackson became very serious in face and in voice. He appeared on the verge of an important revelation, waiting for absolute silence.

"Our system of government—I refer to that envisioned by Washington, Madison, and Jefferson—is a model of justice and equity, holding that the people must decide for themselves what is right and proper. They believed the ultimate wisdom is with the people."

He spoke evenly, but with a semblance of excitement never seen by his students in Lexington, "The Confederacy and the Union considered the same situation, one wants to be left alone, the other decides war. Obviously, the politicians control the one for they know not the horror of war."

Jackson warmed to his subject, became visibly excited as he continued beyond his initial intent, "Our decision to join the Union carried with it the choice to leave the Union. Our freedom to do that is denied. Our Constitutional right to consider what is correct and proper is denied by Lincoln and his minions. They have illegally denied us our freedom and our heritage."

Embarrassed, he fumbled with his napkin, raised it to his mouth, and coughed into it. Colonel Boteler looked pleased for he had never seen him so voluble, so ready to talk.

"I'm sorry. I was carried away." Jackson shuffled awkwardly in his chair.

His hostess smiled graciously, "Please. No apologies. We find both wisdom and pleasure in your words. I am doubly grateful to you, sir, for I believe our girls have benefitted from your words, as have we."

"Oh yes! Mother. I have. I have," Racey agreed fervently.

"Mrs. Morrow, thank you for your kindness. And you, Miss Grace. Few have an interest in justice and reason these days—or in self-discipline. Thank you for having me to dinner."

Jackson pushed from the table, "Colonel, we have dispatches to prepare." Henry accompanied him into the foyer.

Alex Boteler lingered, "Sarah, General Jackson likes you all very much Never, since I have known him, have I heard him speak so freely. He truly likes being with you."

"The honor is ours, Colonel Boteler."

"Please, good lady. I'm Alex to my friends.

"You represent what is most dear to him, family and home. He sees in you what he desires most in this world; he sees you in dire peril, your family, and your home. He has experienced war and its devastation offends him."

"I understand."

"Sarah, I hope you can be his friends. He is so lonely for Anna and their home in Lexington."

The next morning, the Stonewall Brigade formed column, the last leg of their march to rejoin their beloved General Jackson in his new command. Looking forward to another joyous welcome, their stride was light and the miles to Winchester easy. They marched past the toll gate, Abraham's Creek, and Milltown into Winchester. Brian hitched up the strap of his Yankee canteen.

Citizens gathered on Loudoun Street to greet them, waving hats, kerchiefs, and flags hidden during the Yankee occupation. Their huzzahs rang out, a wave rolling ahead of the marching men.

"It's Jackson's men!"

"The Stonewall Brigade!"

"It's Jackson's own!"

Past Hollabeck's Hotel they marched, and Sacred Heart Catholic Church, past Courthouse Square where Brian saw his father. He resisted an impulse to break ranks and run to him. He wanted so much to have his approval.

They marched by Taylor's Hotel toward the town line, and Mr. Rouss's shop, where the owner stood at the curb showering them with plugs of good tobacco and small cakes, accepting their cheers with both arms waving high. Catching and retrieving the gifts meant a sacrifice of discipline and decorum in the ranks, but in the festive reception no one noticed.

They passed half a dozen taverns, cheered at each one, Amick's, Waller's, Lamb's, Massie's, and The Red Lion built in 1753 by Peter Lauck. Near John Linn's, Jed spied Betsy.

Tossing his musket to a soldier on the outside file, he ran to gather her in his arms. Soldiers cheered. She nestled into him, laughing and ignoring joyful tears. The soldiers cheered even more lustily.

Falling in with a company following his own, he carried her past the bank on the corner, through the next block and the next. Those around Jed learned her name and started a singsong chant.

"Betsy. Betsy. We love Betsy."

Their rhythmic accolade spread through the ranks up and down the line until all ten companies of the 2nd Virginia had taken it up. It spread into the regiments ahead and behind.

"Betsy. Betsy. We love Betsy."

Each of them did. For that memorable moment, each of them did.

Colonel Allen, riding at the head of the 2nd Virginia with his aides, turned in his saddle, seeking the reason for the high jinks. He smiled widely for it was good to see such spirit. He side-stepped his horse half a block, adding to the camaraderie.

Briefly, the shadow of military discipline flitted across his mind: Old Jack will have my hide. But Colonel Allen did himself proud, ignoring the decorum of a proper colonel.

"What the hell," he said to his aides, "if this isn't worth it, nothing is."

Approaching the old fire house, Jed left the column again, and set Betsy gently on her feet.

"I want ta marry you. Soon's we can."

Her joy caught him as he ran to join his company, "Yes, Jed! Yes!!"

The brigade set up camp four miles north of Winchester, not far from Stephenson's Depot where the rail line made a wide turn east toward Harper's Ferry.

The weather turned bad almost at once. Cold rain, sleet, and freezing winds beat on the tents. The men suffered. Influenza and measles broke out. Many afflicted with "The Virginia quick-step" headed repeatedly for the bushes.

In an order that made life even more miserable, General Jackson put Winchester off limits, no passes to town except on official business. But man-made rules were made to be broken, and break them the men did.

They forged passes. They slipped between sentry posts. A few concocted family emergencies to convince officers sympathetic enough to look the other way. One group marched snappily through a guard post on the pretext they were the provost guard ordered to Winchester to round up miscreants without passes; another simply charged through, intimidating the candy-ass sentry. The worldly pleasures of Winchester were not to be denied.

Jed was one who missed the first night at Camp Stepherson. Eluding the guards, he walked into Linn's tavern soon after dark. Betsy wasn't there. She had left directly after supper serving. Yes, they told him, she still kept the same rooms.

He was half way up the steps, when the door flew open and she was in his arms, "I knew you would be here tonight."

Smothering her with kisses, he picked her up easily. In the room they knew so well, they lost themselves in an embrace too long denied.

Then Betsy leaned back, arching naturally against Jed's arms. Automatically, he tightened them about her waist. She tilted her head back, extending the graceful curve of her back, framing his face in her hands, blinking ecstatic tears.

"Oh! Jed! I am glad you're here. I've waited so long.

"I even told Uncle John I wasn't feeling well and left early. I knew you'd come tonight. I had to be here for you."

She blinked new tears, looked at him lovingly, longingly, as if to absorb him before he could go away again. She rested her head on his chest and squeezed him tight. Then she teased him.

"Now, tell me again. What was it you said this afternoon when you set me down in the street? I didn't quite hear you."

Her teasing was lost on Jed, "I said I wanted us to get married. That's why I'm here now. We have to make plans."

"Any other reason?"

"To see you. But you haven't answered me, Betsy."

"I did. Of course I will. You know that."

She stood on tiptoes, kissed him hard, both arms tightening around his neck. He lifted her clear off the floor, she nuzzled along his neck and into the hollow of his shoulder. She murmured softly, "Mrs. Jedediah Morrow. That sounds nice.

"Jed?"

"Hmmm?"

"I've answered your question."

"Uhhuh."

"An' you've seen me."

"Uhhuh."

"Any other reason you're here?"

"Because I love you and want t'be with you. And because y're Star Queen, the one I'm gonna pick up and fly t'the North Star."

"Any other?"

He saw the answer in her eyes.

"Might be," he teased.

"Jed, I love you so much."

And together they moved toward the bed.

XXII

GRACEY'S QUESTIONS

In early December, the Stonewall Brigade met its new commander, Richard Garnett, assigned by Richmond. Men were unhappy, wanting one of their own colonels appointed, but they quickly changed as they saw Garnett's concern for them and his ability as a field commander. Jackson thought he pampered them, would in January request Richmond to replace him, and two months later relieve him of his command under charges. Their situation was as cold and bitter as the weather, which felled many, including Brian.

Laid low with influenza, Brian convinced Captain Morrison to send him home. The new company commander also detailed two men to escort him.

Sarah wrapped him in a cocoon of warm blankets, at regular intervals spooned into him her own remedy, whiskey and cider heated just short of boiling, laced with lemon juice and sweet butter. "Ma's tonic" enjoyed its own reputation. She supplemented it with motherly attentions and, as her patient improved, conversation and company.

For Brian's stubborn fever, she added two of her famed onion treatments: breathing the fumes of onions baking in the wood stove and wrapping newly-cut slices to the soles of his feet. She had her own ways to decide which to use, dry fumes, steamy fumes from onions boiling, either of which made sense, or the foot treatment that didn't. On the third day of the compound therapy of tonic and onion, Brian was sitting up in bed, taking tea and clear soup, and listening to Racey's chatter.

"Oh, Briney, I'm glad you're feeling better because you're the best brother in the whole world."

"I'll bet you tell that to all your brothers."

"I do," she answered cheerily, "because they are."

Knees drawn up under her chin, her back against the blanket rail, she reported happenings of the past year, speeding through the good and the bad with equal fervor.

"When Pa read your letter about enlisting, he turned red and yelled at Jed. When Jed left he yelled at Ma and stomped out of the house.

"Racey, is he still angry with me and Jed?"

Racey puzzled, then answered brightly, "Gee, Briney, I don't know. He doesn't talk about it, so it's hard to tell."

She skittered again, "Oh, I wish you were here when General Jackson had dinner with us."

"The general was here!"

"Oh yes, he is so nice. He called me Miss Grace, talked to me like an adult. He knows David. He knew right off where he was, said he was a fine officer and had the most beautiful stallion he'd ever seen. Oh, Briney, David was so handsome on Sable. I'm so lucky with the best brothers in the world."

She changed the subject abruptly without a pause, her eyes sparkling with excitement, "There's so many soldiers in town. They touch their caps and say 'hello', I say 'hello' back and smile. I don't see anything wrong in that, do you? Some are very bold, but I smile anyway and keep walking like David said to do.

"Sometimes it's hard because some of them are so handsome. Besides, I like to talk to them."

Brian picked up the clue, "It sounds like you don't always keep walking."

Racey rattled on, "David told me to be careful of the soldiers, that most of them were just lonely but some could be dangerous and it was hard to tell them apart."

She hesitated, not certain that she wanted to continue.

Brian waited.

"He didn't say it right out, but I knew what he meant."

In a way, Racey did know, but needed confirmation. She needed to hear the words, to say them herself to somebody she could trust. It was part of the excitement of growing up.

"He meant getting into bed and taking my clothes off so they could have me. That's what he meant, wasn't it, Briney?"

Brian choked on his tea.

"Racey, for goodness sakes!"

"That's what he meant, isn't it," she pressed.

A flushed Brian sputtered, "I-I'm not the one t-to answer g-girl questions, Racey. S-sit down with Ma—or Ruth. They know more about . . ." Brian never had a chance to finish.

"Come on, Briney, that's what David meant, didn't he?"

"Well, uh . . ." Brian sipped at his teacup. Racey looked him square in the eye and waited for an answer. He had no escape.

"Yes, Racey, that's what he meant. And you could be hurt very badly."

"That's what David said.

"Briney," Racey looked through her lashes at him, "have you ever been in bed with a girl?"

Brian thought immediately of the morning he had wakened in Betsy's bed, with her and Jed. He laughed aloud at the memory, and in the humor lost his embarrassment. Seeing his sister as she was, no longer the little girl, he answered.

"Yes I have, Racey, but not the way you mean."

"How else is there?"

"You can be unconscious, like I was, from being exhausted from marching and drinking too much beer," Brian laughed.

He expected her to laugh at his joke. Instead, she asked more questions, phrased as though she were practicing the words.

"But what happened to the girl who was in the bed with you? Was she naked? Did you wake up and—and—enter her?"

Brian gulped and recovered, "Gacey, for all that is holy, you have too many questions for me. Like David said, just don't be too anxious to be friendly. You just want to be friendly.

Some think it's an invitation to do whatever they want.

"Racey, save yourself for someone you want to spend your life with. You have a precious gift to give. Don't waste it.

"Hmmmph! As if I would do something like that."

"You might not be given the choice. That's what David meant when he said to be careful. Now, take this cup and let me rest."

Brian stayed at home for almost two weeks, gradually throwing off his illness. Except for Pa's reticence, the time was good, an opportunity for re-connections and renewal after a year's absence.

"It seems years ago," he mused one day toward the end of his illness remembering Washington College and Lexington in December the festive atmosphere, joyous holiday greetings, and the gay parties that encouraged flirtations with pretty girls. Conjuring visions from that innocent time, he saw President Junkins' entryway festooned with twinings of ground pine, the altar of Dr. White's church decorated with red-berried holly, and distorted reflections in a silver punch bowl.

He tried and tried to recall the name of the girl with the capricious eyes. She had promised much and laughingly denied it all. Somebody's sister's friend visiting from Charlottesville. Strange he thought, to remember Charlottesville and not her name.

Gracey and he spent hours together, she playing the piano for him, singing together. One afternoon they read aloud portions of Romeo and Juliet. Racey puzzled over some of the phrasing, was moved by others.

"Oh! Isn't that beautiful, Briney? I could just cry!"

He visited with Ruth, became reacquainted with his niece and nephew. Sensing a melancholy about her, he made an effort to help, but with one exception when she made a remark about no man around the house, she kept him at a distance.

He spent hours with Sarah, talking of the army, guard duty at General Smith's headquarters, and Jed's deception at Blackburn's Ford. He didn't mention the battle on Henry Hill, except to say they chased Yankees back to Washington. He expressed his concern for Ruth. Ma said 'Yes, she has changed. I've been trying to keep her busy'.

Brian felt she was overly optimistic, hiding her real concern, but he said nothing. Ma had always done that. Most always things had turned out as she expected.

Toward the end of his furlough, he had a talk with Pa. He had tried on three separate occasions, but each time Henry closed off the discussion before it began. Finally, Brian had used a club, "Pa, you've got to talk to me. I leave tomorrow.

"We may not have another chance."

Henry had grunted, motioned him to follow into the office. As soon as they were seated, Brian started.

"I know you disapprove my joining the army, Pa, but I need you to understand."

"I don't understand—doubt I ever will," Henry snapped, "I don't understand you and I don't understand Jed. This isn't your war."

"I thought you'd be proud of me, joining the army to fight for what I believe in. The same as Grandfather Jedediah did in the Revolution."

Ignoring, or more likely never hearing Brian's plea, Henry cut in, "Brian, I'll tell you what I told David. You shouldn't've enlisted until you finished your school."

"But, Pa, the war might be ov . . ."

"You should have finished your schooling," Henry interrupted, "Closed that out, so you had something when you moved on. That's what I've done all my life and it's worked damn well. I always closed out whatever I was doing."

Henry caught himself, suddenly feeling very old. The habits and rules important to him seemed out of date, strangely unrelated to today's world.

He had always felt confident drawing on his own life to teach his children, but now his experience and beliefs seemed to belong to the past, important to him but no longer relevant to them. His whole life seemed tuned to other years, years made obsolete by this damn war that was changing everything.

For the first time in his life, Henry Morrow was unsure, knowing that the old ways were sound, but how in the hell did you make your sons see that? Why couldn't they understand? As a father, he wanted to help his children avoid the troubles, guide them, set them on the right track, to help Brian, but it was too late. He was already in the army, a crazy-ass idea that could get him killed. He should be in school. Brian was one to use his brain, not run around shooting, being shot at. Damn, it was so obvious. Why couldn't he see it?

Even so, he felt a great need to say something, hopefully something of importance to this son who was the smartest, brightest of them all. If he could just find the right words to replace the old, Brian would remember them and be influenced by them. A father owed that to his son.

He spoke slowly for starters, reflecting his belief that a man accepts what he's been given, accomplishes what he can, no wasted energy or tears as to what might have been.

"I think you should have graduated, Brian, but you already know that. The fact is that you didn't. There's no changing that. You're a soldier now. That's your job.

"All I can say is do the best you can in the army, Brian, the very best you can. You be the best soldier you know how t'be.

"You learn everything you can. You never know when it'll come in handy. Whatever you're given t'do, do the best job you can. A man owes it t'himself, Brian, else he's not a man."

As he said the words, Henry realized that an important part of his life wasn't obsolete at all, that at least two of the tenets he lived by were as true as they had ever been.

"Like you're doing, son," he said with a tinge of pride and a bushel of reluctance. He pointed to Brian's corporal stripes.

"And that Yankee canteen. The strap is a work of art. You wrote about it after the Manassas battle, I remember."

"Yes, that's the one. I was reaching for it and Jed stepped on my hand. I thought he was a Yankee about to do me in. I'll never forget that day if I live to be a hundred."

Henry Morrow looked tenderly at his youngest soldier, "I guess you learned something there. Just keep learning and doing your best."

"I knew you'd agree with me," Brian said, smiling relief.

"Don't get me wrong, son. I don't agree that enlisting was the right thing. I don't agree t'your giving up your schooling." Henry hesitated, weighing his words with care, "The only thing I agree to is that we've been squeezed into a corner. General Jackson said as much a few weeks back, sitting at our dining table, that we had no choice."

"That's the whole point, Pa. There was no alternative that was honorable."

"But not you and Jed!" Henry hit the desk top with his fist, "Virginia got backed into the corner, not you and Jed. You had a choice. You're not soldiers, not you, not him."

Immediately, Henry regretted his outburst. Move on, he had always said, don't waste energy on what might have been.

Brian noticed, too, but said nothing. Pa had come a long way for Pa. While he hadn't given his approval to his enlistment, he was doing the best he could to accept it.

The next day, Brian reported for duty.

The whole brigade had just returned from a 4-day mission to destroy dam #5 on the Potomac, one of several that shunted water into the Chesapeake and Ohio Canal.

On their return, the Liberty Hall Volunteers were assigned again as guard company, part of Jackson's headquarters. Since he had moved to a small cottage in the northern part of town, they anticipated a good winter, close to Winchester's attractions.

A week later, their expectations were destroyed by an order from the general: draw five days' rations, cook one day's food, be ready to march before dawn. As Napoleon, Jackson believed a winter expedition healthier than the idleness of winter quarters.

New Year's day broke bright and clear, more springtime than winter. The column swung easily down the road toward Bath, four brigades and militia troops, 10,000 strong.

As the sun climbed the sky on January 1, the temperature rose deceitfully, the men dropped coats, tents and blankets for the baggage wagons to pick up. By noon, the wind had shifted northwest, and they leaned face-first into zero temperatures and slashing sleet that turned to snow.

They hunkered down for the night with no shelter and little food, the wagons bogged down somewhere behind. Most, as usual, had eaten their rations early in the day to lighten their loads. The second day was more of the same, wind shrieking, snow swirling about them, and no sign of the wagons.

Brian and a dozen others accompanied Jackson's own wagon at the rear of the column, manhandling it along the treacherous road. Horses balked on the upgrades, wagons careened down the descents skidding crossways, overturning.

Encouraging the others, Brian pushed and hauled, five steps ahead, three back, two sideways. When wagons jammed completely, impossibly bogged down, they could only stomp their feet, swing their arms, and wait in the cold.

On the morning of the third day, they went to work again, one wagon at a time, push, pull, shove the wrecked ones off the road. They did get the train moving, to bring the column coats and tents, and its first food in forty hours.

They chased the Bluecoats out of Bath, and on January 7, started south for Winchester. Mean weather continued, a full-blown, blinding, swirling blizzard. Snow and sleet fell heavy, tramped quickly into an icy sheet.

Jed wrapped his boots with strips of an old blanket for better footing. The wrappings worked well for a few yards, until they became slick with their own ice. He tried evergreen boughs. They did the same.

"I coulda tole ya it wouldn't work," a soldier snickered.

"Nothin' like tryin'," Jed responded amiably.

Men and horses, unable to keep their footing on the treacherous road, fell and suffered cuts, contusions, and broken bones. Badly injured horses were shot where they fell.

Brian's friend, Lieutenant Lyle, wrote of the homeward march from Bath, "Such a tramp it was; something like Napoleon's crossing the Alps. The mercury was below zero, and the northwest wind cut like a knife. . . . Neither men nor horses could keep their feet and were falling constantly. . . . The brink of the road had to be shunned, to avoid a slide like a toboggan down the side of the mountain. Men's rumps were continually hitting the road. . . ."

They camped at a place called Unger's Store where their suspicions were raised.

"Brian," one asked, "where they sending Lieutenant Lyle?"

"Home with the rest of the sick ones. He's got jaundice."

"Why don't they stay with the column?"

When the farriers heated iron cleats, they knew their winter ordeal was not over.

As the column formed up, a man asked Jed, "Wherethehell's that crazy man takin' us now?"

"Don't rightly know. Guess he has his reasons," Jed answered brusquely hoping to cut off further conversation. He had little interest in criticizing the general, or the army, and less in listening to anyone's complaints.

Brian's company, moved out first, crossing Shenandoah Mountain the first day, marching into Romney by mid-morning the next.

If the road from Bath had been a trial, this one was even worse, inexorable in its wintry garb, every bit as slick, even more treacherous as they climbed into the mountains. The accumulated snow deepened, the temperature dropped, gentle slopes became precipices. Lieutenant Lyle's "toboggan rides" could become life-threatening glides into oblivion.

Rough-shod horses slid and fell. Men with smooth, slippery shoes shouldered wagons and gun carriages along. Increasingly, struggling horses needed help, exhausted teams had to be unhitched and led. Weary, panting men became the horse power, some harnessed to ropes and chains. By evening on January 14, they occupied Romney on the South Branch of the Potomac. The Yankee force had evacuated it four days earlier.

"When we marched into town," a comrade of Jed's in the 4th Virginia wrote home, "every soldier's clothing was a solid cake of ice, icicles two inches long [were] hanging from the hair and whiskers of every man."

Nine days in Romney did much to restore the spirit of Jackson's men for the long return march. On January 26, they reached Winchester, making 43 miles one day for the general was anxious to see his wife. Jed was delighted for he was every bit as anxious to see Betsy.

XXIII

A FAMILY EVENING

After nearly a month of exposure in the western mountains, the Stonewall Brigade settled for the winter in its camp north of Winchester. General Jackson resumed his headquarters in town, in the same six-room cottage he had used before. Brian's Liberty Hall Volunteers were close by, still his guard company. They had an excellent time of it, living close to the town's attractions.

Some of the young soldiers shared a large house near headquarters. A few cooked for themselves; others took meals in a nearby private home where they were served extravagantly by "a lot of pretty girls" one of them bragged to the home folks.

Those with family or friends had an effortless entry to the town's social life and introduced the others. As students and sons of Valley families they were accepted and entertained in the best parlors, singing, playing piano and guitar, reading Dickens and Bulwer aloud. They played chess and backgammon, tobogganed down icy slopes, skated wherever the ice was smooth. And they attended church services with their new friends.

They wrote home of the families and attractive daughters, of their cousins and relatives. Some sought entertainment elsewhere, wrote shorter letters, mostly about the army.

One met a buxom, young widow who fell madly in love with him. She ran an inn at the edge of town, and fed him regally. She offered all the applejack he could drink, and a warm bed, which happened to be her own. On the occasional nights he spent in camp, he was the target of many an earthy joke.

Another boasted of spending a night with two of Winchester's most desirable ladies, but betrayed his strained recuperative powers when he stayed in camp for the next seven days.

Jed visited Betsy whenever he could get a pass, even more often when he couldn't. One evening he brought her home to meet Henry and Sarah.

He and Betsy had discussed the visit at length, mostly whether or not to announce their plans to be married. Jed was reluctant, predicting his father's instant objection and another stalemated argument. Betsy was insistent.

"It just isn't right that they don't know our plans," she argued, "it would be like we're ashamed of what we're doing."

"Besides, I want to meet them."

Jed recognized the ultimate of feminine arguments and gave in. Still uneasy when they entered the house on Wolfe Street, his introduction was anything but gracious.

"This is Betsy—uh—Elizabeth Dearing and we're plannin' on bein' married."

Caught completely off balance by Jed's sudden announcement, Henry managed an unsmiling "Pleasedtameetcha" that inadvertently sounded gruff and uncaring; it angered Jed, for knowing his father to be an hospitable man, he took it as a continuation of his implacable obstinacy. Sarah provided the family welcome.

"It's so nice to know you, Betsy. May I call you Betsy? It sounds friendlier than Elizabeth."

"I would like that, Mrs. Morrow."

Sarah reached for her hand, and together they walked into the parlor. Intuitively, she was drawn to this pretty, young girl that Jed had chosen. She sensed a depth and seriousness that confirmed her initial reaction when Ruth announced the Manassas trip. Her son had chosen well.

Jed and Henry followed them silently, with not a word passing between them. Each still felt the tension of Jed's secretive departure from home, and a sense of disappointment at the other's action. Neither had the desire to echo old attitudes worn weary and tattered. The apparent antagonism in Henry's greeting had not helped.

To the father, Jed's abrupt announcement of marriage was just another of his thoughtless notions. To the son, Henry's greeting and ensuing silence reflected another disapproval. Each was too much entangled in their unresolved argument to make a conciliatory move, or for that matter, even to recognize what was happening.

Sarah glanced sharply at her husband. Failing to get his attention, she made another attempt, one he couldn't ignore.

"Henry, I need you in the kitchen."

Left with Betsy for a moment, Jed muttered his displeasure, "He's still stubborn as a mule. I shouldn't have brought you. Damn it!"

"Don't say that, Jed. Your father needs time. He's still puzzled that you left as you did, and your abrupt announcement really took him by surprise. Be patient, love."

She went on quickly, "Your mother's adorable. She is so sweet. I—I wanted to hug her and call her 'Mother' right away."

"Why didn't you then?" he asked peevishly.

Betsy looked up at him with glistening eyes, "You big idiot. Everything's simple, and right to the point with you—isn't it?

"Most times it is."

"Most times! Jed Morrow, tell me one time when it wasn't. Tell me one time that you didn't have a simple answer. Even with your father you have a simple answer, without the slightest idea of what he's thinking. Try to understand how he feels, for goodness sake."

Sarah and Henry came back into the room, one smiling radiantly, the other following as though he had been chastised. Henry's changing expression gave him away. Betsy knew immediately he had overheard the end of her scolding.

"You've put your foot in it, now!" she reproved herself. She felt the warmth rising in her cheeks. Sarah saw the blush, smiled at its innocence, for she, too, had heard Betsy. She made it easier for both of them.

"Henry, I would like a glass of sherry. Betsy?"

"Wh-what? Oh, yes, ma'am. That would be nice."

"Why not pour four glasses, Henry? It would be more sociable if you and Jed joined us.

"Now, Betsy, it is high time that you and I became better acquainted."

The two women moved to the horsehair love seat across the room and sat, half facing each other, hands folded in their laps.

"Ruth told me about your visiting her in August, and the time you've spent with her since. She said she almost shut the door in your face the first time you called?"

"I remember how puzzled she looked when she saw me standing there. I don't blame her, seeing a stranger at the door."

"She also said how happy she was that she hadn't shut you out. She couldn't recall a thing you said, only that being with you somehow lightened her sadness."

"It was Jed's idea. He wrote me a letter about her husband, and suggested I visit her."

"Jed and you seem to get on very well."

"Oh, yes, Mrs. Morrow! When we first met, we knew it was special. We both felt it."

"I can believe that, for Jed is a very sensitive person."

Betsy expanded the thought with increasing verve and enthusiasm as she spoke.

"I've seen the same tenderness in him. And imagination, consideration, generosity. Dreams for the future. A love for the land and nature. For God."

She stopped thoughtfully, blinking at the moisture in her eyes. Then very softly she smiled and added, "And Jed can make me feel like the most important person in the world, Mrs. Morrow. I like that. I try to do the same for him."

"You bring back memories. A wonderful feeling, isn't it."

While their women talked, Jed had asked his father about Ezekiel and the farm. Receiving only monosyllables for answers, he had switched to his own experiences in the army.

"I never saw men suffer the cold like we did. Marchin' through all that sleet and snow to the Potomac, then gettin' into the freezin' river t' chop the dam.

"Leastways, I didn't have t' do any choppin'.

"Then we were marchin' into the wind and snow over the mountains. To Romney in Hampshire County. My God! I never saw such wind. And the snow was swirlin' so that we couldn't see one end of the horses from the other. Could hardly tell which was head and which was rump."

"Sounds bad."

"It sure was, Pa, it sure'n hell was."

Jed shook his head slowly, from one side to the other, hardly believing his own memory.

"When we got there, the Yankees were gone, and we spent all our time tryin' t'keep warm."

As Jed's story unfolded, Henry became caught up in it.

"You mean they lit out before you got there?"

"That they did, Pa. Vamoosed. Skedaddled. Blown away with the wind for all I know."

"Hmmm, maybe this war won't last as long as I thought. Not if those people keep runnin', it won't."

Sarah had paused for a moment, then returned impetuously, as if driven, to the earlier conversation.

"Ruth was shattered at Jonathan's death. I was very worried about her. She neglected the children. She neglected herself. Refused to see her friends. She wouldn't even leave the house. I thought she would get over it, but she didn't. Finally, I asked Mam to stay with her.

"It was about that time that you called on her. And then that trip to Manassas."

"I wish I had known earlier."

"You did just right, Betsy. Any earlier would have been too soon for Ruth. She probably would have shut the door in your face. I'm so happy that you have become friends."

"I am, too, Mrs. Morrow."

"I've always wondered. Whatever did you find to say to her?"

"Nothing important. Usually, I stopped at Christ Church on the way, and I talked of that. How beautiful and peaceful the church is. How safe I felt there. Like I really belonged."

Betsy hesitated before she went on.

"I feel safe with Jed, too, Mrs. Morrow. Like I belong with him. One time, I talked about him with Ruth."

The shadow of a smile gave her face a radiance as she continued, slowly, pensively.

"I remember the day. It was so beautiful. Bright and sunny.

"I had just received Jed's letter about being married. I told Ruth about it after I swore her to secrecy. I was so happy I just had to tell someone.

"Suddenly, the happiness was gone."

"Whatever could spoil such good news as that?"

"I hadn't considered her feelings at all, Jonathan and all. It was very thoughtless of me."

"I'm sure Ruth understood," Sarah said gently.

"I'm afraid I was carried away. His letter was such a surprise! We had talked about it before he left, but he thought we should wait. Until the war was over. I was so excited. And I had no one else I felt I could tell.

"I'll always remember his exact words. 'As soon as I get home', he wrote, 'and I hope you feel the same way'.

"Then I thought of Jonathan, how bad I must be making Ruth feel. I wanted to apologize, but I didn't.

"Instead, I just took her by the arm and said, 'Lets make cookies for the children'.

"We had a good time baking, mostly that I saw her smile for the first time."

"Maybe your own happiness made her smile. Being with a happy person can be catching. However you did it, dear, you helped her. I'm glad you were there. I know Ruth is, too.

The two sat in quiet thought, as only close friends can, without embarrassment or discomfiture, without the need to fill the silence with manufactured talk.

"I'm so glad Jed is home."

"I fear for him when he's not here."

"And I, too."

"I worry first if he is safe. Then if he is hungry, sick or cold, or unhappy."

"Betsy, what will you do if he is hurt?"

"Or if he is—or if, he doesn't come home at all? Have you thought about that?"

"Oh, Mrs. Morrow, I try not to. I say a prayer every morning and every night. First I ask God to keep him safe, then I thank Him for the happiness we have had. Sometimes I lose faith, then I pray for myself."

Sarah persisted gently, "But you haven't answered my question. What would you do?"

"Yes, I have thought about it, but not for long."

"Not for long! I—I don't understand."

"It's just that I didn't have to. I will care for him as long as he lives. I knew that at once. No matter what happens. No matter what he needs." She looked directly into Sarah's eyes.

"And the other?—If he—doesn't—come home?"

Alone, Betsy had tried to face this worst eventuality of all. She had failed. She tried now and failed again.

"If he is k—," Betsy hesitated. Stiffening perceptibly to maintain her composure, she held on almost long enough to finish her thought.

"If he doesn't come home, I don't know what I . . ."

She bit on her lower lip, clenched her fingers ashen. For a tiny part of a moment, her eyes widened, came more white than hazel, then clamped shut behind protective fingers. Limply, her head sagged forward.

Sarah caught her breath behind quick finger tips. She had ventured into a forbidden area.

From across the room, Jed saw what had happened and jumped up to go to Betsy. Sarah saw him and signaled to stay where he was, that she had everything under control. She hadn't, really, but she realized at once that the situation was hers to handle.

She leaned forward, a tentative hand Betsy's shoulder.

"I'm sorry. I didn't mean to—I've known you only a few minutes, and here I've invaded your privacy."

The younger girl dabbed at her eyes, her words catching in her throat, "It's all right."

"Betsy, I am sorry, so sorry. I'm afraid I let my own fears get the better of me. I get so worried. I hope you understand."

Controlling her concern for Jed, Sarah apologized yet again, augmenting it with a gnawing sensation she felt compelled to share, "I am sorry Betsy, I want you to know that. And I want you to know this strange feeling I have about us, about you and me. It's as though we have known each other for a very long time. Despite the difference in our ages, I feel as though we have had a happy and loving friendship all that time. I felt very close to you, and took advantage.

"I did a very selfish thing. An inexcusable thing."

Betsy smiled through moist eyes, leaned closer, inside Sarah's arm. She shifted slightly on the love seat, relaxing her body into the older woman's, head on her shoulder.

"It wasn't that at all, Mrs. Morrow," she said softly.

Slowly, Sarah stroked Betsy's long, auburn hair, a reprise of times past when she had comforted her own children when they were small. Memories of trying times flooded in, fleeting, shadowy pictures of small ones, feverish or frightened in the night. Now, a generation later, her healing fingers soothed the anxiety again, just as they had then.

She was at peace, comforting this new daughter with whom she shared a great fear.

In a whisper, she broke the spell.

"Betsy?"

"Yes?"

"Please call me Mother, or better still, Ma—as my—other children do."

Betsy tilted her head momentarily. She spoke softly, as if to share a confidence.

"We have been friends, for a long time—Mumma."

Sarah stopped her stroking, hand in midair, "It's strange you should say that. Jed called me 'Mumma' when he was small."

The two sat close without further conversation, without a move except for Sarah's soft fondling of auburn tresses.

Jed had watched them anxiously, wanting so much that they like each other. Although he couldn't make out the words, he knew at once their conversation had taken a serious tone.

"Well, I'll be! Looks like Betsy and Ma have hit it off and become friends."

"Seems so," Henry answered non-committally, still nursing the sulks from Sarah's chastisement.

Unwillingly, Sarah stirred. Savory smells from the kitchen demanded attention.

Betsy remained quiet, reluctant to relinquish the security and warmth the older woman offered. She murmured, her voice muffled as she nestled closer.

"I could stay like this all night."

Sarah's voice was almost a whisper, "I know, dear, I know."

She remained motionless, holding the moment as long as she could. Then she turned toward the men, slowly and gently so as to leave Betsy undisturbed for a few extra ticks of the mantel clock. She addressed her husband quietly.

"Henry will you escort our lovely guest to the table. Dinner's ready."

Betsy roused. She smiled up at Sarah.

"That was nice. Thank you—Mumma."

Henry looked surprise toward his wife, raising his eyebrows in a crooked question mark at the unaccustomed formality. He lumbered across the room to the love seat, made a stiff bow from the hips, and ceremoniously offered his arm.

Betsy curtsied gracefully, glancing through long lashes, "Thank you kindly, sir."

She rested her fingers on his arm just above his wrist, pressing ever so slightly. In each of her words and actions was an innocent coquetry that radiated the ingenuous charm of a small child. She had caught his attention earlier when he overheard her admonition to Jed, now her reactions were winning him over.

On the way to the dining room, he leaned close so that no one else would hear, "You are right about Jed. He doesn't know at all how I feel."

Then he added, "I'm glad you came, Betsy."

"And I am, too. I've been wanting to meet you for some time, but it never seemed to work out. I know that Jed has wanted to talk with you, too. He's so wonderful, Mr. Morrow."

Henry thought 'stubborn and pig-headed, too'. But he said nothing.

XXIV

OCCUPATION!

Nature's springtime in the Valley was as beautiful as ever in 1862. Redbud trees and dogwoods floated orchid and snowy white through the forests. Maple trees showed baby leaves, translucent yellow-green in the sunshine, and apple trees unfolded blushing blossoms.

To Henry and Sarah Morrow, the joyous expectancy of renewal was subdued, its natural beauty dulled by the threat of invasion. Springtime was the warriors' season, the time for armies to uncoil from winter camps, to yawn, to stretch, to tramp the land. Even last year's springtime seemed joyful in retrospect, despite the birthing of a new country Henry had not wanted. Now, stories from Harper's Ferry told of a Yankee army violating Virginia's border at the Potomac. Some said it was marching for Winchester; others, that it was led by Nathaniel P. Banks, erstwhile Speaker of the House of Representatives and governor of Massachusetts, now Major General, United States Volunteers. The stories were true, and more.

Some 13,000 Union soldiers had indeed crossed George Washington's river, seizing Harper's Ferry and Sheperdstown, a dozen miles upstream. Also true were rumors of another army marching from western Virginia to link up with Banks.

Woefully outnumbered, three to one by Banks alone, Jackson wrote prophetically to Henry Morrow's friend, Alec Boteler in the Confederate Congress, "If this Valley is lost, Virginia is lost."

Henry Morrow knew nothing of Jackson's letter of course, and very little of the threatening armies and the inadequacy of the defenders. He had nothing but his own acuity to assess the fact, the fiction, and the questionable.

His apprehension grew as Federal soldiers approached Winchester and occupied Bunker Hill, only twelve miles out. He and all Winchester were relieved when eye witnesses reported Jackson marching north, apprehensive again with first-hand reports of Jackson's quartermaster loading wagons with high-voltage profanity. One meant Winchester defended, the other Winchester abandoned to the Yankees. Henry pondered how best to protect his family.

He saw others scurrying frantically to pack a few pitiful belongings on their wagons and close up their houses, shutters and doors. He saw their wagons rattling toward the Valley Pike.

Henry Morrow went home, worn down by the dilemma those in the wagons had resolved: should he move his family out or stay put? Which? Which? As he shut the iron gate, he made his decision, arbitrarily, angry that he was forced to choose between two such alternatives. Either could drive a man daft with worry.

"But, Sarah, I can't let you stay here. The way the Yankees are treating the women!"

"Henry Morrow, you don't know how they're treating the women. All you know is the stories you've heard and who knows which are true. Maybe none of them."

"It may be that all of them are," he snapped back.

Sarah handled the possibilities with that confident irrationality that can be so charming even when danger lurks in nearby shadows, "Of course we're staying here. This is our home."

"If I was by myself it would be different. But I'm not. I Have you t'think of, and Gracey, Ruth, Mam, Betsy. I feel responsible for her, too. I'm telling you we have t'leave."

Puzzled at first by what appeared a sudden decision, Sarah saw his predicament, "So that's what's bothering you! You really want to stay. And you think you have to leave for us." She poured coffee into thick mugs.

"Maybe we should talk about what's best to do."

"It's all settled, damnit!" He stirred his coffee fiercely, slopping it onto the kitchen table. He stirred more slowly as he recognized the situation. It was not a new one.

Sarah had poured him coffee thousands of times over the years, had suggested talking of 'what's best' hundreds. Each time she had combined the two, she had dug her heels in to fight. He knew the pattern. He knew her obstinacy. He had never prevailed, not one time, when she primed him with coffee and talked 'what's best'.

"Sarah."

No answer.

"Sarah," he started more loudly, "What do you think?"

Jed and Brian had a brief conversation before they moved out toward the Federal army. Brian's Liberty Hall Volunteers, under ex-sergeant now Captain Morrison, were still assigned as Jackson's guard company.

"This looks serious, Jed. I just heard that Banks was moving this way and collided with Ashby's cavalry. I hope the estimate of his army is exaggerated."

"Leastways, we don't have cold and snow like we had two months ago at the dam."

"Jed, you take care of yourself out there, you hear."

"You, too, little brother! See you in a day or two."

Citizens milled around Courthouse Square, seeking assurance in the company of friends and neighbors whose anxiety levels were every bit as high. Exhausting the helter-skelter rumor of the street, they repaired to the taverns.

Even those who remained loyal to the Union felt danger in the unknown. Living in Virginia, they were target for the Northern soldiers. With close economic and family ties across the Potomac, they were suspect to the Confederates.

Henry Morrow thought it a day for men only, "Sarah, I'm going t'the courthouse and see what's going on."

Sarah disagreed, "Wait for me. I'm coming with you."

On the way, she chided him, "Whatever made you think I was going to stay home on this of all days? If we're to be overrun by Yankees, I want to know about it."

"Oh, now, Sarah, it doesn't pay t'jump t'conclusions. You told me that yourself, more than once."

"Henry Morrow, don't talk to me like I'm one of your children. Things aren't good and you know it."

"I told you we ought t'pack up and leave."

She cut him off, "We've already decided to stay."

They crossed Main Street to the public square. In the excited crowd, Henry spotted the young clerk from the Valley Bank of Winchester.

"Christopher, what are you doing here?"

"Trying to make out what's happening, Mr. Morrow, just like everyone else."

"But, the bank. Why aren't you working?"

"The bank's closed, Mr. Morrow. First time its ever closed on a work day."

"Closed? There's nobody there?"

"No sir. Colonel Brighton, he locked the door an hour ago. Said he was going to Strasburg."

"Strasburg! When's he coming back?"

"Don't rightly know. He just said he wasn't staying here for the Yankees to rob his bank. He cleaned out the vault and left. He said tell everyone don't worry, their money would be safe."

"But I need the bank open."

"That's all I know, Mr. Morrow. Sorry."

Christopher hustled into the crowd.

Visibly upset, Henry shouted after him, "What the hell am I supposed t'do for cash?"

"Now, Henry, don't fret. Things will work out."

"Damnit, Sarah, Brighton just lit out. Didn't even wait t'see what was gonna happen."

They learned that the doors of other banks were locked as well; also, that friends had left town and more were planning to. Here and there they saw a house shuttered tight in the middle of the day, a store locked and boarded.

"Henry, I want to go to John Linn's to see how Betsy is." They edged out of the crowd, Henry leading the way.

The tavern bustled with people as they came in from the spring sunshine, benches taken, standing room jammed, everyone talking excitedly. In the babble, they had trouble attracting Betsy's attention. Finally, she waved a greeting, and worked her way through the crowd with a tray held high. On it were a tankard of ale and a delicately stemmed glass containing sherry.

"How nice to have tailor-made service. You remembered."

"But of course, Mumma, how could I forget?"

She stepped closer and hugged Sarah briefly.

Betsy glanced quickly around the room.

"I'll see that you get the next bench."

"Betsy, we aren't planning on staying that long. Just stopped t'see how you were getting on."

"Fine, Papa Morrow. Very busy, these last few days. Uncle John is worried about his stock with everyone saying supplies from Harper's Ferry will be cut off. Prices are going up, double and probably triple."

"I wouldn't be surprised.

"Betsy, I want you t'promise me something. I want you t'promise you'll come t'the house before any Yankees get here."

"Oh, Papa, I'll be all right."

Characteristically, Henry showed his impatience, "No argument, now, just do. . ."

Sarah held a hand toward him, cut him off with a glance.

She turned to Betsy.

"We know you'll be all right, dear, but we want you with us. It will worry us to death if you're alone in a town full of Yankee soldiers."

"All right, Mumma, if that's what you want. I promise."

"That's what I meant," Henry mumbled apologetically.

Betsy stepped closer to him. She stood on tiptoes to kiss him on the cheek.

"Thank you, you old bear," she cooed sweetly.

"I must get back to work. Thank you both." And she was gone.

Henry and Sarah sipped their drinks slowly, listening to the conversation around them.

Without any real information, men were filling the void with opinions and rumors that stimulated more rumors.

"Where are they now?"

"Just heerd outsahd they's at Littler's Run."

"More's at Stephenson's."

"They can't be that close, they just left the Fay-ree."

"Y're wrong as hell. They left yester . . ."

"Don't make no difference enyways," Hans Schroeder broke in, "we got no cause fer alarm."

Hans did business with a brother in Philadelphia, shipping wagon-loads of tanned hides and grain, bringing back coffee, tea, sugar, and molasses. He waved no flag for the Confederacy.

Sarah and Henry moved through the room, catching snatches of other exchanges.

"—hide the silver plate."

"—daughters to Strasburg."

"Pack up an' leave 'fore they git here."

"—be boozin' it up an' all hell'll bust loose."

"I seen it in Mexico. They fornicated with ever' woman they could get their hands on. Y'think yer wife'll be safe? Ha!!!"

Henry took Sarah's hand and shouldered sideways through the crowd. They made slow progress through the hubbub.

"They wuz aw right in Charlestown."

"Like hell they were."

"I heerd they wuz aw right there. What'd they do?"

The question birthed yet other opinions.

"Y'cain't trust them sonsabitches."

"—cash an' jool'ry . . ."

Just short of the door, another group blocked the way.

"Y'all 're fergettin' the officers. They'll keep 'em in line."

"Hell they will."

"They ain't all bad. The good ones'll . . ."

"Shit. They ain't no good Yankees."

"Yes, they is."

"No, they ain't."

Henry pushed his way through.

Outside, he turned to Sarah, careful of his own language as apology for the cursing she had heard. Sorry for that, he realized that profanity sounded worse when someone else used it.

"Not much t'learn in there."

The crowd on the street had grown larger and louder. Most of Winchester's 3,000 people seemed to be milling about.

Toward one side of the square was a large group of free blacks, watchful and anxious as they observed the growing tension. Winchester had some 600 free blacks, accepted as townsmen, but still apart. Most cheered the Yankee approach privately, and all had more immediate apprehensions as they watched the mounting tension among the white folks. What little conversation they had was unobtrusive, guarded.

Henry put a protective arm about Sarah to guide her through the crowd, through still more rumors. They heard that Banks was within a mile of town, that a farmhouse beyond Darkesville was burned, that another Yankee army was approaching from Martinsburg. They were shocked at the particulars of Yankee mistreatment of women in Harper's Ferry and Charlestown. They had no way to sift out the chaff.

At noon the next day, the Liberty Hall company was stationed north of town on a fortified hill called Fort Alabama. From the high ground, Brian kept watch with his friends for approaching Bluecoats, fearful of the imminent battle for control of his town and authority over those he held dear.

Yankee columns closed the distance; Confederate cavalry darted in to delay the head of the column. On his spectacular white charger, Colonel Ashby stood out among them all. The blue columns slowed their advance. They stopped.

Outnumbered as badly as he was, Jackson knew his only fight was to stay put, be assaulted in his prepared position. He held fast, challenging the Federal general, wanting him to attack.

As Brian kept watch at Fort Alabama, Banks refused the gauntlet, waiting for the column from western Virginia. When it joined he would outnumber Jackson five to one.

At 5 o'clock that evening, Winchester citizens who had been in the streets all day heard commotion to the north, toward the town line. Those on the fringes ran for Main Street and the public square. They fell silent for the first time that day, hearing the rumble of marching soldiers, louder and louder.

Waiting, waiting, they stood absolutely quiet watching down Main Street, anxious to see their future. A few made for home. The rest stared in disbelief. A column of Yankee blue would have been less of a surprise to the people of Winchester.

There was no mistaking the nondescript uniforms, felt hats and butternut, as Jackson's army topped the rise, all but a small rear guard. Eyes downcast, they tramped past the courthouse on their way south, neither pleased nor proud to be retreating. Gradually, the citizens recovered and took up a cheer; it rang hollow, far short of the raucous huzzahs of October.

As he had done in the autumn when he carried Betsy along, Jed Morrow broke ranks. He ran to the tavern to warn her.

"She just left, not five minutes ago. Said she would be with your Ma and Pa," John Linn offered.

Jed thanked him and ran to catch his company, a rage of mixed emotions. Disappointed at missing her, happy she was safe in the house on Wolfe Street, angry that delays had kept them apart, and boiling-hot angry that they were retreating at all.

He spat his opinion, "Damn fool thing t'do! We should stay and have it out."

Others, grumping along with heads down, glanced up in surprise for they knew Jed not as a grumbler, but as the steady optimist when others complained. Bitching was not his way—ordinarily. Vacating Winchester, however, was hardly ordinary.

He was irate at the order, resentful of having to leave not only Betsy, but his family and his town to the mercy of the invaders. Leaving them unprotected in the midst of thousands of Yankee soldiers was sheer villainy.

"Desertion, damnit, nothin' but plain runnin' away that makes us all into cowards."

At first, he had listened indifferently to the report of the Bluecoats' superior manpower as any other of the "reports" that filtered down the line; he had simply shrugged his shoulders and smiled indulgently. Most likely, just another empty rumor, or at worst an exaggeration. True, false, or in between, however, this one had forced them to turn their backs and run.

"Goddamn it, stayin' t'fight, even bein' killed would be better."

A soldier behind him, "Jed, let it go. The general . . ."

"T'hell with the general," he raged, "you heard the stories. The goddamn Yankees take what they want, food, liquor, women."

He steamed black rage, his foul mood palpable in the heat of smoldering eyes and black beetle brow, in his bearing, his stride, in the white knuckles of a fist locked around his musket barrel, the other clenched on nothing but itself.

His shoulders hunched as he stomped southward, his chin pulled in low against his chest as a bare-fisted fighter. Leaning forward from the waist, he clumped along with bent knees and short, off-beat steps as though he were climbing a steep hill. Walking with the heaviest feet in the column, he mumbled again.

"Nothin' but a goddamn big mistake. The whole thing stinks. Let the bastards take the town and do what the hell they want. That what we're supposed t'do?"

Jed didn't realize he had spoken aloud. He was jarred back by a soldier alongside.

"Bet your ass on it 'cuz that's what th'army sed."

Shamed and dishonored by the only choice he was given, Jed could only refer to the whole affair as a smelly pile of barnyard dung. Every time he heard "outnumbered," or "Yankee superiority," he snapped the same earthy epithet, accent on both syllables.

"Bull-shit!"

Up ahead, Brian bristled with the same anger.

They trudged through Winchester with heavy hearts and heavy feet, past Linn's tavern, the Red Lion, the Frederick County courthouse, and the Taylor Hotel with its outside stairs and tiered verandas.

Many were leaving homes and families; others, good and generous friends. Most were silent and sullen, but not all, for scattered shouts could be heard through the column, promising a better day to the subdued townspeople lining the roadway.

"We'll lick them Yankees yit."

"Y'all take care."

"We'll be back."

Spectators became fewer as they marched through town, the soldiers, angrier as they retreated south into open country and across Abraham's Creek. They came to the toll gate which, as all toll gates, was always the occasion for joshing officers, "Who's payin', colonel?" "Today's your turn, cap'n."

Not this time! They plowed through without a word.

Bivouacking near Strasburg that evening, Jackson called a council of war for his lieutenants to approve a daring plan he had concocted earlier. He had protected its security by telling no one, a habit he held sacrosanct that frustrated his subordinates out of their minds, causing one at least to call him "crazy as a March hare."

He described his plan at the council, fall back a short way as if they were leaving Winchester, only a short distance, enough to make the retreat appear genuine, then turn around and launch a pre-dawn attack on the unsuspecting Banks. His veteran troops, he said, and the sheer daring of a night attack would surprise the green recruits Banks commanded and send them flying.

At the meeting, he learned that an egregious error had been made. Leading elements of his army had not stopped at the outskirts of Winchester as he had intended, but had kept to the road. By now, they were miles beyond town, and the supply train that had started earlier was even farther away. Jackson was furious!

He ordered the army turned around at once. There was still time to make the attack, he fumed. His officers, including General Garnett of the Stonewall Brigade, took exception. Jackson argued, as reluctant as Jed and Brian to give up Winchester without a fight. Finally, he acceded gracelessly. His eyes flamed fury as he closed the meeting and snapped, "That is the last council of war I will ever hold."

And it was.

While Jackson's soldiers bivouacked near Strasburg, the Liberty Hall Volunteers were given a special mission that began with a short march to the tracks of the Manassas Gap Railroad.

Brian looked without confidence on an engine of questionable fortitude, its stack crooked, its sheet metal dented and rusty. Steam shot from a dozen places, curled lazily and vanished; smaller leaks spit and dribbled. The engineer and his fireman cat-napped in their high seats, worn out from long hours on duty. Brian shook his head doubtfully, and squeezed aboard the rough boxcar coupled behind.

The engine coughed, snorted, and chugged eastward out of Strasburg. It wheezed along uncertainly, closing with the North Branch of the Shenandoah River and negotiating the narrow shelf between river and Massanutten Mountain.

Brian and his friends detrained near Front Royal, marching to the Shenandoah River bridges they were to destroy. At the confluence of the

North and South Branches, they first set fires to the railroad's 450-foot trestle.

Entranced, they watched the separate fires burn brighter and larger, and grow together into spectacular, leaping flames.

Angry timbers cracked and popped. Showers of sparks danced high into the night sky on currents of heated air. They caught the acrid scent of fire, but only faintly, felt nothing more than a pleasant warmth, for the smell and the heat caught the swirling currents, too, vanishing upward into the night.

The young soldiers celebrated their success pointing to the largest of the flames, cheering, shouting, laughing.

As they congratulated themselves, the flames became huge sheets that engulfed the railroad's trestles. Geometric sections of trusses appeared as shadows within the fire, shimmering like live beings. Then, one by one, two by two, the segments trembled, slipped, and fell in on themselves. Without supports, the weakened bridge collapsed into the cold water, hissing at its tormentors, steaming its fury, leaving blackened debris to show where it once stood.

The soldiers hiked a quarter mile up the South Branch to a covered bridge that connected the highway, river's edge to river's edge. Again, they piled tinder on the worn flooring, primed it with turpentine, threw their torches. Flames burst from the tinder and snaked along the dark stains of turpentine trails. The fire inched laterally along the old timbers of the floor until it all burned, turpentined or dry, reached the thinner side-planking and sprang to the trussed roof.

The bridge itself became a flue, sucking air to feed the flames and hasten its own destruction. The unnatural wind thrived and grew, fanning the fires until they filled the old covered bridge, spewing onto the opposite highway.

Flames chewed slowly at the underbelly of the sloping roof, ate through, suddenly burst forth, a geyser of sparks erupting high into the night sky. For a few minutes, sky, sparks, and covered bridge merged into one.

Then the people's bridge crashed, charring the water with debris, separating neighbors one bank from the other.

Brian watched the bridge die and became very still, no longer cheering, no longer shouting. Soldiers around him turned quiet too, bewitched by fire as their Stone Age ancestors had been before them.

As he stared, the kindly, old bridge and its flames became the war itself, soiling the Union, dividing the people. Confounded by the symbolism, for it seemed right and the war wrong, a third sobering wave washed over him, the realization that he was a part of the great destruction. He felt heavy with remorse and melancholy.

Should not bridges be built rather than wrecked, he pondered, for they connected people across rivers. And people needed such connections. As they needed food to survive, so, too, did they need bonds of friendship and love. He thought of Ma and Pa, his brothers and sisters, of the learned men at Washington College, and yes, of the men in Company I, named the Liberty Hall Volunteers for the birth name of their college.

Brian looked at the young soldiers around him. They were quiet as he, and he knew that they, too, had been touched. Absently, he reached for the Union canteen from Bull Run. He fondled the intricately tooled strap.

Harsh orders interrupted, "Company, form up. Fall in over here. Fall in!"

Another rattley, jolting, train ride returned them to their bivouac.

The rear guard of Jackson's little army marched through Winchester the next day, followed finally by Turner Ashby's hardy riders. Within the hour, blue-coated troops marched in.

Citizens loyal to Lincoln greeted them, some jockeying for interviews with General Banks to curry favors. Henry Morrow was not a proponent of the war, but neither was he of a mind to do business with the Yankees. He and others not anxious to deal with the invaders moved quietly to their homes. By nightfall, the town was shut tight, houses dark and watchful behind closed shutters and locked doors. The gas street lamps remained unlit.

As the army of Nathaniel P. Banks, Winchester's first army of occupation, took over, Turner Ashby watched closely. He would not leave until the final minute, literally when the invaders were within musket shot, then he would stick close to give Jackson frequent scouting reports.

The occupation by a Union army was the first of 72 times the Valley town would change hands, Confederate to Yankee, Yankee to Confederate. The townspeople rode waves of despair and elation, and learned to live with what they had. They learned that people who were injured and shell-torn were neither blue-coats nor butternuts, neither Yankee nor Confederate. Winchester women shared what they had and nursed them all equally.

What was a new experience to them this day would become more and more a part of their daily routine as the war dragged on. Many with strong ties to families and states across the Potomac acclimated more easily to Yankee rule, some making money off their sentiment. More remained loyal to Virginia and the Confederacy, supporting as they could the labors of Jeff Davis and his soldiers. All of them, whatever their sentiments or politics, lived with an unremitting fear for the safety of their loved ones, young sons at home, parents, and grandparents, wives and daughters dreadfully available to renegade soldiers, and for sons and husbands in one or the other of the warring armies.

Immediately on settling into his headquarters, Banks issued an order to his troops: treat the citizens and their property with respect. Political appointee and poor combat commander though he might be, the general was a good and decent man.

Despite his efforts, he couldn't control every soldier every hour, and some overstepped the bounds. Some drank too much, carousing on the streets, stumbling into private yards and homes, making lewd suggestions to the womenfolk. A few went beyond insolence, snatching what they wanted, liquor, valuables, and women. Winchester folks, enduring their first occupation by a hostile army, were outraged.

In the early days of the occupation, Henry Morrow placed his confidence in the authority of the Union officers. Graduates of the Military Academy or successful in politics and business, they would surely respect Winchester and its citizens, controlling their soldiers. He was horrified as the obscenities accumulated.

For the first time in his life, he carried a weapon hidden in the folds of his coat. He set rules for Racey, prohibiting her leaving Wolfe Street without a proper escort, and absolutely no talking to soldiers, not even a simple greeting.

"But I'm old enough to take care of myself," she pouted.

"You do like I say," Henry ended the discussion more brusquely than he intended.

His transportation business was reduced drastically by the occupation. In applying for passes for his wagons, he had to admit to three sons in the Confederate army, and was denied all schedules moving up the Valley. However, Banks' provost did grant him permits to run east and north to the Potomac, with the proviso that he do no public business with the Confederacy or its armies, and that he carry Union loyalists and freight without prejudice. Other businessmen in Winchester fared better.

Hans Schroeder, who had hauled leather and grain north made out very well. With an outspoken Union preference that predated the occupation, he was looked on with favor.

He signed the required loyalty oath, hauled all sorts of goods, paper and pencils, dry goods, playing cards, coffee, tea, molasses and delicacies and fresh fruit. Cannily, he sold no alcoholic spirits to the troops, for drunken soldiers could be a problem to headquarters and in turn to anyone with a military dispensation. He was more obliging to influential officers.

Very quickly, he became the biggest sutler in the lower Valley. His son, Willie, was his first clerk and not averse to taking goods for himself to augment his meager wages.

Selling to the Union army hardly endeared the Schroeders to the Southerners, and certainly not to the Northern soldiers who paid their exorbitant prices. A very unhappy Henry Morrow led the list.

"They're getting rich selling t'Yankees," he growled, "betraying us all, t'say nothing of the State of Virginia."

XXV

BAWDY HOUSE BACKFIRE

David Morrow spent the winter near Centreville on picket duty. He rode daily with Jeb Stuart posting and inspecting the string of outposts guarding against hostile activity.

In November, his friend from the Academy, John Pelham, arrived to command Stuart's innovative Horse Artillery.

"Pelham! I don't believe it. What are you doing here?"

Pelham grinned broadly, "Come up to show y'all how to shoot these guns, and how to gallop them to where they're needed most. Flying Artillery some are calling us."

"Good name. And you're just the man for it."

"Thanks, Dave. Damn but it's good to see you. Hear Tom's around here with the N'awleans Artillery.

"Saw him yesterday. Has his own company. Detailed to us.

"He made captain, too," indicating Pelham's insignia, "congratulations!"

"I have uh greeting from Alabama for you."

"For me! But I don't know anybody...," the light dawned, "that cousin of yours!"

"Right! She says no gentleman would treat her as you did."

"But, I didn't even meet her."

"That's just it. She said a gentleman would have made the effort. She says to tell you she's mighty put out."

"I am sorry about that. But let's have a drink. I'm free for the evening if you are."

A few minutes later, they were raising tin cups. David toasted, "To eyes as blue as the summer sky, and golden hair like new corn silk," he intoned. "That's how you described your cousin on the sidewheeler when we left The Point."

"You remembered!! From over a year ago! I will surely have to write her."

"As long as you identify me as the gentleman from Virginia."

David's long winter of surveillance paid off on the 7th of March when he was able to report activity in the Union camps around Alexandria. Mr. Lincoln's army, now commanded by General McClellan, filled the roads in a ponderous march south. The move suggested another attack on Richmond via Centreville, a repeat of McDowell's fiasco almost a year ago.

From his positions behind the Occoquan River and Bull Run, Joe Johnston watched the sluggish advance for two days, then left Manassas for a new line along the Rappahannock.

David stayed behind with Stuart to observe and report McClellan's advance. The cavalry also had orders to destroy the huge piles of supplies and personal baggage abandoned at Manassas Junction. David despised the waste, a million and a half pounds of meat and rations and uncounted personal trunks and boxes from homes across the Confederacy. An effort was made to move everything south, but Johnston had delayed too long for the single-track railroad to haul more than a token.

Everything in the path of the Yankee steamroller was set afire, meat, corn, wheat, rations, blankets, ammunition, personal belongings. Rashers of bacon stacked house-high went up in smoke, teasing families for miles around with the pungent aroma. Even privately owned corn cribs were destroyed, all the way to the Rappahannock. Barrel upon barrel of whiskey was axed and allowed to gurgle onto the ground, all lost except for what the soldiers were able to scoop into canteens and slurp from the puddles. And two barrels David made off with, "For Doctor Fontaine by order of General Stuart," he told the guards.

On March 10, Stuart's troopers departed Manassas Junction. They rode glumly, hunchbacked under blankets and sheets of India rubber against the icy rain and beating sleet. Horses plodded along, heads canted against the wind.

The next day, McClellan's advance troops captured the Junction with its smoldering supplies and a deserted defense line with blackened logs to simulate field cannons. Quaker guns they were called, and Northern generals were hard pressed to explain their trepidity. How, they wondered from up close, had blackened logs looked so lethal. Adding their embarrassment to the rainy cold, they shuffled another 25 miles, down the Orange and Alexandria Railroad to Bealeton station.

With hand-picked men, David shadowed the Yankee advance and reported daily. After dark, he and Tom Rafferty, the corporal with him at Falling

Waters, crept through loose perimeters into the Yankee camps. They joined groups around the fires, lingering on the edges, avoiding the circle of firelight.

On one of their infiltrations, just south of Warrenton Junction, they ransacked an officer's tent, looking for order books, dispatches, letters, anything of intelligence value. They found none. Instead, they liberated three bottles of imported whiskey, two boxes of Havana cigars, and about three dozen tiny vials of French perfume wrapped protectively in roller bandages.

Corporal Rafferty looked quizzically at the small bottles. Opening one, he sniffed at it cautiously.

"What the hell is this stuff doing here?" he whispered.

Rafferty was intrigued with the perfume, "Captain, you suppose he's got a girl stashed somewheres around?"

David continued his search of the portable desk.

Rafferty's third question piqued his interest, "Maybe they got a lady officer, huh?"

"Not hardly, Rafe."

"Then what's it for?"

"I'd guess he's a shrewd one who has campaigned before."

"What d'ya mean?"

David cocked his head and chuckled, "Come on, Rafe. Yankees are like any other soldiers! At least, we have an honest man here, willing to pay for services received."

"Think we oughta take it?"

"Hell, yes! No Yankee deserves all that service."

Rafferty fumbled with a small vial. The stopper stuck. The fragile glass shattered.

"Damnit!"

Perfume leaked onto his hand and shirt, filling the tent with its aroma. He scrubbed the offending hand on his rough trousers. He rubbed it in the dirt floor and on his shirt. Nothing would kill the flowery redolence.

"Oh, shit!"

"Let's move, Rafe, and you'd better let me go first." David grinned broadly, "Soldiers'll be sniffing after you, and I have no interest in sharing their disappointment if they catch up."

They packed their loot in a haversack, circled wide around the campfires to their rendezvous. Fortunately, Rafe attracted no followers, but a short distance beyond the Yankee guard post, it did evoke catcalls from their own party.

"Thought y'all wuz scoutin' Yankees!"

"Smells like ya run into a frien'ly bivouac."

"She got a sistuh?"

"A perfume raid, huh?" Their adventure had gained a name.

A few days later, David reported changes in talk around the campfires, "Yankee grapevines work just like our own, sir. The truth gets mixed in."

"What's your point?" Jeb Stuart answered.

"Just this, sir. Their talk has changed. I've heard complaints about marching since The Point, but when I heard 'marching for nothing' my ears pricked up."

"Probably just some soldier with sore feet or blisters."

"Could be, general, but what if you heard 'Carolina' and 'Fortress Monroe' at the same time?"

Jeb Stuart came alert at once, "You think it means a feint here, an attack there."

"Yes sir, that's what I think, but I'd want more before I started moving the army."

"Hmmm. Could be. It's worth passing on."

Richmond read Stuart's report with interest, for it fit with intelligence from Washington concerning an unusual number of ships gathered at Alexandria.

Then David observed the Union army halted at Bealeton Station, despite light resistance.

"Why stop there?" he asked Stuart when he next reported, "you'd expect they'd keep moving toward Richmond as long as they could—one more thing. The trains aren't supporting any all-out effort. Not nearly enough wagons for that."

Stuart pressed him, "You sure you're reading the signs right? McClellan's never hurried in his life."

"This is no build-up for an attack. I'd bet six months' pay it isn't. Sir."

"You bet that horse of yours against my last offer?"

"No sir, but I'll match it if you really want to bet."

Stuart's booming laugh rang out, "Get out of here, captain."

David's next report was unexciting: the Yankees still holding at Bealeton. Then came the clincher.

"Yes sir, they're falling back"; and the next day, "The van cleared Centreville. No sign of their stopping."

McClellan's march was nothing more than a diversion, clumsy to start, questionable in its spirit, and in the end, transparent. The overland route to Richmond was not in McClellan's plans.

Joe Johnston moved his army to counter the Peninsula threat, leaving the Rappahannock in weather that continued miserable. He hurried through Richmond on to Yorktown. The cavalry followed.

Basking in Stuart's commendation for his reconnaissances, David was in a mood to celebrate. Camping near the capital the first night, he hailed a friend, "I hear Richmond is full of liquor and relaxation. Want to check it out?"

"Thought Richmond was supposed to be a sleepy town."

"It was until it became the capital. The politicians moved in and their entertainment followed."

They picked up a third officer, then a fourth.

"Come on along," David perked with camaraderie and expectation, "a couple of drinks,—who knows what else."

The Spotswood Hotel was their first stop, as it always was with officers in town for fun. Or to meet influential officials.

They never noticed a short, well-dressed man leave his chair as they crossed the lobby. Vigilant, he had marked them at once, young officers with money and a night to spend. He followed them into the bar, ordered rum. Standing next to David, he spoke tersely through thin lips, and confidentially for he had been escorted out of the Spotswood more than once.

"Name's Rufus," he said, "you want women? Six blocks east and one left to Franklin. The Exchange Hotel. Mention my name."

He scanned the room furtively and glided silently back to the lobby. David and his friends finished their drinks.

"Why not?" one of them said.

"It's been a long, cold winter," another rationalized.

"No need to leave. The Spotswood has everything we need."

David broke in quickly, "Too much brass here. What I do on my own time is none of their business."

Rufus followed them outside, "If y'all want colored, I can take ya t'-Cash Corner."

A few seconds of silence was all he needed for an answer. "The Exchange is closer," he acknowledged agreeably and was gone.

"Cash Corner, that's down the hill in Shockoe Bottom," one of David's friends offered, "never was there myself, but I had a sergeant that like to get himself killed there. He was in a very vulnerable position when he got clubbed in the back of his head."

At the Exchange Hotel, a night clerk thumbed indolently toward the back of the lobby where rooms had been subleased to a wartime entrepreneur. One of the ornate double doors opened to their knock. A middle-aged mulatto in a maid's uniform smiled pleasantly, "Evenin', gentlemen." She stood aside as they stepped into an overly-decorated reception room.

Beckoning from the opposite wall was an enticing picture done in oils, a provocative nude on her painted couch. For all the world, she looked like she should be lounging on the room's own sofa pampering herself amongst the soft, satin pillows. Endowed with natural red hair that the artist had highlighted delicately, she seemed to pulsate, alive in the subtle strokes of his brush work. Sly shades of purple, dark greens, and deep blues blended into shadows that played like fingers about her body, diffusing, yet focusing her sensuality.

"Please be seated, gentlemen. What would you like?"

David ordered bourbon. The others followed suit. He sank into the softness of a settee toward the center of the room and let the painting tantalize him.

He broke the spell to take in the other decorations and furnishings, draperies of rich maroon edged with ball fringe of black, bell pulls of rich, red yarn thickly braided, a well-stocked bar on the wall opposite the red-haired lady, gas jets inside glass globes that caught the light in their etched designs. The assorted upholstered chairs and side tables were all arranged for the convenience of the more analytic viewers wanting to study the portrait in detail.

"Not like Northern Virginia and living in tents," the young troopers luxuriated, tossing off their drinks. They ogled the painting, drinking in her generous proportions. The maid refilled their glasses, "She's beautiful, isn't she?"

"Good evening," a voice interrupted their fantasies from the stairway at the end of the room, "you-all look lonesome." A quartet of girls descended the remaining steps, the third in line wearing a satiny, dressing gown. She held it graciously, daintily, raising the front a few inches to avoid stepping on it. Or was it to show her slender ankles? She came at once toward David, stirring a memory within him.

He took in her beauty, almost breathing it, smelling, tasting it, hair the sheen and rich brown of Sable's polished leathers, and eyes of smoky blue. He glanced quickly down her graceful neck and shoulders, along rounded bosom, down the shallow S-lines it formed with waist and hips, one pinched curve the mirror of the other. He enjoyed each part of her, intrigued with her hands, small, long-fingered hands that made him think of butterflies. How did she control them so lightly?

He sensed, too, an evanescent sadness held under control; it came and went, appearing and vanishing, mostly in her eyes.

That he had known her before weaved vaguely through his consciousness, an elusive impression that he had walked with her not very long ago, perhaps here in Richmond. It's the liquor, he thought, but the feeling persisted.

She sat by him on the small sofa, hands folded properly in her lap, close enough to suggest touching but not so close as to appear immodest. They sat quietly, David puzzling at the familiarity he felt.

"You may call me Carrie," she purred as a permission granted only to a favorite.

Her three companions joined the other troopers, were served by the mulatto maid, red wine in delicate, bell-shaped glasses. They chatted gayly, accepted a second glass of wine as the soldiers' glasses were refilled a third time. Laughter and giggles punctuated the conversations from across the room, emphasizing the silence between David and Carrie. With his drinks from the Spotswood, he struggled to concentrate on this girl. Where had he met her?

"You are not pleased with me?"

Startled, David responded badly, "I was thinking of something else."

"Then it is true. You are displeased with me."

"Oh no! Quite the opposite. You are very lovely. But you seem familiar. I know I haven't met you before. Or have I?"

"I'm sure you haven't."

One of the other couples walked toward the staircase.

"Carrie? Is that your real name?"

He finished his drink, and the maid refilled his glass at once, bourbon and pieces of ice.

"That's what I've gone by since I've been here."

"How long would that be?"

"Not very long. Would you like to go upstairs now?"

David persisted, "How long have you been here?"

The others made for the stairway.

"Almost a week, in Richmond that is." The young girl spoke softly, reluctantly, looking down into the dainty handkerchief she carried, "but we have to go upstairs now, or I'll be in trouble."

"I'm ready when you are, Carrie." He stood up. The room went askew and he fell back onto the sofa. She offered a butterfly hand. It seemed even smaller when he took it in his own. It was soft and warm, made for caressing.

The corridor at the top of the stairs was a short one leading to six rooms, three left, three right. She passed two pairs of doors, stopped at the third, on the right. David reached to open it for her. She hesitated, stiffened slightly, and walked through. David followed, into a tired, old hotel room lighted by two gas jets turned low.

The dim light revealed wallpaper of faded morning-glory blossoms, woodwork that had turned dark years ago, and indifferent furniture. A bedstead stood just inside the door, its iron showing hard usage in its chipped white paint and bent spindles. The inward slope of the mattress suggested a shallow saucer. A chest of drawers was too small for the wall to the right, and a foggy-mirrored dressing table too large for its cramped corner, extending a hand-width past the window frame. Another corner held a wash stand with pitcher and wash basin glazed white with a blue pattern. Threadbare areas of an upholstered lounge had apparently absorbed much of the room's business. The worn carpet showed remnants of color that wearied into dirty gray in front of the lounge and became even thinner near the bed where raggedy ends left a lop-sided circle of bare floorboards.

David squinted at the daguerreotype of a young man on the dressing table. About Carrie's age, he mused dully as the untarnished silver frame went in and out of focus. When he turned from it, Carrie was on the bed, her hands clenched into fists at her sides, her eyes squeezed shut as if she expected a blow she could do nothing about.

"Whatever are you doing?" David wanted to laugh aloud, but thought better of it.

"I'm—I'm—This is what we're here for isn't it?"

"Yes. I guess it is. But don't you think you'd better take your stays off first."

Large eyes popped open, more smokey than blue. She sat bolt upright. Then jounced off the bed.

David walked to her, feeling the full impact of his last drink. He took her by the shoulders, "Now, Carrie, or whatever your name is. Tell me what's going on. You haven't been here long, that's obvious. How long have you been here? In this house, not Richmond."

She looked at him apprehensively, frightened, "Since this morning."

"I thought so. What are you doing here?"

She stammered, "This is my first night."

He cupped her face, so soft to his calloused hands.

The booze added a touch of sentimental tenderness to his sincerity, "Carrie, you don't have to be afraid of me. I won't hurt you."

"I was afraid you might. I was afraid of what you were going to do."

He tilted her face up to his, speaking deliberately as he tried to concentrate, "I just want—to know—to know what you are doing—here?"

"Uh uh. I have to."

"You don't—have to—uh—do anything."

Aware that he had spoken the words brokenly, he paused to let his brain catch up. After a moment, he repeated the question, hesitating between each word, "What are you doing here?"

The beautiful, young girl broke down, trying desperately to control her sobs before they were heard beyond the room. With difficulty, she confessed, "I came to Richmond to find someone. A nurse from the hospital wrote for him and I came to take care of him. He was a soldier. Wounded." She forced herself to say it, "He died and I was out of money."

"The man in the picture?" He pointed oafishly in the general direction of the daguerreotype. She nodded.

"So you came here."

"I can take care of myself."

"You don't belong here," flinging his arm around the room. The quick motion linked his head with the booze in his stomach. He fell back, onto the lounge.

For her effort to help, Carrie received only a growl, "You think you can take care of yourself, but you can't. You don't know soldiers. You can get hurt bad, Racey. You do what Pa says."

Snapped out of her own discomposure, Carrie looked at him wide-eyed, "Racey! Soldiers! Whatever are you talking about?"

No answer from David, flopped rag-doll on the lounge. She poured water from the white and blue pitcher, bathed his face, "That feel better?"

Assorted groans and moans, then eyes that focused normally signalled David's return. For a moment. He clasped his mouth, gurgling urgently, "Basin." She jumped to get it. Just in time.

She set it and its sour contents outside the door.

She turned at the door to look at him, sitting upright on the lounge, not only chagrined, but deflated by the sudden conflict of emotions. Carrie moved closer, assuming he still wanted her. She opened her dressing gown, "You'll have to unlace me first. Remember? The stays."

Surprised, he gazed on her for one delightful moment, imagining round hips freed of their restraints and the fullness of breasts partially freed already. She was very desirable.

He looked, but the association with Racey was too much for him, "I'm sorry, Carrie, but not tonight."

"I thought you were feeling better."

"I am."

"Then," she hesitated, "then let me—let me take care of you. They know we came upstairs."

"I can't, Carrie. I see Racey when I look at you."

"Racey! That's what you said before, when I said I could take care of myself."

David started, "Racey said the same thing. My younger sister, Grace. That's why I felt I knew you downstairs. You remind me of Racey.

"I'm sorry, Carrie. Maybe another time will be different."

At last she understood. And understanding, she felt concern and warmth in his change of heart. He was substantially more than the pleasure-seeking customer she had seen downstairs.

This young soldier had truly affected her, tall but not too tall, wide shoulders, narrow waist. He had shown concern for her she had never expected to see in this house, and love for a sister more important than his personal indulgences. And those dark, sad, tender, smiling eyes! She could fall into them.

"I'm sorry, too. You were my first—my very first and I was beginning to like you, enough to hope it wouldn't be so bad.

"Now I like you even more," she looked up, through her lashes, directly into the eyes that had intrigued her so. "enough to think that it would be nice to—to—know you better."

David took her hand gently, "And I like you, Carrie. It would have been very nice." He pressed banknotes into her hand, "They'll be expecting something."

"Oh, I couldn't."

"Oh, but you can," he mimicked. "There's enough for the whole night. You can have a good sleep. I'll be back in the morning." Already, David knew what he had to do.

The next day, Stuart's cavalry paraded through Richmond. Blooded horses prancing and dancing through the Confederate capital. No parade-ground cavalry this, but troopers hardened by battle and a year in the field. They had trained, skirmished, fought, raided, stood picket duty from the Shenandoah Valley to Northern Virginia within sight of Lincoln's capital.

Yankee equipment and weapons they carried reflected their successes; shabby uniforms and leathers told the hardships. Citizens that day saw none of the wear and tear, only heroes and high-spirited, Virginia-bred horses as they cheered and waved small flags and dainty handkerchiefs. Men shouted approval and women dabbed at joyous tears. Many offered up garlands of flowers. A few broke into the streets to walk alongside a loved one. Brushed and curried to a high sheen, the horses showed off better than their bedraggled riders.

Riding their first parade through the capital, the troopers soaked up the ovation, holding their serried ranks and stern expressions. Very quickly, the cheering crowd destroyed the discipline; they relaxed, smiling, saluting and greeting spectators unknown. Here and there, a rider on an outside file broke ranks to lean from his saddle for a hearty handshake, or to lean even further for a tip-toe kiss. David Morrow and his glistening black stallion drew particular attention.

"What's his name?" people shouted.

David beamed at the notice, "Sable," he shouted back laughing, "what's yours?"

Down Franklin Street to Capitol Square they rode, each horse and rider an heroic unit of the feted army. Just past the State House, David broke from the column to enter the Exchange Hotel. He went up the stairs again to the third door on the right.

"I was going to buy you a stage ticket so's you could go home, Carrie, but it occurred to me you might want to stay here in Richmond." He handed her a package wrapped in newspaper. "If that's what you want there's enough to live on until you can get other employment. All I ask is that you find another room."

The young girl demurred unconvincingly, "I can't take this. Why, I don't even know your name."

"It's David Morrow. And you will take it. Pay me back after the war," he added carelessly.

Her eyes filled with tears as she accepted the package, "How can I ever thank you?"

"By doing what I ask—one more thing," he handed her an envelope, unsealed, "here is a letter to introduce you to a friend of my father's. He's a member of our Congress here in Richmond. His name is Alexander Boteler and I've asked him to help you find work. In the envelope, too, is an address on Church Hill where you can find a room. It's near St. John's Church with a view of the river."

"I will. I will," her words were muffled against him as she stepped closer and hugged him innocently around the waist. He held her, too, and momentarily, just momentarily . . .

He squeezed her tight for an instant, then released her quickly, "I hope you'll be there when I get back."

"I will say prayers for you, David Morrow."

She glanced down modestly, "I want you to know," her eyes teared with joy and gratitude as she looked him full in the face, "I would like you to know, before you go, that the picture is my brother. We are—we were—twins and very close."

A few minutes later, he was once again at the head of the column alongside Jeb Stuart.

"Last minute good bye, captain?"

"More like last minute business, general." As soon as the words were out David regretted them, for he feared they were taken with a different meaning than that intended. The playful twinkle in Stuart's eyes confirmed the fear.

Enjoying the accolades every bit as much as his men, Jeb Stuart danced his horse at the head of the column and waved a black-plumed hat. He swung his regiments onto Broad Street and climbed Church Hill. David looked wistfully at the well-kept house he had suggested to Carrie. It slipped past, along with all the other houses, along with St. John's, where Patrick Henry had demanded liberty or death, the white hospital tents of Chimborazo, and the winding decline that took them to the low ground beyond.

Their day in the sun was over, a moment of cheers and glory for them all, and for David, a bittersweet memory.

XXVI

COUNTERMARCH
MARCH, 1862

Brian squinted into the first rays of the sun, cranky and in the sulks, as most of Jackson's army, for leaving Winchester open for a Yankee army of occupation. None of them were aware, of course, of the general's plan for the surprise night attack, or the logistical bungle that made it impossible. They only knew he had deserted Winchester and marched them until midnight.

Brian and his student company from Washington College, the Liberty Hall Volunteers, had been ordered at once to Front Royal to destroy bridges before the Yankees could use them. The early morning bridge-burning had left little time for sleep, and that had been disturbed by the same despair that plagued Jed: they should not have deserted Winchester. That was not commendable.

Nor was the destruction of the railroad bridge or the covered bridge for people and wagons. Even though Brian accepted it as a military need, it had niggled at him. The demolition just wasn't right.

And the Zouave he had shot at Manassas! He could justify that, too, but with little satisfaction. For weeks he had nightmares of that killing and the fancy-uniformed soldier whose face he had blown away. The dreams had stopped, but the sense of wrong remained.

Frayed by the lack of sleep and bitterness, he failed to see Captain Morrison exiting Jackson's headquarters.

"Morning, Brian."

Brian's discomposure was such that he spoke without the salute that marked the day's first meeting with one's commander.

"Captain, am I wrong to think we've deserted Winchester?" Morrison squinted a warning. Mention of the retreat within earshot of Jackson was off limits for it meant botched orders and failure. Had he heard it, the general would have considered it a double abomination for it also concerned his military plans which he kept to himself. He forbade even conjecture on his intentions for a lucky guess might prove accurate and tip his hand to the Yankees.

Brian persisted, "What do you think?"

Surprised at the unseemly question and Brian's manner, Morrison chose his words judiciously, "You're entitled to your opinion, Brian. I'm sure you saw the wagon trains."

Brian fidgeted, testy at Morrison's empty response. He waited for more. Henry Morrison busied himself with his saddle, fussing with buckles and straps.

Brian pressed again, less circumspect than he might have been with a better night's rest, "Yes sir, but moving the wagons means we're to follow—that means deserting Winchester." Deep concern for loved ones painted his next words with unintended surliness, "What makes even less sense is for us to give up without a fight!"

Captain Morrison looked up sharply, his mouth compressed, his eyes bristling. He snapped his words.

"Corporal Morrow!! Your ill temper is out of line! Your stripes carry responsibilities,—one of them has to do with confidence in your officers."

"Yes sir, but . . ."

"You stand at attention, corporal, and you listen good."

Shocked, Brian stiffened, guts in, chest out, "Yes SIR."

"The general knows what he's doing. It's not your place to doubt him. Do you understand that, corporal?"

Taken aback by the heat of the captain's reproach, Brian backtracked feebly, "Yes, sir. I didn't mean . . ."

"Damn what you meant. You hear my words good."

"Yes, sir."

"—and you remember 'em."

"Yes, sir!"

Brian held his rigid stance, eyes focused on the stone house behind the captain. Henry Morrison turned to his horse again, concerned himself a second time with the same straps and buckles. He left Brian standing at attention. Minutes passed, long minutes interminable for both of them. Brian stood severely correct. Captain Morrison fiddled with the tack, hesitant to speak as a friend yet knowing he must.

"Brian, I can tell you I sympathize with your concern for everything we've left, family, friends, home. But as captain of this company, I can't afford to consider the personal misery of this war. I'd like to, God knows, but I can't."

Brian's response was softer too, "Yes, sir."

Captain Morrison wanted badly to be understood, "I have to look at things from the general's point of view. The army is not a debating society."

"Yes, sir."

"If I know Old Jack, he'd have my hide if he heard 'skedaddle' or anything resembling 'skedaddle' in my company.

"He'd have my scalp, and before he got through all of us would wish we'd never heard of this man's army."

"Yes, sir, I understand, sir."

Having done his duty, Captain Morrison once more became friend and mentor, "Brian, sometimes a man has trouble with being a soldier, trying to match the decent qualities of one with the life-and-death requirements of the other. I've known you long enough to appreciate the fine man you are. I want you to know that."

"Thank you, captain. I'll remember what you've said. That's a promise."

Henry fretted as he drove down the Valley Turnpike in silence. He had watched Hans Schroeder's fawning overtures to the Yankees, and never again would feel the same about the merchant who had been his friend. Turning into the wagon-track that led to the farm, he mumbled, "Damned old Dutchman!"

Alongside him on the high seat, Sarah heard and smiled to herself, "So that's what's been bothering you.

"Mr. Schroeder thinks the war is wrong, just as you do."

"Damn right it's wrong!"

"Both your families have roots in Pennsylvania."

"Damnit! I have sons in the army. And he's already peddlin' t' those who would do them harm."

"Henry, I dislike that as much as you. They're my sons, too, you know."

Henry ignored the precipitate rejoinder, "I don't want any truck with Yankees, sons or no sons."

Mattie heard the wagon as it rumbled into the barnyard of the smaller house she and Ezekiel had chosen to occupy.

"It's Henry an' Sarah, 'Zekiel, Grace an' Betsy's with them."

She was first to welcome them, "G'mornin', y'all. Thought you might be comin' today. I said so t' Zekiel not a hour ago didn't I 'Zekiel, even put a pot of coffee ta cookin'. An' I just took fresh bread out. Needs ta cool a bit before it's cut."

Seated in a kitchen of yeasty fragrance, they stirred sugar and fresh, sweet cream into steaming cups. Henry was still enmeshed in Hans Schroeder's catering to Yankees.

"Nobody ought to be making money off this war, "he mumbled, "this town and this Valley's going t'hell and there's people gettin' rich off it. That isn't right. It just isn't right."

Henry, I'm sure you and Ezekiel have more important things to talk about."

"That's important, damnit, people truckling t'the Yankees. A man stands with his friends."

Racey and Betsy exchanged looks, excused themselves. They wanted to see if there were new kittens in the barn, they said.

Ezekiel pushed his chair back from the table, "Don't know about Yankees esept they're about like everybody else. They need watchin' before trustin'.

"Got somethin' ta show you down the cellar hole, Henry."

At the top of the steep stairway, he lit an old lamp. Sooty smoke puffed out until Ezekiel adjusted the wick and fitted the glass chimney. The familiar pungency of the oil flame remained. "Watch those steps. There's room enough for a heel and a mite more, that's all."

The warning reminded Henry of his first descent into this cellar more than a quarter of a century ago. He had been deceived by the narrow treads and thrown off balance by a toe left hanging in mid-air. A quick reflex and a lucky handhold had saved him.

Now, he twisted on his heel, and with sidling steps took one narrow step at a time. As they descended, elongated shadows danced brokenly over the stairs behind them, then along the dirt floor, climbing the boulders and stones of the foundation walls. Distorted by the cellar's angles, they slithered across floor boards above and jumped around the edges of hewn hickory joists. Delicate spider threads flashed gold in the flickering light.

Two walls were lined with rough shelves holding glass jars, the green glass shaded gray with the winter's dust. They held the balance of last season's preserves: tomatoes, corn, three kinds of garden beans; apples, peaches, cherries from the orchard; jellies and jams in smaller jars.

Ezekiel manhandled a section on the shelving from the wall, ostensibly a rickety section that had been repaired. Shadow's jumped lively as he passed the lamp to Henry, and again when he took it back. Stooping, Ezekiel held it at arm's length to a low tunnel. They crawled through into a small room.

"Dug it out in case we have ta hide."

"Well, I'll be! Even a broom."

"T'sweep the scuff marks when I pull the shelves inta place. Cut the handle short so's I can reach through. With eatables and water we could hole up for a while."

"Well, I hope you don't have to."

"I hope so, too, Henry. I was lookin' at the root cellar in the big house,—figger on doin' some work on it, too."

"Appears you have enough t'do without all that diggin'."

"If somethin's important, you have ta work for it. You told me that in Washin'ton. And this may come ta be important."

Replacing the rack, Ezekiel hand-smoothed the dirt floor. He led the way up the narrow stairway. The shadows danced again.

Sarah and Mattie were loading the wagon with garden vegetables, last year's cabbages, carrots from storage, potatoes from the bin, dried apples and rashers of bacon from the smokehouse.

"Gracey! Betsy!

"Time to go."

Stonewall Jackson methodically opened the dispatch from Richmond. "Hold Banks'army in the Valley," the message read, "risk no defeat." Feeling free to define tactics for himself, Jackson knew exactly the best way to carry out those orders: get close to him so he couldn't afford to be caught on the march, strike a good blow, good enough to guarantee victory.

Proud and pertinacious, Jackson never forgot the abortive council of war and the aberrant order that took his wagon train way beyond the rendezvous point. Without the train, his plan for the night assault died. He had no choice but to continue the retreat up the Valley with failure throbbing in each heartbeat. Being neither a forgetful nor a forgiving man, Thomas J. Jackson churned for revenge. The dispatch was his redemption, the chance to regain Winchester, maybe chase Banks clear out of the Valley, away from Richmond.

Had Jed and Brian known his frame of mind, they would have slept more easily, and Brian might have avoided Captain Morrison's scathing blast.

Betsy had stayed with the Morrows for about a week after the Union army marched in, then, after the initial shock of occupation, suggested she move back to her rooms.

Sarah and Henry insisted that she stay on with them.

"Go back to work, if you want," Sarah told her, "but I'd feel better if you brought the rest of your things here.

"We'll arrange for an escort home after dark. Or maybe you can work daylight hours."

"Oh, Mumma, you worry too much about me."

"Nobody knows how long Mr. Banks will be with us. And nobody knows when his men might turn nasty."

"All right, but I still think you worry too much."

Henry had listened to the conversation and saw his chance to allay the uncertainty that had nagged him, too.

"That's it, then. I'll get a wagon and we'll move your things in the morning."

Betsy did move to the Morrow's, into Jed's old bedroom.

She did go back to work at Uncle John's tavern. From the very first, serving Bluecoats gave her a unsettling sense of disloyalty to Jed.

The tavern was threatening and dangerous, mostly strangers in uniform, some in mufti, opportunists following the army for whatever they could get, unprincipled and irresponsible in their anonymity. Amidst these ruffians and scoundrels, the regular customers were not themselves; those who Betsy knew as jovial and cheerful became almost strangers themselves. Always expecting an outbreak of fisticuffs, or a fight with deadly weapons, they were suspicious and watchful. Some regulars simply stayed away.

The friendly banter Betsy had known was gone, its innocence destroyed by pawing hands and crude offers of money for favors. Grimy fingers held out silver coins, mostly quarter dollars and halves. Betsy's appeals elicited only guffaws.

"Give you the best you ever had."

"Two hours and its yours," one held out a silver dollar.

Another offered a Spanish coin, once called a piece of eight, "A piece of this for a piece of you."

There was no dealing with these barbarians.

She appealed to her uncle, who with a glance and a shrug signaled his sympathy and helplessness. He was a prisoner in his own house, forced to abide the vile behavior or risk his property, perhaps even his life. He could do nothing.

Seeing her uncle so reduced, the same who always had control of his domain, Betsy realized there would be no change as long as the Yankees controlled Winchester. She snatched off her apron and left, amidst jeers and foul remarks of her availability.

As she passed Courthouse Square, a young, clean-cut soldier smiled pleasantly, raised his hand to his kepi in a respectful salute. Betsy stopped in front of him, tears of fury streaming down her face. She glared wet fire. With all her pent-up anger slapped him reeling against the fence. She stared hatred at the young soldier, then ran for home, white petticoat flashing down Wolfe Street.

"Oh, Mumma, it was terrible," she screamed hysterically in Sarah's arms, "the soldiers said horrible things and offered me money and grabbed at me and Uncle John couldn't stop them, those horrible men so dirty and mean and nasty and—and . . ."

"It's all right, Betsy, it's all right now."

"I kept thinking of Jed, Mumma, how nice he is to me. Oh, I love him so much."

Thoughts of the tavern overwhelmed her again.

"Oh, Mumma, I felt so dirty."

She dabbed at flooding eyes.

"I know, dear, I know," Sarah soothed in a singsong lilt. She gently lifted the tear stained face, "Look at me, Betsy. Listen carefully." She smoothed the rich brown hair lovingly, "It's the soldiers who should feel dirty, not you. You did nothing wrong, dear. The soldiers did the wrong. Their behavior was as much an insult to themselves as it was to you. Some day, they will come to see that and be sorry."

Gradually, with the soft words, she controlled her sobs.

"They will remember you longer than if you had accepted their offers," Sarah continued, "in years to come, they will look at their daughters and regret their vulgarity."

Betsy listened, trying to assimilate the profound truth in Sarah's simple words. Then she thought of the young soldier at the courthouse. She remembered his open smile and respectful salute and wondered if perhaps she had made a mistake.

Lieutenant Lyle called Brian to the company tent, "Find Captain Morrison. Colonel Ronald requests his presence. At once."

"Yes, sir."

Waiting as close to the regimental tent as he dared, Brian heard the order to his company commander, "Prepare the company to march. General Jackson is heading out within the hour, ahead of the main column, and wants his guard company with him."

The Liberty Hall Volunteers formed up at once, stepping out at half past three in the afternoon. Much to their surprise, for they expected to be retreating even further, they headed not south, but down the Valley, back toward Edinburg, toward Strasburg and Winchester. Smiles were everywhere, for they weren't running away after all! They were going back to fight.

Old Jack was, indeed, taking them back, for he had in hand Ashby's latest scouting report: above Strasburg, Federals had faced about, were moving north, toward Winchester. The backtracking of Shields' Division suggested that at least part of Banks' army was preparing to leave the Valley. Jackson's orders were to prevent that, keep him from reinforcing McClellan who threatened Richmond. The chance to seize the initiative suited Jackson well, pursuer now instead of pursued. Move in close and find weaknesses to exploit.

Jackson wasted no time with a council of war, asked neither opinion nor advice from anyone. He made his own assessment, his own decision, and issued marching orders: he would leave at once with his headquarters company of Washington College Students. The main body would march at dawn. He sent dispatch riders to his commanders, Fulkerson to the north at Woodstock, Burks to the south near Mount Jackson, and an aide to General Garnett and the Stonewall Brigade just across the road.

Enthused at Jackson's show of resolve, Brian's company marched the Valley turnpike with a will, covering eleven miles to Woodstock in a brisk two hours twenty minutes.

For the moment, Brian forgot his black thoughts. He strode jauntily over the macadamized road his father had built more than twenty years ago. As he marched the gravel Henry had hauled, Captain Morrison's words echoed in his head. One matched the cadence of his stride, CON-fi-DENCE, CON-fi-DENCE.

The general did indeed deserve his confidence, for he was taking them back, wasn't he? Sure he was, Brian celebrated to himself, the general was taking them back!

He yelled out, "Let's hear it, boys! The Old Gray Mare."

He sang a few bars, until his enthusiasm caught those around him. Their steps lightened, as though they foresaw the future, and the nom de guerre soon to be theirs, Jackson's Foot Cavalry,

By early afternoon the next day, the college company reached Strasburg, bivouacked near Jackson's headquarters, the same store house he had used a week ago on the cheerless road south. Immediately, some of the boys mounted guard duty; others were free to rest, massage tired feet, and bathe in the North Branch of the Shenandoah. Some listened to firsthand accounts of Yankee thievery. One of Brian's friends wrote in his diary.

"The citizens here are all down upon the Yankees . . . when their horses, cattle, money, chickens, etc. were plundered . . . the hearts of these honest people became filled with loathing for the contemptible Yankees."

One day behind, Jackson's main force shouldered muskets, marched north, Fulkerson's small brigade leading the column from his advance camp at Woodstock, Burks' Brigade bringing up the rear from its camp above Mount Jackson, Garnett's Stonewall Brigade in between.

Garnett's five Virginia regiments marched twenty-six miles to Cedar Creek before it bivouacked. As it tramped past Jackson's headquarters, Brian and his friends shouted from the roadside, cheers for their own Colonel Ronald and his 4th Virginia.

With three canteens slung over his shoulder, Brian waited anxiously for the 2nd Virginia and Jed's company. Spotting him up the road, he waved furiously and hurried against the direction of march. The older Morrow smiled thanks as Brian handed him the Yankee canteen he had found at Bull Run last summer.

"This one's fresh spring water to drink now, Jed. I have two more for you to keep, one water, one stronger."

Thirsty and dusty, Jed nodded a quick thanks and drank at once of the sweet water. In ecstasy, he closed his eyes as the cool liquid soothed his throat, and murmured an attenuated little sigh, like the whistle of a distant train, "AHHhhhhh—"

Sparing a handful to wash over his head and face, he used the last of it to soak a kerchief he took from his neck.

The brothers walked in silence. Together for only a few minutes, they found little to say, as if the time was too precious to waste with words. It was good just to be together, to walk side by side knowing the other was safe. North of town, beyond the town line, Brian broke the silence.

"I'd better be getting back." He reached for the empty canteen, "I'll trade you two full ones for it. This one's stronger. For later."

"That's the one from Bull Run." Jed observed as he handed it back, "the one in the mud."

"Your lesson saved my life, Jed."

"You're a life saver, too, little brother," indicating the full canteens. They pressed hands as they marched along, and Brian dropped off the pace.

Jed half turned in the road, lifted an arm. A stranger might have seen indifference in the gesture, but to Brian it was affection, the desire to extend contact for another moment.

Jed faced around to the direction of march, and clumped doggedly toward the Yankee invaders. For the first time, Brian saw his brother as destructible, mortal as everyone else. His eyes misted, he whispered reverently, "Take care of yourself."

Drinking in Jed's broad back and shaggy hair, Brian held his hand high, watched him disappear in the light dust of springtime. He stood quiet, staring to the space where his brother had been. Other shoulders entered and exited Jed's space, but Brian saw only the familiar back and shaggy hair.

He remembered last summer and the Bull Run ford where Jed had scared him half to death, where they had wrestled in the sweet forest earth laughed at Betsy's innocent joke, and the memory of her in bed between them.

He remembered their goodbyes there on Bull Run had been made with expectations of going back to their regiments for a few hours to whip the Yankees. A quick victory would end the war, and they could go home. That's what most were saying. For a brief time, Brian had made himself believe it. For that was what he wanted to believe.

That had been a lifetime ago. He and Jed had won their battle, yet the war wasn't over. Even now, eight months later, it still wasn't over. The Yankees hadn't quit. He and Jed hadn't got to go home. He knew now that the war would be short only for the unlucky, a long one of many goodbyes for those more fortunate. Surviving a battle would be nothing more than a ticket to the next one, the next, and with good fortune to the one after that. Living was until the next fight, nothing more, possibly less.

His melancholy was not for himself, but for Jed and Betsy, for the bridges he had burned, the Zouave he had shot at Manassas, the man with no face. As he had done so many times, he wondered about the man's mother and of his father. Did they even know their son was dead?

The end of Jed's regiment passed him by. He remained yet a few moments staring after it, unwilling to break the fragile connection, fearful that it might be gone forever.

"Father in heaven, let thy goodness shine upon him. Protect him with your love. Protect Betsy. Protect their love. Amen."

He dug hard knuckles into his eyes, swiped roughly at streaked cheeks. He murmured once more down the Valley, toward Jed, "Take care of yourself—big brother."

He let his hand drop. He turned back toward Strasburg.

Up ahead, Turner Ashby skirmished above Winchester, and sent spies to citizens who had given useful information in the past.

Only four regiments of Bluecoats were left, they said. Those were to leave on the morrow for Harper's Ferry. Most of Banks' army had already marched east via Castleman's Ferry and Snicker's Gap to join McClellan.

Banks himself was en route to Washington, they said. Jackson's quarry was slipping away.

By early afternoon, all but one of Jackson's eleven companies had arrived at Kernstown, a crossroads village four miles above Winchester.

One question concerned the soldiers, "Do you suppose he plans to open a fight today?"

"Not likely. He thinks it wrong to fight on Sunday."

Jackson had indeed planned to respect the Sabbath, and to rest his road-weary soldiers. He felt he could afford to do that since Ashby said only four Federal regiments opposed him.

Then, seeing Union artillery on high ground looking down his throat, able to lob shells, he changed his mind. He learned, too, that Federal reinforcements could return before morning. The Lord would understand and forgive his breaking the Sabbath peace.

He made his plan, simple and sound, a diversion on the right, artillery to protect the center, and an all-out assault on the left covered by woods and high ground.

Three batteries opened fire. Quickly his attack bogged down as Federals shifted to meet it, substantially more than four regiments. Jackson realized that Ashby's intelligence was faulty, perhaps the result of deliberate misinformation.

He sent aide Sandie Pendleton out to investigate. Finding a high knoll overlooking the Yankee resistance, Sandie made a quick estimate. He galloped back to Jackson.

"There must be 10,000 of them."

"Say nothing about it," Jackson replied, "we are in for it."

XXVII

KERNSTOWN

Ezekiel had been uneasy since dawn. Attuned to the natural rhythms of the Valley, he was aware of something foreign, an underlying ferment in the pastoral serenity, an arythmia in nature's heartbeat. As country folk are wont to say, he just felt it in his bones.

He watched birds suddenly spooked from their roosts in the trees, sensed alarm in their frenetic flight. Ordinarily, they flew in graceful, patterned flocks with great looping turns and lyrical undulations; this morning the formations were in disarray, the birds in turmoil, perplexed beyond their instincts.

Ezekiel thought it odd that still other birds, singly and in small groups, were flying from the east so early in the day.

When he heard scattered gun shots floating in from the direction of Kernstown, his disquietude was validated.

"That isn't any hunters," he told Mattie, "too many for hunters. Besides, I heard big guns a while back. Thought it might be thunder, but I know now it wasn't."

"Come on, we got work ta do."

They rounded up what animals they could, horses, cows, mules and pigs. Driving them deep into the woods to the west, Ezekiel hoped they would stay hidden from the Yankees without wandering too deeply into the wilds of Little North Mountain. He figured them to stay close to the water of Opequon Creek, close enough to be rounded up when the danger was over.

Except for two hams and a side of bacon, they cleaned out the smokehouse, secreting the cured meat in Ezekiel's newly dug room in the cellar. Best leave something for the soldiers to find.

Having done his best to preserve food supplies, he wormed his way under the porch of their small house. He pushed ahead of him two small bundles wrapped in worn sheets, three bottles of whiskey in one of them. Best to hide the popskull from marauding soldiers.

The other sheet held jewelry and silverware that Henry's father had given Mam many years ago in Washington, treasures she had passed along to her son and Mattie for a wedding present.

As valuable as they were in the marketplace, they had greater worth to Ezekiel and Mattie as the tangible side of a family history. Family was important to them, the heirlooms were something to pass on. Stories and legends, tales of Washington, D.C., Mam and Henry's father, Jeremiah, of Winchester, the Shenandoah Valley, of Ezekiel and Mattie, and one day, God willing, of war and invaders, and digging holes under a front porch. The small collection of things and tales was important for they were memorials touching on immortality.

Ezekiel dug holes several feet apart, one for each of his wrapped caches. As he worked, Mattie hissed to get his attention, tossed a leather pouch of silver and gold coins they had put away over the years, "These, too, Ezekiel."

Covering them level, scattering enough debris to hide his work, Ezekiel crawled into the open. He dry-washed his hands of the dirt, slapped it from his trousers and shirt. He looked toward the east for telltale signs of dust, then a quick glance around the yard. Nothing more could be done. It was consternation time, time to go inside and wait.

Mattie had drawn and latched the shutters, first floor and second. Bolting the front door and the back, she poured coffee from the flame-blackened pot. They sat at the kitchen table, waiting for whatever the Good Lord had in store for them. Ezekiel considered using the secret room, but decided against it.

Maybe whatever was happening wasn't all that dangerous. Even if it turned out to be serious, there was always the chance it would pass them by.

For the rest of the evening they waited tensely, alertly, listening for approaching danger. Repeatedly, Ezekiel cocked his head to judge the gunfire better.

"It's not comin' any closer."

"Doesn't seem ta be."

They waited until the sun sank behind Little North Mountain and the kitchen grew dim and dark. The gunfire thinned, became sporadic as the light waned and at long last came to an end.

"Thank the Good Lord that's done."

Mattie answered him with a long sigh, "Amen."

As Ezekiel and Mattie rounded up the stock, Brian's regiment, the 4th Virginia, formed in a cleared field and waited for orders. Up close, Brian heard the same gunfire that had driven Ezekiel and Mattie to work so frantically. For 30 minutes, he stood under heavy artillery fire from Pritchard's Hill. The colonel's horse bolted, throwing and so injuring him that he had to be assisted from the field. His replacement received the awaited orders, pointed his sword across the field and shouted.

"At the double quick! Forward. MARCH!!"

Brian crouched and ran through the clearing. Artillery shells continued to explode around him, finding hapless targets in Company I and the rest of the 4th Virginia. Most of the regiment angled away from the danger, to the left where a copse of cedars offered a fragile protection. Too far from the cedars, Brian with a few others were left isolated when Yankees exited the woods across the clearing to run for a stone wall. He joined up with another regiment racing for the same wall. The prize for the winner was protection; the penalty of losing, bare-assed vulnerability out in the open. He learned later he had joined the 27th Virginia.

Somewhere an officer yelled unnecessarily, "Fire! Fire!"

A ragged volley exploded from the Virginians' side of the wall. Blue-coated soldiers dropped by the dozens. Sheer momentum carried a few onward.

Biting furiously into a paper cartridge to reload, Brian stuffed the wad, poured powder, and was ramming the ball home when a Yankee came shrieking over the wall, bayonet first. Brian side-stepped, squeezed the trigger. The ramrod could have been an Indian arrow except for the round tamper on the notch end.

The shriek was cut off in mid-air, as the ramrod penetrated the attacker's chest. He clawed at it uselessly. He gasped for air. He drowned in his own blood. Fortunately for Brian Morrow, the Yankees pulled back from the wall.

He stood motionless, staring at the body, a young boy, peach-fuzz on his chin, sprawled grotesquely. John Lyle shoved him toward the copse of cedars, "Come on, Briney, run."

In the brief lull that followed, he and the other Liberty Hall boys rejoined their company in the trees.

Yankee reinforcements filed into the line and kept coming, from the other side of the turnpike. Finally, the Federal commanders across the pike had tumbled to Ashby's diversionary threats and feints, and ordered troops to the main battle along the ridge line. They accumulated an attack force opposite the stone wall opposite Fulkerson's demi-Brigade, two Virginia regiments holding Jackson's left. They extended beyond Fulkerson, threatening to turn it.

Still, Jackson had hopes for a victory. He ordered the regiments into position to meet the coming onslaught.

"Second Virginia. Double-quick. Forward!"

Jed heard Colonel Allen's order and raced forward.

From his flimsy cover, Brian moved up, too, behind the partial cover of a snake fence. Over to his right, another regiment was deploying to the stone wall, Jed's 2nd Virginia. With his comrades Jed ducked behind their sanctuary breathing hard. The 2nd filled a gap between the 27th and Brian's 4th.

"Prepare to fire."

"Fire!"

The quick volley caught the Yankees by surprise, convinced them to back off. For an hour, the lines spit fire, the Northerners waiting for reinforcements, the Confederates behind the wall ducking chipped stone and lead balls.

Then the Yankees launched successive attacks, one close after the other. The Confederates hung on by their fingernails, refusing to give in.

Jed fired, reloaded and fired again, grimy, sweaty and black around the mouth from biting cartridge papers. He smelled and felt the acrid powder, strong and gritty; he tasted it on his tongue and in his throat, smelled it, and felt it on his teeth, lips, and hands.

Jed and his companions, Brian and his, held their ground, but lost the initiative. Jackson's turning column on the ridge line was bogged down.

Jed sensed that all was not well, and kept close track of his regimental flag; if Colonel Allen called for a retreat, he wanted to know it. Last summer at Manassas, he had seen men get left behind in the mid-day confusion. He saw the flag fall, then wave high again as another soldier selflessly rushed in to rescue it. He was shot down, too, along with five more gallant flag bearers on that holy Sabbath day at Kernstown.

The invaders were not only frustrating Jackson's battle plan; they were within a whisker of stealing it, overlapping and turning his flank as he had planned to turn theirs.

Blue cavalry slipped dangerously around the Confederate left, and opened fire. With infantry support, the cavalry sortie could spell disaster.

Fulkerson's men, on the flank, and Garnett's to his right held their ground despite the threat of being turned, but their men were running low on ammunition. A few who had already shot their last rounds scurried among the dead and the wounded, risking their lives. At each body, they ducked like long-billed birds feeding in shallow water, snatching paper-wrapped cartridges for soldiers still able to use them. Their commander looked in vain for reinforcements from the turnpike.

The firing slackened noticeably as more and more men ran out of ammunition. Finally, Garnett made the decision most abhorrent to every combat commander.

Twenty-one years out of the Academy, veteran of the Seminole Wars and the western frontier, the old warrior smelled annihilation of his brigade, growled, and pulled it out of the line. The withdrawal exposed Fulkerson's flank, and he too had to fall back.

Jackson was irate. He believed adamantly that any leader worth his salt maintained contact until he had specific orders to break it off,—bullets or no bullets, Garnett had broken it off without orders.

He shouted to his brigadier, "Why have you not rallied your men? Halt and rally."

He shouted to the men who had stayed to their last cartridge, "Go back and give them the bayonet."

Over and over he exhorted them.

He grabbed a drummer boy, hauled him to a slight rise in the ground, the better to be seen.

"Beat the rally," Jackson shouted, and the young drummer rattled the drumhead with his sticks. The message of defiance and challenge resounded over the battlefield, but to no avail. The retreat had gained its own momentum. The battle was lost, Jackson's first and only defeat.

More than any other leader, more than General Lee himself, Jackson had a mystical love of battle. Transformed by its imminence, many close to him remarked on the strange, otherworldly brilliance of his eyes as he made his preparations. His soldiers swore the normal gray pigment changed color, and formalized the phenomenon in a nickname, "Old Blue Light."

At Kernstown, his battle passion brought him to the arena and then betrayed him with inaccurate information. Empty cartridge boxes sealed his fate.

On the retreat, the Liberty Hall Volunteers scampered for the protection of a nearby wood. Brian saw a man up ahead stumble and fall. He ran to him and knelt. It was Sergeant Nelson, "Help me, Brian, help me."

John Lyle, 30 yards behind them, yelled a warning.

"Move, Brian, move! They're on our tail."

Brian turned to see Yankee cavalrymen surround Lieutenant Lyle and Captain Morrison. He wanted to help them, but John was already breaking his sword, and the captain had his hands raised in surrender. Trying to help them, he would only be taken himself. Or shot in the attempt.

He screamed in the sergeant's ear, "Run, Charley, run."

"Come on, man, stand up. Damnit! Stand up and run!"

Nelson tried but reeled like a drunk man, "Too dizzy. Everything's whirling about."

"Never mind. I'll carry you."

Nelson only moaned, "Help me." Blood coursed down his face. Quickly, Brian steadied him with an arm around his waist. He grabbed a wrist, and braced the wounded man's arm across his shoulders. Charlie's heavy brogans trailed a pair of wavering lines behind as Brian pounded for the woods.

They were lucky, for the pursuers gave them a free gift of time when they stopped to concentrate on Lyle and Morrison, not much but enough for Brian to race through the covering sanctuary of the treeline.

For another 35 yards, he staggered under his load, around trees and through underbrush. He hauled his load as far as he could, and simply dropped it. Nelson fell limp. Brian stumbled two more steps and collapsed.

He sank to his knees, fell forward onto his hands. There, on all fours, he vomited into the sweet earth, spewing from his mouth and dribbling from his nose. The soup burned terror in his nostrils, vile, sour, and suffocating. He choked and gasped as vomit and air collided in his throat. Alternately and involuntarily, he gulped one and ejaculated the other as they competed for the single passage. His frantic lungs gasped for oxygen. His heart boomed in his head.

Then, the worst was over, paroxysms reduced to spasms, chills and coughs. Gradually, the violent heaves and poundings subsided as lungs and heart approached normal rhythms. Through accident, sheer good luck, or the Grace of God, no vomit had violated his lungs.

Still on all fours, he stared back under his arm at Nelson. Like a rag doll, his body sagged over a low shrub of laurel, head and arms limp at one end, legs askew at the other, foot over ankle. Brian marvelled vaguely that he was alive. For the moment, it didn't make any difference.

He tucked in a shoulder, rolled easily onto his back, away from the ground he had soiled. Raising his arms lazily, he stared through aching fingers, let them fall as they would, out of sight, somewhere behind his head.

With eyes closed in blessed relief, he lay still for several minutes, savoring a warming sense of peace and safe haven. The war and danger were gone, out of sight, out of feeling. The sourness in his mouth and nose intruded and the war came back.

A vision stirred within him, of John and Captain Morrison captured but still proud, hands raised only enough to keep from being murdered. He remembered the last time the captain had chastised him, at the Hawkinstown camp near Mount Jackson.

"Responsibility, and confidence in your officers."

He stood up, moved quietly to Nelson, lifting him gently, lowering him to the ground. A quick inspection of his head discovered a grazing wound, not serious intrinsically but a bleeder. Brian bandaged it as best he could with a clean sock from his pocket held in place by a sleeve torn from his patient's shirt and tied tight under his chin.

"Charley, Charley, you sure as hell look like you have the mumps," he joked as he felt for a pulse. After a moment he found it, steady enough but faster than normal.

"Mumps! Christ, that's all I need."

"Hey, I'm joking. You're doing fine. Pulse is normal, a few extra beats due to the excitement.

"On your feet, Charley. We have to get out of here, to a hospital."

Sergeant Nelson nodded, "Yes. To a hospital." He tried to stand, reeled some, kept his balance with Brian's help. He pointed to his shirt pocket, "Address. If I don't make it."

"Come on, Charley, you'll make it. I promise you that."

Brian peered into the late twilight to get his direction and headed for the rear. Walking unsteadily, Charley Nelson would have fallen had not Brian supported him. No path guided them through the deep woods. The twilight had given way to darkness.

"We'd better stop. I can't see a thing." Brian groped for a tree, propped his patient against it.

"How you doing, Charley?"

"All right, I guess."

Brian rustled in his haversack, "Here eat this. It'll give you strength." Charley reached for the hardtack, fumbled it, dropped it to the ground. Brian groped for it in the darkness, put it in the other's hand.

"How's your head doing?" Brian felt around the shirtsleeve bandage, "Bleeding seems to have eased. Feels like its congealing. Let's rest a while and decide what's best to do. I'm not even sure where the turnpike is in this darkness.

"Maybe it'd be best to wait for morning, or at least for the moon to come up."

"That sounds good to me. And—thanks, Brian."

"Try to get some sleep while you can."

Brian was startled by the rustle of leaves. He came awake immediately, reached for the musket by his leg. Moonlight penetrated the woods enough to show him the source of the disturbance. The sergeant had toppled from his sitting position. He rushed over to him, checked the bandage. It seemed all right, less bleeding than before. He felt for the pulse, "Oh, shit!" It was rapid now, weaker than it had been.

"Come on, Charley, time to move. We've got to find the hospital." The sergeant moaned weakly.

Standing him on his feet, Brian stooped low so that the wounded man flopped across his shoulders. With the moon as a guide, he headed for the rear as fast as he could go. That rapid pulse worried him.

"You all right, Charley?"

"Uh huh."

Brian stepped along faster than he knew was safe, but he had to get to a hospital. He picked his way quickly, avoiding the most obvious obstacles and holes, taking his chances with the rest.

"Won't be long, Charley. We should find a doctor soon."

Charley moaned.

He continued his chatter, "You're lucky. Get a sawbones to fix you up and maybe you'll get to go home. You might even get out of the army with a head wound. I've heard of a couple of guys that got out on head wounds. One of them faked it by losing his balance every time they examined him. Finally the doc said the hell with it and sent him home. Charley, that man danced all the way and never fell down once.

"What are you going to do when you get home? You have a girl waiting for you? I know you're not married. Or are you? Last I knew you weren't. Are you married, Charley?" Brian waited for an answer. None came.

"Come on, man, don't pass out on me now. We're almost there."

Brian was out of the trees, looking at the Valley Turnpike shining silver in the moonlight.

"Charley, we're almost there. My father worked on that road. He hauled gravel for it when they built it. He helped build it, he did, set up his own company to use it after it was completed. Charley, you'd like my father. Sometimes, he's hard to understand, but he's tough as nails and honest as a cock's crow at daybreak. Jed tried to explain why he needed to enlist in the army but Pa never budged an inch. 'Damn the war,' he said, 'you're a farmer not a damn soldier. Better to get back to building the country instead of tearing it down.' Jed took off anyway, Charley. He's in Colonel Allen's 2nd Virginia. He must have been fighting today—uh, yesterday—but I never saw him."

Brian talked his patient through the night and carried him into the dawn.

"God, I hope Jed's all right. Here he is my brother, Charley, and I don't even know if he's dead or alive. Maybe Pa's right about this war. Yes, goddamn it, he is right."

Brian stopped in his tracks. He lifted his head to the sky and shouted, "Goddamn this whole stinking war. Goddamn this whole stinking war. Goddamn this whole stinking . . ."

"You need help, corporal? There's a field hospital right over there in the chapel." The stranger had appeared like an apparition in the grey dawn. He pointed toward the turnpike.

"I'm an orderly there—saw you coming across the pasture. Men have been staggering in all night. God only knows how many are still out there."

"Field hospital? Where?"

The orderly pointed again, "Let me help you with him."

Brian ignored the offer, shifted his burden to ease screaming muscles, and set off.

"Charley, we made it," his voice was ecstatic, "I told you we'd make it, Charley. We made it! There's the hospital. You'll be fixed up in no time. We made it! We made it!!"

"Bring him inside, corporal. There's an empty pew up in front." Brian climbed the board steps, walked toward the altar. He lifted his eyes to the hewn, wooden cross behind it.

The doctor followed, "Over there to the right."

Brian knelt in front of the pew, lowered a shoulder and let Sergeant Nelson roll gently onto the plain bench, "Easy does it, Charley."

He stood up, stretching muscles and back. He rubbed neck muscles as the doctor tended his patient.

"Corporal, this man is dead."

"He can't be!"

"I tell you he is. No heart beat. No breathing. Look for yourself."

"He can't be!! HE CAN'T BE!!!" Brian shouted furiously, "I carried him all night. I bandaged his head—carried him all night. He can't be dead." He rushed to kneel once again at Charley's pew, "Charley, tell him you're not dead. Tell him, Charley."

He shook the body shouting, "Tell him. Tell him." He shook the body again, demanding, "Tell him, damn you, tell him."

The doctor put an arm around Brian's shoulders. His voice was low and comforting, "He can't, son, he's gone. There's nothing we can do. God has him now, my boy."

Brian did look like a little boy ready to burst into tears, "But he's my friend. I carried him all night."

The doctor led him away from the pew, away from the rough cross and altar, down the board steps to the trampled grass.

Brian looked bewildered, "But I bandaged his head. The bleeding was almost stopped."

"I'm sorry, son, you did all you could. Scalp wounds as serious as your friend's will bleed to death every time."

"But I didn't," Brian mourned, "I should have bandaged him sooner. I could have saved him if I bandaged him sooner."

"That would have made little difference. He might have lived a few minutes longer, that's all. He needed sutures and someone to sew him up."

Brian's guilt overwhelmed his reason, "He would have lived long enough for you to fix him."

"That is simply not the case. Your friend expired at least an hour before you got here." The doctor reached a friendly hand to Brian, wanting badly to ease his pain but forced to accept reality.

"Others need me," he disappeared into the chapel.

Stunned, Brian squeezed his eyes tight needing to shut out the world, "I should have bandaged you sooner, Charley. I let you die. I let you die."

He made his way down the weather-beaten stairs, across the churchyard to a stone wall edging the little burial ground. There he collapsed, face in hands, sobs racking his body.

"I let you die. Charley, I'm sorry. I'm sorry. Forgive me, Charley. I let you die. I didn't mean to but I let you die."

He slumped against the wall until the tears dried and the sobs shut down, until the lashing words ran out. Limp, exhausted, he stumbled away from the chapel. Like a homing pigeon, he headed toward the Morrow farm and Ezekiel.

XXVIII

NIGHT VISITOR

Mattie shook her husband's shoulder. "Ezekiel! 'Zekiel! Wake up 'Zekiel. Someone's scritch-scratchin' at the door."

Half awake, not hearing her at all, Ezekiel rolled over, nuzzled her, resting a hand on her breast.

"I was just dreamin' about you. Aksin' if you wasn't wantin' a little poontang."

"Zekiel, stop your messin'! Someone's at the door."

"There it is again. Go see who it is. 'Zekiel, I'm fr . . .'"

"Just you stay easy. Everythin'll be all right. If anybody was out there, OleHoundawg'd be barkin' and I don't hear him."

"But he did. He barked just once before I heard that scritch-scratchin'. You suppose somebody . . ."

"Shhhh," Ezekiel warned. His desire for Mattie vanished.

He slipped out of the warmth of the feather bed, reached for the club he kept handy, rock maple it was. Barefooted he slipped down to the kitchen. He listened at the back door. Nothing.

In a hissing whisper, "Who's there?" Silence.

"Who's out there?" Still no answer.

He glided through the house to the front door. Listening as he did before, he hissed again, "Who's there?"

No answer, again, but the latch rattled softly.

"Anybody out there?" he asked loudly, "who's out there?"

He raised the club head high, half expecting to hear rough shoulders batter the door, or a bullet come crashing through.

" Zeke, it's me. Brian. Let me in, Zeke."

Shaken and relieved all at once, Ezekiel let the club drop. He opened the door. Brian was leaning exhausted against the door jamb. Close by sat

OleHoundawg, the contented watchman who had barked until he caught the familiar scent. Brian pushed through the door, put out both hands in greeting.

"I thought you were a Yankee lookin' ta do mischief. Damn! if I wasn't ready ta clout you with this club."

"Just what I need." He had never heard Brian so glum.

"Scat, you!" Ezekiel shooed the dog trying to sneak into the house. He closed the door.

"Now, let's get some light in here and get a look at you."

"No! Might be Yankees about."

"The blinds are shut. I'll keep it low."

Guarding the lamp's sooted chimney, he held the light to Brian.

"My, if you don't make a sight."

Mattie padded into the kitchen, "Lawdawmighty! What in the world you been doin', chile?" She looked closely, "where in the world you been?"

"Hello, Mattie."

Shaken by his tone, she took over, "But it don't make no nevermind. Y're here. Ezekiel, pour some water so's he can wash. He's thirsty, too. And I know y're hungry."

In short order Mattie had food on the table, rich milk from the spring house, slabs of her own bread, ham that smelled of hickory, half an apple pie left over from supper.

Brian ate without relish, bread and ham, no pie. He drank milk though, two glasses, answering questions with monosyllables. Mattie and Ezekiel flashed worried looks at each other for this wasn't the buoyant Brian they knew. Almost another person, disheveled, dull. Mattie noted too, he had no jolly compliment about her food as he usually did.

Brian ate in silence. Once finished, however, he started to talk. His voice carried little enthusiasm.

"I wanted to see you two weeks ago, when we left Winchester. But we marched right by. To Mount Jackson and turned around and marched back. We had a fight at Kernstown. They whipped us. Bad."

"Mattie and I, we heard it didn't we, Mattie."

Across the table, she nodded, "Sure 'nuff did."

Brian talked on, "Too many Yankees. All over, like . . ."

The word he wanted was within reach, but he didn't find it.

"Like bees in clover," Ezekiel interjected.

Brian never heard him.

"We marched up the turnpike and turned off into Yankees. We won some ground and they brought up more troops. We fought them off three, four, five times I lost track. Near dark we ran out of cartridges. I ran into the woods, carrying Charley. John Lyle and Captain Morrison were captured. Yankee cavalry cut them off."

"You were lucky, Brian."

"Yeh lucky, Charley was shot in the head," Brian answered flatly, "I put a bandage on it."

"In the head? He still alive?" Mattie asked innocently.

Brian's face clouded. For the first time, he showed spirit, "Damnit he was. The sawbones said he wasn't. I kept telling him but he wouldn't believe me. I carried Charley all night."

His voice became confidential, secretive, "Charley wasn't hurt bad. Only the skin broken. I bandaged him—carried him all night to a hospital. In a church with a wooden cross. I carried him—talked to him all night— he answered me, and he was alive."

Brian stared vacantly into his plate, "The sawbones said he was dead".

They waited for him to continue. He didn't.

Ezekiel scowled, sending frown lines up his dark forehead. He and Mattie locked eyes, exchanging their anguish. She parted her lips to speak, but he stopped her with a nod.

Brian stared blankly through the empty plate, all the time fingering the strap of his canteen. A graveyard hush descended on the kitchen, absolute but for Brian's constant fingers massaging the tooled leather. Mattie saw the tiny moves and with her eyes queried Ezekiel, "What's wrong? What can we do?"

Silently he replied, "I don't know."

"Brian."

She spoke very softly trying to break the spell.

His fingers continued their work. They had found another world and carried him into it.

"Brian," she rested finger tips lightly on his hand.

He looked from his work to her hand on his, and up to her face. Anything he said would have been welcome.

"Mattie, can I have a piece of pie? And milk?"

"Of course, chile."

She cut a double piece, placed it before him with a full glass of milk. He ignored them.

"After dark, I headed for the farm. It was close enough to pay you a visit. Besides," he grinned shyly, "I knew you'd feed me before the army would. Most of those fellows won't have much to eat this night."

Brian's voice was no longer strained. He adjusted the canteen strap on his shoulder, rested both hands quietly on the table. He smiled as if seeing them for the first time, "Now tell me how things are. Is everyone at home all right?"

Ezekiel exhaled a sigh of relief to be on familiar ground, "All right, considerin'. Your Ma, she goes like always, smilin' and cheerful. And your Pa, you know him! But I guess he has reason ta be upset. They're makin' it hard for him ta run his wagons and he's worried about . . ."

"Charley Nelson talked to me."

Ezekiel stopped in mid-sentence, puzzled. It wasn't like Brian to ignore family news. He frowned at the disconnection, looked at Mattie for assurance. She glanced back, revealing the same question. They waited. Their Brian had left them again.

"I carried him off the hill and he talked to me. Sawbones said he was dead." Brian's voice rose, "He wasn't dead when I brought him in. The goddamn doctor killed him."

He looked frantically around the room, from one corner to another and back. He jumped up from the table. The chair rasped on the floor boards. "Where's the goddamn sawbones?" The chair crashed backwards. "He killed Charley. Goddamn him, he killed Charley." Brian pounded his fist on the table top. "The goddamn sawbones killed Charley."

He looked through Ezekiel, through Mattie, without seeing either of them. As the full force of his guilt hit him, his face reflected his own confusion of Charley Nelson's demise, "No, not the doctor. I killed him. I should have bandaged him sooner. I fell asleep—I should have bandaged him first.

"I killed him. Oh, my God! I killed Charley." He sagged over the table, pounding it with his fist.

"My poor, poor boy," Mattie cooed as she came to him.

"He doesn't belong in the army, Ezekiel, he just doesn't belong there. He's just a boy, not tough 'nuff for the army."

Mattie's words hit home in a way she hardly expected.

"The hell I'm not. I'm tough as any of them. I've got to be getting back." He headed for the door.

Ezekiel intercepted him, "Briney, you aren't finished with your plate. The pie you aksed for is waitin'."

He obeyed as a small child, sitting again at the table, eating calmly, without any trace of the violence that had possessed him. Finished, he stood up, reached for his haversack.

"I'm all right, now. Sorry to carry on so."

"Maybe you should stay. Get a good night's sleep."

Brian sloughed off the suggestion, "I'd best be getting on while its still dark. Best supper I ever ate, Mattie."

"You be careful. There's no tellin' what's out there."

"I will, Zeke,—thank you, Mattie, for the extra food."

Brian slung his loaded haversack over a shoulder and slipped through the door into the early morning darkness.

At sun up, Winchester was dusty with confusion. Soldiers in blue with weapons, soldiers in gray, captured and disarmed, wounded soldiers of both colors carried on stretchers or helped along. A few citizens intermingled, seeking information of loved ones, inquiring, examining, searching ambulances, not entirely certain they wanted answers to their questions.

Henry saw Lieutenant Lyle and Captain Morrison amidst the shuffling prisoners. He knew neither of them, but recognized the brass "LHV" on their caps. He fell in alongside.

"Brian Morrow. Have you seen him? I'm his father."

John Lyle answered, "Not since the end of the battle. He was all right then. Escaped into the woods."

"Thank you. You are?"

"John Lyle. This is Captain Morrison. Tell Brian good luck."

"No palaver with the prisoners," a young voice rang out straining to sound tough. A boyish soldier in a coat much too big came toward Henry.

"You need anythin' write me. Henry Morrow Winchester."

"Get back there, y'damn rebel," the guard jerked his lowered bayonet toward the gutter. It flashed close to Henry's middle.

Seeing the contempt cloud his face, Sarah gasped a little scream, ran to him, embracing him tightly, saving the young soldier at least one blow, and Henry perhaps his life.

The column of prisoners and its young guard moved on.

Sarah clung to him, trembling.

"It's all right, sweetheart, it's over," he soothed until she relaxed. Try as he might, he failed to hide his anger.

"Henry, we have to forgive and forget. He's just a boy.

"The wounded ones need our help."

He was furious at the disdain of the young soldier, "Let the goddamn army take care of them, they're so goddamn smart. It's not our doin'."

Immediately, he was sorry, not for the sentiment but for the disrespectful use of profanity in Sarah's presence.

"Henry Morrow! I never thought to hear you say such a thing!

He argued day after day against her becoming involved with the wounded soldiers, fussing, fuming, resorting to a scowling silence when he ran out of words.

"We just can't do nothing. Those poor boys need help."

"Let the army take care of them. And the politicians. They're the ones that wanted this war."

"We've already had this discussion, Henry. You know you don't mean that."

"Hell, I don't," breaking again his own rule.

"Somebody has to step in."

"It doesn't have to be us."

"Yes, it does. There is nobody else."

"Sarah, you can't do it. You don't have the room, no supplies, no medicine, no anythin'. You aren't even a nurse."

"Henry Morrow," his wife shrilled, "how can you say that after the hours I've spent caring for the children. And the times you were ill and hurt. I've taken care of all of you, and no one has died. You had good and loving care, if I do say so myself."

"Now, Sarah, I didn't mean—you know what I mean."

Sarah pressed the advantage. "No, I don't know what you mean. Except that you don't want to help these poor boys. They're hurt, in need, and I intend to do what I can.

"Even though I am not a nurse," she snipped, walking from the room to clean bedrooms and rearrange them into sick rooms.

He persisted until she talked of Brian, "They are so pitiful. Some of them are no more than boys, no older than Brian. What if he's hurt somewhere and nobody helps him?"

A picture of Brian, suffering alone, crashed through Henry's obduracy, "All right, Sarah, all right. Do what you have to."

Sarah marshaled her family, Gracey and Betsy first, then as more wounded arrived, Ruth and Mam. Other households did the same, opening their homes and hearts to soldiers of both sides. They started by sharing food and cool drinks, milk and buttermilk until it ran out, then water; and by comforting them, propping heads, providing shade, bathing faces and hands; and by dealing with mangled flesh and blood despite their queasiness.

The Battle of Kernstown proved only the beginning for Winchester's generous people. Their strategic location in the lower Valley put them not only in harm's way, but also in mercy's path. The women became accomplished nurses as the floors of public buildings and private homes soaked up more and more American blood, Northern and Southern.

Sarah's days after the Kernstown fight were busier than she had ever known, far beyond the years of raising children. At first she had furnished simple refreshments to the soldiers, and almost at once found herself with a house full of the wounded.

She hadn't even poured coffee for Henry and said, "Let's talk about what's best to do."

With no choice he accepted, reluctantly and without grace, but also with love in his heart. When he saw her lugging extra furniture, he mumbled churlishly, "Here, I'll do that." He still groused, but from that day on he looked for ways to help.

The day after the Kernstown battle, Sarah was caring for three wounded soldiers, all Confederates. A Yankee doctor had found them on the battlefield.

"I couldn't just leave these three," he explained pitifully, through nightmares of all those who were left. He wrote an affidavit for each, attesting to wounds serious enough to keep them from ever fighting again. Two with shattered bones needed no such papers but he wrote them anyway; the right leg had been sawed off one, the left, off the other. The third affidavit was for a young man of the Stonewall Brigade who had survived the artillery fire on the hill. Afterwards, he was found smiling and working his mouth, but saying nothing.

"A shell that exploded too close," the doctor said, "better he had caught the shrapnel and died.

"Perhaps my testimonies will be of benefit to you—keep your patients from incarceration. Bless you." And he was gone.

That had been only the beginning.

By the next day, Sarah had two in each room, then three, Yankees and Confederates both. She ministered to them all the best she knew how, using what she had learned and what she felt. She cleaned their wounds not because she understood infection, but simply because clean was better than dirty. She fed them, talked to them, treated fever with onion poultices, and poured whiskey and kerosene on suppurated flesh.

Henry prowled about, muttering of the smells in 'that damn hospital' and of a wife too tired to take care of her home.

Still, he brought blankets from town, left them in the upstairs hall without a word to anyone, moved furniture, and told Betsy that both she and Sarah worked too hard.

"Get her to rest, Betsy," unable to tell Sarah directly.

"I do, Papa, but she shushes me."

Henry kept a wary eye on Gracey, reluctant to have her too close to the wounded soldiers. For the most part, his fears were unfounced for she disliked being around them. Their clothes smelled bad and they smelled bad. Their wounds were unpleasant at best, disgusting at their worst. For a time, she rolled bandages in the kitchen with Mam, avoiding the filth and stink.

She was able to accept only one of the wounded men, the young man of the Stonewall Brigade who had lost his hearing and worked his mouth in that silent, heart-rending way. At times he shook and hit his head, but Gracey seemed to see beyond. When he was upset, she was the only one who could quiet him.

A natural rapport existed between them, she accepting him as he was, and he aware of the gift she offered. She could get him to sit still, to wash himself, even to smile a bit. She could lead him by the hand when he would keep his distance from others. They walked to the verandah and across the lawn and he was tranquil. By signs, expressions, and pantomime, she talked to him. He responded in kind.

One day she gave him paper and a pencil. Write to your family, she pantomimed, and he did. She learned he was from New Market, not far up the Valley from Winchester, was in an all-Irish company of the 33rd Virginia, the Emerald Guards.

He followed her one day when Sarah called her from upstairs, "I need hot water and cotton batting."

"Here," Gracey stopped at the door of the bedroom. She extended the requested items at arms' length to Sarah.

"Bring them here."

Gracey clenched her teeth and inched toward her mother.

"Long as you're here, you might as well help. Put your things on the chair and hand me a piece of cotton."

Gracey obeyed.

Sarah worked loose a bloodied rag from a soldier's arm.

Without looking she held out the filthy dressing, "Take it," she ordered, swabbing with a piece of clean linsey. Gracey gaped at the raw flesh.

Sour stomach juices rose in her throat. She swallowed hard against them, ran from the room, brushing against Sarah and losing her finger-tip hold on the bloody rag. The young soldier from New Market ran after her. On the staircase she felt sticky blood on her hand and her stomach revolted again. Her young friend supported her and helped her to the kitchen.

Mam saw her dismay at once, "What's the mattuh, chile?"

Gracey worked her jaw, but "I've got blood on my hand" just wouldn't come out. All she could do was point, frantically. Mam could have laughed at the antics. But she didn't.

"My, my, isn't that somethin' now," she said lightly as she led Gracey to the sink and washed the soiled hand.

Two days later, Gracey's young soldier friend left with his father who had received the letter and come to take his son home.

"May the Blessed Virgin bless you, mam, bless you and yeer family," the father intoned in his brogue and burred "r's." He swiped roughly at his Irish tears and left.

Henry heard his words and went to Sarah. He put his arm around her, "You were right about nursing the soldiers."

Another day, Sarah threw on a shawl and stomped out of the house to General Banks' headquarters. His guard blocked her way with musket and bayonet.

"Young man, put that silly thing up." She pushed it aside like a small toll gate and was by him before he recovered.

The orderly sergeant leaned back at his field desk. "What's the . . .?" he tried to take charge, but Sarah cut him off.

"I need to see General Banks. And I will see General Banks."

"Mam, the general is busy."

"And so am I, young man," addressing him no differently than the guard who had followed her whining, "She barged in before I could stop her."

"Outside, soldier. See if you can keep the stray dogs out."

"And now I'll see the general, young man."

"The general is too busy to see anyone."

At this point, General Banks himself opened the door to his office, "What is this commotion, sergeant?"

Sarah waited for no answer but stepped close to the general so that he had to back a couple of steps into his office. She stepped across the threshold, too, almost breast to chest. Somewhat flustered, he retreated again to the safety of his desk.

"I am Sarah Morrow," she began.

"I know. I know who you are, Mrs. Morrow,—I know of your work. I also know Mr. Morrow, who has given me harsh words regarding licenses to operate his wagons."

"Then you know, sir, that I am caring for your soldiers in my home as well as General Jackson's men. They have received equal treatment, and now, sir, I ask the same of you. I need bandages, medicines, daily visits of a doctor. Not any doctor, mind you, but the best one you have. These young men deserve no less. I have one who needs morphia, and I have exhausted my supply. I have another with a leg turning black. I have done all I can, and now he needs a surgeon to amputate. If I knew how, I would do it myself."

"I believe you would, ma'am. Are these men yours or ours? I've heard tell you make no distinctions."

"General Banks, if you had been listening, you would have no need to ask. Furthermore, your question is un-Christianlike. I have given you that information, but I will say once more I do what I can for whoever needs help.

"Now, where do I go to get what I need? And I want an order from you for the doctor. Your best one. By name."

The general smiled. Despite what most Valley folks thought of him, he was a decent man, not a good general but a decent man.

"Mrs. Morrow, I have heard of your house of mercy. You shall have what you want, bandages, medicines, and my best doctor, for daily rounds as you have asked.

"Now if you will grant my headquarters the chance to return to its ordinary bedlam, and me the time to write your order, you shall have everything you ask."

"And when might I expect delivery, sir?"

"Within the hour, my good lady, within the hour."

General Nathaniel P. Banks was as good as his word.

XXIX

ROUNDABOUT RETURN

Brian rejoined his company at Newtown, an hour before Jackson's little army continued the retreat south, up the Valley. Jed found him and marched with the Liberty Hall Volunteers.

Many shuffled along with vacant, downcast eyes, mindlessly following the feet ahead, here and there a makeshift bandage. They carried their muskets for the least discomfort, at high angles and low, canted right and left, aimed at the ground, heaven, and in between. Jed carried his across both shoulders pincered between neck and raised arms that flapped like buzzards' wings; Brian, at an angle over his shoulder, stock skyward, fingers hooked loosely over the barrel.

"Yesterday was a bad one, Briney."

"Yeh."

"The artillery most drove me crazy. Thought they'd never stop. We shoulda been moles."

They walked in silence.

"One shell came so close it covered me with dirt from head t'foot. Came down like rain. When I looked up I saw this soldier dancin' one foot t'other and punchin' himself in the ear. Never saw anythin' like it."

Again they fell quiet. Jed puzzled at his brother. Briney was tuckered out, he figured, just didn't feel like talking. He chattered on to shorten the miles.

"Then waitin' at that stone fence, and the attacks. Just like Manassas waitin' for them t'come. Then they came one more time and we beat them off again. We were out of bullets and General Garnett pulled us out."

As he walked, Brian felt the pressure building again, like last night with Ezekiel and Mattie. He tried to control it, thinking of Washington College, home, a pitch black wall without light or sound, nothing but sheer blackness. Charley Nelson expanded in his head, and crashing bridges, faceless Zouaves, and another skewered with a ramrod.

His brother's voice grew in volume, louder and louder, until he could stand it no more.

"Jed, why in hell are you yelling like that, telling me all that. I was there."

"Briney, you feelin' all right?"

"I'm fine, damnit, just fine."

"Doesn't sound it t'me. You feelin' sick?"

"Just let it be."

That night, they finished Mattie's rations at Mount Jackson without conversation, one unhappy with himself, the other hurt with the anger.

In the weeks following the Kernstown fight, Jackson rested his men. The regiments filled as the sick and wounded filtered back. Toward the end of April, Jackson was reinforced with another division, Ewell's. He was ready to make his move.

Keeping his destination to himself, he marched off to the southeast, toward Richmond. At Mechum's Station, he pulled a surprise, turning west along the railroad instead of east as everyone expected, past Staunton and into the mountains beyond.

At McDowell, on May 8, he defeated a Federal army, pursued it a fruitless thirty miles through brutal country. Then, having marched 175 miles in fifteen days, he wound his way out of the mountains and angled northward through the foothills. Clearing the mountains, his men camped in their Valley and celebrated. They were going home!

As before, Jed marched and bivouacked with Brian.

"Jed, I'm sorry for the argument we had."

"What argument, Briney?"

"When I lost my temper. Marching up the Valley."

Jed had not forgotten, "I'm glad you left it behind."

"It was my fault. I was tired and fed up with the killing."

"I'm glad you got it out of your craw."

"But I'm not sure it is, Jed. I need to talk to you."

"Shoot! That's what I'm here for."

He motioned with his hand at the lounging soldiers around them, "Too many ears. Let's take a walk."

They followed a pretty run back toward the mountains until its tranquility became raucous, splashing over rocks, rushing its way toward the valley floor.

Jed heard music in it, "I wish Betsy was here."

"She'd make better company than me."

"I agree. You seem like you're sick or somethin'."

To Brian, the noisy water was insurance against eavesdroppers. He looked up at his brother, his dark eyes round and sad that brought to mind Ezekiel's Olehoundawg. His words were subdued, tinted with alarm, painted with resignation.

"Jed, I've got to get away from this."

The older brother started as if he were shot, reminded of himself almost a year past, "What do you mean, Briney?"

"Just have to get away. This army, Jed! it's too much."

"Briney, get a hold of yourself. We've marched a lot of miles—you're just tired. Runnin' off won't do any good."

"But, I can't—I don't know. . . ." His voice drifted off.

"I know exactly how you feel. Remember last summer when I felt the same way? I told you in John's tavern. You remember that, Briney?" Jed forced an answer, "Remember that?"

"Yes."

"I'm ready t'tell you now, I was wrong t'run off. I hadn't thought it through. What I'm tryin' t'tell you is t'think it through."

"There's nothing to think through. Charley Nelson is dead and I'm wearing his stripes," Brian's voice rose, "he's always with me. I can't get rid of him."

His voice fell to a whisper, "I can't forget him."

"You got to, Briney, you have t'let him go."

"I'm telling you I can't," his voice raced on, "I want to, but I can't. I can't get rid of him. I can't get rid of any of them. I should have bandaged Charley sooner but I didn't and he died. Every time I look at these sergeant's stripes I know they're his. They still belong to him and I killed him."

Jed startled at the distress he heard, "Damn it, Briney, get that out of your head. You didn't kill him."

Knowing his brother's problem was beyond the relief of whiskey or a night's sleep, he reacted intuitively, touching Brian's shoulder. "Everythin' will be all right, Briney, everythin' will be all right," he intoned as he had quieted overwrought horses in better days. He drew him closer, murmured softly, "It'll be all right, Brineyboy."

He patted Brian's shoulder, whispering,

"You need some time t'rest and forget.

"You need some time, little brother, just need some time."

He patted again, softly.

"Just need some time t'forget."

He held his brother for many minutes, patting, soothing, comforting with the metrical phrases he used with horses. He felt Brian's tension drain away.

He chose his words carefully, spoke compassionately, as firmly as he dared, hoping Brian would listen, "You can't run off, Briney. You'd be runnin' from Pa and Ma,—mostly from yourself. I don't believe that's what you want."

Jed pressed gently, "Briney, think it through—promise me you won't do anythin' without talkin' t'me first."

Brian agreed, mechanically, with little conviction.

Jed took him by the shoulders, "Look at me, Briney, eye to eye." He spoke more sternly, unintentionally sounding like Henry when he was displeased, "Brian, I mean it. No ifs or maybes. You come t'me first. If you leave, I'll hunt you down and—and—carry you back in a grain sack."

He chuckled at the vision he had suggested.

"What the hell's so funny?"

"Just the thought of you stuffed and tied in a sack, with your head stickin' out like a Thanksgivin' turkey." And his soft chuckle became a full fledged belly laugh that caught Brian.

He smiled despite himself, "Thanksgiving—! Jed, you're a turkey yourself." He had never felt closer to his brother.

Then Jed became serious again, "Just talk t'me when you need to, Briney. Promise?"

"Promise."

Too worn to continue and too proud to quit, Jackson's soldiers lurched down the Valley turnpike on sheer grit. Men dozed on their feet. Many simply collapsed, the spoor of an exhausted army dragging its way to battle. They had been on the road for seventeen hours, nipping at Banks' rear.

In the past few days, they had marched more than a hundred miles, fought at Front Royal, engaged the Federal rear guard near Middletown, and drove now to catch the Federal main body before it reached the Winchester heights.

They might have caught it, too, had it not been for the abandoned goods along the Valley pike, sutlers' stores, bottled wines, whiskey by the barrel, and wrecked supply wagons marked "US." It all proved irresistible to soldiers whose last meal was yesterday's breakfast.

The macadamized road was dotted with the fires of burning wagons, and the silhouettes of others simply deserted. Even Jackson stopped to munch on hardtack he found. Up ahead, new fires flared as scurrying Yankees torched still more wagons.

In the peripheral darkness, muskets flashed suddenly, popped, and were gone, riflemen harrying the pursuers.

At one o'clock in the morning, May 25, they drudged along.

"Press on, men, press on."

More men dropped. The army was a broken snake of a column, the van two miles south of Winchester. The colonel of the 37th Virginia reined up before Jackson and pleaded, half his regiment had fallen out of ranks. Rest the army, he said, or we'll have none to fight come daylight. Jackson's implicit apology was as close as he would ever come to making one, "Colonel . . . I am obliged to sweat them tonight, that I may save their blood tomorrow." Then, in the dark night above Winchester, he yielded and ordered a one-hour halt.

The commander of the 5th Virginia was up ahead, alert, seeking signs of the Federals. Joining him, Jackson listened, too, and stood sentry duty over his sleeping army. Maybe Banks had to halt, too, he hoped, and was strung out unprotected on the road; maybe he could still be caught.

At 4 o'clock, the respite was over.

"Press on, men, press on."

Jed moved cautiously into the darkness, straining to see ahead, to check the ground for his next step. When a hole threw him off balance he mumbled, "Damnit," and when wet ground sucked at his shoe, mumbled again, "Shit." He kept moving, as best he could in the dark, pretty sure he had the right direction.

Assigned as skirmishers for this attack on the Yankee-held hill, his company stretched across the low ground, out ahead to feel for the enemy. The early morning darkness curtained off each man. Their extended front increased the sense of isolation. An eerie sense of lonely suspension fell over the skirmishers. "Where the hell is everybody?"

Every one of the Winchester Rifles felt the loneliness and the growing tenseness that gripped Jed. Uncertainties of direction and distance plagued some as they advanced. Taut imaginations gnawed at others, creating distortions of who, what, and where. Tension wrenched at them, inviting graveyard panic.

As they moved forward, tiny noises became alarm bells, broadcasting their approach. The slightest crack of a twig or swish of long grass made a crashing boom, raising visions of an enemy within knife range, stealing the breath from their lungs, echoing hollow in pumping hearts.

The light of dawn helped some, but the early mists rising from Abraham's Creek created their own ghostly illusions.

Jed was the first to climb the gentle incline that ranged north as Bower's Hill on the edge of town. From the top, he looked east to the turnpike, a scant half mile away, and north where the pike entered Winchester and became Loudoun Street, Main to the oldsters. The square tower of Christ Episcopal Church broke the dawn-wet canopy of trees. To the west of town he saw the high ground where Banks had dug in during the night. Peering closely, he counted twelve, spooky guns taking shape, emerging in the dusky light of the new day. Beyond was Apple Pie Ridge.

He looked to the east where a pencil line of gray pushed at the darkness, climbing wider and coloring blue. Enchanted, he soaked up the new day. Soon eastern clouds glistened pink; the radiance flowed up and up and up.

When he looked again, he marveled as always at the miracle of the expanding light, for the whole sky was there to be seen, golden daylight now in the eastern arc, darkness turned azure in the western, a spectrum of blue connecting one to the other. As Jed watched, a bit of sun edged the horizon. It reached northward along the shadow of the Blue Ridge and southward, and grew fat. He looked, admired, and forced himself again to the business at hand. He inspected Banks' hill again, half expecting an attack.

While Jed wavered between the brilliant sky-scape and Yankee tactics, Jackson advanced his Division, his own brigade with Jed's and Brian's regiments on the right, closest to the hard-surfaced Turnpike. General Winder was its commander. On his left, to the west, was Campbell's Brigade, then Taliaferro's. Taylor's Louisiana Brigade was held in reserve.

Brian's regiment, the 4th Virginia, was closest to the turnpike, Jed's 2nd Virginia and Winder's other three regiments extending westward from the 4th. They splashed through Abraham's Creek at the foot of Jed's hill, dressed their lines and started up. As he climbed, Brian looked in vain for his brother.

A half mile to the east, Ewell's Division was on the plank road from Front Royal closing on Winchester.

Winder's Brigade advanced, following Jed and the skirmishers up the hill. Their line bent as only the strongest kept the pace, showed gaps and broke where those of weary muscle and waning lung power lagged. It sagged uneven as men slowed to angle around obstructions, straightened again when the strongest halted at the military crest, allowing others to catch up.

White clouds puffed from Yankee cannons opposite. A year ago, the men had puzzled at the silent puffs of smoke, but they had learned. The delayed booms thudded in, then the shells. The pounding increased as all twelve Yankee guns went into action. Brian crouched in the wheat field occupied by his regiment.

Two rifled guns careered past Jed, unlimbered, and returned the fire. A battery of Napoleons joined them, smooth-bore twelve-pounders, then another. The guns dueled.

Jed thought of moles and Jonathan, puzzling the combination. Then he remembered turning to Jonathan at Henry Hill, saying something about moles and digging into the earth.

He watched a Yankee battery deploy to its right, supported by sharpshooters behind a stone fence. Their advanced position gave them an oblique angle on Taliaferro and the Confederates beyond him, threatening enfilade fire. A direct hit on a Confederate gun increased the advantage. The oblique fire pinned Jackson's troops to the ground. His attack was stalled.

Jackson sent his reserve brigade, Taylor's Louisianans, around to his left to get those Federal guns. They used the defile of Abraham's Creek across the rear, and emerged on the flank. Yankee guns on the hill redirected their fire.

The Louisianans were a hard lot, recruited along the waterfront, led by a commander who, if anything, was even tougher. When they flinched under the heavy cannon fire, Taylor halted them, threatened to hold them for an hour if there was any more of it. Exposed with them, he bawled his threat, and then ordered the advance to continue. The colonels shouted to their regiments; the captains, to their companies. The men dressed their lines, stepped off as if on the parade ground, despite the barrage. They climbed the hill in normal cadence, ninety steps a minute toward the guns. Jed watched respectfully as they payed their dues.

Two stone fence rows broke their line. Scrambling over, they straightened the line and continued up the hill, completely exposed, into the guns. They controlled the urge to hurry on, holding their formation at the cost of casualties and tortured nerves. Tension built to explosion level. The guns fired at point blank range. For God's sake, general! Turn us loose!!

The general knew his men, knew their limitations and fears as if he read their minds. He was proud of them, and they, of him. Proud, hard, and tough were the general and his men, and primed to fight. He raised his sword. They anticipated his order.

"Forward, double quick, CHARGE!"

The Louisianans stormed forward, overlapping the Federal flank, and fought hand-to-hand at the stone fence.

Released from the terrible barrage, Jed and Brian charged with their comrades, giving new life to Jackson's attack from the west and the south. The Yankee position was threatened.

Now the Louisianans fought amongst the guns. Jed and his Valley folks, Brian and his College students pushed into them adding to the pressure. The Yankees fell back. Confederates captured several of the guns, tried to turn them on their previous owners.

The Yankees regrouped. Countercharged. They fought again among the guns with fists and clubbed muskets. Yankees regained partial control, hauling off what guns they could. Confederates spiked the rest.

Across the turnpike, 1,500 yards east, old curmudgeon Isaac Trimble, of Ewell's Division, howled his brigade forward, leading the attack down the Front Royal road. He met resistance at the Indian Springs, even more at Camp Hill, but Jackson's success across the turnpike threatened to flank these Yankees and they had to fall back.

Jed charged down the face of his hill, into the environs of Winchester and eastward to Main Street. He continued north. Up ahead, Yankees stopped in the street, turned to fire to the rear, ran some more.

Those ahead had set fire to Winchester's Market House and other buildings appropriated for Union warehouses. A few of the bravest piled makeshift barricades to defend the intersections. Other stalwarts made a stand in courthouse square, only to be surprised by Winchester soldiers familiar with the alleyways and hidden passages.

Block by block, Jed advanced watchfully, not hanging back but happy enough when Bluecoats up ahead melted away. Muskets popped. Lead minie balls hummed close and splatted harmlessly into brick walls. A hundred yards ahead he saw a jury-rigged barricade, a farm wagon on its side, barrels and planks piled to the brick walks. That could be trouble.

A few, grim-faced citizens ventured into the streets to fight alongside their soldiers. Others fired weapons from second story windows, threw knives, chamber pots, and boiling water. Jed hoped they knew Confederates from Yankees.

Suddenly, he felt a thud in his left leg. It gave out—he went tumbling. "Whatthehell?"

He looked at the leg without understanding, made an effort to stand on it. It wouldn't hold him. He lay in the street contesting the pain and the blackness.

He moaned and writhed, barely conscious as the hot pain traveled his entire body, searing his leg. He stared dully. Somebody was slapping his face.

He wondered about the hole near his knee. Woolen thread ends stained red. Abruptly, he knew he'd been shot. He objected.

"It can't be."

The stains spread. The pain grabbed his leg, up and down, stinging, throbbing. And he knew.

He grabbed the stain with both hands, held tight. People were gathering about him now, men in homespun without blanket rolls or canteens, women in bonnets and aprons.

"My God! It's Jed Morrow." The voice was familiar. Jed concentrated on it, trying to identify the owner. Josiah Dunbar the butcher. A memory of him on referendum day a year ago flashed across Jed's brain.

The leg pulsed, excruciating, hot to the touch, making Jed's head swim, "Mr. Dunbar? That you?" And Jed Morrow lost his bearings again.

"Come on, boys, we gotta git 'im home."

"Where's he live?"

"Wolfe Street."

"First lemme wrap that leg tight so's it don't bleed."

Meanwhile, Brian had crossed the turnpike and came into Winchester two blocks east of Jed, near the end of Kent Street. He zig-zagged west, north, and west to Main Street where he turned north again. He had missed Jed by minutes.

With the Liberty Hall Volunteers, Brian pursued the fleeing army past the courthouse. Just north of the town line, he raised his musket and fired at a group of Bluecoats up ahead. One dropped, thrashing in the weeds that lined the road. Behind him, ecstatic citizens emerged from their houses and cellars.

They embraced their own soldiers and hindered the pursuit, but they didn't care. Smoke from Yankee fires filled half the town, but they didn't mind that either. They tore down the barricades, formed bucket brigades to fight the fires, saved stores in boxes marked "USARMY," foodstuffs, clothing, and more medical supplies than they had ever seen. They filled the streets with their shouts and laughter, dancing, and celebrating. This was their day of liberation.

In the house on Wolfe Street, Henry Morrow laughed and gave in to his women, "But just in the front yard. You can see enough of the excitement from there."

Of course, they weren't satisfied and pestered him again. "Oh, Pa, the celebration is over on Main Street," Racey pleaded.

"We can watch from Uncle John's tavern, Papa Morrow. We'll be safe there," from Betsy.

"Yes, Pa, let's go to the tavern. Everybody will be there," Ruth echoed, "Mam can manage my little ones."

Two blocks east and two south, Josiah Dunbar ran for a make-do stretcher. Despite their opposing politics, he and Henry Morrow were still neighbors, and his neighbor's son was in need.

"Henry, my love, you're outvoted—don't be so glum about it. This is a day for celebration. For the whole town to dance, laugh, and rejoice."

"But, Sarah . . ."

She could see nothing but joy and liberty in their future, and that demanded a gala festival to bury the memory of uninvited Yankees, "But nothing, my darling."

Henry flashed surprise at the endearment, for it was one she seldom used. He was even more surprised at what came next.

"It's Camelot, my darling. It's Camelot,—the good knights have defeated the bad infidels, they're running and we're safe again, and we can all sleep peacefully tonight."

She danced lightly alongside him as he gave in, holding his hand, smiling radiantly. She hugged his arm and snuggled close. She stopped at the red oak that marked the corner of their property, twisted him around to face her, and lifted her face to his. Right there on Wolfe Street, she kissed him on the mouth. "I love you, Henry Morrow."

"I can look for Jed and Brian," Racey read the signs correctly and tested further, hurrying ahead.

"Stay together!"

"Yes, children, do as your father says." Sarah tucked her arm through his and leaned into him. Racey waited.

Back on Main Street, Josiah Dunbar dropped an old door alongside Jed, "Here. This'll do." He took Jed's blanket roll for padding. "One of you take the weight of his leg. Gentle now! He hurts enough." They headed down Main Street with their burden.

Henry and Sarah walked down Wolfe Street, crossed Braddock, a short block from Main. The three girls had raced ahead again.

Sarah came back to earth. She squeezed her husband's arm, seeking confirmation for her own joy, "Do you think it's over, Henry? Oh, I have prayed so for it to be ended."

They saw a small group of men turn the corner, "Why! It's Josiah Dunbar. Haven't seen much of him lately."

They came closer.

Betsy screamed, "It's Jed! Mumma. Papa. It's Jed!"

XXX

REUNION

While Stonewall Jackson schemed to disrupt Nathaniel P. Banks' future in the Shenandoah Valley, McClellan planned strategy on a grand scale, no straightforward advance on Richmond through Manassas as Mc-Dowell had done. Instead of that, he petitioned Lincoln with a plan worthy of his generalship, a march up the peninsula between the James and York Rivers. Lincoln was skeptical, but ultimately approved the plan.

First, "Little Mac's" army would have to be transported from Alexandria to Fortress Monroe guarding Hampton Roads. A veritable armada would have to be assembled to carry it 175 miles down the Potomac River and Chesapeake Bay, more than 100,000 men with all the wagons, cannons, equipment, and supplies to support them—also horses, thirty to forty thousand of them, with adequate forage. And shovels.

Stanton's Assistant Secretary of War, John Tucker, was hard-pressed to charter the seagoing vessels necessary, but he did his job well, signing 289 steamships, schooners, and barges. McClellan loaded, unloaded at his destination, and started his army northward.

Twenty miles up the peninsula from Fortress Monroe, John B. Magruder, known as "Prince John" for his love of pomp and theatrics, guarded Yorktown. With a single division of 11,000 men and an active imagination, he created the illusion of a much larger defense force, marching the regiments in and out of sight. Prince John's fakery bought enough time for Joe Johnston's army to reinforce him. Stuart's cavalry was with him.

McClellan watched the tactical stage play, enter left/exit right, counting, recounting, over-estimating his opponent. He would prove the perennial exaggerator of opposing forces, with or without theatrics. At Yorktown, he put out feelers and decided against an attack. Instead, he would dig in and besiege the place.

For a month, he entrenched, collected supplies, and bombarded, badgered Washington for more men, and watched from aloft. His observation balloons were an historical first.

Finally, reports indicated that the Confederates had vacated the York River town, inviting occupation by anyone willing to make the effort. McClellan walked in on May 6, three days after Magruder pulled out. The Confederates fell back, joining other forces on the defense line named for Williamsburg.

From Yorktown, McClellan advanced slowly, the delayed start of a two-month campaign to take Richmond.

After Stuart's parade through the cheering crowds of the capital, his troopers trotted down the peninsula, 1200 strong. David and John Pelham enjoyed the pretty countryside and shaded road past Shirley, Berkeley, and the other James River plantations, through Williamsburg and beyond. For two weeks Stuart covered the extreme right of Johnston's Warwick River line as far as Blow's Mill.

In early May, he formed his troopers on Telegraph Road to harass the advancing Yankees. The area was low and swampy, funneling the huge Yankee army into a few narrow roads. Stuart positioned Pelham's flying battery on the left where it had a clear field of fire into a division of cavalry hindered by the swamp. Pelham made full use of his advantage until the Federals brought up larger guns. He had to fall back, along with Stuart's main body. Stuart sent David with a situation report for Johnston up near Williamsburg.

A short distance out, David ran into a Federal column coming in from the right. Without hesitation, he reined Sable about and galloped back to report his discovery.

"Too big a force for us," he advised.

Stuart accepted his estimate, evaded the threat by angling toward the James and the river beach that skirted the danger. Dawn brought them to Johnston's line and an easier day.

While infantry fought in the mud, defending the Williamsburg line and its crucial Fort Magruder, the troopers were held in reserve. Stuart himself rode to army headquarters, making himself available as necessary.

Aide-de-camp David Morrow went with him. He had little to do until late in the battle when he was summoned to deliver an order to the Washington Artillery to fall back.

"Major Walton and his guns are near Fort Magruder," Jeb Stuart added. David galloped off.

Unexpectedly, he rode into Tom Rosser's Second Company, hard pressed near the fort. Rosser was busy laying one of the guns.

"What the hell are you doing up here?"

David laughed, "I'm reserve force. Ready to save you. But first I have orders for your major to pull back."

"Save hell! We're holding our own. Hey, Duffy," Rosser called one of his men, "Captain Morrow has a message. Take it to battalion." Sweaty, hard-pressed, serious as usual, he attended to his gun, then turned again to David shouting, "Over there, number two gun needs help. You remember anything about real guns?"

"Yes, sir," in mock deference. David raced to the gun and fired off half a dozen rounds before his message cleared Major Walton and came back to Rosser.

"Battalion's moving," Rosser yelled in his battlefield voice that could be heard a half mile when he wanted, "limber up and move."

"Tom, you know where to find me if you need help again," David grinned and rode off. Rosser's response, not entirely unfriendly, followed after him, "Go to hell."

McClellan moved inexorably up the peninsula to West Point, his right wing on the York River. Like angry bees, Stuart's troopers stung at him repeatedly, keeping him off the Confederate rear. Every day, early dawn into the dark, David scouted, unaware that his cadet friend, George Custer, was in the area mapping routes for the Yankee army.

After a sharp fight at Eltham's Landing, three of McClellan's divisions and his reserve artillery continued up the Pamunkey River, camping on the broad fields of Cumberland. The two-story plantation house overlooked green fields that sloped to a picturesque bend in the river, folding it into lush woods upstream and down.

While McClellan rested three days at Cumberland, Johnston dug in around Richmond, close enough to hear the city's church bells. He had fallen back as far as he could.

McClellan inched his way toward the city.

In the Richmond environs, Stuart named his camp Quien Sabe, "Who knows?" His choice was a fitting one at this stage of the war,—for David, too, whose thoughts had gravitated more and more to Carrie as he drew closer to Richmond. Until he saw her, he could only wonder, "Who knows?"

Was she still in Richmond? Did she move as she said she would? Was she still interested in seeing him? Maybe. Maybe not. Who knows?

At the end of May, Johnston was wounded at Seven Pines, and Robert E. Lee assumed command of the army that would ever after be known by the name he himself had used unofficially. Beauregard had called it the Army of the Potomac; Jeff Davis, the Army of Richmond. To General Lee, it had always been the Army of Northern Virginia.

His preference surely must have been born in a dream of taking his army back to Arlington County, as it was known then, and recapturing Mrs. Lee's columned birthright on the hill. His lyrical label stuck, exciting the image of ragged and proud men swinging loosely down the road.

At "Quien Sabe", David drew up an order for the outposts, "For your approval, general." Stuart scratched his signature.

"A personal request, sir?"

"Yes?"

"Permission to go into Richmond. Be back before reveille."

"Come on, captain, I'll race you part way. I have business at the War Department."

Breaking off on Church Hill, at the house near St. John's, David told himself he only wanted to see how that young lady was getting on. He thought of her that way to keep her at a distance, but her name kept popping into his head, Carrie, Carrie. As he mounted the stone steps from the sidewalk, he couldn't deny his excitement. Nagging thoughts tweaked yet again, what if she wasn't there, what if she hadn't even moved from the hotel. He lifted the door knocker.

"No, she's not here, young man," a gray-haired lady snapped. She tilted her sharp chin ever so slightly as she raised a silver lorgnette to inspect David and his uniform. She looked closely, a veritable inspector general.

"Just so you understand my rules, visitors are not allowed," she paused, enunciating crisply, "beyond the front parlor."

David flashed his most appealing smile, "I'm happy to hear that, ma'am, very happy indeed."

The gray-haired lady, not an inch over five feet tall, was visibly surprised at his reply, for men in uniform, she thought, were nothing but rascals, rapscallions, and rogues. Ne'er-do-wells, every last one. She knew how they carried on. Like a body wouldn't believe.

"Will you tell her I'll be back? My name is David Morrow."

"As long as you obey the rules," she sniffed.

As David thanked her, another voice tugged at him from behind, a familiar one that pulled at the corners of his mouth, "Why don't you tell her yourself, David Morrow?"

He turned, to see Carrie, one hand extended, the other holding a reticule. Butterfly hands, he remembered, and reached for the one

"What a surprise!" she gushed, breathless from excitement or from running, no way to tell which, "whatever are you doing here?"

Always sure he would try to see her, the question surprised him, "To see how you were getting on. I said I would, didn't I."

"I wasn't sure you meant it. People say things."

Her doubt surprised him, "Now you know me better."

She should have known. As he had always known.

Carrie's landlady reached for the reticule, "Let me take that inside, dear. Maybe you would like to sit on the swing."

"Why thank you, Mrs. Burgess."

She pulled David toward the wide swing chained into the verandah ceiling. They sat, David stiffly with his hands on his thighs. They let the swing rock to and fro, one not sure that he should be here, the other sorry her words had unsettled him.

"David, you really did surprise me. Maybe I feared I would never see you again, afraid to raise my hopes. Anyway. I am very glad you're here."

"To be honest, I guess I had doubts, too. I wasn't completely sure you'd leave the hotel."

"Now I'm upset," she pouted.

"I'm sorry, it's the first I've been in Richmond since I saw you. I've been on the Peninsula."

"Was it bad? I read about it and thought of you every day."

Her hand brushed over his ever so lightly, lingering. He watched her graceful fingers, "You did!"

"Of course," she lowered her eyes modestly, "I was worried."

Not quite sure of herself, she moved to withdraw her hand. David gently stopped her.

"Many had it worse than I did. I was at Williamsburg and Eltham's, but mostly I was just riding and scouting, trying to keep the Yankees away from our army."

"I read about those. It sounded terrible, especially Williamsburg. Oh, David, I hoped so that you weren't there."

"I was there all right, but just for a short time. Not as long as some of my friends. But tell me about you, everything since I left you that morning at the hotel."

"Oh, wasn't that awful. I am so ashamed of being there, even if it was for only one night. David, I am so ashamed."

"Don't be. You moved out didn't you. A good night's sleep anywhere is nothing to be ashamed about."

"I did sleep well that night, soundly and happily thanks to you. I want to tell you again that I will repay the money you left with me."

"And I want to tell you again, 'Forget it'."

She smiled, "We've had this conversation before—nothing has changed. I will repay it."

"If you insist. Just stick to the original terms. Pay me when the war is over. That was our agreement.

"Now tell me all that you've done."

As she turned toward him, her breasts strained against the bodice of her dress, creating starbursts of calico darts. Below, her hands fluttered, playing with his fingers.

Peripherally, David caught the fluttering, thought butterflies again. He flicked his eyes from the rise and fall of her breathing, forcing himself from the twin curves. Staring like a damned schoolboy, he berated himself, maybe she hadn't noticed. Her first words floated in from some far off place, boring into his thoughts, "I did just what you wanted me to do. First thing that morning, I packed my things and came here. Luckily, a room was available. Mrs. Burgess is like a second mother."

"So I gather," he shook his head approvingly, "no visiting beyond the parlor. She really means that, doesn't she?"

"Indeed she does," Carrie sighed not without a note of dissidence, "no second chance. More than one has been told to leave since I've been here, one in the middle of the night along with her guest."

"Not like the Exchange Hotel," he teased, "sitting in Mrs. Burgess's parlor is pretty old-fashioned by comparison."

Her smoky blue eyes darkened, less blue, more smoke, "That was not nice, not nice at all."

Contrite, he agreed, "You're right! It wasn't. I'm sorry."

Without hesitation, she gave it right back to him, flirting outrageously, "Sorry about what you said, or sorry about Mrs. Burgess's rule? Sorry about the rule is what you are, David Morrow, and sorry you can't take me upstairs."

He answered altogether too quickly, "Oh no. It's just that—just—uh—well—uh—it just sounds old-fashioned that's all."

They let the swing sway gently for several minutes, David embarrassed at his less than unblemished thoughts, Carrie uncomfortable with her memories of the Exchange Hotel. Meeting there as they had, the idea of walking into a bedroom together was not difficult to entertain, but there was a growing friendship to consider, one that had become important to each of them.

"David, now I am sorry. I shouldn't have said that. After all, we've only known each other for a short time."

"No, don't apologize. I was the one who started it. I was trying to be funny and I didn't stop to think. Carrie, I've thought of you since I left, wondering what had happened to you. I didn't even know if you were still in Richmond,—that was the worst part. I was afraid I would never see you again."

"Isn't that strange. For I've thought of you, too, and wondered if I would ever see you again."

She twisted her little handkerchief, "I was afraid, too. Now you'll have to leave again, and I'll be afraid again."

"Young man," Mrs. Burgess appeared in the front door, "I know you must be hungry. All young men your age are."

David demurred, "Oh no, I'm fine thank you,"

"Fine or not, I have the tea steeped and sweets on the table," she opened the door wider and waited. Her stance left no room for refusal.

David held her chair at the dining room table, glancing quickly at a table set very properly, sterling tea service in front of her, a silver tray of 'sweets', scones and tarts, linen tea napkins, delicate china, and gleaming flatware all precisely in place. He hurried around to hold Carrie's chair.

Mrs. Burgess poured, "Sugar? Milk?"

Elegantly, she extended her fingers toward the tray, "Please help yourself. The scones are Scottish, not like most you find nowadays.'

The conversation was agreeable, as it should be for tea, on rising prices, the gentlemanly South, the shameful North. Gradually, other concerns crept in as Mrs. Burgess went on to query David.

She started with tactful questions concerning his family, worked her way toward her real goal. Was he good enough for this attractive girl who had become a second daughter to her? David recognized the inspection for what it was. He had no objections for he quickly realized that her efforts were to protect Carrie. Quite the contrary, he knew that Carrie had found a home.

"She has taken a liking to you," Carrie said later as they strolled East Broad Street toward the temporary hospital at Chimborazo.

"She did seem to warm up a bit. Her greeting would have scared a bear."

"She whispered to me that you said you were happy with her 'no farther than the parlor' rule. You impressed her with that."

"I meant it, Carrie, for her concern is for you as well as for her own sense of propriety. She surely has your welfare at heart, judging by the questions at tea. It reminded me of West Point and some of the interrogations I went through as a cadet."

They turned the curve that had hidden Chimborazo's make-shift hospital, tents and wooden buildings. Seeing them, Carrie stopped short as if she had run into an invisible barrier.

"No further, David. That's where my brother was. Where he died." She turned back. David caught up.

"I'm sorry. You told me about him, and I should have known better than to walk you here."

"I did?"

"The first night we . . . ," he hesitated, "his picture was on the dresser. You were twins, you said, and he was wounded. You came to Richmond to care for him. Then he—was gone. And you were left alone, no friends, no money."

"He died, David, I've made my peace with that.

"We were so close, not just brother and sister, but really twins. We liked the same things and laughed at things together, sometimes when no one else did. We were happy together and unhappy together. We thought alike and often knew what the other was going to say before he said it. That was eerie."

Carrie lapsed into silence. David respected her need, walking alongside her quietly, giving her the chance to remember and recover. He did seek her hand, holding it gently as they walked back to the house.

"Thank you, David."

"For what, Carrie? I didn't do anything."

"That's what I thank you for, understanding and being patient. I haven't been very good company."

"On the contrary. You've been excellent company. Nothing wrong with quiet. Most people talk too much, anyway."

She smiled at his gentle humor, "I haven't even told you about my job."

"You took a job! That's wonderful."

"Thanks to you and your letter to Mr. Boteler. He was so nice. He said, 'I know just the place', scribbled a note and sent me to the Secretary of War's office. Mr. Walker asked for a sample of my handwriting. When I gave it to him, he hired me right away as his clerk—with a desk right down the hall from his office."

"Carrie, that is wonderful. I am so happy for you."

"Mr. Walker is such a busy man. He has to work far into the night. Too busy for his own good health.

"Thank you for your letter to Mr. Boteler."

"I'm glad he could help. He's been a friend of my father's for a long time. From the first day my father was in Winchester. Even before he met Ma."

"He waves to me sometimes on his way to the Secretary's office."

"You surely have impressed him, else he wouldn't do that. So you see, you won your job on your own merit. Working where you are, you probably know more about the war than I do."

"Not from sitting in a chair and reading things. I am very busy, but you have been there.

"David, was it very bad?"

"Not so bad that it won't get worse before it's over."

"Do you think it will be worse?"

"Yes. Most think one big battle will put an end to it. But I'm not sure. Lincoln is strong for the Union, and I don't see anything that looks like a change of mind.

"McClellan's close to Richmond, ready to fight. That's going to make the last few weeks look like child's play. If he's successful, maybe the war will end with one big battle.

"With Richmond gone, northern Virginia is lost and more than likely the Shenandoah Valley. Without the Valley, Richmond will starve to death."

"Oh, I hope it doesn't end like that. David, I hope not."

"Carrie, I want you to promise me one thing."

"But I do want it to be over soon."

"Carrie, listen to me. I want you to promise."

"Yes?"

"Whatever happens, stay right here with Mrs. Burgess."

"But, David, maybe if it happens like you say, it would be safer to move south. Get away from the Yankees."

"The problem with that is that I may never find you again. People get moving around and they drop out of sight. One of us has to stay put." Suddenly his face clouded.

"David, what is it?"

"Nothing."

"Of course, it's something. David, what's bothering you?"

"Maybe it's because—oh, nothing," he stood, "I have to be getting back to camp."

"David Morrow, you are not leaving on that note. Tell me what's bothering you. What is it?"

Caught for the moment in his pessimism, he searched for the right words, "Carrie, it just struck me that—that—maybe you aren't as anxious to see me again, as I am to see you."

She lifted from the swing, standing in front of him. She clasped his hands, "David Morrow, you are a goose. Of course I want to see you again. I want you to find me, just as you did today. I do promise that I will be here, just as I have been every day since you left, waiting for you."

She hesitated a moment before moving toward him.

They didn't notice the flutter of the curtain in the front window. Behind it, Mrs. Burgess smiled serenely. A well-set, afternoon tea had always been her favorite kind of party.

XXXI

CASUALTY

Sarah stopped short, frozen to the street by Betsy's scream. What was she screaming about? Who yelled for Jed? Was that her? Wounded. Who was wounded? Jed couldn't be wounded. Not Jed. Only other sons were wounded. Not mine. Not mine. Only others'. Not mine. Henry! Henry! Why are you running? Betsy, where are you going? Gracey! What's the matter with everybody? Jed wounded? Not Jed. NO! NO! She turned frantically to Ruth, eyes wide, hands raised in supplication.

Everything had been so right, everyone so happy. I was filled with joy, as if I had shed half my years. It can't be true. God! make it not true. Make it not true!

She felt Ruth's arms about her.

Betsy and Henry crowded close to the makeshift litter. Gracey followed. She slowed, then hesitated, not sure she wanted to see.

Josiah Dunbar tried to help, "Jed'll be all right, Henry. It's his leg. Listen to me, Sarah, he'll be all right."

"Thanks be to God. And to you, Josiah," Henry forgot his enmity. "You hear that, Sarah? Jed's going t'be all right."

Sarah heard neither of them. She spoke in a soft voice, "I have to see my son." Ruth walked with her.

Henry stood at Jed's head; Betsy, at his side holding his hand. Languidly, Jed raised an arm, "Hello, Mumma."

At his voice, she ventured a tiny smile. Briefly it curled about and dissolved as quickly as it came. With caressing fingertips, she touched his hand, tears in her eyes. She clutched his hand to her breast, wanting to hold him close as she had when he was small and helpless, clasp him tight to her own body, soothe his hurt. She felt again what she had felt then, that if she could hold him close enough, her love would flow from her body into his. And her love would heal him.

A memory of a fiery fever flashed in her mind, one that had gripped him as a child, turning his small body crimson and causing delirium. For two days, she had fought for her son with all her energy and all her love. Exhausted, she had dropped to her knees by his bedside and prayed.

Now in the middle of Wolfe Street, she remembered and repeated the Lord's Prayer. Her child needed her again.

"Heal Your son, Dear Lord, heal him and make him whole."

Then she went to work to help Him.

"Ruth, get Jed's bed ready. See that the ropes are tight.

"Grace, tell Mam to heat water and tear some linen bandages. Then get Doctor Holliday. Tell him it's an emergency. Hurry!

"Henry, you walk with me. Jed is in good hands with Betsy alongside."

Then it was Josiah Dunbar's turn, "All right, boys, go easy with him. Careful not to jounce him."

They carried Jed to the red brick house on Wolfe Street.

Sarah pointed to the wide space on the front verandah, "Put him down there, please." She knelt and stroked his forehead.

"Now we'll see what we can do until the doctor comes.

"Henry, get me the large tailor shears."

She kneaded the leg as gently as she could. She felt and knew at once it was badly broken.

Mam appeared in the front door with a blackened kettle, "This was boilin' already. And heah's cotton battin' and bandages from befoah."

Sarah scissored Jed's pant leg, around a bloody rag of a circle, to his knee and above. The wool fell open but for the remnant stuck in the thickening blood. Henry clumped up the steps with an old table from the storeroom, "T'save your knees."

Sarah stretched a kink from her back as men lifted the makeshift stretcher onto the table.

Warmed by Henry's concern, she touched long fingers to his face; she let them linger. Their eyes coupled in profound affection, hers shimmering with the intensity of the moment. She embraced him, letting her lips glide into the pucker of a kiss. She held it for a moment and let it go with a soft pop. A soft moan broke the spell. Sarah turned to her son.

"Get me the whiskey, Henry."

Three of the men who had carried Jed home drifted down the street. They were strangers and had done what they could. Josiah Dunbar stayed, as did one other, a corporal of The Winchester Rifles. He and Jed had been friends from school days.

Henry came back with whiskey, cotton batting, and a pan of water floating a small cake of ice.

Sarah picked gently at the lopsided circle of wool left imbedded in the wound. Jed winced, squeezed Betsy's hand harder; his forehead glistened with perspiration. The material was stubborn in the clotting blood. It had helped to slow the bleeding, but now it was a time-consuming hindrance.

Sarah wet the batting with hot water and sponged the edges of the rag. She worked painstakingly, soaking and testing with gentle tension on each obstinate thread, soaking and testing, soaking and testing. Careful to avoid the wound itself, mindful of Jed's misery and the risk of more bleeding, she soaked and swabbed and pulled gently at the threads. Bit-by-bit, she dissolved the bond and worked the material loose. Only a few threads were left, driven into his leg by the bullet.

"Almost done, Jed."

She pulled easily at the stained wool, evenly, gently, more and a bit more until it let go. The blood started again, but she was ready with a clean bandage to clamp tight over the wound.

"The whiskey, Henry. Not too much."

She glanced quizzically at him when he hesitated, shook the clean batting at him. He poured. Its redolence made her giddy. She swabbed inward from sound flesh, as before. Jed tensed as she came closer to the bloody wound, perspired and clutched at Betsy's hand when whiskey seeped into it. She cooed at him, stroked his forehead, murmured endearments, "I love you, my husband." Henry started when he heard that, but said nothing. He held out the iced water.

With a brief smile of thanks, Betsy bathed Jed's forehead and face.

"Henry," Sarah nodded at the whiskey bottle. He vacillated. Impatiently, she made a rotating motion with her wrist signaling, "Pour it."

Henry stepped toward Jed, then pulled back, handed the bottle to his wife. She tipped it quickly, not a tavern serving, or even a half serving, but enough to cleanse the wound.

"God all mighty!" Jed Morrow bolted upright, grabbing at his leg, rocking back and forth, straining to squeeze away the agony. Drained of energy, of caring, of everything but the racking torment in his leg, he collapsed back on his door-stretcher.

"That will have to do until Doctor Holliday gets here."

Betsy bathed his face. Sarah applied a bandage, and Josiah Dunbar helped to carry him upstairs, into his old room, the one Betsy had been using.

His generous sleigh bed was turned down and ready. Piled at its high headboard were a half dozen pillows Ruth had gathered for her brother's comfort. Betsy stayed alone with her husband.

At the front door, Sarah turned, "Thank you, Mr. Dunbar. We are grateful to you." She brushed at a wisp of hair that had fallen over her forehead.

"Not at all, Mrs. Morrow. I'm glad I could help."

Henry came from the staircase with his right hand offered in friendship, "Josiah, you and me, we've had our differences, I know, but I want you t'know I'm obliged."

"No need. You'd do the same."

Sarah and Henry Morrow fell into the hand-fashioned rocking chairs on the verandah, so finely balanced they almost rocked themselves. Sarah needed quiet time. Henry wanted to talk.

"Sarah, do you think Dunbar was different today?"

"No."

"He was different. More friendly. Seems t' me he's changed."

"Maybe it's you who've changed, dear."

Henry lapsed into silence. Sarah relaxed her head against the chair, closed her eyes to the easy arcs of the rocker.

Now that things had quieted, she felt relief in having one of her soldier sons home in his own bed. Wounded as he was, she could tend to him herself and see to his well-being. She trembled that he could have been hurt far away amongst strangers, or worse yet, captured and perhaps had no care at all.

"Sarah, did you know Jed and Betsy were married?"

"Why no! Why do you ask that?"

"When you were cleanin' his leg, Betsy was talkin' to him and called him her husband."

"I didn't hear that."

"You were too busy, I guess."

"It doesn't surprise me," Sarah closed her eyes again, drowsing for a full ten minutes before the heavy front door clicked open. It was Betsy.

"Is Jed all right?"

"Oh yes. He's sleeping."

"That's good. It's the best thing for him."

"He quieted down after the whiskey sting wore away. He seemed comfortable enough and just dropped off."

"I don't know how many times I've done that for cuts and open hurts. Its painful, but it seems to keep them clean."

Henry added his bit, "I'll say so. I'll never forget the time I ripped my leg open and you poured it on me."

Sarah saw the opening and jumped, "Is that why you gave me the bottle? So you wouldn't have to do the same to Jed?"

Henry hesitated a moment too long, and Sarah good-naturedly pushed her advantage. For years, she had teased him about his innate tenderness and his need to cover it up.

"Why Henry Morrow! You're nothing but a faker. A big faker."

"Now, Sarah . . ."

"If you're not why don't you ask Betsy the question you asked me just before she came out." Henry never saw it coming.

"What question, Mumma?"

"Henry?"

Henry shifted in his chair. "Well . . ." He shuffled more. "Just before you came out, we were talkin'—Sarah and me." He hesitated. "And I was . . ." He coughed. "I was tellin' her about what I heard." He rubbed at his chin, which he often did when perplexed. "I wasn't listening." He felt like a trespasser in territory not his. "Just happened to overhear it."

"Oh for goodness sakes, Henry.

"Betsy, are you and Jed married?"

"Oh, Mumma . . ."

"You were upset and talking intimately to Jed. Your words carried, that's all."

"I knew we should tell you. Jed wanted to wait for a better time."

"We all wait for a better time to do things, Betsy."

"I'm sorry. I truly am. I wanted to tell you in January, when I first met you. When we had dinner with you. But we didn't, and Jed kept saying wait for a better time. Then—then he was gone." Betsy was close to tears.

Henry had been feeling guilt pangs ever since he had seen Jed was wounded. "It was my fault. I was mad with Jed for running off. He was hoping I'd get over it."

"Oh, Papa, don't blame yourself."

They sat in silence for several minutes.

"When were you married, dear?"

"That same night. The night of the dinner. We had decided to wait. But when we left here, Jed said let's get married right now. He said he had talked to one of the chaplains. He said no, but when Jed told him how long we knew each other he said all right. I have the certificate upstairs. With his name on it."

"We don't need the certificate, Betsy."

"Jed tried to tell you after dinner. He wanted you to be there. And I did too. I know he feels sorry—so do I."

"Betsy, you've been a daughter to us since that dinner. I hope you know that. Hasn't she, Sarah?"

"Yes, Betsy, you certainly have."

"I didn't want you t'think I was snooping."

"I would never think that. Papa."

Henry stood up and opened his arms wide, to both Sarah and Betsy. They came into his big bear hug together.

"Welcome to the family, daughter. And I'm sorry I didn't say it before." He tightened his hug around them, and with a twinkle in his eye, added, "I was just waiting for a better time."

It was just about the same time that Brian shot the Yankee soldier near the town line. The others skedaddled, leaving their wounded friend in the weeds. By the time Brian reached him, he was dead. He stood over him, dazed and remorseful.

Brian had shot impersonally into the small group, and watched as his bullet hit. The soldier had looked directly at him wide-eyed with surprise. Brian had seen censure and a death stare.

"Come on, sergeant, we got 'em on the run."

Brian was a moment tearing himself away from the man he had killed, assimilating the fact that he was the sergeant being addressed. He choked back his regret, followed the others mechanically, without firing another shot.

They stopped, one wrote later, only "when we were so tired we could not pursue farther." Camping near Mrs. Carter's orchard, they found water, looked longingly at the apple trees, wishing the green fruit was ripe enough for eating.

Up ahead, Banks' army hurried along to Martinsburg, rested briefly, and scurried on to Williamsport. There, it crossed the Potomac, leaving the Shenandoah Valley to its own.

For the first time in a month, Jackson's army relaxed, two full days to catch its breath, mend clothing, and patch worn shoes; to renew friendships and closer alliances with Winchester's young ladies; to sleep, bathe, drink and eat their fill. The general had it better, too, with his headquarters in the Taylor Hotel. For a change, he knew where he would sleep.

Food was plentiful in Winchester and uncommonly tasty. Jackson's men found a dazzling windfall of staples and delicacies compliments of the Federal commissary, coffee, molasses, oranges, lemons, figs, dates, oysters, pickles, lobsters, sardines, sugar, cheese, ham, fine brandies and wines

They fitted themselves with Yankee shoes, which they kept, and new uniforms, which they didn't. The blue tunics proved irksome when their own cavalry shot at the them.

Sarah softly opened the bedroom door, and looked lovingly at Jed, stretched in the sleigh bed. Betsy was sound asleep in a chair, one arm crooked into a pillow for her head, the other extended protectively across the coverlet toward her husband. It's strange to think of you as husband and wife, Sarah thought, strange but nice. You do seem to belong together.

She touched Betsy's shoulder, "Doctor Holliday's here."

Betsy jerked upright, "What is it? Is Jed all right?"

"Yes, dear, everything's fine. The doctor is here."

"Oh, I must have dozed. What time is it? I heard the clock strike midnight."

"It's only a few minutes after. The doctor delivered a baby over near Round Hill and came directly here. Poor man's about done in. He's in the kitchen with a cup of coffee."

Jed moaned and came partly awake.

Betsy moved immediately to him, "It's all right. Mumma's here with Doctor Holliday to look at your leg."

"My leg? Why's the doc here? What's wrong with my leg?"

"You were hurt yesterday in the fighting."

"Hurt? Yesterday? I don't. . . I just fell down and then I was on the verandah. And the smell of whiskey. I remember the smell of whiskey. And I remember you there. You held my hand."

"Everything will be all right, sweetheart." Betsy leaned forward. Their lingering kiss was interrupted by Sarah and the doctor, one with a pan of hot water and the bottle of whiskey, the other with his small, black satchel. Betsy turned up the oil lamp, and lit another for good measure.

Doctor Holliday went to work as if he was just starting his work day. In reality, he had been going for eighteen hours, "Now let's see what we've got here." He rested a hand on Jed's forehead, "Mmmm," and threw back the coverlet. He cut Sarah's bandage, exposing the wound, "Hmmm." He pressed the area around the wound, and "Hmmm-ed," again. Jed bit down on a knuckle.

"Looks like you had some expert attention, son."

He kneaded the lower leg as Sarah had done, frowning as he detected the smashed bone. He nodded to her in the affirmative, "You were right." He looked at the wound again.

"Seems clean except for the bullet. No suppuration. Some see it as a part of healing, call it laudable pus, but I don't. It's too nasty to be good. Now let's get the bullet out. And take a good look at that leg."

Betsy moved one of the lamps closer, reached to hold Jed's hand. He squeezed tight, managed a tighter smile, and shut his eyes. She whispered, "I love you."

Sarah stood perfectly still. She had seen other doctors extract bullets, but this was her son. She held the hot water and whiskey bottle for immediate use, so tight her knuckles went white. Doctor Holliday noticed.

"Take a little whiskey and swallow it slowly. Not a gulp. Just a bit at a time. You, too, young lady."

He waited as they drank. "Now. No heroics. If you feel faint sit on the floor at once. I want no more patients this day."

He reached for his bag. He washed the short-handled forceps in the hot water and held it out for a whiskey rinse. Sarah obliged. Unobtrusively, he noted that her hand was steady, her face a better color. He leaned over Jed.

The end of the instrument disappeared into the wound. Jed stiffened, stifling a cry. Betsy held him tight. Sarah stood taut but controlled, ready to help. The doctor probed delicately through damaged tissue and bone. He scraped metal.

A deft twist of his wrist gripped the bullet, "Got it." Extracting it slowly, he held it for all to see, and dropped it with a plop into the pan of water.

"One more thing and I'm done." Dousing fresh batting with whiskey, he warned Jed, "Hold on for one more minute."

His energetic swabbing attested to his relative values of cleanliness and comfort. Jed went rigid in the bed, clenching Betsy's hand until she winced.

"Now, I'd like another cup of coffee," Doctor Holliday announced, "while you two young ones enjoy each other's company."

Sarah caught his tiny nod and led the way downstairs. Henry was at the kitchen table, elbows on its worn surface, chin cupped in his hands. "How's Jed, doc?"

"I extracted the bullet, Henry. Sarah had the wound cleaned up fine. But there's another problem. I wanted Sarah to hear this too. I had hoped for better." He hesitated to let them prepare. Then, because he always had trouble announcing bad news, he rushed ahead nonstop, "The bone is too shattered to mend.

"Jed's leg has to come off. The tibia is in too many pieces to put together. It won't heal itself enough to be of any use—there's no way it can be set. Without an amputation, you're risking a serious infection, maybe gangrene."

Henry tried to fight the inevitable, "How can you be so sure? I've seen broken legs and they always healed."

"Henry, you haven't seen limbs broken by shells, shrapnel, and Minie balls. That's what hit Jed, a lead Minie ball. Those damn things are heavy—two ounces or more. When they hit a bone, they don't break it, they shatter it. The lead spreads like a mushroom and smashes the bone into pieces."

"But maybe it—"

The doctor's exhaustion showed, "Henry, I've told you all I know. All any doctor knows. If you want to risk that boy's life with no chance of getting a good leg back, that's your business."

Sarah held up a hand, straining to control her muffled sobs, "Stop it, the two of you. My son is hurt and you stand there arguing. Stop it and take care of my son."

Henry heard her anguish and slumped as if he had been kicked by a horse, "Sarah, I'm sorry," his voice came in a whisper, "I just can't see Jed like that, without a . . . Bein' one of them."

"It's not good, Henry, but it's the best there is. I'm not happy with it either. I'll save as much as I can."

XXXII

LOSS AND GAIN
MAY–JUNE, 1862

The new day dawned as flamboyantly as yesterday, the one Jed Morrow had celebrated on the hillside. At first glance, the Blue Ridge looked the same and the Alleghenies to the west and the Great Valley between. But differences were there, obvious changes as well as subtle distinctions that went unnoticed unless one knew what to look for.

The sun burst from the ridge line imperceptibly to the north of yesterday's rising, a tad earlier by the clock; trees rustled differently in the ever-changing air currents; the night's rain had darkened the plowed ground. More obvious were the birds that yesterday had raced and dived so frantically; they were unruffled today. And Jed Morrow lay in his bed less half a leg.

Last night, Betsy had stayed when Doctor Holliday came upstairs to apply his skill and tools. A quick glance at her set off his alarm, "Maybe you'd better wait downstairs."

"I'll be all right, doctor. I have to be with my husband."

"If you do as I say." he scowled impatiently for a response.

Both she and Sarah started at the curt statement.

"Well?" Doctor Holliday was feeling yesterday's fatigue.

"Why—yes. Yes of course."

"Then get the whiskey bottle and pour a drink.

"Now sip it slowly like you did before."

Betsy was surprised but did as he said.

"And now you, Sarah, for insurance."

He poured for her, and a half portion on his hands, washing them slowly, all the time watching the two women. He noted that Betsy's ashen anxiety was gone and color back in her cheeks. Sarah was less of a worry for she had proved her strength and strong stomach assisting him with an amputation after the Kernstown battle. But this was her son.

"If you feel faint, you know what to do. Sit on the floor before you fall. Head between your knees." They nodded.

"Ready?"

Betsy remained through the surgery, satisfying a profound need to be there. She fought the desire to go somewhere alone and weep. The thought nagged, but she stayed because Jed was part of her, and she, a part of him. Because the shattered leg was hers. Because she and Jed were forever.

She smelled the cloying sweetness of the chloroform, watched the knife and heard the saw. One sent icy whorls through her heart; the other's grinding rasp lifted bitter bile in her throat. When it was over, a scant fifteen minutes that seemed hours, she collapsed in the chair near the bed, the same chair she had dozed in earlier when Jed's future seemed simpler.

Even through the measured dose of morphia and the residual fog of chloroform, Jed twitched with shadow pains that throbbed along bone and tissue no longer there. He cried out that his knee hurt, but the knee was gone, and he moaned of misery in a leg no longer his.

Betsy fought to stay alert but the night had been long. She rested her head on the pillow of her arm, the other across Jed's chest, and was asleep.

In front of Richmond, McClellan methodically prepared to attack. With McDowell from Fredericksburg, he would have 150,000 troops, virtually ensuring the fall of the Confederate capital. As Washington officials cheered McClellan's success on the peninsula, they also had reason to fear Jackson should he decide to cross the Potomac.

And fear they should, for Banks' decision to retreat north was inviting him to do just that via Harper's Ferry, into Maryland, even to the Federal capital. Jackson was not one to miss such an opportunity.

Washington's mood changed. Newspapers predicting Richmond's early capture now screamed bold headlines that the Federal capital was endangered. Wires buzzed to General Banks and to the small force defending Harper's Ferry.

The telegrams and their replies reflected the confusion and concern: "Please answer immediately"; "All communication is cut off"; "Have you heard anything from Banks . . . Answer immediately"; "We are left in extraordinary state of uncertainty"; "Lynch says 'they' are retreating from Winchester, without saying who."

Lincoln himself was dismayed and sent off a wire to McDowell, "[lay aside] the movement on Richmond . . . put 20,000 men in motion at once for the Shenandoah. . ."

Thomas Jonathan Jackson had thrown the fear of God into the Federal leaders, generating not only confusion, but sufficient uncertainty for them to cancel out a major portion of McClellan's planned additions. Jackson added to their anxiety when he issued his marching orders for Harper's Ferry.

Just after midnight, intelligence came that could change everything. He already knew that a Federal army commanded by Fremont was in western Virginia; Fremont could come into the Valley behind him and cut him off. If he were a lesser commander, he would have cancelled the marching orders and hurried up the Valley toward safety.

"A gentleman is outside with a report," an orderly wakened Jackson's aide, "he says it's important."

"Bring him in," the young captain groaned, not pleased to be disturbed. Too many civilian reports were of whole cloth.

"I have ridden far to see the general," the stranger began.

"And?"

Authorities in Washington are in a near-panic, the stranger said, that Banks was being chased out of the Valley, and are convinced that Jackson is strong enough to invade Maryland, perhaps even the capital. To stop him, he continued, McDowell has been ordered to the Valley instead of to Richmond; Shields' division is already within a day's march of Front Royal and two divisions follow directly behind.

"I saw Shields' column on the road," he concluded his story, "and didn't stop until I arrived here."

Soon after daybreak, he repeated his story for the general.

The story was important for Shields could link up with Fremont's western army and cut off Jackson at Strasburg.

Even though Fremont was already closer to Strasburg than he was, Jackson boldly decided to hold to his Harper's Ferry ploy. First, he would throw a real scare into Washington. Playing on Washington's jitters, he could ease the pressure on Richmond still more, and still have time to extract his army, he calculated. He would deal with that problem in its turn. Thomas Jonathan Jackson was no ordinary commander.

He sent General Winder with the Stonewall Brigade, Brian's 4th Virginia and three other regiments, off toward Harper's Ferry, toward opportunity, into danger.

Washington pondered. Would Jackson cross the Potomac?

As if he were reading their fears, Jackson gave them more reason to worry about it.

Would he attack the capital?

Jackson would do all he could to make them believe it.

Who knew what he might have in mind beyond chasing Banks out of the Valley? He played on their fears as an accomplished violinist hypnotizes his audience.

He confounded Federal officials with tactics, swift marches that led them to estimate the size of his army at 40,000 men, triple what he had. He was not a peril at all but a phantom of their own apprehension, and their bogeyman estimates.

The Stonewall Brigade played out the charade, scrapping Yankees near Charles Town and Bolivar Heights.

Shields' division continued its advance, and Fremont was still headed for Strasburg. If they came together, Jackson and his men were in for it.

On picket along the Potomac, Brian and the Liberty Hall Volunteers missed the morning's skirmishing. Things being quiet, they enjoyed a swim and a bath in the clean water.

Almost a year ago to the day, they had marched from Lexington, exuberant, confident, and innocent of the ways of war. Since then, they had become soldiers, seeing the elephant at Falling Waters, victory at Manassas, winter marches and winter mountains, defeat at Kernstown. They had seen death, by wounds and by disease. They had been through a great deal and changed much. They had learned to sleep when they had a few minutes, enjoy what was offered at the moment.

This Friday morning in May was one of the good times. They made the most of it, splashing and cavorting in the river. All except Brian who sat alone on the bank. Still in his head was the ghost of the Yankee soldier he had shot north of Winchester.

Over and over again, Brian watched him writhe alongside the road, and stain the weeds red. He would bleed into eternity, it seemed, and bear the agony of his wound forever. Henry Morrow's scholarly son couldn't purge the incident from his brain.

It deepened his melancholy as did Jed's disappearance from his regiment. After the Winchester fighting he had searched for his brother. Unable to find him, had conjured visions: Jed wounded, dying alone; Jed already dead, unburied, chewed by wild animals; Jed black and bloated, a balloon of noxious gasses ready to explode. Then he found a soldier of The Winchester Rifles who had seen Jed fall.

"He was runnin' through the street an' he jest fell down. Five, six men come up an' one of'm got uh old door. Still had a iron latch on one side. Then they carried him off."

"Did he move? Or say anything?"

"Not that Ah know."

Then hesitantly, wanting, yet not wanting an answer, "Was he still alive?"

"Seemed t'be. But Ah cain't say fer sure."

Brian pressed for more, but that was all the soldier knew.

That had been four days ago, the day after the battle.

The next day, a Tuesday, Brian had a visitor, a corporal in Jed's company.

"Heard you were worried about your brother."

Brian looked up eagerly, "Yes. Yes. What do you know about him? I heard he was shot in Winchester."

"That's what happened all right. I helped carry him home. I knew Jed in school. Know your Ma and Pa, too."

Brian glowed with excitement, "Tell me. Was he all right? Was he hurt bad?" He grabbed the corporal's arm, "Tell me."

"Bad enough. We set him down on the verandah. Your Ma cleaned him up. She's a strong one."

"But was he hurt bad?" Brian shook the corporal's arm.

"Not as bad as I'll be if you squeeze my arm any harder. You trying to break it off?"

Embarrassed, Brian dropped his hands, "Sorry. It's just . . ."

"Your Ma cut his pants and cleaned his leg."

"He was shot in the leg?"

"Just the once I think. But I couldn't say for sure."

"I hope you're right."

"I stayed for a while. Your Ma poured whiskey on it and Jed yelled like a banshee. Then they carried him upstairs and I left.

"Couldn't help but notice the pretty girl that held his hand the whole time. A real princess."

"That must have been Betsy."

"Yes, Betsy, I heard someone call her that. How did Jed come by somebody like her?"

"That's my brother! I sure do thank you, corporal."

"The least I could do. Sorry I didn't see you sooner, but I never knew Jed had a brother in the army until this morning. Name's MacDonald. Tom, to my friends."

"Tom MacDonald, I'm Brian Morrow. I owe you."

"Know how you feel. I've got family with the rangers."

Brian offered a hand, "Stay healthy, Tom. Thank you."

"Keep your head down."

As soon as Tom MacDonald left, Brian thought of other questions he should have asked. He really didn't know much more than before, except that Jed hadn't been shot dead. Maybe the leg was infected. Broken or shattered beyond use. Maybe gangrene set in, or the red streaks that shot up arms and legs. Men recover, then die. The thought of Jed's dying was too much.

He ran for a copse of trees where he could be alone, flung himself on the ground, and sobbed until there were no more tears.

"Damn this army! And goddamn this rotten war!!"

Couriers galloped to Jackson: Shields was almost to Front Royal; a column was closing on Berryville; Fremont was on the Strasburg road; McDowell himself led a column toward Winchester, not true, but too ominous to ignore at the time.

Exploiting the jitters in Washington, Jackson had with 15,000 men tied up four times his number, keeping them from the Richmond front. But his string was running out. Leaving General Winder and the Stonewall Brigade in front of Harper's Ferry, he ordered the rest back to Winchester. He promised his namesake brigade he would wait for them there—if he could.

Having done all he could for the time being, he went sound asleep under a tree. A brief rest and he boarded a train to Winchester and slept again. At Winchester, word came that Shields had driven into Front Royal, only a dozen miles from Strasburg. Strung out twenty to forty miles from that crucial point, Jackson could well be trapped, even if he marched at once.

He notified Winder to march immediately,—should Winchester be occupied head west, he advised, use the Back Road or go into the mountains and join me farther up the Valley.

The situation was made even more severe when the courier lost his way. The delay cost several hours when minutes were precious

At once, Winder recalled the 2nd Virginia on Loudoun Heights. Lacking a better crossing, they held horses' tails and were pulled across the Shenandoah River. The regiment came up with the brigade near Halltown, and without rest or breakfast, headed for Winchester. "We decamped with undignified haste," one wrote.

They slipped and slogged through mud, tied make-do scarves over hats and necks, flung blankets across shoulders and heads against the rain. Wind-driven, it soaked blankets and clothes to the very skin, accumulating into irritating and chilling trickles on back and belly. They blinked water from their eyes, only to be half-blinded by more.

Across the miles and through the hours, they leaned against wind and rain, staring mindlessly into the mud. They missed nothing for there was nothing to miss.

Winder force-marched his column through the dreary day that mired wagons and tested men's legs. Twenty miles and more they marched, dragging through a deserted Winchester at dusk. Hungry, tired and wet, many slipped away to find friends, a meal, or a dry corner. Brian was one of them.

Worn out and determined to get home, he dropped out as the column shuffled past the courthouse. He needed a respite. Even more, he needed to see Jed. How badly was he hurt?

Unfortunately, Captain Hugh White, brother to the first captain, saw him break ranks, "Sergeant Morrow, we'll have no stragglers from Company I. Rejoin the column immediately."

Brian kept walking.

"Sergeant, halt where you are," Captain White bellowed. Brian seemed in a daze, neither running nor stopping.

White drew his revolver. "Sergeant Morrow!"

The company commander shouted once more, "Sergeant Morrow! Halt at once!!" Brian walked on.

Captain White raised the revolver.

"Goddam. I don't believe it," another student-soldier mumbled. Then he screamed, "He's gonna shoot him."

"For the last time, Sergeant Morrow, HALT!"

The sudden shot startled every man of Company I, those ahead and behind. Some prepared to defend themselves. Others dropped in the roadway. Brian fell to the ground.

Captain White ran to him, kneeled and turned him over.

"What happened?"

"I couldn't let you walk away. Every man in the company wants to do the same thing."

"But I heard a shot."

"You ignored my warnings. I shot over your head."

"I didn't hear you. I wanted to see Jed. He was wounded."

"I know, Brian." It was not Captain White speaking now, but Hugh White who had been studying for the ministry when the war demanded his services, "We all have someone we worry about—all of us have been sorely tried by this day."

He put his arm protectively around his distressed sergeant and together they made their way back to Company I.

"Are you all right, Brian?"

"Yes, sir. I guess so," he mumbled without conviction.

"Let's say no more of it. We all have our duty to perform."

Meanwhile, Jackson's main force had made it almost to Strasburg where it bivouacked. He was determined to hold the road open for Winder's men, even as Fremont was within ten miles on the Wardensville road

The Stonewall Brigade dragged through Winchester and up the turnpike. Hundreds strayed from the column, or dropped on the road. The rest endured, some dozing as they walked.

For another five miles they plowed through the darkness. Until 10 o'clock they trudged, the clock around and more, covering twenty-eight miles, Jed's 2nd Virginia seven miles more than that. They were still fifteen miles from Strasburg and safety. Most were beyond caring.

General Winder conceded the exhaustion, called a halt despite Jackson's order to be in Strasburg by 7 o'clock the next morning. The damned order was impossible anyway!

Brian was not with them. He had slipped away, dropping by the roadside, hardly daring to breathe lest Captain White stop him again.

When the tag end of the column passed, he trudged back to the gate up the lane to Zeke and Mattie's house. He stumbled onto the back verandah. Too tired to knock, he staggered through the door, into Ezekiel's arms. Hearing the faltering steps, Ezekiel had opened the door to investigate.

"Lawdawmighty!" Mattie gasped, "he's worse off'n last time."

She fussed and sputtered as Ezekiel led him to a chair at the table, "What's this army do ta my boys, anyhow. Wear 'em out. Shoot 'em like Jed. I never, never, seen anythin' like it."

"Mattie! Pour him some coffee."

"What's that you said about Jed, Mattie?"

"He was shot, Brian, that's what."

"I know that. How is he? Is he all right?"

Ezekiel broke in, "Saw him yesterday,—I don't know." His voice trailed off vaguely.

"What do you mean, you don't know, Zeke? How is he?" Brian grabbed his arm as he talked.

"Well his leg is healin', but he isn't himself."

"Not himself? Goddamn it, Zeke, What does that mean?"

Mattie stewed again, "That's another thing this army does. Teaches boys ta cuss with the Lord's name—who knows what-all other kinds of sinnin'?"

Ezekiel talked right over her fussing, "Just isn't himself. He doesn't laugh, doesn't talk much at all. Never talks cheerful, always down in the mouth. Hasn't been outa bed at all."

"Hasn't been out of bed! But I thought you said his leg was healing. He could be sitting up in a chair by now—walking a couple of steps to it."

"Jed isn't walkin'. Not on one leg, he is'nt."

"On one leg!"

"Had ta take it off. Doctor had ta take it off at his knee."

"Oh my God. Not Jed on one leg." Brian sagged.

"Afraid so, Brian, that's how it is."

"I've got to see him." He started from his chair.

Mattie put a heavy hand on his shoulder, "You stay where you are. First you eat. Then you sleep. But first of all get out of those wet clothes. Or you'll be down like your brother."

Brian gave in and shed his wet shirt. He hesitated.

"Stop lookin' like we-all are strangers. I cleaned you up when you were small—I know what you look like."

Ezekiel rolled his eyes upwards, showing white.

"My, but don't he embarrass easy."

Brian lifted his hands outward, palms up in a what-can-I-do gesture. He unbuttoned his trousers.

"Get him a blanket, Ezekiel while I tend the stove." She busied herself stirring an iron pot that steamed happy aromas. "Left from supper. Enough for you and a tad for Ezekiel."

"Smells like heaven, Mattie."

"Just some old soup. Big bone and vegetables like always. Been simmerin' since yesterday mornin'."

Ezekiel came back with a woolen blanket, "Here, Brian, this'll cover you."

Mattie continued her stirring, long enough for Brian to wrap himself snugly. She marvelled at men's vacillation when it came to being without clothes. She chuckled to herself.

"What's so funny, Mattie?"

Her chuckle grew to a hearty laugh before she answered, "Zekiel, I've seen you the same way, embarrassed as a school boy ta get outa your clothes. And other times when you couldn't shed 'em fast enough."

Late for its 7 A.M. rendezvous with Jackson, the Stonewall Brigade formed for yet another day of forced marching. Stragglers had filtered in all night. Dulled with fatigue and hunger, the ragtag column trudged on. On and on and on.

During the morning, a soft rumbling from up ahead pricked their numbness. Distant thunder, perhaps, but it continued, too persistent for thunder. Only gunfire rumbled like that, General Jackson fighting to keep the road open for them. Perhaps they were already too late to escape the Yankee pincers. They picked up the pace. Winder sent an aide ahead.

The gunfire swelled. A rumor burgeoned, Shields' eastern column had joined Fremont blocking their path. Winder's aide galloped back, "The road is clear."

Jackson had worked a miracle.

XXXIII

PATIENT AND PRISONER

Jed Morrow stirred in his drug-induced sleep. Betsy wakened at once, listened from the smaller bed Henry had moved in for her. She had insisted on sleeping close by.

Sarah suggested they alternate nights, but Betsy was adamant, "Mumma, I can do it. I'll get more rest near him than in another room worrying. If it's too much, I'll let you know."

"It will not be easy. I'm afraid you'll exhaust yourself."

"I won't. I'll tell you if I need relief."

"I know you mean it, but you never will." She questioned with her eyes, "I'll agree if I have your solemn promise."

"You have it, Mumma."

"Promise me you'll keep your promise."

They smiled at the unexpected humor and embraced.

"I know what you mean, Mumma. Please don't worry."

That same morning at Ezekiel's and Mattie's, Brian came into the kitchen. Cooking hung in the air, the yeasty aroma of fresh bread and the smokey hickory of sizzling ham. He wore different clothes, from the humpbacked storage trunk under the eaves.

"Morning, Mattie. I'm glad you made me stay the night. Never realized how tired I was."

"One look was all I needed ta know that."

"What time is it? I know it's late."

"Late! It's awmost afternoon. Ezekiel's been in for his mornin' coffee hours ago. Almost time he was comin' in ta dinner."

She put slabs of ham into the iron spider, "Gets like shoe leather with too much cookin'. Sit down, Brian."

"You never spoiled a piece of ham in all your life, Mattie."

Breaking four eggs into the same frypan, she spoke seriously to Brian, "Ezekiel and I think it best you don't go home." Ezekiel tramped across the back verandah and Mattie waited a moment to confirm his words.

"Isn't that what you said, Ezekiel? Not to go home, but we can't stop you."

"Yes, that's right."

"You know I've got to see Jed. And I've got to see Pa, too."

"We all know that. That's why we been plannin'."

"Planning! What in the world is there to plan?"

Mattie put Ezekiel's dinner in front of him, turned back to fill Brian's plate with breakfast, and her own dinner.

"You tell him, Ezekiel."

"Brian, you can't just walk home plain as day. You're walkin' away from your own army. Yankees are about and they'll arrest you, or your own people will. So we decided you should ride in the wagon, under sacks or somethin'."

"I'd rather go cross country. I'd be helpless in the wagon."

Brian crammed the midday breakfast into his mouth, eating ravenously as he spoke with Ezekiel.

"Brian Morrow, you are eatin' like you never saw food."

"I'm sorry, Mattie, your cooking deserves better."

"Slow down, child. Take time ta taste it."

"Yes ma'am," deliberately obedient, Brian put his knife and fork down, sat ramrod straight in his chair, and remained quiet. He was rewarded by their quizzical expressions.

"Just slowing down, captain." he smiled.

"Cap'n Mattie!" Ezekiel slapped his knee in glee, " if that don't beat all."

Brian folded a slab of warm bread, took a large bite, "I could eat like this all day."

Ezekiel brought the conversation back, "Up the back way, huh? That might do. Through the north field toward Bower's Hill and across the creek. You want me ta get a horse ready."

"No thank you, Zeke, I'll be less conspicuous on foot." Brian finished the eggs, the ham, and the fresh bread. Lingering over the last of his coffee, he grinned shyly, "Mattie, I could carry a piece of that special bread and eat it on the way."

Pleased with the compliment, she demurred, "Just plain old bread like always." She cut thick slices for him.

She hugged him tight, "You be careful, Brian. Already got one child hurt bad. Don't need any more."

"Thank you, Mattie. I will be. Promise."

Ezekiel followed him down the back steps and walked with him to the north corn field. Brian sensed his discomfiture.

"All right, Zeke, what is it?"

"Somethin' been botherin' me since you came in last night. I see trouble because y're figgerin' on leavin' the army. You figgerin' on leavin' aren't you, Brian."

Brian stopped in his tracks. "Zeke, you're still doing it!

"You did it when I was a boy. You saw things in the woods I never saw, read my mind like you were in my head. I asked you how, and you said you had eyes in the back of your head."

"I remember that. Said it ta all you boys."

"Zeke, you don't know how I searched the back of your head for years looking for those eyes!"

Ezekiel laughed his ample laugh, "Jed told me the same."

Brian turned serious again, "I don't know about the army. First I have to see Jed and Pa."

"Don't do somethin' you'll be sorry for."

They shook hands. Ezekiel stood alone, watching him cross the field. Brian turned. Each lifted an arm in a farewell salute.

Brian tramped the field toward Bower's Hill. The turned soil stuck to his shoes, but his steps were light. It would be good to be with everyone again. See Ma, straighten things out with Pa, talk with Jed, tell stories and listen, and laugh with those he loved. He'd have to think of a prank to get back at Betsy.

At Abraham's Creek he stopped to eat the last of Mattie's bread. Bower's Hill lay directly ahead. He had seen nobody, just the way he wanted it, meeting no one, being seen by no one.

Reaching the hill, he skirted along its eastern foot to the Academy building where he had gone to school as a youngster. Its shadow stretched long in the late afternoon sun. From here he could reach home in ten minutes, five if he ran.

"Hey, Morrow. Brian Morrow."

Brian murmured a single word, "Damn," and stood stock still.

The call came again, from the direction of the Academy, part way up the hill, "Morrow. Wait." A pudgy figure hurried toward him, covering the ground in a strange combination of running and waddling. The feet seemed to skim the ground for he didn't bend his knees; his leg motion was all from

the hip, pendulum like, front to back. Other than that he was oriented not
to the front but to the sides. His toes pointed sideways, his arms swung sideways, and his body rocked sideways.

"Thought you were in the army?" The question was probing, challenging. Brian ignored it with a challenge of his own.

"Hello, Willie, I thought you Schroeders were busy, peddling to the
Yankees."

"We're patriotic as any."

"Glad to hear it." Brian couldn't resist needling him, but now that he
had, wanted only to get free of him, "G'bye, Willie."

"You going home?"

Brian walked faster, "Good bye, Willie."

Willie was not deterred, "You are in the army. I saw you march into
town in your fancy uniform. What are you doing here?"

"Willie, don't press at me. I don't have the time."

"I'll bet you don't. In the army with those old clothes? Where's your
musket? You're taking French leave."

"Willie Schroeder, let it be."

The fat, young man turned mean, "Maybe you're a deserter." He was
shrewd like his father, Hans, but not smart.

Brian was on him in an instant, gripping the fat throat. They fell to the
ground. Hatred overcame Brian, and a sense of power he had never felt before. He pressed his thumbs. Schroeder struggled. Brian pressed more, saw
him turn purplish, watched as his eyes bulged. He was transfixed.

Figures floated across Brian's mind, Charley Nelson with a stained
bandage on his head; the dead Zouave, stumbling blind without eyes, without a face; a blue-uniformed soldier soaking his trousers, wide-eyed at a
ramrod in his chest; another staring at him, writhing bloody in roadside
weeds.

And Brian saw himself. Reloading his musket.

"Oh, my God," he moaned, and released his grip on Willie Schroeder's
neck. His face dripped with perspiration.

"You crazy? I'm only joking. Can't you take a joke?" Willie's voice was
scratchy, harsh, little more than a whisper.

"Damn you, and damn your jokes, Schroeder." He clutched a handful
of Willie's shirt, threatened him again with a clenched fist. Brian's arm trembled with the struggle to restrain himself. "You never saw me. Understand?"

Willie Schroeder stood up, breathing hard, rubbing his neck. He mumbled invective at Brian's back as he walked away, too subdued for Brian to
hear, and a threat also too low to be heard, "I'll get even for that."

Brian walked straight north, not turning for Wolfe Street as he had planned for Schroeder would be watching him. There was no telling what he might do for he was a mean-spirited one.

He kept walking, trying to clear his head of Willie Schroeder. The quartet of ghostly soldiers appeared again, dogging his steps, plaguing him with their silent reproach. Twisted fingers accused him, pointing at him from Henry Hill and Kernstown and the ditch north of Winchester. Charley Nelson had joined them in their phantom world.

Hollow, transparent bodies whirled, sucking the air around them in great eddies. Smothered, Brian flailed wildly against them. He ran. He fell to the ground, sobbing and spent. He lay there beside the Petticoat River that flowed down from the mountains, eastward into Winchester.

The phantoms faded into the distance, yet still within eyeshot, quiet now, perplexed, each pointing to his own wound, each gesturing to Brian for an explanation. Why? Why?

Brian tried to blink them away. They remained. He splashed the pure, mountain water to his face and arms. With cupped hands he scooped and slurped at it, threw it over his head and neck, letting it run where it would.

With trembling in his heart, Brian raised his head. The preternatural beings gestured again and retreated, vanishing into some hidden crypt under the water and over the mountain. He kept vigil but they did not return.

He dipped his canteen into the sparkling water, letting it gurgle full, remembering the first time he had seen it at Blackburn's Ford, remembering the fright Jed had given him. Drinking again from his cupped hand, he looked with misgiving toward the mountains for his ghosts. Relieved, he walked north.

The Pughtown Road was just ahead. Between it and the mountain stream, closer to the river than the road, Brian found a grove of hickory trees where he would be hidden from sight.

For what little was left of the daylight, he watched for signs of Willie Schroeder. That weasel of a human being meant trouble, and was no more preferable than the apparitions. He had upset everything, accosting him like that. Bad enough that he had raised such a tumult but Brian feared he would deliver him to the Yankees, or turn him in to his own army, just for spite. The visit to Wolfe Street had taken an ominous turn.

Be smarter to return to Ezekiel and Mattie, he thought, circle around to the west, closer to North Mountain. But he wanted so badly to get home.

"Too late to give up now. Just be careful," he told himself.

He had covered half the distance, almost to the surveyed ground at the end of Wolfe Street.

"Halt! Who goes there?"

Brian froze, hardly daring to breathe, hoping to meld into the darkness. But whoever it was had him spotted. Four men came toward him, carbines at the ready. To run would be suicide.

"Schroeder was right," he heard one of them say. They stopped twenty feet away. "All right, reb, hands up, high up—no tricks." He could only obey.

"Who are you? I have no gun and no uniform. I'm just on my way home, to Winchester."

"You sayin' you ain't a soldier, Brian Morrow?"

"That weasel. He even gave you my name."

"If I was in yer shoes I'd agree, but he's got his uses."

"Shut up, Jaybird," a burly sergeant bawled, "al'ays chirpin' for chris-sakes. Shut th'hell up for once."

He walked to Brian, "We kin do this one way or t'other."

"I don't know what you mean."

"It ain't that complicated, son. Y'kin give us yer parole and go free er y'kin be stubborn an' walk t'prison camp. Y'kin eat breakfast with yer family, er be hungry with yer comPATEreeOTS. Either way, the war's over for you."

As anxious as he had been to get away from the army and the war, Brian couldn't bring himself to accept the terms of parole. Agreeing to cease fighting Yankees was no problem, but declaring his loyalty to the Union was quite another matter.

"I'll stay."

"Suit yerself." The sergeant motioned with his carbine and ordered the others, "Skirt the edge of town t'the fair grounds. We'll wait there for the lieutenant."

As it turned out, they waited most of the night. A small group came in about midnight, but it was four hours later before a lieutenant in charge of the cavalry reconnaissance rode in. He had scouted from Martinsburg for General Banks, who wanted assurances that the area was clear, that Jackson was not planning more surprises. Near Redbud Run he had divided his detail to cover a wider swathe to Winchester and southward. Separating, his patrols he had picked up a dozen Confederates from Jackson's army, all of them from the Stonewall Brigade.

The lieutenant shouted for his sergeant as he rode in, the same one who had captured Brian, "Sergeant Grime."

"Yessir."

"Have your men ready to ride at dawn. Mine need a breather. I'll catch up to you."

"Dawn. Yessir."

"And I want a messenger to report all clear to the General."

"Yessir."

Brian heard it all, and had a question when the lieutenant left, "Where's Banks, sergeant?"

"At Martinsburg, waiting for us t'report. But it won't do you no good. An' I'm tellin' ya now don't try t'run."

Brian watched for just such an opportunity, but the guards gave him none. As the night wore on, homely scenes visited him, vignettes from his last trip home. Ma's onion treatments for his fever during the winter. Only five months ago? God! It seemed years. The fruitless discussion with Pa, the complete failure of his talk with Racey. What questions she had asked!

Another scene appeared from the last peacetime Christmas a year and a half ago. He was in the swaying stage coach from Lexington, straight up the Valley Turnpike, through festive towns, Staunton, Harrisburg, New Market, on into Winchester. On the opposite seat, riding backwards, was a traveler who had talked of impending war and had offered Brian his bottle.

"Maybe South Carolina smashed the Union, young man, but Lincoln sure'n hell will unsmash it."

How innocent he had been to reject the idea of war between the states, how foolish to refuse a holiday drink; and later, how childish to accept a musket in the name of liberty without a thought of bloodshed and suffering.

The image of Captain Morrison insinuated itself, Captain Morrison surrounded by Yankee cavalry at Kernstown, and Lieutenant Lyle shouting, "Run, Brian."

No, that's not what you yelled, captain, not 'run', something else that meant the same thing. What was it you shouted, John, what the hell was it? And what the hell am I in for now? Bedeviled, discouraged, and exhausted, he sat through the night hunched over his Yankee canteen fondling the strap.

At dawn on Tuesday, guards prodded Brian to his feet along with the rest of the prisoners and surrounded them, herding them like cattle. In the early light, Brian saw a friend.

"Tom! Tom MacDonald. You told me about my brother. Charles Town a week ago.

"Brian Morrow. Sure, I remember you!"

"Thank you again. I didn't know if he was dead or alive."

"Glad to do what I could. It wasn't much."

"It was a lot to me. What are you doing here?"

"Nothing that I like. I could ask you the same."

"I was going home to see Jed. Should have stayed with the column, but I was ready to drop. God but I was tired. We marched all day and half the night."

"I know what you mean. I dropped off, too, I guess. I was walking along and next thing I know this Yankee's poking me with a carbine. How's Jed?"

"I'm not sure. They picked me up before I saw him. That's where I was going when I ran into a little weasel that turned me in. I'll kill him if I see him again."

"Don't blame you. So you didn't see Jed?"

"No. I learned they amputated his leg. He's not doing well."

"I'm not surprised. When I was carrying him home I saw the bullet hole. It was in the middle of his leg, right over the bone. One of the men, the one that got the door to carry him on, said his leg wasn't broken but it looked it to me."

A guard bellowed, "Quiet! Now move," he pointed north. "Try t'scape and you're dead."

The hodgepodge of prisoners and guards stirred piecemeal, those at one end moving toward Martinsburg behind the lieutenant, the others sauntering behind. Tom and Brian walked together.

"I can't imagine Jed with one leg. Don't know what he'll do. Zeke said he was black as thunder."

"Who's Zeke?"

"He's Pa's friend," Brian's answer evolved into the tale from Ezekiel and Pa as boys in Washington, to Ezekiel and Mattie's moving to Winchester to run the Morrow farm.

"As if it were their own. They were second parents to us."

The telling passed the time, eased the shock of capture.

"Not many friends like that, Brian, black or white."

Taken by the story, Tom had a suggestion, "You and me, we better stay together. Don't know what's liable to happen."

"Good idea." The two of them clasped hands warmly.

They had walked all day, almost to Martinsburg when a rider approached from the north, the messenger sent last night to Banks. Perfunctorily, the lieutenant returned his salute.

"Might's well stop here, sir. Gen'l Banks'll be marchin' right at you— if he ain't started awready."

"Thought he might be doing that," the officer said glumly.

"He sed take the prisoners to Harper's Ferry. No use bringin' 'em to Martinsburg."

"What the hell am I? A mind reader?

"Sergeant! Banks expects a report. You bivouac and head for Harper's Ferry in the morning if I'm not back. Southeast to the railroad then follow it. Keep an alert guard on the prisoners."

He cantered into the growing darkness as the rest made camp.

In the morning, the soldiers boiled coffee, softened hardtack in it, passing equal portions to the prisoners. They reached Harper's Ferry by dusk, almost a hundred, fed and penned up for the night in the old firehouse with its shadows of John Brown and his son. Brian and Tom McDonald huddled together.

"Where do you suppose they'll send us?"

"The closer the better."

During the night, they were routed out and herded into rough boxcars of the B&O; by mid-morning, in Baltimore, marching from the Washington Station between armed guards. Citizens gathered along the route, many of them saddened for this was a divided city. Brian and Tom managed to stay together. Forty miles north they detrained in open country, lined up and marched for two hours into a village on upper Delaware Bay.

"Oh, God," one of them cried, "it's to Fort Delaware they're takin' us. In the middle of the bay."

From the tiny steamer Brian and his friend caught the first sight of the low island not more than a mile from shore. Story had it that Pea Patch Island was nothing but mud and debris collected around a sunken ship. A 10-year old stone fort stood at the eastern end.

Guards barked orders, pointed, and prodded them along. Senior officers were culled and marched off to the fort.

"The rest a' you bastards over here." Brian, Tom, and the others were marched to the opposite end of the island. They held rags to their faces against the stench.

Theirs was a space with a ramshackle barracks, unevenly alop as it settled into the mud. The "pens" it was called, divided by a ditch of noxious water for washing. Dividing the ditch was a board fence fifteen feet high, separating junior officers and enlisted men, a narrow walkway along the top for the guards. 5,000 prisoners packed the pens.

The "new meat" was corralled to face a captain standing on a raised platform. He eyed them with contempt. Brian imagined he had risen from the noisome slime of the island itself.

A whisper wafted to him, from someone with the same dread he felt, "This sonofabitch can kill us if he wants."

"SILENCE," the sonofabitch bawled, "Shut your damned rebel mouths," and with corrupted logic added, "and address me as SIR." They were registered by name, company and regiment; then searched roughly and completely, patted down and turned out for weapons, money and valuables. A few of the guards were decent men confiscating only weapons. Most took what money and valuables they found; others, letters, pictures, everything. Brian cringed when one of the uglier ones searched the beardless youngster next to him, leering as he patted insultingly. Brian heard his vile hiss, "Y're mine, reb."

The sonofabitch smirked at the unnatural obscenity, and shouted for torches as it had grown dark. The flames danced in the breeze, dropping little showers of sparks, throwing an eerie glow that strained the sense of reality. Brian remembered other camps when similar torches threw a friendlier light.

The sonofabitch started sarcastically, "I'm the adjutant general of this here post. I want you should know the rules."

He put his thumb alongside his nose, snorted it toward the prisoners. Then the other side, wiped across his sleeve, back and forth. Each motion spewed disdain. He proceeded through a long list of proscriptions, many flagrant violations to the accepted treatment of war prisoners.

"Come six feet from the deadline and you're dead. Disrespect my guards and you're dead. No talking in my yard, the mess hall, after 8 o'clock, or whenever else I say. No messages in or out without my permission. Same goes for packages. No runnin'. No sick call. No refusin' my work details. No work, no ration.

"And one more thing, he sneered, " There ain't no standard penalties, each case decided as I see fittin'. DIS-MISSED."

Brian found himself herded through the darkness, stumbling along amidst mumbled cursing and scattered sobbing. Somehow he funneled through the single door at the end of a barracks and found a place to lie down for the night.

Alert to the new day, Betsy lay in her bed, pondering what more she could do to speed Jed's recovery. The amputation wasn't a worry, the stump was healing fine, no infection, no fever, no complications. Physically, he was healing as expected.

Her concern was with his attitude, something ugly and black that had taken possession of him. She should talk to Sarah about it, but put it off. Things would get better, she told herself, and lived with the dark looks, the permanent scowl, the silence or animal grunt that answered anything she said.

Trying to understand, she made excuses for him, that he lacked energy, had a terrible shock, needed time to regain his strength. One day she rationalized that he was lonely for the army and his soldier friends, for the excitement and the camaraderie. He will get over it, she tried to convince herself, be his old self. Each day, she started afresh with renewed hope.

"Good morning, Jed." She came to his bedside, kissed him on the forehead, "Did you rest well?" She smoothed the coverlet.

No answer.

She went to the window, opened it to the freshness of the morning air. The feathery curtains lifted. She raised them apart, inhaled deeply, "It smells so good this time of day, like the air has been rinsed in dew. Can you smell it, Jed?"

No answer.

She filled her lungs again, exhaled, half-turned toward him on the bed, "It's so fresh and clean. I'll bring you some."

She cupped her hands toward the window, tripped lightly to Jed, playfully careful to avoid spilling any of it, "Here, sweetheart, it's all for you." She flung her hands wide.

Jed had only a scowl, mean, tortured, frozen to him forever it seemed. He twisted violently away from her, howled in pain, "Ooooh! Goddam leg jesusgodalmighty."

He sat up grabbing the remnant of leg. Blood oozed between his fingers.

"Mumma! Mumma!" Betsy screamed, "Mumma. Come quick."

She ran to the stairs screaming all the way, colliding with Sarah on the landing. Henry was right behind her.

"Jed's bleeding. He's bleeding. Mumma, Jed's bleeding."

Sarah rushed past into the bedroom, gasped at the blood stains. Betsy saw, too, and screamed hysterically.

Sarah grabbed the bandage, applying pressure over the red smear. Her voice betrayed her concern, "Henry, send someone for Dr. Holliday. Betsy, help me out of my apron—fold it over to cover the dressing. Quickly, girl, quickly."

Betsy reacted at once, pulling the ties of the apron, folded it in half and twice more. Sarah applied the make-shift bandage, keeping pressure on the bleeding stump until her hands cramped. Betsy took over, and Sarah again, spelling each other until the doctor puffed into the room. Inspecting the torn flap, he lightened the concern as usual, "Why did I rush? Everything's under control. Just needs a few stitches which you could have done, Sarah."

"Maybe someone else if I had to. Not Jed, doctor."

"Just like sewing a patch on boys' pants."

Relieved that it was over, Sarah responded in kind, "Maybe so, Dr. Holliday, but I'm happy for you to do it.

"Will you have breakfast with us?"

"Thank you, but Mrs. Holliday has it ready for me."

When he left, Sarah motioned Betsy into the hall.

"You and I, young lady, need to talk. I have never seen you unravel like that—I take it to mean that you are tired out and need help. Jed's been home a week and two days. My guess is that you haven't slept a full night in that time. You and I are going to share the night duty from now on."

"Mumma, I'll be all right."

"I know you will, Betsy, because tonight you will take yourself to one of the empty rooms, David's, Brian's, Ruth's, take your pick. And you will do the same every second night. Now, are we all agreed?"

"Yes, ma'am."

"One more thing. Within the next hour, I expect to see you curled up on one of those beds for the rest of the morning. And no arguments. We can't afford two invalids in the family."

XXXIV

A STRANGE BED

For security's sake on June 12, the reveille bugle was replaced by sergeants' guarded voices at Quien Sabe, Jeb Stuart's camp on the edge of Richmond. David Morrow rolled stiffly from his blanket, his legs aching dully. He heard Jeb Stuart, "Gentlemen, mount up in ten minutes."

Tugging on his heavy boots he felt dizzy. He ignored it as he pulled blanket and saddle over Sable. This raid was a big one.

The order for 1,200 men and three days rations had alerted them all, two regiments and a section of flying artillery. Troopers enough to crash through any likely opposition; two guns for an emergency.

Only Stuart and General Lee were privy to the details: scout north and east to discover the vulnerability of McClellan's flank across the Chickahominy, secondly, look for signs of an attack on Richmond and targets of opportunity.

To mask his route, Stuart led his men north on the Brook Road. At a nondescript crossroad called Yellow Tavern, he turned westerly, crossing the railroad and the upper Chickahominy, where David dismounted to splash cooling water on his face and arms. The column turned north again, then a large zigzag west and north to skirt Ashland. David regained the head of the column.

Stuart couldn't resist joshing him, "You having trouble holding the pace, captain?"

"No, sir, I'm fine."

Stuart puzzled, for in a full year together David had never fallen behind or failed to rise to his banter.

At the South Anna River, Stuart turned east, recrossed the railroad and bivouacked near Taylorsville. He sent scouts ahead. He apologized to the Winston family for imposing his column on them and their fields.

"I'm afraid that's not all," he added, "I have a young officer who is ailing. He's too ill to continue."

"Say no more, general, we're happy to be of service."

The next morning, the troopers were wakened again without bugle calls. His scouts reported a clear road to Old Church. Quickly, they formed column and cantered into Hanover Courthouse at 9 A.M. A small force of federal cavalry holding the town rode off toward Mechanicsville. Stuart chased Federal cavalry across Totopotomoy Creek, where they made a brief stand before falling back. The scouts had been too late in the day to espy the daily patrol from Old Church.

Meeting up with no infantry, Stuart knew the Union flank to be exposed. He had turned it. His primary mission was accomplished.

Riding on toward Old Church, he skirmished again, losing Captain Latane in a sharp skirmish. Old Church meant decision time, keep going or go back the way he had come. His judgment was to continue, rather than retrace his route. Riding around Little Mac's army had a ring to it, good fuel for future campfire stories. Even more important, it seemed less hazardous than returning through country already alerted to his presence.

The ride was indeed storybook, productive and dashing. He had discovered McClellan's flank to be vulnerable, in the air, an opportunity for an energetic commander. Like his friend, Thomas Jackson for one. He had captured wagons of stores, skirmished repeatedly, feasted on Yankee delicacies and wines, gallantly passed by a Yankee hospital, and fired at a supply ship on the Pamunkey. The flooded Chickahominy furnished a dramatic climax barring the way to safety.

For three nervous hours, they cobbled together a wrecked bridge as Union cavalry inched closer. Finally, his two guns and captured wagons were able to rumble across, rattling and shaking the jury-rigged structure ominously. Troopers clattered after them, too slowly for those following. They set fire to the rickety bridge.

The rear guard pulled in, fighting all the while for their diminishing bridgehead. The flames spread. They rode through, only minutes ahead of their pursuers. They watched the flames consume their bridge. They had built for one crossing only, their own.

Shooting continued from the north bank.

They turned toward Charles City Courthouse where they rested in safety, men and mounts. Stuart hurried ahead to report to General Lee.

Some thought his 4-day reconnaissance theatrical, but Stuart's easy response was that riding around was safer than returning through country alerted to his presence. His report gave General Lee what he needed and the feat made him the toast of Richmond.

Meanwhile, in a quiet bedroom at the Winston farmstead, David soaked in steaming water, drank a potion of hot whiskey, and plummeted into deep sleep. He was wet with fever.

Eighteen hours later, he felt a cool cloth on his forehead and sensed shadowy undulations. The refreshing coolness was his only reality until the floating billows became lace curtains lifting to the summer breeze.

"Can you manage a bit of broth?" The voice was soft, lyrically soft, honeysuckle sweet.

"Unt uh."

"If Ah help you?"

Before he could form an answer, a warmth soothed his lips, flowed salty into his empty stomach.

"That's all," the voice purled, "Would you like more?"

"Unt uh."

He mumbled "thank you," rolled away from the piquant voice, slept again, through the evening twilight and through the night.

He stirred momentarily, throwing off the suffocating bedclothes. He dozed, slept, twisted, and perspired. He slept restlessly, hearing, yet not hearing the noises of the night. Obscure rapping and tapping filtered through the darkness, soft, loud, close by, nonsensical. As did a dog's sharp bark, near the house or far off, faint, then gone, back again louder. A door squealed on its hinges. Cows lowing. Thunder off in the distance. Or was it gunfire?

Momentarily, he sat up in the bed, vaguely sensing that he had to be somewhere, aware of distant daylight. Trance-like, suspended, he flopped back into the abyss, dreamed of fire and hot coals searing his body. The darkness came again, then the light and he was awake.

The latch on his door clicked. A face slanted through the opening. Long, golden tresses fell free on one side.

"Ah you awake? Ah heard noises as Ah was passing."

The voice, David knew, was the same one that had spooned broth into him, musical, refined. He pulled the quilted bed-cover up around his face, reluctant to be seen in so disheveled a state.

He blinked from his covey, entranced at her beauty. He knew as he spoke that his words were witless, "I was sleeping."

"Really?" the question mocked playfully.

For the moment, he saw nothing but eyes. Blue they were. No, green. Bluish green, mostly green, with a sparkle that broadcast liveliness and love of excitement.

"You have no need to be bashful. Ah do have brothuhs."

"It's not that. I'm just not—uh—presentable."

"Do you feel bettuh? When we put you to bed, you were not exactly Prince Charming."

"You put me to bed!"

"Ah pulled off youah boots," she teased, and generously ended his incipient embarrassment, "mah uncle did the rest. Actually he's mah great uncle." David remembered honeysuckle.

"Youah clothes ah hanging in the armoire, washed, pressed, and mended. Ah did do the mendin'.

"If it's of interest to you," she flirted.

"Of course it is. Thank you very much. I'm David Morrow."

"Ah know."

"How do you know?"

"Mah uncle told me?" she inflected as a question.

"How did he know?"

"Ah b'lieve the general told him."

"Oh.

"What time is it?"

"Early aftuhnoon. Half past one."

"I slept all night and half the day?"

"Oh no! Moah like two nights, then the half day. Ah've been in and out to make shuah you were still among the living?"

"Two whole days! I don't believe it."

She looked at him coyly, "Ah wouldn't lie to you."

"I know you wouldn't. I'm sorry for the implication."

"Ah accept youah apology, suh," Vicki dipped a curtsy, "Ah'd be happy to prepare a tray. You must be hungry."

"Oh no, I've been too much a bother. I'll come down."

"Bed's the place for you. To build youah strength. You haven't taken a bite since yestuhday. And then all you had was a bit of broth."

"Yesterday? I thought that was just a few minutes ago."

"Fevuh does that to people," she came to the bed to put a hand on his forehead, "the fevuh's down, but you are pale as a body can be

"Best stay abed fore now."

At the doorway she turned, "By the way, Ah'm Victoria. Mah Papa owns this farm."

"Happy to know you, Miss Victoria." His voice trailed off as she left the room.

David dressed, stopping more than once to let his head clear. Maybe she was right, he thought. The fever had left him too washed out to do much of anything quickly.

He managed the hallway and half the stairs, to the landing where the staircase took a right-angled turn. Lightheaded from the effort, he had to sit. Victoria with the blue-green eyes found him there, against the newel post.

"Oh! You should be abed. You are not ready to walk about."

"I'll be all right,"

"Let me help you," she held out a hand.

He took it in his, but remained seated, longer than he was ready to admit.

"May I call you Vicki? Miss Victoria, or even Victoria, sounds so— don't think me rude—so formal."

"Ah think our customary formalities valuable, when they ah appropriate that is. But Ah also think Ah would like you to call me Vicki. Aftuh all, Ah did take youah boots off."

Steps clicked across the verandah.

David stood, supporting himself on the carved bannister. He negotiated the rest of the stairs without mishaps. Victoria, Vicki, took her hand back decorously as the front door opened.

"Betty, what are you doing here this late in the day?" Victoria embraced her cousin, "it is good to see you. But what ah you doing heah?"

"Papa thought I should visit for a few days, until those dreadful Yankees leave."

"Until the Yankees leave?"

"Yes, they've been around the courthouse. Just yesterday some of them rode their horses right up to Courtland. As if they had the right!"

"To youah house? Y'all must have been terrifahed."

"Papa spoke sharply to them about it, and they rode off. One of them, a lieutenant I think, was respectful enough. He saluted—said something about 'orders'. He apologized, too, in a mannerly fashion, but papa thought I'd best come over here."

"How is Uncle William?" Without waiting for an answer, Victoria put her hand to her mouth and gasped a little gasp in mock astonishment, "And Ah have forgotten mah mannuhs.

"Betty, this is David Morrow, Captain David Morrow with General Stuart's cavalry.

"David, mah cousin, Miss Barbara Winston."

"Captain, it is a pleasure to make your acquaintance."

"Miss Winston," David stood straight, heels together. He bowed slightly from the waist, "The pleasure is mine, ma'am."

The bow, or the standing, cost him another dizzy spell, and he had to sit again on the stairs.

"Oh mah! You must get back to bed."

Embarrassed, he objected with a feeble wave, "Just give me a minute. I'll be all right."

"You have ovuh-done, David. Heah, take mah hand."

For the second time, he accepted, leaned toward her lightly. Very lightly, but more than he needed. Vicki seemed not to object to the closeness as they climbed the staircase.

When she came down, her cousin gave her a sly smile, "David it is. You've never said 'David' quite like that before."

Vicki smiled coyly, "Maybe because the Davids we know ah all so—so—young!"

"So young! And you only eighteen years old! I do declare"

"Eighteen is not young," she huffed, "it's not young at all. Why, Ah have friends who married at eighteen, and at seventeen—so have you." She ended her statement with a declaration of independence, "Eighteen is old enough to—to do anything a body wants."

"Now, Vicki, don't be so riled. Tell me more about your captain. What's he doing here?"

"Isn't it exciting! He's been heah three days. Was with a cavalry troop, or army, whatevuh it was and sick with fevuh. The leaduh was so nice, General Stuart. He even apologized for ecamping in ouah fields and having to leave David.

"Isn't he handsome, Betty! Ah just adore him, He has such a nice smile and his teeth are so white.

"Not juvenile like the boys we know," her inflection reduced her contemporaries' ages by half.

In bed once again, David was feeling less mature than he was being portrayed, not able to bow even slightly without losing his balance. Why had Cousin Betty chosen this particular time to visit anyway? Another thought piqued him, too, something about—having to do with—Captain David Morrow reached for it, but was sound asleep.

He spent two more days in the quiet bedroom, satisfied to rest, happy to keep embarrassing dizzy spells private, renewed a bit more with each meal Vicki brought. In between, she swished into the room with cold lemonade or tea, with wild strawberries, yeasty bread right from the oven, and juicy-ripe tomatoes still sun-warm.

"Stuart, it's good to see you back."

"General, it was a rollicking good ride. Right around him."

General Lee was fond of Stuart, liked his exuberance, daring and gay nonchalance, but he wondered if his cavalier trooper might be tempted sometimes to use the war to fulfill his fondness for enjoyment.

He cocked his head expectantly, "Are you sure you didn't plan to circle McClellan from the beginning?"

"Well uh, General Lee, uh, the possibility existed from the beginning, of course. But, sir, uppermost in my mind was the safety of my men. I thought it less dangerous to continue on since we had raised the alarm behind us."

"I see. Decisions made at the scene have to be respected. Now, what have you learned about the Yankees? Here, show me."

Indicating a rough circle on the spread map, Stuart began,

"This is our route, sir. We met our greatest opposition at Hanover Courthouse and Old Church," he pointed, "a regiment of cavalry, out there to patrol. No infantry at all. That part of Hanover County is open," splaying his fingers, "all the way to the Pamunkey. McClellan's flank is in the air, sir, ready to be turned."

"Hmmmmm. As I suspected. Your confirmation is valuable."

Anticipating Jeb Stuart's report, Lee had written to Jackson twice in the past week, first about uniting "at the decisive moment with the army near Richmond" and subsequently, about sweeping "down between the Chickahominy and Pamunkey. . ."

Now with Stuart's report, an anxious General Lee wrote a third time: "the sooner you unite with this army the better. . . The present, therefore, seems to be favorable for a junction of your army and this . . . the sooner you can make arrangements to [join me] the better."

He called for a courier, "I need to talk to Colonel Boteler. Find him if it takes all night. Find him!"

Early next morning, Colonel Boteler rode out Nine Mile Road to Lee's headquarters, the same Alexander Boteler who, in 1834, had talked with Henry Morrow at Taylor's Hotel, and last winter had dinner at the Morrows' as aide-de-camp to General Jackson. He entered the Dabb house as he had yesterday to deliver Jackson's request for more troops.

General Lee stood at a small table studying the map that spilled off one side. He interrupted his reflections to offer a folded paper, "Colonel, this dispatch is for General Jackson. It is of the utmost urgency. And discretion, of course."

"Yes, general, I understand."

"As to his request, please tell him this is not the time to be looking across the Potomac. Not yet. Not yet."

He addressed Boteler again, "Jackson has done a first-rate job in the Valley. He's like a right arm to me."

"I shall inform him of your compliment, General Lee. He will be pleased, I am sure."

David awakened early, stronger, ready to rejoin Stuart.

"I wouldn't count on that," Vicki's uncle said, "you don't know where he is. He could be back in Richmond by now—the Yankees are scouring the countryside for him. They've operated out of Hanover Courthouse for three, four days, so it's reasonable to say you are cut off in that direction."

"Then I'll have to return by the way I came," David responded but added almost at once, "that's probably just as bad. They'll be watching that, too."

"Captain, I don't want to intrude into your military matters, but I have a thought that may be worth considering."

"Of course, sir. I am overly indebted to you as it is."

"What I have in mind is to do nothing for a day or two, maybe three. I have some very dependable hands that I can send out to see what they can. Then we decide what's best."

"My thought, if I may, is to return by way of Ashland. That looks closer than going around McClellan's other flank. Perhaps cut it closer to the railroad if it looks clear."

"We are in agreement then, captain. Good. Another two or three days will hasten your recovery."

David was happy at the extra time with Vicki, even though he had shared her with Cousin Betty for two days. They were on the verandah, Cousin Betty with them, attending her embroidery hoop as Victoria sat close to David. They were, Cousin Betty observed, much taken with one another.

"And your brothuh, the scholarly one?" Vicki was asking, 'you haven't said much about him, othuh than he was at Washin'ton College, and now he's with General Jackson."

"Well, Briney read everything he could find. Curious about everything. When he read Sir Walter Scott, he made a study of the knights. That led to King Arthur, the Crusades, gunpowder. That's his way. Interested in one thing and then a half dozen others."

"He sounds nice," Vicki sighed wistfully.

"I haven't seen him since before the war," A fleeting melancholy touched him.

"I'd rather talk about you. You're nice, too."

"Oh, David, you ah just sayin' that."

Painstakingly, Betty folded her needlework, preparing to leave, yet not wanting to, "I think I'll walk down the lane." With a twinkle in her eyes, she paused, "Anyone want to join me?"

Looking up to answer, Vicki saw the telltale warning and pointed. David saw it, too, and made for the front door. The tiny horse and rider unrolled a dust trail in the still air. Yankee or Confederate? The man and his mount grew in size, showing a flying tail and stretching legs, a wide-brimmed hat flat in the wind. As they closed the distance, a harmony of horse and rider emerged, and a sense of urgency.

Galloping up the lane, the rider flashed between the trees lining either side, pulled up at the verandah steps. Glistening, the chestnut danced nervous, mincing steps in her excitement.

"This the Winston farm?"

"Yes. And who are you?"

"I'm Corporal Rafferty, ma'am, lookin' fer Captain Morrow, ma'am. They said I could find him here."

He gave a half salute as David came through the front door, "Hello, captain. Hope you're feelin' better." The corporal patted the mare's neck, cooing to calm her.

"Rafe, what are you doing here?" He grasped the corporal's hand, more friend for the moment than superior officer. "What's the general up to. Expected him to come back through here, until the rumors came. Is it true he went around McClellan?"

"Clear around, by Go—" he glanced at the women, "by gosh. All the way around, an' Richmond's been cheerin' him since."

"Sorry I wasn't with him. But that's not why you're here."

Vicki stood motionless on the verandah, blue-green eyes wide, finger tips pressing into soft lips.

Rafferty glanced significantly toward the two girls.

"Vicki, Miss Betty, excuse us please."

The two soldiers walked across the lane into an open field, their shadows long in the day's late sunshine.

"Now, what is this secret message you have?"

"Captain, somethin's brewin'. General Stuart's been t'see General Lee three times. When he came back this morning, he wrote this message and told me t'bring it here."

Rafferty fished a small paper from his boot.

David read quickly, "Hope you're feeling better. Stuart."

"You galloped a blooded mare half to death to deliver this?" David spit the last word.

"No si—, yes sir," Rafferty reversed himself, "that 'n another message General Stuart said don't write down."

"Well, what is it, man?"

The corporal looked suspiciously about, "He said for you t'meet General Jackson. If you were up t'it, he said."

"Of course I'm up to it. What else?"

Rafe lowered his voice, "General Jackson will be in Gordonsville t'morrow."

"Nobody ever knows that much about Jackson's whereabouts except when he's within eyeshot."

The corporal lowered his voice almost to a whisper. "They do this time, sir, General Stuart said you can bet on it. He said for me t'go with you if you wanted."

"Of course, Rafe. Only one thing. The mare needs time to cool down. A breather and water."

"She'll be all right," Rafe answered quickly, his fear of being left behind greater than that of an extended ride. He would follow David anywhere, horseback or shanks' mare.

David returned to the verandah, wondering how best to announce his departure. He needn't have worried.

"You have to leave, don't you?"

"Afraid so, Vicki. I have orders from General Stuart."

"Oh! Ah knew it. Ah just knew it when Ah saw the dust," Vicki chewed a knuckle.

Cousin Betty broke in, "Uncle was looking for you. He said he'd be around the barn."

"Ah'll help you find him."

"That would be nice, Vicki."

As they walked, he felt her fingertips on the back of his hand, tentative and inquiring. Only when he clasped them gently did she look up at him, glistening eyes more green than blue. As he had done on the stairs pretending more weakness than he felt, she leaned against him ever so lightly. He leaned back, without pretense this time. They met Vicki's uncle as they rounded the corner of the house.

"I have good news, captain. The road to Ashland is clear. That will allow you to circle around to Richmond. My man could have missed something, but I don't think so."

"The information is just in time, sir. I have orders to report to headquarters."

"I thought that rider might be looking for you. General Stuart is a fine man. Give him my regards." His host made the reasonable assumption as David hoped he would.

"Yes, sir, I surely will."

Vicki's uncle glanced at the intertwined fingers. David feared he read disapproval. Vicki blushed. They squeezed hands for courage.

"I thank you for your many kindnesses, Mr. Winston."

"Not at all, captain. Happy to do what I can for the cause."

"Night's coming on. I suggest you wait until morning."

XXXV

TWO SLEEPLESS NIGHTS

"Thank you again, Mr. Winston, for all you have done. I'd better look to Sable if I want to get an early start."

"Not at all, Captain Morrow. It has been our pleasure, hasn't it, Victoria?"

"Oh, uncle, you!"

"I'll come with you," Vickie offered, adding coyly, "if you like?"

In the barn, they found Tom Rafferty rubbing down his mare, Princess.

"That Mr. Winston is sure a nice man," he volunteered, "he had one of his men bring a bucket of oats."

"My uncle loves his horses. When he saw your mare come in so lathered, he was concerned that she be taken care of at once. Right away he said she needed to be rubbed down, watered and fed. With a generous portion of oats."

"Tom, I didn't know you were familiar with this area."

"I'm not, captain, I'm from the Valley like you—Frederick County. But I had a young fellow who lives near Hanover Courthouse—he guided me. He sure did know the country, trails that only he and the deer knew about. We stayed off the main roads, gave all the houses a wide berth. He said you could trust most of the people, but it wasn't fair to even talk to them. It could put them in danger."

"How about the Yankees? See any of them?

"Not a one. Not where we came through."

"This guide of yours sounds like a good man to know. You know where to find him?"

"Have no idea, captain. He left me a few miles out, with directions how to get here. Said he'd probably stop to see his folks, get a good meal, then wait for dark to go back across the Chickahominy."

"You suppose we could find his folks? Sounds like he could be useful. Something big is brewing. A man who knows the country could be mighty important. The one map I've seen is almost useless."

"Golly, I'd have no idea where to look for them. Somewheres this side of the swamp is all I know."

"That's not much help."

"Sorry, captain, I should have thought of that myself."

"Don't fret it. I'm sure there are others. Better get back to that mare—make sure she's ready for a long day tomorrow."

"Yessir. G'night, sir. G'night, ma'am." The young trooper headed for the other end of the barn.

Vickie stood close watching David brush Sable, moving step by step as he moved about the big stallion. He brushed with care, inspected Sable's coat minutely for soil and telltale blemishes. He brushed down each leg, larger than most but still fragile-looking, examining knees, hooves and shoes with particular care. He was sitting on his heels, looking closely at a fore hoof when Sable nudged, setting him on his backside. Sable tossed his head, neighed in apparent delight.

Vickie laughed, too, dropped beside him, an arm across his chest, her face close to his. She was too inviting not to kiss and he, too attractive. They came together.

"Oh, David, I've been wanting you to do that. Kiss me again."

"You are so beautiful, Vickie." He touched her face lightly, her neck and shoulder tentatively, allowing her the freedom to deny him. She didn't. He kissed her again as his fingers explored.

Uncle's voice interrupted.

From somewhere in back of the barn, he was shouting instructions to one of the hands.

David stood quickly, held a hand for Vickie.

"Oh, David."

They brushed roughly at bits of clinging straw.

"Vickie, I'm . . ."

She put a finger to his lips, "Later. Finish brushing Sable for now.

"And brush me if I need it," turning about for his inspection.

Discreetly, he flicked bits of hay from her skirt and blouse, "You're fine."

She laughed again, "I know that. Is there any left?" She turned again, slowly.

"Not now."

Smoothing her skirt, she drew herself erect, hurried toward the barn door. She turned back and mouthed, "Later."

With two hours of darkness left, David and Tom Rafferty were on the road, hoping to be well clear of Yankee patrols by dawn. Despite the report of clear roads, Yankee cavalry could well be prowling about. They felt a bit safer when they crossed the tracks of the Virginia Central Railroad.

The night faded to gray. They were in open country beyond Ashland, reasonably confident they were out of danger. David was quiet, preoccupied.

"That's a nice family you were with, captain."

"Appears so, Rafe, surely does appear so."

Rafe tried again, "Glad you decided t'wait until this mornin' t'leave, an' Princess here," patting the mare's curried coat, "is, too."

They trotted another quarter of a mile without conversation.

"You feelin' all right, captain?"

"Yes, I'm fine."

"You aren't gettin' the fever back, are you, sir?"

"No, Rafe, I'm fine."

Riding cross-country at times, they guided on the Virginia Central, northwest through Beaver Dam Station and Bumpass turnout, through Louisa Courthouse and into Gordonsville.

A few questions, each one narrowing the location, brought them to Jackson's headquarters. David had asked them prudently, without any mention of the general.

"Captain Morrow, isn't it?"

"Yes, sir," pleased at the recognition, but puzzled at the tone of the greeting. It was anything but friendly.

"I'm happy to be with you again, general."

"Sir, I am surprised to see you here, very much surprised indeed," Jackson frowned his irritation that someone knew where to find him.

Four days he had kept his own counsel so that even some of his staff and senior officers were unsure of their location, and none yet knew their destination.

"General Stuart's compliments, sir. He thought I could be of service."

"How'd you know I was here?"

David knew from experience that the question was not really a question at all, but Jackson's pique at the apparent lapse of security. It was best met with brevity.

"General Stuart, sir."

"How did he know where I was?"

"I can't say, sir, but I know he's had frequent meetings with General Lee over the past few days."

"Hmmmm. Your corporal. I've seen him before."

"You have, sir, at Falling Waters. Corporal Rafferty, general. You met him there when we made our report on General Patterson's advance. Just before the fight."

Jackson looked less severe, pleased with his memory perhaps, then scowled again.

"I suppose he knew, too."

"Yes, sir. But he's no tongue-wagger, sir."

"Nobody's a tongue-wagger, but information gets out. I want information kept close. The fewer that know, the better chance for surprise. Surprise 'em, surprise 'em, . . . It worked in Mexico, it will work here." Jackson changed the subject, "you familiar with this area we're going?"

"Not every nook and cranny, sir, but I've ridden through."

"Ridden through? What does that mean? How many times have you 'ridden through'?"

"Once, sir. Today."

"Hmmm." He had been impressed before with this young cavalry officer and his positive attitude. It reminded him of his own rash confidence as a young subaltern at Chapultepec.

"Only one time! In that case maybe I'll find someone who has ridden through it twice'n put you to training troops again," he gave voice to a series of controlled screaks, his own strange way of laughing. "Report back in one hour."

David looked at his pocket watch, "Yes, sir," saluting smartly.

General Jackson casually lifted a hand toward the cracked visor of his ancient forage cap. He looked tired, very tired.

David mumbled to Rafferty as they left, "Ridden through twice! You think that's funny, Rafe?"

"Not especially, sir, but I guess the general does. He surely has a funny way of laughing."

They watered Sable and Princess, gave them the last of the oats from the Winston farm.

"Better keep them separated, Tom. If he gets her smell, you just might find yourself with two horses to take care of."

His thoughts wandered back to Vicki and a walk with her just last night. It seemed ages.

After supper, he had gone back to the barn to finish with Sable and make a final inspection of his gear. An early, very early morning departure was essential. He had checked Sable, his tack, carbine and revolvers when he heard Vickie call from the barn door.

" 'most finished?"

"Be right there. Just need another minute."

The evening was pleasant, for this time of the year, with a trace of refreshing breeze. They strolled to the well, where they drew water, cool and sweet. Perched on the well cover, they watched the sun disappear behind the low hills, enhancing the blue of the sky, burnishing the horizon and the bulging clouds with its orange and gold. As they watched, its wide blaze across horizon narrowed, changing orange, red, cerise.

"Lovely, isn't it, David?"

"I never tire of watching it. Sunsets and sunrises."

In the darkening twilight, they walked the entry drive. lined with magnificent oak trees. She leaned against one of them, back to the rough bark.

"Ah'm sorry you are leaving."

"Thanks to your expert nursing care."

"Will Ah ever see you again?"

"I hope so, but who knows? With this war and all. It might go on for years."

"And you will be a famous general and fo'get all about li'l ole me."

"I will always remember how kind you have been to me. Besides, I'll probably be back to see you in a few days."

"Oh, do you really think so. Ah'd love that."

"It's like I said. Nobody knows, but you have to think things turn out for the best. No other way to get through a war."

"Ah wish Ah could do that. Sometimes, it seems Ah'm jus: goin' to die an old maid."

Daintily, she sniffed, reached for a tiny square of a handkerchief. She dabbed at her eyes.

"Vickie, you won't die an old maid," he grinned, "if I have to come back and save you myself. I'll rescue you from your tower room and we'll ride off into the setting sun. Isn't that the way it goes?"

She looked coquettishly through long lashes, "Now you are laughing at me."

"I wouldn't do that."

"What would you do, Captain Morrow?"

"Why, anything. Anything at all to make you happy."

"Anything? You really mean that? Anything at all?"

"We—ell, you know, anything within reason."

Having danced along the edge of the unknown, they walked back toward the house in silence. They had started something, each knew, left it hanging, like a dance only half finished when the music stops. It demanded a finish, either now or later.

Now or later? They needed time to think about that, but the circumstances indicated there may well be no later.

She steered him toward the gazebo on the lawn. They had sat there on the previous evening, talking, holding hands. They held hands as they had then. David felt a familiar excitement. He wondered if Vicki felt the same, until she pulled closer. Then he knew.

She tilted her face into the light of the rising moon, kissed him. She led him up the steps into the gazebo, and as they had not done the evening before, moved into its flimsy protection.

She removed pins, shook her blonde hair out to its full length; it fell just below her shoulders. In the shadows, they kissed again. She leaned into him, breasts flattening. Ever so slightly, she relaxed, pressed again. The contact excited them both.

"Touch me," she whispered, "oh, there, yes, there."

They felt and shared the rising excitement. It became passion and the passion, abandon. He slipped buttons free and slid the sleeves from her shoulders. Her white skin glowed in the moonlight, soft to his lips, inviting him to do more. When he hesitated, she moved his hand back to her breast, inhaled deeply against it, inviting it into her wondrous softness. Gently, he caressed. Ever so softly, she answered his advances.

"Love me, David, love me and let me love you."

David hesitated, "Are you sure, Vicki? Maybe we . . ."

She purled her answer, "Yes, yes, and yes."

They separated, enough for hands to undo buttons and belts, laces and hooks, his and hers, trousers and shirt, dress and shift, boneless corselet, down to underthings long, medium and short.

They separated a bit more, to look at each other in the moonlight, marvel at what they were about to share. David cupped her face in his hands, framing it in handsful of golden hair. The remaining long, medium and short fell between them, covering nothing but their toes.

Tenderly, he kissed her, lowered her to the floor of the gazebo. He knelt and lay beside her. He held her giving mouth to his, taking, submitting. He caressed, massaged, murmured cryptic love messages into her ear, preparing her, moving between her legs, slipping smoothly into her.

She stretched to accept him, moaned her pleasure and very slowly withdrew most of what she had given. He closed the space, opened it again for her to fill, closed again, opened, closed until the rhythmic undulations took on an existence of their own, lithe, slow, giving, receiving, plummeting now, withdrawing, plunging beyond control, entangling, melding into one flesh, one mind, one brain, bursting forth in a symphonic coda, allegro, molto vivace, molto . . .

Joined, they whirled deliriously into space, into a final marriage of ecstasies that left them breathless, limp and radiant. They lay quietly, letting their fervor subside, their blood cool.

Vickie nuzzled his ear, whispering, "My! how you do marshall the troops! You should be a general, David, at least a general."

"And you, a queen. So the people would have an exultant king to govern over them."

For several minutes, they lay quietly in each other's arms, imagining their behavior as the world's grandest monarchs. Vickie squirmed closer.

"Do you think we could do it again?"

The question was answered in the gazebo, but never in David's reverie, for Rafe interrupted it, "You asleep, Captain Morrow?"

"What are you doing here, Vi . . ." David caught himself. The voice was wrong. He forced himself from the illusory vision of the gazebo in the moonlight, "Er—who's that? Rafe?"

"Just thought you might want to eat before the general sends for us."

"I'm all right, Rafe. You go ahead."

He lay back, head on his saddle. Vickie's words came back to him from last night, after their second love-making and before they prepared to leave the gazebo. "Ah you asleep, Captain Morrow?"

They returned to Jackson's headquarters just as he was concluding his orders to General Ewell, "—early Monday, east down the railroad tracks. Use the trains to pick up the men in the rear—keep the column closed up." Ewell saluted and left.

The small escort waited, David, Tom Rafferty, and three of Jackson's aides "From this moment call me 'colonel'. No one is to know my identity."

They coaxed horses into a box car of the Virginia Central, boarded the car ahead. Rattling into Fredericks-hall Station that Sabbath dawn, they made immediately for the home of Nathaniel Harris to rest, and to conceal Jackson's presence. They remained until after midnight, for the general considered it important to give the Lord His day.

At 1 o'clock in the morning, the small party mounted up for the last forty miles to Lee's headquarters. On this final leg, David took the lead so the 'colonel' could remain inconspicuous. A few miles out, Jackson quietly asked Corporal Rafferty and the others to drop behind. In a voice still lower, addressed David. "Do you know where we're going?"

David had an accurate guess, but thought it better to respect the general's penchant for security, "Not really, sir. I could guess but I'd rather not. The army has enough rumors flying about without mine."

In the dark, David didn't notice Jackson's nod of approval, but did hear his reaction, "Good! Good!"

Jackson almost whispered, "It's Richmond we're headed for. Richmond and General Lee's headquarters. We'll need directions."

"I know headquarters, sir, the Dabb house. Least it was ten days ago,— there's no reason to think it's been moved."

By mid-afternoon, they were on Nine Mile Road almost to the farmhouse where General Lee had called the meeting of his senior commanders, Pete Longstreet, A.P. Hill, Daniel Harvey Hill, and of course Jackson.

Worn from his whirlwind success in the Valley, exhausted from four days with little sleep, the South's new hero dismounted slowly, rested against a rail fence. In another minute, he would have been asleep on his feet had not General Lee called his commanders into his temporary headquarters.

"Gentlemen," he addressed them, "General Stuart on his recent reconnaissance confirmed the vulnerability of the Federal right. My plan is predicated on his observations. General Jackson will march from Ashland to the vicinity of Cold Harbor, turning McClellan's left flank, forcing those people to fall back. That will clear the way for an attack en echelon. A.P. Hill will cross Meadow Bridge, advance on Mechanicsville, clearing the way for Harvey Hill to cross the lower bridge, which in turn, allows General Longstreet to cross below that."

The commanding officer left the room for his lieutenants to discuss the plan amongst themselves.

Longstreet suggested Jackson set the time for the attack since he had the greatest distance to travel. Completely fatigued, Jackson answered absently, "The morning of the 25th." Longstreet thought it too soon. Jackson gave himself another day, "the 26th then."

General Lee rejoined them. The council broke up at dark.

"Thank you for your assistance, Captain Morrow. You may return to your command."

"With all due respect, sir, I request permission to escort you back, at least part of the way. The roads can be confusing, especially in the dark."

"I'm sure that Major Harman and the rest of the party can manage to find our way. But I thank you anyway."

With that, Jackson rode off to rejoin his Valley army which should have advanced to Beaver Dam Station, fifteen miles north of Richmond. He spent another sleepless night in the saddle.

David slept in the open and made his way to the cavalry camp by mid-morning.

XXXVI

FORT DELAWARE

For most of that first night on his prison shelf, Brian lay wide-eyed, struggling to come to terms with his fate. Never, never had he been so close to evil such as this. He had been overcome with it, from the moment he set foot on the stinking slime of Peanut Island and heard the brutish adjutant. The depraved corporal added to his misery, as did the stinking barracks and pestilent sleeping rack. He hadn't slept for more than an hour when the outrage started all over again.

"On yer feet, you rebel bastards. On yer feet I say."

Guttural voices filled the barracks as guards tromped the center aisle.

"Fall in!"

"Line up!"

"Damn new fish!"

Prowling the aisle, four guards smacked feet with the flat of their bayonets.

"Off yer ass an' on yer feet!".

Not asleep, yet not fully alert to his new surroundings, Brian lingered in the obscure world between. Harsh voices quashed his uncertainty. A fuzzy shadow loomed ominous.

"Outa that bunk," a cracking blow whacked his foot.

A sting echoed up his leg.

"Line up, cracker, NOW!"

The shade moved off.

Jarred into reality, he scrambled, reaching for his canteen with the tooled strap. He sought it not for the dregs of any water that might be left, but automatically, simply for the feel of something he knew and trusted. It had become his amulet of reassurance and temporary relief in this horrible place.

He blinked in the gray light making out an aisle that ran lengthwise through the middle of the room. A rusted wood stove presided at one end. Two tiers of rough boards lined each side, five feet apart, one the ceiling for the other. A hundred feet long, the sleeping shelves had no mattresses, only wisps of straw and tatters that at one time might have been clothing. Here and there was a crumpled blanket marking a new fish.

Brian saw the young soldier standing at his sleeping space, scratching. Brian scratched at his own lice, and gagged at the mixture of human gasses. He motioned, "Move up here next to me."

A sharp voice rang out, "Wherethehell you goin', sonny?"

Brian spoke for him, "He's my cousin and . . ." He cut it off fearful of suggesting vulnerabilities the guards could use.

"You forgot yer manners, reb."

The voice rattled with mucus, unclean, familiar to Brian.

He had heard it last night, the pervert who had leered at the young soldier. He saw the two chevrons on his sleeves.

Slime-voice put his face into Brian's, exhaling heavy, vile vapor.

Brian winced at the stench, realizing for the first time the enormity of the wickedness surrounding him.

Abruptly, the brute leered, swung his bayonet, flat-side to Brian's head, "Didn't hear no respect and that ain't nice." He grinned brown teeth and black spaces.

"Apologize, reb. Stand on yer bunk and sing out."

The bayonet drew slow loops about Brian's face, cobra-like, swaying, swaying. A maniac with a sharp knife.

Fearful for his very life Brian froze. Only his eyes moved, moving as the blade moved, watchful, watchful.

He glared his hatred.

"You hear me?" the voice menacing, "on yer bunk."

Brian did as he was told.

"Louder! So's yer friends kin hear," the corporal taunted.

The bayonet weaved its cold rhythm.

Again Brian obeyed.

"And that cousin uh yers, I'll be back fer him," the devil bared his rotted teeth again, walked off, "nuthin' but fresh fish an' dumber'n hell. You bastards better learn quick."

The guards counted heads, stomped out as the sun broke the horizon. Brian stood rigid, feeling ice in his soul, knowing that death had brushed very close.

Then the trembling started. The cold shakes.

Sweat glistened into tiny balls and flowed rivulets.

Tom McDonald crossed the aisle in three steps, "I thought you were going t' take a swing at him."

Brian whispered unintelligibly. The trembling increased.

Tom grasped him by the shoulders, "Settle down, Brian. It's over." He continued to hold him until the shakes diminished and stopped.

"Damned if I didn't think you were going t' hit him."

Brian mumbled numbly, "Almost—almost."

He quieted.

Tom rested his hand on Brian's arm, "You all right now?"

Brian nodded as he sank to the edge of the crude shelf.

"I don't know about you, but I have t' piss."

Tom shouted as he walked the length of the room, "Guard."

Cracking the door, he yelled to the outside, "Men need the sinks."

A musket shot rang out.

A miniature, pink cloud puffed briefly near the doorway as a bullet splatted brick. Wild laughter screeched, "Hang it out the door so's I kin shoot it off."

Brian exploded off the shelf mindlessly, running for the door, "You animals! Brainless, vulgar lunatics! Fools! Animals!"

Tom caught him by the arm.

"Beasts! Bastards!" Brian slammed the door open, screaming insanely, "Bastards! Bastards!" "Bastar . . ."

The musket popped again, another thud, softer this time.

A stillness washed over the room. Prisoners craned pop-eyed at the heap just inside the door, Tom and Brian intertwined. As they watched, Tom gripped his friend's arms against another suicidal run, lifted him, walked the length of the room, a second time and yet again before he spoke.

"Come on, Briney, we just got here—there's a long way t' go. Nobody'll make it without trying."

"I've taken all I can. Soon as it's dark I'm getting out."

"Now you're talking crazy."

"Crazy or not, I'm leaving tonight."

"The way you're talking, you might at that. Not like you mean but by getting shot dead. Chances are you'll get a hole in the ground and nobody knowing what the hell happened to you."

"Who the hell cares?"

"A lot of people," his voice rose, "if its sympathy you want, I'll give you sympathy. For starters, I care," he plunged on, "your mother cares, your pa cares, all the people you've talked of care. Ezekiel. Your brothers. Sisters. All of us care.

"I'll give you more sympathy. Your friends in I Company care, the ones you enlisted with, the Liberty Hall Volunteers."

Brian looked up suspiciously, "I know what you're doing.'

"Good! I'm glad you understand. Now you got your sympathy, you can start talking sense."

The two were silent for several minutes, Tom giving time for his words to sink in, Brian ambivalent. He was wrong to claim no one cared, he knew that, but it didn't help.

"Tom, it's how I've felt since Manassas. It's worse now.

There's no sense left. See these stripes?" he pulled his sleeve around, "they belong to Charley Nelson and I killed him."

Tom ignored the chevrons, "There's a lot of sense left, not here maybe, but it's there. You have t'keep looking for it."

"Look where? All I see is blood and bodies. It's insane."

"Look toward Winchester—the Shenandoah Valley—home. Look t'next year, Brian. Next week. Tomorrow."

"I see Jed in Winchester, and," his breath caught. He sobbed into guilty hands, "—and bodies."

Tom stayed nearby, watchful to protect him from himself.

At midday, the prisoners were routed out for their daily ration. One of them dug a lead slug out of the door. From older inmates, the new ones learned that the morning's coarse humor was for them, the fresh fish, the raw meat. A typical greeting. Guards had their laughs, then resumed the morning sink calls.

Brian looked at his meal in disgust, a piece of salt pork, a chunk of bread, dirty, more stale than fresh. Tom was beside him, "Toward home, Brian, look toward home."

Tom remained vigilant through the day, the night, into the next day when Brian volunteered, "I guess you are right."

"What do you mean?"

"About people caring."

"I know I am, Brian. We'll get off this Peanut Island or whatever the hell it's called. You and I'll keep looking until we find a way."

Brian Morrow clung desperately to that hope.

That night the young soldier, Samuel Turner, approached him, "I'm sorry if I caused trouble for you. I didn't mean to."

"You're not the problem, Sam. It's that reprehensible guard."

He looked a question, "You know what I'm talking about?"

"I should, that's why I ran away and joined the army."

Brian gulped, "That's why you ran away!"

"That's right. My Ma and Pa were killed by bushwhackers and I went to live with my uncle. He was all right for a while—then he started pestering me. Touching me. I ran away—they wanted soldiers for the army so I signed up."

Brian had heard the stories, but disbelieved them all. Maybe in Biblical days, Sodom and Gomorrah, but not here in this day and age. Now he had seen it. He was stunned.

"But your uncle . . .—you're not old enough to enlist."

"I lied about my age. They didn't seem too particular."

"Just stay close to me. Don't get alone with that animal."

He lived one day at a time, reveille, head count, sick call, work call, the day's one meal, head count, and taps. Sick call was cancelled for a short time, then re-instituted when Richmond threatened equal treatment for Yankee captives.

He and Tom volunteered themselves and young Sam Turner for work details for the chance to survey the grounds against their escape. The work was boring and filthy, a bit of it tolerable, none desirable.

Every few days, he had a quart of watery bean soup, slopped into his cup. Some without cups slapped dirt from shapeless, felt hats, held them out for their ration.

Despite the routine, the prisoners had much idle time to fill. Finding an anthill in the yard, they collected lice and set them to fighting the ants. Brian watched briefly, until he saw the irony of prisoners abetting a war for entertainment.   Some spent hours making rings, ladies' pins, watch chains, carvings, all sorts of handwork that guards bought for a pittance and smuggled out, doubling and tripling their money. For a price, the guards passed tobacco, whiskey, money, letters to the prisoners.

One prisoner they worked with was a master at maintaining an optimistic outlook. He told them his secret, how he shoveled out the sinks in one temporary camp he was assigned to. He was happy they didn't have to shovel them out here since they were on a pier extending into the bay. "Look on the bright side," he said.

As the days and weeks passed, the prison sapped Brian's strength. He volunteered less often. The poor food cost him pounds he couldn't afford to lose, taking him beyond the gaunt, gray look of all prisons. Purple patches appeared under his eyes. Above and below, long, wild hair added to his haggard appearance.

Once a week he bathed in the bay—if the sonofabitch adjutant didn't cancel it. Those were the best days, washing and drifting innocently with the tide until guards shouted him back.

Brian made a sullen truce with Fort Delaware, precariously balanced on hopes of escape. He wrestled his ghosts, guarded young Sam Turner. And found new hope in a Yankee guard.

From New York City, Sean Murphy who burred his rrr's and spoke with Erin's own musical lilt took to him at once.

"So yer name's Brian. An honorable name it tis, carried by me own brotherr. He was named for Brian Boru of the Royal House of Munster, begorrah, Brian Boru. Was crowned king in the year one thousand and two he was, and a dozen years later fought his men at Clontarf near Dublin. He saved Saint Patrick's green isle itself at Clontarf, nothin' less. On Good Friday it was that Brian fought and on that same blessed day that Brian died, turnin' it into a curse. Blessed and cursed that day was."

Sean Murphy was silent, then mumbled it again, "Blessed and cursed."

He continued, "He was murdered in his tent Brian Boru was, by wild north-men, on the same day Our Lord Jesus, was nailed to the cross." He kissed his thumb, made the sign of the cross. "Brian saved Ireland, lad, dyin' in the effort.

"That's the truth, lad, as related by me old da before he died. May the good Lord keep his soul." Sean Murphy crossed himself again.

Murphy hated the authorities who had drafted him, ending the job that let him save passage money for his wife and children.

" 'Tis unfairr," he railed, " 'tis unfairr to be keepin' a man from his loved ones. Why, the countrree is no frreer than is Ireland acrross the seas."

One day, Sean Murphy motioned Brian to follow around the corner of the barracks, beyond earshot and out of eyeshot.

"By the Holy Motherr, Ireland was nivver so hot," he burred and rolled. He mopped at the perspiration, glancing furtively left and right as he slipped Brian a soiled paper, folded small.

"From an officerr across the fence, Brian."

"I don't understand," Brian stalled suspiciously. Guards had been known to entrap prisoners then turn them in.

"Take it, lad. I swearr by the holy relics of Saint Patrrick, it's no Yankee trick. Tell him it's from Morrison, he said, not darin' t'put his name to it."

"Captain Morrison! My company commander." Brian celebrated the first ray of light in this wretched place.

He read the note.

"He says you'll carry an answer back. What's he doing here?"

"Brian, ye're askin' what I don't know. Me friend guarrdin' the fence says can I get a paperr to ye. I says yes. That's all I know, lad."

"He and John are still together. John Lyle's my friend."

"I'm happy for ye, Brian Morrow, begorrah I am," Sean smiled his wide grin, looked around nervously, "but sure'n they'll not be happy should they discoverr me loit'rin'."

"Sean, not yet. You have to tell me how I can see them."

"You want a meetin', Sean Murphy kin arrange it. Now quick wi' ye, write up an answer if that's what ye're wantin'."

It was August before the meeting could be arranged. Brian's spirits soared, "He's done it, Tom, Murphy's arranged for me to see Captain Morrison and John Lyle. He's really done it!"

"You sure everything's all right? Nothing fishy going on?"

"Not with Sean, Tom. He's in by the draft—doesn't like it one bit. So he's taking his pleasure in outsmarting them. He has an officer over the fence that he'll sneak across to take my place in case there's a head count. I'll be him.

"Only one detail left. We need someone to bring my stand-in back here to the barracks. You're the only one I can trust."

"You know I will."

"Then it's done. You're a good friend."

"And you. When does this come off?"

"Next heavy rain at seven in the evening. We'll meet near the kitchen building. Two hours later we'll switch back."

Before the week was out, Brian had his heavy rain. Surreptitiously, he was led to the officers' quarters. His substitute went off with Tom McDonald. The reunion of the three Liberty Hall Volunteers was a complete success and more, hidden from all but the two guards. Brian related what had happened at the Kernstown battle after the others' capture.

"We fell back by stages, all the way to Swift Run Gap. Everybody thought we were going to Fredericksburg or Richmond, but we went west into the mountains. We beat Fremont at Bull Pasture Mountain and headed back into the Valley. Damn! we were happy." He told of the victory at Winchester, skirmishing at Harper's Ferry, and the long march to Strasburg.

"Where'd they capture you, Brian?"

"Near Winchester," he hedged, "I dropped out of the column, into bad luck."

"Wonder what's happened since?" They fell into silence.

"Captain, hadn't we better tell him now?" John whispered.

Morrison nodded, "It's why we needed to see you," he looked around furtively, "to tell you our plans to get out of here."

Brian had trouble containing himself, "When, when?"

Captain Morrison restrained him, "Stay calm, Brian, calm and secret. John and I have been working on it for some time."

"Count me in—if you can, that is. In any case your plan is safe with me."

"We know that. We want you to know what we've done." The two officers leaned in close. Brian did the same.

"We've been collecting cans from the officers' mess."

"Cans?"

"Tomato cans. All kinds of cans. We seal them."

"Seal them? What with?

"Candle wax as much as we can. Short of that with anything that will hold the water out for a while, rags, rope, old leather. With enough of them a man can get to shore."

Lyle moved in even closer. Brian followed suit to hear the low whisper, "There's a loose floor board directly beneath me. What cans we've saved are in a hole under it. We need more."

"How many? What day? When?" Brian whispered back.

"Not yet. The grapevine says a prisoner exchange is coming up,—we want you to know about the cans if we both are on the list. Now, we'd better be getting you back where you belong."

The "grapes" proved accurate. Through Sean Murphy, Brian learned that his two Liberty Hall friends were exchanged. The news cheered him enough to write his first letter from Fort Delaware.

Dear Ma and Pa and all, I almost visited you, but I was picked up by a Yankee patrol and sent here to Fort Delaware near Philadelphia. I'm fine so don't worry about me. Nobody is shooting at me, and I sleep indoors every night. It isn't too bad here except for the food so I hope you can send me a package of food and some clothes socks and drawers and a shirt. Also some money. I am able to buy some things here if I have the money. There isn't much to write about because mostly we talk about when we get out of this place and hope everyday that there is news of being exchanged. Sometimes you don't know about that until the last minute, and then sometimes they change their minds. I hope this war is over soon. You can write me Prisoner of War, Fort Delaware, Delaware and put VIA Flag Of Truce on the envelope. Your son Sergeant Brian Morrow

XXXVII

THE QUESTION

"Captain Morrow."

David lifted the flap of Jeb Stuart's tent, "Yessir."

"Like you to carry this order to Colonel Rosser."

David's surprise was explosive, "Who?"

Stuart glanced quickly, surprised at the uncharacteristic lack of official poise; David was never that informal unless the general himself encouraged it.

"Colonel Thomas Rosser. I believe you know the colonel."

"He's here? A colonel! Tom was captain last time I saw him."

"Then you haven't seen him for a while. He made lieutenant colonel of artillery a few weeks ago, now he's commander of my newest regiment. Fifth Virginia."

"Colonel! I'll be damned."

Empathizing with the lapse of military courtesy, Stuart leaned back in his chair to rest a spurred cavalry boot on the very edge of the small table. He seemed to want to talk.

"You two appeared pretty fair friends in Fairfax County."

"Yes, sir," David responded properly, "we crossed paths last fall and lifted a few. Before that, five years at The Point. Good years they were, from Benny Havens' tavern to Ferrero's dancing lessons. We resigned—came south together, us two and Pelham."

"Ahhh, Benny Havens. I remember him well. Craggy face, white hair as wild as he was. What would we have done without him?"

"It's hard to say, general. The stories about him, smuggling whiskey and women across the river. Chasing the constable through Buttermilk Falls with a club. They broke the mold when they made Benny Havens." Laughing easily, Stuart drifted back ten years.

In a few seconds he returned to the present, still smiling.

"Benny must be a friend to most of the officers in this man's army—to those fighting us, too. You're right, David, they were good years up there on the Hudson."

Stuart let his boot slide from the table, straightened in his chair, "But this is 1862—we have work to do. Hand this order to Rosser personally. He's on the Charles City Road, posted on the far side of Colonel Goode. Toward the river."

"Yes, sir. Fifth Virginia. Beyond the Third. Toward the James."

"One more thing, just for you to know," he lowered his voice, "I'll be off toward Ashland to join Jackson. You know where to look."

"Yes, sir. Anything else, general?"

Stuart looked up with eyes twinkling, "As a matter of fact there is. I'll raise my offer for that stallion of yours."

"I'll ask him again if you like," David smiled at Stuart's persistent efforts to buy Sable. He just wouldn't give up.

The general looked at him with feigned reproach, then broke into a hearty laugh, "The first time I heard that gambit was more than a year ago at Bunker Hill. How many times you used it since?"

"With you, sir? Only twice. Not counting Bunker Hill," and he reached for the flap of the tent.

He found Rosser within the hour. The echo of Stuart's unrestrained laughter echoed in his head, tempting him to engage in humor of his own. He braced, snapped a West Point salute.

"Colonel, sir, message from General Stuart, sir."

He held both the salute and the exaggerated posture until Tom returned it, with his left hand for his right was in a sling.

"Dave Morrow, you old scoundrel."

"Cadet to colonel in? Fourteen months? It's a record."

"Not what I wanted," Rosser grumped.

"You didn't want it! I don't believe it."

"Not in the cavalry. I told Randolph the same."

"Randolph? George W. Randolph? The Secretary of War?"

"One and the same. Told him I'm staying in the artillery. He said take the transfer or leave the army. Arrogant civilian."

"I don't believe what I'm hearing."

"It's the truth. I jumped two ranks from captain. Had my own battalion. Sixteen guns. He said my replacement already had his orders," Rosser's pique escalated to anger, "it's too late to make changes so take it or resign from the army, he said. Transferring an officer without his acceptance!"

"That's not army procedure as I learned it."

"I told him that, and more. If that's my choice, I told him, I resign my commission."

"You didn't!"

"I told him that and walked out."

"Tom, you damned hothead, what are you doing here then?"

"I ran into Stuart at the War Department—he convinced me to go back and accept it."

"And Randolph? How did he take it?"

"All right—why the hell not. He won his point. That's all he wanted. But he did promise me the first weapons to come through the blockade. Would you believe this regiment had only shotguns and dueling pistols the men brought with them?"

"Hunting guns and single shot pistols!"

"That was it. Then I had an order from the armory."

"So now your regiment is armed properly."

"Like hell it is. They gave me lances."

"Lances! Like in Napoleon's lancers?"

"Worse. These aren't even good ones. Green wood, unbalanced, nothing but saplings with the bark stripped off. The damn blades two-foot pieces of farmer's scythes lashed on with rope."

"—they expect you to fight like that?"

"I never thought the cavalry worth a damn, anyway."

"Come on now. You're not that sour."

"The way they use us for messengers and guards? You've heard the real soldiers yelling 'whoever saw a dead cavalryman'."

"They're mad because they have to walk."

"Maybe," Rosser growled.

"Maybe you have a point, but Stuart's working to change all that. He's fought requests for details so's to keep the regiments together. He's building a real corps. Scout, picket, attack, and pursue is his idea for troopers."

"Maybe," Rosser mumbled again.

"One more thing. You've got your own regiment. I'd give anything for my own command."

"I had my own command. Battalion of sixteen guns. Sixteen guns to gallop into battery. That's real soldiering, by God!"

"If Stuart has his way, you'll have just as much excitement wheeling ten companies of troopers. You may be unhappy with the cavalry but I'm not. You, Pelham, and me together again just like we said on the train. We'll have a time."

Concern prompted David, "But what's the sling? Don't tell me you slugged the Secretary of War and broke your hand."

"Hardly. Took a piece of shrapnel a month ago at Mechanics-ville. But don't get the idea I was whipped. I gave as good as I received."

"I'd bet on that. What was the artillery doing there?"

"It wasn't, but I was. Attached to Robertson's 4th. We had a hot little fight."

"Your arm broken?"

"No. Just a flesh wound—a nasty one that's slow in healing. The doctors keep saying be patient it'll mend fine."

"Telling you to be patient? That's a laugh."

David's eyes crinkled with subdued laughter as he gave his friend both barrels, "But the sawbones should know. Just be patient, Colonel, it'll be fine."

"Damned if I wasn't right the first time. Except you're a bigger scoundrel than ever. A big damned scoundrel, Dave Morrow."

"Yeah, I know."

"Talking about friends, you met any interesting ladies? Seems I haven't had much luck, even with this," indicating his wounded arm. "Too many wounds around to be the magic attraction they used to be."

"I never thought I'd hear you resorting to that line."

"Anything that works, Dave, you know that—what about your adventures with the fair maidens?"

"I'd like to be able to say feast or famine, but it's been mostly famine. With one exception." David hesitated.

"Well, don't stop there."

"I'm not really sure how to talk about it, Tom. Two weeks ago I was ready to marry the girl. But now I'm not so sure."

"Marry! You have turned a corner. What's her name?"

"It's a long story."

"Make it short then."

"Well, it started with Stuart's Hanover County raid when he rode around McClellan. The first night out I got sick with a fever, was left at a farm near Taylorsville. I slept for a couple of days—when I came to, here was this blonde angel taking care of me. She wasn't at all bashful in telling me how she had helped put me to bed,—how it was no big thing because she had brothers and all."

"Sounds like she's giving you a message?"

"I didn't really know, Tom. It could have been read one way or the other, but they had been kind to me and I didn't want to presume something that could turn embarrassing."

"I see what you mean."

"They treated me royally for ten days. When it was time to leave I asked Uncle for permission to call on his niece—he asked me a thousand questions and went to bed. Well, Vicki, that was her name Victoria Winston, Vicki and I talked for a while on the verandah, then she wanted to walk in the moonlight."

"Now, that sounds promising," Rosser grinned, "I hope you're not going to hang fire there."

"We came to the gazebo, got carried away, both of us. She was as worked up as I was—before we knew it—well, you know the story from there."

"What the hell was wrong with that? Sounds good to me."

"I thought so, too, but it isn't that simple. I was really serious about her."

"So what's your trouble? I don't see any problem."

"Tom, I'll tell you the trouble. But if you laugh I'll kill you, colonel's stars, bad arm and all."

"It must be important for you to talk like that."

David remained silent, as if he were having second thoughts.

"Well!"

"Tom, as strange as this sounds, she was too—too easy. And she wasn't a virgin. I never felt that was important, but when I found myself thinking marriage, the idea that someone else had known her—maybe more than one. I don't think I can accept that, not for a wife."

Apparently, Rosser had considered the same matter, "But how can a man know a thing like that for sure? Maybe something else happened to her, riding, falling down stairs."

"May be. But like you say, how can a fellow know for sure?"

"Can't, I guess. Unless you ask straight out and hope she tells the truth."

"With a thing like that? Come on, Tom!"

"Yeah, I know."

"I may never see her again, anyway."

"But I have to move. Stuart's on his way to Ashland and expects me to catch up."

He hesitated deciding how much to tell, but one confidence made it easier to share another, "Something's in the wind, Tom, something big. Jackson is out of the Valley. It looks like General Lee is preparing to attack McClellan's whole damn army."

A few hours later, he rode into Ashland.

David spent the rest of June in the saddle, as did Jeb Stuart and most of his cavalry. For two days, they screened Jackson's left as he fumbled for the Federal flank. Then they headed for McClellan's supply depot on the Pamunkey River. By the time they reached it, the white, clapboard house was in ashes, and much of the depot destroyed. On July 1, David bivouacked near Malvern Hill, the final battleground of the campaign. After another three days of scouting and picketing, he had an opportunity to write a letter home.

Dear Ma and Pa and all. I finally have time to write you after a busy week. Can't say if it was a success or failure but we kept McClellan out of Richmond, forced him back to the James where his gunboats could protect him. We had the chance to destroy his army between the Chickahominy and the James but we couldn't get ourselves together. Our army was strung out about as bad as his, some of it a day late. Most of the time, I was with General Stuart, guiding Jackson's column from Ashland and screening his left. We ran into Yankees at Cold Harbor and chased them off. Then we rode to McClellan's supply depot on the Pamunkey River. By the time we got there Rooney Lee's plantation house was burned to the ground. The supplies and munitions burned all night, but we ate well on what was left, fruits, vegetables, wine, pickled oysters, confectioneries, canned beef and canned ham. We had millions of lemons and great quantities of sugar and ice so we drank lemonade by the gallon. And Havana cigars and coffee, more than we could use. While we were there, Pelham (I've written about him) shelled a gunboat. It was a time to celebrate I'll tell you.

Everything's quiet now—I hope it stays that way for a while. Your son David Morrow

After the Seven Days Battles, the army rested near Malvern Hill for a week. Divided, the cavalry alternated between picket duty around the Yankee army and a new camp at Hanover Courthouse.

Stuart used the lull to drill and train his command, expanded now to two brigades with many new regiments. The new units needed to sharpen skills and establish discipline to become part of the cavalry Jeb Stuart visualized. As it was no longer enough for individual troopers to ride off on missions of their own, neither was it enough for a troop to do the same. Companies would have to cooperate with other companies, and regiments with other regiments.

Tom Rosser, as the new colonel of a cavalry regiment, reported the problem succinctly: "[the 5th Virginia Cavalry] had not been drilled and the most of them had never been under fire before. They must be trained to co-ordinate with one another, to discipline themselves to act as a unit. That's where their strength will be."

Jeb Stuart said essentially the same thing to David when he assigned him as drill-master at the new camp.

David was both delighted and perturbed for the Hanover camp was only a half dozen miles from Taylorsville and Vicki Winston. For a few days, he remained in camp to avoid his quandary, but then he galloped off to see her. Be circumspect, he told himself, don't rush things, see how it goes.

Uncle was not there.

Vicki heard him ride up and was on the front verandah when he dismounted. A part of him ached for her, to fold her in his arms, kiss her and hold her tight. Instead, he walked calmly, looking up at her every second as he approached the wide stairs to the verandah. The question of her virginity faded, he quickened his pace, mounting the steps two at a time. Entranced at the sight of her, straining against the emotions that filled him, he stopped on the last tread below the verandah. He could have reached out to touch her.

She waited, an arm half-raised, her eyes misty, showing more blue than green in the tree-filtered sunlight. Her full lips were slightly pursed, apart as if to say hello, or to invite a kiss. David restrained himself, "Hello, Vicki."

"Hello, David," she whispered leaning ever so slightly toward him. When her hand touched his sleeve, his self-imposed restraint vanished.

They were together, embracing as each had dreamed.

"YouarebeautifulandIloveyou."

"AndAhloveyou Ah missed you so much Ah was so worried All that fightin' around Richmond."

"I didn't get a scratch."

"But Ah didn't know. Is Sable all right?"

"Fine but," David loosened his embrace enough to look around, "where's your uncle?"

"He's off somewheahs. Have you eaten?"

"To be truthful, I haven't."

"Then come on," pulling him through the center hall to the pantry in the back of the house where they embraced again, closely, passionately, "Ah you shuah you want to eat?"

"Vicki, I'm starved. I haven't eaten since breakfast."

"Mah mothuh used to say the way to a man's heart is through his stomach."

"Sometimes," David laughed.

"Theah's leftovuhs from the suppuh table, and theah's buttuhmilk in the milk house."

"Everything sounds good to me."

When David had eaten, she exhaled softly, "Anything else you'd like?"

"Just to sit here and look at you."

"Nothin' else?" She walked around to the back of his chair, leaned over him so that her breasts shaped to his head. She pressed closer, "The gazebo is close by."

"Vicki! It won't be dark for another half hour."

She looked through her lashes, challenged, "We could go upstairs to my room. No one will bothuh us theah. Come on, David." Grabbing his hand she pulled him through the center hall.

Here again was the boldness he had seen in the gazebo and the answer to earlier subtleties. Her behavior was unusual, at least in the girls he had met; and disconcerting, it made him uncomfortable. Unsure of himself, he demurred at the staircase, trapped between desire and visions of Uncle bursting in on them.

"Vicki, I just don't think it wise. If your Uncle . . ."

"Uncle won't be back for hours," she purred.

"You can't know that for sure, Vicki."

"Oh? You didn't worry about him befoah. What's changed since then? Is something botherin' you, David?"

"Oh, no, nothing's changed."

She saw through his dissembling at once, "But something has changed since Ah saw you last. What is it?"

She was right on target and David realized it. Something had changed, indeed it had. He had known, and now she knew. No denial was possible, only the choice whether or not to confront her with the direct question about her virginity, as Rosser had suggested. It had sounded pretty impractical then, but now it seemed a better alternative than some mealy-mouthed evasion. The words did not come easily.

"That night in the gazebo. That wasn't the—you weren't—I wasn't the first was I?"

"Why! David Morrow," she ruffled, "Ah'm shocked at such an impertinent question."

"It's important to me."

Vicki was furious, sputtering the start of a statement she couldn't finish, "If you think Ah am going' to ansuh . . ."

"I agree. I've been presumptuous. I risked asking because it is important to me. I'm sorry, Vicki, but that's the way it is."

"Well, it's not that impo'tant to me, Mr. David Morrow. As far as Ah am concerned it is impertinent; it is trivial. Maybe Ah should ask you how many women have you had befoah me? But Ah won't ask it because Ah don't give a damn. That wasn't youah first time. And it wasn't mine."

Now that David had his answer, he wasn't so sure he wanted it. She had been kind to him. She had nursed him back to health. She had waited on him and catered to him, had sponged his face and arms to allay his illness, used precious ice for him, fed him soup and sun-warm tomatoes. She had offered much to make him comfortable. Then, she had given herself.

He knew that her anger was justified, her counterpoint question a fair one, yet he couldn't get past the fact that another man had been with her.

"Vicki, I'm sorry."

"And so am Ah."

She ran up the staircase, petticoats flying. David never saw her again.

XXXVIII

"IT DOESN'T TAKE TWO LEGS"

"Jed Morrow, it's been over a month since you tore your leg open. I've done all I can, and you're still acting like a child."

Turning away, Jed mumbled, "If it was you . . ."

"Like right now. A little child hiding from the world. With Ezekiel you're different. Even with him, you're not yourself, but at least you don't scowl and grunt like you do with me."

Jed growled, "If it was you without a leg . . ."

Tears of despair coursed down Betsy's cheeks. Had her back not been to the doorway, she would have seen Sarah, and controlled her temper, "Without a leg! Without a leg! That's all I've heard for weeks. If you want to be babied, cry on your mother's shoulder. She's the one for that, waiting on you hand and foot. Not me."

The floor creaked behind her. Betsy cringed.

"Oh, Mumma . . ." Her breath caught in a quick, little gasp. She ran from the room. Sarah and Jed heard the front door slam.

"What's eatin' at her?" Jed mumbled.

"She's just tired I suspect," Sarah answered generously, despite her surprise, "I've brought you lemonade, son. With lots of ice." The tall glass was slippery with water droplets.

Setting it down, she fluffed pillows, heisted Jed against them. She smoothed his hair, patted his face.

"Extra lemon, the way you like it," she smiled handing him the glass, "anything else you'd like?"

Jed nodded one time, right, left.

Turning to the door, Sarah's smile disappeared. Betsy's words rankled. I don't baby Jed. Or do I?

Downstairs, she motioned Henry to follow. Closing the door to his office, she wheeled on him point-blank, "Do you think I baby Jed?"

Over the years, Henry had become wary of answering questions prematurely, "Now, Sarah, who's saying that?"

"That makes no difference," she snapped, "I asked simply for your opinion. Do you or do you not think I baby our son?"

"I heard Betsy run downstairs and slam the front door. I take it she thinks you do. "

"Yes. That's what she said. I was just going into the room and she had her back to the door. Well, do I or not?"

"You want my opinion, flat out, that it?"

"Yes, that's exactly what I want."

"Then, yes, sometimes you do."

"All I want is for him to . . ." Tears welled in her eyes.

Henry went to her kindly, put an arm around her shoulder.

"Come now, love, it's not that bad. We all want what's best for Jed. You. Me. Betsy. All of us."

"But he can't do for himself. He needs help."

"Of course he does. It's just that he needs t'do what he can. Do as much as he's able."

"Maybe I should leave him alone. Let Betsy do it all."

"Sarah, you don't mean that. Just let him do what he can."

"It's so hard for him."

"And for you, Sarah. It's like raisin' him all over again. We ached t'save him, all of them, the trouble we've had and at the same time know they have t'learn for themselves. That's where Jed is, needing t'crawl before he can walk. It's hard for fathers, Sarah, even harder for mothers."

Sarah dabbed at her eyes, "I still see our little boy."

"Nothin' wrong with that. So long as you let him grow."

She hugged him, close against his chest for a moment, "You're an honest man, Henry Morrow. Sometimes difficult, but don't ever change."

Running directly to Ruth's house, Betsy fell into her arms sobbing, "He just wants somebody to take care of him. I can't let him do that, Ruth, he'll never recover."

"Sometimes, men have to be boys, get their own way, pouting when they don't. It's their nature. I saw it in Jonathan."

"I never saw Jed pouting."

"Maybe you just never noticed."

"I think I would have. But that's not all! I made a stupid remark about Mumma's babying him, and she heard me."

"I'm sure she understood."

"Oh, I hope so, Ruth, I was so angry."

"Betsy, stay for the night. We'll open a bottle of wine and talk. We haven't done that since Manassas and Falls Church.

"I'll never forget you for making that trip possible."

"I remember. You didn't see how you could do such a thing."

"Pa was so angry."

"Mumma must have said something for him to change his mind. He still wasn't too happy about it."

"Without that visit to Jonathan's grave, I'd still be holed up, here in this house. Mourning him. Wasting away, thinking of the times he turned his back to me."

She fumbled in the cavernous, oak sideboard coming up with a bottle of imported Madeira, "I've been saving this. Jonathan used to call it a man's wine. Whatever that means. I say if you like it drink it."

Her light mood turned serious, "Seems only yesterday Jonathan and I had wine together."

She re-crossed the room, "As mean as it sounds, maybe it's better that he's gone. I could never tend to him like you do with Jed."

"You'd do what you have to do, for as long as you could.'

"Then what?"

"Cry, scream, as I did. Talk to a friend. Then go back to what needs doing. That's how it is when you love someone."

Pouring the wine into delicate glasses, Ruth hesitated, "Maybe—it may be that my love was just worn out."

Surprised, Betsy sipped at the wine. That Ruth was not going to add anything became obvious.

"This is delicious, Ruth."

"As good as that we had in Manassas?"

"Oh, yes. Maybe a wee bit better." Ruth poured again.

They drank slowly, Betsy with thoughts of Jonathan's grave; Ruth, with a livelier memory.

"I wonder where that Yankee lieutenant is. Matt Garland. I'd forgotten all about him."

Betsy sparkled, "You haven't forgotten him at all."

"Maybe not," she teased coyly. "For all the good it will do. I'll probably never see him again, the way things are."

"Betsy blurted without ceremony, "You're wrong about being killed. I'd rather have Jed as he is than not at all." Her voice shrilled, "I'll push at him until he comes around, and scream and shout if I have to."

"Like now?"

"Like this and more."

After the outburst, she sat silent taking thoughtful sips at her glass.

Ruth gave her a few moments.

"Then what?"

Betsy tilted her wine glass stem up, draining it. She held it out for more, smiled, "Then I'll come over to talk with you. And drink your wine."

"Any time," Ruth invited, "any time at all. My brother's a lucky man, Betsy. I hope he comes to know that."

"He'd better, or I'll—I'll . . ."

They sipped and talked far into the night, and went to bed with their serious concerns submerged in French grapes.

Back on Wolfe Street, Betsy found Sarah at once, "Mumma, I'm sorry for yesterday. I shouldn't have spoken as I did."

Sarah ignored the apology. "When you left, I asked Henry for his opinion," she hesitated, "he felt as you do."

"I am really sorry I caused unpleasantness."

Sarah offered both hands, "Don't be, Betsy. Your concern is for Jed. As is mine. But I have to spoil my son—just a bit?"

"Of course, Mumma. I do love you."

Dr. Holliday finished his examination of Jed's stump, "It looks good to me, young fellow. No reason why you can't leave this nest of a bedroom— there's another question."

"What other question, doc?"

"Whether you're ready to face the world with half a leg."

Jed winced. Betsy recognized his uncertainty and was happy, for it was better than the despair of early summer. Since then, especially since her outburst, she had been more demanding, less patient, literally forcing him to accept his injury, cajoling, humoring, nagging him inch by inch, minute by minute.

"Jed Morrow, it's time you did some things for yourself," she said one day, "like giving yourself a bath." She handed him basin, soap and towel. His little-boy pout reminded her of Ruth's observation, but he did as she said.

Another day it was, "Jed, you've got me wondering if you still love me. All scowls and grunts. It's time to smile again, Jed Morrow, smile because the sun is shining—you haven't lost both legs—life is good and you have me to bother you."

Jed had responded with a tiny little smile that was huge in importance. It was his first since the injury.

Another time she tickled him lightly. Gauging his objections half-hearted, she badgered him, "A smile isn't enough any more. You've got to laugh, damn it, laugh yourself silly."

She worked him step by step toward independence, to smile, to laugh, to self-respect again, and love. She exhausted her imagination and herself, helping him, forcing him to cope. Two steps ahead, one back as he withdrew behind the curtain of self-pity, but his retreats became shorter and the intervals separating them longer.

Oftentimes, in the evening, after she stretched the bed clothes smooth and settled him for the night, she stood by the open window drinking in the night's tranquility. The brief solitude relaxed taut muscles and over-wrought mind. One night, she did not want to be alone.

Walking barefoot to the bed, she remembered a similar night a week ago when Jed refused her and she had slept restlessly dreaming of a frantic search through a garden of North Stars. Each was empty until the very last one, where an old man with a long beard said, "He's not here," and vanished.

"Jed."

Getting no answer, she perched on the edge of the big bed, whispered again, "Jed." She whispered a third and fourth time very close to his ear.

Finally, a sleepy reward, "What is it?"

She lay her head close to his, "Jed, hold me."

Turning, he brushed a bare shoulder, "No nightdress?"

She sensed his doubt and uncertainty, "Just hold me, sweetheart. Nothing more until you want to."

He massaged her back in small, slow circles until she purred contentedly, "Do you know what this reminds me of, Jed?"

"No."

"The night that Brian spent with us in my old bed."

Jed chuckled at the memory, not his raucous, belly laugh but cheery enough to please Betsy, "How could I ever forget it."

They lay close, remembering.

"Make love to me, Jed."

Abruptly, he turned from her, "I'm just a damned cripple."

Betsy attacked furiously, "Not in this bed you're not. Nor out of it either. What I'm asking doesn't take two legs. Or even one."

He mumbled into his pillow to hide the doubt, yet wanting her to hear, "But I feel like a cripple, like half a man who should be dead and forgotten."

"Jedediah Morrow," she sat upright in the bed oblivious to her nudity, "I want never to hear you say such a thing again. I'm glad you're alive. I'm glad you're here with me. I'd be happier if you didn't feel that way, but even if you do, don't you ever, ever say that to me again."

She pulled at his shoulder, "Do you hear me?"

He turned slowly onto his back at the very moment she stretched over him for an eyeball to eyeball answer. As they rolled the counter-turn together, a satiny softness grazed his arm and was gone. He caught his breath, stiffened, quieted. He lay there on his back, Betsy suspended over him in the dim light. The little oil lamp flickered in the night breeze, white curtains fluttered their blessing.

Betsy quieted, too, for she knew she had won her long battle. She had Jed back. She relaxed against him, half her fullness conforming to the curve of his chest, the other half suspended in supple invitation. Discreetly he accepted, clasping her in his square, farmer's hand, fondling, kissing, feeling her heart pumping so near.

He lifted her enough to take both breasts, one in each hand.

Betsy pressed excited nipples against his hands, squirmed against his good leg. She wriggled between his hands flattening against him again, nibbling along his chest and shoulder. She snaked higher to kiss his neck, ear, forehead, and along his cheek. She let her lips play down his face to his mouth. Throwing a leg over him, she offered everything, her breath coming faster as he held her to the kiss. She inched down his body, sliding her leg along his injured one, reaching with her toe to caress a foot not there. Then she remembered, but he never gave it a thought as he guided himself into her.

He clasped her tight, hands on her buttocks pressing and lifting. Her hips matched his rhythm.

"More, Jed, more."

Her breath quickened as she set her own pace—hurrying, dashing, pumping faster. Jed felt the pulsations ripple through him and squeezed. He arched to fill her, deeper and deeper.

"Jed, Jed, . . ." Betsy opened wider with a vision of more and more.

She convulsed once—the waves overtook her as he crushed her hips into him and burst deep inside her. She held her breath, holding, holding to capture all of him, just one more moment, one more. She trembled, gasped for air and finally yielded, panting, exhausted, limp.

Jed, too, breathed hard under her.

Fulfilled, they lay together, Jed's hand on her back, tracing the same slow circles.

She snuggled into him, "Jed, I love you so."

"I love you, Star Queen."

She managed a sigh of contentment, a muffled murmur, "Am I too heavy?"

For an answer, he tightened his embrace.

Betsy shifted her weight, he rolled with her, together as before but staying face to face and front to front. She nuzzled into his shoulder, a happy prisoner locked in his arms.

"Betsy."

"Uh huh."

"I'm glad I'm not dead."

She squirmed even closer, dreamed again of the bearded patriarch on the last of the North Stars. He was running to her, shouting, "I found him. I found him. He's back."

Betsy wakened early the following morning, wakened with a song in her heart for this was truly a new day. She listened to Jed's deep breathing, watched the slow rhythm of his chest, rise, fall, rise, fall. He really hasn't grown up completely, she thought as she looked at him. Part of him was still little boy.

In the morning she smiled at the thought of her little boy, "But not last night, Jed. Last night you were all man."

She chose one of her prettiest dresses, brushed her hair a hundred strokes, pinched her cheeks for color even though they didn't need it. Sarah and Mam were in the kitchen.

"My, don't you look pretty this morning."

"Uh huh," Mam chirped emphatically, cheerful as a chickadee.

Betsy dipped a petite curtsy. She felt the warmth rise in her cheeks as she just knew they sensed last night's lovemaking.

"Jed ready for his breakfast tray?"

"Mumma, he's coming down for breakfast."

"He is!"

"Well, not for a few minutes yet, he was just waking up. He doesn't know it yet, but I know he will."

"Is there coffee left? I'll take him some."

Back upstairs, she put the steaming mug close to his nose. "Mmmm. That smells good. I knew it was you."

He sat up against stacked pillows, blew on the coffee, sipped noisily, "Mmmmmm." He sipped again.

"Come sit by me," he offered the mug, "want some?

She sipped almost as noisily as he had.

Gradually, the slurps subsided as they blew and the coffee cooled. When the cup was empty, she put it on the candle table.

"This is nice, Jed, being here with you."

"Good as last night?"

"Yes. In a different way."

"Betsy I'm sorry for the trouble I've given you."

She touched a finger to his lips, "Shhhh."

"No. I want you to know . . ."

"Shhh. All I need to know is that you love me."

"You already know that."

"That's all I need."

She held his big hand to her cheek, turning into it, kissed each finger-tip, "That's all I'll ever need."

She stood up, "Come on, lazybones, breakfast is ready. It's time to get dressed and go downstairs."

"Downstairs!" his mood changed at once, "Betsy, I can't go downs . . ."

"Today you can. Today is my magic day."

"Same as yesterday'n the day before." Like a thunder-head boiling over the mountain, despair swooped over him. He plopped down, pulled the covers around his ears, turned his back.

Betsy ignored him, laying out clothes on the foot of the bed. Light-heartedly, she danced to the bed with drawers, with trousers, with shirt. Putting one slipper out for him, she stood up and twirled so that her skirt flew high.

"This is my magical day, Jed, my day for a miracle. I can feel it."

Coming closer, she humored him, "Time to get up, lazybones."

"No," the little boy rode the thunder-head.

She kept her gay mood, "No what? At least you could say, 'No, sweet-heart'."

Jed grunted.

"I thought we were over the grunts and mumbles." With a suggestion of a pout, she added, "you said you loved me."

"What's that got t'do with it?"

"Everything."

"Nothin'. Got nothin' t'do with it."

"It has everything to do with it. Didn't I tell you this was my magic day?"

"Magic day. Magic day. Talk sensible for God's sake."

"Jedediah Morrow! How can you say that and still say you love me and take my magic day away from me."

"I'm not takin' anythin' away from you."

"You are. You're taking my day. And you don't care. You just don't care." Her voice said tears were close behind.

"Aw, Betsy."

"Don't 'aw Betsy' me. You don't even care."

"Yes, I do."

"Then show me," she challenged.

"All right I will, damnit."

Scowling through his black cloud, he threw the covers back and, without a word, sat up in the bed. Gruffly, he hiked himself to the edge. His injured leg extended short.

Betsy kneeled by him, an arm about his waist. Her eyes shimmered with genuine tears as she looked up at him. Jed melted.

With her help, he dressed, balanced on one foot and hopped toward the doorway. Almost there, he stopped, "Betsy I can't."

"Two more steps and you're there."

"Steps? More like hops. Hoppin' like a damn rabbit."

They reached the door.

"Rest for a moment, sweetheart," letting loose his arm.

He glanced up and down the hallway.

She looked up at him thoughtfully, wondering, debating, deciding: Should I say it? No. Yes. Why not?

"Even rabbits have to rest."

He stalled, feeling both irritation and amusement at being likened to a rabbit. Then a third possibility occurred to him, bringing light into his eyes and a tiny smile, "Come t'think on it, I'm not so sure they do rest. There's so many little ones."

Waves of hilarious laughter filled the room.

Jed was the first to quiet down, "I haven't laughed like that since the night Briney was in bed with us."

More peals of laughter broke out.

"What in the world are you two doing up there?" Hearing them, Sarah had come to the foot of the stairs.

"Nothing, Mumma," Betsy managed, "just coming for breakfast.

"Ready?"

He leaned on her again.

At the top of the stairs, he sat down, still with Betsy's help, half squatting on his good leg, toppling sideways onto the other. She could have cried, so hurt was he, so vulnerable.

He bumped down the steps one at a time toward Sarah.

"Suppose we could eat on the verandah?"

"Of course," Sarah almost danced to the kitchen.

Betsy pulled him onto his good leg, steadying him through the front door to the wooden rocker just outside, "You're not leaning on me as much."

"Gettin' the hang of it, I guess."

Settling into the chair was easier than the awkward acrobatic at the head of the stairs.

"Jed, thank you."

"For what? I didn't do anythin'"

"But you did, sweetheart. You gave me back my magic day."

They caught the smoky aroma of bacon as Sarah and Mam came out with two plates, one piled high, one with normal portions. It did indeed seem to be a special day, for at noontime they were still on the verandah to greet a visitor.

"Jed, it is good to see you out and around," Doctor Holliday called as he came up the brick walkway. He made a quick inspection of Jed's stump, "I'd say it's time for Pinocchio."

"Pinocchio! What's that mean?"

"Oh, it's just my way of saying, it's time to think about the wood. Crutches and a new leg."

Betsy felt Jed stiffen as if to ward off a blow.

Doctor Holliday sensed it, too, but went on optimistically, "You'll find the crutches easy to manage. They'll give you mobility which you didn't have getting down here. We can talk about the rest later."

"Yeh, later."

Betsy would have been pleased with more enthusiasm, but the dull answer was still a far cry from yesterday's growl.

From the doorway, Sarah called, "Doctor, will you have dinner with us? It's almost ready to put on the table."

He begged off, pleading other patients to see as Henry approached the front gate, home for the mid-day meal.

Jed stood without help, before Betsy could get to him, leaned on her shoulder lightly and hopped through the doorway and hall into the dining room. Henry followed, grinning broadly at everyone, nodding approval at Jed's efforts.

"It's good to have you at the table again, son."

"Thanks, Pa."

So taken by surprise he could think of no other way to express his happiness, Henry repeated, "It's really good to see you downstairs. And at the dinner table. Good to see you, son."

The Morrows' dinner that day was a holiday from the usual sedate and proper meal. Gracey took advantage of the relaxed discipline, babbling about friends and adventures. Betsy chattered about her magic day, enchanting everyone. Sarah gushed about her morning in the kitchen with Mam; Henry, the Valley's respite from the war and his morning at the courthouse.

Into the middle of it all came Ezekiel, excited as a young boy. He forgot his two drawings when he saw Jed at the table.

"Lawdamercy if you aren't downstairs. Praise the good Lord."

"Howdy, 'Zekiel."

Sarah broke in with her priority question, "Have you eaten?"

"Had an apple on the way. That'll do until I get back."

"Sit down then and have dinner with us," Sarah pushed her chair back to get another plate, "there's plenty."

Henry took charge, "Gracey, move down t'make room."

"Didn't mean ta disturb your dinner but I thought you could use some veg'tables."

He looked at papers in his hand uncertainly, "And I had somethin' ta show Jed. Some drawin's I made—for crutches. "

For the second time Jed went rigid, failing this time to keep his anger to himself, "First the doc and now you! Twice in the same day!! Seems you can't wait to get me on crutches."

He looked daggers at the papers Ezekiel was handing across the table Ezekiel hesitated.

Henry filled the gap, "Didn't know you for an artist, Zeke. Let's see how good you are."

"They aren't much, but I figgered you'd be needin' them."

He became more excited as he presented his original design. "Top one's the way I've seen them, just three pieces. A long pole, a handle, another piece on top. Other one's the way I'd make it," he glanced down self-consciously, "my own plan, ash poles split halfway with a handhold in between. "

Mam ended his embarrassment with a heaping plate of food.

"Thanks, Mama, it looks mighty good."

Jed glanced at the papers, wanting to crush them, destroy them, make them go away, but he couldn't offend Ezekiel.

Betsy spoke for him, "That's kind of you, Ezekiel. It's a blessing to have friends who care."

"It's nothin'."

"Ezekiel, don't belittle yourself. You were there for Ruth. Now you're concerned for Jed. You are a good and loyal friend." It had taken someone outside the family to say it.

Seeing the nods of approval, Jed regretted his reaction to the drawings: how could he be so blind to Ezekiel's gift, stupid enough to fight the truth? Rabbit hop or use crutches.

Dinner over, the three men retired to the verandah, while Sarah and Betsy worked with Mam on the after-meal clean-up.

"How in the world did you get Jed to come downstairs? Yesterday he was impossible. Today you get him to slide down the stairs on his backside. Whatever did you do?"

"I just told him this was my magic day and don't spoil it."

"Just like that? Told him a fairy tale and he agreed? That's not Jed. Maybe when he was a little boy, but not now."

"It wasn't quite that simple," Betsy wondered if she was blushing again, "but it worked and that's the important thing."

"Yes it is. You have been wonderful with him since—since his injury. Even telling him I coddled him too much."

"Oh, Mumma, I should never have said that."

"On the contrary. It needed to be said—I love you for whatever you did with him. Without you he'd still be in his bed."

"And, Mumma, without you he wouldn't be here at all. Let's just say he's fortunate to have the both of us."

Sarah smiled gently, "How do you do that?"

"Do what?"

"Say just exactly the right thing."

"I've been lucky lately," she knew she was blushing now; she knew Sarah sensed last night's lovemaking.

"Betsy, thank you for healing Jed."

She reached out and Betsy took her hands. They stood silently, mother and wife, their eyes reflecting love for one another and for the man who was son and husband.

XXXIX

"WITH SOLDIERS LIKE THIS"

Dear Ma, Pa and all I can't believe August is almost over. General Stuart has kept me busy. I've really lost track of time. On the 16th we rode the cars to Orange Courthouse. Men rode on the roofs and in the tender. I remember the 16th because that is Ma's birthday. Happy birthday, Ma! I wish I could have been home to celebrate with you, also to stuff myself with the cake I know Mam will make for you. I can smell it from here. Maybe I wouldn't stuff it, at that, but just put it on my head and smear it all down my face, chocolate icing and all. I guess that's all for now—the general is calling me. I am fine, so is Sable. Happy birthday, Ma, even though I'm late, tell Pa to kiss you for me. Your loving son David Major since July 25.

The day after he wrote, David was off again with Jeb Stuart and 1,500 troopers to raid Catlett's Station, 25 miles behind the Union's Rappahannock line.

They rode almost that far upstream to round the Yankee flank, crossed the Rappahannock at Waterloo Bridge, turned east to Warrenton. Occupied briefly by Yankees threatened constantly, the entire town turned out to welcome its own with food and lemonade, flirting, and dancing in the streets. Old friends kissed and hugged. Here and there, strangers formed instantaneous friendships, hugging and dancing, too. The frolicking was over all too soon.

"Forward. HO!"

Citizens crowded both sides of the street. Handkerchiefs fluttered at their departing heroes. Tears welled.

"Come back!"

"Don't forget me!"

"Take care of yourself."

A bearded gentleman wearing a Mexican War medal called, "God bless you, boys."

Stuart doffed a very ordinary felt hat, for he had lost his fancy one with the black, ostrich plume at Verdiersville.

David danced Sable as he had in Richmond. The citizens admired the big stallion and his faultless rider. As they had then, they called, "What's his name?"

Proud troopers high-stepped their mounts, waved their good byes. Hooves clip-clopped, equipment jingled, and they were gone. The memories of that day were written into the diaries of young ladies, and recorded in Warrenton's history.

David waited on the road for Rosser and his regiment.

"Hello, colonel, nice weather for a raid."

"David! I knew you wouldn't miss this one. Heard you made major. By personal recommendation of the general, no less."

"At the end of July. Haven't had time to get the stars yet. You don't have a couple I could borrow, do you?"

"As a matter of fact, I do, somewhere in my gear. Consider them yours."

David scanned the regiment still armed with lances.

"Randolph never got your weapons through the blockade!"

With his dark eyes and complexion, and almost black hair, Rosser's scowl was fierce, "No! Damn the Secretary of War. He probably forgot his promise before I was out the door! Dammit, Dave, here we are raiding enemy country with lances, crooked damn lances for God's sake. You wonder I argued to stay artillery?"

"It's a disgrace! Pikes against carbines and colts?"

"Oh we'll fight, all right. My 5th is good as any."

"I believe it. We'll drink to it when this ball is over."

David saluted the scowling colonel, not only in recognition of his rank, but because he was a respected friend. He spoke in a low voice to cover the familiarity, "Good luck, Tom."

Rosser saluted back, "Luck, Dave."

As they left Warrenton, roiling black clouds churned over the Blue Ridge. The turbid sky chased them eastward and, three hours later overtook them, unloading buckets. As they closed Catlett's Station, the heavy rain continued.

Rosser's 5th Virginia led the column, its only real weapons a small number of shotguns and dueling pistols. The lances had worried Stuart, too. He rode up to Rosser.

"You must give place to a regiment that is better armed."

Hot-tempered Rosser took offense, refused.

Stuart's tone changed, good-natured to peremptory, "Halt your regiment, form it on the side of the road and allow the column to pass."

"Sir, you know I am not under your command from choice, that my regiment is not armed is more your fault than mine. To yield the post of honor would be cowardly. It would disgrace me and my regiment."

"Do you refuse to obey me?"

"Yes sir. You may arrest me for disobedience of orders but you sha'n't disgrace me or my regiment."

Jeb Stuart stroked his beard, deliberating. Without another word he rode off. David followed.

Stunned, David saluted smartly, thinking it best to go by the book, "General, request permission to go in with the 5th."

"Denied!" Stuart roared. Reflecting, he recanted, "No, go ahead. Rosser is impulsive. He needs watching."

David sensed trouble, "Sir! That's not what I had in mind. He is my friend. I don't want to be interrogated when this is over—Sir!"

"Understood," Stuart snapped, "that wasn't my intent. Just do what you can."

"Yes, sir."

Rosser huddled with his advance party, "I want all shotguns and pistols in the regiment collected. Arm yourselves with them, and leave the damn lances in the ambulance."

He saw David, "Why the hell are you here?"

"You asked me the same at Williamsburg. Sir."

"Stuart ordered you!" Rosser roared.

Thunder roared louder, lightning flashed on the ugly scene of friendship gone awry. David spit back, "That's a hell of a thing to say. You know me better than that."

The storm lashed their anger.

"Well, what then? if not to spy on me?"

"I wanted to go in with you. No more, no less. Stuart agreed. No strings. No conditions."

Dour and waspish, Rosser stalled, "You men there! hurry up!"

"You want me to leave, I'll leave."

Rosser pulled irritably at a gauntlet, "Sorry."

David gripped his friend's hand, "You should be."

The words were querulous; the handshake, restorative. defusing the nasty situation. They rode on.

A challenge rang through the night, "Who goes there?"

Rosser was ready, "Scouts from the 5th Indiana."

"Advance to be recognized."

They advanced as ordered, indistinguishable shapes huddled against the storm. They captured the entire picket.

Blinding lightning flared incessantly, furnishing fleeting views of the trail, stepping stones to glory. Or destruction.

Through the driving rain, they came on another guard who lowered his musket at Rosser. David stood in his stirrups, swung his saber almost beheading him. They were inside the camp. The lightning betrayed a Union regiment a few yards from its stacked muskets. The riders cut off the weapons, captured the men.

Another flash from the heavens betrayed a parked wagon train across the railroad tracks. Up the embankment David urged Sable, and across the tracks. Rosser followed, his men close behind. The guard ran.

Other Yankees were more resolute. Their hand guns flashed in the storm as they fired into the darkness. The troopers countered as best they could with their limited weapons. They fought better after they took over the wagons.

The Yankee train did what the Confederate Secretary of War could not, furnishing the entire regiment with sabers, carbines, pistols, ammunition, horse blankets and new saddles. David added a brace of Colt revolvers to the pair he carried and a factory-new carbine. Rain covered their withdrawal.

From out of the gloom, a shadow sprang at Rosser who aimed his revolver. Click! It was empty, good only to parry the bayonet thrust. Alongside, David took aim and fired twice. The assailant dropped into the mud, one bullet in his heart, the other an inch away. Rosser was badly cut, wrist and hand. David wound it tight with a makeshift bandage.

The 5th Virginia Cavalry had come into its own, armed with weapons worthy of its mettle. No more lances for the 5th Virginia.

Four days later, on the 26th, David scouted ahead of Jackson sweeping around the Federals to Bristoe Station south of Manassas Junction. Among the first to reach the railroad, he wore Rosser's major's stars, a memento of a life-saving saber thrust and two pistol shots at Catlett's. Two stars, one for each redemption.

He pitched in with troopers raising a barricade, scavenging the right of way for railroad ties, rocks, debris. It was dark when they heard a steam whistle down the track, wailing loud, falling to nothing, rising again.

Hot, sweaty, David stood by the helter skelter obstruction. He peered into the dark, momentarily in The Valley hearing a happier whistle. The locomotive's pulsing boiler brought him back, pounding toward the barricade, louder, nearer, louder.

Dim light flickered off the trees. David watched it unfurl across the embankment, across the track as the engine rounded the curve. He saw the swaying lantern, its beam exposing the danger ahead. Steam hissed angrily. Sparks flew from locked wheels.

The barricade burst into flames skyward and sideways, like a giant chrysanthemum exploding at the end of its iron stem. In the center of the blossom, the mass of iron lifted beyond its flanged wheels. They spun out of control and dropped, tearing up roadbed, wrecking tracks. The locomotive plunged down the embankment, pulling cars after it, all but the last three.

David saw red warning lights still burning on the last car, heard the whistle of another engine close behind. As he listened, he caught the pounding THUMPTHUMP of its boiler.

Spurring Sable along the wreck, he smashed his saber into the warning lights, only seconds ahead of the thumping boiler. The big light of the on-coming train washed around the curve, over horse and rider as they reached the trees. Without the red lights to warn him, the engineer pulled at the brake lever much too late. Sparks flew as before from screeching wheels.

Sable reared, terrified by the sparks and the piercing shriek of iron on iron.

"Whoa, boy, easy now, easy," David countered the nightmare of feral screech and flying light. He leaned over Sable's withers shouting again. The thunderous crash drowned him out.

The locomotive plowed into the first wreck, jack-knifing the three cars still on the track. It tilted precariously, balancing a delicate tiptoe. It strained uselessly, gave up. Over it went, iron plates, pipes, levers and valves atangle. Wheels spun crazy, idiotically horizontal. The firebox belched flame. Steam hissed.

Sable reared a second time at this new bedlam. Fearing the big black would go over backwards, David stood in the stirrups, pressing close. Sable was going out of control.

"Easy now, easy boy, settle down now, easy Sable, easy, boy, easy." He shouted to regain the upper hand. The big horse reared again, screaming his fright.

David kept at it, using everything he had to reestablish his authority, voice, reins, knees, patience, muscle. He had seen good horses go out of control and be worthless afterward. He tightened the reins, fearful of wounding Sable's tender mouth but refusing to give in. Relentlessly, he applied the pressure.

Sable pawed the air, settled on all fours, reared again. David hit him with his fist, between the ears. Sable came down on all fours and stayed. David hoped him ready to consider a truce.

He let up ever so slightly on the reins, then more as Sable settled down. In the firelight, both he and the stallion glistened in their exertions. His wet shirt stuck to him, sopping trousers to saddle and legs. Pain coursed his arms and legs and up his back. He was used up, drop dead tired Zeke would say.

Despite the aches, despite his absolute exhaustion, he leaned forward over black withers, whispering the same soothing words, but with a cooing quality, softer, rhythmic, comforting, man-to-man. Dismounting he stretched his own taut muscles.

He rubbed the long nose; Sable nuzzled the familiar hand.

"Don't you ever do that again. EVER, EVER. You hear me?"

Sable shook his head side to side. David stroked the long nose again, patted the wet neck. He let his hand linger along the shining coat before he mounted. Riding into Bristoe Station, he removed saddle and blanket, dried the big stallion and brushed him clean in the starlight. He stayed with him through the night. The next day, he reported back to Stuart near Manassas.

"Major Morrow," Jeb Stuart shouted from his tent, "round up what men you can. We ride in five minutes. Longstreet's coming through Thoroughfare Gap to reinforce Jackson."

Trotting west toward Longstreet's column, David ventured the obvious question, "What's up, general? Emergency?"

"More likely a brush fire. But it could flare up. A scouting report puts cavalry near Haymarket directly in Longstreet's path. We're making sure he's not surprised—we'll clear the way for him if they don't outnumber us more than three to one."

Jeb Stuart threw back his head laughing at his own temerity. His men knew he was not joking, for he had always accepted odds.

Before nightfall, they did find Union cavalry at Haymarket, skirmished indecisively and withdrew. Dismounting, Stuart spoke to David guardedly, "I want you to ride to Longstreet. Warn him the Yankees are restless, both cavalry and infantry. He needs be cautious—give him Jackson's location. You know where he is."

"I did this morning, sir. At the old railroad cut north of the Warrenton pike. But he's been hard to track these last few days."

"He's still there. Longstreet will be coming in on his right near Groveton. Stay with him and guide him in."

"Yes, sir. Permission to take Corporal Rafferty?"

"Anybody you want. One more thing. Scouts put Yankees in your path. Elements of Ricketts—maybe his whole division. Go around them or through. It's your choice."

Riding west in the darkness, the two riders pulled up.

"What do you think, Rafe, straight ahead or around? Straight through you may find another perfume cache." For a moment, he thought of the Exchange Hotel and the lovely girl named Carrie.

"Don't remind me, major."

He pulled Sable around, away from Princess, the corporal's mare, for he had caught her scent.

"Let's go through. We can bluff our way."

The corporal pulled his hat tight, "I'm with you."

"Good. If we're challenged, we're scouts with important information for General Ricketts."

He pulled Sable's head around again, for the big stallion was more interested in Princess than Yankees.

Both laughed and kicked gently with their heels.

"Go, Sable. Go, boy!" He pranced a small arc, lifted on his hind legs, enough to show his frustration.

"Yaaa, Princess!"

They were challenged twice as they galloped along the road. Twice they raced by gaping guards, yelling, "Dispatches for General Ricketts."

Five hundred yards beyond the second guard, they slowed to a walk to save the horses.

"Suppose there's any more, major?"

"Figure on it," David snapped, peering into the blackness ahead, "be ready to run through."

Squinty-eyed vigilant, pulse-pounding tense, they covered another mile without incident.

Suddenly from up ahead, "Who goes theah?" The voice was rough but touched with magnolias.

"Couriers from Stuart's cavalry."

"Advance, an' keep youah hands wheah Ah kin see 'em."

Minutes later, they were at Longstreet's headquarters.

"Bring 'em in," a voice boomed from the tent.

David took a couple of steps, turned to shout at the guard "Keep those mounts apart."

Inside, they found themselves before a solidly built, barrel chested man, full beard, sandy and thick. David and the corporal saluted.

"You're from General Stuart?" a suspicious Longstreet asked.

"Yes, sir." David answered

"When'd he graduate from The Point?"

"1854, sir. 13th in his class."

"What's his wife's name?"

"Flora, sir"

"His horse?"

"Skylark, sir. Another's Lady Margrave."

"Where'd you see him last?"

"Three, four miles down the road, sir, near Haymarket."

"Haymarket! What the hell's he doing there?"

"Investigating reports of gathering cavalry. We lit into them before dark, but there weren't enough for you to worry about. Bigger problem is infantry about a mile in your front."

"I know. They pecked at us coming through the gap."

"We were in Haymarket and heard your fight."

"Now, what's this you have from Stuart?"

Boots scraped the floor behind them. Recognizing General Lee, David snapped his best salute.

Lee lifted a hand, tired but no less involved with them, "Those people are just up the road? How did you get here, son?"

"Just galloped through them, sir."

"Galloped through them? Just like that?"

"Yessir. Shouting 'dispatches for General Ricketts'."

He looked to Longstreet, "With soldiers like this, Peter, how can we ever doubt our victory. What's your name, major?"

"David Morrow, sir. From Winchester." Thinking of Rafe's joy at meeting Jackson, "May I present Corporal Rafferty, sir.

"General Longstreet, Corporal Rafferty."

More salutes, Tom Rafferty's by the book, Longstreet casually touching his cap, Lee's a tired half salute as before.

"And now your dispatch from General Stuart, major."

"No dispatch, sir. He said don't write it down."

"Well?"

"Two points, sir. Approach cautiously because the area is alive with cavalry and infantry. You may stumble onto them."

Longstreet looked up sharply, "If I *stumble* on to them, sir, I'll have somebody's scalp."

"My words, general. Only to emphasize the unusual activity we've seen. We've been scouting the area for three days—have never run into so many Yankees. They're all over the place, marching and riding this direction and that."

"Go on."

"If I may use your map. I am to show you General Jackson's position. And, guide you in. You are to deploy on his right fl . . . Sorry, sirs. No disrespect intended."

"I see no reason for an apology, major. Do you, Peter?"

"None whatsoever, sir."

David drew a finger along the map, "This was his position this morning. Along a partial railroad bed with cuts and fills. He intends to draw Pope in before he gets reinforcements."

"Good! Good!" General Lee suddenly gained new life, "That man needs to be suppressed."

The following day David guided the column through Haymarket, relinquishing to Jeb Stuart on the Gainesville road.

"Morning, General."

"Halloo, major. See you're taking good care of that stallion of ours," he chuckled.

"Yes, sir. Equal care to both halves," he laughed back.

"Like you to scout ahead," Stuart turned serious, "reports put a Union force toward Manassas. That could put them on Longstreet's flank if we bring him in as planned. Find out if we've got trouble there."

"Yes, sir."

"I've ordered your friend, Rosser, over that way. He may have a fix on them."

David waved to Corporal Rafferty to follow and was off. They hadn't gone but a few miles when they sighted dust clouds ahead. They slowed to a walk. David warned, "May be Yankees, Rafe."

Topping a small rise, they saw a column of cavalrymen a quarter mile off. Yankee or friendly? Could be either, uniforms and horses coated with the dry dust from the long branches and saplings they dragged. David squinted for a long minute.

"Oh, for God's sake. It's Rosser. He's riding on the left of the column about halfway back."

David waved, flicked his heels gently to Sable's sides.

"Hello, colonel, didn't expect to find you here making like Birnam wood."

"Hello, Dave," Rosser returned the salute, "No, Macbeth's witches can take care of their own prophecy."

"Then what in the world are you doing, dragging trees?"

"Pretending we're infantry on the march. Trying to bluff the Yankees over there," he pointed toward Manassas, 'maybe a whole damn corps. Maybe we can fool them. At least slow them down."

"First Corps is coming in on the right. They'll be looking down Pope's line if he attacks Jackson. Stuart's concerned that Longstreet may be vulnerable the same way, from this direction."

"If this column behind me comes in, he damn well will be. But it could stop or turn back, no way of telling. Yesterday, Yankees attacked Jackson at Brawner's maybe to soften him up. They stood eyeball to eyeball, no one backing down. We tangled with cavalry a while ago that could be screening for them."

"Sounds logical."

David turned to his corporal, "Rafe, you hear all that?"

"Sure did, major."

"Then repeat it all to General Stuart. Important thing is we're not sure what the Yankee column is up to. I'll report myself as soon as we know, maybe an hour or two."

"Yes, sir."

Stuart sent Rafferty on to Longstreet, but it was too late; leading elements had already reached Jackson's right. By mid-afternoon, Longstreet's entire First Corps was in position, a two-mile line in an obtuse angle with Jackson, 22 batteries massed inside the angle. Rosser's contrived dust cloud seemed to have an effect for the worrisome Yankee column turned back. David wrote of the battle a few days later.

Dear Ma and Pa and All I've just learned that a Mr. Richardson is preparing to leave for Winchester so I'll write quickly to let you know that I am fine and Sable is fine too. We had another set-to with the Yankees at Manassas. This one lasted two days, it was strange being on the same ground as before. It was infantry and artillery with the cavalry very busy before and after, two days of Yankee assaults, opposing battle flags separated by ten yards. Jackson's men fought them off with muskets, rocks, whatever they could shoot, swing, or throw. Artillery from Longstreet hit them from the flank. The next day, Jackson repulsed more attacks, and Longstreet came in. He drove them onto Henry Hill where I was a year ago, and Jed and Brian. I was not in the heavy fighting. I guided Longstreet's Corps to the field. General Lee was with them. I think I wrote before that he is a true gentleman, very kindly and considerate. By nightfall, the battle was over and the

Yankees pulled back to Centreville. Then it was time for the cavalry. We chased them back to Washington and captured more than we could count. Word has it that we are about to cross into Maryland. I hope it's true so that we can take the war out of Virginia. You have seen more than your share of it. Mr. Richardson is ready to leave. I don't want to keep him waiting. Love David

XL

A CRAZY PAIR

David trudged the steps of Mechanics' Hall where the Secretary of War had his offices. Ordinarily, he would have taken them two at a time, but he was weary from a night on the cars, Manassas to Gordonsville, an interminable wait for an engine and only catnaps flayed by bumping, clacking and tooting to Richmond.

The uncertainties about Carrie had gnawed at him through the dismal night. Is she still in Richmond? Maybe she doesn't want to see me again. She seemed friendly, but then she got crossways. Upset about my coming back, or that I thought she wouldn't expect me. Or something. Maybe she's upset about the money. She has to be there so's I can at least find out what's troubling her.

Yesterday, he had expected to cross the Potomac when Jeb Stuart summoned him, "I have papers for Richmond, Secretary Randolph."

The name whipped up the ultimatum to Tom Rosser. Accept my orders or resign? Unbelievable treatment of an officer!

Stuart continued, "Hand this envelope to him personally. If necessary, tell him you have orders to sit in his office until you get an answer. He can be a devil when he chooses."

"I've heard as much, sir."

The cavalry commander raised an eyebrow, "From Rosser? I'd like to hear that tale from him! A real hot-head."

He recalled Rosser at Catlett's Station, how he had flared up at Stuart just before they went in. Colonels just don't do that to generals, especially when the general is one's commanding officer. David wondered again why Stuart had backed down that night in the rain.

"Your friend has a hair-trigger, but he knows how to fight."

"Yes, sir," maybe that was it, Stuart would accept the verbal onslaught to keep the fighter. "He has a powerful sense of honor."

David sighed as he reached the top of the stairs.

As he entered the Secretary's office, a tall, slender man brushed by him, calling over his shoulder, "Yes, Mr. Randolph. Right away, sir."

"I'm Major Morrow, sir. I have papers from General Stuart."

"I just sent him a Whitworth. What's he want now?" Randolph snapped. The man apparently held common politeness in low esteem.

"I can't say, sir. He didn't tell me," David's pique showed. The older man looked up sourly, tight-lipped over tiny, oval spectacles perched low on his nose. He peeled them from his face, one wire earpiece to the other. He threw them on the desk.

"Damn headache." He squinted myopically at David, "What are you waiting for!"

"The general ordered me to wait for your answer, sir."

"The general! The general! Everybody says 'the general'. The general wants this. The general wants that. I have ten generals for every man, weapon, and gun I can raise. Get out of here!"

"Yes, Mr. Secretary, but I'll have to check back. General Stuart's orders." He hesitated, seeking the right words.

"General Stuart speaks very highly of you, sir, and expresses his gratitude for your help. Especially the Whitworth. He said 'Tell the Secretary it is put to good use'."

With that, he saluted, faced about, and left, hoping his flattery would neutralize this caustic old grouch before he returned. He clicked the cover of his pocket watch, planning to return in an hour.

Damn the delay!

"Excuse me, sir," a slender, scholarly man stopped him, "I saw you in the Secretary's office," he too looked at his watch, "just 9 minutes ago."

"Yes. I remember you. You didn't appear too happy."

The observation was ignored, "You are Major Morrow of General Stuart's command."

"Yes?"

"I overheard your self-introduction to The Secretary. May I introduce myself? John Jones, clerk to Mr. Randolph."

David accepted the offered hand with reserve.

"When I heard your name, it seemed familiar."

"Well?"

"Oh, I am sorry. I think we have a mutual friend, I'm curious to confirm my suspicions, I have waited for you."

"Yes?"

"I have a young lady working for me."

"So?"

"She's been with me now for three months—let me think—since June 2nd, three months and two days, to be exact."

"Mr. Jones, that's all very interesting but I fail to see how it affects me."

He digressed again, "You young officers! So eager to rush, rush along. Too busy to look around, to notice the details."

David took a deep breath, and with time to kill, acquiesced to this meticulous observer of fact and detail."Sorry, sir. Now, who is this friend that we share."

"As I've said, a lovely young lady who writes a beautiful hand. She earns every penny we pay her. But I try your patience."

"She was referred by Congressman Boteler, and carried a letter of yours, I believe. Unless there's another David Morr . . ."

"Carrie Nash?"

"One and the same. Her name as it appears on the payroll."

"Mr. Jones! I am indeed sorry for my impatience."

"She has spoken very highly of you, Major Morrow. But why waste more time. She is just around the corner."

"Just around the corner!"

Mr. Jones extended a hand, palm up, "If you will follow me?"

Copying a document, Carrie dipped her pen into the glass inkwell. He watched. She looked up. Open-mouthed, she stared in disbelief. Her steel pen and its wood holder slipped her fingers, spattering drops of ink.

David stared, too, for the girl he saw was far beyond Mr. Jones description, a surprised princess, sparkling with childlike wonderment, unspeakably lovely despite her drab surroundings.

Her eyes were the smokey blue he remembered; her hands, tapered, delicate as the butterfly wings he also remembered. The sheen of her chestnut hair was the same, although she wore it differently, the front brushed to waves of soft magic. A snood held the back.

She screamed delightedly, "David!" and ran to him.

Throwing her arms about his neck, she embraced him as a favorite brother after a long absence. He wrapped strong arms around her, brotherly —like until he caught the scent of summer evening in her hair, a Sirens' potion of hollyhock, lilac, and magnolia, clover, and fresh mown hay. Enchanted, he held her closer, whispering as no brother ever did, "Carrie."

All his questions of the night vanished. Woosh!

She sensed his feeling, hoped he saw that she too had remembered only the good things between them. Her eyes held him, unblinking smokey sapphire with violet speckles reaffirming the blue.

Mr. Jones cleared his throat genteelly.

Embarrassed, Carrie slipped from the embrace, "Sorry, Mr. Jones. We haven't seen each other since the 25th of May."

"The 25th of May. Hmmm, you have a remarkable memory."

Mr. Jones smiled innocently, "Miss Nash, you look pale. I think a touch of fresh air would refresh you."

"But, Mr. Jones! The copies of the Secretary's report."

"Miss Nash, that's one part of my job. Another is the well-being of my people," his eyes twinkled, "now, off with you."

He watched their jaunty strides down the corridor.

"David, whatever are you doing here?"

"The general had urgent papers for your Mr. Randolph."

"I am impressed, major, by your promotion and your friends."

"Hardly a friend. I'm just a courier with papers for him."

"I'm still impressed. You're a major. Meeting with the Secretary. Why, he talks every day with President Davis."

"He pulls his pants on like everyone else, one leg at a time. But I want to talk about you. Your job. Everything."

"Oh I love it! It's so exciting! I don't know where to begin. I started on June 2nd," she rattled on, "I took your letter—thank you again for writing it—to Mr. Boteler—he wrote on it to Mr. Jones. He's such a nice man and told me I was to come back to him if Mr. Jones didn't have an opening—if I needed anything else to let him know," she went on breathlessly, "that was on a Thursday but Mr. Jones couldn't see me until the next day. So I came back—he asked me if I could start Monday and I did. Oh, it is so exciting. I have you to thank. It's all your doing. Thank you, David, thank you. And you're a major!"

"Carrie, you're absolutely radiant."

She turned misty eyes up to him, "How can I ever repay you?"

"By having supper with me tonight."

"I'd love to, but my hours are until 6. Often I work later."

"I'll wait."

Carrie took his hand. Looking him full in the eyes, she pursed her lips, as if she were about to say something. Instead, she lowered her glance, caressed the back of his hand lightly, "I really should be getting back." Watching her go, David knew she was about to tell him something important.

She was the girl he remembered, yet how much she had changed. No longer did she remind him of Gracey. What was it that she had wanted to tell him?

David went back to the Secretary of War's office, but Randolph was elsewhere. He sat and waited. And dozed.

"You're back again." The sour voice startled him, "Come back in the morning and I'll have an answer for your general."

"I was hoping to return today. Sir," David said rising.

"You heard me, major, tomorrow."

"Thank you. I'll be here. Early. Sir," emphasizing the last two words more than he had intended. He started for the door.

"One more thing, young major."

David stopped in the doorway, turned a quarter turn, "Sir?"

"Thank your lucky stars that poor health recently forced me to resign my rank of general. Else, I'd have you up on charges."

"Thank you. Sir." David turned and left, mumbling impolitely about sons of bitches masquerading as Secretaries of War.

He still steamed when Carrie met him.

"Whatever are you raving about?"

"That ass, the Secretary of War. I could kill him!"

Stopping in her tracks, Carrie snapped, "Someone killed my brother. It solved nothing."

"Carrie, I am sorry. I didn't mean to upset you."

"Well, you did. He could be ill, you know."

"By gosh, you could be right. He did mention a headache. Maybe it's the aches and pains that make him so sour."

Leaving the building, they walked up Ninth Street.

"I owe you an apology too. I have no right to scold you." He put fingertips toward her lips, "Shhh, tell me more of you."

"Well—I make regular deposits from my pay envelope."

"What in the world are you talking about?"

"To repay the money I owe you."

"Oh for goodness sakes. Forget it! I have."

"Well, I haven't. You loaned it and I'm going to repay it."

"That's not necessary. I gave it to you to get you out of that place, that's all."

"But that isn't all. It was a loan and I will repay it."

David heard the iron in her voice, "All right, if that's . . ." That's exactly what I want."

David took her dainty hand, "All I meant was that what you call a loan, excuse me, your loan isn't due yet."

"A loan, that's exactly what it is. You can't talk me out of it."

"I am not trying to. But it isn't due until after the war. Those were the terms after you refused it as a gift."

"You didn't mean that."

"But I did." He touched her cheek lightly, "Keep making the deposit —think of it as your rainy day money."

"But I want to repay you."

"You can. When the war is over. Nobody pays bills before they're due. Would you like to eat?"

"David, can we walk for a bit? To enjoy the evening air."

"Of course."

They strolled along the tree-lined paths of Capitol Square, past the hexagonal bell tower, toward the columned portico of the capitol. Carrie seemed preoccupied. He was about to question her.

"David, I'd like to talk about that place, as you call it."

"There's no need to."

"But there is. I want you to know how ashamed I was when we were in that horrible room."

"I knew you didn't belong there."

"I don't know how I agreed to such a thing."

"Carrie, don't blame yourself. You did what you had to do."

"I could have worked, like I'm doing now," she fought tears.

David tried to comfort her, "But nothing happened."

She shook him off, "I still shouldn't have been there."

"You did the best you could. Times have changed—you see things now you had no way of seeing then."

She ignored him, "I was frightened. David, I didn't have anyone to turn to. I was so afraid." She looked him square in the eye, said unabashedly, "I've never been with a man, David, and I was terrified you would hurt me."

"I'm sorry for that. But I'm glad I was your first—almost your first, that is. I'm just happy I came along when I did."

"So am I."

For several minutes, they were content to watch the river and the western sun settling into the tree line.

"Is that what you wanted to tell me in the corridor?"

"Yes."

He took her hand again, "Did you know that Thomas Jefferson designed a dome for the capitol?"

Carrie interrupted, "Shhhhh."

"What is it?" David whispered.

Carrie pointed as softly as she spoke, "Over there."

He moved close to her, ostensibly to sight over her arm. Just over her outstretched finger, he saw the redbirds, the brilliant one feeding a seed to his mate. She took it without hurry, daintily as though thanking him. Together they flew away.

Carrie responded very softly, "No. What happened to it?"

"She accepted his seed. Do you know redbirds mate for life?"

"Not the cardinals, silly," playfully ignoring the double entendre, "Jefferson's dome for the capitol."

"The dome was turned down, but Jefferson had his way. His dome is in the attic under the roof." Standing up and leaning against a corner pillar, David pointed to the hidden dome.

Carrie joined him at the pillar, "Are you joshing me, Major Morrow?" She emphasized his higher rank.

"No, honestly. It's there."

Carrie laughed, "It isn't!"

"Well, I haven't seen it myself. But that's what they say."

"I believe you," she laughed lightly.

"Would you believe me if I said I love you?"

David put an arm around Carrie's waist, tentatively drawing her to him, ready to release her at the slightest resistance. Far from objecting, she nestled into him, and David kissed her long and sweet. She returned his kiss, when he relaxed to end it, she melted into him, pursing her lips against his and mumbling as best she could, "Mmm think so."

They held each other while the sun dipped below the trees, and the redbirds came back. The male fed his mate another seed, and a hundred miles north, ragged soldiers sloshed through the Potomac into Maryland.

They kissed again, softly, "I've loved you, David, from the very first," she smiled, "even if I didn't show it."

"Maybe you did show it. When you washed my face?"

"You were like a little boy in need of help."

"When you look like that I don't feel like a little boy."

Amused, she put him off, "Get on with you, David Morrow."

"Now that's settled, would you like to walk to the Basin? It's always exciting with the barges loading and unloading. There's a man who makes daguerreotypes. Would you have one made for me?"

"If you'll do the same for me."

They walked down the capitol's front slope and Tenth Street to the Great Basin. It was not quite the hubbub David expected for the day's work was over, except for a single bateau loading. They watched and learned it carried stores for a blockade runner moored at Rocketts, a mile downstream.

They found the photographer's shop. It was locked. His neighbor, in a chair tilted against the unpainted building, pointed, "Takes his supper in the ordinary. Next block."

It was a raucous place catering to those who worked the canal, rough men unaccustomed to seeing women like Carrie around the Basin. David pried the photographer loose from his supper offering a double bonus to get the likenesses at once.

His shop had an ancient mirror where Carrie smoothed her hair and pinched her cheeks, all the while fussing she should have worn a dressier dress.

The photographer loaded the glass negative, waited for her, and at last ducked under the hood to focus his camera.

"Ma'am, this pan has phosphorus in it for light. Now hold still until after it flashes. Try to ignore it."

David intervened, "Wait! Can't she smile?"

"Sure. If she can hold it without moving."

"Ma'am, a big grin most always comes out bad. I'd suggest a small smile, just the corners of your mouth. No strain. Just natural, now. That's fine. Beautiful. Hold it just like that."

High above his head, the narrow pan flashed. Carrie jumped. He changed plates, "Perfectly still this time. Hold it."

David sat for the third plate.

They wandered hand in hand about the Great Basin, looking at everything and at nothing. In no time at all they were back at the photographer's, looking at themselves in little leather cases, Carrie's smile a meld of restraint and explosive energy.

"I love it," Dave raved, "it is the very expression you had when you were watching the redbirds."

"And yours is so handsome. David, you should be a general!"

They backtracked along the Basin to Eighth Street, Main and into the dining room of the Spotswood Hotel.

"I'm ready for supper. Are you?"

"Starved."

"I could eat a horse."

"Please! I'm in the cavalry."

"Will you order for me? Whatever you have."

"You're easy to satisfy."

"I'm satisfied just to be here with you."

After supper, for which their waiter apologized, "The war you know," David pulled his chair around the table to sit close to her. He reached to take her hand in his.

"It's wonderful to see you again."

"And to be with you, David."

Glistening in the gas lights, her eyes seemed darker, no smoke, just very dark blue.

"Carrie?"

"Yes?"

"Would you be surprised if I asked you to spend the night with me?"

"No, I wouldn't."

"Wouldn't be surprised or wouldn't spend the night?"

"I would have been surprised if you hadn't asked me, David. I have felt it, too, and have been arguing with myself. I want very much to be with you, but . . ."

"But what, sweetheart?"

"It's not right. I want you, too, but it's just wrong."

Carrie's plain answer was that of the common sense girl he had come to love so quickly and so dearly, the face-the-world Carrie who accepted the cost of survival and still lived her beliefs to the fullest. He squeezed her hand.

"I agree with you, dearest. I shouldn't have asked."

"I would have been disappointed if you hadn't," she leaned toward him, "but what if we did and I had a baby? With you off to wherever, I'd be alone, David, and then—you may be—you may never come back—gone—forever," she buried her face into his tunic, "and I love you so."

He pressed her even closer, vaguely sensing that other diners were looking, assisted her to the street. She caught her breath, trying valiantly to suppress sobs.

David found a barouche waiting for a fare, gave the driver the address of the rooming house on Church Hill, Mrs. Burgess's. Settled comfortably in the leather seat, Carrie gained control of herself, "I'm sorry I spoiled our evening."

"You spoiled nothing, sweetheart."

At Broad Street, the driver guided his horse to the right.

"Driver, the lady and I are in no hurry."

"Yes, suh!"

"Being at the Basin reminded me of Pa telling us about the canal in Georgetown. He had a warehouse on it years ago. Ezekiel worked with him and sang us the mule skinners' songs."

"You speak so well of your family. Who's Ezekiel?"

"We are close, Carrie—you'll meet them all, Ma, Pa, Jed, Brian, Gracey, Ruth, Ezekiel—he and Pa grew up together." "I'd like that, especially Gracey," she cocked an eye at him, "will you tell them how we met?"

"Of course. I'll add what Pa told Ma, that you are the right one for me. And they will love you, too."

"David, you're talking so seriously."

"I am serious. Riding the cars last night I was afraid I wouldn't find you. Maybe you'd left Richmond and I'd never see you again. I've never felt for anyone what I feel for you. I just want to be with you. All the time. And I've made you sad."

"I'm not sad," eyes of violet mist peeked at him, "not with you so much as with myself." As before, she looked directly into his eyes, unblinking and unashamed, "I would like to be with you all the time, too. I would like to spend the night with you, and every night. But for now, I can't."

"I know."

"I feel it's not right—I know it's not practical. It would be beautiful, but I know I'd be sorry. Oh, David, I just don't know. I want so much to say yes."

He felt her trembling against him, reached out to comfort her. Holding her gently, absorbing the sobs and shivers, nuzzling her soft tresses until she quieted and tilted her face upward.

They kissed long and lovingly.

Carrie dried her tears, laughing through them to cover her desire, "First, you turn me down. Then I turn you down—in between you give me a pocketful of money for nothing. David, we make a crazy, crazy pair."

He jumped at the opening, "Crazy enough to be married?"

"David!! Are you serious?"

"I've never been more serious in my life. What have I been talking about half the day?

"Driver, stop this carriage at once. You are the witness."

David knelt on the floor of the carriage, close to Carrie's legs in the limited space. His voice was very low, somber, "Carrie, I will love you forever. I want to take care of you forever. Will you marry me?"

A trace of a smile came and went, joy and melancholy. Her eyes glistened sapphire and violet, shimmering in the mist and smoke. She cupped his cheeks in her hands, and whispered as she touched his lips with hers, "My crazy Major Morrow."

XLI

A VISIT HOME

Next morning, David waited for her as she came out of Mrs. Burgess's. He had the same barouche, the same top-hatted driver.

"David, what a surprise!"

"My intention exactly, milady," he intoned, bowing with a flourish, "the royal carriage awaits your pleasure."

Carrie loved the make-believe, raising an imaginary lorgnette with regal detachment, "How nice."

He crooked an arm at chest level to accept her hand, "Milady?"

Butterfly fingertips touched his forearm.

Bright teeth flashed as the driver grinned his approval, doffed his stovepipe hat, held it at arm's length. He made a sweeping circle with it as he bowed low.

At the curb, David became Major again, sweeping Carrie off her feet, "The cavalry has arrived! Prepare for action!"

Hands twining about his neck, Carrie lifted her face to his, "Prepare for action yourself!" Their eyes embraced in a message only lips could seal.

In the window of Mrs. Burgess's home, a lace curtain fluttered ever so slightly. The driver snapped his reins.

They touched hands all the way to The War Department, but neither trusted himself to speak. The carriage stopped.

"God keep you, David. I will pray to Him every day to keep you safe until we are together again."

"And we will be, love. We have a wedding to attend."

They parted in the corridor, quickly before tears, she to her work, he to Randolph's office. The secretary gave him a sealed envelope. He detoured to Carrie's door.

His lips formed words of love. And he was gone.

He rode the cars back through Beaver Dam Station, Bumpass Gordonsville, through Orange Courthouse, Catlett's and Bristoe's that he knew so well, into Manassas Junction.

Retrieving Sable, he hurried on to Dranesville, querying stragglers whose druthers were to remain in Virginia, "They was headin' fur White's Ford an' Marylan'."

At the Potomac, David dismounted, watered Sable, splashed his own face and head. He filled his canteen, and crossed.

He cantered through countryside untouched by war, hay fields ready for a second mowing, lush acres green and high, flourishing apple orchards, peach and cherry. Not like parts of Virginia he thought. Soon after dark he rode into camp at Urbana.

"Halloo, major, you made a quick trip of it," Jeb Stuart greeted him, ebullient as ever, anticipating action,

"Too quick for me, sir."

Stuart broke Randolph's seal, "Good—uh huh—good—hmmm what's this?" He read aloud, feigning disbelief, "Your Major Morrow needs to be taught respect for his superiors?"

"I tried to cover my irritation."

"Unsuccessfully it seems. But no matter, he says he'll give Pelham more guns as soon as he can."

David smiled, thinking of his politic phrases to Randolph.

Stuart, "What are you smirking at?"

"Even the devil is susceptible to flattery, sir!"

Jeb Stuart shook his head with pleasure.

"You haven't missed much here. McClellan has command again—has stayed close to Washington. Learned today he's finally moving. We've patrols out, watching him."

Bursting to talk of Carrie, David interrupted, "General, I want you to be the first to know. I'm engaged to be married."

"Married! I thought you liked your freedom."

"I do—did—until I met Carrie."

"I know. I know. It happens to all of us," Stuart chuckled. "My hearty congratulations."

"Thank you, sir. I was surprised myself, but she's so . . ."

"Please! Spare me the details," Stuart held up a hand in mock impatience and raced on. "You're in time for our first festivities in Maryland. Von Borcke is arranging a ball."

"A ball? Here?" David's tone registered disapproval.

"Tomorrow night. You don't sound enthusiastic."

"With due respect, sir, I'm not. It seems trifling and dangerous here in Yankee country."

"It may be. But we have many friends here. Our arrival calls for a celebration. Soldiers need pretty girls and music. They need to dance and laugh. Maybe not you with your new love, but the rest of us do."

Stuart stood pensive for a moment, staring at the floor, "As for me, I ask only to fight with honor—enjoy convivial people when I can. And if necessary, to die game."

David was about to reply but lost the chance as Stuart chuckled, "Well! That's today's lesson in command."

"I see what you mean, general. But, I'd—no offense, sir."

"Go on."

"I'd rather it be held in Richmond."

Stuart's Prussian aide, Heros von Borcke, planned the ball, using troopers to clean an old academy building, decorate it with battle flags and flowers, collect hundreds of candles, and carry invitations about the countryside. Unschooled in local mores, he opened with a rollicking polka. His lady, a visitor from New York educated him, "Proper ladies dance polkas only with family."

With aplomb, Von Borcke halted the musicians to substitute a quadrille, a genteel promenade that required no body-touching other than fastidious fingertips, quite different than the whirling polka in which impulsive overtures were possible.

David stood on the sidelines halfheartedly for his thoughts were of Carrie: Carrie whirling in the candlelight, Carrie feted by his friends, Carrie bewitching General Stuart and pretending chagrin at his prolonged hand-holding; Carrie, Carrie, Carrie.

A pretty, red-haired girl intruded, "Why so somber, major?"

"Is that how I look?"

"Like you'd rather be somewhere else."

"I would."

Gunfire erupted in the distance. David ran to a window. The girl followed, obviously apprehensive.

David couldn't resist, "And why are you so somber?"

She clung to his sleeve, "What is it?"

"Nothing to worry about," he reassured her, "maybe a picket with the jitters. Best leave the window, though."

A trooper clattered in, "Federals have attacked an outpost!"

Ladies gasped. Troopers donned spurs and weapons. Among the first, David raced toward the gunfire. They fired at musket flashes in the dark and the raiders drifted off. All but David returned to the ball. He remained with the pickets.

For the next ten days, he and the far-flung cavalry scouted McClellan's gingerly advance and fought twenty actions.

On September 17, David stood on Nicodemus Hill looking east toward Antietam Creek. The early morning fog lifted as a blue line advanced. He maintained his watch as the Confederate left resisted hours of furious attacks. David lost count of them. Before noon, the battle drifted away. A lull. More blue lines cleared the woods onto Lee's center. The battle was one of infantry.

"ANTIETAM" rode the wild winds of the North; "SHARPS-BURG", the fiery gales of the South. Horror followed, hissing, "Dunker Church", "Corn Field", "Bloody Lane," "West Woods." Americans shot down 26,000 Americans on that September day in 1862.

David saw nothing of the mortal struggle for a stone bridge to the southeast. Defenders held for hours, protecting Lee's right and rear until Bluecoats turned them via a ford downstream. Reports reached Lee. Lee summoned Stuart. Stuart bellowed for his aide with the cavalry's fleetest stallion.

David sensed the urgency, "Yes, sir!"

"Powell Hill is marching from The Ferry. Intercept him—guide him to the lower bridge. If we lose it, we're flanked. Go!"

"With your permission, sir. Ten seconds to make sure," David scratched lines and arrows in the dirt, "Our line. The bridge. From it, they have a straight shot to our flank and rear. Hill is coming like this," pointing, "I'm to guide him to the bridge."

"Either that, or onto the Yankees if they've crossed."

"One more thing. Send Rafferty after me. Just in case. Sir."

"Good idea. Now let that black giant out."

David did reach Hill's Division and brought it in. Not to the bridge but to the Yankee flank for they had crossed and headed for Lee's rear. Hill hit a good blow, saving a disaster.

David was cited once again in Stuart's battle report for his unerring instincts and immediate grasp of the situation that guided the critical counterattack. General Lee repeated Stuart's citation in his own report to President Davis.

The following day General Lee waited in vain for McClellan to resume his attack. After dark, he commenced an all-night withdrawal, back to the Potomac and across, into Virginia.

David and the cavalry were the last to cross, even then had no rest, for as the rifle companies established camps along Opequon Creek, the troopers manned outposts to guard them.

Back in Virginia, well within a day's ride of Winchester, David went about his duties stubbornly. Longing for Carrie, he asked leave to go to Richmond. Stuart turned him down. He filled the emptiness with reports, outpost inspections, and grooming Sable.

Camp was west of Charles Town at the Dandridge estate, where officers spent an idyllic three weeks amidst "a house full of daughters and nieces, all grown and attractive." They ate of loaded tables under a canopy, where a stream of newspapermen encouraged their tales of derring-do.

David kept to himself.

Stuart surprised him one afternoon, "I'm riding into Winchester in the morning. Plan to spend the night if all stays quiet. Maybe more. Accompany me, and do the same."

David accepted with enthusiasm, "Yessir! The usual escort?"

They left early, David light-hearted for a change.

"I'm happy to see you smiling again."

"It's good to be going home. I have a lot to catch up on. That stallion of ours senses something. I swear he's smarter than some officers."

"He's been on this road before. How about it, Sable? You know where you are?"

After a few miles, David dropped off the pace. "I'll catch up," he shouted, heading for a copse of trees. He dropped the reins near a stand of tall grass. When he picked them up a few minutes later, Sable nudged him as if to say, "Let's get going."

David agreed in sheer happiness, chattering like a jaybird on a fence-post, "Yessir, we're going home. Going to see Ma and Pa, Racey and everybody, talk and eat Ma's cooking. Sable, we're on our way home. Celebrate, Sable, celebrate!"

For a moment, they stood there in the road as lovers might. Rich, brown eyes solemn, Sable pawed gently at the ground.

"You have an itch?" David stroked the long nose, "that what you're saying?" The stallion pushed against the hand rubbing his bone-hard nose. Flat-handed, David smacked the solid neck muscle, swung into the saddle, "EeeeeeYAH."

The big black shook out his feathery mane, reared high, pumping his forelegs, springing forward in a great leap. David leaned low, gave him his head, "Go, boy, go."

Sable flew, head and tail flat on the wind. Shoulders and legs pumped so effortlessly, so elegantly that only the tiniest of dust feathers marked his course. Too quickly did they reach Stuart and his party for they felt like running forever.

"Saw you coming hellbent. Thought Yankees were chasing you."

"Nothing like that, general. We're just celebrating."

"Never saw a horse run like him. Sure you won't sell him?"

"You've seen how he feels about that. Sorry, general."

Across Red Bud Run and the railroad tracks, they angled onto the Martinsburg Pike just north of Winchester.

"Damn that's a pretty sight. General, mind if I ride ahead?"

"Catch a smell of the barn did you?"

"Yes sir. Think Sable has, too."

"Go on, major. Let him out."

No one saw David's signals, but Sable felt them. Maybe he smelled his old barn, for he exploded into a flying gallop.

"Look at that black beauty run," Jeb Stuart said to no one particular, "that is one beautiful horse. Even from the rear."

At the town limits, David slowed to a trot, and to a walk. Here and there he saw injured soldiers, bandaged, splinted or on crutches. He rode by more and more of them. Wagons had hauled thousands of injured soldiers from Sharpsburg to the lower valley. They and the walking wounded filled Winchester.

He had looked on the Antietam and its vast slaughter, but was unprepared for anything like this, casualties everywhere, trudging along, sitting against walls and fences, lying prone in private yards. The public square, every nook and corner, every available space was filled with wounded in their soiled, bloodied bandages.

Among them, he spied occasional doctors by their aprons; women, men, and children administering as they could. Winchester's people had turned out en masse to care for Lee's battered army.

Approaching the house on Wolfe Street, he saw Sarah in one of the verandah rocking chairs. He waved, but had no response. Drawing closer, he waved again. Still no response, for she had her eyes closed. Very strange for Ma to doze, he thought, instead of working with her needle and thread, mending, darning, working threads into colorful pictures. He took the steps, two at a time.

Sarah stirred, "David? Landsakes, what are you doing here?"

"Came home to see my best girl," he laughed as he bounded up the steps and to her chair in the time it took her to stand.

"Mercy," she gasped, "you'll squeeze the breath out of me."

"That's what best girls are for." He tightened his hug.

Sarah clung to him, her own codetta of love for her soldier son. When she let him go, she blinked moist eyes, "I've watched for you, afraid I'd find you." She wiped at ungovernable tears.

He was startled, for Ma never gave way like that. Never had he seen her so drained, so emptied of joy. Her hair was more gray than he remembered. He felt the chill of war's un-tallied cost.

Sarah let him go, dabbing at tears that had slipped through.

"I'm sorry, son," she forced a smile, running her hands lightly over his face and arms, "Are you all right? Of course you are, I can see that. But you need to eat. You must be hungry."

Ma was pushing herself, David realized, pushing herself to keep the war away, to keep things as they were.

"You look tired, Ma. Is everything all right?"

"Everything is fine. We've been busy caring for the soldiers we have with us, but everybody helps so it's not so bad."

"The soldiers you have with you? Here in the house?"

"Of course. Everybody has taken them in."

And David Morrow learned more of the cost of war.

"I saw them as I rode in, Ma. Courthouse Square was full. I supposed they were waiting for wagons to take them to hospitals."

"The army is overwhelmed, David. They do their best, but there are too many. Winchester is a hospital—the whole town is one big hospital. Every place is full, the courthouse, churches, schools, the marketplace, our homes."

"Sheltering them is one thing, but who cares for them? Dresses wounds? Feeds them?"

"We do. There's no one else."

"You do, Ma? That's the army's job."

"I know."

"Pa? Where's Pa?"

"In the back, I suppose." Sarah sounded tired, more than that, exhausted.

"Close your eyes again and rest. I'll be right back."

He led Sable around to the barn, where he found Henry repairing a saddle, "Hello, Pa."

"David! Sarah said you'd be along. How are you, son?"

"Fine, Pa, fine."

"No injuries?"

"Not a scratch."

"Sable looks good."

"Try to brush him every day. Haven't missed many."

"That's good, son," his voice was subdued, almost reverent.

"We were there, Sable and I but not in the fighting."

"Was a bad one, huh."

"Very bad, Pa."

More discussion of the war was painful, so each waited, David for his father, Henry for his son, each adrift in the emotional undercurrents, unsure of their landfall. Henry fussed with broken leathers. David unsaddled Sable, fed him oats, started to wipe him down.

Then their eyes met and the uncertainty disappeared. They came together with a bone-crushing handshake that was sanctified at once with a third hand and a fourth.

"It's good to have you home, son."

"It's good to be with you, pa."

"Pa?"

"Yes."

"Is Ma all right?"

"All right? What do you mean?"

"She looks bad. Tired, worn-out, sickly."

"The damn hospital is what it is."

"The hospital?"

"The Morrow hospital on Wolfe Street," Henry spat the words, "she did the same thing after Kernstown in March."

"Two or three wounded soldiers shouldn't wear her out like that. Not with Mam to help, and the others."

"Two or three!! There's a damn-sight more than two or three. Must be twenty or more."

"Twenty!"

"Could be forty. Or eighty. Or a hundred and eighty if I hadn't put my foot down. I told her, 'No more, damn it, not one more, Sarah'. I thought she'd ignore me, but she didn't. Thank God for that. David, she'd kill herself if she had her way."

"I know. You did what needed doing, Pa."

"She doesn't think so. You'd think I'd closed the door to her own sons. Like I'd told you three boys t'stay away."

"She knows you wouldn't do that."

"That may be. But she keeps sayin' 'what if Brian or David was hurt and needed help', and 'what if Jed got shot again'."

"Again? Jed was shot? How bad? When? Where is he?"

"We wrote you about it."

"I never got the letter, Pa. Tell me."

"Somebody talkin' about me?" Jed appeared at the edge of the barn's wide doorway.

Overjoyed to see his brother, David spoke before he assimilated what he saw, "Jed!! Damn it's good to see you. Pa . . ." The crutches hit him in the stomach like a club, then the pinned-up pant leg. Jed with a pinned-up pant leg!

David felt his stomach collapse. The locomotive was coming at him again, the nightmare locomotive of Bristoe Station—he was backed against the wrecked train, against the red warning lights that he had smashed but was trying to light again, the locomotive was crashing into his stomach, and he was watching it all from scrubby growth alongside the track.

"I—I—" David was crushed, beyond words or understanding. This was Jed who could work the day dawn to dark, and do the same the next day and the next. Jed the tireless, the indestructible. Jed who knew what to do with soil and seeds and animals, who read the weather and the seasons, who respected God's forests, and God's nature and God's ways with man.

"Jed, I—I don't know what to say."

"Just say 'how did it happen'—I'll tell you and we can enjoy the rest of your time home."

"All right," David tried but failed to sound confident, "how did—it—happen, Jed?"

"Was back in May right here on Main Street. Got hit in the left leg, below the knee. Doctor couldn't save it and Zekiel made me crutches. He's thinkin' on how t'make a wooden leg."

Jed hitched his way to David, put out his right hand, "David. I am glad y're home. Danged if I'm not."

The brothers held a long handclasp, feelings with no words.

"Jed, I'm sorry."

"Hey, big brother, we're past that."

"I know, but I had to tell you," he held up a palm toward Jed, "but that's all."

"Good! Have you seen Ma?"

"She was on the verandah when I rode up. I was talking to Pa about her as you came in." He turned toward his father.

"Pa, what can I do? I'll be here for two or three days."

"Don't know of anything."

"How about hiring someone to live in? I'll send money."

"David, help isn't the problem. Mam's always here, and Mattie has come from the farm until things settle down. Betsy is a wonder. Ruth and Gracey pitch in. Gracey has surprised me."

Jed hobbled over to Sable, "He looks good, David, want me to brush him some?"

"Please do."

David turned back to Henry, "What do you mean, Pa?"

"Gracey's really changed. She was a little girl when we had the Kernstown casualties, shocked with the blood and disgusted with the smells. She wouldn't have anything to do with them. Now, with the whole town turned upside down, she pitches in, washing them, dressing wounds, emptying slops. She's her mother's girl, a real nurse. She'd be a good doctor if women could be doctors."

"That doesn't sound like the Gracey I saw last."

"She was heading for trouble with the soldiers."

"I know, Pa. I talked to her. I didn't think she heard me."

"You never told me you talked to her."

"It was our secret. I hoped putting it that way would make her feel grown up. Less need to prove anything."

"Maybe you started her thinking."

"Sounds as if something did. That's what counts."

Henry looked closely at the stirrups and stirrup straps, "Have to replace the straps. They're looking worn."

"What about Zekiel, Pa? How's he getting on?"

Henry tossed the stirrups over the saddle, sat on a wooden keg, "He's fine, but he can't go on forever. I worry about what's gonna happen t'the farm. I won't be here forever, and Zekiel's older than me. You want the farm, David?"

"Pa, I'm no farmer."

"Then who? Brian'd be reading a book during planting season. Jed's on crutches. He can't work it like we planned."

Jed paused with the brush in mid-air, "Pa, Zeke's gonna make me a wooden leg."

"He never told me about it," Henry grumped.

"He says he'll make it so's I can do anything."

"Maybe he can and maybe he can't. So far I don't know of any farmers with wooden legs—that's what I've got t'go on. As of right now, today, there's nobody t'help Zekiel and fill in behind him. If there's anything left t'fill in after this war."

Jed threw up his hands in resignation, went back to brushing Sable. David was about to side with him, tell Pa he had to look on the bright side, but seeing Jed's gesture, decided it better to back off.

"Where is Brian, Pa? Have you heard from him?"

Henry looked old when he answered, old and perplexed, as active men often do when their hands are tied, "We don't know. We haven't heard from him in months."

"Nothing? Nothing at all?"

"Only one thing. In June, he was at the farm. A week after General Jackson took Winchester back. Zekiel thought he might be leavin' the army—on his own."

"Not deserting! I hope not, Pa."

"If it isn't that, he's been hurt or captured."

"Maybe he decided to go back to his regiment."

"I don't think so. Zeke told him about Jed's being shot and he said he had t'see him, He left in the afternoon. Was coming through the fields t'avoid being seen, Zeke said," Henry lowered his voice almost to a whisper, "that's the last we heard."

David put a hand on Henry's shoulder, "Pa, you have to think the best."

Jed jumped back into the conversation, "You sound like Betsy. And Zeke. You know what Zeke told me?"

"To water the horses and plow a straight line," David joked.

"Yeh. He said that. And he said to use the crutches he was gonna make, or lean on somebody for the rest of my life. And bump down the stairs on my ass."

"Zekiel always did say things flat out."

"He was tellin' me not t'give up an inch without fightin' for what I wanted. And, by God, he's right."

"He made the crutches? I've only seen them as poles with a piece across the top. Never saw crutches split like that."

"Made them from his own idea."

"I'll be."

"He figgers with a wooden leg I'll be able t'walk without them. Maybe one crutch for a while, until I get the hang of it. Betsy thinks so, too."

"Ma wrote you married Betsy. The Betsy I met at the tavern in Falls Church?"

"One and the same. I'll never forget when you leaned her back on the bench and kissed her, square on the mouth."

Puzzled, Henry looked from one to the other, "Falls Church? You met your brother's wife and kissed her in a tavern?"

David laughed, but focused on the importance of the wooden leg, he unintentionally brushed off the question, "That's another story, Pa." He never saw the thundercloud that claimed his father's face, and turned to his brother.

"That's wonderful! If you get this wooden leg, you'll be good as new."

Jed's face brightened at once, "Betsy and I have been talkin' about the farm. Livin' in the big house, and workin' with Zeke like I did. Betsy says everyone needs t'look ahead. Have a dream she calls it, and she's right."

Enthused as they were, they talked right past their father—never saw the signs, first the cloud, now the scowl, the tight eyebrows, the pulsing jaw. Henry was not accustomed to being brushed aside.

The reminder of Brian's enlistment without his approval had started the black mood. Now, the shenanigans in the tavern, kissing Jed's wife like that—the business about a wooden leg, that had caught him by surprise. The new hope for Jed's working the farm should have been good news, but in his pique the wooden leg meant nothing except another case of his family's doing things without him. Even Ezekiel.

Unaware of Pa's turmoil, David walked right into it, "Everybody needs to look ahead, Jed."

Henry looked daggers, "Meaning me, I suppose." He made for the wide doorway.

"No, Pa, I was thinking more of myself," David called after him, "Pa . . ." Henry disappeared around the corner without a word.

David would have started after him had Jed not put a restraining hand on his arm, "Pa's been touchy, David."

"He was fine. We were having a good talk, then . . ." he gestured toward the door, "he walks out."

"He's upset with Ma for takin' in the soldiers. Thinks she's runnin' herself into the ground. Betsy told me she did the same thing after Kernstown and Pa was madder than a hornet. He didn't talk t'anyone for . . ."

A compelling screech penetrated the barn. David ran for the house. Jed crutched after him. In the kitchen, Mam pointed, "The parlor. The front parlor."

Running, he heard muffled, excited voices between the screams, "Hold him." "I can't." Ma was at the front door.

Across the room, two young girls struggled with a soldier on the floor, trying to pin flailing arms. David recognized Gracey.

Shoving roughly between them, he fell on the soldier's chest, grabbed his wrists, and held.

"Something to tie him. Bandage. Anything," he snapped, "you, Gracey, sit on his knees." He failed to recognize Betsy as she handed him a tourniquet. The soldier went limp. David probed his neck. No pulse. The room was quiet.

Sweaty with exertion, David was aware of furniture pushed to the walls, stacked to make space, other soldiers, two rows of them side by side, feet toward the center of the room, a narrow aisle between. One was on a small day bed, the screamer and the others on mattresses and pads on the floor.

A soldier in the next space cackled crazily, "You killed him you killed hi . . ." A dark figure loomed above him.

Disappointment made David as dangerous as he appeared, for instead of a joyous reunion, he had come home to a family in tatters, battered by exhaustion, argument, and pessimism, worn down by mangled soldiers they didn't know, would never see again. Surely, the winds of war had blown down Wolfe Street.

David kneeled at the cackling soldier, gripped his chicken neck with one hand, hauled him up, face to face, eye to eyeball. He hissed cold fury, "You shut your mouth or I'll rip your goddamned throat out."

"David, let him go," Gracey screamed, tugging at his arm, fearing what he might do. She pleaded, "Let him go, please let him go. David! Please, please. Betsy, tell him. David. David."

She saw the taut ridges of his hand loosen and the sharp angles of deadly fingers soften as his rage lost its heat.

"Come on, David," still gripping his arm, Gracey stood up, encouraging him to do the same. She led him from the room.

In the center hall, she threw her arms about him, "Thank you for what you did in there."

David's shirt was soaked with sweat, his dark hair plastered to his forehead. He held his sister close, uncertain of who he was becoming, and more than a little bit frightened.

Almost murdered a man in there. Get a hold of yourself. He heard Jeb Stuart's words, "You take what comes and move on, able to handle the hardship and strain." I thought so, too, but now?

He released his grip on Gracey, breathed deeply, "That crazy fool. None of you deserve that, the way you're working."

"He hasn't caused trouble before."

"Once is too much."

"He didn't know what he was doing. We could have handled it. Are you all right now?"

"I'm ok, Gracey." He spoke sadly for he remembered his little sister, full of joy and innocence. She had grown up.

In the parlor, Betsy pulled a sheet over the face of the dead soldier. She gagged at the foul odors that pervaded the room from apertures in human bodies, normal and inflicted, holes that bled, rotted, belched, and farted. From her apron pocket, she took a small bottle of lavender water, sprinkling some on the still-warm corpse and some on herself. The delicate fragrance was not nearly enough.

Wobbling and pale, she looked ready to collapse as she left the room. Jed reached her first, "Sit down. On the floor."

He held her arm, awkwardly trying to help, as Sarah lowered her to the floor, "Now put your head down, between your knees."

A few minutes later, the blood was back in her face, she smiled at the two brothers, "Silly thing to do."

The large foyer of the Morrow house became a tableau as everyone regained his composure, Betsy sitting on the floor outside the parlor, the others staring at her, Sarah and Jed on either side, David and Gracey together near the front door, Henry next, Mam and Mattie in the doorway leading to the kitchen.

Mattie was the first to move, quickly crossing over to Sarah, "You all right, Sarah? You need to sit."

They headed for a chair near Henry.

David had walked close to the edge, but was ready to move on, just as Jeb Stuart had described him, "Betsy, if your husband wasn't here, I'd give you a Falls Church greeting."

"Hello, David," Betsy matched him word for word, "if my husband wasn't here, I'd go look for him. To protect me from dangerous soldiers who don't even know who they're kissing."

"Touché, sister. If you ever get rid of this guy of yours, let me know."

"Not a chance. But you make a very nice brother." She took a step toward him to emphasize her sincerity.

David shrugged his shoulders toward Jed, "What else can I do? Certainly I can't insult your wife now, can I?"

He did hug her with enthusiasm, brotherly enthusiasm, and kissed her a brotherly kiss, "I know I'm late, but—welcome to the family, sis."

Henry lumbered down the steps, "I'll get a wagon."

"I'll go with you, Pa," David offered.

Together, they loaded the body and rattled off to the dead house. Henry nodded toward the shrouded figure behind them.

"That's what I mean. No reason for Sarah, no reason for any of them to be involved in such—such nastiness."

"I agree, Pa. But one thing I've learned is to reconnoiter, then decide whether to attack or fall back."

"You telling me t'back off? Let your mother work herself t'death? She would, you know. She'd take all of them in."

"But she didn't, Pa. You said you put your foot down and she didn't take any more. She told me how much you helped, that she didn't know what she'd do without you."

"She's told me that, too, but I never payed much attention."

"Maybe she was thanking you for saying 'no more soldiers'. She knows when she's at her limit. She can't refuse them, and needs someone else to do it for her. You've done that, Pa,—you've given her room to do what she needs to do."

"I'd be happier if she didn't have any of them," he growled.

"But she wouldn't be. You honored that. Damn it, Pa, give yourself credit."

They discharged their cargo and rattled toward home. Henry had seen the development of his soldier son over the years, his keen intellect and ability to go directly to the heart of a problem. He understood David and respected him.

"You really think that's what your mother meant?"

"I think she meant that, and more."

They rode the rest of the way home in silence.

A soldier galloped past them, was waiting when they arrived. Recognizing David, he saluted, took a handwritten note from his boot top, "From General Stuart, major. He's leaving within the hour, wants you to accompany him."

David rode from Winchester in a far different mood than he had felt that morning. Carrie had changed the war for him, and this visit home changed it even more. What the hell good were the battlefield victories, the excitement, the glory, when it meant torn-up families and absence from loved ones? When it meant being home, not saying a word about your bride to be?

XLII

ESCAPE

The moon passed through its last quarter. Brian Morrow lay on his shelf, absorbing the night noises, alert to dissonances. A tiny noise that didn't belong could be the harbinger of black isolation in 'the hole' or the final proof of his mortality.

He had decided this was his last night on Pea Patch Island, one way or the other. Tom McDonald tried to coax him out of it, "Wait for another exchange. It's safer."

Brian would have none of it, "I've already waited too long. I'll go alone if I have to. The moon is black. No more delay." He fingered the canteen strap.

Sean Murphy had given life to the escape plan by reporting the sinks ready to fall into the bay. He had damaged the rickety structure as part of a scheme he hatched when he learned of John Lyle's cache. There was only one reason for saving tin cans.

"Fix it," he was ordered, "get a work party and fix it." He named off Brian, Tom McDonald, Sam Turner.

As he marched them about for boards and tools, Sean put on a show of harshness, scolding in his indelible brogue. From a distance, he appeared a hard taskmaster; from up close, quite the opposite. The glimmer in his eye and the wry turn of his mouth were dead giveaways. They gave him the look of an overgrown leprechaun enjoying his droll joke on authorities too dull to believe in pranks or the little folk.

"Git ta worrk ye worrthless rebels.

"You therre, you want a week in the hole?

"Ye're enough t'try the patience of Saint Patrrick himself." Only his work party was close enough to hear the interspersions, mumbled sotto voce for safety's sake.

"Drraft me into yourr stinkin' arrmy will ye. Ha!

"The Lorrd's ways are just. Blessed is the Lorrd."

They rebuilt the sinks, secreted the cans there. Extra boards lay unused, extra to anyone else perhaps, but important to Brian and his friends. Sean Murphy looked with satisfaction on the finished project, including the extra lumber.

"By the Sacred Motherr, 'tis finished," he crossed himself, turned to the conspirators, "I am of the opinion we have indeed been blessed."

Brian had waited one night for rain that never came. This was the second. An hour passed, two. Brian fussed, "We'll go without it if we have to."

"Be patient. Rain will be good cover."

Just before midnight, the rain did come, gentle, then heavy. Three shadows slipped from the barracks. A familiar brogue surprised them, "Hold me shirrt tail. Oy'll lead the way."

"Sean, what in blazes . . ."

"Shhhh," the brogue again, "tain't no time fer quarrelin'."

Sean went ahead, making for the sinks and the sealed cans, Brian next, Sam Turner, and Tom. Concealing rain pelted them.

Rounding the corner of the kitchen building, Sean stopped. He mopped his eyes, squinted into the rain. He felt danger.

"Murphy, I knew you wuz up t'somethin' on them sinks." The voice was unmistakable, the corporal who coveted young Sam.

He leered, "With my boy an' his cousin!" Rain hid the knife in his hand.

"The saints presarrve us!"

"Haul yer ass outa here, Murphy, you an' him," indicating Tom, "I ain't seen you an' you ain't seen me."

He turned on Brian, never suspecting Sean's rebellion, "Stealin' my boy what I been savin'! Want him all fer yerself, maybe?" He lunged forward, slashing upward with the knife.

Sean Murphy, unwilling draftee, lonely for his loved ones, swung his musket with fury. Brian pounced, hands diving like talons for the corporal's neck. Curled thumbs dug into the throat crushing the yell for guards. It gurgled, still a mortal danger. The knife slashed Brian across the arm. The talons closed down. Palpable hatred flamed from the corporal's eyes. Then fear as the thumbs dug deeper.

He thrashed, rolling left and right, jerking his head wildly against the death grip, flailing, fighting now for his life. Tom grabbed the knife arm. The other smashed Brian's side. His breath caught. He dug deeper into the devil's throat, squeezing, choking off the alarm. The corporal's eyes bulged frantic. He writhed in mortal fear.

He lurched again, catching Brian along the same ribs.

Mud-slippery now, Tom wrestled the knife arm; Sam Turner, the other. Brian held on, through slime and blood.

The corporal sagged limp.

"Let him go. He'll give no trouble for a while."

Brian snarled, jammed taut skin. Suddenly, his thumbs broke through. Bone cracked, softer parts slipped silently. The corporal's body jerked once and lay still.

Brian felt nothing, not broken throat, not rain, not mud, not the corporal's blood or his own now mingled forever. Nor did he feel Tom pull him to his feet and lead him to the sinks.

Sean Murphy unfolded his own plan,"I'm goin', too."

"Sean, no. You can get shot for desertion."

"Desarrtion me ars! It ain't my warr."

"Take one bunch of cans then. Sam, you take the other. Brian, you and me share the third. Grab a board, too. Off the pile," he pointed.

They waded into the muck of Delaware Bay, knee-deep, chest high and neck. In the cats and dogs rain, Tom hissed them close mostly for Sean, "It's a mile to shore and the tide has started to run out. Keep the current to your right—stay together." Hand-paddling, they inched away from Pea Patch Island.

Very quickly, Tom and Brian fell behind, Tom paddling for both. He paddled one-handed, all the time holding his friend, towing from ahead, pushing from behind to spell arms and legs, now unsure of the tide and direction.

Hours later, Brian gasped, "Can't breathe right. Take the boards—leave me—you'll never—make—it—if—you don't." Brian forced the words, his breathing shallow.

Tom held his grip. He saw white, fluffy clouds ahead, paddled on. Catch them, they'll carry you. He reached. Nothing.

"Tom—the cans—dragging."

He ignored the voice, preferring the comfort of the clouds.

The voice prodded a second time, "The cans—getting heavy." "The clouds are so beautiful."

Clouds, time. The night merged, seeking the morning.

"Tom! Tom!—wake up—the cans."

"Uh huh." He heard a child's voice, "They will find you." Dimly, he reached for a can, lifted it. "Too heavy" jarred him awake. He tested the others. Each had leaked water.

"Hold the boards, Brian."

"Go—leave me."

"Hold the goddamned planks."

Brian moaned. Tom un-lashed the cans'. Holding Brian to the boards, kicked and paddled mechanically. He was unaware when the tide went slack. Soon it would be carrying them up the bay.

The clouds were gone when his feet brushed the bottom. The eastern sky hinted a new day. He sank into the putrid mud, into the beautiful, heavenly, stinking ooze. He could stand up! He could keep his head above the water! His shoulders lifted clear, then chest and hips as he climbed the sucking slime.

"We made it! We made it!!" He towed Brian toward shore.

The water lowered to his knees and feet. He looked behind at the drifting mud trail. He lowered his friend to the narrow beach, "Guess we steered pretty good." Brian didn't hear him.

Dr. Edward Ruggles, 1811 graduate of Maryland's College of Medicine, practicing physician for 51 years, yawned as he sat on the edge of his bed. He stretched stiff muscles. At the window, he watched the low sliver of first day stretch its arms just as he had, lifting, lengthening the sky brighter and bluer.

"A fine day," he observed, reading the signs.

The good doctor had moved to St. George's three years ago after turning his practice over to his son. For years he had run off to this hideaway and its prime fishing grounds, three hours from his son in Baltimore, two from Philadelphia's culture.

The only doctor for miles about, he still practiced. On the first day, shelving books in his front-room office, he had a knock on his door and rode off to deliver a baby. From that day, he was important to the people for miles around, and they to him. He had sought a quiet haven, found a second career.

His farmers and watermen paid mostly by sharing food from their kitchens, the harvests of their fields, gardens, and Delaware Bay; by hauling and splitting fire wood for him; by repairing and cleaning his small house. He kept no books.

In the office/examining room, he displayed two documents of the many he had accumulated, his sheepskin from medical school and a scrolled citation for service at Fort McHenry 50 years ago. He loved the two testimonials as evidence of a life devoted to others. He hated the warfare that spawned the one.

Doctor Ruggles put a raggedy paper on his door, FISHING BE BACK SOON. Anyone needing him knew where to find him.

Not far from his house, the dirt street became a wagon track through weedy growth, then a footpath to the beach. Turning right he walked into the rising sun. Momentarily blinded, he stumbled.

Brian's body startled him despite the years of death and cadavers. He dropped to his knees in the sand, ready for another one. A half century of viewing untidy remains told him this one was still alive, no death smell, tell-tale gray, waxy hollowness.

"Thank God." He exhaled, and saw Tom stretched prone.

"And another! What have we here?" A canteen near one suggested the army. The clothes confirmed his suspicion.

He felt one pulse, over 100 and weak; then the other, slower and stronger. Tom McDonald stirred.

Dazed, he mumbled, "My friend needs help."

"He's not conscious. What can you tell me?"

Tom raised on one elbow, shook his head to clear the wool, "He had trouble breathing. He needs a doctor I tell you."

"I am a doctor, son. Has he been sick? Fever? Chills? Cough? Headaches? Vertigo? Soldier's quickstep?"

"No. But he was in a fight. Got an arm cut."

"Oh?" Dr. Ruggles lifted Brian's arm. Nothing. The other showed a bad gash that oozed blood even as he looked.

"How long ago?"

"About midnight, maybe half an hour earlier."

"A long time to be bleeding."

"I tied it tight as soon as I could."

"I see that, son, you probably saved his life."

With a roll of clean cotton from his tackle box, the doctor expertly wrapped over Tom's make-shift bandage, folding it into itself to keep it tight. "That'll do temporarily." He lifted Brian's shirt, saw the purple bruises. The doctor examined gently with educated fingers, "Broken ribs. At least two. Give me your shirt." Brian twinged, moaned.

He ripped the shirt down the middle, gently worked it under Brian, pulling it snug, tying the sleeves, "That should hold him for now. Need something to carry him on. He pointed to the boards they had floated on.

Tom staggered as he dragged them from the water's edge.

"You're not a picture of health either."

"I'm all right. It's my friend needs the help."

They eased Brian onto the boards, doubled for strength. The doctor used his jacket for a cover, tying the sleeves under the make-shift litter. He stripped off his belt, buckling it to hold Brian's legs. He checked respiration and eyes again.

"My house isn't far." He stooped to the make-do stretcher.

Tom stopped him, "Let me take this end. It's heavier."

The doctor didn't argue. As he moved to the other end, he picked up the canteen, "Beautiful leather work. Yours?"

"My friend's. He's carried it ever since I've known him."

"Must be important to him." Doctor Ruggles ducked his head through the canteen's strap, and picked up his end of the board.

They mushed along the soft beach and the weedy trail, resting twice. The wagon tracks afforded better footing.

In the examining room, Brian was moved onto the narrow, wooden table where Doctor Ruggles cleaned the arm of its dirt, swabbed the open wound, bandaged it again. Reexamining the rib cage, he wrapped it tight with similar bandage, coarse and tawny. He checked pulse and temperature.

Tom fingered the bandage, "I've never seen that kind."

"Osnaburg. From Germany. It's made of linen." He waved aromatic ammonia under Brian's nose.

"Glad to see you back, son. How you feeling?" No answer.

"Watch that he doesn't roll off the table."

Soon he was back with two steaming mugs, "Chicken stock. Drink it while I get some into your friend. Then I want the two of you to sleep. After you've shed those clothes."

"You're going too fast, doctor. You've been very kind, but before we go off to sleep, I want you to know who we are."

"I already know. Not your names of course, but you've been prisoners at Fort Delaware. A cut above the ordinary, for you have somehow managed to escape."

"Then you know we're at risk. This isn't exactly friendly country for us. How do I know you won't turn us in?"

"You don't. You won't know any more whatever I say. People around here tend their own business but some have kin in the army." His inference was all too clear.

"What about you? We can mean trouble for you."

"It's little enough," he tossed off a hand to show his indifference, "Edward Ruggles is my name. What's yours?"

Doctor Ruggles turned pensive after the exchange of names. Tom sipped the broth, sensing more to come.

The doctor spoke softly, sorrow in his blue eyes, pain in the memory, "I served in the war with England.

"I was a young man, one year out of medical school, sewing, patching, and sawing. I'd never amputated a limb before that.

"For fifty years I've carried the memories. Fifty years I've lived with those soldiers. The blind. The halt. Those cursing God. Boys with one arm, one leg. Others turned to the wall to die alone. And those who sobbed for their mothers. I prayed to God I would never see another war."

He stared back through the years.

"Now—we do have another war—and it all comes back. I'm an old man, with still more soldiers to mend. Brushing at his eyes, he sighed, "As it was then and ever shall be."

Tom started to apologize for his mistrust. The doctor waved him off, "Soap's on the pump out back. I'll get towels—leave those rags in the yard, all of them."

Brian, conscious after the whiff of medicinal ammonia, was strangely quiet, passive, without will as Tom led him outside to the pump. He shed foul trousers halfheartedly and washed. Tom led him back. Going upstairs he winced, one foot up, drag the other, one up drag the other, a child too small for the risers.

Upstairs, Doctor Ruggles pointed to the first door on the left. He had laid out clean nightshirts.

Brian's last thought before he slept was of their two friends, "Tom, did Sean and Sam make it?"

"I don't know, Brian, they drifted away from us."

The sonofabitch adjutant at Fort Delaware screamed his guts out.

"HOWTHEHELL COULD THIS HAPPEN?"

"Don't know, sir," the corporal of the guard whimpered, "one of my men jest found him."

"SERGEANT! GET YER ASS IN HERE."

"Yessir," the clerk saluted as he tumbled through the door.

"Put this man in the hole. Thirty days. AND CUT OFF HIS GODAMNED STRIPES."

"But, sir, I didn't . . ."

"Shut the hell up, PRIVATE. Get him outa here. And find me that bounty hunter."

"Scroggins? Sir, I'm not sure where . . ."

"THEN FIND 'IM, DAMNIT. You know what that means? YOU find 'im. No one else. YOU. Don't come back alone."

"Yessir," the sergeant backed meekly out the door. It was almost a week before he came back.

The adjutant had a characteristic greeting for him, "Where the hell you been?"

"Lookin' for your tracker, sir. The bounty hunter."

"Find 'im?"

"Yessir. In Wilmington. Drunk in a whorehouse. Had t'promise $20 now, 'nother twenty fer each one he finds. In gold."

"WHAT!!"

"Sir, he wouldn't come fer less."

The adjutant grinned malevolently, "Sergeant, I know you're willin' t'do yer part. So you pay 'im from what y'make offa the pris'ners." He cackled laughter through rotten teeth. spewing his stinking breath across the room, "Bring 'im in."

Tom McDonald stretched luxuriously in the first bed he had pressed since Winchester, "Ahhhhh." Soft, white, scented with lavender, the sheets were a sacrament, given for weary bodies.

"Brian. You smell that?"

No answer.

While they slept, Doctor Ruggles had gone back to the shore to cover any signs of the escapees. Twenty yards beyond their landfall, he found tin cans tied with twine, hemp, and rags. A jumble of footprints marked the beach as though men had shuffled about, waiting. He examined the cans, "That's how they made it, sealed cans and those boards." He buried the cans, transplanting clumps of marsh grass over them. The boards were ordinary flotsam. He brushed the beach of the foot prints.

Satisfied, he rested, looking to Pea Patch Island, pondering man's inhumanities to his brothers. Retrieving the fishing gear left earlier, he headed home.

When Tom wakened in the late evening, Doctor Ruggles told him of the cans and his burying them.

"Sean and Sam!" Tom elated, "it's their cans! I sank ours in the bay. We started together, but got separated. They made it!"

"Sean and Sam?"

"Yes. Sean was a guard. Sam a prisoner."

"A guard? He deserted?"

"He had to." Tom told of killing the corporal, Brian's seething hatred of him, of Brian's growing aversion to war.

"I wondered about him. He seems dull, disconnected, more than his injuries would cause."

"He was that way in prison. No interest in anything except escape—and protecting young Sam from the corporal."

"The same one he killed?"

"Yes. Brian went crazy, killed him with his bare hands."

"Why didn't he call a guard. Stop the escape."

"Brian was strangling him. He knew he had to kill him, but it was something more. Like the devil himself driving him. Called him an animal and pushed his thumbs right through his neck."

"We may have a problem bigger than broken ribs. I say 'we' since I seem to be his doctor and you're his friend. He's too withdrawn for his injuries, vacant. My guess is that he's one of the tender ones who saw too many men die. It wore him down. Then the horrible choice of strangling the corporal or dying himself. Maybe something snapped. Bare hands like that. Thumbs. Ugh!"

Doctor Ruggles stared at the floor, trying in vain to fathom Brian's suffering, to conjure a treatment. "Strange," he mused philosophically, "what if I hadn't gone fishing this morning, or walked away from the sun instead of into it."

He spoke more to himself for he had no answer, no remedy, "Some are like that, can't stand the suffering and killing, or the scoundrels who use war to visit their evil on others. They get scraped raw. One more thing and poof! They're gone. We've learned a bit of the human body, but nothing of the mind.

"Maybe God gave me Fort McHenry for a purpose."

He glanced up self-consciously, "All that must sound terribly pretentious. 'What a pompous ass,' you must be thinking."

"Not at all, sir, not at all."

XLIII

A LETTER, A DREAM

"Sarah, Sarah, come here."

The urgency in his voice alarmed her. She hurried from the kitchen, wiping her hands on her apron. In the front room office, his broad smile eased her worry.

"Henry Morrow! Here I thought you had a problem and I ran in here to see the biggest smile I've seen from you in two years. What in the world . . .?"

He held a letter up to her. She beamed, too, for happy looks are catching. For a moment, they simply looked one to the other, each pleased with the smile he saw and the joy. Celebrate every blessing, their hesitation declared, make the most of every chance to suspend worry and war.

Henry was pleased, for Sarah was looking better than she had for weeks, color in her face, purple shadows gone, fewer lines. He was especially pleased with her hair, which he always said had attracted him in the first place. She had been brushing it faithfully, as she used to before the days of her "hospital." The sheen was back, the soft waves replaced the tight bun she had worn as a "nurse." It was more sanitary that way, but hardly more attractive.

She had gained a few pounds, filling out the angles of sunken cheeks and gaunt arms. Sagging dresses had rounded pleasingly.

Henry's disposition had improved with her appearance, as well it might for he had been mightily concerned for her well-being.

For over two months now her nursing duties had diminished as the wounded soldiers in her "hospital" had been carried farther up the Valley, even to Lynchburg and Richmond. Only two were left, too badly hurt to be moved. Gracey, Betsy and Mam saw to it that she had little more to do for them than look in on them.

She nodded at the letter her husband held, "What is it, Henry?"

"A letter from Brian. He's a prisoner at Fort Delaware."

"Oh, How wonderful!" she bubbled before he had finished. Her hand covered a quick gasp, "prisoner? He's all right isn't he?"

"He's fine."

"Delaware? Prisoner! Is he really all right? Henry, tell me he is all right?"

"He's fine, Sarah. Sleeps indoors every night, he says, and nobody's shootin' at him. He wrote it over two months ago."

Sarah read eagerly, hastily as if to take in the entire letter at once. Once through, she sighed.

"Well, that's a relief."

Then she read it again, more slowly, letting each precious word sink in. Finished, she touched loving fingers to the paper, caressing it lightly as if to absorb her son's words.

Dear Ma and Pa and all, I almost was able to visit you a month or so past, but I was picked up by a Yankee patrol and sent here to Fort Delaware. It seems I've been here closer to a year. The war is over for me, at least for a while. I am fine and in good health so don't worry about me. Nobody is shooting at me, and I get to sleep indoors every night. It isn't too bad here except for the rations so I hope you can send me food and socks and drawers and a shirt. Also money. I am able to buy some things here if I have the money. There isn't much to write. Everyday we hope for an exchange. We aren't told until the last minute, then sometimes they change their minds. Captain Morrison and John Lyle from my company were exchanged a few days ago. They said Pa talked to them in Winchester after they were captured and was almost shot. I hope this war is over soon. Your son Brian Morrow July 15, 1862

"We'll have to pack him a box. Henry, take a wagon to the farm. Or is there enough here? Henry, do you have a packing box?"

"Now, Sarah, this doesn't have t'be done right now."

"But it does. Brian's hungry. We need to send it today."

"Sarah! His letter is dated July 15. Goin' on three months ago."

"All the more reason to hurry."

"That's a fact," he humored her, "let me work on it."

He sat at his desk, read the letter aloud as Sarah thrilled to the words, confirming together what each had wondered to himself, protecting the other, feeling that to say the words or even to ask the question would make it more real.

"Yes, sweetheart. Yes, darling. Our son still lives. Brian is alive!" As before, the words remained unspoken.

Instead, they came together in silent sacrament, mother and father, man and wife, hugging tenderly, so thankfully that they let the tears flow, smiled, and held each other close.

"Thanks be to God," Sarah whispered.
"Thanks be to God," Henry echoed.
As one, they relaxed their embraces.
In unison, they sniffled, wiped eyes.
They smiled. They kissed.
Henry turned to the door, "I'll be back soon."
Sarah followed him to the front door. He was back soon just as he had said, within the hour.
"Pack the box for Brian, Sarah. It can go out tomorrow."
"That's wonderful," she sang, "how did you manage it so quickly?"
"That's my business. Remember? Moving people and freight."
"I remember."
With one of her impish smiles that he remembered so well, she moved toward him, "Thank you, Mr. Freight Man."
They touched hands, then embraced there in the entryway, in perfect view of anyone who happened to be looking.
"Just for you. It's good t'see you happy."
She cuddled into him, "I'll thank you properly later."

Forty miles northeast, David put the final touches on a report for the general's signature. Orders to clean up the paper work was a sure sign of impending action. He cleaned the steel nib, setting the candle stub to flickering, and wrote again.

Dear Jed, It looks like the general has plans for us so I want to write while I have the chance. It was good to see you—all—especially you and Betsy with your plans for the future. I want you to know how much I admire your spirit. I've seen men with lesser wounds moan about how they'd be better off dead. You two make a beautiful couple. I hope I'm as lucky. I plan to be married soon. My intention was to tell everyone before I left, but things happened too fast. I had pictured everyone at the dinner table for my news, just like the old days. Pretty dumb! God, how things have changed. I met Carrie, that's her name, in Richmond last spring. She'll kill me if I tell you the whole story, but I will anyway.

Next time I'm home. I'd like to help Ma but don't know how. She looked bad.
Any ideas? Give my love to everyone Your brother David Morrow

That evening, it was October 9, he gazed longingly at the cobalt sky. The air was autumn crisp, clear enough to touch a star. Did the Richmond sky excite the same enchantment?

"Which star would you choose, Carrie?"

"David," a disappointing voice in the dark, "You alone?"

"Why, ah, uh. Yes, I'm alone."

"Thought I heard you talking to someone."

"I'm alone. Enjoying the evening, Channing. You must be looking for the report," he added quickly to Channing Price, Stuart's acting adjutant, "it's ready."

"Good. The general's asking for it."

"When and where, Channing?"

"When and where what?" Lieutenant Price asked innocently.

"Don't play fox with me, my friend, the signs are all there. The general doesn't catch up on his papers just to continue this endless picketing."

The young lieutenant drew close with an air of secrecy, "Sooner or later we're going into Pennsylvania, that's my guess. Sooner unless something happens to delay us."

"Pennsyl . . . ," David started in surprise but his companion shushed him at once. He spoke in undertones.

"That's only a guess. The order prohibits pillaging and requires proper receipts for property taken in the name of the government. It also reads that property in Maryland is out of bounds. If Maryland is out of bounds the receipts must be for some place else. Where else but Pennsylvania."

Indeed, Channing Price was right, for the morning saw eighteen hundred troopers rendezvous at Darkesville, ford the Potomac before daylight, reach Chambersburg, Pennsylvania, at 8 o'clock that very evening. In a drizzling rain, Chambersburg surrendered without resistance.

David took shelter in a private home, he and a hundred others before the night was over. They were served food in a friendly enough fashion, coffee and tea until supplies were exhausted. David dried by the open fire, enjoying good conversation, politics, the war, its battles and generals.

Their gracious host wrote of the evening in the Philadelphia newspaper he owned, "They spoke with entire freedom upon every subject but their movement into Chambersburg. . . . Most of them were men of more than ordinary intelligence and culture and their demeanor was in all respects eminently courteous. . . . They did not make a single rude or profane remark even to the servants."

Mr. McClure was impressed, writing, too, that they politely asked permission to get water, to enter the house and the library with its fire, and offered to pay for what they ate.

At dawn they saddled up in the continuing rain. Soaked again, they rode through Gettysburg, Cashtown and Fairfield, Emmittsburg at sundown, on into Maryland.

Near New Market at midnight, a dozen miles east of Frederick, the tireless Stuart hailed David, Pelham and others of his staff, "How would you like to see the 'New York rebel' tonight?"

They had given the nomme de guerre to an attractive visitor at von Borcke's grand ball in Urbana a month ago. Daring cavalier that he was, Stuart had promised to visit her and her pretty cousins very soon. This was the night he kept his word. They had been in the saddle for the last eighteen hours.

They clattered into the yard, wakened the ladies, visited for half an hour, and galloped off. Such was life with Jeb Stuart, riding, fighting, frolicking outlandishly. He could go without sleep forever, it seemed to the men who followed him.

With no respite, they reached Hyattstown at dawn on the 12th and continued on to the Potomac. Bluffing Yankee defenders at White's Ford, they splashed through the river to safe haven and on to Leesburg.

They had covered 170 miles in three days. They could boast a thousand horses bought with notes of promise, destruction of an ordnance depot and $250,000 of public property, railroads, thirty prominent hostages carried off to exchange for Southerners held by the Union, and a social obligation promised in September.

David wrote of the raid, mostly about his fantasy on the last night in the saddle. Exhausted, he had imagined that Carrie was with him.

My dearest Carrie We have just returned from Pennsylvania. Maryland and Pennsylvania are so beautiful, with farms that are clean and prosperous, not devastated as Virginia's. We covered eighty miles the last day to reach the Potomac, most of us asleep in our saddles. Sometime during that endless night, I thought you were with me riding double. I had to hold you tight to keep you from falling off. Then you said you were cold, that you'd take the reins if I would wrap my arms around you. After a few minutes, I said why don't we stop so I can warm you up good, and you said all right if somebody could marry us first. So I took

*the reins back—we galloped to General Stuart and I asked him to marry us—
he said he couldn't because he had to visit a friend of his we call the New York
rebel. Maybe she can marry you, he said. When we got to her house she did and
you and I hid in the barn when it was time to leave. Carrie, you were so beautiful. After a while I said we had to catch up with General Stuart,—you said not
yet love me again. Sable was there, too. He kept shaking his head up and down,
agreeing with you. So we stayed longer there in the hay—you kept whispering
how nice it was to be my wife, over and over you whispered it, then you clutched
me tight, trembled and wouldn't let me go. I could hardly breathe. Then I was back
with the column. You were gone, I was alone, holding Sable's reins. I can't believe
that we have seen each other only three times. So few hours. It seems that I've always known you. Carrie, I love you forever*

Two weeks after the raid, McClellan crossed the Potomac east of the
Blue Ridge. For a full week, David shadowed his general, intermittently
rode with Tom Rosser, seeing more than his share of action in Loudoun
County, near villages and hamlets with country names, Mountsville,
Union, Upperville, Markham's Station, Barbee's Crossroads. In contact
daily, they fought it out when the odds were right, strike, run, strike
again.

"Heard you have a brigade, Tom."

"Don't get excited, Dave, it's only temporary. Wickham was wounded
so I'm filling in."

"What do you think McClellan's up to?"

"Who can tell what he's doing? They're saying Lincoln's upset with
him again for moving so slow. One of the men brought in a newspaper from
New York. The Tribune, I think."

"I'll bet McClellan caught hell if it was The Tribune."

They spent half the night, talking politics and the war. As usual, Rosser
broke out bourbon and his box of Cuban cigars. His source of both continued a secret for David.

Jeb Stuart wrote General Lee urging the creation of a fourth cavalry
brigade, recommending Rosser for its brigadier and David Morrow for
lieutenant colonel.

On the 10th of November, Stuart's request for the new brigade was approved. Tom Rosser was not promoted, but David Morrow was, changing
his insignia to the double stars of a lieutenant colonel.

"Two stars look good on you, colonel."

"Thank you, General Stuart. I appreciate . . ."

Stuart held up his hand, "No need for that. You earned it. You'll pay double now that Burnside has replaced McClellan."

On Saturday, December 13th, the morning fog swirled from the Rappahannock, hiding Fredericksburg, overflowing onto the flood plain, sending tendrils toward the high ground. The sun, warm and bright on a glorious winter day, soon melted it, revealing Federal troops downstream ready to drive on Jackson's line.

The I and VI Corps, comprising the Left Grand Division in Burnside's new organization, had taken two days to lay pontoon bridges and cross. They established a bridgehead, right and left flanks anchored on the river and Deep Run. To their front was high wooded ground and the inestimable Jackson.

The attack began at 8:30 A.M.

Federals crossed a ravine, advanced through woods to Jackson's hill. About the same time, Jeb Stuart and David rode up to the intersection of the Hamilton's Crossing and Bowling Green roads where the cavalry brigade guarded the flank. John Pelham had a bronze Napoleon out front. Another 12-pounder rumbled up to him, a Blakely, more accurate with its rifled barrel.

"General, Pelham can use an extra hand."

Stuart nodded, then raised his binoculars again.

David hesitated before getting his attention again, "Sir?"

"Yes?" still looking through the glasses.

"Will Sable be safe if I leave him here with you?"

Stuart swept the glasses to the two pontoon bridges and then to the far ground. Again, he answered without lowering them, "Oh, I don't think the Yankees will bother us here. They'll get enough from Old Stonewall to keep them busy."

"It wasn't the Yankees I was worried about, sir."

Now David had caught Stuart's complete attention. He took the binoculars from his face, "What then?"

"You, sir," David laughed, "can I depend on you not to run off with him?" Before Stuart could answer, David dropped the reins, ran down the incline to Pelham and his guns. Stuart's hearty laughter followed after him, mixing with his own chuckles.

From their gentle elevation, David and Pelham looked across the panorama of Yankees advancing across the flood plain in Napoleonic lines that extended into the distance.

Pelham loaded solid shot, elevated slightly, and fired.

The 12-pound iron ball ripped a furrow through Bluecoats. They closed ranks and continued the advance, past the two guns.

"Pelham," David grinned, "I never saw this before. We can hit them in reverse."

They did just that, sweating on this winter morning as they worked. Gunners backed off as the lanyard was yanked. A small puff of smoke from the touch-hole, a cloud from the muzzle, and a deep-throated BOOM. Another shot for freedom. They fired so rapidly that a Union general reported them as a full battery. The Federal line halted until the murderous fire could be stopped.

Artillery on the heights across the river opened up, four batteries, fifteen to twenty guns. The Blakely was put out of action. A gunner fell. Men swabbed, loaded, and rammed. Pelham laid the gun meticulously, small changes left, right, up, down.

Stuart sent von Borcke with a message, "You can withdraw whenever you like."

Pelham brushed him off, "I can hold my ground."

David shouted, "Yeah! We've got 'em." Infected with battle fever, the two ex-cadets, West Point friends, ignored the increasing danger and worked their gun, fighting an entire Yankee division with a single 12-pounder, just the two of them with a handful of gallant gunners. They moved it repeatedly to thwart Yankee gunners across the river. With his keen eye for subtle dips and undulations in the terrain, Pelham picked one spot after another that seemed invulnerable. Yankee gunners observed, corrected their elevations and azimuths. Pelham moved again and again. Shells burst around them, but never a direct hit. Neither he nor David received a scratch.

Stuart sent another rider with the same message, "You can retire." Pelham refused. David yelled, "HELL, NO."

In his elation, he screamed as if he were galloping Sable, "EEEeeeYah." He had felt the battle fever before, on Henry Hill for one, but it was nothing like this. He was invincible, beyond mortality, crazy delirious, intoxicated. No hatred for Yankees. No anger with their efforts to kill him. Only joy, orgiastic joy and gratification. Duty, Honor, Country. Swab, load, ram. Left fifteen yards! Up ten! He shifted the gun. FIRE!

Fighting a whole division!! A whole division with a single 12-pounder. He whacked Pelham, "Goddamn it, Pelham, a whole division! We're fighting a whole fucking division!"

Federals found a break in Jackson's line and went through, fanning left and right. The colonel of the 37th North Carolina responded at once, skillfully and bravely. He refused his three companies closest to the breakthrough, dropping them back into a right angle to his original line, changing his front to meet the threat. If credit went to anybody for saving the situation, it had to go to Colonel Barbour of the 37th.

Not until a third messenger arrived did David and Pelham break off their action. Hanging on to limber and emptied caisson, they jounced through the explosions of Yankee shot and shell, victorious and lucky.

David rode a short distance up the hill and jumped off, running to retrieve Sable. He threw his arms around the stallion's muscular neck, "Did you see us, boy? Did you? We gave it to 'em, damn if we didn't give it to 'em."

Stuart was never prouder than he was that day of John Pelham and David. He never mentioned the two orders disobeyed.

XLIV

A NEW HOME

Doctor Ruggles and Tom spooned cups of chicken broth into Brian, innumerable cups of chicken broth and water from the well. As he gained strength, beef broth with slivers of meat was added to his diet.

The doctor had a long-time belief in this trio, having used it for years back in Baltimore for convalescing children as well as adults. He also prescribed quiet and plenty of bed rest to cure the body's ills.

Following Doctor Ruggles' regimen, Brian did regain his strength and healthy color. The malaise, however, proved a more stubborn adversary, clinging to him like ivy on a brick wall.

He was encouraged, cajoled, ignored, and threatened, but nothing seemed to work. He remained in his blue funk, talking nothing but the killing the war brought, and the bestial behavior that existed in Fort Delaware.

He could find pump, bedroom, kitchen, and the four-by-six foot outhouse that to him was still 'the sinks', able to get around, but spiritless, without motivation or interest.

"What do you think, Tom? Was he always this way?"

"Just the opposite when I first met him, doc. He was so eager to be in the army, to learn everything he could, for news from home, everything. Never knew one with more energy. Quit college back in Virginia t'enlist."

"You notice any problems?"

"I didn't think so at the time. He was scared, but we all were, proud of the uniform, proud of his brother who had been at West Point, enthused like a boy out of school. But then he changed. One time he talked of burning bridges and got real sad. Near Front Royal. And he was sad about a soldier he killed. I tried to tell him the soldier was trying to kill him, it was either one or the other. But it didn't make any difference."

"He was in the 2nd Virginia, and I was in the 4th with his brother so I didn't seen him regular. Mostly, I knew him through Jed. I carried Jed home when he was shot in Winchester."

"Hmmmmm. Would you say he was smart?"

"Strange he rarely talked of them after that."

"Talked of who?" following Tom's disconnection.

"His family. He wrote them, but didn't talk about them much after Jed was shot. Except Ezekiel. He talked about Ezekiel."

"Like he'd forgotten the others, son?"

"Yes, but I'm sure he hasn't. Is he off in the head, doc?"

"Oh, I don't think so. One thing I know, we can't do him any good by thinking that way. Now what about my question?"

"What question?"

"I asked you if you thought he was smart."

"Everyone's smart in something."

"You know what I mean. Book smart."

"Oh, yes, he knew Latin and Greek."

"Tell me more about him."

"Like what?"

"Anything. Anything at all. His family. Friends. Anything."

"Like I said, they're a close family. One brother at West Point resigned. Sister's husband was killed at Manassas in '61. Father had a business in the Valley. Mother a real lady, able t'take charge. I saw her when I carried Jed home."

"Any problems that might have weighed on him?"

"Not that I know," Tom hesitated, "oh! Jed did say their Pa was madder than a hornet when he found out he was in the army."

"Who? Which one?"

"Both of them, Brian and Jed. Madder than hell he was. Wanted Jed t'stay on their farm, and Brian t'finish school. But Brian changed and was thinking of getting out of the army."

"How could he do that?"

"Just walk away, I guess."

"Why? That could mean trouble."

"Jed told me one time that Brian shot off a man's face and had nightmares about it."

"Hmm. Hmmmmm."

The older man smiled sadly, "This is beyond me. His arm and ribs will mend. His pulse is stronger and his lungs, clear. But your—our—friend needs more than any physician can give. A part of Brian is blocked and needs to be cleaned out with something that would purge him of his malady. Like ipecac or tincture castor flushes an obstructed bowel. This," he tapped his head, "can be a bigger problem. He needs to make peace with himself, and with his God. No one can do that for him. All we can do is stand by. Be his friends."

It was the following day that Ray Chesley banged on the door and shouted an alarm, "A stranger snooping around the beach. A dirty bugger. Looks t'me like one of them waterfront bums."

It was, indeed, a waterfront bum, the adjutant's bounty hunter that Ray had seen, hired to track down the escapees. By the time he reached the Ruggles cottage, the doctor and Ray were playing an innocent game of checkers on the front porch.

The man approached warily, eyes flitting here and there taking in everything.

"You're right," Doctor Ruggles agreed under his breath, "he is a dirty one."

The stranger held his hand up in a sign he meant no harm. As he did, the filthy shirt gaped where buttons had once held it together. His belly pushed out, dark with hair and accumulated dirt. What he meant for a disarming smile came off badly, an animalistic leer of pig eyes and missing teeth, "You see men from the fort?"

"We've seen no one, chief. Look around for yourself."

The tracker's derisive laugh caught the edge of phlegm in his throat. He spat, "You let me search." It was not a question.

Doctor Ruggles stood up. Ray Chesley reached for the shotgun leaning against the weather-beaten table.

The tracker raised hands palms forward. "Just doin' my job."

The doctor was about to shout him out of the yard, but reconsidered. A controlled tour might allay his suspicions.

"Sir, I am a physician and will not have my honesty doubted. I don't know who you're looking for, but you won't find him here." The doctor looked him square in the eyes.

"Prisoners escaped from the fort. Three and a guard."

"And a guard, you say. What do you think of that, Ray?" He turned back, "I have no truck with this war, either side. I had my fill 30 years ago. You want to search the house? Come ahead."

Doctor Ruggles led him through every room, talking loudly to warn Brian and Tom. Ray Chesley followed. With his shotgun.

"Look for yourself. Under the bed, in the armoire there," He opened its two doors wide. "That's about it."

"You forget attic. Where's door to attic?"

"Why, I haven't been up there for years. There was a trap door in the hallway. Never used it so I nailed it shut."

The bounty hunter stood on a chair and pounded on it to test the doctor's word. He looked closely at the nails, and jumped off the chair, agilely for a man his size. He glanced back at the ceiling, then at Ray and the shotgun.

Doctor Ruggles read him perfectly. This man would be back.

"You want to look in the cellar?"

They descended the steep ladder into the dank hole, five feet high forcing them to stoop, dirt floor, no place to hide.

Finding nothing in the barn either, he peered at the house briefly but long enough for the doctor to notice. He grunted his thanks boorishly, and headed toward the beach.

"I thought I'd bust when you said t'open the armwar, doc. What if he asked t'move it out from the wall?"

"If he had, I figured you were there with the shotgun."

Ray moved a man onto the king row, "Crown me."

Preoccupied, Doctor Ruggles moved a man, and Ray jumped on him at once, "You just lost the game."

"He'll be back. We have to get those two to safety. And be very careful doing it."

After dark, Brian and Tom followed Ray to his house. Doctor Ruggles followed, ostensibly taking the air by himself. He passed his neighbor's house without stopping, but not without noticing the shovel thrown carelessly on the front porch. He couldn't resist a smile at Ray's prearranged signal.

The blade of the shovel overhung the porch by half a length, concave side up, wooden handle pointing in the direction of the doctor's own house. Ray and his two charges were safe inside.

Doctor Ruggles walked on for five minutes before turning back. The shovel had been turned, its business side down. Ray had watched after he went by and seeing no one following, flipped it over. The doctor continued his surveillance past his cottage, to the beach, and home again to sit in the shadow of the oak tree.

At an hour past midnight, he hitched 'Gray' to the four-wheeled buggy, loaded his doctor's bag and picked up Brian and Tom. He and Ray spoke in whispers, all the time watching and listening for signs of danger.

"Haven't seen a thing, doc."

"Good. I'll be back before dark tomorrow.

"Today," he corrected himself, "thank you, Ray. God bless."

"If I spot anythin', I'll fire the shotgun, two shots quick as I can load."

Raised hands said a silent good bye, and Ray started his vigil invisible in the shadows.

The buggy swayed along a canal in soft rhythms of wheels and harness. Not an hour down the road, Tom jerked alive. He moved close to the doctor to whisper in his ear.

"Somebody's back there. I've heard it twice now. Thought it was an animal at first. Listen." They sat with cocked ears, listening, straining. Nothing.

Doctor Ruggles whispered, "Raymond didn't fire his gun."

Tom did the same, "He could have circled around. I'm going to drop off. Keep moving just as we are. I'll catch up."

"It's too dangerous alone. Stay here."

Tom McDonald was not one to run from danger, "Like General Jackson says, 'move fast and secret. Surprise them.' That's what I intend to do, surprise the hell out of him."

"You don't know what he looks like."

"Anybody following us this time of night is no friend."

"Tom, I don't like this."

With grim humor, the young soldier had the last word, "Cheer up, doc, at least you'll be warned if you hear a commotion."

Tom slipped to the road easily, disturbing none of the soft cadence of their passage. The light slaps of harness leathers faded into silence, then the rattles and pops of the buggy.

Tom crouched low, straining to see into the darkness. Dirt, road, sky, trees, and underbrush melded together, black and threatening. With patience he waited, watching, listening, even sniffing the air. He stretched his neck to see through the night. His senses converged and sharpened. His heart was double-loaded cannons in his head. Boom. Boom. Boom.

Hairs on his neck bristled; the army had taught him to respect them. He read their alarm even before the vague sense of someone moving toward him. The warning simply came, out of the night, a vibration, a change of air pressure, an aura, or maybe a preternatural spirit assigned to sit on Thomas McDonald's shoulder and protect him from evil.

He drew the knife from its holster, kneading its shaft for comfort. Night noises fell into a rhythm of their own. He waited. A brushing sound interrupted the pattern, a tiny repetitive crunching, and then the wheezing of labored breathing. A denser blackness materialized in the road, a manform, an apparition. Perfectly still, Tom let the figure go by.

He rose gingerly from his cover in the low brush, stalking the shadow, creeping closer, knife poised to strike. The shadow halted, half-turned. Tom froze. The shadow moved on.

Tom sprang.

The other sensed danger at the last moment and turned in time to deflect the blow.

The knife cut across his forearm.

"Yeeeowww!"

Tom slashed again, backhanded.

The shadow jumped back, out of range, cursing to the night.

"Sonofabitch."

The dark hulk grabbed across its belly, struggling to free the revolver from its belt. Tom came at it again, lunging to get under its guard, to stab low. The shadow side-stepped, swinging its wounded arm wildly. It had the revolver clear.

Intuitively, or maybe the guardian spirit on his shoulder warned him, Tom kicked. The revolver fired. Its split second flash created a macabre canvas of good and evil alongside an indifferent canal.

The kick was straight and true, spoiling the aim and sending the gun flying. Tom heard the whirr of the bullet, felt a tug at his shirt and its heat as it nicked the skin on his shoulder.

Without its weapon, the shadow backed off, compromised only by its heavy, phlegm-filled breathing. Picking himself out of the dirt, Tom inched warily toward the telltale throat-rattles.

A raspy voice snarled, "Damn you. Before I'm through, that fort will look good to you. You'll wish you never left it."

The voice was farther left than Tom had estimated. He stooped for a handful of dirt and pebbles.

"You're so tough," Tom challenged, "come closer so's we can finish it now. Right now, you Yankee pimp, whoremaster, bastard."

Quickly, he sidled silent steps to the right.

"That trick won't work, sonny."

Tom faced to the voice, and slipped more to the right.

A sudden rush! He would have been bowled over, or worse, had he not moved. Now he could make out the shadowy hulk, furtive in the dark, confused, twisting this way and that to find him.

"Sonofabitch."

Tom crouched, ready to leap. He tossed the handful of dirt and pebbles to his left. The shadow pounced for the tiny noise. Tom was on its back in an instant, plunging the knife deep into its side, again and again. The shadow collapsed, legs stretched wide in the roadway, head toward the scrubby growth alongside.

In the dark, Tom dragged him by an arm, through the weeds, deeper into the tall grass, enough, he hoped to keep him hidden. Catching his breath, he trotted down the road.

Doctor Ruggles started when the buggy jounced under the additional weight. Reaching for the single-shot derringer he had taken at the last minute, he hissed, "That you, Tom?"

"Yeh, Doc."

"Are you all right?"

"Fine," he fingered the damaged shoulder of his shirt where the bullet had torn through, "only a scratch."

"Better let me look at it. I was worried when I heard the gun go off. And shouting. I'd know that rough voice anywhere."

"He was a nasty one, all right. Never did see him clear, but I sure smelled him."

"Tom, did you kill him?" Edward Ruggles was trapped between his Hippocratic oath and their personal safety.

"Doc, I stuck him enough times, and deep enough, too. I've seen men killed by bayonets that weren't stuck so bad. And he never grunted or groaned when I dragged him off the road. I was sure he was dead, but it was too dark to see. Never thought to feel for his heart beat. Guess I should have, huh?"

They rode along in silence, wondering about their pursuer. Was he dead or not? Brian was quiet, too.

Abigail Ruggles Cooper lived in the tiny village of French Town, west of St. George's, on a road that few travelled. Nearby was the Elk River, flowing into Chesapeake Bay, and the farm of the Cooper family.

Abigail was the doctor's niece, married twenty-one years to Cyrus, a life-long Quaker who had introduced the doctor to St. George's for a day's fishing.

Cyrus valued his independence and looked with skepticism on authority of all kinds, including his own church. He followed a bygone preacher named Hicks who held the unorthodox view that the Holy Spirit revealed truths to individuals rather than to elders. Cyrus realized Preacher Hicks was also saying that Abigail too was a recipient of God's truth, for Quaker tenets held women equal to men. He found his wife's independent thinking a trial at times, but loving her very much, learned patience and respect for her judgment and wisdom.

They felt a state of grace when their union produced a girl baby in 1844, a pink, healthy, and happily cooing child. They insisted she be called by her full name which they selected from the Old Hebrew, Hannah meaning Grace.

Hannah had thrived in her wholesome environment, nourished with the farm's bounty, nurtured by loving parents. She learned her letters and numbers, and a thousand skills of Mama's work and Papa's daily chores. She observed Quaker tenets to serve the Lord and one's fellow man, swear no oath, reject tithing, warfare, and the ex cathedra proclamations of priests.

Blue-eyed and rosy-cheeked, she had grown up a plain girl, innocent and robust of body with tawny hair braided and pinned. She loved to let it fall free, down to her waist, and brush it with long, lazy strokes. Velvety soft, it smelled fresh as the morning's dew, and glistened as a wheatfield in the sunlight.

Because Hannah had learned to control her enthusiasm and her emotions, she appeared more subdued than she felt. A few were blind to her liveliness and fascination with the world and God's living creatures. They thought her apathetic.

Why, Cyrus could tell of the day she was hilling corn and came across a hurt bluebird. Alarmed as she reached for it, the little bird made a frantic effort to escape, but once in her hands, he saw what the few had missed and rested easily.

His feathers matched her eyes, shades of blue that changed with the light even as she held him. She wept for the little bird, and Cyrus told her to take it home and care for it.

"Fix a nest, Hannah, and give it water."

And Hannah did what Papa said, attending her injured friend and praying for him when she knelt at her bed at night. The little bird responded to her ministrations by hopping onto her hand, and then one morning flying off to perch on the old pump in the yard. For months afterwards, Hannah saw a bluebird in the yard, sometimes around the barn, sometimes on the pump handle singing its song. Later in the summer she saw two of them and knew it was her bluebird and its mate.

It was to the Coopers in French Town that Doctor Ruggles brought Brian and Tom, where, the good doctor prayed, they would be safe and Brian would find release from his haunting devils.

Just after sun-up, they turned into the Cooper's lane, to a flurry of handshakes, hugs, and kisses. Safe after a trying night, Doctor Ruggles opened his black bag and prescribed a tonic for himself, a double dose of whiskey followed by a single.

"Need your help, Cyrus, Abigail."

"Anything, Edward, anything at all," Christian names were important to Cyrus, "thee has no need to ask."

Doctor Ruggles introduced them, "Brian and Tom here are Virginians. They escaped from Fort Delaware. If you want to know more, please ask them. I'm sure they won't mind. Tom?"

"Not at all. Neither of us has anything to hide," adding with a shy smile, "from friends, that is."

"I expect Tom will be heading home in a day or so."

"No, doctor, I'll stay with Brian as long as he needs me. We'll go home together."

"Tom, you're a good and loyal friend," Doctor Ruggles turned to his niece and her husband, "I'd prefer to send both of them home, but it's not possible yet. Maybe when Brian recovers and the authorities get tired of searching."

As he talked, Abigail watched the escapees, "You-all have seen your share of hardship. I can see it in your eyes."

Turning to her uncle, "Have you written their families?"

"No, Abigail, it's too big a chance. A letter addressed to Winchester could easily arouse suspicions and get into the wrong hands. I'm not even sure that mail moves across the line."

"His mother must be worried to death."

"I know, but short of sending someone we trust, there's little we can do."

"There must be something you—we can do."

Although she had adopted her husband's religion, Abigail retained her childhood use of the pronouns, except at times when she was upset.

"Please come into the house."

Hannah stepped closer to Brian, "Would you like a cold drink? They say our well is sweeter than any around."

Brian stroked the canteen slung over his shoulder. He looked at Tom uncertainly, a shadow clouding his face that could have become panic had Tom not been at his side.

"It's all right Briney," using the family nickname, hoping to strike a chord, "she's a friend. Aren't you, Hannah?"

"A friend, yes, a friend, Briney," picking up on the name. She took his hand, "the pump is over here."

Sensing her warmth and concern, Brian left his hand in hers, letting her draw him to the well.

She worked the iron handle once, twice, three times, enough to see that the pump needed no priming.

"You do it," she invited lightly, putting his hand on the iron handle. Momentarily, the shade of doubt crossed his face again, but he did as she said until her tin cup overflowed. She offered it to him. Hesitantly, he took it, and drank.

Tom watched every move, apprehensive lest Brian knock the cup to the ground, or even break and run. Elated when he did neither, he forgot his manners, "I'll be damned. He took it."

"Thomas. To be damned is to lose thy soul. Do not be so quick to wish it upon thyself." As her mother did, Hannah too reverted to the speech of her father's people when she was upset.

As tender and caring as this young girl appeared, somewhere deep in her make-up was a confidence and faith, a strength and conviction that could never be stifled.

XLV

DOCTOR RUGGLES' PLAN

After that first visit in October, Doctor Ruggles avoided another trip to French Town for fear of being followed and compromising Brian and Tom. Staying away was difficult for him as he had developed a close friendship with the two escapees in their short time together. He grew more and more anxious to know their situation, especially Brian with his very serious problems. Tom, he had learned, could take care of himself. A glorious day in March convinced him it was time to check up on them.

He decided to wait two days during which time he could ensure that he was not being watched by someone hired at Fort Delaware. The word was that no one had ever escaped from that miserable place, and he could easily imagine the fury of a commandant who had a reputation to rebuild.

Doctor Ruggles had neither heard nor seen anything to give him alarm. Nothing since the tracker who had searched the house. And he, presumably, was dead. Otherwise, the good doctor thought, he would have showed up here or around French Town. Even so, other bounty hunters, more patient and clever enough to remain hidden, could well be out there. Fort Delaware would not give up the search easily.

The next two days brought nothing to arouse his suspicions. "I don't know, Ray. I'd like to think the search is over, but something keeps nagging at me. I keep thinking there's someone out there watching, just waiting for me to make a mistake."

"Doc," his good friend and neighbor offered, "you ever think mebbe they just declared them dead and wrote down that they buried 'em. That would cover the escape."

Doctor Ruggles knit his brows as he considered this new possibility.

"Ray Chesley, you're a good man. That surely would explain why we haven't seen anything suspicious."

He pondered more, "You could be right. Let me think on it a bit more."

Later, he walked the short distance to Ray's house, "I'll leave in the morning," he said, "with precautions.

"I'll be visiting friends near Baltimore—if anyone asks.

"And, Raymond, the flag?" Everyone knew about the flag, royal blue with white letters MD, the doctor available when it was flying, day or night.

"If I take it down, and if someone is out there, they'll know for sure I've left. I'd as soon leave it up for a while after I'm gone.

"Good idea. Flag flyin' means you're in the area."

"I think I'm going to forget to take it down."

"I'll take it in—" Ray added conspiratorially, "If you forget.

"Say hello to our friends."

Early next day, Doctor Ruggles slid his medical bag onto the floor of the four-wheeled buggy, harnessed the mare and backed her between the shafts, "Back, Gray, back up." She was a gift from grateful patients, a Christmas gift four years ago to replace his aging gelding.

He had no more flicked the reins and clucked her down the lane when he pulled up mumbling, "Damn brain is turning to oatmeal." He climbed down, clumped back for his carpetbag still at the front door, right where he had put it. He scowled his way back to the buggy, grumping about forgetful old men. As he drove out, he double-checked the flag. It was flying in all its glory.

Doctor Ruggles drove 5 miles along the canal connecting the upper reaches of Delaware and Chesapeake Bays, then branched off to intersect a small stream. The route was the same he had travelled six months ago. Halfway to the creek, close to Tom's mortal battle with the tracker, he felt the chill of last October. Even in the warm sunshine of spring, October's crispness penetrated his bones again. He heard the bounty hunter's raspy voice as he had heard it then, and the gun shot echoing through the stillness. Shuddering at the recollection, he peered right and to the left, behind and ahead. Would that he could pierce the foliage for hidden peril.

As he made toward the unmarked line dividing Delaware from Maryland, the road came onto cleared land and his mood lightened. He passed the time thinking of the thousands of birds on the flyways to northern hatcheries. He recalled the cacophony of shrill calls and splashes as they settled to rest and feed in the wetlands, railbirds and plovers, ducks, pintails, teals and wigeons; he heard the drumming wings as they lifted still again, refreshed and eager to follow their instincts into New England and Canada.

He felt the enchantment of the long-necked geese in lissome Vee's and weaving echelons. French Town was another five miles.

"It is good to see thee, Edward," Cyrus's sincere welcome was a broad grin and calloused hand, "come stretch thy legs."

Abigail waved as she opened the back door, "Uncle Edward! I had a feeling this warm day might bring you."

In October, Cyrus had objected to his leaving money, "Thee knows our beliefs, Edward. Our bounden duty is to share earthly goods with those in need." This visit, he had an offering not of money, but of citrus.

Cyrus held up the sack of fruit, "See what Edward brings, Abigail, apples and peaches. Thank thee, Edward, thank thee."

"Yes, a real treat, Uncle Edward, thank you. The first we've had in months." She shielded her eyes against the late sun, "Your boys are around here somewhere."

The doctor hugged his niece, "Don't call them. I need a few minutes alone with you."

"I have fresh buttermilk to wash the dust from your mouth?"

"Sounds wonderful."

"Then into the house with you. I'll be along in a moment."

Abigail headed to the milk shed, neat and newly whitewashed. A wooden channel tumbled water into its cooling tank and out. Abigail poured from the earthen pitcher she carried. Doctor Ruggles drank long and slow, savoring the rich flavor and bits of butter, "I swear, your buttermilk is the best."

"You always say that."

"Only because it is," offering his glass for a refill.

"I wanted a few minutes to talk of Brian. How is he? Remember, I haven't seen him for several months."

It was Abigail who answered, "Uncle Edward, I'm not sure how to answer. As you saw when you brought him last fall, he's perfectly at ease with Hannah."

"How about with you and Cyrus?

"He's been helping in the kitchen. He's always been ready to give Hannah a hand with her chores, but lately, he's offered to help me. Washing vegetables from storage, chopping fire wood, that sort of thing. And twice a week, he bakes four loaves of bread."

"That's progress. Maybe an indication that he's mending."

"I think so. I've learned a bit about healing from him."

"How do you mean?"

"Well, the first day I was in the pantry scooping flour and he and Hannah offered to help. When I mixed the milk and eggs and all, he said that he had helped his mother bake. When I added the yeast, he said, 'now you have to knead it. My mother used to let it rise three times and knead it each time'."

"Good! A positive connection for him to make."

"Since then, he and Hannah have done the bread-baking."

She slapped her husband playfully, "This one says their bread is better than mine."

"Now, now, Abigail, thee knows full well I only josh."

"How about you, Cyrus? He still standoffish with you?"

"Still the same, Edward, he keeps his distance.

"Edward. Does thee know anything of the canteen he carries?"

"Only that he had it when I found him. Why do you ask?"

"A few days ago, I admired it and asked if I could inspect it more closely. I believed I could encourage friendship."

"And—"

"He cringed and shrank, clasping it tight. He was close to panic, Edward, outright panic."

"I'm not surprised. I never saw him without it. Then what?"

"I simply raised my hands, slowly to show I meant no harm. He seemed to understand."

"That's good. Maybe you laid a plank in the bridge."

"Plank? A plank in the bridge?"

"Between you and him. He's separated himself from all but Tom and Hannah. Now he seems to be gaining confidence in Abigail. Maybe you're next. If only we knew Hannah's secret.

"I'll never forget that first day, the way he trusted her. I wish we all could do what she does so naturally."

Doctor Ruggles shuffled in his chair, "Do you think Brian could get along for a couple of weeks without Tom?"

Cyrus stroked his long beard thoughtfully, "Hard to say, Edward. What does thee have in mind?"

"That he go to Winchester to Brian's family."

"To Winchester!" Abigail blurted out in surprise.

The doctor put a finger to his lips, "No need to bother the others if we decide it's a bad idea. Tom could let Brian's family know where he is, and see about getting him home. He's strong enough and it's as safe now as it ever will be. I expect the effort to find them has cooled off after five months."

"I am convinced, Edward."

"And I as well, Uncle. Brian would be all right, I think, with Hannah here. But there's another thing."

"What's that?"

"Thomas. You said you hadn't talked to Thomas."

"Of course."

They heard steps across the planked porch.

"Hello, Uncle Edward," Hannah greeted him affectionately.

Her light-hearted exuberance warmed his heart.

One time he had suggested, "I'd like to take her to Philadelphia. Just for a few days and show her how enjoyable life can be. Attend the theater. Buy a new dress."

"Thank thee," Cyrus had responded stiffly, "but it is better she remain at home."

That had been three years ago, and the thought occurred to Edward Ruggles that maybe Cyrus would be more receptive now that she was almost twenty years old.

"Sweetheart, it is nice to see you so happy."

Pleased with the compliment, yet not entirely comfortable with it, she interlaced her fingers. A thimbleful of smile washed across her face as she lowered her hands to her waist.

"And you, Brian, how are you feeling?"

No answer.

"Tom, I can see you've been eating and living well."

"Yes, sir. Better than the army."

Brian's small move wasn't much but the doctor caught it, a motion that in other circumstances would go unnoticed. He had eased away from his questioner, enough so that a shoulder was partially hidden behind Hannah. He pointed timidly.

"Who's—he?"

Doctor Ruggles and Tom interrupted each other trying to answer, "I found you—"; "He's the one—"

Startled at the small confusion, Brian withdrew, fondling the canteen strap, seeking an answer. Finding none, he pleaded silently with Hannah to save him, all the while folding the strap over and over until it filled both hands.

And save him she did, gently, soothingly, "It's Doctor Ruggles, Briney. You know him."

"No. I don't."

"Then I'll introduce you.

"Brian, this is Doctor Edward Ruggles. He's my great uncle and a very good physician. Uncle Edward, this is Brian Morrow."

"I'm happy to know you, Brian Morrow."

Cautiously, Brian reached for the proffered hand, "How—do—you—do?"

"Very well, thank you." The doctor's congenial expression faded into one of reflection. Later, he drew Hannah aside, "Why did you introduce Brian and me as if we didn't know each other?"

"But, Uncle Edward, he didn't know you at that moment."

The answer took him by surprise, but only briefly as her wisdom registered. Why hadn't he been as perceptive and accepted Brian as she had? He had missed what she recognized, he reflected, despite his years of training and experience.

"Uncle Edward, will Brian be leaving us?"

"One day he will go back to his own family."

"Soon? How soon?"

"Oh, I don't know, child. He's strong enough, but the road would be hazardous. And by no means should he go alone.

"Why do you ask?" he asked compassionately.

"I heard you talking with Mama and Papa about Winchester."

"Hannah," he took her hand in his, "What you have done for Brian—are still doing—is wonderful. You have touched him, but don't let yourself get too close for one day he will leave."

"I will miss him—very much."

Hannah's attraction to Brian disturbed Doctor Ruggles enough to keep him awake half the night. He could see all sorts of trouble ahead if she was as taken with him as she appeared to be, difficulties stemming from her own innocence to Brian's instability. Upbringing, education, experience, religion, this confounded war, Brian a fugitive, Hannah tied so close to her parents, everything pointed to disaster. Hoping he was exaggerating the whole thing, he pulled the bed clothes to his chin and finally fell asleep.

Meanwhile, Tom lifted himself from his chair on the front porch and yawned, "Guess I'll turn in. Coming Briney?" As usual, Brian stood up too, silently prepared to follow him.

Hannah stopped him, "Don't go in yet."

Brian looked from one to the other, uncertain in the change of routine. Always, he had followed Tom. Never before had Hannah asked him to stay. Distraught and unable to choose, he started from the chair, anxiety boiling and spiralling. His fingers tightened on the hard tin of the canteen and its supple leather, and he sat again. Tense and fragile on the edge of the chair, he held the canteen close, caressing the softness of the strap.

"Briney, it's ok if you want t'stay," Tom let him off the hook, and disappeared into the house.

"Briney, are you going to be leaving?"

He hesitated, "Leaving? Leaving—here?"

"Yes."

"Where—would—I—go?"

"Why, home of course."

"Home?"

"Yes. To Winchester. Where your mother and father live."

"Oh, yes—Winchester. I could help my mother bake bread."

Neither spoke for several minutes.

"I could go with you."

"You can't do that."

"Why not? I could still be your friend."

Brian looked furtively toward the house and whispered, "Cyrus would be angry." He fidgeted and jumped up. "No. No. Cyrus would be very angry. I have to go to bed now."

The next day, a baking day, he showed no signs of recalling the incident. He was content to be working with the redolent dough.

Doctor Ruggles took Tom aside, along with Abigail and Cyrus, to discuss the proposed trip to Winchester.

Tom was all in favor, "I agree. We have to get Brian home."

"You don't like us here?" Abigail joshed.

Embarrassed, Tom tried to make amends, "Oh no, it isn't that at all. I mean yes I do. Yes I do like you, but we've stayed long enough. I mean we've bothered you long enough."

"Thomas, you have been no bother."

"Thank you, ma'am, for saying so, and—thank you for everything."

Doctor Ruggles picked up the sidetracked deliberations, "You can ride to Baltimore with me, and get the B&O to Harper's Ferry. From there it can't be too far to Winchester. And one other thing," he conspired in good humor, "I'll write you a pass. Why do you want to go home?'

"How about to my father's funeral?" Tom chuckled, "a bogus pass to a make-believe burial."

"That has a ring of consistency. Now give me a town and a name. Something not well-known."

Tom thought for a minute and smiled, "How does Hanging Rock sound? Nobody outside the county knows Hanging Rock. And Clark's a common name."

Doctor Ruggles wrote a 10-day pass for Captain William Clark of Hanging Rock to go home for the funeral of his father. He hen-scratched a name over 'colonel and adjutant general'.

"This will give you something to show if needs be. Avoid any town big enough to have a telegraph."

"Never thought I'd be a captain, doc."

"You'd better have a talk with Brian to reassure him. He has to know that you'll be back. Otherwise, he may well get it in his head to take off after you."

"He'll be all right."

At the noon dinner table, their optimism died when Doctor Ruggles complimented Hannah, "You have the keen sensitivity that others respond to. It's a mystical thing, a gift of God."

Brian jumped, upsetting his chair. "There is no God," he shouted, "I killed him. I shot off his face."

He ran from the room, yelling, "I killed him. I killed him." Hannah followed at once.

To the well she followed him, kneeling over the iron pump, embracing it, racked with tears of pain. She knelt beside him. Reaching an arm around his shoulders, she pressed lightly her message that she was there for him. They knelt together for several minutes. Brian's shoulders heaved with his lamentation. He had killed God!

He leaned toward her, letting his head fall against her shoulder. Hannah said nothing. She caressed his face, and felt the tension ease. She wiped his tears, "Would you like to walk?"

Obediently, he rose. Hand in hand, they crossed to the corn field and along its grassy edge. She pointed.

"When I was a child, I found a bluebird over there. He couldn't fly." She related the whole story as they walked.

Back in the house, Tom voiced his concern, "I can't leave now. Not before he settles down."

Doctor Ruggles said, "Let's wait to see what happens. He's been upset before and come out of it in short order.

"Tom, did you ever see him react like that before?"

"Not that I can remember. But I wasn't with him much before we were captured. Most of the time he was just quiet-like, you know drawn in on himself, not much to say."

"How about at Fort Delaware? Any upset there?"

"Mostly just quiet, like he was somewheres else.

"But there were times—"

"What times?"

"Well, the first morning there, he went screaming for the door and would have been shot if I hadn't stopped him."

"What was he shouting about?"

"The guards. Calling them animals and er—uh—other names." Cha-grinned, he glanced quickly at the Coopers, mother and daughter.

"What set him off then?"

Uncomfortable, Tom wriggled and delayed, "Well—we were treated pretty bad. Cussed at and slapped awake."

"It must have been more than that."

"Some of the guards were plain nasty, they wouldn't let us go to the—sinks. And one especially who—"

"Go on."

"Doc, I can't—" he glanced at Hannah and Abigail again, "it's just too—"

Doctor Ruggles had caught Tom's embarrassed glances and understood, "I think I understand.

"What you're saying is that Brian couldn't accept the vulgar behavior of the guards."

"Yes sir, that's about it. He couldn't believe people could be like that."

"Hmmmmmm.

"Let's wait," he repeated.

An hour later, Hannah and Brian, peaceful now, returned, to the relief of all, particularly Hannah's parents who had seen her walk off with, for all they knew, a raving maniac. They didn't join the others, but sat on the front verandah quietly and contentedly.

"What do you think, Abigail? Cyrus? Think it would be all right for us to leave. Things seem to have settled down."

Cyrus was not that sure, "Does thee think he will stay quiet, Edward?"

"Tom here has given us the clue. Brian is no worry until something comes up that is intolerable to him. Without that extra strain, he seems to manage all right. Not at his best, but enough to get by. The secret is to give him chores that he finds satisfaction in, like making bread, cutting wood, that sort of thing that you know give him pleasure. Keep him occupied like that and avoid the ugly things.

"Brian is scholarly, a student and sensitive to the beauty in the world. He has been badly hurt, and needs to be protected from ugly people and ugly situations.

"I want to talk with my son about him, he may have some ideas, and I want to see Tom on the train to Harper's Ferry, then I'll be back. I won't be gone but a day, or two at the most.

"Now, Tom, why don't you explain to Brian that you'll be back soon. I would emphasize that you want to see his mother so she will know he is all right and won't worry about him any more. And I would say as little as possible about his father, so as not to rile him. If you talk with him and feel we should stay, tell me."

Shortly later, Doctor Ruggles and Tom left to catch the Baltimore train.

XLVI

DEATHS

Alex Boteler, Confederate legislator and temporary aide to General Jackson, approached the Morrow home without enthusiasm. His long-time friend, Henry, had asked for help.

Brian is a prisoner, Henry had written, and all our letters have been ignored. I know you must have your hands full and am sorry to add to your problems, but I have run out of string. Sarah says don't bother you. We would be most thankful for any bit of news as to his present whereabouts and situation. Sergeant Brian Morrow 4th Virginia Infantry, prisoner at Fort Delaware. You are our last hope. I trust, he ended petulantly, that our prison camps are run with more concern.

Colonel Boteler had replied: Don't apologize. I've posted inquiries to Fort Delaware and to an army friend in Washington. We have known each other for many years, and if anyone can do it, he can.

Henry opened the door to his old friend, "Alex! Alex Boteler! I hope the new year finds you well."

"Hello, Henry, it has been too long."

"Come in out of the cold. Sarah will be happy t'see you."

Colonel Boteler removed his hat, gloves, and, military cloak. The three stars of a colonel adorned the collar of his uniform.

Henry shook his hand again, "It is good t'see you. But come, warm yourself." Henry steered him back to the morning room where Sarah had drawn close to the warmth of the open fire.

"Colonel Boteler, what a delightful surprise. What news do you bring from Richmond?"

"Sarah Morrow, such formality. Tsk. Tsk."

"I was dazzled by your uniform, sir." She offered a cheek for a friendly kiss.

He moved closer to the hearth, turning his backside to the fire, "What news do I bring? What do you want first? Lincoln's emancipation speech? Negroes celebrating jubilee in Norfolk? The fighting at Murfreesboro? The President's speech to our Congress?

"And there's Fredericksburg. All Richmond still talks of our glorious victory there. A secret communique from Washington says Burnside is out. Hooker will be named his replacement."

"That's not surprisin' is it, the way they go through generals. One of these days, Lincoln will get one he likes."

"Bobbie Lee would agree with you, Henry. He was happy with McClellan; always said he knew pretty well what he'd do next."

Their friend turned to the fire, rubbing his hands toward the flames, putting off the real news. More polite talk was too transparent, yet he hesitated.

Sarah glanced anxiously at the two men, first her husband, then his friend, "You have news of Brian."

"Yes, Sarah, I do. I received a note from Washington."

"You have bad news." She stated flatly.

"Yes, I am afraid so. But first I want to emphasize my information is unconfirmed. It might very well be inaccurate. With the war's confusion, and all, we get reports every day that are negated the next day. I can't overstate the confusion that exists. So, please, Sarah—and Henry—take this with a grain of salt. It may turn out to be entirely untrue."

"Alex, my friend, I—we—appreciate what you're trying to do. I think we know your news."

"All my friend has is what he called 'a very sharp response' from the adjutant at Fort Delaware. Saying that Brian—is—is—reported as deceased."

The words rang through the room, bounced and reverberated off the walls, echoed in Sarah's head. Her hands flew to her mouth, her eyes wide. "Brian is—? BrianBrianBrian."

Henry jumped to embrace her but she felt no comfort.

"Oh no. He can't be. We had this letter—he was safe."

Henry, "Alex, are you sure? Can you be sure?"

"No, Henry. Listen to me, both of you, listen to me. This is what I've been trying to tell you. No, I can't be sure. All I have is this note," he laid it unfolded on a side table. "No confirmation. No other evidence. Only the word of the adjutant at Fort Delaware. Names get mixed up. Maybe the adjutant has made a mistake, maybe he's lying for reasons of his own."

"Sarah, did you hear that? Alex isn't sure."

She ignored him.

Alex Boteler coaxed, "Sarah, listen to me. Please listen to me." She ignored him as she had her husband and left the room.

"Henry, I'm sorry. It would have been better to say I had received no news. "

"No, Alex, no. Sooner or later, we would have to face up to things."

"My friend, your good wife did not hear what I said. Nor did you. This is unconfirmed and may not be true at all. There is still room to hope."

"I know, Alex, I know."

Sarah Morrow fashioned from black crape a floriform symbol of mourning for the front door. And then she withdrew, into herself.

Sarah sequestered herself after Alex Boteler's visit, gray in face and gray in spirit, without energy or emotion. At first, she had stayed abed. When she did get up, she rocked dully in her chair, staring at the open fire that offered neither warmth nor comfort. Henry stopped trying to convince her to leave their bedroom, and one day simply took her arm and led her downstairs. She neither resisted nor accepted, only went with him, a half step behind.

Betsy paused at the door of the morning room with a tray, tea and dainty quarters of fresh bread slices red with strawberry preserve. She felt so awkward with the new life inside her.

"Mumma, I've made tea. To take the chill off." Betsy sat stiffly on the edge of the plain wooden chair, "shall I pour."

Sarah nodded. Absently, she raised the tea cup to her lips. Vacantly, she spoke her first words in days.

"The good china."

"I thought you'd enjoy using it."

"Yes," Sarah sipped again. "Yes. Thank you."

Betsy wriggled back in the chair, gingerly, first one hip then the other. She sighed deeply.

"I will be happy when spring comes. Only six more weeks."

Sarah's melancholy remained, "It's been a long time since we had a baby in the house. God's ways are strange. He takes one and provides another."

"Mumma, we all miss Brian. Jed wishes it could have been him. He said that and he meant it with all his heart. Jed would take his place if he could, Mumma."

A brief light came into Sarah's eyes, the first since the report of Brian's demise, "Henry said the same, dear.

"What is it these men of ours? Do they think we love them less than Brian?" She sipped the tea and reentered her private world.

The routine repeated the next day and the next, Henry's persisting that she come downstairs, Betsy's visiting with a tray with tea and a sweet. His solicitations and her attentiveness worked as an antidote to her gloom, slowly and undramatically and as surely as the moon's phases over the Blue Ridge.

The determined attentions gently helped Sarah work out of her self-appointed seclusion, until one day she emerged from the black hole to reenter the world. She was in the morning room with Betsy, and for the first time since Alex Boteler's visit, she offered something of herself. A dream proved to be the mechanism that finally brought her around.

"I don't know that I should tell you, but I had a dream last night," she said into the china teacup, poised at her lips. Perched on the edge of her chair, she sipped to cover her indecision.

Betsy leaned forward eagerly, "Please do, Mumma."

Encouraged, she finished the cup, and spoke as she reached to put it on the tray, "It was a strange dream. Brian wasn't in it but I had this feeling it was about him. Like he was in the next room, trying to come to me. Everything was happy and we were all together again."

"What else, Mumma, what else?"

"That's all. Nothing but an overwhelming sense of joy somehow connected with Brian."

"What's this about Briney?" Jed crutched into the room.

"Mumma and I were just talking. Having tea and talking." Betsy hitched forward in her chair, "Sit with us."

"No. I'm expectin' Zekiel. Said he'd have my new leg today."

Jed smiled broadly at Betsy's rounded middle, "You're lookin' better every day. Isn't she, Ma? Better and better."

"Bigger and bigger is more accurate," she wriggled back in her chair again, "any bigger I'll have to stay in bed."

Jed cocked his head. "With me?" he started to say, but glanced at Sarah and changed his mind.

"Where's Pa? Thought he might be in here by the fire."

"Not your father, Jedediah, not in the middle of the day."

"You sound better today, Ma, You feelin' better?"

"Yes, son, I do. I have this wife of yours for company. She's brewed tea and we've talked. I do feel relieved."

"She's good for me, too, Ma," Jed leaned across his crutch to touch his fingers to Betsy's cheek.

In the dark before dawn, two cavalrymen hurriedly threw saddles on their horses. One of them spoke in hushed tones.

"We'd better make tracks before Stuart changes his mind."

"I agree. He's refused me leave for two months," David Morrow answered, "Orange Courthouse isn't Richmond, but it's better than nothing."

"What do you mean! Orange Courthouse is a wonderful place."

"For you maybe, with Bessie Shackleford nearby."

John Pelham laughed, "You can inspect my gunners while I visit her. You ready?"

Swinging up, they rode into the dark. An hour later they stopped at one of Pelham's Horse Batteries, "Dave, I thought we might get breakfast here, but now that I think on it, I'd rather keep going."

"How about five minutes to give the horses a blow. Maybe they have coffee in the fire."

"OK. But no longer."

Pelham's instincts were on target for Jeb Stuart at headquarters expected his two young officers to be at breakfast with him. When he learned they had left, he ordered a rider out to bring them back. He never caught up with them until they had reached the county seat, and by then it was dark, too late to return. They would at least have one night.

The next day, a train pulled in from Culpeper with news that the Union cavalry was gathering across the Rappahannock, not just a troop or a squadron but regiments. No reason for such activity unless some general had ideas in his head for a sortie across the river.

"Stuart's scheduled to be in Culpeper for a court-martial session," David observed, "we can take the cars up there and meet him. We'll be closer to the action, too, if Yankee troopers have been ordered to cross the Rappahannock. And one other thing."

"What's that?"

"If Stuart finds himself in a fight with them and we're not with him, he'll be madder than a hornet. Pelham, we just picked a bad time to visit Orange Courthouse."

They did catch their train and connect up with Jeb Stuart who was not happy with them, "Where have you two been? I had the provost beating the bushes for you."

"Sorry, sir," Pelham spoke up first feeling that their badly timed ride was his idea, "things were quiet and I thought it a good time to look in on some of my gunners. Dave here—er Colonel Morrow—agreed to come along."

David broke in, "Sir. we caught the cars from Orange Courthouse as soon as we learned of the build-up at the ford."

"We'll sort this out later when things quiet down. From now on, I want the both of you available."

The intelligence proved true. Soon after daylight, 2,100 Federal cavalrymen pulled up at the river bank fronting Kelly's Ford, both banks obstructed with felled trees. The right, south side, was guarded by butternut sharpshooters, some sixty of them in rifle pits and weathered farm buildings. Their job was to stop any small reconnaissance force that might venture the crossing, hardly an attack of this size.

It was a complete surprise. They fought for an hour before the Yankees forced the crossing, and then pulled out, those that could. Half the defenders were captured.

Meanwhile, Jeb Stuart led a column out of Culpeper, David and John Pelham sticking close like his shadows. They trotted past the Shackleford house, where Pelham's friend, Bessie, stood on the balcony waving her handkerchief.

The Yankees advanced a half mile from the river to the protection of woods and a stone fence. An open field was to their front.

"With your permission, sir," John Pelham pointed at one of his advancing batteries.

Stuart understood at once and with a wave, gave his approval.

Pelham galloped off to guide Breathed's Battery into position.

With his quickly marshalled regiments, Jeb Stuart deployed for attack. David reined alongside him.

They galloped through a cultivated field, past a farmhouse, 400 yards now from the Federals, 300, 200, and less.

"OPEN FIRE!" Carbine fire from Yankees behind the stone fence took a heavy toll. The 3rd Virginia, close on Stuart's flank, fell back, every man for himself.

Stuart rallied them, "Don't leave us, men. If you do we'll be here by ourselves!" The Virginians responded. Behind a sod fence, they deployed for another attack, reached the Blue line, fought saber to saber, fell back again.

Yankees countered with an attack of their own, in a column of fours down the road. Sabers rang as the 2nd Virginia met them head-on. The melee broke into smaller fights along the roadway and in the clearings on either side.

David rode with an order for Tom Rosser's 5th Virginia, "Swing left and hit their rear."

Rosser did his best, but ran into heavy flank fire from a stone wall and two Pennsylvania regiments in front. Overmatched, the 5th had to retreat. Rosser sustained a serious wound, but stayed on the field until the fighting was over.

Meanwhile, David had returned to Jeb Stuart. Stuart pointed, "Pelham's back there with Breathed. Tell him the Yankees are bringing up guns west of the road, three batteries, maybe more. He'll know what to do."

Pelham was already unlimbering three guns.

"They're bringing up at least a dozen," David shouted, "you'll need more."

Pelham laughed good-naturedly, "That makes it about even. Remember Fredericksburg?"

He turned to his men. "Colonel Morrow here thinks twelve guns is too much for us," he shouted, "what do you think?"

A chorus of denials lifted to the sky.

The Yankees opened fire. Pelham's men responded, swab, load, fire, swab, load, fire, not a lost motion. As at Fredericksburg, the devotion between them and their young leader was grand. No one could inspire a gun crew as could Pelham.

Shells burst around them, closer as Yankee gunners made small corrections. Pelham started to shout, an order to move that David anticipated. A shell burst overhead.

David heard part of the order. Why hadn't Pelham completed it? David waited.

When he looked again, Pelham was on the ground, still.

"He's dead," someone shrieked.

David dropped to the ground next to him, gently lifted his head. Wildly he protested, "No, goddamn it, he isn't dead. He can't be. Pelham. Pelham."

"He's still breathing. Unconscious, but still breathing"

Blood stained David's hand and forearm, blood from the back of Pelham's head. David took command, ordering one man, "Get a horse, limber, anything to carry him," another to help lift him, and to no one in particular, "Get a surgeon."

The battle went on without them.

David knelt by his friend, dazed by the suddenness of it all, Pelham laughing, encouraging his men, shouting an order; Pelham lying on the ground, silent, still.

They took him to the home of his friend, Bessie Shackleford.

David remained with him, pacing the sorrowful room, stopping to massage his friend's hand. He prayed as he touched Pelham's boot. He paced, he prayed, he cursed. He prayed for the doctors, and cursed when they nodded with long faces.

"Do something, goddamn it, he can't die."

Clocks ticked the seconds. The sun said the day was done.

"Yea, though I walk through the valley of the shadow—"

Pelham lived through the sunset and through the sunrise.

"Give us this day our daily bread—"

David stayed with him, never giving up, maintaining his vigil and his hope. He refused to accept the clinical opinion, "You can't give up. You can't let him die."

But John Pelham did die, despite the hopes, prayers and curses, despite the best efforts of surgeons. John Pelham never recovered consciousness.

David shed tears for the engaging cadet who two years ago had cheered him out of the doldrums as they sailed from West Point. For the young officer who fought his guns with joyful abandon, the "Gallant Pelham" as General Lee honored him after Fredericksburg.

Never again would they share confidences, or gallop off on a lark as they had only two days ago.

"The Lord bless you and keep you. The Lord make His face to shine upon you—"

Jeb Stuart wept openly, shattered as David by Pelham's death, for he had been one of his favorites, " You loved him too, David. You knew him longer than any of us. It is fitting that you escort his remains to Richmond."

In the Confederacy's capital, Pelham's corpse was transferred from its plain box to an iron coffin, and moved to the capitol with an honor guard.

David draped the coffin with the flag of Virginia, drawing it to the small window above Pelham's face. He smoothed a tiny wrinkle in the flag and looked on his friend's boyish features.

With love and sadness, he touched fingertips to the cold glass, lingering, unwilling to break this final contact. Moments accumulated into minutes, two, three, five and more. The honor guard stood by respectfully, ready to assume its duties. David stood transfixed, fingertips to glass, eyes wet and glassy.

Not the slightest sound nor the tiniest movement disturbed the stillness. David remained motionless.

The tableau might have gone on forever had not a venerable clock imposed itself, chiming Westminster tetrachords, pausing, then striking the hour.

The tones beckoned and David quivered for he was chilled through. He gazed on the draped coffin again, and looked on the face of his beloved friend. It was time to say good-bye.

He snapped to attention, braced as he had so many times with Pelham at West Point, and saluted precisely as they had been trained. He stood rigid for a full minute before dropping the salute, hesitated for one sculptured moment, and executed an about-face.

"Sergeant! Post the guard."

His official responsibilities were over.

XLVII

A WEDDING

" Colonel, it's 'most seven o'clock," the sergeant of the honor guard touched David's shoulder, "you said don't let you sleep later'n seven."

David stretched the kinks, "I'd rather sleep on the ground."

"Yes suh, stone floor's mighty unforgivin'."

"Everything all right last night?"

"Bah the book, suh."

"Thank you, sergeant, for your help. And your men, too.

"I would like you and them to do something for me."

"Yessuh," he smiled tentatively, "long's it's not agin' reg'lations aw the law."

David held Confederate currency to him, two paper certificates, "For you and your men."

"Oh, no suh. Last naht's duty was an honuh ta all of us. We-all knew of Majuh Pelham. How he stood his ground at Fredericksburg an' Gen'l Lee called him 'The Gallant Pelham'."

"Then I want you to take this money and next chance you get, drink a toast to him. To 'The Gallant Pelham'. Now take it, sergeant and drink to his memory."

"Puttin' it that way, suh, 'twould be an honuh. An' one othuh thing, suh."

"Yes?"

The sergeant whipped a textbook salute. "It's an honuh t'know you, suh."

David caught a ride on a wagon going east on Broad Street. Unshaven, unwashed, and dishevelled, he looked more scoundrel than Lieutenant Colonel, C.S.A.

"Good morning, Mrs. Burgess. Remember me?"

Carrie's landlady peered suspiciously through her lorgnette, "Can't say as I do." Scowling, she made a move to shut the door.

"Carrie Nash's friend. Please excuse my appearance."

"A friend of Carrie's you say? Not the friend I remember. He was handsome, and a captain. And he hasn't been here in months."

David smiled, "That's my only redemption. I was promoted."

"Did I hear my name mentioned?" Carrie appeared at Mrs. Burgess's shoulder. She gasped in surprise.

"David! Oh, David," and she was in his arms, laughing, laughing and sobbing, "it's been so long. I didn't know where you were. I was afraid you—oh, I didn't know what had happened."

Frantically, she held to him, alternately clutching and stroking his uniform. She looked him full in the face, and kissed him hard on the mouth. Then she broke and wept tears of relief.

Mrs. Burgess, "Come inside, for goodness sakes."

She had come to love Carrie, learning of her brother killed in the war, and of David and their intention to marry. David's long absence had made her skeptical, "Soldiers! all the same."

However, Carrie's constancy had gradually won her over, and David's return won her over completely.

She swung the door, urging them inside, "Take your young man inside. Such a public exhibition and you a colonel, for goodness sakes. Into the parlor with you and shut the door behind you."

"Colonel! David, I never noticed. I was just so happy to see you. Colonel, private, general, I don't care as long as you're here. Oh, David, as long as you're here."

All too soon, Mrs. Burgess was rapping on the door, "Carrie! I'm sure your young man would like some breakfast."

"Yes, mam." Muffled in their kiss, Carrie's voice hardly carried through the door.

When they had eaten, the elderly lady had another surprise, "Show your young man to the room next to yours."

"Upstairs!"

"Certainly upstairs. We can't have him bathing down here, can we? I have hot water on the back of the stove." And to David, "Put your clothes out so we can get them washed."

"Thank you, Mrs. Burgess."

"And one more thing. I've laid out trousers and a shirt, and a razor, brush, and strop. My late husband's, rest his soul. His soap cup is gone so you'll have to use regular."

David thanked her again.

Upstairs, in the room David was to use, they turned to each other and embraced again. Carrie sighed and melted into him, "It's been so long."

"Too long, sweetheart."

"Mrs. Burgess surprised me. In all the time I've lived here, there hasn't been one man on this floor."

For several minutes they stood close, perfectly content in each other's arms, saying not a word.

"Maybe I ought to get the hot water. She's been so sweet, I wouldn't want her to get the wrong idea."

Nuzzling her neck, David teased, "What idea is that?"

"Oh, you!"

A clatter on the stairs announced Mrs. Burgess's maid with the cradle-shaped tub. Slipping from David's arms, Carrie helped her through the doorway. While the two of them scurried for heated water, David tugged at high boots and stockings.

"Don't take too long," Carrie kissed him lightly.

David tossed clothes out the door and luxuriated in the steaming water until it cooled. He toweled, shaved, and donned borrowed clothes, rolling shirt sleeves and trousers, waist and cuffs. Waiting at the stairs, Carrie burst out in laughter.

"Those clothes!"

"What's the matter with these clothes?"

"You look like a rag doll who's lost half his stuffing."

David went rigid, transfixed in a moment. He collapsed on the stairs head in his hands.

Carrie shrieked, "David! What is it?"

She guided him to the parlor, "What is it? What happened?"

Tears streamed down his face. He nodded denials, I don't know or don't ask me or leave me alone. She couldn't tell which.

Sitting with him on the sofa, she ached to help, suffering his suffering. She held him tight to her breast, and rocked gently, allowing him the time and freedom to regain his composure as he would. She hummed softly, close to him without intruding.

Bit by bit, David quieted, "I'm sorry."

"Don't be sorry. Just talk to me when you're ready."

He brushed his face and moved away from her, toward the edge of the sofa, "It was 'rag doll'. You said 'rag doll' and I saw Pelham again hanging loose over a saddle, his arms and legs swinging limp. Pelham was killed."

Carrie gasped, "Oh, I'm so sorry. Your best friend."

"Him and Rosser. For seven years. We resigned from The Academy, the three of us, to come south. Seems like yesterday.

"We were together in Stuart's command. At Manassas together and Sharpsburg and Fredericksburg.

"God, Carrie, you should have seen him at Fredericksburg! General Lee called him 'gallant'. I was with him for part of it, fighting a whole division with one gun. God, I'll miss him."

Carrie remained silent, hoping he would continue. Get rid of it, David, get rid of the hurt and pain.

"That's why I'm in Richmond. To escort his remains. He's lying in state at the capitol."

"That must have been very difficult."

"I've said my farewell. It's done. Pelham's dead."

The episode was closed. David had dropped the curtain, and the room became suddenly hushed. Carrie waited, stroking the back of his hand, sensing his turmoil, loving him, knowing he had more to say. She rested her head on his shoulder. She waited.

How could she know that she herself was part of the turbulence that wracked him, she and the recognition of his own mortality. Always before he had skirted around his own dying with the happy sentiment that he was too young for that.

Abruptly he came alive, almost shouting, "Carrie, marry me." "I've already said I would. Have you forgotten so soon?"

"No. I mean now, before I leave."

He clutched her by the shoulders, "Today. This morning."

"This morning! David, we can't. I do want to, but—"

"But what?"

"But everything, a minister, the banns, your family, a place to live, my job." Her eyes came wide.

"My job! Oh, David, I'm late already," she jumped up, ' I have to go. Yes I'll marry you, but right now I have to go to work. Mr. Jones will be wild."

"Carrie, sweetheart, will you? Today, before I leave," he followed her halfway up the stairs, calling after her as she disappeared into her room, "tell Mr. Jones it's my fault you're late. I'll make what arrangements I can and be at Mechanics' Hall before 6 o'clock. What church do you go to?"

She called through the door, "I'm sort of Episcopalian."

"That's a coincidence. So am I. What else should I know?"

"Not much else to tell," as she rushed down the stairway.

David blocked her path, "Now I want a proper answer. Will you marry me?"

"Of course I will. Yes. Yes. Yes."

"Today?"

"Yes, my love. Today."

"I'll have to know your real name."

"My real name?"

"Yes. You told me Carrie was just a name you were using because you liked the sound of it."

"I did?"

"At the Exchange Hotel. The first time I met you."

"Oh, that! Well, Carrie is my real name. I've been Carrie Nash all my life."

She kissed him and was gone.

David did make the arrangements, with Mrs. Burgess's help. A lifelong parishioner of St. John's on Church Hill, she asked The Reverend William Norwood to officiate, "without all that falderal.

"There's nobody to object, and he has only today."

He did object, "But we have procedures. We have to follow procedures. The Bishop would be most distressed."

She reminded him of her long service, tithings, special bequests, "I do so hope to continue," she cooed sweetly.

David purchased a wedding ring, hired the same carriage and driver they had almost a year ago. He paid a premium for a corner room at the Spotswood.

At 5:30 o'clock, he was at Mechanics' Hall. He apologized to Mr. Jones, "wars and weddings have no respect for the clock, sir. We would like you to attend." And to encourage Mr. Jones' continuing good will toward Carrie, he slipped in a reminder of an influential friend, "I want to ask Colonel Boteler, but I haven't been able to find him or General Stuart. Both of them are in town today."

"I'll make an effort to locate them. My congratulations to you both. And rest assured, I'll be there."

Hand in hand, they ran laughing to the waiting carriage. The smiling coachman remembered them, "Seen a passel uh perposals in this ole car-r'age, weddin' an' othuh-wise. You-all's the fust t'come back fer the ride t'the church."

"David, I can't believe this is happening."

"Believe it, love, in two hours you'll be Mrs. Morrow."

She burrowed under his arm, contented and secure for the first time in many months.

"Dearly Beloved: We are gathered together here in the sight of God . . ."

Carrie edged closer, unobtrusively seeking David's hand, entwining his fingers with hers. Her smoke blue eyes misted over. Later, she recalled only bits and pieces of the ceremony:

". . . as long as ye both shall live?"

Her answer, a whisper solemn as if she were talking to God Himself, "I will."

David's strong voice making the same promises, to love, comfort, honor and keep her . . . forsaking all others.

And then.

"I, David, take thee, Carrie, to my wedded wife, to have and to hold . . . to love and to cherish . . .

". . . I, Carrie, take thee, David . . . in sickness and in health . . . until death do us part. I plight thee my troth."

". . . I pronounce that they are Man and Wife . . ."

What she remembered most vividly was David's embrace and whispered pledge before God's table, "I will love you forever."

Crossing the lobby of the Spotswood, the new bride flushed, "I feel so conspicuous. Everyone's looking at us."

"A glass of wine will take care of that. Are you hungry?"

"Starved."

"Dining room? Or be more private. Have dinner upstairs?"

Carrie colored again, "Would you mind the dining room?"

"The dining room it is."

They were greeted at the entrance.

"We have a reservation." David beamed as he added, "Colonel and Mrs. Morrow."

"Yes, sir. A table in a quiet corner, I believe." With practiced elegance, the maitre d'hotel raised a hand, "Your waiter is Steffan, our very best."

"Please send the sommelier to our table."

"Certainly, colonel. Congratulations to you and your lady."

Carrie blushed crimson.

At their table, David conferred with the master of wines.

"Yes, colonel, I believe I can find something special for you in our cellars. The blockade has cut into our stock, but I have a Chateau Lafite saved for so worthy an occasion."

Returning in a few minutes, he offered David the aged label attesting to year and origin, and poured a bit for him to sample. David swirled the ruby wine, tested its bouquet and taste.

"Splendid."

David raised his glass, "To us, Carrie, my love."

"To us, sweetheart."

Steffan refilled the crystal glasses, "May I suggest the shad, sir, served with the roe?"

"Carrie?"

"You choose for both of us."

"Steffan, I'm going to leave it up to you."

"I don't understand, sir."

"You select for us. Everything. As if it were for yourself and your true love."

Steffan looked surprised for a single, fleeting moment. As he recognized the compliment, he beamed, "Of course. My pleasure, indeed, sir." Refilling delicate glasses he left for the kitchen.

"I remember the last time we were here."

"I asked you to spend the night with me."

"And I refused. David, I wanted to be with you so much. Later, in the barouche—"

"I know. I had the feeling I could change your mind."

"But you didn't."

"But I did," he smiled, "it just took a little longer."

She sipped from the fragile glass, and held it to him to be refilled, "Thank you, David, for taking a little longer."

"The way it should be, Carrie."

Steffan's dinner was delectable, she-crab soup subtly spiced, the shad sweet with roe browned just so, salad crisp and iced, a French pastry, tiny and rich, redolent coffee, a creme de menthe frappe'. Steffan served with a panache he hadn't used since Paris.

"What would you like now? How else can I pamper you?"

Almost imperceptibly, Carrie nodded her answer. Her eyes locked with his across the table, smoky blue and violet searching for another question. Without waiting for him to ask it, she reached for his hand, answering it herself, answering it in her glistening eyes, and in the air of anticipation and excitement she projected.

David pushed away from the table. Steffan was there at once, angling Carrie's chair as she arose.

"It has been a pleasure to serve you, Madame. Sir." He added conspiratively, "I have found another Chateau Lafite."

"Why, thank you, Steffan. Thank you very much."

Together, very close together, they left the dining room.

As they climbed the broad staircase to their room, neither of them could avoid thoughts of their first encounter at the Exchange Hotel, David amused, Carrie chagrined.

"I can't wait to tell our children how we met."

"Don't you dare! David, you have to promise me."

Their room was everything he had ordered and more, an arrangement of spring flowers on the table, champagne in a cooler of cracked ice, the gas lamp turned low, extra pillows on the bed. A bottle of Chateau Lafite rested against the pillows.

The bed itself was a four-poster, high enough for a step-stool. It had been turned down, displaying a triangle of pure white. Carrie glanced at it quickly, then turned to a window.

The room faced south and west with a window on each of the two walls. Looking from one, Carrie was delighted, "Why there's the War Department building, only a block away."

David came up behind her, encircling her within his arms, "I thought you'd like a corner room." She rested her head back, against his shoulder.

They stood at the window watching a potpouri of pedestrians in uniforms, mufti, bonnets, and hooped skirts hurrying through the cheery circles of gas lamps. Carriages, some with oil lamps on the sides, and here and there a soldier on horseback added to the bustle. A dog barked from the direction of Capitol Hill.

"It's all so wonderful, David, I can't believe it. You're here with me. Together in this room, just the two of us."

David nuzzled her hair, and her ear and cheek as she lifted her head to him. Slowly, inside the bracelet of his arms, she turned to him and clasped her hands behind him. She squeezed and stretched tip toe to kiss him hard on the mouth. David tightened his arms and lifted her, clear of the floor.

Carrie squirmed in his embrace. She mumbled into his lips, and pulled back.

"Oh! you take my breath away. I can't breathe." She held a hand to her breast.

She inhaled deeply, swelling the bodice of her dress.

He had noticed, "Now you take my breath away."

They gazed steadily at one another, each a prisoner of the other's eyes. Slowly, David reached for her. She guided his hand across her breast. Lost in one another, entranced, unblinking, their eyes remained locked as he undid buttons. Her gown fell from her shoulders. She wriggled it to the floor. He looked at her as he had before in another hotel, another life.

"Would you rather do the rest yourself?"

"Uh uh."

"Never knew you wore so many things."

Still, he undressed her slowly, whispering his love, stopping to caress and kiss her, to put her at ease, to let her set the pace or stop if she so wished. He waited a moment before removing her shift and corselet. She squirmed her consent. He dropped them to the floor and gave her another moment before lifting her bare breasts, caressing, kissing them each one.

Removing his own clothes, he held her close, and she, him, only her pantelets between them. He slipped them past her and past him and they were together. They toppled onto the high bed, she on her back, legs dangling, he over her. Carrie made room for him, and he eased into her with restraint for she had never lain with a man before.

He lay perfectly still, "All right?"

She pulled him ever closer, "Uh huh."

He lifted tentatively. She followed, anticipating, matching his rhythm now and more, now breathless, and more, more and more. An hour later, they were dreamily awake, stretched proper, full lengths on the bed. David burrowed an arm under her, and she turned to him and squirmed close. Safely cuddled against him, she found the courage to speak of an important change of heart.

"David, I want to have your baby."

"You want a baby!"

"Not any baby. I want to have your baby."

"But you said—"

"It's different now."

"Different? How?"

Raising on an elbow, she traced a fingertip down his nose and around his lips. In the dull light, her eyes were less smoke than sapphire, begging him to know the depth of her feeling.

"I don't know how or why or what. It's different, that's all, just different. Oh, David, I love you so much."

She collapsed on his chest, crushing her breasts to him, clutching him frantically, doing her best to stifle the sobs she felt. Holding her and soothing her, David realized he wasn't the only one living on the edge of his mortality.

He held her until she quieted, and kissed her tears.

"I would like that, my love, I would like you to have a baby very much. I could tell him, and his brothers and sisters stories of the war."

"Or her? What if he's a her?"

"I could tell her and her brothers and sisters stories of the war. How you and I met."

Carrie smiled ambivalently through her tears, "You wouldn't do that. Or would you?"

He teased, "Maybe."

"One thing you haven't thought of, my love."

"I remember that night like it happened yesterday. Every detail."

"You would have to explain how you happened to be in that awful place."

"I'll make up something."

"There is nothing to make up."

"Hmmmm. I haven't mentioned this before, but that day I had orders from the provost. To investigate The Exchange and two other hotels in that district. You know, poke around and see what was going on there. The provost said, 'Maybe they ought to be declared off limits for the soldiers'."

"Why, David Morrow, that is a downright lie. You would lie to your own child?"

"No, I would not be lying to my child. I would be telling of an occurrence during the war. And you know how war stories go."

Carrie stretched, "No. Tell me, how do war stories go?"

"Well, they take on a life of their own. You know that."

"Yes, I do. Like you and me, making it up as we go along.

"They go on and on," she purled deamily into a diminishing rhapsody, "and on—and—on—and—"

She turned as did he, unto him, unto her.

"—and—on—and—on—and—

XLVIII

DEAD OR ALIVE?

The heavy door knocker reverberated through the rooms of the large house, foyer, dining room, into the kitchen. Sarah Morrow frowned at the interruption, wiped her hands on her apron, frowned again, and hurried through the hall and foyer. She opened one side of the double front door. And gasped audibly, finger tips to mouth.

Bristles covered the stranger's face; untrimmed, unkempt, wild hair fell over his forehead. Raggedy trousers and shirt belonged on the cornfield scarecrow.

He clutched the crown of a shapeless felt hat, sliding it sideways from his head. Awkward as the move was, its boyish innocence eased Sarah's apprehension.

"Mrs. Morrow? You probably don't remember me, but I was here a year ago."

Not entirely relieved, she replied somewhat sharply, "No, I'm afraid I don't."

"I helped carry Jed home. My name is Tom McDonald."

The two stood awkward at the open door, Sarah waiting, Tom unsure. How do you tell a mother her son is—that her son has spells?

Sarah broke the impasse, "That was a bad day. I'm afraid I didn't thank you for your help with Jed."

"No need. I was glad ta. How is he?"

"He's around here somewhere. Would you like to see him?"

"That would be good, but that's not why I'm here."

He fidgeted, obviously ill at ease.

"Why then, Tom McDonald? You did say 'McDonald' didn't you?"

"Yes, ma'am."

"Why are you here then?"

Tom blurted the words, "I'm a friend of Briney's."

"Brian?!"

Her face paled. Her breath stuck.

"Yes, a good friend. Mrs. Morrow, are you all right?"

Sarah floundered in that awful memory, the report that her son was dead, her dream with its aura of joy and inference that he was safe, the overwhelming desire to accept it. For a while, she had held faithfully to it, but time had niggled at her and eroded her belief, "Brian's—gone."

"Yes, they took him away. He was captured last summer. Same time as I was."

"I know. He wrote from Fort Delaware. We sent him a box."

"He never got anything."

"You were there with him?"

"Yes, all the time. I'd have known if he got a box."

"Then you might know what happened to him."

"Yes, he and I—"

"Henry, Henry, come here," Sarah literally screamed for her husband, "Quickly. Henry! Come here."

Henry Morrow scrambled from his front room office, steamed through the generous foyer prepared to fight off an intruder, "Get the hell out of here!"

"No, Henry, no, no," Sarah restrained him at the front door, "this is Tom—," the last name wouldn't come, "he knows Brian. He even called him Briney."

"A friend of Brian's?"

"Yes, sir. I'm Tom McDonald. We were prisoners t'gether."

"Then maybe you can tell us what happened to him."

"I'm not sure, sir. Doctor Ruggles thinks he's just seen too much war and suffering."

"Too much war and suff—," Henry Morrow enunciated incredulously and blew sky high, "A boy is killed and the doctor thinks he's seen too much war? What kind of stupidity is that!

"I was against his enlistin' from the start."

Surprised, Tom answered, "But Briney wasn't killed, sir."

"We had word. Back in January. Brian's dead."

"But I was with him a week ago. Brian's not dead."

Sarah turned ashen white. Henry paled, too. He jerked his head toward his front room office, "Follow me, young man."

Sarah hurried after them through the foyer into his private sanctuary, standing just inside the sliding cherry door. Henry sat at his desk.

"Now, young man, tell me what this is all about. If this story about Brian being alive is some kind of cruel jest, I'll have your hide. I have learned otherwise. From a respected member of our Congress."

"Brian was alive when I left him, Mr. Morrow. We escaped and he's in Maryland, alive and safe."

"One week ago, you say?" Henry wanting so badly to believe, needing to hold this gossamer thread of hope.

"Yes sir. I wouldn't joke about a thing like that. Briney is alive. Leastways, he was when I left."

"We were told he was not. Information right from Washington to Congressman Boteler. You have a message from him? A note? Anything? "

"No, sir. All I know is I left him alive and kicking. I can take you to him."

"You can!!" Henry shouted the last of his skepticism

"Sarah, do you hear that? He can take us to Brian. Brian's alive, Sarah, alive and well."

Sarah remained speechless, her eyes darting from one to the other. Agitated fingers worried a dainty handkerchief.

Henry bounded from his elegant leather chair, around his desk toward her, "Brian's alive!"

She became perfectly still, "I heard you, Henry, but I'm afraid. I don't know what to believe."

Henry touched her arm, "Tom, here, says he was with him a week ago."

"But maybe he's wrong. Either he's wrong or Alex Boteler is. Which one, Henry? Who's wrong and who's right?"

Tom spoke first, "Mrs. Morrow, Brian was alive a week ago. You'll just have to believe that because it's the truth."

Sarah's eyes welled. Tears flowed. "Oh, I want to. I want to so much."

An uncertain smile played around the corners of her mouth, tasting the tears. Her eyes pleaded to know the truth. Sobbing, she clutched at Henry's arm, searching his eyes for reassurance, one and the other, back and forth, back and forth.

Gently he held her by the shoulders, "It's all right, Sarah. Brian is still with us." And she knew he was right.

The baby smile emerged, lighting her face, "My dream, Henry, my dream was right. I knew it was and I believed it for a long time. Oh, Henry, my dream was right!"

"What dream, Ma?" Their second son, Jedediah, clumped into the doorway. He leaned on a single crutch to ease the weight on his wooden leg, a stranger unfamiliar and repulsive. Betsy, his lusty wife, stretched to look around him. Gracey, his nineteen-year old sister did the same, "Dream?"

"My dream that Brian was alive. I felt for so long that it was true. But I gave up hope. And now we learn that my dream was true. Brian didn't die at the prison. He is still among the living. He escaped. This is Tom and he escaped, too. Brian is alive!"

"Oh, Ma, how wonderful!!" The two girls ran to Sarah, entangling her with hugs.

An hour later, Tom McDonald mopped bacon grease and eggs with a chunk of bread, "And that's the story, the first prisoners t'escape from Fort Delaware. We were lucky, having Sean Murphy to help us, he was a guard, and floating t'shore on all those tin cans. And then having Doctor Ruggles find us on the beach."

After the session in Henry's office, the three of them had gone to the kitchen, Jed following, and Betsy and Grace. Unlike her mother, Gracey was not put off by Tom's stubbly beard or shabby clothes. Greeting him, she had seen a depth in him that she liked. And, feeling her empathy, he was attracted to her.

"You were more than lucky," Jed interposed, "havin' that doctor find you on the beach like that. And the Irish guard. Without him, you'd still be in prison."'

"Good old Sean Murphy. Never saw him after we all waded into Delaware Bay, not him nor Sam. But they made it safe to shore, Doctor Ruggles found their boards and tin cans.

"Sean had a good job, saving passage money for his wife and young 'uns to come over from Ireland. But then he was drafted into the army and out of his passage money, which made him very angry. He was spoiling t' get even, and back to his old job.

"Sam was just a youngster who should never have been in the army in the first place. Brian kind of took him under his wing."

He popped the last of the soaked bread into his mouth.

Jed had been impressed with the story, "I heard stories of that Fort Delaware. Pea Patch Island I think they called it. Word was nobody ever escaped from that pile of mud."

"You're right," Tom McDonald grinned, "until we did.

"Jed, I'm glad you're getting on. You weren't looking so good last time I saw you."

"Had some good doctorin'. Figger t'be a lot better with this leg 'Zekiel made. Still need a crutch t'take some of the weight."

"Briney talked a lot about Ezekiel. I feel like I know him."

Abruptly, suspiciously, Henry cut in, "Why didn't Brian come home with you?"

"Doctor Ruggles thought it best he stay where he is."

"That's no answer. Why didn't he come home with you?"

Alarm wrapped Sarah's face. She waited, stone still. Betsy reached to Sarah, to offer encouragement, to be reassured herself. Gracey glanced anxiously at her father.

"Brian is fine," Tom started, searching for the right words, "he had a pretty bad cut on his arm, but that's all healed."

Everyone waited for him to continue.

Henry fidgeted impatience.

Tom hesitated, seeking the right words. Nothing came.

Henry scowled and drummed on the table.

Tom met the inevitable head-on, "He gets spells."

"Spells! What kind of spells?"

"Not often. He was worse in prison, and when we first escaped. For the last few months he's been much better, ever since he's been with the Coopers. Honest, he's been much better."

"What kind of spells?" Henry pushed him again.

"Sometimes, he just stares into space. Other times, he goes wild, like he's having a nightmare. He's seen too much war according to Doctor Ruggles. Doctor Ruggles says, 'what he needs most is rest, quiet, and good food'."

"Henry, we have to get him. Bring him home at once."

"That's the other reason I'm here. I'll guide you t'the Coopers. If you'd like."

"We'd appreciate that," Henry nodded, not anxious to be creating an obligation for himself, but without a choice, "We'll start in the mornin'."

"Mr. Morrow," Tom started uneasily, "There are details."

"Details? We're goin' after him. That's all I need t'know."

"For one thing, I haven't been home yet. They think I'm still in prison."

Henry's mood switched still again, "Yes, son, you should. Thank you for comin' ta us first."

Tom took charge, "I'd say leave a week from today."

"A week!"

"Yes, four days back and forth, time with my folks."

"What else is there?"

"For one, t'go by wagon or train, the way I got here. That's faster, but a wagon would be safer. Both are dangerous, through Yankee country the whole way."

"A wagon it is then. What else?"

Tom took a deep breath, "You, Mr. Morrow."

"Me? What about me?"

Sarah reacted to his brusque tone, "Now, Henry, don't you get your back up. Tom knows more about this than any of us."

"But, Sarah—"

"No buts. Just listen before you disagree."

Henry slumped on the kitchen chair. The others waited expectantly.

Tom picked his way, "It's just that Doctor Ruggles thinks Brian needs t'be quiet, away from upset and argument."

"Doctor Ruggles this! Doctor Ruggles that! Who the hell is this Doctor Ruggles anyway?"

Tom threw caution to the winds and looked Henry square in the eye, "Doctor Ruggles is a good man, Mr. Morrow. He risked his life for us. Without him, we'd have been caught. Without him, we could have died right there on the beach, both of us!"

The room was tombstone still as the confrontation jammed in on them. Only Sarah talked that way to Henry. And not often.

The young soldier shattered the quiet, booming despite his efforts to stay calm, "Brian knows how angry you are with him for joining the army, Mr. Morrow, and it's bothered him a lot."

"It's bothered me, too," Henry grumped.

Tom wanted to shout even louder, "Goddamn it, you're part of his problem. You've hurt him bad and he's never gotten over it."

Red to the point of explosion, Henry vaulted from his chair, strode half way to the door.

"Henry Morrow, where do you think you're going?" Sarah shrilled.

"Of all the—in my own house—I won't be insulted in my own house. I love my son."

Sarah walked to him, taking his hand. She spoke softly.

"We all know that, dear. We all love him. And Tom is probably the best friend he's ever had.

"Tom went out of his way to bring us this news, dearest, and I'm sure he means only the best for Brian.

"There has been trouble between you and him, and Tom has done us all a favor by speaking openly of it. We ought to know what is troubling

Brian, whatever it is, not to blame anyone but to help him get back to himself."

Sarah held both her husband's hands, looking him square in the eye, "We all want the same thing, dear. Me. You. All of us. Whatever needs to be done I know we can do it. We have to, for Brian's sake."

Henry controlled his anger, and controlled his tears as he let Sarah lead him back to his chair. He slumped into it, without a word.

"Tell us everything, please," Sarah addressed Tom, "whatever we should know."

"Doctor Ruggles asked me a lot of questions about Briney, about his family, studies, friends. How he felt about the army, the war. All sorts of stuff.

"And then he said maybe he was too sensitive for the army. He said he needs time to make peace with himself. Like he keeps blaming himself for things that aren't his fault."

"What kind of things, Tom?" The question was Jed's.

"Causing disappointment at home for one."

No one responded.

"And another thing, his nightmares after shooting the Yankee at Manassas. I learned of that from you, Jed. I told him he had to forget it or he'd drive himself crazy.

"He told me of burning bridges, how exciting it was at the time, how bad he felt after. He was real angry when he told me and yelled, 'We oughta be building bridges, not burning them'."

Henry bolted upright in his chair, "My God, Sarah, he sounds like me." Visibly shaken, he left the kitchen.

Sarah followed him back into his office. She closed the door.

"At last you're beginning to understand your son."

Habit was too strong, and Henry reverted to his patterned reaction, "What I understand is that he's beginning to get his thinkin' straight. Too bad he didn't start sooner."

"Henry Morrow, how can you talk like that? Brian's always been the most serious of our children. The most serious and the smartest."

"How come he enlisted in the army then?"

She mocked his sarcasm, "How come you left Washington?"

"That's got nothin' t'do with Brian."

"But it does." She pressed again, "Why, Henry? Why did you leave Washington?"

"The doctor told me to."

"You never did anything because a doctor told you to."

"Sarah, that was a long time ago."

"Why, Henry? And don't tell me it was to seek your fortune."

"It just felt right, damn it. It just seemed right."

"Well, thank you, Henry Morrow. Now you know why Brian joined the army."

"But t'fight a war? He was riskin' his life."

"You did the same. You could have been killed on the road.

"Henry Morrow, for two years I've listened to you carry on about Brian. First Jed, then Brian. We thought we had lost him, and now we have him back and I won't listen to any more of it. Brian did what he felt was right, and I am very proud of him. It's high time you felt the same." She turned on her heel and marched from the office.

Her words echoed in his head. Sarah was not one to carry on like that without good reason.

Damn it, I'm proud of him, too. He's a fine young man. Build bridges instead of burnin' them, hmmm. Henry smiled to himself. Damn, if he hasn't come t'think like me.

And Henry mourned even as he smiled: I'm sorry we had problems, Brian, you did what you thought was right, just like we taught you, your mother and me. She's a good woman, your Ma."

In the meantime, Sarah sat on the verandah alone. She had only a few minutes before Betsy sat quietly beside her.

"Your dream has come true, Mumma."

"Seems so," absently.

"I remember when you told me about it. We were drinking tea from the good china. You said you had dreamed a feeling of happiness. Brian wasn't in it but somehow connected to the joy you felt."

"I remember. The feeling was truly inspiring."

"And now it's come true, Mumma. Your dream has come true. And my prayers have been answered."

"You've been praying for Brian?"

"In a way. I prayed that the joy you felt was for real. I prayed for a miracle, Mumma, and I think we've seen one."

Before the week was out, Tom McDonald was back at the Morrow house. Clean shaven and decently clothed, he looked a different person. He had bad news.

"I won't be able to go back to Frenchtown like we planned. My father's had an accident and they need me."

"That's too bad. Hope he's not hurt bad.'"

"Nobody knows, Mr. Morrow. Something's wrong with his back, and he's hardly able to walk. Can't tell how long he'll be laid up."

"Backs can try a man's patience. I know."

"I'm sorry to beg off this way, but he and Ma need me."

Tom handed him a paper with a rough map drawn in pencil, Winchester to the left, Delaware Bay and Frenchtown to the right, "The 'X' marks the Cooper's house, just outside of town. Folks there will be able to direct you."

"Well," Henry rubbed his chin, "this changes things."

"Yes, sir. I'm sorry to let you down, but I can't help it."

Always impatient with changes in plans, Henry managed a modicum of composure."It's just that we decided t'have Ezekiel go with you t'get Brian. Now I'll have t'go. There's no one else."

Tom hesitated, flustered by adverse pressures, his father's injury, Brian's friendship, Mr. Morrow's testy nature, and not least, his own interest in Gracey. Needing to help Brian, wanting acceptance, unsure of Henry, he fidgeted. Did Mr. Morrow fully understand what he had been told the other day?

"Mr. Morrow."

"What?"

"Briney needs understanding." In his consternation and desire to help, he talked of himself.

"I told Briney he had to spit it all out, everything that was eating at him, but he can't. Easier said than done I guess. Every so often, he gets caught in it again."

Not quite ready to face the issue, Tom waivered, "Even Doctor Ruggles doesn't know what to do, except what I've said." He felt his chance slipping away. It was now or never.

He looked directly at Henry, "Everybody has to be patient and wait for Brian to find his own answers in his own time. Nobody can do that for him, Doctor Ruggles said." Tom hesitated and plunged ahead, "He needs your patience, Mr. Morrow, and—and—not your anger."

Henry's scowl convinced him he had said enough, especially since Brian wasn't his only interest in the Morrow family. It was time to speak more softly.

"I'm sorry to run my mouth, sir. The other day, too."

"Young man,—" Henry started harshly. Surprisingly, he stopped shaking his finger, "I don't like what you've said, not one bit," his voice softened, "but I do appreciate your loyalty to my son. And maybe what you've said isn't all bad."

"Not all bad! I don't understand."

"If I am t' go after him, and now it looks like I'll have ta, I should know everythin' about him, shouldn't I? Everythin'."

Sarah joined them, "I thought I heard your voice, Tom. It's nice to see you again."

"Hello, Mrs. Morrow."

"I had Mam set a place. You will have dinner with us?"

"I can always eat," he smiled, "thank you very much."

When they had eaten, he spoke falteringly, not anxious to stir up Henry's gruffness again "Mr. Morrow—uh—and Mrs. Morrow—there's—uh—something else."

They waited expectantly for him to speak more of Brian.

He surprised them, "I'd—I'd like your permission to call on Miss Grace when I have the chance."

XLIX

THE CANTEEN

Breakfast on this last day of April was a very solemn one for Henry and Sarah Morrow. Henry handed her Tom McDonald's map to the Cooper's, "I have this in my head. Put it in a safe place."

Earlier, he had secreted a LeMat in his saddle bag, careful that Sarah caught no sight of it for she would be upset. Weapons of all kinds made her nervous, especially the huge LeMat with its two barrels, the 8-shot cylinder feeding the upper barrel plus a single grapeshot charge below. As he packed it away, he thought of another day, almost three years ago when he and Ezekiel had ridden into the mountains. Then, he had carried a pair of derringers. Before nightfall, he had killed a moonshiner with one of them. Neither he nor Ezekiel had spoken of it since.

Sarah took Tom McDonald's map, folding it slowly, "I'm glad you're not going alone." Gratefully, she nodded at Ezekiel, finishing his second breakfast for the day. He had driven from the farm at dawn in a high-seated farm wagon, chosen for its strength and lack of elegance. It would attract no untoward attention.

At the door, Henry and Sarah embraced, "I'm glad you feel better about Brian. He's grown to a fine man, Henry."

Less sure of his feelings, he answered a gray 'I know'.

"A fine man like his father. I'll miss you, dearest."

"I'll miss you, too," Henry whispered, and immediately shied away from his feelings, "Don't look for us before two weeks, maybe closer t'three."

They embraced again, "Be careful." He climbed to the high seat alongside Ezekiel. Sarah waved. And he was gone.

Ezekiel guided the horses north to Stephenson's Depot and on to Harper's Ferry, paralleling the railroad most of the way. They stayed the night with friends of his.

The next day, as the horses plodded the road to Frederick City, Henry asked about the folks they had just left and learned things of Ezekiel he had never known.

" 'Zekiel, I didn't know you had friends at The Ferry. How come I never knew that?"

"I guess because I didn't talk about 'em."

Henry waited for him to go on. Ezekiel remained silent knowing full well the delay was whetting his friend's curiosity. They rode a half mile or more before Henry gave in.

"Well?"

"Well what?" Ezekiel teased a bit more.

"Your friends. How'd you meet them?"

"In the railroad," Ezekiel replied nonchalantly.

"You were in the underground railroad! You never told me."

"Henry, I didn't want you mixed up in it. You had too much ta lose."

"Damn it, man, you could have lost your life. You should have told me."

"It wasn't somethin' I planned. One night this young couple came ta the house. Wanted ta get married, stay t'gether. They said they'd seen me before dark, and figgered I'd he'p 'em. Hid 'em in the woods and found those folks at The Ferry who'd take 'em in. Turned out they were part of the railroad and knew the next station north. After that, others showed up and Mattie and me took care of 'em the same."

"I'll be damned!"

"The war ended most of it. Henry, I just didn't want you messed up in it. Figgered it was better that way."

" 'Zekiel, you know how I feel about slavery. I would have helped."

"I know that, Henry, that's why I kept you out of it. Like I said, you had too much ta lose."

They rode another distance in silence.

"My friends gave me a family near Frederick City where we can stay tonight."

Losing time to heavy rains, they crossed Maryland slowly, through Westminster where they heard of heavy fighting back in Virginia, and across the Susquehanna River at Havre de Grace where they read in a newspaper of a battle near a country crossroad called Chancellorsville. Henry hoped stories of General Jackson's wounding were not true. On through Elkton they rattled, finally into Frenchtown.

An hour of daylight remained when they reached the Cooper's farmstead. They took it all in, an orderly, clapboard house painted white, a porch across the front, substantial barn, a barnyard free of trash, fields turned and newly planted.

"There's a man knows farmin', Henry."

"Looks so, doesn't it."

As they came closer, they saw two figures sitting on the porch steps. Henry squinted to sharpen his vision.

" 'Zekiel!" he shouted excitedly, "it looks like Brian."

As he spoke, one of the figures rose and went into the house. Ezekiel turned the team into the lane.

Stiff with riding, Henry eased forward on the high seat. One hand on the splashboard, the other on the seat for support, he inched around, dangling his rear in mid-air. Bent over and numb-legged, he used the wheel and hub for a ladder and lurched to the ground. "Gettin' creakier than the damn wagon."

A girl on the steps shaded her eyes to see them better. When Henry looked again, a man and woman stood beside her, one tall in farmer's overalls and a black, broad-brimmed hat low in the crown. He wore a full beard the color of oak leaves still hanging in January. The woman had a girlish figure. She, too, shaded her eyes.

"Thee has ridden far, I believe." the voice a soft baritone.

"Name's Henry Morrow. From Winchester. This is my friend, Ezekiel Brown."

"I am happy to know thee, Henry Morrow. And thee also, Ezekiel Brown. I am Cyrus Cooper. Been looking for thee these past few days. Thomas did not return with thee?"

"He felt obliged to stay. His father was hurt."

"Sounds like Thomas. A good man. True friend to thy son."

"Where is Brian?"

"He's in the house. This is my good wife, Abigail, and my daughter, Hannah."

"Have you eaten?" Abigail asked simply, her cheery voice hospitable, that of a pretty woman settled in a good marriage, rebel before her time. Abigail made a point of avoiding the customary pronouns and had taught her daughter the same.

"Thank you kindly. We found a tavern as we came through Elkton. Tell me about Brian. He ready t'go home, you think?"

"Come up and sit," Abigail skirted the question, adding with a smile, "or maybe you would rather stand for a few minutes. A wagon can be a torture."

"That's a fact," Henry clambered the half dozen stairs.

Hannah went inside, "Briney, it's your father. Come out and say hello to him."

"No." He held tight to the Yankee canteen he had found at Blackburn's Ford in '61, fingering the intricately tooled strap.

"But he's driven a long way," Hannah offered, "I'll stay with you."

"What does he want? He's angry with me, Hannah."

"He didn't seem angry. Come, Briney, take my hand."

"You won't leave me?"

"I said I would stay with you."

Hand in hand, they came through the front door.

Overjoyed to see his son, Henry started for him, his impulse to hug him and tell him everything was all right.

He had thought of this moment as they had rattled along the road, planning so that everything would go right. Tom's warning rang loud, "He needs quiet, Mr. Morrow"; and Sarah's chastisement, "It's time you were proud of him, too."

He restrained himself. He held out his hand, across the distance between them, "It's good to see you, Brian."

Brian stopped in his tracks and winced, unintentionally offending his father. Henry felt the old exasperation, but held his tongue. At Hannah's gentle urging, Brian reached tentatively, eyes lowered to the floor. Touching hands briefly, he clasped the strap of the canteen and backed away.

By design, Ezekiel ended the awkward moment, "The horses have had a long pull. I better take care of 'em."

And it was Hannah who sensed his motive, "We'll help you. Come on, Briney."

They disappeared around the corner of the house.

"I understand thee are opposed to the war, Mr. Morrow."

Henry misunderstood Cyrus's effort to establish a common interest, "I was opposed to Brian enlistin'."

"Thomas spoke a small bit of it. I do not envy thee."

"I'm mighty obliged, you takin' him in and all."

"No obligation is necessary. It is how we serve the Lord."

"Do you think Brian is up t'the ride home?"

The Coopers exchanged quick glances. Abigail answered.

"Seven months ago, when he and Thomas came to us, I'd have said 'No', but now I'm unsure. He is much improved. Yet—"

"And yet what, Mrs. Cooper?"

"I don't know. Even Uncle Edward is baffled and he is a very good doctor."

"Your uncle is the doctor? Tom spoke of a Doctor Ruggles."

"Brian and Thomas were half dead when he found them on the beach. He treated them and brought them here."

Cyrus broke in, "Thee has seen Brian for thyself. Is he ready to go home?"

Henry chuckled, "You bring t'mind a man I met years ago in Washington. From Vermont he was, and he never answered a question other than by askin' another one."

"I've heard tell of the practice," Cyrus smiled.

"Mr. Morrow, may I make a suggestion," Abigail asked.

"Of course."

"Stay a few days, see more of your son, understand him. Returning home is really going to be up to him, isn't it?"

"No, ma'am, it isn't. I came t'bring my boy home. Take him off your hands," he added to muffle his irritation.

Abigail stiffened at Henry's intrangency, but said nothing.

"Never knew until now how hard it is t'see sons grow up."

Cyrus Cooper acknowledged his agreement, "With thee it's a son, with us, a daughter.

"It's agreed, then? Thee will stay, as my good wife has suggested? Get to know thy son."

"Mr. Cooper, I already know my son."

"Not to argue, Mr. Morrow, but thee may find him different than the memory in thy mind."

"I think not. Brian's Brian."

"Please." Abigail countered the growing tension, " 'Mr. Morrow' and 'Mr. Cooper'! So formal. 'Cyrus' and 'Henry' would sound so much better. And I'm Abigail.

"At least stay a day or two to catch your breath before starting back. And rest the horses."

"Well, I suppose," Henry acceded gracelessly.

Meanwhile, near the barn, Ezekiel had unhitched the horses, "Want ta water 'em, Brian? You and Hannah water 'em together."

Hannah was impressed with this gentle black man, "May I call you Ezekiel? Has Mr. Morrow come to take Briney home?"

"Home! Take me home? Away from here?" Brian's eyes flitted from one to the other, then behind him as to avoid an ambuscade.

Ezekiel answered evenly, "We came hopin' you'd go back with us, but nobody's goin' ta make you go if y'don't want."

"Pa's angry with me, and he'll yell for me to go home."

"I don't think so, Brian. He said he was proud of you for doin' what you thought was right."

"Pa said that!"

"And I told him it was about time."

Hannah had never seen Brian so animated and pleased.

"You two goin' ta water the horses now?"

On the next day, a Sunday, Henry and Ezekiel declined invitations to attend weekly meeting. Brian did go, not to attest his faith but because he felt safer with the Coopers. Clucking at the horse, Cyrus waved as did his passengers. All but one.

"That was nice of 'em, aksin' us ta go along."

"It was, 'Zekiel, it was. How does Brian seem t'you?"

"Can't surely say, Henry. He seemed all right takin' care of the horses. But I wouldn't rush things."

"Seems all right t'me, too. We'll leave t'morrow. It's a good time t'check the gear. The hubs were squeakin' pretty bad."

Busy inspecting hubs and tack, they were surprised when the Cooper's wagon rolled into the yard.

"Somethin's wrong, Henry. Look who's drivin'."

"I see. Why is Cyrus on the back bench with Brian?"

They ran to meet them, "What happened?"

"It's Brian!" Abigail Cooper answered as she brought the horse to a halt, "the meeting was over. He wouldn't leave his chair. He just sat, blank, staring, not saying a word."

Sitting on the high seat between Hannah and her father, Brian appeared not at all insensible, but wild and ready to run. His eyes flashed, feral, brilliant, and darting.

Jumping to the ground, Cyrus took charge, "Hannah, hold his arm; Abigail, steady the horses; Henry, catch the bridles."

Cyrus and Hannah led Brian onto the porch to one of the rocking chairs. Head down, he sat, mumbling incoherently, hunched over his canteen, rocking back and forth, back and forth.

"Briney," Hannah touched his hand, "it's all right."

Henry glowered, knowing for certain he had to get his son home. Morrows do not sit like beat dogs. A bit of firmness was all it would take, a strong hand to snap Brian out of this foolishness. He started up the steps.

Brian rocked faster as his father came nearer; a death-grip on his canteen raised veins and tendons from wrists to finger joints. Hannah had seen him upset but nothing like this, seething, smoking hot, a volcano ready to blow its plug. She squeezed his shoulder, knowing she should get him away and at the same time, that it was too late.

"Briney," she whispered, drawing closer.

Henry reached the top step, "Brian I want you t'get hold of yourself. I know you been through a bad time, but you need t'put it behind you, forget it. You can do it because you're a Morrow and the Morrows are strong. Strong enough t'do anything once they set their minds. You've had plenty of time t'get over this—this—whatever your problem is.

"The Coopers have been mighty kind, done more than their share. Now it's time t'leave and stop botherin' them. I want you t'be ready t'leave in the mornin'."

Brian uncoiled from his chair, pointing accusation at his father, into the sky, and around the porch. His voice spread over the others, low and menacing, then agitated, disappointed, screaming, whispering, and finally, an entreaty for forgiveness.

Waggling a finger and leering, Brian hissed, "I know you and what you're up to. I know what you're doing."

One by one he pointed to the devils that plagued him, his father first, "You," he spit out, "so angry with me for enlisting you hate me. You used to love me and now you don't. How can you be so angry and not hate me? You don't love me any more!

"And you," he pointed a crooked finger to the image only he saw, "Corporal Fiend who buggers helpless boys. You son of a bitch, I cracked your neck with my bare hands." His breath came shorter and quicker, as though he were climbing a steep hill.

"And you. I killed you, too, playing God in your fez and fancy uniform, shot your goddamn face off. And you who cut me first, I carved your putrid guts out of your belly," screaming, slashing, lunging with musket and blade no longer his, "twisting my bayonet in you, rifle butt to the side of your head. Blood ran that day, and pieces of brain. Dying. Wasted. Oh! My God!"

Brian stopped, puzzled as he reached the top of his hill and faced into a different world. He reached for the canteen at his side, looked at it lovingly, saw a smiling face in it. His voice came low and reverent.

"And you, Charley Nelson, my friend. You were bleeding and I carried you all night to find a doctor. I talked to you all the time, and you answered. My legs gave out and I needed to rest, and you died because I stopped to rest. I just stopped for a minute.

"Just for a minute. ONE GODDAMN MINUTE!"

"I screamed at the doctor, 'you killed him', and then I got all mixed up. You became God. I had killed God," Brian buried his face in sweaty hands, shrouding his words, "but you were Charley Nelson. my friend. I killed my friend."

Sobbing, Brian raked his face, drawing blood, let his hands fall limp. His voice unmuffled now, was clear, subdued, "I was so tired, Charlie, so tired."

"And just because I closed my eyes to rest you're dead."

He pleaded, "Charley, I only closed them for a minute."

He looked at his father, at Hannah and Ezekiel and the Coopers, not seeing any of them. He moaned and whispered.

"And someone else might die if I sleep again."

His moist eyes pleaded for forgiveness. His lips moved in a supplication of last resort, administering his own final unction.

"Charlie, I'm sorry, I'm—so sorry. I'm—, " His voice faded to a murmur, a whisper, to nothing.

His chin sagged to his chest. Raising the canteen to his face, he leaned into it lovingly, caressed it with his cheek.

He sank to the floor, on his knees, swaying slowly, murmuring, "My friend Charley Nelson, my friend."

Hannah dropped to her knees beside him, tears staining her face, "Oh, Brian. My dear, dear Brian. It will be all right. I love you, Brian. I want to be with you always." Abigail and Cyrus Cooper heard; Henry and Ezekiel heard.

Shocked at Brian's cursing, transfixed by the horrors in his head, surprised at Hannah's confession, they said not a word.

Abigail was the first to move, running to their children, kneeling protectively, offering sanctuary in her embrace.

Cyrus moved his lips silently, "Thy will be done. Help us to carry the burdens of this life. Protect thy children from evil."

Ezekiel looked to the sky, to speed Cyrus' prayer on its way perhaps. He, too, dropped to his knees. Unabashed, unblinking, he let his eyes fill and overflow.

Henry Morrow stared fixedly at a spot close to his shoes. The Brian he had known was gone forever.

One by one, the three men drifted away, Cyrus to his private place in the barn's high loft where he could smell the hay and reconcile the evil he had heard, Ezekiel to the stables to find relief in currying his horses, Henry toward the Elk River.

Along the river bank he sought but found none of the precise answers he was accustomed to, only the realization that the old ways were gone. As he had adjusted to new situations in his business, so must he adjust to those he held dear.

He found Ezekiel still with his horses. His voice was cheerless, "He's afraid of me, 'Zekiel, afraid of his own father. You saw him yesterday, afraid t'come close t'me. And you heard him today."

"Yes, Henry, he told me he was afraid you'd yell at him ta go home. But it's more'n that," Ezekiel stepped closer and touched Henry's arm compassionately, "it's more than that, my friend."

"It's my fault, no one else's. First Jed, and now Brian. You tried t'tell me about Jed. It's all my fault."

And Henry Morrow lost his composure, Henry Morrow who had proved himself in the competitive business world of Washington, who had walked the length and breadth of Virginia, looked into the future and built a substantial business in The Old Dominion's great valley; Henry Morrow who had raised his children with affection and concern and taught them his own values of honesty and morality, and then, in the turmoil of fratricidal war, failed to comprehend the success of his own teaching.

Ezekiel sorrowed for his friend's pain and guilt, "It's more than that, Henry. Brian is carryin' a bigger load than that."

"He's been hurt by the war, seen more than he was prepared ta see. He marched off ta save his world, and was told ta destroy it in order ta save it. He was told ta kill, when everythin' he'd been taught said it was wrong ta kill.

"Brian woke up screamin' in the night, Henry, Jed told me that. Screamin' he'd shot a man's face off. Brian told me himself, how sad he was ta see the bridges burnin' and how he'd killed Charley Nelson.

"You have ta talk ta him, Henry. Make it up with him. And then you and I can go home."

The following morning, Henry came into the kitchen as Brian and Hannah were finishing their breakfast. Hannah glanced at him anxiously. Brian continued eating as though yesterday's rage had never taken place.

Henry's eyes were red and puffy from lack of sleep. He spoke with reserve and very softly, "Brian, you and I have t'talk."

Brian continued eating, "I'm not leaving here."

"It's not that, Brian, not that at all. I'll be on the front porch when you've finished your breakfast. And Hannah, would you give us a little time alone—please."

A few minutes later Brian joined him, apprehensive lest Henry overwhelm him. He repeated, "I'm not leaving."

"I know that, son," Henry's voice was close to tears, "I asked you for a few minutes t'tell you a secret Ezekiel and I have kept for years."

"Secret? What secret, Pa?"

"You will be the only other person to know what I am about to tell you, not even your Ma. Just Ezekiel, you and me. I trust you, Brian, to keep our secret as we have."

Expecting loud arguments to return home, Brian was taken entirely by surprise, aware that he was seeing a side of his father he had never known.

He reached to touch Henry's arm. He let his hand linger as he spoke with warmth, "Pa, of course you can trust me."

"It was just before the war started. Bein' at that Washin'ton College, you never knew that Ezekiel and I made a trip t'Moorefield t'buy horses and a coach. Well, son, on the way we came on a bootlegger and his son with a broken wagon wheel. They took our offer of help for a sign of weakness. T'make the story short, they started a ruckus and I killed him."

"Pa! You Killed Him?!" Brian's eyes were wide with wonder.

Henry avoided his son's stare, "With your grandfather's derringer. I have thought of that man every day, Brian. It was not an act I'm proud of."

"But it wasn't your fault, Pa. You said he started the fight"

"So he did, son. I was fightin' for my life, and that's important. The law says you can protect yourself, but somehow that doesn't make it right. Especially in the middle of the night when I wake up and see him again, all bloody, falling in the dirt." Henry finished with a whisper, 'How many times do I have t'kill him?"

Brian moved close offering both hands for comfort. Henry took them. And they were silent, sharing their trials, their sins.

"Pa, I'm glad you told me."

"Thank you for listenin', son. We have much pain t' share, you and I. I hope you find peace."

"And you too, Pa."

They sat many minutes without words, father and son holding hands, eyes misting and overflowing. After a while, Henry spoke.

"Ma and I would like you t'come home, we want you t'know that. But I realize, it's not the right thing, not yet. It's not the right time."

Still affected by the story, Brian spoke quietly and seriously as Henry remembered him, "The right time? The right thing? What's that mean, Pa? I thought I was doing the right thing when I signed the company roll, and it was all wrong."

Henry laid a hand on his shoulder, "Things may have gone off the track, Brian, but you didn't do wrong. You did what you had t'do. Your Ma made me see that before I left Winchester. She saw it all along, and she is very proud of you for that. You and I both, we did what we had to do."

He looked directly at Brian, "Somehow I missed it. I was so furious with this war, that I missed it with both you and Jed. And I missed it with David, too, faultin' him for leavin' the Academy. All of you were doin' what you thought was right, what you had to. Nobody can ask more than that, Brian. I didn't begin to see it until your Ma told me how proud she is. And then I didn't see it completely."

Henry hesitated before going on, "And I'm proud of you, too. I've never been prouder of anythin' in my life—son."

Henry Morrow's eyes welled as he stood dignified in his confession, unashamed of his tears, satisfied and at peace. Brian smiled, too, recognizing the love in his father's words and the love in his tears.

Relieved at last of the anguish he had caused his father, he reached his arms and hugged him tight, a little boy again, without nightmares, without war, only happiness and warmth and safety in his father's arms. He clung to this man he loved so much. And Henry clung to him.

Brian's words were muffled, "I can't come home yet, Pa. Not now. Maybe someday soon."

Henry whispered in his anguish, "I know, son. It's for you t'decide. Whenever it is, your ma and I will be there for you." In the barn, Ezekiel climbed aboard the wagon. He snapped the reins and steered from the shadows into the sunshine. Son and father must have heard, but they ignored the creaks and rattles that meant departure and separation.

They remained locked in each others' arms, father and son together.

"Ready ta go, Henry." Ezekiel jumped from the wagon to bid farewell to the Coopers and to the boy he had helped raise, "Brian, Mattie and me'll be waitin' and OleHounddawg, too. Everythin's gonna be fine."

"I know it will be, Zeke. After you leave, tell Pa I love him. And Ma when you get home. And Mattie and Mam. Tell Mattie I plan to eat a bushel of her biscuits."

Their handshake became a teary embrace, "I love you, too, Zeke."

The Coopers' farewells were most gracious: Cyrus, "God go with thee, Henry, Ezekiel"; Abigail, "Visit us again, anytime. Don't fret. Brian will be fine"; and from Hannah a loaf of bread, "To eat on the way. Brian and I made it special."

At the last minute, Brian yelled, "Pa."

Brian walked to the wagon, his head high and his shoulders back. His voice had a new ring of confidence and joy, "I would like you and Ma to have this."

He handed up the canteen he had rescued from the red mud of Blackburn's Ford and the stream named Bull Run. He had carried it through the war, through prison camp in the middle of Delaware Bay, through his escape and his sojourns with Doctor Ruggles and the Coopers. It had served him well. It was time to send it home, and perhaps some day find the Yankee soldier who had lost it.

The visit had started badly, but Brian's load had been eased. By the love of family, by the love of the Coopers, or by the love of God? Who knows? The answer lies in each of us.

Ezekiel clucked. He and Henry turned to wave as they topped the small rise that led into Frenchtown. Brian answered in turn as did the Coopers. The wagon disappeared and Brian turned to Hannah.

Joyously, he lifted her in his arms, and danced through the neat yard in the sunshine. He twirled her around and around until her simple bonnet went sailing in the wind, and her pinned hair fell free about her shoulders. He danced her to the verandah and half way to the barn, then back again, Cyrus and Abigail Cooper watching with surprise and happiness.

"He's never been so happy since he came to us, Abigail. God be praised."

"Yes, my husband, thanks be to God," Abigail moved closer taking his hand in hers.

Brian twirled Hannah close enough for all to hear, "And thanks be to you-all, too. And to Pa and Ma and Ezekiel. And to Jed and Betsy and Racey and Tom and Sean Murphy and Doctor Ruggles and—"

Throwing his head back, he laughed raucously to the heavens, and shouted with abandon, "And to everybody. Thanks be to everybody. I love you all.

He touched Hannah's cheek tenderly, moved close to look into her eyes, "Hannah Cooper, my special thanks to you. I will love you always.'

L

A BATTLE, A FIGHT

Unbeknownst to its citizens, the sleepy college town of Gettysburg, Pennsylvania was in for a disturbance. No one knew any more than they, including the commanding generals both North and South, for the battle was a quirk of war, capricious and contumacious, neither planned nor anticipated.

During the afternoon of June 12, David Morrow led his two squadrons from Front Royal to Winchester and the upper Potomac. Jeb Stuart had detailed him to Ewell's Second Corps, "as far as Winchester, no further" he told both David and General Ewell.

He also told Ewell, commanding Second Corps, "He's alert and capable, and knows the ground, a good man to have up ahead."

General Ewell had assigned David commander of his forward screen, made up of Marylanders and a Company from the 14th Virginia. Outranking the units' own officers, David was received with reluctant deference. He quickly won them over.

Milroy's Union army had occupied Winchester since January, destroying buildings, arresting citizens and denying them food and firewood for refusing to sign oaths of allegiance.

The Morrows still mourned the death of Stonewall Jackson, Gracey shedding copious tears for the man who had called her "Miss Grace" at the dinner table, acknowledging her questions with courtesy and tenderness. She would never forget him.

In the growing darkness, David ran onto Federal cavalry and drove them back. He gathered his officers, "Let's call it a day, gentlemen. Major, you're in command. I'll be back before dawn." He yearned for Carrie, but she was far away.

He rode cross-lots to avoid pickets, through familiar country west of town, not far from where Brian had fought with Willie Schroeder. Slipping along the stream to the Morrows', he stabled his big stallion. Stealthily, he stole to the back door and crossed to the hallway lighted faintly from the sitting room. He heard the murmur of voices. A board creaked under him. "Anybody out there?" Henry challenged.

"Nobody but me." He stepped into the cozy room.

They rushed to him, Sarah, Ruth, and Gracey, burying him in embraces. Wrapping all three in his arms, he twisted a hand to Henry. He had impressions of Jed's pushing from his chair, Betsy beside him holding a small bundle, and a figure on the fringes.

"Welcome home, David." The world's most beautiful words.

Jed saw the double stars on his collar, "We've got a colonel in the family. He'll be general before the war's over."

"Just lucky, Jed, the right place at the right time."

"Not as lucky as me," he moved closer to Betsy.

Betsy remembered their other meetings, in Falls Church and here in this house. She flirted outrageously, "Don't I get a kiss from the colonel?"

David laughed, "Of course, now that I know how pretty you are. Don't tell me I'm an uncle again."

Betsy held her bundle for David to take. He hesitated.

"Take her. She won't break."

Very carefully, he settled the baby in one arm and slipped the crocheted blanket from her face. She remained fast asleep.

Marvelling at the tiny fingers curled at her chin, David whispered solemnly, "She's beautiful. What's her name?"

"Sarah Elizabeth."

"You two are so lucky." Betsy wondered at the wistful tone.

Jed broke in with a chuckle, "As you said, David, some of us are in the right place at the right time."

"Jedediah Morrow!" Sarah reprimanded mildly.

Ruth had a surprise, "You remember Matthew, don't you?"

David started at the sight of a blue uniform.

"Captain Garland. He's had a promotion, too."

David's mind reeled and settled down, "Of course. Taylor's tavern. Fairfax Bourbon. Matt Garland! What are you doing here?"

"Courting your sister," the two officers shook hands warmly.

David recalled his straightforward manner at Taylor's.

"Courting Ruth?"

Sliding closer, Ruth took Matt's arm affectionately.

"Yes, she has accepted, but Mr. Morrow has objections."

"I can see why. My God, Matt, it makes everyone suspect."

Happy with David's agreement, Henry interrupted, "Not objections t'you, Matthew, but t'the circumstances. Without this war, I'd be the first one t'give my blessin'."

Henry paused. He liked Matt Garland and could see a good match for Ruth, but his family had been hurt by Bluecoats, "I've got two sons hurt by Yankees, and you wear the uniform. Besides, we'd all be suspected of aidin' and abettin' the enemy."

"I'm sorry for your sons, Mr. Morrow, but there's nothing I can do about that. As for aiding and abetting, I've lived with that for six months."

"Six months! You've been arguing this for six months."

"My regiment has been in and out of Winchester since January. I always remembered Ruth. And you." Matt grinned.

"Early on, I knew Ruth was for me, just as I felt you and I could be friends, David. The way she fired up at my uniform, and the way you reacted to Sergeant Folsom."

"I hope he's not here in Winchester," David spit the words.

"I'm afraid he is, my friend. So far, he's behaved himself."

Matt Garland was the first to see the fierce hatred in David's face. The snarl revealed it to the others.

"I should have killed the wretched bastard."

Nothing in the conversation had prepared them for the shock of a David they had never before seen. Never, ever had they felt such icy, cold-blooded hatred. Betsy held the baby closer, and the other women shivered at the taut fury in his voice.

"Easy, my friend," Matt spoke softly, "after tomorrow you will be able to sleep easier. Our army will be gone."

They turned to him in surprise.

"You've all heard the rumors. Lee's army has crossed the Blue Ridge. David's part of the vanguard."

Matt Garland lowered his voice, "I could be shot for this, but I am shamed by the incident at the tavern. Units have been ordered to fall back to Main Fort, north of town. Others are ordered to Star Fort, beyond that. That means we're leaving.

"Folsom will be gone, David, beyond any mischief here."

"He's capable of more than mischief," David growled.

"Who is this Folsom?" Jed asked aggressively.

"An evil man, an animal."

"He better stay away from here," Jed scowled.

"David is right," Matt agreed, "I apologize for talking of him. I wanted to put you at ease, knowing he'd be gone. Now I'd better leave so you can enjoy your reunion."

Matt Garland said his good-byes to each in turn, with special messages for Henry and David.

"Mr. Morrow, I feel much as you do about this war. I will be back to marry Ruth, I hope with your approval, sir."

"David, seeing you was certainly a surprise, a very pleasant one for me. Good luck."

Preoccupied with the shadow of Sedge Folsom, David said nothing, but grasped Matt's outstretched hand warmly.

"Jed, Betsy, Mrs. Morrow. God be with you."

"I'll come to the door with you, Matt." Ruth grasped his arm and they left the room. The others heard the front door close.

"Ruth, I'm sorry your father feels as he does. I would have liked you to wait for me as Mrs. Garland."

Ruth stepped close, "I wanted that too, Matt."

She lifted her hands to his chest for a moment and snaked them around his neck. She felt his arms about her waist, urging her closer. Curling into him, she lifted her chin for the kiss that could be their last. Forever, forever, rang in her head. Passion erupted, passion and panic.

Ruth clutched at him, trembling, "Don't go, Matt. Hold me." She kissed him desperately, eyes, face and mouth, whispering frantically, "I want you, Matt. Stay with me. I need you."

He held her, trying to calm her, trying to calm himself. He had better leave now. If he didn't—.

"I'm afraid, Matt."

Tilting her head, he looked into glistening eyes, "Don't be, sweeting. Nothing can keep us apart."

"I want you so much."

"And I want you, sweetheart. I will be back."

Matt Garland galloped wildly down Wolfe Street, lashing his mount as if beating the whole stinking war.

Ruth remained on the verandah, alone with a promise. "Come back, Matthew. Please, God, let him come back."

Meanwhile in the sitting room, David was taken with his little niece, "You got yourself a beautiful baby, Betsy."

Jed touched his daughter lightly, wearing his pride as a new hat, "Isn't she somethin'! Picture pretty, like her mother."

"Carrie would love her."

Betsy saw through him at once, "You sound serious."

Henry asked bluntly, "Carrie! Who's she?"

"A girl I met in Richmond."

Betsy looked up skeptically, "The colonel is being coy."

David laughed, "You were already taken so I married Carrie."

"Married!"

"When?"

"How'd you meet her?" Henry asked pragmatically.

David knew from Pa's tone what he was really asking.

"The Exchange Hotel, Pa. Her brother was shot and she came to Richmond to nurse him. Carrie Nash she was then," he went on quickly, "we had an Episcopal service. You'll love her."

Not interested in the least, Baby Sarah Elizabeth squalled her hungry cry, and Betsy left to accommodate her. Jed followed.

Alone with the elder Morrows, David had his first opportunity to talk seriously, "Pa, Ma, I feel bad you couldn't be at the wedding but there just wasn't time."

Sarah responded quickly, "We understand. Don't we, Henry?"

"I guess so, Sarah," he answered diffidently, "God knows I'm tryin' t'understand all that's happenin' t'my family."

Anxious to finish before they were interrupted, David rushed on, "I've told Carrie that she should come to you if she needs to. She has no one else to turn to."

"Certainly, David. She should consider this her home. We all have to make emergency plans and pray we never need them."

"Of course," Henry added, "The same as with Betsy. Tell her this is home and we're her family."

"Thank you both. Maybe she wouldn't want to leave Richmond, but I have to know she has someone to turn to.

"She has a position in the War Department. Colonel Boteler put in a good word."

"Alex recommended her?"

"That's right, Pa. And says she's doing a fine job."

"Hmmmm." Henry respected Alex Boteler and his opinion. Like her. She's like Betsy, holding her own with folks. And a worker, too, asking no favors of anyone."

"I'll have to admit to some surprise, David. Mothers always like to think they know more of their children than they do."

"Ma,—

"Mind you, I'm not complaining. Just saying how it is with mothers. Now the war makes it worse. It's difficult, David."

"I know, Ma. It separates all of us from those we love."

Just inside the front door, Ruth dabbed the last of her tears and returned to the sitting room, "I'd best be getting home. The children are probably pestering the life out of Mam."

"I'll walk with you," David offered.

Only a few steps from the house, David put his hand on Ruth's arm, "Shhhh. Keep walking." He glanced quickly behind them as they turned the corner onto Washington Street.

At the front door, he gave her a brotherly kiss on the cheek, "Good night, Sis. Lock your door."

He ran up Washington Street, disappearing into the shadows of the corner house. A moment later he emerged across the street from Ruth's, shrouded in darkness. A sliver of light widened as her front door swung open; Mam bustled out and scurried for home. David stood immobile, invisible, watchful as the night stars revolved around Polaris.

For an hour he watched, and more as clouds covered the North Star, bringing wind and rain and lightning. David kept his vigil, huddled against the driving storm, circling Ruth's at intervals, checking doors, windows, nooks and crannies. His thoughts wandered to Carrie, warm and soft in her bed.

A shadow crossed the street at the corner, stopped at Ruth's gate, studying the house. Easing a Colt from its holster, David slipped silently toward it.

"Hands in the air, you bastard."

Henry Morrow nearly choked, "What in tarnation?"

"Pa! What are you doing here?"

"Damnit! You said you'd be right back. It's after midnight."

David told of the suspicious noises, "So I stayed."

"Anythin' t'do with this sergeant of Matthew's?"

"Everything. He's a vile man, a worse reputation. I had trouble with him. I wish I had killed him. "

"Reputation? What kind of reputation?"

"Not nice, Pa."

"I gathered that. Women and drinkin', I suppose."

"Yes, Pa, women that refuse him and make him angry He's bragged openly about hurting them. And young boys."

"My God!"

"He's mean, Pa. It's not only Ruth, but Ma and Gracey and Betsy, even Mam, anybody!"

"Damn Yankee pigs!"

"Pa, it's not only Yankees. Every army has its share."

"Hard t'think of our people bein' like that. Y'hear the talk, but never quite believe it's true."

"Believe it, Pa. Believe it."

Father and son stood in the rain, silent in their disgust.

"Pa, there are good Yankees, too."

"I know."

"Matt Garland is one of them. He loathes Folsom, every bit as much as I do. Don't separate him and Ruth, Pa."

Henry looked at him sharply, resentful of being given an order by his son, colonel or no colonel.

"He's educated and from what I've seen, considerate and kind. He surely is taken with Ruth."

Henry remained quiet. Accepting a Yankee into his family?

"And Ruth seems taken with him, Pa."

"Maybe."

David had no idea what his father meant.

"Ruth's lights went off an hour ago. Everything's quiet."

"Seems so."

Lightning flashed and its thunder continued to rattle Winchester. Wild winds lashed the rain into sheets. ". . . the artillery of heaven shook the earth" a Yankee wrote home.

"Folsom won't stay in this."

David and Henry circled the house one last time. Sopping wet, they felt it safe to go home.

At 4:30 the following morning, deep-throated cannons boomed reveille for Winchester. Within 1,000 yards of the Morrow house, Confederate guns fired and advanced, softening Bower's Hill for an assault. By 9 A.M. the Confederates held the hill and David rode to the crest with generals of Second Corps. He overlooked the Yankee-held forts Matt Garland had spoken of.

To the east, he could see a bit of Wolfe Street, but foliage blocked the house; north and west, the road to Romney, and beyond, the two forts and trenches. Union soldiers improved earthworks guarding their western approaches. Farther out was Little North Mountain commanding the Union positions.

David read their minds, "I can lead a column up that mountain. I grew up right over there." He pointed vaguely.

He was ready for the generals' questions.

"Five miles, sir, maybe six, allowing for the zigs and zags.

"Yes, sir, concealed all the way to that area they've cleared," pointing again, "could be on them before they knew it.

"Artillery? Maybe need prolonges up the worst slopes, but nothing we haven't done before."

"I'd allow six hours, sir."

His last answer brought an explosion, "Six hours! We could attack from here in one."

"Just what they expect," Ewell objected, "we'd pay dearly."

"Excepting the first mile, sir, it's cross-country, through woods, mostly uphill."

Experience had taught him generals barked at subordinates who offered details they could see for themselves; it reflected on their reputation. Stick to facts they couldn't be expected to know. The generals looked wise. Ewell nodded, "Go."

The sun was descending when David looked from his copse of trees onto the westernmost fort. Just as he had said, he was above it, looking down on the sweaty shovellers. Under orders to remain quiet, the lead elements rested in the woods. Within two hours all units were up and deployed.

Field guns rolled into the open, twenty of them. They opened fire. Surprised at first, the Yankees recovered, manhandling their own guns into position.

For forty-five minutes the artillerists duelled. The assault brigade advanced from its protective cover, maintaining an acceptable line through a tangled abatis of brushwood, climbing the steep slope of the defenses. They drove the Yankees from their unfinished earthworks and stood down until morning.

Riding for home in the dark, David rode within shouting distance of Main Fort and its southern trenchline, hugging the base of the hill. One mile, instead of the roundabout route of the morning, took him to Bower's Hill and home.

"Where's Ruth? Isn't she here?"

"Didn't expect t'see you again so soon, David."

"Where's Ruth?" more urgently.

"She decided it was safer t'stay home with all the gunfire."

"Pa, have you seen her today?"

"Just before dark. Mam has been with her most of the day. She came back half an hour ago with the two children. She said Ruth would be over as soon as she put a few things t'gether.

"You worried about the noises you heard last night?"

"I sure am. She shouldn't be alone."

Sarah joined them, "David, this is wonderful, seeing you two days running. Were you in the fighting?"

"It didn't amount to much."

"Well! It was too close for me. Have you had supper?"

Henry broke in, "Want me t'go with you?"

"No, Pa I'll be all right."

Sarah touched his arm, "Go where? You just got here."

"To Ruth's, Ma. I'll bring her back with me."

Tensely, he checked the grounds as he had before. Everything was as it should be, until he came to the back door. It was ajar. He stepped lightly over the threshold. Not a lamp showed.

He made his way through the first floor rooms. At the bottom of the staircase a floorboard creaked. He froze, drawing his captured Colt from its holster.

Hearing nothing, he started up, slowly, one step at a time, back to the wall where the stairs were tightest. Half way up he heard in quick order a muffled mewling and unmistakably the hard slap of a hand on bare flesh, seconds later the strident rasp of tearing material. A harsh, familiar voice chilled the air.

"Shut up, bitch. You can fuck Garland you can fuck me."

No time for stealth now. And no need.

David burst into the room as the large figure sprang from the bed, nothing more than a shadow in the dark.

David roared, "Folsom, you goddamned animal."

He fired the Colt.

"Yowww," the shot drew blood.

Its flash illuminated the Yankee sergeant for a snap second, freezing him in a picture of palpable evil: black hair, narrow forehead, close, deep-set eyes, splayed nose and rotten teeth; rounded, sinister shoulders and ape-like stoop. Blood was on his face from parallel scratches down his forehead and cheek. His animal stink saturated the room.

Folsom crouched low and charged.

David fired a second shot as Folsom hit the revolver sending it flying. They grabbed and grappled in the dark.

Folsom came up hard butting David under the chin, snapping his head toward oblivion. A punishing knee to the groin put Folsom on the floor, grabbing himself, doubled over in agony.

David's brain went limp, leaving him drifting, sliding into a void, comfortable, and tranquil.

Folsom writhed on the floor, momentarily incapacitated.

"David!" Ruth's scream stunned him back.

He shook his head to ward off the abyss. Not a moment too soon, for Folsom, too, had recovered enough to get to his knees, a beast trapped in its cave. He ran at David, long arms poised to grab. David moved inside, pummeling with both fists. Folsom took the blows and came down on him with a bear hug that locked tight.

Gradually, Folsom squeezed. David smashed him against the wall time and again. He couldn't break out. His hands were tied helpless against his sides. His breath came harder. Folsom was literally squeezing the life out of him. He kicked and thrashed. Folsom leered close to David's face, displaying black, decayed teeth and foul breath. He couldn't resist a moment to gloat.

"I swore I'd kill ya, ya rebel sonabitch. An' yer sister's gonna watch. Too bad you won't see how a real man fucks." His ugly laugh rattled phlegm in his throat.

David felt the slight relaxation as Folsom laughed, a small unintended gift at the last minute. He turned slightly, enough to raise a heavy boot. The heel slammed onto Folsom's instep. It broke the death hold. Folsom yelled again.

They grappled, overturning a chair, stumbling through the doorway, Folsom attacking again and again to regain his lethal bear hug, David warding off each attack, sparring, weaving, feinting to set up the bigger man for jabs and crosses. David hoped he could wear him down. Already his opponent was mouth-breathing heavily. They struggled across the upper hallway, crashing into a highboy, wrecking a horsehair loveseat. They fought to the edge of the stairs and back.

Ruth lay on the bed, on top of her dress and underthings torn from her body. She hurt in so many places, head, face, breasts, wrists, legs. She struggled with obscure obscenities.

She remembered calloused hands, squeezing and twisting until she screamed. She felt the burn on her wrists and felt again the rough hands pinning her helpless to the bed, vile breath in her face, hard boots forcing her legs apart.

She had bit and scratched and fought while the hands controlled her, exploring, ravaging. She collapsed and the hands moved to the neck of her dress, gathering in its material. A yank snatched it from her body and ripped away underthings, leaving her cold and naked with hard boots gouging her legs, forcing them wider. A shout and an explosion rocked the room.

David's voice! David had shouted! The need to be doing something struck her. She struggled to focus on it.

Of course! David was there. He had come to save her.

Ponderous and powerless in her state of trauma, she fought in sheer desperation, struggling to move arms and legs. She must help David. In the dark, she crawled from the bed and along the floor to the armoire, her arms feeling in front of her like the geniculated antennae of a giant insect.

The duelling pistols were in the armoire, the pair she and Betsy had carried to Henry Hill and Sudley Church. Pa's words rang in her head: get close enough so's you can't miss.

In the hall, David and Folsom circled warily looking for an opening, one lithe and quick, the other, brutishly strong. David knew he was no match physically, that his fight was to out-think this monster, spar, frustrate him, tire him.

Folsom came at him. David sidestepped and whirled, pushing him as he went by. Folsom crashed into the wall. He turned and snarled. Glowering, he reached to his boot top for the old Bowie knife ground to half its original size. He crouched, breathing heavy and foul, snorting against the blood that plugged his nose. He held the knife at arm's length, low, level to his knee.

Lowering an arm to protect himself, David waited for the onslaught, knees flexed, weight forward on the balls of his feet.

They glared across the hall, Folsom a taunting grimace that David had seen before, a battlefield skull laid bare by rain.

The brute charged, slashing upward, cutting into sleeve and forearm. David caught the wrist with both hands and swung the arm pendulum-like, one way and suddenly the other, twisting and lifting it hard against Folsom's back. The knife dropped. David jerked upward. A pop and a crack told him what he needed to know. The arm dropped limply. Folsom yowled in pain.

David backpedaled, his lungs heaving. Folsom turned slowly. Eyes red and flaming, the beast cornered, wounded with no escape. One arm dangled uselessly. He took a step toward David, and another, and a third, swaying side to side. David waited.

At the last moment, he sideslipped around the worthless arm. Hurt though he was, Folsom was still dangerous.

They turned again toward each other, two professionals in mortal combat. For the first time in his life, one of them was fighting with malice in his heart, fighting to administer condign retribution, to kill an enemy he abhorred. Never had he wanted to hurt another human, torture and kill slow to suffer as his victims had suffered. David was losing himself in hatred.

He realized it and sensed danger. He could afford no more mistakes, no emotion, not even hatred for this brute, nothing but cold calculation, speed and vigilance. He warned himself, unaware he was talking aloud.

"Stay alert. You've got him. Don't lose it. Think. Think."

"Talkin' ta yerself, sojer boy. Come on," he waggled his good hand enticingly, "come an' git it. What's the matter? The little man's scared? Scared shitless of a man wi' one arm.

"Fuckin' officers, no fuckin' good fur nothin'. How about it," and here he sneered, "colonel. Come an' git it."

He leered the grimace as the unearthed skull, taunting, "like yer sister said ta me, 'come an git it'."

His fingers danced again, slowly, beckoning, inviting.

David's hands twitched, too, with the tension and pressure of restraining himself. He brushed blood from his face, and suddenly saw victory in Folsom's own tactics.

"Folsom, you're a mockery to the service. No army in the world would have you, save Black Abe's. You're a coward, afraid to face the truth. You're a coward on the battlefield, afraid to fight, afraid to face us Southerners, afraid of all of us. Except the women and boys too small to refuse you."

David talked louder, "Sergeant Folsom, the great soldier who's not afraid of any woman on this earth—or any boy. Big hero! They're listening to me, sergeant. Your whole regiment's listening and shaking their heads. You're a yellow-dog coward, and your regiment's agreeing with me. Coward! Coward! Coward! I can hear them. Listen," David cocked his head as though listening, "listen. You'll hear them, too." He continued in a low whisper, "Coward! Coward! Coward."

Enraged, the brute took the challenge and charged once more. Straight on he came. The staircase behind him, David side-stepped again, but Folsom grabbed as he went by, and they crashed to the landing, through the railing.

They landed in a heap, face to face, Folsom's good hand searching for David's throat. Heavier, he rolled to his back, carrying David with him, and kept rolling until he was on top, smothering, overwhelming, just what David had fought to avoid. He thrashed to break out, kicking, squirming, flailing, gaining enough to grab a handful of thick hair. He forced Folsom's head back. His other hand found Folsom's face and eyes. The ignoble sergeant twisted and beat indiscriminately with his single fist, kicking wildly, snapping as a mad dog. David held on, for his very life. Folsom's efforts slackened as he tired, and then resurged, driven now by sheer panic. David strained against him, forcing the hated head back, bit by bit.

He found an eye socket and gouged with a thumb. Folsom jerked.

David felt the soft ball, felt its resistance for the briefest part of a moment as it flattened and came loose. Like a grape quashed from its skin, the eyeball popped out and dropped to the floor. With a yowl, Folsom grabbed his face and collapsed on the floor, spent and broken.

David stood over him, chest heaving as he gulped air between words, "Now you sonofabitch, SUFFER."

Blood stained him and his clothes, Folsom's and his own, drying and darkening, mixed together, not distinguishable save for that on David's thumb and hand. It stood out from the rest, still red and shiny, not dry at all.

Behind him, Ruth descended the stairs silently. Wrapped loosely in a thin blanket that had slipped from one shoulder, she carried the duelling pistols, one in each hand.

"No, Ruth, don't," he shouted, "let the bastard die slow."

"Close enough so you can't miss," she was saying as she leaned over Sedge Folsom, exposing a breast round and full.

With his good eye, Folsom stared at it closing in on him. Reaching for it with his good arm, he babbled, pleaded, "Closer. Closer."

And then it was gone, lost in the explosion and smoke of black powder.

LI

FAILURE
JULY 3, 1863

Once again, Winchester celebrated the departure of a Yankee army. Hearty shoulder slaps and handshakes were the order of the day, broad smiles and joyous imbibing. Even as they reclaimed the streets and taverns for their own, muffled battle noises drifted in from the northeast. "Near Stephenson's," they said.

Worn from his own combat, David lay in his bed at home. Dim visions crashed in and out, a gap-toothed leer, a shout to Ruth.

Firing the little pistols, she had stared at Folsom, mesmerized by revulsion and exhaustion; her stomach heaved sour and she vomited onto his marred face. David drew the blanket about her, and held her close until the violent trembling eased.

He had hauled Folsom's body through the night with neither respect nor ceremony, dragging it by one leg as a rabid dog, through mud and over rocks. He dumped it beyond Bower's Hill, an apparent casualty of yesterday's fight. He spat his disgust. David squirmed restlessly, moaning and dreaming of purple grapes pinched from their skins. A great pressure hit his chest and he wakened with a shout.

A gentle hand reassured him. Carrie.

"You're finally awake?" The voice could only be Carrie's, soft and sweet. He reached for her, indistinct against the light. He reached for Carrie, and saw Betsy.

Not fully awake, embarrassed, he apologized weakly, "I thought you were someone else."

Betsy put the breakfast tray on the table, "Carrie?"

"How did you know?" He mumbled sleepily.

"You mentioned her the other evening. As a matter of fact, you announced you had married her."

He sat up gingerly, "Before I met her I never thought of dying. And last night I was that close," holding a thumb and forefinger slightly apart, "my God, I ache."

"No wonder! You stumbled in last night hardly able to stand. Ruth told us of that horrible man."

He spoke even more softly, "Never to see Carrie again. No baby like you and Jed." He sank back on the pillows.

"It must have been a terrible." Betsy watched the rise and fall of his chest. Breakfast would have to wait.

She watched him for several minutes, tears misting her eyes, empathetic tears not only for him but for a Carrie in Richmond waiting for her husband, never knowing, never knowing.

While he slept, more hours in two days than in some weeks he could remember, news came that Second Corps was crossing the Potomac. David's temporary duty with Ewell was finished.

He felt he should return to his command, but everyone prevailed on him to wait. "Don't rush it," they said.

Jed had advice, too, "Enjoy it while y'can, big brother." Being home was a tonic, from the yeasty redolence of warm bread to Gracey's new seriousness. Jed and Betsy's talk of moving to the farm touched a chord, their homely chatter a warm blanket.

With Pa, he talked family, Ma's health, Brian and the trip to Frenchtown. They groomed Sable. "He looks good, son."

"He's charmed, Pa," rapping on the wooden stall, "nothing more than scratches. It's sad the blooded horses killed."

"All that time and care wasted."

"Pa, I should leave Sable home. Get another mount."

"Oh no, I didn't mean it that way. You want the best horse you can find. Your life might depend on him one day."

"I'd hate it if anything happened to him."

"So would I, son. Just do the best you can."

"I'd like to buy him. I know business is not good."

"We're fine. You need your money. Now that you're married!"

"I have a balance with the paymaster. And Carrie won't take any from me. Fact is, she's saving to repay a loan I made her."

"A wife payin' back a loan!"

"She insisted. When I said it wasn't due until the war was over, she said, 'That gives me time to save it for you'."

Henry thought that over, "Sounds like you found a wife with a lot of gumption, son. You make me anxious t'meet her."

"You'll love her, Pa."

They sat in comfortable silence.

"Seems like Brian's just where he belongs, Pa, with people who love him, and work to do as he feels up to it, no more war. One day he'll be coming home."

"I hope so. Be nice t'have him home again. And you. Maybe you oughta go in. Spend some time with your ma."

"I've enjoyed our time alone, Pa."

With Sarah, David expressed concern for her health and was reassured. He listened to stories of her "hospital," and Gracey's penchant for nursing. "She would make a fine doctor, David, Maybe after the war—" Sarah let the future hang.

He listened to Ruth bubble about Matt Garland, a gentleman, cultured, knowledgeable, handsome. She would go to Massachusetts if he wanted. How she could be so cheery after Folsom's attack, he puzzled. Maybe that was her way of handling it.

"He's a fine man, Ruth."

She was indeed covering up, "Thank you for being there." "Sooner would have been better. I'm sorry I wasn't sooner."

"I'll never forget what you did. Pa told me how you stood guard in the storm."

"He was with me most of the time."

She reached for his hand, "You risked your life for me."

His voice turned low and pensive, for he had thought much on life and death and Carrie, "Maybe God has been with me, too."

The next day, he dawdled over breakfast, wanting to stay, needing to leave; so little time left, not enough to say what was in his heart, too much for comfort.

Pa took his hand, "I filled a sack with oats for Sable."

Sarah had the last word, "God protect you, son."

Hugs, kisses, a cadet salute. What is meant to be will be.

He rode south, past the old Indian springs, and east through Ashby's Gap in the Blue Ridge as the sun dipped low. Beyond Upperville he learned that Jeb Stuart was just down the road. Ten minutes later, Stuart greeted him with enthusiasm.

"How was Winchester? I thought you'd enjoy a visit."

"You sent me there for that? To visit my family?"

Jeb Stuart's eyes twinkled, "That and other things. You did find some action with Dick Ewell I hear."

"Yes sir, I did."

"Heard you led a few men around their flank," Stuart enjoyed his own understatement.

"A few, sir," David knew his general. "I would have been back yesterday but—"

"Ewell crossed the river yesterday. I looked for you then."

"I would have been, but a personal matter needed attention." He glanced at his bandaged arm.

'Matters that needed attention' were commonplace. Stuart charged ahead to the business at hand.

"You're just in time. Yesterday, Hooker moved north toward Washington. Looks like he finally suspects something. He sent Kilpatrick's cavalry to break into the Valley, but Rosser and Munford stopped him just down the road at Aldie.

"Have that arm dressed."

"Yes, sir. And, general—"

"Yes?"

"Thank you for the time at home. You'll never know how important it was for me to be there."

"Glad you made good use of it, colonel. As I said, your return was timely. Another ten minutes and I'd have had the provost marshal after you," his laughter rang.

David was indeed just in time, for the scrap at Aldie started a week of cavalry actions for the mountain gaps, Federals trying to force through, Confederates fighting to maintain their screen. Horsemen tangled daily at Middleburg, Aldie, Upperville, Haymarket, Thoroughfare Gap, and Dover Mills.

The Army of Northern Virginia stretched a hundred miles as the crow flies, Ewell's Second Corps in Pennsylvania, Stuart's horsemen in Virginia, First and Third Corps in the Shenandoah Valley, ready to cross the Potomac. Hooker's army was east of the Blue Ridge, tents and campfires stretching 20 miles.

In a blue uniform, David scouted Hooker's army for a full week, gliding inconspicuously from camp to camp, listening and observing. He reported gaps between divisions and corps, "Large enough to take a cavalry column through, general."

Stuart looked up sharply, for he had been toying with that very idea, slip through Hooker and cross the Potomac east of the Blue Ridge, "You don't miss much, do you, colonel?"

"Try not to, sir."

"How's our horse doing?" he joshed.

"Strong as ever, sir."

"Good. He has a long ride ahead. Across the Potomac and north. I want you up ahead with the scouts. No surprises."

"Yes, sir."

"You know the situation. Do whatever you have to do."

"I understand. One thing more, general."

Stuart raised an eyebrow.

David smiled, "You sure do have a liking for excitement."

"That's what life is for," he laughed merrily, returning David's salute.

Stuart ordered three brigades to rendezvous at Salem, the other two to remain with Lee's main force.

David rode out with the scouts before 1 A.M. June 25. Six thousand troopers followed, through Glasscock's Gap in the Bull Run Mountains and northeast across desolated farmland.

Near Haymarket, David cautiously rode through a thick wood, leading Sable the last few yards. From the trees he peered on a Yankee column, surprised for the area had been clear. He sent a messenger to Stuart, who came up to see for himself.

Frustrated at being blocked, Stuart observed, "too many to fight, but we can give them a scare." He ordered up field pieces.

As they waited, Stuart asked bluntly, "How'd you know I was considering this move through Hooker?"

"Mostly a lucky guess, sir."

"That's all! A lucky guess?"

"Reminded me of your ride around McClellan a year ago."

Stuart smiled at the memory, "That was a good ride indeed."

When word came that the guns were up, Stuart gave his instructions, "Let the rear of the column pass and then fire. When they form to attack, fall back."

Stuart lost a day at Haymarket, detouring around the Yankee column. More delays accumulated to a week's separation from Lee's main force, until July 2. The battle of Gettysburg was in its second day. David witnessed Lee's greeting, the only time he ever saw Stuart embarrassed, 'General Stuart, you are here at last."

Stuart briefed his lieutenants on the plan General Lee and he worked out, "Infantry to assault Cemetery Hill. We will flank them beyond Culp's Hill, cut through and improve the opportunity, turn the retreat into a rout. Colonel Morrow has our route."

David spoke confidentially to Stuart.

"Of course," Stuart turned again to the others, "we hope to surprise them. Jump them before they know it."

David rode east on the York road, guiding two brigades, Ferguson and Chambliss. Fitz Lee's, where Tom Rosser and his 5th Virginia rode, and Wade Hampton's were to follow.

Two miles out David turned on a lane to Cress's Ridge. From its wooded crest, he looked on the fields and farmsteads of the Rummel and Lott families and beyond, to the Low Dutch Road held by Federal cavalry. He and Stuart assessed the defenders.

"What do you think, sir? Swing wider to get around them?"

Stuart pulled at the gold chain looped across his stomach and looked at the large watch he carried. He clicked the cover closed, "No time left. We'll have to force a route here." He turned his horse and left the ridge. The day was hot and humid.

David felt his excitement building for it appeared that they outnumbered General Gregg's cavalry, an advantage they seldom had. Rummel's barn would be a good place for sharpshooters.

Regiments deployed on the reverse slope of Cress's Ridge. a Confederate gun galloped along the crest and unlimbered. Its crew fired a shot. Yankees returned the fire.

David frowned, "What the hell! Stuart said surprise them."

Stuart offered no explanation.

More guns came into battery on the high ground and across the fields. The firing increased to a full-blown artillery duel. A Confederate gun on the ridge took a direct hit.

Stuart and David watched as Ferguson's dismounted troopers advanced to Rummel's barn. Yankees advanced to meet them.

A fire-fight erupted around the barn and fences, escalating into the mid-afternoon, as dismounted troopers were fed into it. Cavalrymen of both sides advanced and fell back, as more men tipped the balance. The fight raged back and forth, hand-to-hand for the same fence in one sector.

Rifle fire flared in one area and another, as if men were settling private contests. Cannons boomed, the lethal glue that bound the isolated actions into one.

Three friends from West Point converged this day: David Morrow, Tom Rosser with his Virginia regiment, and 24-year old Brigadier George Custer, who four days ago was a captain.

At 3 o'clock, gunfire fell off as men were captivated by the riders on Cress's Ridge. Transfixed by the spectacle of deploying regiments, they became spectators in their own unfolding drama. Those closest heard Confederate officers bark orders.

Fascination became concern as squadron after squadron formed in close column of squadrons, the classical attack formation. As the reality hit home, Bluecoats scampered for safety. Custer's Fifth and Seventh Michigan raced from their exposed position, angling to the sides for safety.

To Generals Gregg and Custer, watching from the Low Dutch road, Stuart's intent was obvious, nothing less than an all-out effort to smash through, no feints, diversions, or hokus-pokus. They knew his squadrons had the power to do it, and once done, who could foretell the outcome? Drastic action was needed.

Custer had orders to return to his division down near Little Round Top. Knowing the danger here, he disregarded them.

Gregg rode to Custer's First Michigan and ordered it into attack formation to meet the charge, one regiment against those of three brigades. This was Custer's veteran regiment, steady and dependable, and fresh having been held in reserve. Even so, how could one regiment stop the Confederates?

George Custer galloped to its front as he always did, for to him leadership meant leading. When men in his command attacked, he set the example, doing no less than he asked of them. It was his credo, from his first independent action, only yesterday on the Hunterstown road, to his last at Little Big Horn.

He tossed his hat, letting his long hair fly in the wind.

On Cress's Ridge, a small group of mounted men caught Yankee attention. One sat a magnificent black horse, regal and strong. As they watched, he shook out his flowing mane and pranced lightly toward the center of the group. His rider saluted.

David asked of Jeb Stuart, "Permission to join the attack, sir?" and answered it himself, reining about even as he spoke,

Observers saw the giant stallion wheel and gallop diagonally across the face of Cress's Ridge. They murmured their approval.

"Look at that black devil go!" one said with respect.

"He's flying," from another, awestruck.

"Never know he's touchin' the ground."

Sable slowed to a trot as he angled gracefully to join an officer on the left. His run took mere seconds, but he etched a permanent vision in the minds of all who saw.

Side by side, David Morrow and Tom Rosser nodded their friendship. They scanned the scene ahead, squinting to size up the small formation coming out to do battle.

Suddenly, David pointed. The figure in front had caught his eye. Only one man let his golden locks grow that long.

Excited, he shouted, "Look, Tom, it's Fanny. Fanny Custer."

Rosser squinted, "Damned if it isn't."

"We're going to fight Custer!"

Instantly they recalled a scene at West Point: cadets innocent of war pondering resignations. What would they do, they had asked, if they met as opponents on the battlefield.

Sadness had infused the question, sadness and an obscure conjecture of doing one's duty. David side-stepped Sable.

"It's strange, Tam," using Rosser's cadet nickname, "how we thought of fighting against friends. There isn't any question."

"No question at all."

"There is one thing left, though."

"What's that?"

"The sadness. It's no less than it was then."

The two formations approached at a walk, one so badly outnumbered. As their adversaries, but without the depth, Custer's Michiganders were formed, too, in close column of squadrons. Nobody doubted a one-sided fight.

The columns drew together, slowly it seemed, ever so slowly.

Confederate officers turned in their saddles, proud of what they saw, their men steady with the confidence of born horsemen.

Knowing the effect of unsheathed steel, officers shouted advice, "Keep to your sabers, men, keep to your sabers."

The men heard and loosened swords. They reacted to experience, too, and eased pistols in their holsters. The saber was their weapon, but saber plus pistol was better.

"Draw sabers!" came the shout, and calloused hands reached right to left. Sibilantly, the steel cleared scabbards.

Some murmured a quick prayer; others cursed; a few did both. They wiped sweat and spat brown and jammed their hats tighter.

Officers barked orders to quicken the pace, "Steady—Dress on the center—Trot."

Sable went out a length ahead as if he anticipated the words. Other riders kicked rowels, drawing even with him. David patted the muscular black neck, "Let's get 'em, boy."

Leathers snapped, irons jingled. Cold steel flashed hot sunlight. The separation between the columns shrank.

Custer responded with the same order.

The Confederates kept their parade ground precision, each line arrow straight, every interval exact; just as precise was the pattern of shadows obliquing to their front.

Crackling, snapping, regimental flags were held high to the sun, proud with ground-in dirt, with rents and stains of battles fought. Their reds, blues, and golds stood out in brilliant relief against nature's earth colors. The time for training, for polishing, and for preparation was gone.

Company and regimental commanders turned once again for a final glance at their men. Some raised their sabers in the knight's salute. Silently, lovingly, the captains and colonels admired their young troopers, their constancy and fearlessness in this bloody business. Who could ask for better?

Looking on with admiration, too, were Union troopers for they knew they were witnessing the world's finest horsemen. For a brief moment, Bluecoats shouted cheers and huzzahs, losing track of the deadly game, appreciating such mastery of their own trade.

One more order, "Steady, men—at the gallop—CHARGE!"

The lines burst ahead as one, a thousand sabers alongside horses' heads, a thousand throats screeching the rebel yell, hats flying in the wind. Thunder rose on the breeze, the thunder of shodden hooves, a thousand doubled and doubled again.

"EEeeeYAH! CHARGE! CHARGE! CHARGE!"

The column came on, larger and larger. Iron shoes pounded the good earth. Battle flags crackled. Riders shrieked.

Sporadic rifle shots cracked on the flanks as they thundered into range, fire from the Fifth and Seventh Michigan, the Third Pennsylvania, the First New Jersey, Maryland men, and men from Massachusetts, Maine and New York, from all those who had fought at Rummel's fences and fallen back.

Artillery commanders sighted down gun barrels, and gave the most difficult order of all, "Hold your fire."

The column came on.

"Wait, men. Let them get closer. Steady, steady, not yet."

For the gunners it was waitin' time, sweatin' time.

"Hold your fire, men."

Closer the Confederates came. Wait. Sweat. Closer. Closer.

"FIRE!"

"FIRE!"

"FIRE!"

Batteries exploded in flame and smoke, left and right. Horses and men went down, leaving ugly holes in the parade ground formation. The column closed up.

"Swab—Load—FIRE"

"Swab—Load—FIRE"

Gunners poled gun barrels, rammed home powder and shot, yanked lanyards, swabbed again. Guns spit, ripping the oncoming squadrons. They closed the gaps, mending broken lines.

Riflemen prone and kneeling in the long grass added their sting, aiming to destroy that which they had admired. The lines shivered. Custer took advantage of the hesitation.

"Forward—Gallop—CHARGE!

Standing in his stirrups, he challenged his men, "COME ON YOU WOLVERINES!" He outstripped them by four lengths, waving them on, spurring them even faster, "COME ON YOU WOLVERINES!"

Columns crashed together, Custer and his single regiment, Rosser no safer for all his fellow riders, and David maneuvering off Rosser's flank as he had done so many times with Jeb Stuart. No time now for academic questions of friendship or loyalty, only time to fight, shoot, slash, recover.

They were on each other, screaming and keeping to their sabers, firing huge horse pistols at close range. Men screeched pain and fury; horses, pain and fear. All stood to their work.

The collision of forces took on a life of its own, breaking and reforming a kaleidoscope of local fights, changing and whirling. David fought alongside Rosser, but was soon separated.

"Left, Sable, LEFT, LEFT," David screamed automatically, and they avoided a mean blow. David was unaware he had yelled, and they came out on the edge of the melee, safe for a few seconds in their coating of dust and sweat. David holstered his empty Colt and dug for its mate, fully loaded.

"Ready, boy? EEEyah." The fight swallowed them again.

Dust rose over the battle and settled around its edges. David choked its dry pall, and grunted as he cut down into a shoulder. A saber came at him from the other side, high in the air, a saber and a blue-clad arm. Sable pivoted away from the blow. David twisted in his saddle and lunged, penetrating blue uniform and soft belly. The high sword came down across Sable's flank. David saw gold chevrons on the arm, three of them, and cursed all sergeants in blue. He saw the wounded man topple from his saddle as he parried another thrust.

Others reacted to Custer's infectious elan and joined his charge, dashing into the maelstrom, ignoring orders to hold defensive positions, discarding caution.

General McIntosh sent his adjutant to two squadrons fresh from the Rummel line with orders, "Mount and charge"; he shouted to an aide, "Collect anyone and everyone. GO TO CUSTER." Then he himself led his staff to Custer's aid.

Adjutant Newhall delivered McIntosh's order and rode with the squadrons when they hit the Confederates on the right, near a color guard. Newhall made a grab for the flag, and was speared in the jaw by the standard bearer.

Captain William Miller, commanding a squadron of the Third Pennsylvania, had orders to hold a position near the Lott farm in case of a Confederate breakthrough. He saw a better use for his men and charged Fitz Lee's left flank, narrowly missing David and Rosser. Congress voted him the new Medal of Honor.

Captain J.H. Hart, also part of the last ditch force, followed Miller, en echelon, smashing the column near the first line, where some of his men struggled with the Confederate color guard, along with the Newhall squadrons. David was in the middle of it again, fighting Miller's and Hart's men.

Sabers flashed cruelly in the hot sun. Pistols popped. Hand-to-hand, men struggled on horseback and off, slash, lunge, cut, fire, grapple, charging, whirling, countercharging, fighting again. Good men bled and died. Horses whinnied their fright; those with empty saddles ran blindly for a way out. Rippling battle flags pointed high and proud.

The telling artillery fire and Custer's inspiring assault, was enough to stop Jeb Stuart's column. The promises of glory, so exhilarating in the morning, went up in smoke and grime. The afternoon saw not only a cavalry fight lost, but the end of hope. As the troopers were stopped below Cress's Ridge, so too were the gallant men of Pickett and Pettigrew stopped even as they reached Cemetery Hill. Flotsam marked the high water line as the tide turned.

In the waning sunset, General Lee lamented, "All this has been my fault. It is I who have lost this fight . . ."

LII

RETREAT

After the collision at Rummel's, Jeb Stuart held his ground below Cress's Ridge, thereby claiming a victory. At dusk he pulled his regiments back to the York Road and bivouacked. David spent the night with Sable, as he always did after a dangerous day. Currying him, he found blood on his flank, the first wound either of them had suffered.

He relived a moment of the battle, a wild horse and a saber raised high, a blue sleeve with three chevrons poised to strike.

He cleaned Sable's flank, finding the wound less serious than he feared. As he massaged animal grease into the raw flesh, he was overwhelmed by the thought that Sable, or both of them, could have been killed. They had been lucky.

So many battles, so many fateful meetings and so many instances of good luck: today's battle, Brandy Station, Manassas; fighting Folsom; meeting Carrie, finding her again. He fancied their hurry-up wedding and their glorious time together. Simple good luck was insufficient. Surely, he was blessed.

"It's time we gave proper thanks, my friend."

Lovingly, he rubbed Sable's nose. He dropped to one knee. Head bowed, he remained silent and motionless. Sable watched quietly, his brown eyes rich with understanding.

Gettysburg left General Lee with an army in enemy country, and Jeb Stuart the job of covering it to the Potomac, forty miles away. Four solid weeks of marching and fighting with no let up.

"From General Lee, sir." The courier saluted by the book, taking no liberties with an angry general.

Uncharacteristically, Stuart was on a short fuse. Yesterday had been a trying day, and the interruption made him impatient.

"Now what!" he bellowed, snatching the dispatch.

He turned to David. "That was a damn fool stunt, riding off like that yesterday," David had never heard him curse.

"Sorry, sir, I thought I had your permission."

"Next time, be sure." Stuart didn't have the heart to rake him more for he understood the motivation.

"Yes, sir." David made a move to leave.

Stuart held up a hand as he read General Lee's order. "Well, there it is. Back to Williamsport and across to Virginia tonight. A column of supply wagons and ambulances by way of Cashtown and Greenwood. Hill, Longstreet, and Ewell by way of Fairfield and the South Mountain passes."

"The cavalry, general?"

"Will escort both columns, two brigades each. I want you to find out what you can at headquarters. And no more escapades."

At Seminary Ridge, David saw row upon row of wounded, lying helplessly in the heavy rain, waiting to be loaded into wagons. *Poor devils, you'll suffer more on the roads to the Potomac.*

Others held their line on the ridge, grim, expecting an attack. Otherwise, he learned, they were to pull out after dark, a skeleton force of cavalry to feed fires and convince Yankees a formidable line still opposed them. David reported to Stuart.

"General, if you want volunteers, I'll stay behind."

"Denied," Stuart answered gruffly, "you ride with me."

And David did stay with Stuart, fending off Federal cavalry until they crossed the rain-swollen Potomac on July 14.

At the Dandridge's estate once more, David unsaddled Sable, "Now you get a rest, old boy, and some new shoes." He brushed, inspecting the black coat as he went. The wounded flank had closed neatly, with little scar tissue and no sign of gray or white to mar the ebony coat. The grease had done its job.

My Dearest Carrie The past month has been a bad one, no time to write, for anything except keeping Sable clean. I just worked an hour on him and he looks better than he has in months. He was hurt at Gettysburg, but healing well. He's such a fine horse, Carrie. We crossed the Potomac this morning into Virginia and made camp 30 miles from home so I hope to get there. I tried to get to Richmond, but couldn't.

I did get to Winchester for a few days. Jed and Betsy have a new baby girl and Pa said he loves you already. He was half won over when I told him how you had impressed Colonel Boteler. He, and Ma too, said for you to consider Winchester your home. I'll be happy when this war is over and we can be together but nobody seems of a mind to talk peace. I think of you every day and every night, you are always with me. I give thanks every day that you're my wife. I love you very much, pumpkin. I will ask for leave, but the general is tense. Hope with me. David

In the meanwhile, even before Lee started his retreat, a lone rider galloped into Winchester, bedraggled, tired, his horse lathered. People dressed for church this Sabbath morning gathered about him as he reined up at Courthouse Square.

Most feared news of approaching Federals, with a repeat of the hardships under Milroy. A goodly number loyal to the Union hoped for the very thing their neighbors feared. Instead, the rider brought confirmation of a terrible battle.

"In Gettyvania. Pennsylvania," he said, "Lee got hisse'f whupped. He attacked three days arunnin', and is retreatin'. They say he lost 10,000 men, mebbe more. Nobody knows."

"Ten thousand!" one woman gasped, "oh my God."

"Yes mam, that's what they're sayin'. Ten thousand er more."

The distraught woman fainted into her husband's arms.

"We have two sons there," he apologized vacantly.

"They's wounded every place, lyin' face up in the rain, dead ones mixed in. Nobody knows wich is wich 'til they pick 'em up." Sarah prepared her hospital again, marshalling her family and preparing pallets of quilts and blankets. Henry and Jed pitched in, moving furniture and helping with the heavier chores.

When Sarah heard Gracey's "Help me with these blankets, Pa," she held her breath for Henry was not one to be ordered about by anyone, most of all his children. Seeing her apprehension, Henry threw up his hands good-naturedly and mouthed, "What can I do?" Later, with things as ready as they could be, he had serious words for Sarah, "I'm givin' fair warnin' I'll be keepin' closer track than last time. I'll do all I can t'help, but I'm not standin' around t'let you work yourself t'death again."

"You are still my old bear, aren't you. If you didn't growl, I'd think you were sick. Or had stopped loving me." Stepping close, she raised on tiptoes to kiss him on the cheek.

"None of your softsoap, woman. I mean every word."

"I know you do. Thank you, Henry."

The first of the army ambulances arrived the next day. Even as David and the cavalry had fought off the pursuers, drivers whipped and cursed their teams through the treacherous crossing.

Again, as after Sharpsburg, Winchester became a huge field hospital, and its people the orderlies, nurses, and doctors. The courthouse, churches, schools, every public building filled, floors, pews and offices. Ambulances continued to rattle into town, and private homes were soon overflowing. Soldiers were laid out in the yards and open spaces. Virtually untended since the battle, many of them received their first proper care, their first chance to have wounds properly cleaned and bandaged. The walking wounded gathered in the streets and grounds, resting, passing the time, until they could be moved up the Valley to Staunton or Lynchburg. Gettysburg's casualties overwhelmed the county seat, threatening complete confusion. Only the superhuman efforts of good people and their sheer grit delivered Winchester from its trial. They persevered one soldier at a time, each bandage, each washed face, each cup of soup a tiny step forward.

With the house filled, Henry and Jed prepared pallets of hay in the barn and on the wide verandah. Still the wagons came.

"My God, Pa, they must have shot half the army."

"Looks so, son, looks so."

Shrill screams startled them, blood-curdling screams from the house. They dropped armsful of hay and made for the verandah.

"Ma! Pa!"

Gracey ran for them, hair flying, tears streaking her face. "He's too young to die. He's only a boy, not as old as I am."

Henry embraced her protectively, seeking words that wouldn't come. Unspoken messages passed between Henry and Jed who disappeared through the front door. Gracey didn't need to see the body being carried off.

"He—he seemed—all right," she mourned brokenly, "and he—he started to shake—and—he—he went limp and—and—starey—his eyes just went starey."

Henry continued to console her, kissing her hair gently as he stroked it, whispering over and over again, "It's all right, Grace, it's all right."

Civilian and army doctors worked side by side, all too few for the job. They worked desperately between catnaps and snatches of food, luckier this time with a good store of drugs and medical supplies left by the Yankees in June.

Doctor Holliday, who had amputated Jed's leg, spent his time taking off limbs too shattered or too gangrenous to save. "Waited too damn long," he said to nobody but himself, and gave Sarah a quick demonstration of dealing with the corrupted flesh.

"Snip and cut like this, to where it looks good," he said, "leeches would help if we had them. Do the best you can."

Sarah spent the next two hours 'snipping and cutting,' washing, bandaging, daubing herself with lavender water against the stink of rotted flesh. She was just finishing a bandage when Henry appeared with a pot of tea, "Time for a breather."

"Oh, Henry, you're not a moment too soon." With the back of her hand, she wiped straggles of hair from her forehead.

He reached for her to lean against him, "Let's sit outside."

Sarah dropped exhausted into a chair in the weathered gazebo. Tilting her head to the back of the chair, eyes closed, she breathed deeply, "The fresh air is heavenly."

Henry poured from the teapot.

Abruptly, she came alive, "Do you suppose being in the fresh air would help the wounded soldiers?"

"It sure smells better."

"That's what I mean. It seems healthier. I wonder if Doctor Holliday has an opinion. I'll have to ask him."

Doctor Holliday's response was a fascinating tale.

"I'm not surprised you ask, Sarah. I know a doctor who's been at the largest hospital in Richmond. Its called Chimborazo and is built on one of Richmond's hills with plenty of fresh air. He swears it's good for the patients, and says many of his colleagues agree with him."

"Really! It does seem to make good sense."

"Not only seems to, Sarah. He says the recovery rate in the open tents is higher than in the permanent wards."

Henry told of her idea at the supper table that evening and beamed his pleasure, "And doctors in Richmond agree with her."

Betsy read the implication, "Mumma's a smart lady, Pa."

"Yes, she is that. Smart as most doctors I know and smarter than some." Henry's eyes lighted as he drew the logical conclusion, "Damned if she shouldn't have been one."

Following her insight, Sarah ventilated her rooms, windows braced open with sticks and doors with bricks.

The Morrows devoted themselves for weeks, saddened with each death, pleased with every improvement. They were touched by the soldiers' fortitude and stamina, and surprised at their own. Each had his own collection of moments that would ever remain, moments of celebration and of mourning. Gracey, especially, was affected.

It was the death of the young soldier that haunted Gracey, the 14-year-old soldier on the first day. She felt personally responsible, unable to shake the thought that he had died because she didn't know what to do. If she had known more, she grieved, she could have kept him alive, and in her grief a vision was born. Grace Morrow dreamed of becoming a doctor.

"But ladies don't become doctors," Henry observed mildly, wondering if there ever would be an end to the changes of a world turned upside down. His reaction surprised Sarah for she was accustomed to his objections rattling the house.

He surprised himself, too, wondering if any medical school would accept a young lady. It would be nice to have a doctor in the family, he thought, and none of the boys seemed bent in that direction. Maybe it would be Gracey. And why not! She was a Morrow, too.

LIII

RICHMOND
JULY 30, 1863

*M*y *Dearest Carrie July continues to drag along. I asked for time off again and was turned down flat. The general says things are uncertain now, nobody knows what Meade will do. D—it, I could be in Richmond with you. I'm afraid I'm not in a very good mood to be writing tonight. (Next day) I thought I'd better not continue last night so I visited Rosser. He was in a foul mood, too, so we drank a toast to each other. He married two months after we did and can't get home to Hanover Courthouse. Besides that he's been in grade over a year and thinks he ought to be promoted. I agreed with him on the first, but told him that cadet to colonel wasn't all that bad for someone his age. His answer was, "Age h—, that's got nothing to do with it." Then we drank toasts to you and Plum, that's what he calls his wife Betty, lit cigars and we both felt better. That's one solution to a man's troubles, not the best but the best available, a friend, good Havana cigar, and bourbon. I felt terrible this morning with every little noise like an arrow in my head. Carrie, I don't want any arguments about the enclosed pay voucher. I have back pay on the books and want you to buy yourself something special. Rosser may have his Plum but I have my Pumpkin. All my love David*

Not until the end of December, would David get to Richmond.

In addition to his operational duties, Stuart assigned him the Gettysburg report. He wasn't in the army to get ink-stained fingers, or to indulge delinquent colonels, he groused to Rosser, let the general chase down their late reports. Since that wasn't the army way, of course, he wheedled the reports himself.

In mid-August, he turned over the regimental submissions and his own division draft. Stuart could submit it or change it.

Meanwhile, the Federal army followed Lee across the Potomac and came south, east of the Blue Ridge. Lee paralleled it, moving up the Valley. Again, the cavalry guarded the mountain gaps. When the cavalry manned the old Rappahannock line, David knew there would be no leave before winter. Ever lonely, he spent many an hour with Rosser, cigars and bourbon to ward off the emptiness.

August became September and Stuart's reorganization plan was approved, a two-division corps, four new brigadiers. Passed over, Rosser was infuriated again. Stuart had lied to him, he fumed to David, misled him and deceived him and never again could he be trusted. David tried to mollify him, but he would never believe otherwise, even in October, when he was promoted, adding wreathes to his three stars. Stuart seemed unaware of the ill will.

Rosser's choler remained, but was buried in the fighting at Bristoe, Gainesville and Centreville and between the Rappahannock and Rapidan. On December 1, the Federal army turned north, across the Rapidan for the winter. Lee established winter quarters at Orange Courthouse, where the memory of John Pelham haunted David.

The haunting reminder inflamed the ache of lost friends, so many, John Pelham, Redmond Burke, Channing Price, Tom Rafferty, on and on. Corporal Rafferty hurt especially. How alert he had been at Falling Waters and chagrined by the mission dubbed 'perfume raid'. God! a year and a half ago; now Rafe was dead, killed whimsically. Almost anonymously, on a paltry outpost.

Fellow pickets told of night noises, a lull, a single shot, Tom falling, bloody nose, a hole in his head, bloody ear, the night quiet again. Hang all snipers!

No longer the grand adventure, the war had become a giant tumbleweed, rolling roughshod over professional skill, personal ethics and love, destroying and killing capriciously.

Lost in the maelstrom were Christmas turkeys for Stuart's headquarters, called Wigwam. The holiday meal was saved only by the chance discovery of oysters frozen by the winter.

Quashing his sadness, David wrote Carrie of them, roasted in an open fire, succulent, delicious. He wrote of visiting newsmen from England, and the spirited music of the Sweeney brothers, banjo and violin and the pulsing clack of the bones. He wrote of Sable and then, revisited by the ghosts of fallen friends, signed his name, fearful of worrying her with his sadness.

Five days later, the next day was the eve of the new year, Jeb Stuart called David into his tent, "I'm off to Richmond tomorrow. You have anything here that can't wait?"

"No, sir. Enjoy yourself."

"Colonel," Stuart sounded very official, "I know I'm free to go. I asked you if you were."

"Me free to go?" Surprised, David regained his composure with enthusiasm, "Yes, sir. I can leave now."

Enjoying his little joke, Stuart continued it, "There's no great hurry, is there?"

David was up to the challenge, "Don't put off 'til tomorrow is what I've always heard, general."

Jeb Stuart's inimitable belly laugh did justice to his enjoyment. He looked at his turnip of a pocket watch.

"We'll catch the early cars in the morning."

"Yes, sir."

The train clanked and rattled out of Orange Courthouse, smoke billowing from the awkward funnel-like stack, cars swaying and lurching. Demands of one army and depredations of another had taken their toll on the rolling stock, but intrepid engineers patched and oiled their machines, coaxed and cussed and kept them rolling. Always, they strained for more speed.

Down the road at Gordonsville, David and the general transferred from the single-track line to the Virginia Central for the 75 miles into Richmond. Seven hours later, after a delay at the Bumpass Turnout, they chugged through Shockoe Bottom.

"I expect to be at the President's festivities tomorrow. Have you ever met Mr. Davis?"

"No, sir, I never have."

"Tomorrow will be a good opportunity. And," Jeb Stuart's eyes sparkled, "I'll get to meet your new wife. As pretty as you say she is, I won't be satisfied until I do."

"She's that pretty and more, general."

"Then I'll expect to see you both."

"Oh, I don't know, sir. Carrie may have other plans."

"You sure it's her and not you that may have other plans? It's Richmond's party of the year, one you won't forget."

"I'll do my best, general."

The train jerked to a halt at the Central's depot between 17th and 18th streets. They shared a carriage to Mechanics' Hall.

"Until tomorrow," Jeb Stuart strode jauntily off. David went in the opposite direction. At Carrie's door, his alarm blasted! She's not here! She's left Richmond! Her desk was empty, chair slid under as chairs are when not in use. He stood befuddled.

An older clerk saw him, "Can I help you, sir?"

"Carrie Nash—? Carrie Morrow I mean. I'm her husband."

"Why of course. She has been transferred to the Secretary's office. Down the corridor. Turn—"

"I know," he called as he ran, "thank you very much."

Breathless, he pulled up at the door with memories of the haughty George Randolph. So be it, he thought, I'll handle him when I have to. Carrie stared wide-eyed past the uniformed figure standing over her desk.

"David!" She ran to him before he crossed the threshold. Engulfed and dazzled by the sight of her, David felt a vague familiarity with the officer at her desk. Whoever it was didn't matter for she was in his arms and he in hers, laughing and sobbing joy, exchanging smothered Iloveyous, kissing frantically, lips, eyes, hair, nose, ears, erasing the months of loneliness.

"Carrie, Carrie, you didn't tell me. I went to the other office and you were gone. I thought I had lost you again."

And they held each other, eyes closed, earth's only inhabitants, only the two of them and they were one.

Opening the door of the inner office, the Secretary of War, looked on the embrace with an exquisitely quizzical expression. Carrie and David never knew he was there. He and Jeb Stuart, for it was the general at Carrie's desk, exchanged glances and the Secretary motioned him into the inner office.

The stomp of heavy boots on the bare floor was enough to bring Carrie and David back to Mechanics' Hall.

"General!"

"Mr. Secretary!"

Stuart answered, "Go back to what you were doing. It's probably more important than anything you'll ever do."

Succumbing to an impulse, the Secretary of War, aristocrat by birth, man of culture, graduate of Charlottesville's University, respected lawyer, waved loosely at them, fingers pointing to the floor sweeping in a gesture of dismissal, "I agree with the general. Get out of here. Happy 1864."

In the corridor David expressed his surprise, "Who is the Secretary? He's not the grouch I expected to see."

"Mr. Seddon? He's been very nice to me. He replaced Mr. Randolph in November." They embraced again, hungry just to touch.

"Carrie, we have so much to talk about. I have a room for us at the Ballard House. The Spotswood was filled."

"The Ballard!" She broke out of his arms, "across the street from The Exchange?"

David laughed, "I thought it would be nice to be near our first meeting place, maybe visit the old place. See if that robust redhead is still hanging on the wall."

"David Morrow!"

"I'm joking, sweetheart."

She pouted, "You'll never forget The Exchange, will you?"

"I really love the place. It's where I found you."

"I'm surprised you didn't take a room there instead."

"Now why didn't I think of that?"

"Oh, you!" She reached her arms about his shoulders again, pulling his head down to her, "We have so much to talk about. And to do, sweetheart."

And they did.

The first day of the new year was bright, crisp and windy. Carrie held finger tips to a shallow little saucer of a hat. Of velvet and sheer linen, it balanced pertly toward her forehead, its only decoration a baby ostrich plume dyed the rich blue of its materials. They settled in the carriage carrying them to the Jefferson Davises' levee.

"I like your hat."

"I bought it with the money you sent. Mrs. Burgess said the blue went with my eyes. And I love your other gift, too."

Carrie fondled a garnet brooch, "It's beautiful. I'll treasure it always, David." She cuddled close under the lap robe.

"You make it beautiful, sweetheart."

Earlier in the day, she had been distraught at the thought of attending the President's annual celebration.

"David, I can't go. I don't even have a proper dress."

He nodded in admiration and puzzlement, "I do love you."

"I am serious," she frowned.

"So am I. Your first concern with the President's levee is what to wear. Mine is that we should even be there."

"But it's true. I don't have a thing I could wear."

Delighted, Mrs. Burgess had solved the problem, "Of course you'll go. I have just the right gown. But first we eat."

Later, she had disappeared into an attic storage closet to select Carrie's wardrobe. Coming down with her arms filled, she shooed David from the room and spread the clothes on the bed.

"You'll need help getting into these. Do be careful if you sit down," she had warned as she held up the hoop and petticoats, "hoops have a tendency to pop up.

"Maybe it would be better to remain standing, dear. "

The gown itself was a glimmering royal blue satin, yards and yards of it in the skirt, a jacket of the same material with dainty, pearl buttons, a dozen closing the front, and more on the fitted cuffs. From shoulder to elbow the sleeves ballooned loose. A black soutache worked into a flat braid trimmed the jacket; a similar one, wider, edged the skirt. Mrs. Burgess smiled tears as she recalled Mr. Burgess and gala times of her own.

She reached under the hem to flatten a petticoat, "The length is right, but the waist needs to be pinched in a bit.

"Now let's try the jacket. I always liked the way it flared at the waist, just enough to make the men look twice."

"Why Mrs. Burgess!" Carrie feigned astonishment.

She held it for Carrie to squeeze fingers through tailored cuffs. The front gaped wide.

"You will need more room there. You're fuller than I was."

The older lady closed a few lower buttons, "There, that will do for now."

"Oh, it's lovely. Are you sure you want me to wear it?"

"Nonsense. It's yours. I'll never wear it again."

"But I couldn't. I can see how much it means to you."

"You'll charm every man there. I have the coat I wore with it. And gloves. All made to match. They're yours, too. The color goes perfectly with the saucy little hat you bought." And Mrs. Burgess was off to find them, and her sewing basket.

"May I come in?" David asked as he opened the door a crack.

"Only if you behave yourself."

"I'd better not then," he reached a satin jeweler's box around the door, "just wanted you to open this."

"Oh, David, what is it?"

The little box held a garnet ring, set in gold, a deep magenta crystal framed in a rectangle of delicate, pink pearls.

Carrie gasped, and forgetting her state of dishabille, swung the door wide to embrace him, "It's lovely."

David took advantage of her half buttoned jacket before he chided, "to match your pin. You're lovely, too, but we'd better get back in your room if you have designs on me."

"I will always have designs on you."

The carriage pulled up to the Confederate White House on Clay Street. A uniformed doorman with a rich baritone greeted them, "May the year treat you kindly, colonel. And you, Madam."

Mrs. Burgess had been absolutely right, for Carrie did charm every man at the President's party, from the moment she walked through the door. Jeb Stuart was the first to see her.

"David, I am happy you made it." He held out a hand, and turned to Carrie with a sweeping bow, "You are more beautiful than yesterday, even beyond your colonel's rhapsodies."

He kissed her hand and continued to hold it. Carrie glowed in the gallantry of this modern knight, canting her head ever so slightly, inviting a kiss on the cheek. The general made the most of the invitation as he continued to hold her hand.

"Now let me present you to the President and Mrs. Davis."

"May I?" He glanced at both Carrie and David.

"Of course," and he offered his arm with a flourish.

"Mr. President. Mrs. Davis. May I present two of my favorite people? Colonel David Morrow and his lady."

Carrie curtsied elegantly.

Jefferson Davis took her hand in his two, "It is truly a pleasure to meet you, Mrs. Morrow." He leaned forward to see her better, "Pardon my brusqueness, but I have met you before."

"Perhaps in the War Department, Mr. President. I work there and recently have been assigned to Secretary Seddon's office."

"That's exactly where it was. I was there a few days ago."

"It was three days ago, sir, on Tuesday."

"You flatter me."

"You flatter me, sir."

Behind them, the receiving line lengthened as they talked.

"I will have to visit the Secretary's office more often. May the new year bring you happiness."

"And to you, Mr. President." Carrie turned to move on.

"Your colonel is familiar to me. Although I forget the exact wording in General Lee's report of Gettysburg, I was taken with the uniqueness of his citation. I know General Stuart thinks highly of him."

"Why, thank you, Mr. President." She turned to leave him.

President Davis touched her arm, "I like your hat."

"Why, thank you again, sir."

Jefferson Davis smiled and nodded a welcome to David.

"Colonel Morrow, You are a very lucky man."

"God has been good to me, sir."

"My dear," Varina Davis gave a formal suggestion of a smile. "Mrs. Davis," Carrie replied and walked on.

Jeb Stuart was waiting for her. Together they waited for David, their conversation interrupted repeatedly by others, drawn not only by Carrie's beauty, but by the mystery of this newcomer to Richmond's society. The President's lingering cordiality had not gone unnoticed as he kept prominent Richmonders and eminent officials waiting in the receiving line.

Enjoying the attention, but not entirely easy with it, Carrie felt the warmth rising in her face. Its accompanying tinge highlighted the blue of her eyes, drawing envious remarks from behind hand-held fans.

The men had only compliments and nods of approval.

"David is a fine man," Stuart said.

"Your opinion is important to him, general. He has spoken of you with great affection."

"Are you sure? I am aware of his displeasure for having denied him leave. And I must say, after seeing you, that I better understand his disappointment."

"Thank you, kind sir," she dipped in a little-girl curtsy, "he did voice discontentment, but he understood."

Having paid his respects to his host and hostess, David spent a moment searching. There she was, near one of the long windows that looked out on Clay Street, with General Stuart and three other gentlemen, two uniformed, one in high-collared, formal dress. As David watched, the civilian gentleman left for a stout lady who appeared less than happy.

Carrie continued to charm the others, giving full attention to each as he spoke. From across the room, David knew the impact she was having, for he too felt the enchantment, in her gestures as she spoke and in the tilt of her head as she listened. She carried herself so proudly, not ashamed of her statuesque figure but not flaunting it either. Counterpoint to her sensuality were her fingers laced and held so decorously.

Carrie, how lovely you are, how especially lovely in the midst of the festivities, excited to be in the President's house, exciting to those near you, vivacious and sparkling. You reach for the world and the world is yours. Carrie, how I do love you.

He touched her as he came up behind, "Enjoying yourself?"

Her shining face was his answer. Her eyes with their long lashes asked her own question. She pursed her lips into a just-for-you kiss, making him the envy of every man who saw. Sharp-eyed ladies saw, too, and clucked of face paint, decorum, and impertinent little hats they could never wear.

Apologetically, Jeb Stuart excused himself, "I'm afraid I've monopolized your lady, Colonel."

"Not at all, sir," David glanced from him to Carrie and back, "I'm happy you had the chance to talk."

Carrie smiled, "As am I, general. Until we meet again."

"Your servant, mam." And General Stuart herded his fellow officers across the crowded room. Finally by themselves, Carrie and David wandered arm in arm through the gathering, her hooped satin swaying and swishing.

"Look at the punch bowl, David. Isn't it magnificent!"

A gray-haired gentleman noting her ingenuousness smiled kindly. The battleship of a woman anchored next to him peered affectedly through her lorgnette.

Carrie smiled sweetly and nodded as she walked past them.

"Thirsty?"

"Uh huh."

They accepted fruit punch in silver cups, and sampled from a variety of trays, ham from Isle of Wight county, glazed duck, wild turkey, fresh and pickled oysters, cakes, and a host of delicacies. Carrie wrinkled her nose at the oysters, pickled and on the half shell both, and relished the duck with its suggestion of orange, just enough to pique one's palate.

Brushing elbows at the punch bowl and laden table, they chatted cheerily with a number of guests. In the camaraderie, Carrie radiated genteel coquetry, balancing the decorum of a presidential levee with the gaiety of the holiday.

David saw through her subtlety and whispered closely, "You vixen, you're wonderful."

She whispered, too, privately and up close, "Not wonderful, love, just properly enthusiastic, proper for you, enthusiastic for me." Enough men to fill a regiment saw her lips close to his ear and wished he were the young colonel escorting her.

"I wonder how they make the glaze," Carrie asked as she held her plate for still another serving of duck. David offered an iced oyster in its half shell. Carrie refused it. He offered a small serving of duck with a bit of orange. Instead of taking it, as he expected, she opened her lips slightly to receive it.

"MMmmmm. Do you know what you remind me of?"

"No."

"The redbirds on the capitol grounds," she said, "the male feeding his mate. You said something about her accepting his seed."

A few minutes later he whispered again, "Ready to leave?"

"Uh huh," she fluttered her lashes, in a message as old as time.

LIV

YELLOW TAVERN

After the holiday celebration at the Confederate White House, David and Carrie returned to their lonesome routines, one to the difficult combination of winter boredom and vigilance, the other to the problems of war-time Richmond.

Along the Rapidan, David extended his lucky string as he rode the outposts and engaged in haphazard hostilities. Scraps flared suddenly, maturing into skirmishes or tapering off as quickly as they erupted, anonymous little affairs that affected the war not a whit, important only to the families of those killed, and to the wounded who had scars to show.

Carrie continued in Secretary Seddon's office, and with Mrs. Burgess dealt with the vulgarities of war, the casualty lists, high costs, coarse insults and shortages of everything else. She prayed as she read the lists, carried a long hat pin against vulgar approaches (she used it on two occasions), and bargained for necessities. Mrs. Burgess resorted to the newly opened auction rooms, selling an heirloom watch one day, a silver service another, and Mr. Burgess' clothes and boots on a third.

"I haven't used it for years," she said of the sterling, and "the Mister has no need of those, God rest his soul."

Flour that ordinarily had sold for $16 a barrel rocketed to $150 in January and $300 in March; butter, from 50¢ to $8 a pound; a cord of wood, up 500%. The war was good for some.

In March, Ulysses S. Grant was named to command all the Union armies. His strategy was simple: launch simultaneous campaigns, thus denying Lee the mobility to concentrate his forces; attack on the Richmond front, in the Shenandoah Valley, at Petersburg, in the western theater and beyond, in Texas.

One of General Lee's lieutenants warned, "Don't underestimate him. "He will hang on like a bulldog until he achieves what he wants." Another less genteel than his commander voiced his concern, "Find out where the bastards are, and what the hell way they're moving." On the Rapidan, David's boredom was over.

The day was Tuesday, May 3 the day Grant ordered The Army of the Potomac to cross the Rapidan.

On Wednesday, David and a young scout led the small column along the Orange-Fredericksburg Plank Road, through open, rolling piedmont that became a profuse tangle of second and third growth. As he rode, David imagined the towering hardwoods of the 17th century, virgin forest, the western frontier, the wilderness.

And then the axes came, axes and saws to feed the new iron furnaces. The unsullied forest rang as hard men chopped, and burned as hardwood was turned into charcoal, and rang again with the smithies' hammers. They smelted iron and pounded it strong, and turned the pristine wilderness into The Wilderness of the Civil War.

David looked on a snarled chaos of twisted, weather-bitten stumps, scrub pine, blackjack oak; vines, thickets, and briers; sixteen square miles of unmapped, dismal ground, visibility severely limited; natural declivities turned to bogs. Bogs and bastard growth, one more impassable than the other. Interrupted segments of wild pig trails and wagon-tracks provided the only passage. Outsiders did not enter The Wilderness alone.

How could officers ever deploy their men through this nightmare? David wondered. Artillery would have problems, too.

The young scout spoke in a hushed voice, "Did you ever see anything like this?"

Across the narrow track, David strained to penetrate the thick growth, "Can't see a damn thing. Reminds me of stories of my grandfather, arrows flying in and nobody in sight."

"I've been scared before, but this is downright creepy. Christ, even the sun is blocked out."

They rode cautiously, anxiously, eyes darting left, right, ahead; on guard, alert, expecting anything, preferring nothing. The humid air hung heavy, dead and still, new leaves hanging listlessly from branch and bush. Up ahead, all was still. Even the birds, chirping and flitting ahead of them, had disappeared.

They continued on, sweating, itching now from sticky dust and chaff. Sable shook his great head and snorted.

"Quiet, boy. This place gives me the willies, too."

The big stallion tossed his head emphatically, spooked in the narrow roadway. David thought snake, but there was no snake.

He leaned to the black withers, peering, seeing nothing.

He was turning in the saddle to warn Stuart when shots rang out. No warning, just musket shots. And then! Silence.

A half second of silence before the horses neighed and reared, before flapping birds squawked and whirred high.

Riders shouted, bringing their mounts under control. Panic swirled about them, but they controlled that, too, grabbing for pistols, ready to fight if they could see anything to fight.

Stuart's voice boomed out, "Hold your fire."

David shouted, "They're off to the right, General," he pointed, "near that white oak."

"Column left about," Stuart roared, and they reined around, galloping out of The Wilderness, out of the gloom into the sunshine. Their job had been to uncover the Yankee advance and they had done it. Without a casualty.

The armies fought two days in The Wilderness, the Yankee odds of five to three evened out by the tangled ground. Men bit cartridges and fired, sometimes effectively and another fell. The forest caught fire, completing the Devil's job. Other wounded moaned through the night, lost, helpless. They killed and wounded 25,000 of each other.

On May 7, the armies rested on their muskets and late that night side-slipped for Spotsylvania Courthouse to the southeast.

David rode with Stuart's division that blocked the route, fighting delaying actions, mean little fights for the strategic crossroads. When the guns quieted, he dozed in Spotsylvania as reinforcements hurried through the night.

He dined on hard tack and was off again after dark to find the First Corps and lead it in, winning another citation. Four days he lived on cat-naps, and then on the 9th, a day of relative quiet, he collapsed into a deep sleep. Ten days of renewed hostilities and maneuvering followed.

His drive for Richmond blocked twice, Grant sidled to the North Anna River, where Lee took advantage of a bend in the river to set a trap. Evading it, Grant side-stepped to Cold Harbor into the one battle he regretted fighting, on to the James, to Petersburg and west. Grant was indeed a bulldog, as described, a tenacious man who never let go—hammer, hammer, hammer until his opponent broke. "If it takes all summer," he said.

David was duty officer the morning "Little Phil" Sheridan up near Fredericksburg lined 12,000 troopers into a column of 13 miles. With them he snaked down the Telegraph Road for Richmond.

David apprised Stuart, "Have Freed sound boots and saddles, colonel. We'll move out at once."

Shortly, scouts reported a detachment from Sheridan headed for Beaver Dam Station on the Virginia Central Railroad, a major supply depot. On a more personal level, Stuart's wife, Flora, and their two children were at Beaver Dam at the plantation home of Edmund Fontaine. Only yesterday, it had seemed a safe haven for the three in this world he loved most.

With David and a Carolina brigade, Stuart himself detoured westward, crossing the North Anna at Davenport's Bridge. Ahead was Beaver Dam Station capped ominously with a pillar of smoke.

Yankee cavalry was already there, perhaps capturing his loved ones. Stuart put spurs to his horse. David stayed with him, galloping side by side. The Tarheels trailed out behind.

Up ahead, the Michigan Brigade had torched a million rations of bacon, a half million of bread; stores of flour, molasses, liquor, sugar, medicines; two locomotives and a hundred cars. They cut telegraph wires and wrecked 10 miles of track along with culverts and bridges. David's friend, 25-year old George Custer commanded them. They galloped south to rejoin Sheridan's column.

Stuart and David raced as one for Fontaine's.

Flora Stuart greeted her husband, safe and unmolested. They talked quietly for a few moments. The general leaned from his saddle to give her a quick kiss. Farewell, my love.

That night in Taylorsville, David inspected and cleaned Sable. The great horse nuzzled his hand for a tidbit, but tonight there was none; there had been none for several nights. He nickered his displeasure, shoving David with his black nose.

"You mistreating our friend?" Jeb Stuart came out of the dark carrying a small leather bag, "he seems unhappy with you."

"Nothing a carrot wouldn't cure, or a lump of sugar, if I had it. Ran out a week ago, and haven't found a thing since."

The general reached into the bag, "How about some oats?" As if he knew the language, Sable cleaned Stuart's hand. He stood there regally, commanding more.

Stuart fed him another handful. Then, he took off his felt hat, and to David's surprise, removed the jaunty ostrich feather. With sadness, he caressed the long, black plume smooth. He drew it through a brass terret on Sable's bridle, speaking as he did with reverence, without joy, "It has been my talisman. Wear it tomorrow. The fighting will be heavy."

He fed Sable another handful of oats, slapped the muscular neck affectionately, and walked head down into the night.

Touched by his general's love for Sable, puzzled by his melancholy, David found no words as Stuart faded into the darkness. A cheerless Jeb Stuart was most unusual.

He stayed with Sable, rubbing his long nose, staring pensively at nothing until exhaustion overcame him. He lay down with his saddle for a pillow.

In the twilight before sleep, he realized he was in the village where two years ago he had taken a fever and been nursed by an attractive young lady with long, blonde hair. Her name came to him, Vicki, and he wondered nebulously if she was still there in her uncle's house. A memory of their love-making in the gazebo emerged, and he wondered whimsically about her other lovers. How different she was from Carrie, so very different in her giving and in her taking. Carrie, my love, how empty I am without you.

At ten the following morning he was at Yellow Tavern, only six miles from Richmond straight down the Brook Road. Stuart was determined to fight the Yankee cavalry despite the odds.

David was with him when a brigade commander observed, "Sheridan's cavalry is too fast and too big for us."

Stuart snapped, "I would rather die than let him go!"

Shortly before noon, some 10,000 troopers came out of the northwest, down the Mountain Road that angled toward Stuart's position. Custer and his 5th Michigan had rejoined the column after burning Beaver Dam; an over-age trooper by the name of John Huff was in Company E of the 5th. A very ordinary man, John Huff was riding toward the one historic moment in his life.

Stuart deployed his men along the road, dismounted. The adversaries clashed, and a New York regiment circled around to Stuart's rear, between him and Richmond. The New Yorkers attacked furiously. With David at his side, Stuart passed a field gun, several of its crew wounded. He encouraged them to hold on.

"General, you take too many chances," David scolded gently, "as if you love bullets."

"No more than you do, David. I go where duty takes me, come what may. I have no expectation of surviving this war."

There in the confusion of battle, David looked at his commander with surprise, recalling last night's melancholy and sadness. It wasn't like Jeb Stuart to talk that way.

At 4 o'clock the Yankees attacked again, an entire brigade galloping for a battery of field guns on Stuart's left, pounding through it, driving back a good part of the line. The general and David rode immediately for the trouble spot. Another aide fell behind, his horse jaded.

The two of them rallied some 80 men from the broken line, and fought side by side as they had so many times. They fired into the attackers as they thundered by, hitting them flank and rear. Beyond, the 1st Virginia met the charge head on, fought desperately, turned it. Yankees mounted and shanks' mare raced back. John Huff of the 5th Michigan was one of those unhorsed.

As he ran past the small group of Confederates, he saw two officers side by side, one on a huge, black stallion. John Huff never forgot that stallion, rearing and pawing the air. He aimed his revolver. David saw the hole of its muzzle head on, a perfect black circle. He saw the orange flash and winced.

"He was comin' right for me," John Huff remembered, "and I fired. One shot was all I had. After that nothin' but clicks. I threw the empty .44 at him and ran like hell."

John Huff, one-time sharpshooter, had not hit Sable or David, but had shot a hole through Jeb Stuart's right side. Tottering precipitously, the general managed to keep his seat.

David tried to lead Stuart's horse to the rear but the animal was too balky to handle. He helped the general dismount even on the battlefield, and propped him against a tree.

"Get back to the fight," Stuart gasped through his pain, " I fear I'm mortally wounded."

"Sorry, sir. I've been with you too long to leave without seeing you to safety. A surgeon and ambulance are on the way."

David saw his general examined and lifted into an ambulance, then remained with him to Richmond, scouting the road ahead, protecting him through the graying twilight into the night. They had to detour around Yankee cavalry still at Yellow Tavern, north and east to Atlee's Station and south through Mechanicsville, doubling Stuart's suffering for he was shot in vital organs. Well after dark David pulled up at the Grace Street home of Doctor Brewer, the general's brother-in-law.

He, and the medical men around the bed could suggest nothing but applications of ice for the wound. Ice and whiskey to drink.

Jeb refused the latter, "I made a promise to my mother years ago and I have never broken it."

After a night of breath-taking pain, he spent the morning giving last instructions: his personal effects to go to Flora, his sword to his son, a Confederate flag to a woman in South Carolina who had given it to him, his spurs to a friend in Sheperdstown, his bay horse to Major McClellan, another to David.

A crowd gathered around the Brewer house, eager for news of the general's condition, recounting his ride around McClellan. It parted respectfully to allow passage to President Davis. Toward evening, a lightning storm hit and the crowd dispersed. Grace Street was quiet.

David tried to telegraph Flora at Beaver Dam, but lines were down. Finally, a wire did get to her via roundabout routing through Lynchburg and Gordonsville. It reached Flora about noon. With the two children and escorts she left at once on a special train ordered up by Colonel Fontaine who owned the railroad. Two hours later, wrecked tracks in Ashland stopped them.

Transferring to an army ambulance, Flora's desperate effort to reach her husband was delayed by a confusing maze of roads and a vicious thunderstorm, maybe the same one that had drenched the people gathered on Grace Street. Yankee cavalry added to the danger, maybe just ahead, or about to pounce from behind. Flora cradled her children protectively, praying to reach her husband.

Miles ahead of her, David remained with his general as he drifted in and out of consciousness. The afternoon wore on.

Soon after 7 o'clock that evening, Jeb Stuart turned weakly to David, "You have been my friend, David Morrow. God's will be done." He drifted away one more time and was gone, the beau sabreur of the Confederacy, the last of the cavaliers.

Flora Stuart was north of the Chickahominy when Jeb Stuart died, at a bridge site. Just recently, Confederate soldiers had destroyed it to protect Richmond, inadvertently adding to Fora's trial. An empathetic cavalryman offered to guide her to a ford that was passable. She chaffed at the need for detouring a mile to the crossing, but had no choice. Four hours later, her ambulance rattled up to the Grace Street residence.

A dark figure came down the steps and saluted respectfully, "I'm David Morrow, Mrs. Stuart, the general's aide."

"Yes, colonel. My husband is dead."

"He passed away at 7:38 by Doctor Brewer's watch, ma'am."

"I knew it," she said softly, "I am not surprised."

"He spoke of you at the end, Mrs. Stuart. His last request to The Almighty was that he live long enough to see you," David did well to control his emotions, "I am so sorry."

"I have expected it since the beginning, Colonel Morrow. I exhausted my tears long ago."

In the lobby of the Ballard House with Carrie, everybody, it seemed to David, was talking of Jeb Stuart. At the dining room, Carrie felt him stiffen as the maitre d'hotel offered condolences, "We have suffered a great loss, colonel."

David nodded, straining to control the rising anger. Carrie could see it throb at his temple. Seated at last, she reached a hand across the table for his. At her touch, the dam broke.

"Damn it, he shouldn't have died." He slammed the table, overturning his chair as he sprang to his feet. Other diners watched in silence as Carrie ran after him, across the lobby and up the staircase. She closed the door noiselessly as if to compensate for the commotion in the dining room.

"David, I know how you must—"

"Goddamn it," he roared, "nobody knows how I feel. A year ago I brought Pelham here colder than a goddamn mackerel, now it's the general. Stuart was my friend, too, and now he's dead. How the hell many more, Carrie? How the hell many more?"

He fell to his knees, sobbing his fury, calling names from the book of the dead, "Jackson, Pelham, Garnett, Armistead, Rafferty, Stuart. How the hell many more, Carrie. How many?"

Carrie stroked his hair and dropped to her knees with him. She held his face between her hands, lamenting with him, drawing him close. She never loved him more than this moment, this warrior of hers who could still shed tears. They knelt together for many minutes, holding each other.

When his temper subsided, she whispered, "David, do you remember the last time we were together?"

"Every minute. You said you wanted a baby."

"What I said was that I wanted your baby." When no response was forthcoming, she squeezed close and whispered again.

"I still do, more than ever. And I still need your help."

"Carrie, are you sure? I was with the general when he was hit, not two feet away. It could have been me."

Carrie recoiled, her smoky eyes brim full, for the thought had haunted her ever since their greeting kiss in the dark of the morning: it could have been you it could have been you.

She clutched at him frantically, digging into him, sobbing, "That's why, David, that's the reason why."

As he had been comforted, so, too, did he comfort her, lifting her, holding her tight, soothing her until she composed herself, drying her tears. Her fear flashed from moist eyes.

"Love me and tell me everything will be right. Everything will be all right won't it, David? Promise me everything will be all right.

"Promise me, David. Promise me," she whispered as she received him. For a moment, they lay still in their embrace, relishing it, savoring their closeness. He pushed in, even closer, and she lifted tight against him.

"Promise, promise, promise."

The steady, pulsating beat of her demand faded into the healing rhythm of their love-making, and in their love Carrie found the confirmation she sought. Everything was all right. Everything was the way it was meant to be.

LV

MOVING DAY

Jed was awake at dawn, happy and anxious at this day full of promise. Rolling toward Betsy, he kissed behind her ear, "Come on, lazybones, this is the day we've been waiting for."

She purred and wakened slowly.

"Just another two minutes," she answered sleepily.

This was indeed an important day, one they had lived for, the day they were to move to the farm, have their own home, and work the land again, close to Ezekiel and Mattie.

Henry had been dubious, not sure that Jed was mobile enough on his wooden leg, but Ezekiel had taken care of that. He had whittled more on it so that it fitted better, and he had designed a hinged foot-like piece for soft ground.

Jed nuzzled her ear again, "Let's start the day right."

"It's moving day, Jed, and not the way you mean."

"Aw, Betsy."

"Tonight we'll be in our own home," cheerily, she brushed her lips over the tip of his nose, "Alone."

The move from Wolfe Street was hardly that at all, only one trip with a wagon of clothes and personal things. The farmhouse itself took the greater part of the day, uncovering the furniture pieces left by Henry and Sarah, sweeping, scrubbing and washing. It rang with their happiness, Betsy's singing as she worked, and Jed's enthusiasm as he rediscovered the place of his childhood.

"Look what I found," he called with childlike pleasure, holding a child's top to her, "Ezekiel carved it for me. All I need is some string."

Cleaning the crystal chandelier over the dining room table, Betsy paused and looked down from her short ladder. She brushed a forearm across her forehead, "Was that yours? Really?"

"Sure was. See the letters?" he came close to the ladder for her to see, "Zekiel carved them, too, J-E-D."

"We'll name our first son Jed so he'll think it was made for him," she turned back to the chandelier, "it will be nice to live close to Ezekiel and Mattie."

"Betsy?" He moved close to the ladder.

She read him perfectly, "We still have another hour of daylight, enough to finish the dining room and have supper.

"If you want supper, that is," she flirted from her perch, "after that I'm all yours."

Cavalry headquarters was not the same without Jeb Stuart. Gone was the camaraderie, the informality, the evenings of entertainment. Stuart had recognized the importance of laughter and esprit de corps. He recognized the value of relaxation and enjoyment, knowing when to command and when to joke, keeping his perspective and good humor. David missed him, his banter and hearty laughter, his attention to Sable. Another friend lost. Wade Hampton, the new commander, did things differently, as could be expected from a man 15 years older than Stuart, born of a wealthy, South Carolina, planter family. Not that he was a poor leader of cavalry, quite the contrary, but he was patrician, not one to forget his position. Staff duty became strained and tense, tight-lipped and tight-assed. David was not unhappy when Hampton replaced Virginians on his staff with Carolinians.

He informed David impersonally, without rancor; and to give him his due, did ask his preference rather than transfer him preemptively.

"Nothing personal, colonel. Give it some thought."

"Don't have to, sir. Rosser's Laurel Brigade of your old Division is my choice."

"Rosser's a good man. Report to him tomorrow morning."

David did report to Rosser but not as ordered. He was twelve hours early.

"Lieutenant Colonel Morrow reporting for duty, sir."

"What the hell are you talking about?" Rosser scowled, and then thought he understood, "you're here for bourbon duty!"

"No sir. Our new chief asked me to name my poison. He seems wary of Virginians on his staff."

"You mean you're part of the Laurels?"

"Yes, sir. As of tomorrow morning."

Rosser extended his hand, "Damn, that's good news, David. That demands a drink for luck. We'll give 'em hell together."

The first drink led to another, and a discussion of their new commander.

"He's so damned official all the time," David complained, "never lets down, never has time for a laugh, even when things are quiet. Seems to know horses better than men."

"Better than somebody doesn't know what he's doing, killing men without ever knowing it's his fault."

"I agree. Hampton knows his job." David wanted to talk of Jeb Stuart, but remembered Rosser's disillusionment.

"Tom, who ever would have dreamed of this back at The Point, you with your own brigade and us two together."

The very next day, they left camp on a reconnaissance in force behind the Federal right, toward Fredericksburg.

"You stay with me for this one," Rosser directed David, "I may be able to get you a regiment later."

The next few weeks were more of the same, scouting, fighting steadily, Wright's Tavern, Hawes' Shop, Hanover Courthouse, Trevilian Station, a half dozen smaller engagements. David rode at Rosser's side, making a two-man team as he had with Jeb Stuart. Rosser used him as his second in command, much to the consternation of one rank-conscious colonel in the brigade.

May was hardly the merry month of song as casualties mounted, 55,000 Federals, 18,000 Confederates, 300 in the Laurel Brigade. They suffered food shortages, insufficient forage, and a serious loss of horses. Having to furnish their own mounts, many troopers were authorized furloughs to find new ones.

Some relief came on June 1, when Federal cavalry bent on destroying tracks of the Virginia Central drove Southerners from Hanover Courthouse toward Ashland. On duty at brigade, David received Hampton's order to reinforce them, and had buglers blow 'boots and saddles' at once. Rosser came running.

"What the hell's going on?"

"Rooney's in trouble. Hampton's ordered us out." 'Rooney' was W.H.F. Lee, second son of Robert E.

They drove the Federals into Ashland, capturing prisoners, and 200 horses that eased their own shortage. Rosser gave a rare compliment, "I'm glad you joined the brigade, David. It's good to have someone who can act on his own."

Since no one was about, David ignored the formalities, "This one was pretty obvious, Tom. No time to spare."

"That's what I mean. Some would have taken it anyway."

Nothing more was said of his own regiment.

The affair at Trevilian Station, ten days later, saw David and Rosser fighting their old cadet friend, George Custer, as they had a year ago at Gettysburg. Custer had swung around a flank and come up in the Confederate rear, capturing wagons and 800 horses belonging to troopers fighting a half mile north. His daring impetuosity, so often successful, backfired this June 11, getting him into a three-sided trap, north, east, and west.

From the west, David and Rosser with the Laurels thundered down the Gordonsville road in double column, smashing into his troopers. They recaptured wagons and horses about to be hauled off the field. Another column took prisoners and recovered more horses and wagons, including Custer's personal conveyance. Custer himself escaped with his cutup brigade.

Rosser was wounded at Trevilian's, a shot from a carbine that broke his leg. David had a new commander, Colonel Richard Dulany until late August when Rosser returned.

His absence marked hard times for the cavalry, and for David as well, fighting at White House on the Pamunkey, Samaria Church, to Charles City Courthouse, and into the outskirts of Richmond. His hopes to see Carrie vanished when the cavalry crossed the James to join the meager defense force at Petersburg.

Any leave from southside was impossible, David knew that, for Grant's strategy was clear: keep the pressure on, extend Lee's line as reinforcements arrived.

Without Petersburg and its critical railroads that fed Richmond, the Confederate capital could not be held. And Petersburg was being bombarded daily, in greater danger each day as Yankee reinforcements filed into the trenches.

David suspected, as General Lee knew only too well, that he could not win this kind of erosive warfare. Circling his wagons would lead to disaster, and he had little to extend his line as Grant continued to stretch it. Sooner or later, it would break.

In May and June, the Valley Pike had been busy with wagons moving supplies south, but the farm was not touched. July and August saw a Confederate army in and around Winchester, keeping the Yankees at a distance. The weeks scurried by, good to Jed and Betsy in their new home, fine growing weather.

They had worked long and hard since their move, daylight to long after dark. With Mattie's help, Betsy made the house into a home, and Jed and

Ezekiel turned the rich earth for all the seed they could get their hands on. One August evening, they relaxed on the verandah looking over the land they loved.

"Beautiful sunset, Zeke,"

"Brings ta mind a time long ago in Washin'ton. Henry and I watched one just about the same. I'll never forget it," Ezekiel reminisced, "over thirty years ago, in '32. It was Henry's last night before he left Washin'ton for good. We talked a bit and looked out over the canal and over the Potomac River at the sunset. A long time ago, Jed, and it seems like only yesterday."

They watched the sun nestle into the western mountains.

And Ezekiel spoke again from his heart, "Jed, it's good ta have you near. Hardly a night goes by Mattie doesn't say it's nice ta see lights in the big house."

"I feel the same, Zeke, about bein' close t'you-all. And t'smell the plowed ground."

"It is good, Jed. Sweet 'n fresh."

"Somethin' about it, new plowed in the spring, sproutin' and growin'. Like your lights t'Mattie'. I'll never get enough of it." He reached down for a handful of the rich loam, smelling it close to his nose, and letting it sift through his fingers, "Sweet as anythin' I know." He raised his hand to re-capture the aroma.

"You said the same in the spring when we were plowin', Jed."

"And I've thought the same every day since. No mystery in why it's called 'Mother Earth'."

The peacefulness of the evening overwhelmed the knowledge of cannons booming into Petersburg, and for the time being, the war itself. It seemed a long way off. Even as they talked, Lincoln and Grant were discussing the Shenandoah Valley.

General Early's incursion into Maryland and his advance on Washington had panicked the nation's officialdom. Something must be done, Lincoln and Grant were agreeing, to stop the years of fumbling with the Shenandoah Valley. Too long had it served as a highway into Maryland and Washington, as the breadbasket of the Confederacy. The solution, they agreed, was to combine competing military districts. They agreed, too, on a commander, 33-year old Phil Sheridan, brigadier general, aggressive, graduate of West Point in the undistinguished class of 1853, antagonist of Jeb Stuart at Yellow Tavern in May.

His job would be to clean 'em out. Carry off what could be moved, burn the rest, livestock, crops, forage, horses, mills, barns, anything that by the broadest interpretation helped the Southern cause. Warfare on civilians was no longer unacceptable. They could end their misery by surrendering.

The first night south of the James River, David looked toward Richmond, "Carrie, my love, when we were together, I knew everything would be all right. Tonight, I am not so sure."

He bowed his head in silence for several minutes, "God. our Heavenly Father and Protector, I ask forgiveness for making a pledge that only You can make. Protect Carrie. Protect me. Thy will be done." The day was Sunday, June 26.

The next day, he headed for the western extremity of Lee's line to protect the vital Weldon Railroad, one of the two remaining rail links to food sources. Detouring to avoid the bombardment, the column continued on to Reams' Station, seven miles south of the city.

Almost at once, David led a scouting party that found a Federal cavalry division bent on interrupting traffic on the Weldon line. It was the first of many such forays that kept him busy for a month and more protecting the railroad.

After the shortages of food and forage north of the James, the area was a veritable Eden, affording David and his men a plenteous supply, melons and luscious fruit, fine fishing in the streams, and generous welcomes by landholders happy for the cavalry's protection. In addition, many absentees returned, recovered sick and wounded, troopers with new horses.

On the 24th of August, Rosser returned to assume command.

"I'm glad to see you back, Tom. How's the leg?"

"Not very good. It still hurts like hell. How've you been?"

"Busy. I'm afraid Petersburg is our Waterloo. We're caught, unable to accomplish anything where we stand, unable to break clear. We'll be starved out when we lose the railroads."

"Back in the spring, Longstreet said not to underestimate Grant. He's known him for years."

"Knows him very well, I'd say."

The very next day, they were in a 12-hour action at Reams' Station, driving Federal cavalry back to its supports, and then with the help of infantry forcing them from their defense line. The Confederacy was hanging on, fighting desperately for its two lifelines.

LVI

TOM'S BROOK
OCTOBER 9, 1864

On September 14th, David and Rosser took off on an audacious 3-day raid that caught the fancy of the entire Confederacy. They rustled Grant's cattle herd on James River pastureland.

To avoid detection, the raiders rode a 20-mile arc across the rear of Grant's army to Coggins Point, only six miles from his headquarters. They defeated a substantial guard, and drove the 2,500 beeves back to Confederate quartermasters. En route, David had an unusual exchange with General Hampton.

They had crossed the Blackwater River, Hampton riding with the Laurel Brigade, David leading the scouts as he had for Jeb Stuart. Hampton pressed him, "Keep a sharp eye, colonel! Report anything suspicious."

For the first time, David challenged his commander, "I know my job, general." He rode off without a salute.

Hampton took it out on his brigadier, "You may put up with disrespect, Rosser, but I don't. I want that man up on charges when we get back. I'll want you to testify."

"Write him up? I witnessed nothing. Sir."

"No disrespect!" Hampton huffed, "what do you call it?"

"A man proud of the job he does. He's the best. Sir."

Rosser did well to control himself for he disliked Hampton; the new cavalry chief had bypassed him for division command.

On a slight rise a hundred yards ahead, David pulled up and stood Sable on his hind legs. He waved a loose salute.

The symbolism was lost on Hampton, but not Rosser. *Good for you, Dave, give the son of a bitch what he deserves.*

"What are you grinning at?" Hampton growled.

"At one of the best officers I know, sir. He's telling us that his horse knows his job, too."

Two days later, as Confederate quartermasters distributed Grant's beeves, David slammed a newspaper to the floor, "Did you see this, Tom? The Yankees are raising hell in The Valley again."

"Yes, damn it. And more men will head for home."

"Can't much blame them. They're still Ashby's men, recruited in the Valley expecting to protect their own families."

The men of the Laurel Brigade had fumed ever since they left their Valley. Hunter's pillaging upset them; Sheridan's, more. Letters from loved ones and newspapers written by strangers told of the suffering: womenfolk mistreated, their own wives, mothers, sisters; crops, barns, mills burned to ashes; livestock stolen, homes ransacked. Milroy, Sigel, Hunter, Sheridan, damn them all!

They cursed all the Yankees for devils, and their villainy the work of demons. Hatred was in their eyes as they squinted to the Valley; vengeance in the brown, tobacco juice they spat.

"Maraudin' sonsabitches!"

Just as they had felt going into Maryland in '62, they were irate now, fighting for farms not their own, reading of the latest devil in their Valley.

"Sonofabitch!"

A few days after the cattle raid, they heard rumors of a third battle for Winchester. The bad news was substantiated. Once again, the city had fallen under Yankee rule.

Came still another defeat, at Fisher's Hill, and Early's retreat to Port Republic. More suffering for their families. Frustration rolled again over the Laurel Brigade.

Monday, the twenty-sixth of September, was a better day for the Valley men for they had orders to bolster Early. They would be going home. To protect their own.

David and Rosser went ahead by rail to Lynchburg, on to Staunton and Mount Sydney reporting to Early on October 2.

Around Lynchburg, David saw the evidence of Hunter's passage, fields, barns and homes black with scorch, charred timbers fallen in, stone chimneys lonely against the sky. As he went down The Valley, he saw family after family by the roadside dazed by this man-made plague, the children too young to understand, the oldsters too set in their ways to adjust.

"Goddamn the monsters," David cursed to no one particular, "this isn't warfare. Nothing but ignominious scoundrels running amok, preying on helpless people."

Rosser was given one of the two cavalry divisions assigned to the Valley army, three brigades, Payne's, and Wickham's, and his own Laurels reduced to 600 troopers, hardly a regiment. David remained with Rosser in the same capacity he had served Jeb Stuart, aide de camp, scout, and confidant.

As David proceeded to Bridgewater near Harrisonburg, the depredation became a personal affront, heinous and loathsome. Citizens suffering cruel or drunken men was one thing, but this? Ordered and condoned by officers called gentlemen?

"My God," he complained, "Lee prohibited molestation and looting in Maryland. Burning was beyond mention."

At Bridgewater, he saw smoke to the northwest, fires still smoldering. He had no way of knowing that his friend, George Custer, had set them on specific orders from Sheridan.

Perhaps Custer had his reservations, too, for reporting a few days ago of burned mills, barns, and fields, he also wrote, "No dwelling houses were destroyed or interfered with."

On October 5, Sheridan left Harrisonburg to sweep the Valley once more, his cavalry cutting parallel swathes down its 20-mile width. He used all three north-south routes, the Valley pike in the shadow of the Massanutten Range, the Middle Road, and the Back Road, the westernmost. Cutting across streams and spurs of North Mountain, the Back Road was the most difficult.

He had already accomplished much of Grant's order to leave The Valley "a barren waste," and this sweep would finish the job, forcing a crow, he said, to carry his own rations to cross it.

George Custer, leading his new division, was assigned the Back Road, with its ascents and declivities, its fords of clear water purling sweetly from the mountains. The fortunes of war put David, with Rosser and his brigades, on the same road. The three cadet friends clashed again, at Brock's Gap late in the evening of October 6, the first of several actions.

"They're just ahead, where the road rises," David pointed out, "the rear guard."

They attacked, pushed the guard back, but were repulsed when they came onto the main body with artillery deployed on the high ground across Dry River. Custer held until dark, then withdrew.

As they duelled their way down the Back Road, Custer learned who his tormentors were.

"Morrow and Rosser! I'll be damned." He left at least two notes along the way, where he knew they would be picked up.

"Don't expose yourself so. I could have killed you yesterday," one read. After he had captured Rosser's personal wagon, he wrote another, "Tom, next time, have your uniform made smaller so that it will fit me when I capture it."

Custer had indeed captured a brand new uniform and slipped it on to entertain his camp. At 140 pounds, it was an ill fit, made as it was for the 200-pound, 6'2" Rosser.

"He must have tried it on, the little squirt," David offered in good humor.

"Squirt is not adequate for that—," Rosser thundered.

For more than three years he had never really hated Custer, but he did now. He felt this note sheer insolence.

Rosser had orders to continue the pursuit.

At dawn, David resumed his station up ahead of the column. All morning he rode through heartbreak, more barns, outbuildings, and crops burned to the ground; more hollow farmsteads, without crops, food, or livestock, only ashes, ashes and carcasses.

Behind David, the men seethed in their own fury, for the smoldering farms belonged to them and their friends; the distraught wives and children, the bewildered elders standing by the wayside were their neighbors, their friends, their families.

"Every house was visited," David wrote Carrie, ". . . feeling alike the blasting and savage hand of war . . . robbed of every means of sustenance."

The Southern troopers seethed and spat their brown hate.

Between two and three o'clock in the afternoon, the Laurel Brigade was leading the column along the Back Road, just above Mount Jackson. David raised his hand in the signal to halt.

The fire fiends were ahead, slowed by the wagons of plunder and stolen livestock. Now they would have to fight.

Custer deployed his men in a defensive position behind Mill Creek, covering the ford where it flowed gently over the Back Road. Rosser studied the situation.

"David, what do you think?"

"Looks too strong to attack up the road."

"I agree. I want you to scout downstream, cross and attack with the 35th. Better take a squadron from Dulany, too." The 35th was White's Battalion and Dulany was commanding Rosser's Laurels.

Rosser continued, "When you attack, I'll hit 'em in front." "Yes, sir."

David collected his temporary command and set the pace with the acting commander of the 35th. Finding a good crossing, they backtracked along the north bank. A flank guard of Federals blocked their path. David charged, driving them onto their main force on a prominence controlling the ford. After the acres of scorched earth, he blew sky high, screeching wildly, outrunning his men for the enemy on the hill. The 35th, aptly called the Comanches, rode savagely, too, for their frenzy equalled his.

Now Rosser galloped through the ford, the 11th and 12th Virginia in front, screaming their lungs, avenging their families and their Valley. Never before had one of them felt such hatred. The Yankees had truly become the enemy.

When darkness put an end to the melee at Mill Creek, Custer moved off to the north, abandoning the beeves and sheep and laden wagons. Rosser bivouacked where he was, separated from his infantry support by ten miles. He did what he could to return the recaptured loot to the proper Valley folk.

David slid from Sable exhausted, his legs weak and numb, his head reeling. For several minutes, he lay on his back near Mill Creek, too wearied to move. Sable moved slowly to the clear, mountain stream and drank his fill. He looked at David, stood in the cool water a moment, then moved toward him with concern. He nuzzled softly, as if to say, "Are you all right? Wake up."

Sable shook out his feathery mane, nuzzling him again. Together, they splashed through the shallow ford.

Confederate armies had repeatedly chased Yankees out of the lush Valley, Patterson in 1861, Banks in '62, Sigel and Hunter more recently. Each, with a larger army, had been stung badly enough to call it quits. When Custer continued down the Back Road after Mill Creek, Early's prediction that Sheridan would be number five seemed correct: he appeared to be leaving the Valley, too. Accordingly, Early ordered Rosser to maintain the pursuit.

Both David and Rosser questioned Early's opinion, for they knew Sheridan to be no quitter. Nor were his division commanders Merritt and Custer whom they knew well.

They resumed their pursuit down the Valley, reluctantly, vigilantly, dangerously beyond infantry support. Constantly, the road ahead showed ugly smoke. Wherever they looked, they saw fire and smoke; wherever they turned, they smelled the burning.

Leading the column with the scouts, David caught four soldiers at the tag end of Custer's column setting fire to a farmer's barn. His impulse was to shoot them down, but he resisted long enough to ask questions. When one of the family said the Yankees had maltreated the women, David's thin reservoir of patience ran out.

"Shoot the bastards," he yelled, "take them into the woods and shoot them."

One of the scouts tried to calm him, "Sir, don't do it. Let a courtmartial take care of them."

"Soldier, that's an order," David faced him with menace in his voice, "they're damned miserable bushwhackers, bandits, horse thieves. If you don't like it, ride the hell off.

"Now shoot the sonsofbitches. NOW!"

About noon, they were close to the Yankees, but Custer drove his men, increasing the distance. He crossed Tom's Brook and went on toward Strasburg. David continued to scout ahead.

Unknown to him, Custer turned eastward, toward the Valley Turnpike. David, and the column behind him, kept on toward Strasburg. Soon, he realized he had lost contact.

He was uneasy, for he knew the Yankees hadn't been hurt badly enough to withdraw. A Federal retreat didn't make sense, despite what General Early thought. Yet, he couldn't be sure of Sheridan's intent. Maybe he had orders to join Grant. They would have to play it both ways.

David sent a courier back to Rosser, "Tell him we've lost contact with Custer. We're proceeding with caution. The road up here is all too quiet. Got all that? "

"Yes, sir. Lost contact, proceed with caution, things too quiet," following David's procedure to ensure accuracy.

Rosser received the message and answered by way of the same courier, "Keep it slow. We're already too far from our infantry."

Two scouts reported to David within minutes of each other, one riding hard from up ahead.

"Sheridan's making camp at Strasburg," he said.

David knew Early was wrong. If Sheridan were leaving the Valley, he would be taking advantage of the daylight. It was too early in the day to be bivouacking.

The other scout galloped from the open country to the east. His horse was lathered, obviously ridden hard.

"A large body of cavalry, division size, is off to the southeast," he pointed, "heading for the Back Road."

Immediately, David wheeled Sable, waving for his scouts to follow. Galloping Sable full out, he raced for Rosser.

"Tom, we've been duped. Sheridan's camped at Strasburg. And Custer is moving to cut us off, this side of Tom's Brook likely."

Rosser reversed his order of march. "Let 'em out," he boomed, "let 'em out." The column flew up the Back Road, over the ground he had covered so cautiously.

The column and Custer were on a collision course, one racing to establish a roadblock, the other plunging headlong to avoid it. David's wariness had gained the slimmest of margins, just enough to launch a saber charge that caught the head of Custer's column before he could establish his position.

Riding low at a full gallop, they spurred desperately through the Yankees, and thundered the remaining distance to Tom's Brook. They splashed through the shallow ford. Custer did not pursue in the deepening twilight.

In the cool of the autumn evening, David and regimental officers warmed by the fire, discussing the situation. Had they seen Sheridan's thousand campfires in the Shenandoah night, they would have been more vocal about pulling back right then. Even so, several were reluctant to stay where they were.

"We're 25 miles from our support!"

"We'd better withdraw now while we have the chance."

"We know we're outnumbered so why stay?"

"That's the easiest question of all," David answered good-naturedly," because the general said to."

The others nodded, happy to ease the tension amongst them.

A tall figure walked into the circle of firelight, Rosser himself, "I like your answer, colonel. You all know that I have orders to pursue and encourage their retreat from the Valley."

"But, general, we know now they aren't retreating."

Rosser snapped, "But Early doesn't. We can withdraw in the morning if we have to. Good night, gentlemen."

As they were talking, the peppery Sheridan was ranting at his chief of cavalry, "It's time you fought 'em," he told Torbert, "whip the rebel cavalry or get whipped yourself."

The thirty-year old Torbert passed the order to his division commanders, along with the warning that put careers on the line: Sheridan would be observing from high ground.

Custer, still on the Back Road, and Merritt, to the east, moved before dawn to force a fight. Their men had Spencers, seven-shot repeater carbines, and a coordinated command. Rosser's Division and Lomax's, opposite Merritt, had neither.

Rosser deployed along the southern bank of Tom's Brook: Munford's Brigade, that had been Wickham's, held the left from Little North Mountain to the Back Road; Payne's demi-brigade next; the 35th Virginia Battalion, White's Comanches, on Payne's right; and Dulany's Laurel Brigade on the right flank. Artillery overlooked the ford. Dulany would have to watch his flank, for a two-mile gap separated him from Lomax on the Valley turnpike.

Rosser's position was formidable, with six guns on high ground. At the base of the ridge, he dismounted troopers behind a stone fence and barricades of rails and logs.

David was with Rosser about 8:30 A.M. when he spotted George Custer across Tom's Brook. He wheeled Sable and saluted. Custer responded with a low bow. Rosser did the same.

From his own ridge, Custer opened with artillery fire. He sent dismounted cavalrymen and three regiments against the Confederate center along with field guns. Plunging fire disabled two of the guns; the rest withdrew. White's Comanches stopped the mounted regiments. Custer's blood rose at the repulse. He readied regiments to renew the frontal attack, and shifted three others, Pennsylvanians and New Yorkers, to turn the Confederate left. Munford saw the buildup in his front and warned Rosser.

"David, see what the hell that's all about."

David rode back with the courier and saw the dangerous flanking move. He galloped to Rosser.

"Munford's right, Tom, they're too many for him."

Inexplicably, Rosser dismissed the threat with cavalier abandon, "He can hold them."

"No, Tom, there are too many. They'll turn your flank."

Rosser flashed him a stern look.

"At least give me a squadron to help him."

"Can't spare them."

"A company, then."

"Damn it, you have your answer." Rosser would have none of it. He walked away, inflaming David and leaving Munford to take care of himself. Ignoring a danger like this, and rejecting David was not characteristic. David failed to understand it.

"Yes, sir," David answered angrily, "then I'll go myself."

He wheeled Sable and headed for the endangered left.

Custer coordinated his attack beautifully, putting Rosser's entire line under heavy pressure. No chance, now, to shift forces. The Confederate center held, but Munford on the left was turned, just as he had foreseen and David had confirmed. Gunners poured grape and shrapnel into the attackers but failed to stop them. Munford's 1st and 2nd Virginia fell back, exposing Payne's two regiments at the ford.

The weight of the attack forced the artillerymen to abandon their guns. Rosser himself led a saber attack to recapture them. He couldn't do it.

One gunner who had to run, George Neese, wrote that he departed "not a moment too soon, for it was not long after . . . I saw the blue horsemen swarm all over the hill . . ."

Neese and his crew did manage to save their gun and went into battery again on a hill to the south, firing crazily to stem the blue tide. David saw their efforts and joined them.

Over on the right, the fighting was equally fierce, Dulany and Payne holding firm. The Federals attacked again.

Bluecoats rolled up Munford left to right, then the rest of Rosser's line in turn, Payne's two regiments at the ford, White's Comanches, and finally the Laurels, each unable to hold as its left was exposed.

Just before noon, David fell back again, still with Neese's gun, to a third position two hundred yards east of the Back Road. He ran Sable to a large boulder offering relative safety, patted his nose, "Be back soon, old friend."

Rushing back to the gun, he kept it firing, sweeping the ground in front.

A shout pierced the bedlam, "Boys, save yourselves!"

They were on their own, each man for himself.

David raced for Sable.

The gun crew was captured, including George Neese who described the surrender.

"In less than five minutes there were a thousand Yankee cavalryman, with drawn sabers, around us." As he stood with hands in the air, he had been shot at by one of them, "there was nothing left for me to do but excuse him, which I did with the humble grace of a subjugated captive."

David was the only one to get out, running for Sable. Leaping into the saddle, he shrieked, "Go, Sable. Go."

The big stallion sped through the thin woods.

A shot rang out, another, a third, fourth and fifth in quick succession. Only a Spencer fired that fast. David felt a dull thud and a tug at his shoulder. Sable raced for the sheltering trees. David reined him west, into the mountains.

"Our only chance, old boy. This is a damned rout."

LVII

CLAIRVOYANCE IN RICHMOND

As David fought his gun's third and final position at Tom's Brook, Mrs. Burgess poured tea for Carrie on Richmond's Church Hill. Sunday afternoons she had kept the tradition, her bone china, dainty, tatted serviettes, all but her sterling service.

She offered scones.

"Carrie, how did the Secretary take your leaving?" Mrs. Burgess sipped from her second cup.

"Mr. Seddon was gracious enough to say he would miss me. He said Friday would be fine, or sooner if I feel sickly. I think he feels some embarrassment."

She touched her abdomen, "I'm not showing that much, am I?"

"Not so's to cause embarrassment, but that's men for you."

"He did say he would give me a letter over his signature. 'You might have occasion to use it travelling through army country,' he said. He gave it to me that very afternoon."

"That was kind of him, dear," Mrs. Burgess lifted the china teapot, "may I?"

Carrie sipped from the cup and held it toward her landlady whom she had come to love, "I'll miss these Sunday afternoons."

"I, too," Mrs. Burgess looked up from her pouring, "Carrie! What is it!!

Carrie gasped. Her hand trembled. The cup rattled against its saucer.

"What is it? You are pale as a ghost!"

She clutched her throat, moving her lips, trying to answer.

"My heavens! What is it? Are you choking?" Jumping from her chair in alarm, the older lady thwacked her on the back.

Carrie shook her head desperately, darting wild eyes about the room, clawing at her throat, gagging, gasping. She managed a wheezy, little breath of air. And another. Bit by bit, the paroxysm eased and her locked lungs pumped shallow and rapid. She gulped a swallow of air. Gradually the spell subsided.

"Thank God," Mrs. Burgess sighed, "what happened? The tea? The scones?"

"It's David! Sable! Help David—I have to help David!"

Frenzied, she lunged for the door. Her eyes shouted fear and alarm. Her voice shrilled, "David is in trouble! Mrs. Burgess. He needs me. I can't wait. I have to go to him. Right now."

The older lady remonstrated, but Carrie heard only David's call. Something terrible had happened. She had to get to him.

Bereft of all reason, she ran through the foyer, "Don't leave me, David. I'm coming. I'm coming."

"Carrie, stop!" Mrs. Burgess' sharp voice cut through the delirium as she followed. Clasping her arm, she cooed soothingly, "Of course, dear, but David doesn't want you to leave like this."

Carrie let herself be led back into the parlor, "Something awful has happened to him. He's bleeding," she screamed, "he's been shot, Mrs. Burgess. He's been shot!"

West of Tom's Brook, Sable angled into the mountains. At a small run, David pulled up to examine his throbbing arm, to give Sable water and a breather. A very quick stop, for Yankees might be close. Awkwardly, with one hand and teeth, he tied a bandage of sorts. He filled his canteen. Looking to the sky for Polaris, he guided west and north. He was vague about the stops after that first one.

Across the Valley's floor, faint gray of the new day limned the Blue Ridge. Horse and rider descended Little North Mountain into the Shenandoah Valley. Scattered clouds reflected raucous orange from the sun a minute below the horizon, but the weary horseman sagged precariously in the saddle and saw nothing. His horse plowed along, head low, lifting torpidly with each step. They had travelled the whole night, David and Sable, more than twenty miles through the mountains.

Sable's black coat was dull with dust and dirt, stickers and twigs, his quick eyes slowed by fatigue. Every bit as dirty and more weary, David held to the last vestiges of consciousness.

Weakened by the long night and the bullet wound, he was unaware that Sable had brought him out of the mountains. Not until the great stallion stopped at the edge of the forest and the sun flashed along the Blue

Ridge did he realize the night was over. He winced and raised his good arm to shade his eyes.

Forcing the last of his strength, he squinted against the sunrise for a landmark. Nothing. Nothing at all.

Then he caught a silvery ribbon on the edge of the Valley floor. Recognizing Opequon Creek, he rode on. Familiar lines emerged, fences, barns, house and cottage of the Morrow farmstead its limestone more white than blue in the morning light. His instincts, or Sable's, or the hand of God had brought them home.

"Almost there, Sable," he rasped and patted him weakly.

With Mrs. Burgess' help, Carrie left Richmond on Monday, the day after the interrupted tea. Teary-eyed, they embraced. "Thank you for everything," Carrie hesitated, "Mother Burgess."

"Bless you for that. I'll pray for you. And your David. Please write me." Overcome, Carrie could only wave a gloved hand.

A carriage took her to the Virginia Central depot.

That same Monday was a trying one for Ezekiel and Mattie, too. It started an hour after sunrise when OleHoundawg set up a horrendous yelping.

"Lawdamercy, what's got inta that dog?" Ezekiel threw the question away as he went to investigate. He found David and Sable at the barn, David staring blankly from the saddle.

"Mattie! Come here quick!" Ezekiel ran to help David dismount, "Help him inside while I get Sable inta the barn."

She washed David's face and frowned as she inspected his arm. No bones broken. She washed it as best she could, bandaged it, and put him to bed.

"Ezekiel, We'll have t'get Henry and Sarah."

"I want ta look around first. I got a feelin'."

David had slept only a few hours when Ezekiel ran back to the house shouting, "Get Sable and the mules. Quick!"

"What is it, Ezekiel?"

"Yankees comin'! Get them ta the woods, and stay there. I'll get David inta the cellar."

Taking the stairs by twos, he shook David and shook him. He dragged him out of bed, "Yankees comin'. You gotta hide."

Too weak to fight anyone, he resisted, "Hide from Yankees? Damned if I will!"

"David, there's no time for arguin'. They're headin' up the lane. They'll be here in a few minutes."

"Can't help that," David fumbled with one of his holsters.

"David. David. There's too many of 'em. Besides, they find you here, they'll take it out on Mattie and me."

David scowled as he realized the truth. They would indeed molest them, mostly Mattie. "In the attic?"

"Gotta better place."

Ezekiel helped him down the narrow stairs into the cellar, "David, you're feelin' hot. You got fever."

"Just tired, Zeke, I'll be fine."

David watched as he revealed the room he had carved out. He pointed David into it, "I gotta move them shelves back."

"Damnit, Zeke, I don't like leaving you alone with them."

"Better this way. They don't take kindly ta protectin' Southern officers."

Ezekiel slid the shelves back, smoothed the dirt floor and went outside to meet the patrol. When he saw them approaching at a walk he knew Mattie was in the clear. Thank you, Lawd.

"Hey! You, nigger, tell yer master t'come out here. Then vamoose, y're free."

Ezekiel waited for the lieutenant and his men to halt. It had been the soldier riding next to him who had spoken, a leathery-faced man with three large chevrons on his sleeve.

"I have no master, " he answered evenly, "I'm a free man. Been free most all my life."

Frowning at the unexpected reply, the sergeant dismounted and walked close, nose to nose. Ezekiel held his ground.

"You ain't one uh them uppity niggers, loyal t'yer master? You ain't one uh them now?"

"No. I'm not uppity as you call it. I'm lookin' for no trouble, just ta be left alone."

"Don't sound respec'ful t'me." The sergeant turned to the other troopers, "whadda you think?" Suddenly, he spun back, swinging a blow that knocked Ezekiel to the ground.

"You still feelin' uppity, nigger?"

With difficulty, Ezekiel controlled his anger as he got to his feet. He hesitated for a moment, looking up at the mounted men, appraising them. Eight troopers there were, including the sergeant and the lieutenant. Ezekiel chose his words.

"You'll get a fair fight if you give me one."

The sergeant fumed at the challenge, "You damned black scoundrel. Y'need uh lesson in how t'talk t'yer betters."

"Sergeant, that's enough," the officer barked sharply in a voice with more authority than his boyish face.

The two soldiers remained motionless, eyes locked. Deep in his young face, the lieutenant's eyes flashed. The sergeant wavered, and shuffled to his horse.

The other shouted an order to the rest of his men, "Dismount. You know what to do. Jones, you search the house."

He addressed Ezekiel, civilly enough, "Anyone inside?"

"No, sir. A young couple with their baby in Liberty Hall," Ezekiel used the name proudly, remembering Brian's telling how his friends had named it.

"Liberty Hall? What's that?"

"The big house, over there," he answered with dignity.

The lieutenant touched his breast pocket and the letter he had received only yesterday. His wife had written of his new son.

"One more thing," he shouted to his men, "the big house. Stay away from it. And its people."

The soldiers did their job reluctantly for they were farmers who had labored to build similar barns and raise the same crops.

Their fires walked the fields, consuming gold and green, excreting black. Flames flared in stored hay and up the tinder-dry boards of the barns, punching through sloping roofs. All was burned except the two houses, and Ezekiel's stone spring house.

Private Jones tramped through Ezekiel and Mattie's house. Opening one door, he saw a stairway dwindling into the darkness. He lighted a candle and started down, rather carelessly for his heel caught one of the narrow treads. Down he tumbled, a heap onto the dirt floor. The candle snuffed out. Disoriented, he lay still. His wrist hurt and his ribs on the right side.

Gradually, his head cleared. The rectangle of the open doorway came into focus and he remembered stairs, candle, and a helpless moment of falling into darkness.

Groping along the dirt floor, he found the candle, relighted it, held it high. On one knee now, he could make out the boulders of the foundation walls piled one on the other, and the rough-timbers stretched across. He followed the flickering light along the wall to the rickety shelves hiding David's cave.

Private Jones was attracted to the stored jars for he recalled similar ones at home, filled and waiting. Tantalizing memories of brandied peaches and jellies created expectations. He grabbed a jar. It was empty. He cursed and smashed it against the stone foundation.

In his cave, David held his breath, not daring to cock his Colt for the telltale click, but aiming it for the little tunnel.

Three feet away, Private Jones looked into another jar and threw it, and another and several more. Dismayed, he spat two words as one, "Fuggit," and climbed the stairs.

The Yankees completed their job and left.

Ezekiel waited and watched. Satisfied, he brought David upstairs and started for Winchester, stopping at the big house. From the verandah, Jed and Betsy surveyed smoldering outbuildings and fields. Jed would have fought had not Betsy stopped him.

"Just like that," Ezekiel snapped his fingers, "they emptied the smoke-house and burned the rest. The lieutenant told 'em leave the houses alone." Ezekiel shrugged puzzlement, "Mattie got the mules and Sable inta the woods."

"Sable!!"

"I was comin' up ta tell y'all when I saw the Yankees."

"Tell us what?"

"That David's home. Rode in after sun-up."

"David's home? Here? How come Mattie took Sable?" he asked suspiciously, "what's wrong with David, Zeke? He hurt bad?"

Ezekiel answered quickly to ease Jed's concern, "Mostly wore out from ridin' all night. He took a bullet, but he'll be fine."

"Thank God for that." Betsy breathed a sigh of relief, "They didn't hurt you," she hesitated very much concerned, "or Mattie?"

"They take David with them?" Jed broke in.

Zeke held up his hand to slow them down, "No, they didn't find David. I had him hid. And didn't hurt me. Mattie watched from the wood and didn't come back until they left."

With little Sarah wrapped against the fall breeze, Betsy and Jed went at once to David.

Ezekiel continued into Winchester with mixed feelings. He had looked forward to telling Henry and Sarah their son was home, but now he had the burning to report.

"Mornin', Sarah."

"Why, Ezekiel, what a pleasant surprise. I just put the coffee pot on. Almost the last of what the Yankees left."

"Come ta tell you and Henry David come back."

"David's home? That's wonderful!" Then fear hit her, "Ezekiel, why are you telling me? Why isn't he here?'

For the second time that day, he raised his hand to allay worry, "He's all right. Got himself shot, but he's all right."

"Wounded!"

"In his shoulder. Seems ta have some fever. Mattie cleaned it and put fatback on it, but she wants you there."

"That's good, that will help the fever. I'll get my things."

"What things?" Henry greeted Ezekiel.

"The bag the doctor left. David's at the farm and needs me."

"David's at the farm? He's hurt?"

"Not bad," was all Ezekiel could say before Henry erupted, "First Jed, then Brian. Now David!" He shook his fist high.

The past and the present merged, Yankees, Indians, Civil War, frontier massacre, Winchester and Woodstock, called Muellerstadt by grandfather Ephraim and the Painter family. It wasn't only Henry shouting, but grandfather Ephraim across the century. Henry became one with his ancestors.

"Goddamned baby-killers." His voice rose to the feral scream of a mountain cat protecting her young, "Your bloody hands will burn in hellfire. You killed the Painters and their babies. You hurt my sons. You basta-a-a-a-a-r-r-s!" His eyes blazed insanely.

"And we're still fightin' back," his voice rose now in a crescendo of victory, "us Morrows will always fight you savages."

Spent, Henry Morrow slumped to the floor, tears of sheer frustration and tears of victory coursing inseparable down his cheeks. Sarah knelt by him, cradling his head in her arms, caressing the gray hair, loving him more than ever before.

Ezekiel stood by, his head bowed in respect. He couldn't put into words what he had witnessed, but he knew it was good.

Sarah wiped at her own tears, wanting to comfort her husband forever, knowing that others needed her, too.

"Shall we go to David, Henry?"

Twenty-four hours of rattle, jounce, dirt and delay brought Carrie to Staunton. Unable to find transportation down the Valley, she approached a uniformed officer by a small wagon train headed north. As quartermaster in charge of the train, he refused her request impudently; running supplies was problem enough without a woman to bother with. Anyways, women in her condition should stay the hell to home. But then maybe a woman like this—

Carrie took in his open inspection of her, and fished in her reticule. With a rapier look, she presented Mr. Seddon's letter.

"To whom it may concern—It is my wish that you tender your protection and consideration to the bearer, Carrie Morrow. Mrs. Morrow is the wife of David Morrow, Lieutenant Colonel of Cavalry, C.S.A.

James A. Seddon Secretary of War.

Carrie let him have the second barrel.

"Yes, lieutenant, I am going to have a baby. You know about that, don't you?"

Trapped between his misplaced fantasy and an outspoken lady with high connections, the young officer was doubly embarrassed. He felt like an intruder in his mother's bedroom.

"Y—Y—You are Mrs. M-Morrow?"

"Of course," she snapped, "who else would I be!"

Chastised by this lady who read his mind, and reined short by the Secretary's letter, he was eager to make amends.

He saluted his best, "I'm sorry, ma'am. I just wanted you to know that the Valley is dangerous. Only Yankees and trouble."

"I'm sure *they* would not mistreat me," she answered coldly.

The young officer raised his eyebrows, "Beg pardon, ma'am, but Yankees can't be trusted. Their actions have proved that."

"I don't care. I have to get to my husband."

"Yes, mam. I have supplies for cavalry near New Market. General Rosser."

"General Rosser! My husband is with him. He's been hurt. Two days ago, on Sunday, he was hurt."

"Sunday? Probably at Tom's Brook, ma'am. A terrible day."

"Is there a hospital nearby where my husband might be?"

"No, ma'am. He might be anywhere between here and Strasburg. Most likely in a private home if he was wounded. Best to get to Rosser's camp. Maybe they know something."

In New Market, she accepted his arm to climb stiffly out of the springless wagon. She arched her back against the aches, and the young lieutenant discreetly averted his eyes. Escorting her to Rosser's Division, he repeated his apology.

Seeking revenge for Tom's Brook, Rosser had patrols out daily to report on Custer's whereabouts. He was obsessed with "that little squirt," but he greeted Carrie with enthusiasm.

"I finally get to meet you, Mrs. Morrow. If you'll excuse an observation, David didn't exaggerate a bit. He's a lucky man."

"Please, general, it's Carrie."

"I'm honored, ma'am," he bowed his head briefly, "I am also surprised to see you here. How did you know David is missing?"

"Missing!! I know only that he is hurt."

"How can you? The lists are still being prepared."

"General, I just know."

"He is listed as missing."

"Missing? Just missing? That's all?"

"He was with one of the guns when Yankees overran it. Last seen running for that black stallion of his."

"Running away? Not David. David wouldn't do that."

"Desert? Oh no! I didn't mean that. The line was overrun and it was escape or surrender. He would never submit."

"That makes no sense. He simply can't vanish like that."

"I'm sorry, Carrie, no one has seen him since. Not a word. Maybe he was captured. I just don't know."

"I'd like to talk to those who saw him last, if I may."

Rosser sent an orderly for two troopers who had seen David last, but they repeated only what had been said.

"I'm afraid your trip has been for nothing."

"No, general, I had planned to leave Richmond before this came up. David wanted me to be with his family in Winchester."

"I'm sorry I can't be more help. All we can do is wait. Maybe he'll ride in tonight, or someone will bring news, or his name appear on a prisoner list. Waiting is difficult I know."

Carrie dropped onto a camp stool, suddenly very tired.

"I've been a thoughtless host to keep you standing," Rosser apologized, "and I never asked if you had eaten."

"Not since morning," she answered simply.

"Ah, a lady to admire, directly to the point," he smiled, "how many times has David spoken of your lack of guile."

He called for his orderly.

"You're a brave lady, Carrie Morrow. Now, if you will permit a general to exercise his prerogatives, I suggest you continue on to Winchester under a white flag with an escort from the Laurel Brigade. After you have some supper, of course, and a night's rest. My tent is yours. I'll post a sentry."

"I couldn't, general."

"Nonsense! That's an order. And I'll have no mutiny in my camp," he smiled, closing the discussion.

"Now, you have a good rest and we'll talk in the morning. Maybe we'll know more by then."

LVIII

FRIENDSHIP REDEEMED

The sergeant pulled up at George Custer's tent below Middletown, "We caught 'em ridin' t'Winchester, sir, the men are Rosser's, the woman's f'm Richmond. That's all she'd say."

"Rosser's men, hey? Old Tom must be pretty sore at the drubbing I gave him."

Custer stood as he met Carrie, "You're a ways from home," he glanced at her middle and its developing bulge, "Mrs—?"

"Mrs. Morrow, and I demand that you release me at once."

"Morrow? And you're going to Winchester? I had a friend at The Point named Morrow. And he was from Winchester. David Morrow. You related to him by any chance?"

"We married over a year ago," Carrie informed him coldly.

"Dave's wife!

"That's wonderful! One of my best friends and my men capture his wife," Amused, he laughed his infectious laugh and ignored the boundaries of good taste, "and his baby."

"Mrs. David Morrow," he bowed low, "George Armstrong Custer at your service, ma'am. It is a pleasure to meet you."

"I can't say the same, Mr. George Custer."

"Oh, Dave, you have got yourself one vexatious woman," he baited her purposely, smiling, awaiting her next riposte.

"I suppose you're happy, discommoding me as you are."

"I am enjoying myself, but not for that." He turned serious.

"I'm truly happy to meet Dave's wife. Despite differences, I value his friendship. I hope we can resume it one day."

"If it means so much to you, you can let me proceed."

"I'll do better, Mrs. Morrow. I'll guarantee your safe passage if you allow me to accompany you. And I'll find you a more comfortable rig, one with springs and a leather seat."

"I wouldn't dream of troubling you," her sarcasm dripped.

Custer ignored it, relishing the situation, "Anything for the bride of my friend.

"Orderly, find a carriage suitable for a lady," he pointed, "maybe at that farm. Tell them I'll return it. Also, my horse, the chestnut, six men as escort, and a driver for the carriage."

He turned to Rosser's men, "You'll ride with us, but I need your parole. A truce between us and no attempt to escape."

Their senior officer, a lieutenant colonel wearing two stars on his collar, answered, "You have my word, general."

An hour later, the small party rode from camp, Custer in the lead alongside Carrie in her borrowed carriage. He swung in his saddle to motion the senior Confederate to join them.

"Colonel, you should join my army," he said with good humor.

"Not a chance, general. Whyever in the world would I?"

"For one thing, you'd be a major general with your two stars," Custer laughed.

"Yes sir, but I'd have to wear a blue uniform and I have little liking for blue," he countered.

Custer laughed raucously. "I like a man who can make a joke." He turned to Carrie as they approached Abraham's Creek.

"Mrs. Morrow, tell me of Dave. He is well, I trust."

Carrie remained silent, straining to hold back the tears. The day had not gone well at all.

"Please believe me. I would like to know how he fares. I saw him on Sunday last."

"You saw him on Sunday? After the battle?"

"No. Before. He saluted me, him and Tom Rosser, and I returned the compliment."

Disappointed again, Carrie's tears broke the dam.

Custer was truly distressed, "Dear lady, I have no intention of causing you pain."

He saw her safely through the ford and considerately dropped back so she could be alone. He motioned the colonel he jokingly had tried to recruit, indicating to him to drop back, too.

"This is as good a time as any," he said, "for you and your men to disappear."

"I don't understand, general."

"Disappear. Ride off. Skedaddle. Your parole is canceled."

"I can't do that, sir. My men maybe, but not me. I'm responsible for seeing Mrs. Morrow to her destination."

"Southern honor? I'll be damned."

"My men?"

"Keep them, or tell them to ride. Whichever you want."

The troopers elected to stay.

The colonel disagreed, "Damnit, we don't know what's going to happen. Get out while you have the chance. That's an order."

They saluted, each one of them, and rode off reluctantly, for they respected their colonel. They turned west for the mountains before they went out of sight.

"I don't understand this, but thank you, general."

"Call it a gesture honoring friendship. Now tell me about my friend's wife. What's she doing here?"

"She's looking for her husband."

"He's not with Rosser? Obviously she came through his camp."

"He's been missing since the fracas at Tom's Brook."

"Oh, shit. I'll alert my patrols to keep a sharp eye."

The two of them rejoined Carrie, one on either side of her carriage. With Custer's escort following, they rode into Winchester, up Main Street to the Morrows' house on Wolfe Street. "It would be better if you did the honors," Custer conceded to the officer who had remained with him.

"And better if you wait here," he turned to Carrie making ready to exit the carriage. She answered with daggers, but did as he said. With hope rising in her breast, she perched expectantly on the very edge of the leather seat.

The colonel lifted the brass knocker and let it fall.

Maybe David is inside this very minute walking toward the door, Carrie's dream expanded. She was ready to run to him.

Her yearning became almost real, real enough to feel dismay when Ezekiel's mother, Mam, responded to the knock.

"Lieutenant Colonel Sam Hawthorne at your service. This is the Morrows' residence, is it not."

Hesitantly, Mam nodded.

"The home of Colonel David Morrow?"

Mam nodded again.

"Is he here, by any chance?"

Mam straightened to her full height, "If he was Ah wouldn't be tellin'. Ah don't know you."

"You can trust me. That's his wife, sitting in the carriage. She's come all the way from Richmond."

"Why you travelin' with Yankees," she spat, nodding suspiciously at Custer and his escort, "Ah know Yankees when Ah sees 'em.

"You send her up heah so's Ah can look in her eyes."

Carrie climbed the verandah steps on Colonel Hawthorne's arm, her heart pounding to be practically inside David's house. Surely, being so close to him was an omen, a good sign.

Mam pointed to Colonel Hawthorne, who stood respectfully to one side, "He says David and you are married. You his wife?"

"Since March a year ago, Mam."

Mam started, "How do you know mah name?"

"David has spoken of you often. How you and Ezekiel came from Washington. His second mother, he said. I'm Carrie."

The straightforward mixture of fact and emotion impressed Mam. Maybe the man in his fancy uniform was lying but this pretty young girl wasn't, she could see that. With tears threatening, Mam enfolded Carrie in loving arms.

"David wrote about you, Miss Carrie. Henry and Sarah always let me read the lettuhs from mah boys."

She turned to Colonel Hawthorne, "Ah'm sorry Ah mis-trusted you. David's not heah.

"Nobody knows wheah he's at," she lied, loud enough for Custer and his men to hear.

"I understand. And, Mrs. Morrow, I pray you find your husband soon."

"Thank you, colonel, you're a brave man."

He saluted her and Mam, and rejoining Custer, mounted up.

Custer hitched his reins to the carriage and climbed aboard, rocking it on its soft springs.

He shouted cheerily, "Tell Dave I said hello."

Carrie watched him ride off, lounging on the leather seat, waving energetically. She was not sure what she thought of him.

How could he destroy the Valley and remain so untouched, she wondered; he seemed as much carefree schoolboy as general.

Mam interrupted her musing, "Didn't want to say so in front of the Yankees, but David's with Ezekiel at the farm."

Carrie stared wide-eyed, for after so many disappointments, her head jumbled the words. Their meaning trailed behind.

David at the farm? What Farm? Ezekiel? Where's David? Of course, that's why I'm here. To help David. The words sorted out.

"At the farm, Mam? Where? How far? How do we get there? Now? You mean he's with Ezekiel now? Is he all right?"

"Course he is, honey. Ezekiel was heah two days ago and Henry and Sarah went back with him."

"How do I get there?"

"Ah can still hitch up uh horse if Ah have to."

"Mam, can't you go faster!"

"This old mare goin' about as fast as she can. Now, you just sit back, Miss Carrie."

"You sure this is the right road?"

"Been heah thirty years. Should know it by now," Mam cackled her good-natured laugh, "you sure nervous t'see youah husband."

"It's been a long time. Were you ever separated from your husband, Mam?"

"Since 18 and 27. When he died." Mam spoke very softly, "Jeremy was a kindly man. We nevah could get married legal-like, but we were married all right. Stayed togethah 26 years, evah since Henry's Mama died."

The significance of Mam's answer was lost on Carrie, who was pointing excitedly, half standing in the buggy, "Is that the house? Is that it? Hurry, Mam. Hurry."

Ezekiel was out to meet them, "Saw you comin'. Mama, you shouldn't be drivin' like that."

"Wasn't me, Ezekiel. Ah had uh impatient passengah. And besahds, Ah wanted to see David, too. This is his wife, Miss Carrie. This is my son," her voice reflected the pride she felt.

"Glad ta meet you, Miss Carrie."

Carry took his hand, "Ezekiel, I feel I know you already. Is David hurt bad?"

"Hurt, Miss Carrie, but not bad. Sarah's been with him since Monday evenin'. She got the bullet out first thing."

"I knew it! I knew he was shot. She took it out?"

"Good as any doctor. She got plenty practice when the house was turned inta a reg'lar hospital. Gracey and Betsy, too. Gracey's studyin' now ta go t'doctor's school.

"Jed and Betsy are here, too." He started for the house, but Carrie stopped him with a hand on his arm, "Ezekiel?"

He heard her anxiety, and saw it in her eyes as he turned back, "What is it, Miss Carrie?"

"I don't want to be rude, but, Ezekiel—," her voice broke, "I need to see David."

"I understand. Leave it ta me."

"And one more thing, both of you. Please call me Carrie."

They hurried into the house.

Henry stood at a kitchen window, his back to them, hands clasped behind, fingers tapping. Jed sat at the round table.

"This is David's wife. She's awful nervous ta see him."

Carrie flashed a shadow of a smile as Ezekiel hustled her through the room. Jed raised a hand, and started to stand. Henry never heard them, nor did Betsy as they passed the open door to the parlor. She was busy feeding little Sarah.

"First door on the right," Ezekiel whispered at the bottom of the stairs Carrie hesitated, putting her hand on his arm, "Thank you so much." Climbing the stairs, she hesitated at the top, preparing for—she took a deep breath.

The room was fresh and clean, windows open for fresh air, the bed cover a gleaming white. David lay with eyes closed, the coverlet up to his chin. He looked so—so helpless.

Carrie had never seen David like this. Lively, loving, mourning, angry, even intoxicated once, but never like this. Transfixed with fear, she stood in the doorway staring at the coverlet. Its steady rise and fall reassured her.

Two women were in the room, one busy at a bedside table.

"Gracey, you did fine. It's easy to administer too much chloroform. Just as much as you need and no more is the rule."

"I tried to be careful, Ma."

"And you were. You'll make a fine doctor, sweetheart."

Sarah turned at the squeak of a loose floorboard, "Oh! You surprised me. You are—? You must be Carrie."

"Yes, Mrs. Morrow. Is he—all right?"

"He's still sleeping from a touch of chloroform. He seemed feverish and I wanted to probe his wound for anything I might have missed when I removed the bullet. He's fine."

Carrie touched his face and knelt by the bed, her eyes filled with tears of thanksgiving. She kissed him lightly and caressed I love you into his tousled hair. She wasn't aware of Sarah's silent signal to Gracey, nor did she hear them leave the room, or Gracey whisper, "Is she really David's wife, Ma?"

"Shhhh," moments later at the bottom of the staircase, Sarah answered softly, "yes, she really is. And it seems you are going to be auntie again."

"But she lives in Richmond."

"She did, Gracey, but now she's come home. To live with us."

The next day, David's fever left him, and Ezekiel hitched up a mule cart to transport him to the big house. Whether Carrie's presence broke the fever, or Mattie's fatback poultice, or Sarah's care no one would ever know. Or care, as long as it was gone.

Outside for the first time, David sat on the broad verandah of Liberty Hall. He watched Jed and Ezekiel across a hundred fifty yards of burned field, nodding approvals and disagreements. Now and then a muted word or phrase drifted to him, riding a favorable breeze, "damned shame—better next year." At his elbow, Henry rocked contentedly, the war and its sorrows subdued by the glorious, autumn day.

"Seeing Jed and Ezekiel out there takes me back, Pa."

"Talkin' spring plantin' I'd guess."

The October sunshine was good, and the sight of Jed and Ezekiel was good.

Their first night together, in the room and in the bed David had used as a boy, Carrie's insightful, "It won't hurt the baby," demolished his initial restraint, and their love-making was over very quickly.

"My goodness, you are an eager one!"

"And so are you."

Their laughter started with a giggle, then a chuckle, first one, then the other, growing almost to hysteria.

"What's so funny?"

"What's so funny to you? Tell me first."

"No, you tell me."

"No, you first."

Together, they said, "The Exchange Hotel," and shook the bed with their laughter.

"I'll never forget you that night, lying there with your eyes clamped tight."

"And I'll never forget you. You were so sick!"

His shoulder was her pillow after that, and she was content in the circle of his arm, content, sheltered and safe.

The next morning at breakfast, they half-expected someone, to complain of the laughter in the night. For all they could tell, no one heard it at all.

LIX

DECISION WITHOUT OPTIONS
OCTOBER, 1864

On the verandah, Henry's wooden chair almost rocked itself.
"Your shoulder feelin' all right, David?"

"It's stiff," he flexed the arm, "but not bad. Seems looser than yesterday. Ma surprised me, taking the bullet out."

Henry's response started with a slow, serious nod of agreement and admiration. His voice reflected his great respect and even a touch of disbelief, "Your Ma's a remarkable lady."

"More than I deserve."

"I wouldn't say that, Pa, you're pretty remarkable yourself."

"Not like her, workin' and carin' for the rest of us. Up all night, nursin' you little ones when you were sick, then workin' all day. She's done things I could never do, readin' and askin' when she didn't know the answer. Learnin', always learnin'. She has an inner strength that I've seen time and time again."

"She sure surprised me when she said she was going to take the bullet out. And then Gracey, giving me the chloroform."

"That's your Ma, son. Doin' things herself and aimin' others in the right direction. Like she can see the future."

"You've seen ahead, Pa. You were against this war."

"But I don't see like your Ma. I guess I can plan things all right, but she sees the future in terms of people. She can see what people oughta do. Like Gracey studyin' t'be a doctor."

"You talking about me?" Gracey bounced through the doorway.

"Just saying how you've changed. When I was home last. you weren't interested in much but the soldiers. Remember? I was really worried."

"I told you, David, you had nothing to worry about."

"This is one time I'm happy to be wrong," David laughed, "you'll make a fine doctor, sweetheart."

"Oh, I almost forgot! Ma says do you want anything? More apple pie? Or coffee? There's some left from the supper table."

"Not me. I'm stuffed."

"Uh, Uh."

Gracey skipped back inside, reminding David of the skittery, frolicking little sister he remembered.

As they talked, they watched Jed and Ezekiel.

"Look at those two, Pa. Cut from the same pattern."

"They are that, son. Jed has called Zeke his second father, but sometimes they're more like brothers."

"Jed seems so satisfied, Pa. I can't help but envy him. I don't know where the hell I'll be next month, or even next week."

"You thinkin' of leavin' so soon? Returnin' t'the army?"

"I don't know, Pa, I just don't know. What's the point when the war is lost, Any one can see the war is lost."

Henry glanced at his son with surprise, for this kind of pessimism was not the David he knew.

"I've been lucky, Pa, very lucky up to now, but I have bad feelings. Maybe it's being with you and Ma, or having Carrie here, the baby coming, I don't know, it's just bad, bad feelings. Like seeing a black bird light on your window.

"I never believed in omens, Pa, but now I'm not so sure. They say General Jackson's sword fell to the ground the night before he was shot."

"I'd say coincidence rather than omen, David."

"It's the war, I guess," David lifted out of the rocker and walked to the edge of the verandah. He stared across the fields, watching a barn swallow swoop for evening bugs. If only he could catch an answer as easily. His reverie was broken as Jed and Ezekiel headed for the house.

After-supper chores finished, the Morrow women came onto the verandah, five of them, two by birth, three by choice. Mam and Mattie followed. They found chairs, all except Carrie who moved close to David, very close for she knew he would be leaving soon. Even before he did, she knew.

Jed and Ezekiel headed for the verandah steps, their plans and dreams for next year set aside until tomorrow. Near the house, Jed stooped for a long piece of grass, unpretentiously sweet as he pressed it between his teeth. He leaned against one of the simple columns.

"What are you two hatchin' out there in the field?"

"Talkin' about next year, Pa. Next year's gonna be better."

"I hope so, son."

Jed nibbled the grass shorter, "I wonder now why I ever joined the army. Never really knew how much I love this Valley."

He pushed from the column, standing steady on the leg Ezekiel had carved with such care, "You were right about enlistin', Pa. I never should've." He offered his hand.

Henry, too, stood up and gripped his son's big hand, square and calloused, so much like his own, "You did what you thought was right, son."

As they looked into each other's eyes, the clasp became four-handed, even that inadequate for the love they felt, each for the other, and they embraced there on the verandah of the house named Liberty Hall by Brian's student/soldier friends.

"This is where I belong, Pa, on our land, in this Valley.

"This is where we all belong, together on Morrow land."

Jed seemed to have said all that needed saying, for there were no words for several minutes, only rocking creaky chairs. They watched the western sun flaunt its crimsons and golds, close to North Mountain. They looked across fields they knew would be green again.

David swallowed a lump and rose from his chair. He, too, felt the love for Virginia's Great Valley. And for family.

"I'm going to see Sable."

"I'll go with you." Henry started from his chair.

"No, Pa. I need a few minutes alone."

And Henry respected his son's wish, a tad longer than the few minutes asked for. He stopped short of the temporary shed Ezekiel had built, watching David as he talked to Sable and stroked his shiny, black coat. For several minutes he watched, admiring this soldier son and his big stallion, appreciating for the first time the deep bond between them. They had saved each other's life, these two.

Quietly, he observed, respecting them, unwilling to break into their private time. He watched as David ran his hand over Sable's flank that had been cut by Yankee steel. He remembered a few days back when David had shown him the saber wound, proud that it had healed smooth and black, not a trace of white or gray.

"It was simpler when there were only the two of us, old friend. What should we do now that there are four of us?"

Embarrassed at his unintentional eavesdropping, Henry shuffled to disclose his presence.

Sable swung his great head toward the familiar figure, and David faced the issue.

"We were just thinking about the future, Sable and me. It was simpler in '61 when he and I raced off to Harper's Ferry to the new colonel there. I was young and single, and we knew the war couldn't be lost. The Yankees won't fight, we thought, and even if they do, one of us is worth ten of them. We were right and God was on our side. I wanted nothing more than to be a soldier in Virginia's army."

"Nothing wrong with that, son."

"But the rules changed, Pa. The Yankees can fight, and one of them is worth one of us and the war is lost and God is on their side, too. I have a wife now, and soon a little one to think about."

And David did think about his wife and little one, the days to come, and days gone by.

"Grandfather Ephraim settled in the Valley and then went back to Philadelphia. He should have stuck it out, Pa. Stayed and seen it through."

"Just a minute ago you answered your own question, son. The rules changed on him, too. Gran'mother loved the Shenandoah Valley, but was terrified by it after the Painters' massacre. Gran'daddy had to make a choice. You have to do the same."

"But I'm no quitter, Pa. That's desertion, and I've courtmartialed men for desertion. But the war is lost, Pa, everything's lost.

"Stuart. Pelham. Tom Rafferty. General Jackson.

"General Jackson sat at your dinner table, Pa.

"They're all gone, and for what. For nothing, that's what. A waste of good men. The damned war is lost."

David caressed Sable's smooth neck thoughtfully.

"It's a hell of a choice, Pa, a hell of a choice in a war that can't be won."

Three weeks later, his shoulder healed, David saddled his great black stallion. At the end of Wolfe Street, he turned in his saddle, just as he had done more than three years ago, riding off to Harper's Ferry. As he had done then, Sable danced a quarter circle, prancing almost crosswise in the street. He reared on his hind legs as David waved high, palm toward his family, with an extra flourish this time for his wife and the baby she carried. His lips moved with a message to them, "I love you."

He gave a smart military salute, his West Point best, and gently reined Sable toward Main Street and the corner.

Behind him, Henry rubbed his chin deliberately, as was his custom when his thoughts were deep. Hope and a resurgent optimism filled his heart, for he knew the traditional values of the Morrow family were safe with his sons and daughters. They, each in his own way, had earned his confidence.

He closed the wrought iron gate slowly, reluctantly, the final symbol of David's departure. He looked at the empty street, seeing Sable, seeing David as they had danced and saluted their farewell.

"I agree, son. You had a hell of a choice.

"One hell of a choice."